PERSONAL WITNESS

Also by Abba Eban

Heritage: Civilization and the Jews
The New Diplomacy
Abba Eban: An Autobiography
My Country
My People: The Story of the Jews
Voice of Israel

PERSONAL WITNESS

Israel Through My Eyes

ABBA EBAN

G. P. PUTNAM'S SONS
NEW YORK

G. P. Putnam's Sons
Publishers Since 1838
200 Madison Avenue
New York, NY 10016

Designed by Sheree Goodman

Eban, Abba Solomon, date.
Personal witness : Israel through my eyes/Abba Eban.
p.   cm.
ISBN 0-399-13589-8
1. Eban, Abba Solomon, date. 2. Statesmen—Israel—Biography.
3. Zionism—History. 4. Israel—Foreign relations. I. Title.
DS126.6.E2A3   1992   91-15808 CIP
956.94′04′092—dc20
Printed in the United States of America

1   2   3   4   5   6   7   8   9   10

This book is printed on acid-free paper.
∞

ACKNOWLEDGMENTS

This book is the result of deep individual reflection on the events of which I was a witness and participant. The mood is deliberately subjective and the list of acknowledgments is therefore brief. In my narration I have been conscious of the fact that a previous work *An Autobiography* is now out of print. The rush of events in this land kept me in constant pursuit of new horizons of climax. As an Israeli of the first generation, I feel that I have some responsibility for transmitting the emotions and calculations of Israel's founders while they are still vivid in memory.

I owe special and overriding tribute to Gila Eban whose meticulous editing was of the highest professional standard.

Carmel Ross gave invaluable assistance as a researcher. Gwyn Pritchard at Channel Four U. K. and Arnold Labaton at WNET, Channel Thirteen, commented on the TV scripts of my five-part series and thereby influenced the structure of the book while leaving its style and text in my sole responsibility. Autobiography is an excellent method of telling the truth about other people, but I hope that my own perspectives emerge with greater clarity now that I speak in my own voice alone. My thanks also to Neil Nyren at Putnam, who supplied the first injection of encouragement and stoically adjusted himself to receding deadlines.

My wife, Suzy, has been the loving and candid companion of my journey through all the joys and sorrows, the hopes and tensions described in these pages. The causes that we cherished together may now have a chance to renew their vitality, and our hearts are filled to overflowing.

ABBA EBAN
HERZLIYA, ISRAEL
JULY 1992

CONTENTS

To Suzy, Eli, and Gila with love

1

BEGINNINGS

THE GYROSCOPE FACTORY at Lake Success seemed an unlikely place for the recollection of large events when I visited it recently after the lapse of many years. It is approached after a brief ride through tree-lined streets flanked by neat shops that evade the extremes of luxury without descending to shoddiness. The air of mid-American domesticity soon gives way to lush, verdant lawns across which flocks of geese now strut, close to where world statesmen once used to stride. Lake Success is the home of families who wish their lives to flow in easy rhythm, detached from the exhilaration but also from the turmoil of the modern age. They rarely express any longing for the years when their town supplied daily headlines for the international press. "Our Correspondent at Lake Success" was once a title that excited the ambition of reporters and broadcasters of the first rank. They used to gather at UN headquarters in greater numbers and with greater enthusiasm than did their successors who, until the sensation of the Desert War, used to languish obscurely in the sternly efficient structures on the East River. The UN commentators of the first generation were primarily discharging a professional duty, but they made some mental provision for the idea that they might be the witnesses of a new enterprise on whose outcome great destinies would depend. There was an atmosphere of historic tension as they went about their business of reporting the transactions of foreign ministers, ambassadors and others of lesser rank, who liked to believe that they were constructing a new world order on the ruins of the old.

The international media did not see anything pretentious in this assumption. For many decades the speeches of foreign ministers in the UN general debate passed from ministerial lips to oblivion without so much as a temporary resting place in *The New York Times*. But in the first years of the UN, that newspaper would devote two large pages to the wisdom and platitude of delegates across the entire alphabetic range from Afghanistan to Yugoslavia.

At least one television station would broadcast selected extracts far into the weary night.

Lake Success had become an arena of world politics in a strange sequence of events. President Franklin D. Roosevelt, Marshal Stalin and Prime Minister Winston Churchill had worked in meticulous detail at Yalta to formulate a blueprint for an international organization. But these august auspices did not solve the prosaic issue of finding a headquarters site. There was a tentative Soviet attempt to choose Geneva once again, but that city held haunting memories that the addicts of international organization ardently wished to forget. More decisive than this superstition was the European anxiety about the tendency of America to escape back into itself after every war. Would it not be cunningly wise, said the Europeans, to plant the United Nations deep in American soil so that physical departure would be totally foreclosed?

But where in America? There was a tentative move, inspired by the anti-European theme in American history, to prefer San Francisco, where the Founding Conference of the UN had been held in 1945. Many Americans believe that maximal distance from the eastern seaboard is a condition of national virtue. But the kind of Americans who support international organizations tend to be resolute Atlanticists. So, for better or worse, the United Nations would move into New York, which, having lacked a monarchical era, had no plethora of empty palaces. There would have to be a provisional headquarters until a permanent structure could be built. Thus it came about that the gyroscope factory on Long Island would house the secretary-general and the working committees as well as the bureaucracy that had come into the world fully overgrown. Less often, plenary meetings would be convened in a medium-sized auditorium at Flushing Meadow some fifteen kilometers closer to the center of New York. There was nothing in either building to elevate the mind by any degree of architectural distinction. An inexpensive plaque on a building at the Lake Success factory announces unenthusiastically that the United Nations held its meetings there between 1947 and 1951. At Flushing Meadow, now the site of a popular skating rink and the national tennis championships, there is not even a minimal acknowledgment of the UN lineage.

Nostalgia is not what it used to be, and I could not take my journey from that inscription without a pang of personal memory that jolted me into visions of things past. The recollection is of fifty-eight flags that dignified the green courtyard, to which Israel's blue and white banner was added over forty years ago. My hands still retain the feel of the rope with which I pulled the flag to its mast on May 11, 1949. I knew that in that moment the status and identity of the Jewish people were instantaneously transformed. And beyond the flags, I saw the figures of those who commanded the scene— George Marshall, Dean Acheson, Eleanor Roosevelt and a young Adlai Stevenson; Ernest Bevin, Alexander Cadogan and Gladwyn Jebb; Andrei Gromyko, Yacov Malik and Andrei Vyshinski; Robert Schumann, Alexandre Parodi and Jules Moch; Trygve Lie and Ralph Bunche; Lester (Mike)

Pearson and George Ignatieff; Herbert Evatt and Carl Berendsen; Carlos Romulo, Krishna Menon and Zafrullah Khan; Victor Belaunde and Padilla Nervo. And sharper than any of these, the Arab leaders with whom I was locked in combat—Charles Malik, Mahmud Fawzi, Fadhil al-Jamili and Faris al-Khoury—and the Jewish and Israeli delegations with whom I marched in our nation's cause all the way from the post-war agony to the culminating hour of consolation and triumph.

If it was unexpected for an arena of world politics to be revealed in Long Island, it is certain that no horoscope would have dared predict my own arrival there in May 1947.

It was the consequence of an unusually divided boyhood and early youth that had made Zionism the dominant theme of my life. I suppose that my eccentric choice of what seemed a precarious Zionist vocation in 1946 could be held as proof that Zionism in those days could captivate and enlist young Western Jews who had never suffered the indignities for which Zionism claimed to give remedy. To say this, however, would be to generalize a very particular experience. I did not come to the Zionist cause in sudden ecstasy or in response to some traumatic insecurity. These had been the routine biographical experiences of Western Zionists. I, on the other hand, had been born into the very air and soul of the idea. My mother had arrived in London from Capetown with her two children and my dying father in 1916, when I was seven months old. She was bereaved of her husband through cancer less than a year later. She was in need of consolation and livelihood. Neither was to be easily found. One of her quests for employment had brought her to the modest abode of the Zionist Office in central London as a secretary and translator. At first this seemed to be no more than a job, and an unrewarding one at that. But it soon flowered into an extraordinary adventure that was to leave its mark on all of us.

Early in November 1917, my mother had obeyed a nocturnal call from the Zionist leaders to leave my cradle and go to the office on a foggy night to translate the Balfour Declaration into French and Russian. The declaration was then a few hours old. It was a sensational document because, in promising the Jewish people a national home in Palestine, it took the Jews, for the first time since antiquity, into the world of politics and law. It deserves to be acknowledged to this day as the authentic starting point of the process that led to the State of Israel. The translation of a document sounds a modest chore, but it linked my family to an unforgettable drama. Throughout my childhood, the vibrations of this event were transmitted to me through my mother's narrative in quiet but proud recollection. Something unique and exalting lit up my family's sky and the glow of it would never be lost. Zionism had conquered my inner world.[1]

Another impulse that drove me in the same Zionist direction was derived

---

[1] My father, Avram Solomon, died in London in 1917. My mother married Isaac Eban, a Jewish physician, whose name I took and have gratefully and proudly borne.

from an unusual routine in my boyhood years. My maternal grandfather, Eliahu Sacks, had arrived in London from South Africa in the first decade of the century. He appears to have been one of the few Jews who had settled for any length of time in South Africa and left it without any degree of affluence. In London, he had conceived the idea of investing his last years and his vast Hebrew erudition in one of his grandsons. The other candidates for this unwanted distinction were so devoid of Hebraic zeal that the choice fell by default on me. The senior members of my family endorsed this project with enthusiasm; the alternative would have been my grandfather's resumption of business activity with resultant family impoverishment.

He was a man of refinement and quality with a distinguished presence. With his semi-baldness and Hanoverian beard he bore a faint resemblance to King George V or Tsar Nicholas II of Russia, and his stately walk down a street would often invite a double take from passersby. But he was not constructed temperamentally for the world of business and he found great fulfillment in virtually kidnapping me at the age of five from Friday to early Monday every week for a ruthlessly intense immersion at his very modest home in North London in a world dominated by the Hebrew language, of which I learned the alphabet before having fully mastered the English script. Soon I was being guided through the biblical literature (with some furtive omissions of the sensual passages) by a mind never formally trained but lit up by an intuitive scholarship.

Grandfather Sacks never explained what he expected me to do with this heavy cargo of learning except that he was virulently opposed to any rabbinical vocation. He regarded the Hebrew legacy as an adornment of the mind, rather as the elitist British schools looked upon Greek and Latin. It all seemed to have little relevance for a Jewish youngster undergoing a classical education at a British school, with an ambitious eye fixed on Oxford or Cambridge. Whatever the intention, the consequences for me were formative to the ultimate degree. It was the Hebrew weekends, not the English weekends, that came to excite my deepest sources of feeling. My suffering and suspense were of Isaac under Abraham's threatening knife. My sense of awe came to life in the "thunder and lightning and the sound of the trumpet exceeding loud" that accompanied Moses on Mount Sinai. My sense of nationhood was born in the parting of the Red Sea and the defiant Israeli flight from Egyptian tyranny. Pharaoh in my early days was my personal enemy. The frogs, the flies, the rivers of blood, the locusts and the cattle plagues were no more than he deserved, although in my incorrigibly liberal mind I felt that the slaying of the Egyptian firstborn sons carried things a little too far.

On passing from ancient to modern Hebrew studies, my loyalties became linked with more recent dramas—the martyrdoms, inquisitions, massacres, pogroms and, most of all, the quest for remedy and honor now being enacted by the Zionist pioneers, still few and weak but supremely tenacious, hundreds of miles away.

It might have seemed that these emotions would be overtaken by exposure to a university of dazzling prestige and achievement that was celebrating one of its most creative periods at the apex of European science. But I carried my Zionist enthusiasm with varying degrees of intensity through all the years of my boyhood and my student days at Cambridge.

Zionism was not the paramount concern of pre-war Cambridge even in the consciousness of its few Jewish students. There was the larger issue of individual survival. Cambridge in the late 1930s was haunted by the pathos of contrast between the serenity of its majestic buildings and the sulphurous atmosphere of approaching war. In April 1938 the *Cambridge Review* wrote of a debate in the Cambridge Union: "Mr. A. S. Eban rose to propose that 'this House condemns the Chamberlain Government for its failure effectively to uphold the interest of this country in preserving the freedom of Czechoslovakia and of the other independent and non-Germanic nations of Central and Southeastern Europe.' " The report extolled me in lavish terms ("the brilliant speech that we are used to hear from him") and ended: " 'I appeal to the self-interest of the House as well as to its idealism,' said Mr. Eban in a great peroration." The report concluded with a reference to a victorious vote for the cause that I was supporting.

Although I was only dimly aware of it at the time, it is certain that this appreciation of my speech at the Cambridge Union, and others that followed it, had the effect of weaning me away from the obsessive belief that academic life was my only cherished option. The ability to move audiences and individuals to agreement and emotion is a more potent human capacity than to produce a dissertation on an episode of medieval history. At my earlier educational stage in classical and Hebrew studies, I had been captivated by models of declamatory eloquence. The prophecies of Isaiah were formulated as public addresses, and the orations of Demosthenes and Cicero are memorably recitable. Their purpose was to move hearers to entirely new levels of reaction and behavior, not only to aesthetic appreciation.

When I spoke to my Cambridge listeners of "self-interest" as a motive for resisting Hitlerism, I was using a euphemism. The stark meaning was that many of the young debaters would not survive into maturity, for Hitler was well on the road to the fulfillment of his odious visions. The British and even the continental European press were paying close attention to what British students were thinking, especially in the two universities from which British political leaders were traditionally recruited. The Oxford Union, in what was probably more a stunt than a statement, had carried a resolution announcing a refusal by its members "to fight for king and country." Most of the supporters of that idea, which caused exaggerated satisfaction to the Nazi leaders, were later to fight against the Hitlerist armies and many of them would see their service crowned by valor and sacrifice. In Cambridge, the tendency was for polarization of attitudes between routine conservatism and wild embrace of communism, whose zealots were volunteering for battle in the Spanish civil war, where John Cornford lost his life. He was a celebrated student Communist, the son of a celebrated poet, and I knew him well from my duels with him in debate. Others were preparing, as in the celebrated cases of Philby, Maclean, Burgess and Blunt, to carry their talents and sexual confusions to Moscow's service. This group of brilliant aesthetes became known as "the Cambridge spies." The book *Cambridge Between the Wars* mentions me as one of the few Union orators in those years who kept a central ideological and political course in a haunted age.

Cambridge in the mid-1930s scintillated with talents that resonated far beyond the campus limits. This was certainly true of the physicists in the Cavendish Laboratories where Rutherford and Cockcroft were probing and splitting the atom while pretending that their work had no practical import and was merely a beautiful way of describing Nature. It was true of the Economics Department, where John Maynard Keynes held sway with Joan Robinson and Richard Kahn, who promoted their particular form of social empiricism with liberal undertones. The English Department was kept in constant polemical effervescence by F. E. Leavis and the poet A. E. Housman, while the historians Herbert Butterfield and George Macaulay Trevelyan powerfully enunciated their contempt for each other and fought battles about the meaning and purpose of history. Hersch Lauterpacht towered above everyone else in international law. Some of the non-nuclear scientists, such as J. D. Bernal and J. B. S. Haldane, declaimed pretentiously that "scientists, guided by scientific principles, should replace politicians and run public affairs." Bertrand Russell and Ludwig Wittgenstein redefined logic and regarded Oxford with distrust because of its exaggerated devotion to the frivolity of politics. They treated no one as serious unless he was exposed to the "cool reason" of Cambridge, with its rigorous insistence that all things are subject to the discipline of critical inquiry. C. P. Snow, as a don at Christ's College, was in a position to illustrate his theories of the gap between the two cultures, humanistic and scientific, with a novelist's interest in academic gossip and intrigue.

Nothing but the strong pull of Zionism could have lured me away from thinking that this remarkably effervescent Cambridge was my natural and permanent milieu. The idea of Zionism as a vocational commitment rather than as an amateur enthusiasm arose in my mind in 1938 when the political secretary of the Jewish Agency, Arthur Lourie, left London for New York for family reasons and the Zionist leader, Dr. Chaim Weizmann, called me to fill in at his office for a few months. The background for this summons was the fact that my family was known to the Zionist leadership and I myself had written in defense of Zionist policies in leading journals. I duly secured the necessary leave of absence from my Cambridge college and went to 77 Great Russell Street, near the British Museum, where I was courteously received by the Zionist chiefs, including Chaim Weizmann himself. For a twenty-three-year-old Cambridge don saturated in Zionist lore, this was an hour of opportunity and challenge. Nervousness was natural.

Isaiah Berlin has written: "To call someone a great man is to claim that he has intentionally taken a large step—one far beyond the normal capacities of men—in satisfying or materially affecting central human interests." This was the first time that I was in the presence of a man who undoubtedly stood in this category. My awe soon melted away as Chaim Weizmann began to occupy himself with ordering tea and biscuits from his secretary. She turned out, eccentrically, to be an English Catholic lady who had graduated in classical languages at Oxford and did not possess a single Jewish characteristic. I was told that Doris May was an "institution," and Weizmann warned me in fatherly terms that if she asked for anything it would be prudent to comply.

So this was the Dr. Chaim Weizmann to whose humble office my mother had gone to translate the Balfour Declaration twenty-two years ago! He had traveled a long distance since then. I knew his story well, for I had watched it as a hero-worshiping adolescent. He had lived in Manchester as a university lecturer in biochemistry for eight years with a relatively junior position in the Zionist hierarchy, many of whose leaders were stranded by the war in Central Europe. He had managed to persuade some relatively affluent Zionists in Manchester (who later became the lordly founding fathers of the Marks and Spencer chain of popular stores) that if they would subsidize his occasional visits to London, he would cause the British government and, consequently, the other major powers, to adopt the Zionist program for the establishment of "a national home for the Jewish people in Palestine."

At that time this was a typically Zionist idea: ninety percent fantasy and ten percent reality. Weizmann had no money, little English and no social position in a class-ridden British society. But he had a formidable persuasive talent, and he nurtured a vision of a breakthrough for the idea of a Jewish homeland to be promoted by the British capture of Palestine. This capture, however, had not been achieved and seemed an unlikely prospect. Britain had no control of Palestine, which in awkward reality was a province of the Turkish Ottoman Empire. And Turkey was an ally of Germany, which seemed at that time to be winning the war. Why should Britain be expected to sponsor a Zionist movement that seemed to command no real power and that was regarded by the few Englishmen who had heard of it as an exotic and irrelevant fad?

But outside the rigorous disciplines of his laboratory, Weizmann had a special way of dealing with arguments that ran against his aims. He stood no nonsense from them. Within a few years a declaration by the British foreign secretary, Arthur James Balfour, pledged Britain to promote the Zionist program. Later Weizmann secured the assent of all the major powers and the ratification of the Zionist program by the entire membership of the League of Nations in 1922. He was thereafter universally acknowledged to be the architect of this wondrous new turning point in Jewish history, and his leadership of Zionism was assured with few interruptions for three decades.

His crucial aid as a scientist to the Allied war effort gave him wide access to the seats of power. For over a year his patent was the only source of acetone needed for gunpowder, and the relevant ministries in Whitehall could not afford to alienate him. But this alone does not explain his success. He had achieved the kind of status for Zionism that had totally eluded his eminent predecessor, Theodor Herzl, and historians have described his achievement as the "last and perhaps the only instance in diplomatic history of persuasion without power."

I was now to discover that Weizmann was not only the central figure in Jewish life; he was also part of the international diplomatic landscape. From my own table and telephone I could observe how heads of government treated him with courtesy, ministers with apprehensive respect. They stood a good chance of being charmed into an unwanted commitment or exhausted by the tempest of his intense but controlled emotions. But they behaved toward him as though he were already president of a sovereign nation with a status equal to their own. He and they knew that this was not strictly true, but there was something in his imposing physical presence and in their own historic emotion that forbade them to break the spell. He was separated from the masses of Jews by the range and distinction of his contacts, and by his taste for elegance, order and sophistication in daily life. But in style and spirit he was not removed from them. They admired his balanced attitude toward his own political and scientific eminence. In relaxed moods, as I soon found out, he used the Yiddish language to the full scope of its earthiness and irony. His voice, language and mannerisms conveyed the solid culture of the Russian Jews, and yet he appeared serenely at home in the formal routines of chanceries and embassies.

He was six feet in height, taller than most Zionist leaders, with a solid physical appearance crowned by his most singular feature, which was a large head surmounted by a gleaming bald pate and strongly etched features marked by a goatee beard, which caused one observer to describe him as "a well-nourished Lenin." He was always immaculately clothed in a manner that denoted expensive but unobtrusive taste. He had developed the theory that the best way to promote Jewish statehood was to act as if it already existed. When I first encountered him, he was affluent enough, through his chemical inventions and such perquisites as a Rolls-Royce with a liveried chauffeur, to strike the attitudes appropriate to his national ambition. A leading diplomatic historian, Professor Sir Charles Webster, placed Weizmann high above other national liberators of his age because of the vast gap between the large ends that he sought and the pathetically narrow means that he commanded. He could dominate a room by the mere act of entering it. The word "dignity" sprang to the lips of everyone meeting him for the first time.

The arguments that he had deployed successfully in his original appeal to the British Establishment had a certain strategic logic. A strong Jewish position in the East Mediterranean, the argument ran, would help to buttress

British interests. Sponsorship of a Jewish National Home would give Britain a card to play against France, whose leaders thought of their country as the natural protector of Christendom against Islamic domination. It would be more congenial for Britain to base its claim to Palestine on a humanitarian cause such as the rescue of Jews from traditional servitude than to seek rule over Palestine for the sake of its own imperial interests. The trouble in 1939 was that all the benefits accruing to Britain from its original sponsorship of Zionism had already been harvested and digested and could not be withdrawn. In diplomatic life you gain little by telling an embarrassed friend how much he owes you for what you gave him in the past.

Apart from Weizmann, who ruled the Zionist Office by inspiration and authoritative gestures without ever seeming to have a document or file before him, the political team was rescued from banality by two unusual figures. One was a determined Christian lady of Scottish lineage, Blanche (Baffy) Dugdale, the niece and biographer of the very Lord Balfour whose 1917 declaration was the anchor of Zionist hopes and rights. Her Zionism was fervent and almost uncritical except when there seemed to be a deviation from strict probity. On the other hand, she delighted in receiving reports of British Cabinet meetings from sympathetic ministers, which she conveyed conveniently to Weizmann, and she would chastise her own government's increasingly frequent deviations from its original fidelity to Zionism in the tones of a rigorous governess.

The other unexpected figure in what was called Weizmann's "court" was an eminent historian, Lewis Namier. He had the views and prejudices of the British aristocracy whose annals he was compiling with exquisite and austere scholarship. But while his prose was of perfect construction, his accent was abrasively Polish. He was giving his full devotion to the interests of the Jewish people, but he did not seem to like or admire Jews very much. He considered them to have been stunted and disfigured by suffering, segregation and exile, and believed that only by statehood and independent energy would they be cleansed of these defects and become more similar in style and habits to the eighteenth-century English aristocrats who were the subjects of his research. Winston Churchill and Chaim Weizmann were the only exceptions to the comprehensive disfavor with which Namier regarded members of the human race. His bitterness was nourished by the fact that his professorial chair was not at Oxford but in the dank climate of Manchester. This was because Oxford colleges, apart from erudition, required a few qualities that fell short of insufferability. Namier belonged to the category of people, like commanding officers, dentists and headmasters, whom nobody of sound mind would wish to visit unless it was inescapably necessary. But he was an effective scourge of Zionism's numerous adversaries, and I found his ardent defense of the English language to be a common interest. We shared a strong hostility to such "stammers" as "it is unnecessary to emphasize that . . ." Namier would say, "if it is unnecessary, don't emphasize! . . ." My own reverence for Churchill and Weizmann may have protected me against the full effects of Namier's misanthropic temperament.

I came to the Zionist headquarters in Great Russell Street in 1938, when a bright promise had dawned and expired in a single year. One year earlier, in 1937, the British government had adopted the recommendation of a Royal Commission, headed by Lord Peel, to partition Palestine between a Jewish and an Arab state, with British enclaves in Jerusalem and the Negev. Despite the minute dimensions of the proposed Jewish state, Weizmann and David Ben-Gurion had enough lucidity and insight to accept it as the basis for negotiation. The magic words "Jewish state" on an official document were too dazzling to be lightly dismissed, and the case for avoiding the subjection of the Palestine Jews to Arab rule had been expressed by the Royal Commission in moving and eloquent language. It had been drafted by an Oxford professor, Reginald Coupland, whose membership in the Royal Commission elevated its stature.

Coupland, whom I was to know well in later years, explained vividly that it would be idle to pretend the Jews of Palestine and the Arab inhabitants were members of the same nation with shared allegiances. He stressed that they were totally separate and distinct peoples who held no ends in common, so that for one of them to rule the whole country would entail savage repression.

I had attended the 1937 Zionist Congress in Zurich, at which Weizmann made a majestic defense of the partition idea, in harmony, on this occasion, with David Ben-Gurion. My presence was somewhat equivocal, since I was only twenty-two years old and the minimal voting age for a delegate to the Zionist Congress was twenty-four. I held this limitation in deep resentment, since at my new college in Cambridge, Pembroke, to which I had migrated from Queens' in order to fill a research vacancy in Persian and Arabic, it was customary to revere a former graduate, William Pitt, who had entered the University at the age of fourteen and had become Chancellor of the Exchequer at the age of twenty-three.

The historic partition debate in 1937 had been my first experience of high-level Zionist polemics at first hand. A few months later the British government had abandoned its own partition plan. As the specter of war drew nearer, the Chamberlain government's obsession was to avoid irritating the Arabs, not to ensure a harmonious and lucid settlement of the Palestine issue. The British government, having convened a conference in St. James's Palace at which Jewish and Arab leaders were hermetically separated from each other, enacted a virulently anti-Zionist policy in a document that their tradition called a White Paper. This became a black paper for the Jews. It called for an early cessation of Jewish immigration after a paltry flow of 75,000 over the next five years, a Draconian limitation of Jewish land purchases and the establishment of an independent state with an Arab majority within five years. The Jewish National Home was to become a stunted ghetto. It was something like a death blow to the Zionist dream. Churchill denounced it as a betrayal akin to the accursed Munich treaty, but Prime Minister Neville Chamberlain and Foreign Secretary Lord Halifax explained blandly that it was necessary as a pre-war measure. Their logic ran as follows: "When war comes, the Jews will have to support us because the enemy is Hitler. The Arabs will have a choice. Support of Hitler is a viable option for them. Therefore, we must support the hostile Arabs and distance ourselves from the cooperative Jews." Chamberlain and Halifax were men of principle, but one of their principles was expediency.

I had a central view of the tragic era now opening for the Jewish people when I attended the last pre-war Zionist Congress at Geneva in August 1939. The proceedings began with Weizmann and Ben-Gurion assailing the British government for its abandonment of the Jews at the cruelest moment of their destiny. This was expected. But all oratory was transcended when the electrifying news came to Geneva of the Soviet-German agreement signed by the two foreign ministers, Vyacheslav Molotov and Joachim von Ribbentrop. The war that had been probable had now become certain. There is a celebrated photograph of the dais at the Zionist Congress at which Weizmann, Ben-Gurion and their principal colleagues are seated in such attitudes of dejection that their despair seems to cry out through the silent camera lens. As I look at it now, it seems to gather increased pathos from the knowledge of subsequent events. Weizmann, who hated long speeches, uttered brief but memorable words:

> There is darkness all around us and we cannot see through the clouds. If, as I hope, we are spared in life and our work continues, who knows, a new light may shine upon us from the thick, black gloom. . . . The remnant shall work on, fight on, live on until the dawn of better days. Toward that dawn I greet you. May we meet again in peace. . . .

It was much more difficult to get out of Europe than it had been to enter it a few weeks before. My mother and my sister Carmel had accompanied me to Geneva, and we made hasty return to England in crowded trains after a day in Paris, where something of the French disarray was visible even before the war had begun. There was little for me to do in Cambridge except to notice the transformation that had come over the town through the arrival of non-Cambridge guests from London University. It was this that brought Chaim Herzog to Cambridge with other aspiring law school graduates from London University, as well as graduates and students from the School of Oriental Studies among whom I found many distinguished teachers in my own disciplines. These included a celebrated authority on Persian language and literature, Vladimir Minorsky, with whom I took tuition in Persian texts. Many years later I discovered that he had transmitted a Russian accent to me so that when I came to speak Persian, I had become more learned and more unintelligible than if I had never encountered him.

I returned to the Zionist Office at Great Russell Street for another immersion in Zionist diplomacy when I went back there in the late months of 1939, soon after the British declaration of war on Nazi Germany. Research at Cambridge on "Non Muslims Under Arab Rule in the Caliphates" did not seem an adequate response to a period in which German armies were crushing resistance in a devastated Poland, while British and French forces were heavily deployed for resistance to the expected assault on Western Europe. My natural desire was to volunteer for officer training ahead of a call-up, but this was less simple than it sounds. It was like attempting to break into an exclusive dinner party without the appropriate invitation. Letters and telephone calls to the War Office seemed to arouse resentment. We were living what was called "the phony war," and the term did not seem inaccurate as French and British forces waited at the Maginot Line for Hitler to decide on the time and place of his westward thrust.

My daily routine was to set out from my family's home in Harrow each morning and reach Great Russell Street where a ritual known as the "yeshiva" would take place. This name was devised by Baffy Dugdale in a generous Gentile spirit to express a habit of consultation without agenda about the Zionist condition in general and any concrete issue that might demand urgency. When Weizmann himself participated, the atmosphere became at once more relaxed and more charged with commitment. None of his biographers has ever accused him of humility, and great leaders do not have a great deal to be humble about. But under his captaincy, there was no intolerance of dissent, and the discourse flowed freely. Other participants would include Selig Brodetsky, who was also functioning as a professor of mathematics at Leeds University and as president of the Board of Deputies of British Jews, an organization of vague electoral procedures that had contrived by tradition to get itself recognized as the representative body of British Jews. This involved Brodetsky, a jovial, corpulent figure, in a crazy agenda that would make his whereabouts difficult to guess in the pre-computer age. Professor Brodetsky and Professor Namier maintained the kind of unbelievably hostile relationships that are a feature of academic life and that closely resemble relationships between countries at war.

The Palestinian Zionist leadership rightfully feared that our London office was somewhat remote from the atmosphere and reality of Jerusalem and the Middle East. It therefore decided to be represented by Berl Locker, a Labor leader of the old East European school, who achieved extraordinary results in getting the British Labour leaders to embrace Zionist doctrines with a passion that made their subsequent desertion of those doctrines acutely poignant. It became a Zionist truism that our friends were former ministers, while incumbent ministers were our former friends.

One central issue preoccupied us at the Jewish Agency headquarters in the winter of late 1939 and early 1940. It was the effort to persuade the British government to approve the establishment of a Jewish division or brigade. It seemed anomalous that Hitler had proclaimed the Jews as his chief enemy while the Jews themselves were still unable to fight him in their own name and identity. In the early months of 1940 it seemed that a real breakthrough would be possible. The atmosphere in Great Russell Street was suddenly charged with an optimism close to exaltation. British military leaders were taking the idea of a Jewish fighting force seriously. So seriously that by the summer of 1940, under the impulse of Hitler's successful assault on France and the Low Countries, Churchill would be openly advocating the arming of Palestinian Jews in order to release British manpower for Europe and was telling his colonial secretary, Lord Lloyd, that "I do not at all admit that Arab feeling in the Middle East and India would be prejudiced in the manner you suggest." By the early fall of 1940 Churchill told Weizmann that he was in full support of the plan for a Jewish army and Anthony Eden, now foreign secretary, had announced that "the government have decided to proceed with the organization of a Jewish army on the same basis as the Czech and Polish armies." At Zionist headquarters Weizmann and his colleagues were speaking elatedly of a breakthrough "like the Balfour Declaration." They were soon shocked out of this euphoria when the generals responsible for the armies in the Middle East blocked these proposals and obtained Churchill's retreat from his own vision and intent.

I had been involved in the early excitement around this aborted prospect, but by the time that hope had faded into disillusion I was away in the army base at Aldershot training to be an officer and with a hope, not yet sustained by any tangible prospect, that the war would propel me to Jerusalem. Having secured Weizmann's promise that he would use his influence to get me to the Middle East, I departed for a four-month training period at a military base. The descent from my pursuits in London to the bleak realities of barrack life was drastic and, probably, salutary. One week I was accompanying Zionist leaders to talks with Cabinet ministers, including Malcolm MacDonald, the colonial secretary, and lunching grandly at the Carlton Grill with Weizmann and Sir Oliver Harvey, the permanent secretary at the Foreign Office. The next week my preoccupation was how to get another blanket from the army store and how to endure the lack of privacy that is the supreme affliction of army life. Not that my future was without hope. In the letter summoning me to the colors, a War Office colonel had written: "Your training will last three or four months and then, subject to a satisfactory report, you will be commissioned. You would then be employed, if possible, in a part of the world in which your special knowledge would be useful."

To my embarrassment, a sharp attack of flu delayed my arrival at the army base. I feared that I would have to face stern investigations and suspicions of evasion or desertion. Nothing of the kind. The War Office colonel said telephonically: "Don't hurry to Aldershot. Barracks there are bloody cold, old man. The war will last a bloody long time. A couple of days won't matter. Get fit. Flu is quite bloody, isn't it?"

I was too familiar with the class system to ask myself whether an ordinary citizen who was not a Cambridge don would have a direct personal line to a War Office colonel who would supply justifications for lateness in reporting for duty. I had the impression that if I had requested a month for a vacation in Bermuda, it would have been granted without delay. This was all very relaxed and agreeable, but it led to the haunting question whether this kind of approach would generate the qualities necessary to defeat a rampant Hitler. There was a slightly more convincing militarism on display in the army base to which I was sent near Aldershot, and my letters to Cambridge friends in those winter months contain amused but querulous references to the absurdities of barracks life.

I was in no ordinary unit. My colleagues were all Oxford and Cambridge linguists who would one day be sent to perilous places to use the talents for which they had long been trained. On the parade ground, we exercised our individualism profusely. A "Left Turn" order by the sergeant major would generate at least four directional reactions, which he would greet with a screaming bellow: "You may know fifty bloody languages but you can't march fifty bloody steps!"

In mid-May, duly uniformed and commissioned, I made for London and walked up Regent Street, absorbing the salutes of lower ranks with incredulous wonder. In the War Office I was able to elicit what my guardian colonel meant by the promise that I would be employed in a part of the world in which my "special knowledge would be useful." It turned out that the relevant parts of the world existed, but they were not for me. The War Office had discovered that I was "the offspring of Russian born parents and grandparents," and that the work demanding "special knowledge" was too highly classified to be open to citizens of complex genealogies. There was now no recognition of my status as an Orientalist and I found myself assigned to the fourteenth Staffordshire Regiment and thence successively to Hereford in the west country adjoining Wales, and thereafter to Great Yarmouth in East Anglia. I could not hope for salvation from Weizmann, since his own son, Michael, was denied service in Intelligence, whereupon he enlisted in the Royal Air Force where he met a heroic but tragic end.

Few memories of Hereford linger on, and it had seemed useless at the time to ask for what possible contingency of Hitlerite invasion Hereford would seem relevant. Yet it was in the rolling verdure of Hereford that I received the harrowing news of the savage bombardment of London and the triumphant response of the British air force. And it was there that, as the Intelligence officer of our battalion, I got the message of the alert prior to the expected invasion date of September 15, 1940. The function of the duty officer was to be discreetly and intimately aware of the places of diversion or assignation where officers could be found in an emergency, and I found that my conjectures had a high degree of accuracy.

Yarmouth, unlike Hereford, could, by energetic imagination, be represented as an invasion target and the senior commanders, zealous for morale, expressed with certainty that the invasion would commence at Yarmouth. To believe this it was necessary to assume that the Germans would wish to cross a body of water three times wider than that which would await them if they chose to come from Calais or Dover or even Dieppe. This was a transparent illusion, but my service in Yarmouth at least brought the war into the frame of reality. There were German air raids, long periods of listening to Churchillian oratory charged with defiance and hope, and there was need for vigilant watch against possible invasion attempts. As Intelligence officer, I was equipped with a motorcycle with which to scour the Norfolk countryside and also with a green arm band. These assets gave me a status with the feminine sector of the Yarmouth citizenry that it would have been sheer folly not to exploit. But it had no relevance whatever to my Zionist purpose.

My year on the East Anglian coast gave me a macabre insight into British unpreparedness. One morning the brigade commander requested me to cooperate with a visiting expert from General Headquarters. His name was Captain Oliver Messel and he was well known to theatergoers as a skillful designer of scenery for plays. Messel asked me for what he assumed to be my expert East Anglian advice on the possible location of pillboxes and anti-tank emplacements on the hills and beaches whereon Churchill had promised that we would all be fighting. We had no hills or landing grounds to worry about. Messel hastened to assure me that nothing lethal was contemplated even for the beaches. There was no question of real tanks and guns. His task was to create various cardboard structures that would give German reconnaissance pilots an impression of immense and insuperable British power, ready to spring with tigerish ferocity at the throat of an invader. I have often felt that historians have not given due credit to the camouflage artists for their efficiency in deterring invasions without expenditure of ammunition.

The slow mills of influence and destiny were grinding away, and by the end of 1941 I was posted to an anonymous destination that I knew to be the Middle Eastern command. The revolutionary idea that men endowed with knowledge of Middle Eastern languages might be more useful in the Middle East than in an office in London was apparently winning ground even in Whitehall, and Weizmann's office had put in some protectionist words. The letter posting me to the Middle East was a turning point for me.

My journey to the Middle East, with the Land of Israel as its destination, began somewhat eccentrically at Lincoln College, Oxford, where a group of officers were assembled for later embarkation at Liverpool. A glance at the map would not have told us that we would be at sea for five weeks. The alternative to arrival at the Middle East by such a circuitous route would have been not to arrive at all, for the German submarines were rampant, as if to atone for Germany's failure to win command of British skies. This British success meant that there was little prospect of an invading army crossing into Britain. There was an air of pride in London, the like of which had not been known for many years. The loss of 700 fighting pilots, "the few to whom the many owed so much" as Churchill described them, had set a limit to rejoicing, but it was plain that the Mediterranean and Europe would now be theaters for Western initiatives and that the period of defensive entrenchment was over. To leave London for the Mediterranean was not to run away from the war but to move toward it.

Lincoln College, Oxford, is not the most famous house in that university, but it acknowledges Dr. Samuel Johnson as its alumnus and some of the more jocular officers began all their sentences with "Sir" in a genial mockery of Johnsonian diction. The Lincoln College wine cellar would be worthy of better-endowed colleges and I have recently heard that it has not recovered from our depredations to this day. My mother and my sister Carmel, who was then an undergraduate at Oxford before serving in the women's naval service, were there for the farewells and we spent a broodingly silent evening with a ritual theater visit to a trivial Ivor Novello play. The question when, and even if, we would meet again sat heavy in the air but without coming to expression. Five years would pass before I would see my family again.

It was an age of uncertainty in which life held no stabilities, in which personal horizons were measured in short spaces of expectation. There was no recourse but to live each passing day. Nothing, not even survival, could be counted on, but when I embarked for the Middle East aboard the troopship that had recently been the luxury liner *Orcades*, I had the sentiment of spiritual homecoming, not of outward journey.

The troopship *Orcades* on which I embarked at Liverpool was tense with apprehension. It sailed a tortuous course to avoid lurking German submarines. Yet the presentiment of danger was lived in a curious social context. The British caste system was enacted on board without substantial change. The accepted terminology, offensive to both sides, was "officers and men." The officers were the first-class passengers, enjoying luxury liner facilities that few of them would have been able to afford in peacetime at their own expense. The "men," alternatively described as "other ranks," lived in more crowded conditions, but still more commodiously than in the army camps and barracks from which they had converged.

For many weeks the *Orcades* was home. The library was surprisingly well equipped, and I was in no danger of being trampled underfoot by crowds of officers in search of enlightenment. It was on the *Orcades* that I learned about Pearl Harbor on December 21, 1941, from a scratchy ship's radio that later broadcast Churchill's buoyant speech to the United States Congress. ("What sort of people do they think we are?") There was much speculation about where we would land for refueling and supplies. Suddenly one morning the ship's porthole framed a majestic landscape of green hills, white houses and an inconceivable blueness of water in a curved bay. We were permitted to exult openly. We were in Capetown.

I had never taken the fact of my birth in Capetown very seriously. How could anyone show greater indifference than by "deciding" to leave a country at the age of seven months, returning after twenty-six years only in response to a military order? Whatever I knew about South Africa pertained to its Jewish community, composed of Lithuanian Jews who were stalwart Zionists and who, in the event of emigration, were more likely to seek the Land of Israel than some new exile such as San Diego or Houston, which are their popular destinations today. Beyond this ethnocentric Jewish vision I thought only of the tension between the country's splendid landscapes and the volcanic human condition. It was evident that explosion was only a matter of brief time, unless, unexpectedly, it could be defused by statesmanship.

In the event, the four days in Capetown could be spent freely by day on condition of returning by night to what we were now calling "our ship." The unconcealed lights of the vessel were the portent of the warless world to which we wondered if Europe would ever return. For me Capetown was not one city among others. I made a swift reconnaissance of the main streets, which led me to a musty building that announced itself with a brass plate as the Zionist headquarters. Inside, I saw a picture on the wall in the brownish tint of the formal photography of those years. When I drew closer I saw an inscription on the photograph. It was dedicated to my father and mother. The sight of this utter stranger, of diminutive height and serene countenance, who was my father, smiling down at my mother sent a gooseflesh sensation through my body and mind. Avram Meir Solomon, a solid merchant and civic leader, had been a pillar of Zionism in Capetown and it was natural for his fellow Zionists to celebrate his leadership and devotion. It was his ravaged body that my mother had tended on the troopship that slowly sailed with him and her, my sister Ruth, aged two, and with me, aged seven months, on the way to London in the dangerous days of World War I.

A few more telephone calls and I was reunited with an aunt and first cousins. It appeared that on my birth my father's sister had put aside a bottle of wine to be opened ceremonially on my bar mitzvah or on my first visit to Capetown. The number of years that had passed in the calendars was exactly twice-thirteen, and we opened the bottle, pretended to admire the fermented taste of its contents and drank a toast to our common grandfathers and to the joy of reunion. The Capetonian birth had come to life more vividly than ever before. I had always regarded it as a statistical accident, and it has played no part in my life's journey. Israel, Britain and America have nourished me in their different ways, but the photo on the Capetown wall jolted me into recollection of my early orphanhood.

There was neither time nor mood to see anything of the paradox of South Africa's political structure, but war brings curious reunions. Shopping in the business center, I spied a blond head across a narrow street, and there was Teddy Kollek, of subsequent fame as the mayor of Jerusalem, who, unbeknown to me, was a fellow traveler in the same convoy of forty ships, though not a fellow passenger on the *Orcades*. It would be an exaggeration to say that I was surprised, for there is no place on the globe where one would be astonished to meet Teddy, and my own schedules have never been unduly static.

It was hard to imagine that there would be many more episodes of consequence if I spent more days as an officer on shore leave in Capetown. I felt no tug of sentimental regret when the *Orcades* weighed anchor and sailed northward toward the Suez Canal.

Five weeks later we reached Port Said. The SS *Orcades* sailed back toward England. On its way it was torpedoed and sunk. There were no survivors.

Cairo has been described too often to arouse astonishment in a newcomer, but in early 1942 when I first came there, it had attributes that it does not possess today. It was a city of many layers, with divergent experiences set one atop the other without any apparent necessity to modify their separation or even to acknowledge each other's existence. It was an Arab Muslim city, the center of its particular world, seething with nationalist resentments and passions. But it was also a British base whose massive dimensions were illustrated by the abundant soldiery that took possession of its major avenues, its fashionable Gezira Club, its only air-conditioned cinemas, which I would visit in summer for coolness irrespective of the film, and, above all, its famous pastry and ice cream shop owned by the Swiss proprietors Groppi. Together, and yet not really together with all this, was a medley of societies, British, French, Greek, Italian, Jewish and Copt. Each of them knew its place and kept its own counsel within its private domain. There was every gradation of class and rank from indecent luxury to abject squalor, the latter borne with a certain docility by a populace seeming to accept its condition as a kind of legacy that would be transmitted onward pretty much as it had been inherited from an incomparably lengthy past. Egyptians ruling and being ruled by each other, subdued by every succeeding external domination known to history, are profusely documented in literature and art. There is no recorded history of a world without Egypt.

Its modern condition, as I found it, was enlivened by the way in which the diversity of colors, sounds, passions, tastes and smells interacted in the streets without ever impinging on the hermetic separation of homes.

This versatile experience was being enacted in a strange political context. In theory Egypt was a sovereign state, the heart and center of the Arab world and Islam. In practice the British military command felt no constraints arising from the authority of King Farouk and his administration. It was possible that the British had to inform the Egyptian government of an intention to hold superpower summit meetings in Cairo. It was certain that Egypt had no capacity of refusal. Real power did not rest with the king's grotesquely vulgar court or with the Cabinet of Moustafa al-Nahas Pasha, the leader of the Wafd Party, which had led Egypt to such degree of independence as it purported to exercise. It reposed solidly in the British Embassy, which was more like a colonial government headquarters led by the assertive and dominant ambassador, Sir Miles Lampson. On his elevation to the British peerage, Lampson took the name and title of Lord Killearn. It was told that an English lady who had not followed this mutation and had not known His Excellency's outward aspect had encountered him at a cocktail party and asked who he was. "I'm Lord Killearn, the British ambassador," he replied. "Thank God they've taken that idiot Lampson away," came the devout and emphatic reaction.

This epithet did no justice to Killearn's astuteness and intelligence, but nor did he do much by way of tact to conceal the truth about the real power balance. There was the paradox of a double-tiered country with a monarchy and Parliament side by side and yet not contiguous with a foreign power living in a totally separate field. While I was in Cairo, there was a divergence of view and policy between the Egyptian monarch and the British Embassy. Lord Killearn simply conveyed himself to the palace accompanied by a tank. He naturally got his way.

No wonder that a fierce nationalist resentment seethed and flowed in Egypt like a volcanic rumbling under the exterior surface of mutual understanding. We now know how young Egyptian officers, like Anwar Sadat, were preparing their anti-monarchical and anti-British revolt in the rare intervals between their jail sentences. Meanwhile, the proximity of General Rommel's German legions in the western desert, near Tobruk, added to the surrealist pattern. In February 1942, when I first came to Cairo, I felt closer to the deadly Nazi danger than at any time during my military service on the eastern coast of England, when the Nazi hordes were geographically closer but separated from my brigade by a comforting stretch of water.

As the weeks went by I was haunted by the fear that my journey to the Middle East would end in anticlimax with a tedious, prolonged ordeal of useless routine. My Whitehall officer, who had spoken of a place where my special knowledge "would be useful," must have had an unusually mischievous sense of humor. My task, as it turned out, was to censor local newspapers and letters in Arabic from Libyan soldiers serving with the British army in Cyrenaica. Many of my learned acquaintances had experienced the deflationary process of being employed below the level of their attainments. Unlike most of these, I could seek alleviation in a world of kindred spirits outside the military bureaucracy. I used my Cambridge status and my academic contacts to form a relationship with Arab writers. First among these was the novelist and essayist Taha Hussein, whose repute and genius lifted him above his contemporaries in what I discovered to be a fertile period for Egyptian letters.

The wrenching pathos of Taha Hussein's existence springs to life in his own writings. Born in a poor Egyptian village, he had lost his sight in infancy. He sought and obtained erudition by frequenting the discourse of scholars and preachers around the Al Azhar University. His fame had surged with the publication of his autobiographical novel, *Al Ayyam (The Days)*, in which he set out the story of his triumphant struggle to transcend the darkness of his world by brilliant shafts of luminous imagination. I had read and re-searched the life and work of a medieval writer and poet, Abu-l-Ala al Ma'arri, whose blindness suggested the parallel of Taha Hussein. As I sat in Taha's house with him and his beautiful French wife, who seemed to know no Arabic, I felt that I was at the peak and center of a new Mediterranean culture.

Taha Hussein had used his prestige to embark on an audacious attempt to redefine his nation's cultural identity. His book *Mustaqbal al Thaqafa fi Misr*[2] had been published shortly before my arrival in Cairo, and it was a source of passionate and sometimes stormy debate. Taha Hussein observed that Arab culture and Islam did not exhaust or even dominate Egypt's modern destiny. The West, which had enslaved the Arab world by its power, held the secret of Arab regeneration. Egypt's history had flowed not toward the desert in the east, but toward the Mediterranean, where Alexandria had interacted with ancient Athens and thence with Italy and Spain. The institu-tions and science of the West had conquered the world of power. Whatever had subdued Egypt in the past could now be co-opted by the Arabs and open great windows for the future. A synthesis of Mediterranean standards and values with a rejuvenated and tolerant vision of the Muslim legacy could guide Egypt's steps into a new world of sensibility and feeling.

Thus wrote Taha Hussein. I felt that his detachment from the Arab and Muslim context had been stated too drastically, but in general, I was cap-tivated by his vision. He was right to point out that from the Pharaonic period, with its massive and glorious monuments, and later from the era of Hellenism, Egypt had received a legacy that it did not share with other Arabs. Egypt celebrated its Arabism with a certain measure of aloofness. This was even symbolized by its attitude to the Jews and Zionism. There was no doubt about Egypt's reservations and its solidarity with the Palestinians across the Sinai desert, but there was a Zionist office in Cairo and Zionist leaders, including the illustrious Weizmann himself, would routinely sign the distin-guished visitors book at the Royal Palace and sometimes conduct a conversa-tion with Arab leaders without the furtive concealment that would become the rule in later years.

Cairo was not an uninteresting place, and my contacts with some of its writers and newspaper editors saved me from the wasteland atmosphere of my official duties. But these activities and encounters could only partly compensate for the fact that I seemed no closer to a posting in Jerusalem than I had been a year before. The salient fact was that my work in the military headquarters was barren of emotional or intellectual satisfactions. It was at this stage of gloom and despondency that deliverance came.

---

[2] *The Future of Culture in Egypt*

I had written to Moshe Sharett, the head of the Zionist Organization's Political Department, who later became Israel's first foreign minister. He was a close friend of my family. I told him of my proximity to Jerusalem, which made me weep by the river Nile on account of my continued exile. Whenever I met him in London he, more than anyone, had persuaded me to regard whatever I was doing at any particular time as no more than a prelude to joining him in the Zionist service. He was an impressive combination of intellectual energy with a refined moral sense. He was very meticulous in expression.

To this day he is the only one of Israel's eight prime ministers to have graduated in a full course at a university. He rebelled against the autodidactic tradition of Israeli leaders by insisting on precision, very often more persistently than his colleagues, including Ben-Gurion, were willing to endure.

He was also isolated from many of his more passionate contemporaries by his close understanding of the Middle East and his fluent command of Arabic. He did not have the charisma of Weizmann or the power of decision that characterized Ben-Gurion, but he was more likely than Ben-Gurion to weigh the moral implications and the immediate consequences of decisions and utterances. Above all, he was a man of devout fidelity to reason and humane feeling and his personal loyalties were strong.

Sharett answered my letter in warm and intimate tones. He added cryptically that I would hear from him further in a few days. It was nevertheless a surprise a week later when a voice on the telephone announced itself as that of Reuven Shiloah, who had left Jerusalem for Cairo the previous night.

Reuven Shiloah will appear later in this book as my second in command at our embassy in Washington in the late 1950s. But his formal rank has never fully expressed his complex personality. He is popularly and accurately known as the first architect of Israel's Intelligence system. The term "Israeli Intelligence" usually appears in contemporary novels and articles as an intimation of infallibility. My recollection is that our Intelligence estimates informed me in May 1967 that there was no danger of war because Nasser was "bogged down in Yemen" and in early October 1973 that there was no danger of war since the vast Egyptian troop concentrations were there for maneuvers. The unpredicted war broke out in 1967 a month after the affirmation that it would not erupt. In 1973 the estimate was refuted by war twenty hours after the reassuring diagnosis. On the other hand, the Israeli secret services, however weak in analyzing Arab political calculations, have recorded extraordinary achievements in the field of action, such as the rescue of hostages in Entebbe and the precise identification of Egyptian air locations in June 1967.

Reuven watched over the development of the Intelligence community with relentless zeal from its early beginnings. He was willing to work anonymously to the ultimate point of exhaustion, and gave Ben-Gurion his blind allegiance and total service. In the course of his career he developed personal characteristics that conformed with his "cloak and dagger" image. We once hailed a taxi in London and when the driver inquired courteously where he wanted to go, Reuven delayed his reply for an inordinately long time. He clearly regarded the very question as an intrusion into his private life and as a temptation to violate the national security.

When we met the following day at the Continental Hotel, Reuven told me a story that stunned me with its audacity and gave me a redeeming moment of personal satisfaction. It was clear that I might soon celebrate escape from the grim prospect of fruitless routine in the Cairo office. The story began, as did most stories in those days, with Winston Churchill. It appears that Churchill was in deep rage at the ease with which the large British garrison in Singapore had surrendered to the Japanese. There was a similar disgrace at Tobruk during the war in Egypt's western desert. The prime minister had resolved that German armies must pay with many lives, both in countries that they already occupied and in countries that they might overrun in future advances. An organization called SOE,[3] operating under a ministry in Whitehall, would train Palestinian Jews for a scorched-earth and guerrilla operation in the macabre event of a German Nazi conquest of Palestine. Young Jews of appropriate qualifications and origins would be disguised as Arabs to work against the Germans in the event of a German conquest of Palestine; or to be disguised as Hungarians or Yugoslavs who could parachute behind the lines in East European countries where they would join local partisans and reinforce resistance by Jews. This would involve close cooperation between British Intelligence and the Haganah and Palmach. These were theoretically "underground" organizations, but their name and fame were familiar to everybody in the country, including the British authorities themselves.

The crux of the problem was that since the Chamberlain government's White Paper in May 1939, Britain and the Zionists were in relations close to hostility. The position now to be created would be one that could only be sustained in war and only by governments, like the British, of pragmatic temperament. There would be one level of cooperation—between Haganah and British Intelligence—and another level of frank political conflict—between the British high commissioner and the Zionist institutions. The two parties, Britain and the Jews, would be allies in one department and opponents in another.

This subtle and complex operation would need the enlistment of a liaison officer who would command the confidence both of the Zionist leadership and of the British military command. He would have to abstain from revealing the identities of Haganah trainees and would also have to maintain his fidelity to British military structures. While Sharett and Shiloah were ponder-

<hr>

[3]Subversive Operations Executive

ing how to square this circle, they providentially received my letter announcing my presence in Cairo. Reuven Shiloah's job now was to receive British sanction for my employment in this unique capacity and to arrange for my transfer to Jerusalem, where a headquarters of SOE would be established. A camp in the woods of Kibbutz Mishmar Ha'emek would be the assembly point and training ground for the hundreds of Palmach warriors who would be organized, trained and financed by British authorities.

Everything in my personal position was now falling into place. I would be able to contribute to the Allied war effort, to advance a Zionist interest and also to be in legitimate contact with the Zionist leadership. The job seemed custom made.

I was interviewed in Cairo by Wing Commander Domville, the representative of the SOE, and within a single day I was in a train bound for Jerusalem.

There was a springtime gentleness in the Palestine landscape that I saw for the first time when the train crossed the Egyptian-Palestinian frontier at Kantara and ground to a screeching halt at a small village station announcing itself as Rehovot. The intoxicating scent of orange blossom from the dark green citrus orchards and the Hebrew signposts at the station were my first indications of being in the Zionist domain. In England and, as I was to discover, still more in America, the Land of Israel was an issue, a problem, a debate, a vision and a dream. At the Rehovot railway junction it could be sniffed and smelled as a reality. In the deepest emotional and spiritual sense I had come home to the place where Jewish history has its origin and destination. And if the appalling boxlike structures of Tel Aviv put my Zionist devotion to the test of incredulous shock, the scenic beauties of other parts of the land gave large compensation. I was reminded of George Adam Smith's resonant celebration of the landscapes: "Men who looked at life under that lofty imagination did not always notice the details of the country's scenery. What failed them was the sense of space and distance, stupendous contrast of desert and fertility, straight coasts breaking into foam, the swift sunrise, and if these great outlines are touched here and there with flowers or a mist or a quiet pool or an olive tree in the sunshine, it is to illustrate human beauty which comes upon the earth as fair as her wild flowers, and as quickly passes away. . . ."[4]

The reality would not always show itself with gentle face. It was full of ambivalence. The Jewish sector of Palestine seemed surprisingly fragile and limited in the spring of 1942. There was nothing that could be called stability. But Jewish Palestine already communicated an immense atmospheric power. It came from a subconscious intuition in the hearts of visitors that great mysteries had been enacted in that place.

---

[4]George Adam Smith, *A Historical Geography of the Holy Land* (London: Kegan Paul, 1891).

It was already a more impressive reality than could be deduced from the bland slogans of Diaspora Zionism, from which my disillusion was becoming complete. Henceforth, whatever the future might bring for me would be linked with this reality. My personal story would be part of a larger design. The natural contours of the land were gracious, but the human situation was volcanic. The only certainty was that within a decade or less there would have to be a decision that would engage the entire human scene.

2

PALESTINE IN WORLD
WAR II

MINE WAS NO ordinary Zionist arrival. It was not the standard story of a pilgrim or settler landing at Haifa and embarking on a process of what is now called "absorption." I certainly had no problem of employment or housing. An army driver saluted the three stars of captaincy glittering on my shoulders, and took me deferentially from the Jerusalem railway station to a distinguished-looking house in the Talbiya area. I was introduced to the two officers who had established the SOE Jerusalem headquarters. The SOE commander was Major General B. T. Wilson, an Ulster loyalist of impeccable manners. He was a man of few words, which were, however, more than adequate to cover the entire range of his thoughts. The field commander of our operation was Colonel Basil Ringrose, who had to divide his loyalties between the SOE that employed him and the Palestine administration, which was, in effect, our sworn departmental enemy. Ringrose was known for the excitement that he aroused in the feminine part of the British community. This was not surprising, since his debonair, optimistic attitudes and his physical resemblance to such matinee idols as David Niven gave our stern project a misleading aspect of serene hedonism. At one stage we were joined by Captain Anthony Webb, who confessed to me that he had been a law student but had found law to be very boring. I never found out if he changed his mind after serving as chief justice of Kenya.

General B. T. Wilson was both embarrassed and proud to be confused with another General (Maitland) Wilson, who was in command of all the British forces in the Mediterranean. He told me that in his opinion our operation in training Jewish partisans would be "quite straightforward." I thought it premature to express my conviction that "straightforwardness" was just about the last quality that we could expect. We were establishing a small but very official cell of intimate cooperation between a British government agency and the mainstream Jewish resistance organization. These two "partners" were in a state of suspended war in all domains outside our particular operation. Britain was the adversary of the Jews in Middle Eastern politics and their ally in the war against Hitler. Our cooperation would, at best, go forward in an atmosphere of paradox and ambivalence in a country whose government, led by the high commissioner and the secretariat, would be hostile to what we were doing and restrained from overt opposition only by the overpowering authority of Prime Minister Winston Churchill. In our times, if a novelist were to describe the structure and environment of our SOE mission, the critics would accuse him of taking his fantasies beyond the point of credibility.

The exceptionality of my own position was brought home to me even more sharply the next day when I went to Tel Aviv and had meetings with Berl Katznelson, Moshe Sharett and Eliahu Golomb. Looking back, I become increasingly moved by the fact that on the second day after my arrival in Jerusalem I could have serious discourse with three such historic figures. At the ripe age of twenty-seven, I was evidently viewing Zionism from the top. These three were, by any criterion, among the central authority figures in Jewish Palestine. They were all solid men, rooted in the Labor movement that was then—and has never ceased to be—the main source and cradle of Israel's defense leadership.

Berl Katznelson was in a special tradition of Zionist and, later, of Israeli, leaders whose position and prestige were never defined in terms of their official status. His role was rather like that of Mahatma Gandhi in the Indian Congress Party, in that he wielded an influence generated by his moral authority and by the intuitive tendency of his movement to defer to his judgments. But he did not have the Mahatma's pacifist temperament. He had a tragic vision of Jewish history. He believed that the Jewish people was inexorably condemned to accept conflict and struggle as the keynote of its journey and that any gains would have to be arduously won. His strength lay in his ability to articulate Zionist values in the spirit of a secular son of the Enlightenment with a respectful but not orthodox attitude to Jewish traditions. He had a sincere reverence for language and culture. He conceived that his mission was to prepare the ground for a new Zionist leadership, dominated less by East European experience and more by Jews from the English-speaking world, since it was that world, in its British and American expressions, that would shape the Jewish future in the forthcoming decades. He had visited London while I was an undergraduate at Cambridge and Moshe Sharett brought him to our home, which was frequented regularly by visiting Zionist leaders in tribute to my mother's long Zionist connections. With his outrageously negligent habits of dress, his tousled, disorderly hair and his bushy moustache, he was a disconcerting spectacle in London and, still more, when he visited Cambridge in search of recruits for Zionist service. His objective was to cajole or attract young Jews with strong academic attainments and a talent for public service into the service of a rejuvenated Zionist leadership. He had set his eyes on me, on Isaiah Berlin, who had begun to teach and lecture at Oxford, and on a Cambridge economist in the "nursery" of John Maynard Keynes named Richard Kahn, who as Lord Kahn became a leading figure in the Cambridge Economics School. I thought that Berl's ambition to pull Isaiah Berlin and Richard Kahn ashore was likely to fail, largely because they lacked one advantage that I was, by stroke of fortune, able to deploy, namely, a total familiarity with the Hebrew tongue.

Immigrants to Israel from the West have often confessed to me that the language barrier is the greatest obstacle to their integration. "Suddenly," explained one of them, "I became deaf and dumb, unable to communicate my thoughts or to listen to those of others." The greater the conceptual range and the power of abstraction and nuance in a thinker and writer, the less content will he be with the thin diet supplied by intensive courses of colloquial Hebrew. I have no doubt that whatever Grandfather Sacks intended, his eager transfer of his Hebrew legacy to me was the most determining event in my life story.

Berl reflected on these and other themes with intense and rapid spurts of speech in the study of his small house on one of those Tel Aviv streets where the walls of houses had begun to flake almost as soon as they were built. He sighed sadly when I expressed my own impression that while Zionism was the central movement in Jewish life, the bulk of the intellectual and material resources of the Jewish people were still to be found outside the Land of Israel and would so remain except in the event of a Jewish catastrophe in the English-speaking world. Berl, whose contact with Western Jews had been minimal, absorbed this disconcerting realism with a sigh of reluctant agreement, but added in a strangely hopeful air that there was enough catastrophe in the other sectors of the Jewish world to nourish a great flood of immigration if only the doors could be opened soon.

The table and surrounding chairs in Berl's room were flooded with papers and volumes in chaotic profusion. He had a simple method of dealing with this problem: When the table became so overloaded that his head barely appeared above the papers, he would give the mountainous accumulation a gentle push, enabling some of the material to spill onto the floor to make room for newly acquired enthusiasms. When all this was beyond management, he would get up and go for a brisk walk, presumably hoping that one of his many disciples in the party would introduce relative order into the chaos of his home. This was his solution during our conversation. Seizing the cloth cap which was then the symbol of working-class solidarities, he hurried me out into the street toward the house that was Moshe Sharett's family abode during his frequent journeys from Jerusalem.

This was an intimate meeting. Sharett was then Moshe Shertok. The transmutation of his name arose from the later insistence of the nation's founders on eliminating any indication that they had a pre-state incarnation in such places as Russia, Poland or Germany. In some cases, this caused aesthetic relief through curtailment of the "inskys" and "ovitches," but as a general maxim I doubted the underlying logic. I have been more attracted to the pride of the American people in handing down their Dutch, Scottish, Irish, Italian, Russian and other ethnic names in tribute to ancestors and as reminders of a melting-pot tradition. In later years there would develop a ridiculous rumor that Sharett had been deputed to persuade the great Chaim Weizmann to Hebraize his name. Weizmann had replied calmly: "Unlike many others, I have a name to lose." Weizmann ended facetiously by promising to change his name to Degani (a man of wheat) if his dead predecessor, Theodor Herzl, would change his name to "Levavi" (man of the heart).

One of the Labor leaders who declined to follow the name-changing addiction was the first Knesset speaker, Yosef S(h)printzak. I commended him on this, saying that, after all, few people have names that are exactly identical with the sound produced by opening a bottle of champagne or soda.

At our first meeting after my arrival in Palestine, Shertok (Sharett) rejoiced at my "rescue" from the Cairo General Staff and my integration into the strange collaboration with a British Intelligence agency. Sharett was everything that most of his colleagues in the Zionist leadership were not: methodical, precise, punctilious and academically well endowed. He commanded many languages, most of them with accurate syntax though perceptibly accentuated, and his command of Hebrew was a joy to listeners, on condition that he abstained from correcting their grammar. He was not always resistant to this temptation, and not all his colleagues enjoyed the habit. He liked exactitude and clear definitions, remote from the fantasizing habits that had carried Zionism to many disappointments, but also to some successes. He was animated by a profound moral sense, but not to the extent of vanishing into an unreal world. His advice to his associates in politics and diplomacy was salutary and more concise than most of his discourse. He urged each of us to ask himself two questions: "Is my proposed action right?" "What will be the result?" The second question often irritated the more visionary Zionists, who preferred to correct errors, if at all, after they had become almost incurable. Sharett's love of precision and restraint made him very acceptable to practitioners of diplomacy, and his place in history as the founder of Israel's foreign service is beyond challenge.

My first Tel Aviv day was completed by a meeting with Eliahu Golomb, the leader of the allegedly underground military organization, the Haganah. The homes of Labor leaders in Tel Aviv were all of similar austerity, although that of Ben-Gurion would gradually be extended to make provision for the possibility of receiving distinguished guests. Golomb looked and acted as though he had no other ambition than to discredit the conventional view of what a commander of a national revolt should look like. Small of stature, tranquil and slow in movement, ostensibly detached from any conception of power, he looked more like a pale, gentle graduate from a Talmudic academy than like the popular image of an underground leader. With him I had concrete business to transact: The issue was how to protect our project from the general atmosphere of mutual acrimony that surrounded the relations between the British government and the Zionist leadership. I could already foresee a very likely scenario of conflict. What would happen, for example, if Palmach trainees were caught with weapons? To serve the SOE against Hitler involved the carrying of weapons, and this might involve a capital offense against the Draconian laws of the Palestine administration. My signature could transmute a violation of Palestinian law into a virtuous act of service to the SOE. In the twilight between conflicting policies and loyalties I would have the power to release some Palmach warriors from what would otherwise be a danger to their liberty or to their very lives. I saw no reason to apply this unusual authority with excessive rigor.

A few days in Tel Aviv were enough for me to have a sense of attachment. The feeling of escape from academic limitation and bureaucratic routine gave me profound relief. I made my journey back to Jerusalem along a road with seven sharp curves, called the "Seven Sisters Road," which was so tortuous that it seemed to express an unexpected sense of humor in the Turkish government that had planned its course. There were then not even a twentieth part of the million vehicles that use Israel's roads today, and as I chugged along the narrow ribbon of asphalt, I must have been an exotic spectacle. For mysterious reasons, the SOE had provided me, not with a military vehicle, but with a white Plymouth convertible of which the roof could be retracted with a switch on the dashboard. This car was a wondrous innovation in those days, but it looked more like a facility for a young officer's nocturnal flirtations than like an instrument for serious military purposes. It seemed extraordinary that this vehicle could have been considered for import by an allegedly secret organization, since it ensured that my conveyance would be the most distinctive vehicle in the country except for the high commissioner's Rolls-Royce.

Later, in my first week in Jerusalem, I made contact with Palestinian Arabs who had been my neighbors at Queens' College, Cambridge, or my opponents in Cambridge Union debates. I was already able to reflect that my experiences were at variance with the social norms that had prevailed in Jerusalem society for generations—and which, alas, govern the city again today. I hardly ever met anyone else in Palestine in those days who moved as freely as I did among the Jewish, British and Arab worlds.

Jerusalem, so often idealized as a symbol of cosmic unity, is in sad reality a model of eternal divisiveness, irrespective of the successive jurisdictions under which it is held. Never in human history have so many people lived so close together in such an intricate web of mutual antagonisms. All the sects and faiths have jealously guarded their separate social contexts. Indeed, the acknowledgment of their separateness is the basic condition of their peaceful coexistence; always side by side, or one over the other, never intertwined. An Israeli writer, Amos Elon, has penetratingly observed that the "mosaic" metaphor attributed to Jerusalem is misleading, since in a mosaic the various parts make a design, whereas in Jerusalem there is no design, no harmony and no coalescence between the separate parts.

After a brief period of acclimatization I worked with the SOE officers and Jewish Agency representatives on the plan that had come from London via Cairo for action by the SOE mission in Jerusalem. It seemed wildly eccentric, but it was ennobled by a measure of originality that merited respect even from those who doubted its chances of implementation. It was based on the possibility of a German conquest of Palestine. Anyone who looked at a map of the area in early 1942 would have had to admit that this was not a farfetched contingency. The German armies were not far from Alexandria, and I knew enough from my own access to Intelligence reports to understand that a single German armored breakthrough would expose Jewish Palestine to the fate of Belgium and the Netherlands. The author of the plan approved by the British services was Yochanan Ratner, a professor at the Haifa Technical Institute and one of the Haganah's leading advisers. It was called the Palestine Post-Occupational Scheme. The central base would be a camp in the woods of Kibbutz Mishmar Ha'emek, near Haifa, where hundreds of Jewish volunteers would receive training in guerrilla tactics, night attacks, ambush and sabotage. The manpower would be drawn from Palmach, the striking force of the Haganah. ("Palmach" is an acronym for the Hebrew "plugot machats," which denotes "striking force.") Bridges would be mined and caves prepared as guerrilla hideouts, all in the northern area of the country in the vicinity of Haifa and Mount Carmel. In addition, some German-speaking and Arabic-speaking Palmachniks would be trained for espionage tasks. These would not necessarily be carried out in Palestine. There was already talk of parachute drops by Jewish volunteers into Hungary, Romania and Yugoslavia for the purpose of reinforcing partisan groups and making contact with demoralized Jewish communities. The plan conceived by Ratner, spearheaded by the Haganah command under Yitshak Sadeh and nourished with equipment and funding by the British services, had a sweep and dynamism that took it a long way from the ritual context of conventional warfare. I reflected that if this kind of thinking had animated the British and French armies in the early period of the war, the fiascoes of the early 1940s with their Maginot illusions and Dunkirk consolations might not have been the whole story of the war against Hitler. The shocks and humiliations of shameful surrenders by British armies at Singapore and Tobruk were being transmuted under Churchill's personal influence and with the aid of creative eccentrics like Mountbatten into a new dimension of belligerency. At this stage the commando mystique was making headway in military thought. The dividend for me lay in the sophistication of working at a point of junction between two worlds. I enjoyed the challenge of reconciling the British with the Zionist interest.

Above all, I was exposed to an intimate and trustful relationship with a sector of Palestinian youth of which I would have had no direct cognizance in the stuffy debating chambers of Diaspora Zionism.

The first Israeli-born generations were marked by a total dissimilarity between their parents and themselves. Parents and children belonged to different worlds. The parents had been obsessed by sensitive problems of identity and an unceasing search for pride in non-Jewish environments that were usually hostile. Their sons and daughters had no such reflective ordeals; their image of themselves was as clear as the summer sun and just as uncomplicated. They spent little thought in speculating on the meaning of human existence or of Jewish destiny. Their speech was laconic, concrete and down to earth, in manifest revolt against the diffuse and sentimental style of their European-born elders. Yet beneath their restrained aspect they were fervently devoted to their soil and tongue, and those among them who were kibbutzniks had a noble volunteering tradition. If the nation called, they would quietly answer. The great majority of the Palmach trainees whom I reviewed at Mishmar Ha'emek were schooled in the agricultural villages of the Labor movement. The collective principle dominated their civilian lives and made the transition to army establishments relatively serene.

The brief and transitory cooperation between Britain and the best youth of Jewish Palestine left some traces behind. Although it had been agreed that "only 600" men would receive training at Mishmar Ha'emek, I "interpreted" this as allowing that number to be on parade at any given time. Palmach benefited greatly from being able to train without official harassment and with the aid and cover of the very British government that would become their political adversary after the war.

There could be no "enjoyment" for me in the SOE venture, for it was based on the horrific prospect of a German-Nazi conquest of Palestine. In the event of such a contingency, I would remain in the country, directing resistance activities from a secret cave that the thoughtful and scholarly Ratner had designated for me. This arrangement had its logic: as Ratner said to me consolingly, it offered me everything that could be desired except a possibility of survival.

I was moved and impressed by the skill and high morale of the young Zionist warriors. I made some lasting friendships among them, especially with Yigal Allon, who a few years later would be leading military formations in victorious defense of a State of Israel.

Serious military and political historians of the period attest to the substantial service that the SOE project rendered to Israel's strength and survival in the eventual war of independence. The history has been most fully researched by Yehuda Bauer, who has written:

> Partnership with the British was the factor which made possible the development of the Palmach during and after the year of El Alamein. . . .
>
> The English officers with whom they worked were interesting personalities. First and foremost there was Captain Abba Eban, who had previously worked in the Political Department of the Jewish Agency in

London and was of great help when there were quarrels with the British. . . .

The British, of course, only approved a 500 man "reserve." However, the whole Palmach was introduced to the course and the 600 man figure (100 nucleus and 500 reserve) underwent some stretching as the need arose. . . .

I had a lot to do with the "stretching." It is with a measure of pride that I record Bauer's summarizing judgment:

The Mishmar Ha'emek chapter had ended rapidly, but its achievements were lasting. For the first time an independent Jewish force was created. It was to become an appreciable force in the defense of the country. . . .[1]

At the time, I assumed that our project at Mishmar Ha'emek was one of several elements in an impressive network of schemes for bringing an effective Jewish fighting force to birth. Subsequent research tells me that this was about all that existed in that particular field. Pride has grown with my subsequent knowledge of the importance of the Mishmar Ha'emek project for Zionism.

Apart from its contribution to the war effort against Hitler, the Jewish community in Palestine was prudently preparing for its own battle of survival. While British eyes were focused on the Arab Revolt, and were ostensibly indifferent to the rise of Jewish power, the Haganah was increasing its strength. The fact that it was totally rooted in the Labor movement did not prevent it from assuming a national scope and influence. By the time that I arrived in Palestine, it was customary to think of the Haganah not as a secret conspiracy but as one of the elements of power of which all the actors in the drama would have to take account.

The idea of a contractual relationship between Britain and the Haganah had been dramatically expressed in the project that had brought me to the land. I now knew the more romantic figures in what was ironically called the Jewish "underground." (It was the least secret organization in the history of secrecy.) There was Yitshak Sadeh, a former officer in the Russian army and the real founder of the Palmach, who taught ardent young Jews, such as Yigal Allon and Moshe Dayan, the doctrines of ambush and nocturnal raids. There is a picture of Sadeh with a paternal arm encircling Dayan to his left and Allon to his right. During the SOE period I used to visit Sadeh weekly at his kibbutz home at Yagur near Haifa. His position in the Haganah leadership derived from the fact that he was one of the few Palestinian Jews

---

[1]Yehuda Bauer, *From Diplomacy to Resistance* (London: Temple Books, 1973), p. 191.

who had received training in a European army. The reference was to the Russian army in pre-Communist days. His thick eyeglasses, balding head and khaki shorts made him resemble a kindly scoutmaster about to take the boys on a picnic or jamboree. The contradictions in his own position and character came into view as he interspersed his sincere condemnation of war with a discussion of ferocious plans for the defense of Jewish national interests. Sadeh, like Ben-Gurion, was called "Hazaken" (the old man) long before that appellation was statistically justified. This reflected an Israeli tendency to reach out to men and women who could radiate a moral charisma beyond the range of their formal rank and position. Later, when Israel's statehood was won and defended far more rapidly than Sadeh could have predicted, he lived on as a revered military adviser, but his guerrilla doctrines had to give way to a more formal concept of battle, and other Haganah leaders such as Yigael Yadin seized the center of the stage with the formation of the Israeli Defense Forces.

In my contacts with the Israeli resistance I never ceased to hear echo and mention of a man who was not then in the country at all and who was destined never to return. He was historically the founder of Israel's military tradition in its least conventional and most innovative aspects. Captain Orde Wingate's name resonated among the Israeli youth. He was a British officer so consumed with biblical mysticism that his fellow officers thought him to be clinically insane. He was a crusading Christian. He had first arrived in Palestine in 1936 as a relatively junior officer to reinforce the British army in suppressing the Arab revolt, which was then much more formidable than any incipient Jewish insurrection. Wingate had allied himself spiritually to the Haganah, trained its young warriors in the guerrilla tactics for which he was later to win fame in Burma and Ethiopia, and created a legend in Zionist history as a picturesque hybrid of Byron and Lafayette. He was the kind of man for whom armed national revolutions would have had to be invented if they had not already existed. The British military commanders who had given Wingate his Jerusalem assignment later reached the conclusion that he was more devoted to a radical version of Zionism than to his own country's causes and had him sent back to London with the curt recommendation: "not to be posted to the Middle East."

During my second brief service in the Zionist Office in 1939 I had often encountered Wingate at tea in Weizmann's residence in the Dorchester Hotel. He was languishing at the beginning of the war as commander of an antiaircraft battery in Sussex. He was enraged by the neglect of his military capacities which would rationally have fitted him for a dynamic attacking role in a distant exotic land. He accepted Weizmann's elegant hospitality at the Dorchester Hotel with total indifference to table manners and pressed Weizmann with more ferocity than courtesy to bring about his appointment to the command of a Jewish fighting force in Palestine. No prime minister would ever have considered returning Wingate to such a role except the prime minister who eventually did so, although not in Palestine. Winston Churchill was not likely to recoil from promoting brilliant eccentrics. This would have been tantamount to criticizing himself, which was never his habit.

In the latter months of 1941 Churchill had decided to put Wingate's temperament and talents to work in the Far East, and it was thus that I encountered him in Cairo during a break in his journey after my arrival from England. He was now a major general. I had heard of Wingate's eccentricity without ever having cause to experience it. On seeing me in Cairo that day he had greeted me with as much amiability as his lugubrious temperament would allow and had expressed a desire to have a talk. He then reached in his pocket for a diary, opened it with meticulously slow movements and asked: "What are you doing at two A.M. tomorrow?"

I decided to play it his way, took out my diary and said, "I seem to be free at that time."

Neither of us emitted the laugh that alone would have given coherence to that stage of our conversation. I duly presented myself at the appointed hour at Shepheard's Hotel. I found him in his room, stark naked, stroking himself with the bristly side of a hairbrush. "Have you ever considered," he said, "why horses have such sleek skins?" I indicated that I had never found time to give that important question the attention and research that it undoubtedly merited. To my relief, he put on a dressing gown and launched into a tirade, punctuated with accurate prophetic quotations, predicting personal disaster for those in Britain and elsewhere who had allowed their concern for the Arabs to impede the establishment of a Jewish state in the whole area of Palestine. His proposals for "dealing with the Arabs" were so embarrassing that I refrain from recording them here. In writing to a friend in England I said that I did not know whether we ought to weep or to sigh with relief over the decision of Wingate's superiors to prevent his service in the Middle East, where he would certainly have got himself into grave trouble. In Palestine during my work on the SOE project, I felt that the Wingate legend was inspired by a generous and noble spirit that needed no vindication in further performance. The supremacy of legends and ideas over transient facts has always impressed me as the key to the understanding of the Jewish journey. In March 1944 when I heard of Wingate's death in a plane crash near the Burmese-Indian border I felt, with all my grief, that he had always seen his life as a drama and, in that spirit, would probably have given wry approval to the manner of its end.

Wingate, with his verve and creative audacity, was a particular dimension in the emerging structure of what would become Israel's protective shield. Its architect and the driving force in the Palestine Jewish community was David Ben-Gurion. I had been in Jerusalem for several months before meeting him for the first time in his own home. He had spent over a year abroad, chiefly in the United States, from which he returned home in early October 1942. He had no reason to be in a good mood. His main achievement, which he had shared with Weizmann and the American Jewish leaders, had been to secure the adoption of a statement of Zionist aims at a conference in the Biltmore Hotel in New York. The conference decision called for the establishment of a Jewish commonwealth immediately after the war. This was not such a sensational document as Ben-Gurion and his followers believed it to be. Jewish statehood had long been the central Zionist aim, and most intelligent people understood that Zionism would accept partition as a fallback position. In its text the Biltmore resolution implied that Zionism would govern the entire "commonwealth" in spite of the inconvenient fact that the Jews were a minority of the population. The Biltmore text was regarded by all interested governments as a Zionist dream from which the Zionists, in the course of their tactical deployment, would withdraw to the acceptance of a Jewish state in a part of the country. My experience is that once everybody knows your fallback position, you have virtually fallen back to it.

In America, Ben-Gurion had tried hard to get a meeting with President Roosevelt. He had failed to reach any except the second or third level of officialdom, and to complete his humiliation, Weizmann had swept in and secured a meeting with the president at very short notice. Worse, he and Weizmann had exchanged some memorable insults. Weizmann had made little effort to allay Ben-Gurion's sensitivities and jealousies, and Ben-Gurion had clamored for Weizmann's resignation without any prospect of succeeding in that quest. Other Zionist leaders, such as Sharett and Nahum Goldmann, were "plotting" to ensure that the two giants should never be on the same continent again. It was plain that their rivalry would erupt in full fury after the war.

I recalled my encounters with Ben-Gurion at Zionist Congresses and during my short period of work at the London Zionist headquarters in 1938. He was not at his best abroad. In London he was permanently under the overpowering shadow of Weizmann's dominant stature. As he once confessed, with a mixture of admiration and plain human envy, "Nobody who could get to Weizmann would want to speak to anyone else." I later learned that Ben-Gurion was never received by an incumbent prime minister or president until he assumed the premiership in 1948, whereas Weizmann saw anyone that he chose to see. This sense of frustration had weighed heavily upon him in London and had pursued him relentlessly in his recent year in America, but on his own ground in Jerusalem and Tel Aviv it was obvious to me that his burgeoning sense of leadership was too powerful to be ignored. From his demeanor and discourse I deduced that he was consciously preparing for the great hours and supreme challenges that were manifestly awaiting him on an early horizon.

He had a vivid sense of the paradox in the British-Jewish relationship. He complained to me that many of his colleagues and opponents were urging the Zionist movement to wage unrestrained resistance against the British at once. "None of them," he said, "ever answers my simple question: Who is going to stop the Nazis from sweeping into Palestine, the members of the Zionist Executive or the British generals in the Western Desert?" He added ominously, "The first thing is survival."

I was already learning something about this lucid, pragmatic man that was to become even more salient in my appraisal of him over the ensuing years. The gap between his rhetoric and his policies was wide. In his speeches he would give rein to far-reaching generalizations uttered in a rasping cadence that offended every musical sense. He took these addresses much less seriously than did his hypnotized followers. For example, he had said at the outset of the war that the Jews should fight against Hitler as if there were no hostile British policies, and should fight against the British as if there were no war against Hitler. I had thought this utterance aphoristically attractive but logically untenable. The second part of the parallelism was quite out of touch with realities. How could Zionists fight unrestrainedly against a Britain on whose tenacity and anti-Nazi passion they relied for the survival of Palestinian Jewry and for the overthrow of Nazi Germany? And if we were to fight against Britain as if there were no war with Germany, how could Weizmann have gone to the United States in 1941 to strengthen Franklin Roosevelt's pro-British orientation among the Jews of the United States?

It was not easy then, and it never became easy thereafter, to communicate with David Ben-Gurion. He would always be behind a desk, never in an armchair or in any other device indicating relaxation. His large head, leonine features and his inimitable tufts of white hair sticking up like benevolent horns concealed his diminutive stature.

Ben-Gurion spoke to me in staccato spurts in a high-pitched voice like a tap that turns itself on and off without any special rhythm. In later years I would learn that he had unique methods of keeping control of his conversations. At times he would seize the initiative by professing not to have heard what his visitor was saying and himself taking a tangential leap into another subject with a question like "Don't you agree that Marxism is sheer nonsense?" or, more simply, "Have you ever studied Buddhism?" Another method of demoralizing his interlocutors was his habit of writing busily in a notebook in the course of a conversation. He must have been the only man known to history who ever wrote the record of a meeting in the actual course of conducting it. To my relief, his talk with me in October 1942 was marked by none of these procedures. He was haunted by one single question: Did the British command in Cairo have both the will and the capacity to halt the Nazi advance before it would reach Palestine?

All his hopes for Zionism hinged on the question of whether Rommel's armies would be defeated. When he heard that I had been in Cairo, he returned again and again to the haunting question about the outcome of the Middle Eastern war. I had been told that he would wish to talk about his impressions of the Zionist condition in London and Washington, or about the stark news of the Jewish tragedy in Europe where the "final solution" for the extermination of the Jews was in full momentum. British scientists had broken the German government's codes and Churchill was reading and transmitting to Roosevelt everything that the German leaders were writing to each other, not only about the war, but also about what they called "the final solution." Even in late 1942 the horrors of the death camps had not impressed themselves indelibly on the Jewish consciousness. I had been astonished by the relative reticence in Jewish Palestine both about the tragedy already being enacted in Nazi-occupied Europe and about the new tragedy that would ensue from a breakthrough by Rommel's forces into Sinai and Palestine. Ben-Gurion knew that I could not add anything to the first theme, but his eagerness to know whether the British really intended to make a stand west of the Nile Delta consumed his thought. He believed that all other questions were worth considering only if that one was "cleared up." The very existence of the Mishmar Ha'emek project indicated that the collapse of the Palestine base was one of the options that the British were taking into serious account. Ben-Gurion was talking of such existential issues that I was amazed by the calm demeanor that he showed even when speaking about "our physical survival."

Every month that passed increased my certainty that he would soon be offering firm leadership to the Jewish people in the homeland and abroad.

The Zionism that I had known in England was concerned with meetings in undistinguished-looking halls where young zealots gave voice to fervent utterances that were unlikely to change the course of history, or even of their own lives. I doubt if that kind of movement would have engaged my lifelong devotion. But for one who now knew the Zionist enterprise in terms of Weizmann, Ben-Gurion, Sharett, Wingate and Sadeh, all against the vivid backdrop of the land itself, it was an entirely different matter. I may have been led to exalted expectations and thence to criticism of anything that might fall short of my unattainable dream. I was convinced then, as I have been ever since, that my Zionist cause was charged with rectitude and justice. To deny the Zionist claim would have been to affirm that Arabs must be free and sovereign everywhere and the Jews nowhere, not even in the land that past history and contemporary law had designed as their abode. But this robust defense of basic Zionist claims did not mean that I was oblivious of a moral dilemma. To assert that thousands of years of Jewish connection totally eliminated thirteen centuries of later Arab-Muslim history would be to apply a discriminatory standard to historic experience. My contemplation of the land strengthened my belief that it enshrines two histories that must share their future in reciprocal acknowledgment of each other.

For me, a turning point in the moral history of Zionism had come with Weizmann's remark in a majestic speech to a Royal Commission in which he declared that fulfillment of the Zionist purpose would be "the lesser injustice." Injustice—because the Palestine Arabs, were it not for the Balfour Declaration and the League of Nations Mandate, could have counted on eventual independence either as a separate state or in an Arab context acceptable for them. Lesser injustice, because they were not only Palestinians, but also members of an Arab family that was bountifully endowed with territory and sovereignty in a vast domain. I came to understand that conflict was intrinsic to the very nature of our history, and of theirs. It was impossible for us to avoid struggling for Jewish statehood and equally impossible for them to grant us what we asked. If they had submitted to Zionism with docility they would have been the first people in history to have voluntarily renounced their majority status.

It was only when the Zionist leadership agreed to the principle of partition that a moral crisis became transmuted into a classic issue of territorial distribution. I could not have become an assiduous spokesman of Zionism and, later of Israel, if we had implacably gone all out for a hundred percent of territorial and political control for ourselves and zero percent for them. Nor would a single government in the world have raised its voice and hand to recognize a society based on such a principle.

For these reasons, my first contact with Jewish Palestine, exhilarating in so many respects, aroused my reservations on one of the central issues. I found almost no public or national awareness of what was implied in our proximity to the Arab and Muslim worlds. As a youthful Zionist in Britain, I had been fed with a view of the region that I discovered in a few weeks of sojourn in Palestine to be preposterously misleading. The argument was that Zionist immigration to Palestine was objectively beneficial to the Arab population and was opposed only by special interests. According to this view, wealthy Arabs known as "effendis" wished to obstruct Jewish immigration because it threatened their social dominance, whereas the working population, known as "fellaheen," secretly welcomed the economic benefits, including employment, which they derived from the Jewish influx.

Arriving in Palestine after preaching this soothing doctrine for some years, I found very quickly that it was total nonsense. For one thing, I never met anybody who could with certainty be described as an effendi, while a fellah was simply a person who corresponded to the dictionary definition of a peasant farmer. The agitation against Zionism was generally led by intellectuals or urban townsmen who could certainly not be equated with either of these definitions. The idea that a nation would willingly barter its independence for economic benefits was a typical colonialist illusion. If anything, it was the opposite of the truth; as soon as an indigenous population was liberated from acute economic scarcities, it was free from the obsession of bread and open to the longing for a flag. Zionists, even at the summit of the movement's leadership, seemed to assume that we alone were animated by nationalism, while the Palestine Arabs could be satisfied with enhanced subsistence.

This complacency was to take sharp revenge on us in subsequent decades. Palestine had very little headline value in the war years. It seemed a backwater compared with the fearful scenes of slaughter and mass suffering in Europe and with the more distant echoes of awesome battles in the Far East. Conditions of war also conspired to keep our SOE operation away from public knowledge. In any case, the cooperative relationship between the British services and the Palmach could only survive in an atmosphere of mutual interest. This condition no longer existed after the triumph of General Montgomery's forces at El Alamein in July 1942. With the German armies in Egypt effectively destroyed, it was evident that Palestine was not going to be invaded. In early 1943 when allied forces under General Eisenhower landed in Algeria and Morocco and joined hands with the British Eighth Army, the superfluity of the camp at Mishmar Ha'emek was blatant. A project based on the prospect of a German advance into Palestine and the Levant was now a mere fantasy. Moreover, the relations between SOE and the Palmach were deteriorating rapidly and my own position was becoming impossible. A climax came in March 1943 when a Palmach group broke into a British depot and made off with a hundred rifles. I faced a danger of being seriously compromised, as did General B. T. Wilson and all those involved in the honeymoon period of Mishmar Ha'emek. Not surprisingly, the Mishmar Ha'emek camp was disbanded and Palmach reverted to its previous underground status.

All that remained was the small group of volunteers who were fluent from birth in German and Balkan languages. Their existence was borne in mind at SOE in Cairo, and a year later, in 1944, the British, starved of reliable intelligence, cooperated with Haganah in training and enlisting thirty-two Palestinian Jews, including three women, for missions behind German lines in Europe. Some of them were actually parachuted into Italy, Bulgaria, Czechoslovakia and Yugoslavia. Seven of them were captured, tortured and executed. Three of them, Hanna Senesh, Chaviva Reik and Enzo Sereni, have been immortalized in the consciousness of Israelis through vivid literary portrayals of their heartrending ordeals. Of two of them—Senesh and Sereni—I conserve grave and anguished memories. They passed through Cairo during my service there after the disbandment of the Mishmar Ha'emek camp, and I had brief access to them through my SOE connections and my acquaintanceship with Reuven Dafni, one of the survivors of the group, who now keeps the memory of the Holocaust alive as the director of Yad Vashem, the most poignant world center of remembrance.

In late March 1943 I received orders to report back to Cairo for assignment to a new mission, the nature of which remained to be divulged. My year in the Land of Israel had been rich with enduring memories, and I was left with enough time to explore them in full detail. There was no disillusion in my first contact with the Land of Israel, despite the artificially inflated expectations with which I had come. There was the inevitable disparity between my soaring dream and a reality that had to take account of limitations imposed both by human nature and by the hard circumstances in which the Zionist enterprise was enacted. In order to seize the ears and the imagination of the world, Zionism has always found it necessary to employ a Utopian rhetoric. This is a natural condition of new communities established in an atmosphere of revolutionary passion.

In Jewish imagination, the return to Zion has always been presented as a messianic consummation linked to the idea of the "City on the Hill," a symbol in every land and age of mankind's unfinished quest for individual and social perfection. The advantage of a new society is that there is very little on the ground to refute such lavish expectations. The American Founding Fathers, for example, gave their rhetoric free rein and ecstatic expression: "To present upon the theater of the Universe a spectacle hitherto unknown." "Every day we witness the birth of a new Heaven and a new Earth."

The trouble with Utopia is that it does not exist. Writers who have described the ideal society have usually contrived to situate their Utopias on desert islands or on the peaks of inaccessible mountains, thus avoiding the two conditions that make Utopia impossible: boundaries and neighbors. Israel before and since its birth has suffered from oppressive contiguities with neighbors who have seldom been content to leave us alone. It is not surprising that Plato's Republic, having no neighbors, has no need of a foreign policy. As a Jew I have never had any trouble with the amiable Christian doctrine that tells us to love both our neighbors and our enemies. G. K. Chesterton has written that "this is quite logical since they are usually the same people."

When I compared the reality of Jewish Palestine with my visionary expectations, I concluded that in the two decades between the two world wars, the Jewish people had neither squandered its opportunities nor fully used them.

By 1942 there were about half a million Jews in Palestine. Their economic and technological levels were spectacular by Middle Eastern standards but well below the European average. Nevertheless, they were a fascinating and original spectacle for the world and a source of pride for the Jewish people. Here and only here the Jews faced history in their own authentic image. They were not a marginal gloss on other societies. The national attributes were all reflected on a miniature scale but in growing completeness. The salient feature of this society was its Hebrew character. The ancient language, expanded and renewed, was not only the mother tongue of a newborn Jewish generation, it was also the vehicle of an impressive literary movement and was adapting itself successfully to the task of expressing scientific and technical concepts. The Hebrew language, more than anything else, gave form and color to the nascent community. It was also the link with a universally cherished past.

The driving force in Jewish Palestine was the quest for identity. An intense solidarity inspired its Jewishness. Its ideals and priorities were collective, not individual. What mattered was a Jew's service to the growing nation, not his success in self-advancement. Palestine Jewry was gripped by a profoundly moral preoccupation. Life was earnest, austere, responsible, resolute, effervescent, somewhat irrational, a little ponderous and self-conscious. Every first road, street, settlement, school, orchestra and university department was ecstatically celebrated. The Jewish people lived at last with the unique taste of creativity. There was an intensely libertarian climate. Politics flourished with strong emphasis on ideological definitions and loyalties. As I went from one Jewish house to another I never heard anyone ask how much money anybody was making. I did hear questions and gossip about political ideologies.

The most recent accretion of manpower had come from the German Jewish immigrants who had fled from Hitler's domain while there was still time. Their adaptation was not easy. Many of them gave me the impression of wishing that Moses, in the flight of the Israelites from Egypt, had pursued his journey farther toward the west and north so that the Law from Zion would go forth from a distant Switzerland or Luxembourg. They were disconcerted by the heat and by the informality of the new Jewish society, but they were assiduous in their attempts to "civilize" Palestinian Jewry by adding a dimension of civic order and neatness. Anyone who came to the Jewish sector of Palestine in the 1940s would find a cultural climate that was not completely European and yet more charged with European energies than with Middle Eastern tranquillity or fatalism. Many German Jewish immigrants became leaders of Israeli society and of its academic movement, while others were frankly nostalgic for European values and styles. In the thirteenth century, Yehuda Halevi, the great poet of Spanish Jewry, had written: "I am in the west and my heart is in the extremities of the east." Some German Jewish writers, like Arnold and Stefan Zweig, would have said that their bodies were in the uncongenial east, while everything else about them cried out for a return to their familiar western abodes. Most Diaspora Jews then as now bore the separation between their bodies and their hearts with resignation and docility.

This, indeed, was one of my chief impressions of Palestine Jewry in the 1940s. It still seemed marginal to the life of world Jewry despite its pretension to be the cultural and national center. I was surprised, as I toured the country, by the sparseness and fragmentation of the Jewish presence in the Land of Israel. Jewish Palestine was composed of relatively small patches of existence in a general texture that was dominantly Arab. One could travel a relatively long time between one evidence of Zionist development and another, except in the relatively consecutive areas in the coastal plain and in the Valley of Jezreel, where the kibbutz movement proudly paraded its graceful areas of verdure.

The paradox of World War II in Palestine lay in the contrast between the agreeable physical conditions and the anguished sense of imminent and inevitable explosion. The war immunized the Jewish population from the daily consciousness of their situation. While death, devastation, and violence raged all over Europe, the volume of physical suffering in Palestine was relatively minor. There had been one memorable Italian air raid soon after Italy entered the war. The target was the Haifa Refineries, but the bombing killed more than a hundred people along a wide front. In deference to this experience, the blackout was intensified. I scarcely noticed this on my arrival in Jerusalem in February 1942, since the difference between Jerusalem in a blackout and Jerusalem on a normal evening was not easily perceptible. Jerusalemites have never been addicts of nightlife and at that time the city would not easily be detected from the air even without air-raid precautions.

Later, in November 1942 after the dramatic British victory at El Alamein, Palestine was not even theoretically vulnerable and it presented a paradoxical spectacle of normality and comfort. There was no scarcity of food and no rationing of gasoline. Both Jewish and Arab agriculture flourished. The British forces in Egypt had established a great supply center, which utilized Jewish enterprise in Palestine for the creation of new industrial plants. All in all, it was more comfortable to live in Palestine than in beleaguered Britain or anywhere in the European continent. British officials disliked being posted back to London where they would suffer the danger of air bombardment and a decline both in their social status and in their standards of living. In Middle Eastern military terms, Palestine was not a front; it was a leave center. In Haifa and Tel Aviv, soldiers would obtain respite from hot and dusty Egyptian camps and receive whatever delights soldiers on leave expect in their brief days of release from military hazards and routines.

In Jerusalem, the Palestine Philharmonic Orchestra held its concerts, and I would attend typically colonial garden parties at the high commissioner's residence to celebrate royal occasions. A Palestinian Jew could travel to Cairo or Beirut without undue difficulty and could visit the antiquities in Petra and Jerash by normal arrangements in advance. There was none of the choking claustrophobia that Israelis were to know in 1948 and for many years thereafter.

There was even a flurry of political debate. The British Council, a semi-official body organized to diffuse British ideas and culture across the world, held a lecture series on international politics. I was invited to deliver several addresses in this framework. I had addressed meetings in Cairo, both in English and in Arabic, and had been well received. The lectures in Jerusalem were delivered in the YMCA auditorium. This is an unusual structure with an elliptical tower surging upward to a monumental height. One of the British royals who had inaugurated it had created a scuffling of feet among patriarchs and bishops when he congratulated "all those responsible for this noble erection." Something of the atmosphere in the Jerusalem of those days can be deduced from a letter that I wrote to a friend in England in November 1942:

I have been doing propaganda as a sideline and had a successful show last week when the Chief Secretary, the Attorney General, the Chief

Justice, the Mayor and Counselors attended a lecture I gave to six hundred people in the town. You get such a mixed and at the same time selective sort of audience here that the psychological kick of holding forth is vastly greater than usual. . . .

The spacious freedom of debate in the Palestine of those times is illustrated by the theme of that lecture. Here was I, an officer of medium rank in uniform, discussing the major foreign policy of the post-war era a few months after victory at El Alamein had made the idea of a post-war age familiar to the peoples of the Middle East. My speech was in the ferocious spirit of the times:

Hitlerism is but the latest manifestation of a deep rooted trait in the German character. . . . A single lineage of violence joins Charlemagne to Barbarossa to Frederick the Great to Bismarck to Wilhelm II to Hitler. . . . You cannot allow freedom to German industry, German opinion, German institutions; for her industry will generate a wartime apparatus, her opinion will breed a hideous spawn of fanatical self-assertion, her institutions will merge into a Nazi Brown House. . . .

No one could have predicted that two decades later I would be standing in an Israeli Parliament advocating the establishment of diplomatic relations between a sovereign Jewish state and the Federal Republic of Germany.

The deceptive "normality" of daily life in Palestine was made plausible by the fact that the major political confrontations were in abeyance. There had been a very ugly mood in Jewish-British relations in December 1941 when a totally unseaworthy ship, Struma, drifted perilously in the Mediterranean because neither the British nor the Turkish government would give it permission to land, even temporarily. The ship sank with the loss of over seven hundred lives, including more than three hundred women and children. The sheer malice and fanaticism of British opposition to Jewish immigration had come to expression in similar incidents, but never with such a volume of tragedy. Thereafter the Haganah abstained from attempting openly to run the British naval blockade and instead developed what the British called "illegal" immigration through small vessels arriving on the Palestinian coast by night. The Jewish refugees at this stage were not struggling for Zionism but against torture and death of themselves and their children. The refusal of the Western democracies, especially the United States, to give them refuge and shelter is second in infamy only to the slaughter and persecution themselves.

Apart from these abrasive encounters, the British and the Jews argued with each other about the future settlement and cooperated with each other in organizing the defense of the region against the common and cruel foe.

The Arab situation was more complex. The Arab revolt against British rule and what they called "the Zionist danger" had reached its peak in the summer of 1936. It became muted to a large extent after the appointment of the Royal (Peel) Commission and was renewed at a high pitch of violence in 1937 in response to the partition plan and subsided again in 1938. The Arabs were intimidated by the massive scale of British military power. Moreover, they seemed to have won their case against Zionism. The Chamberlain "White Paper" of May 1939 had virtually promised them independence and majority rule, with the Jews reduced to a subsidiary status. The moral drama of the confrontation between Western democracy and Hitlerism did not touch their leadership in the smallest degree. As in Egypt and Iraq, Arab nationalism in Palestine during the war was virulently anti-British. In Syria it was anti-French. The effort of the Chamberlain government to purchase Arab support by its own anti-Zionism had failed. Arab leaders seldom asked themselves whether German domination of their countries might not be even less tolerant of Arab nationalism than that of Britain and France. In Arab eyes, British and French rule was a reality while the alternatives were distant and hypothetical. In the period leading up to the war the Arab nationalists in Palestine suffered more from Draconian British suppression than the Jews were to experience even at the height of their resistance to British policies. Hangings of Arab nationalists were frequent, and the temporary detention or exile of activist leaders of the rebellion made organized Arab resistance difficult.

The acknowledged leader of the Palestine Arabs was Haj Amin al-Husseini, whose religious title was mufti of Jerusalem but whose major activity was the incitement of the Palestine Arabs to violence against the British and the Jews. In 1937 Haj Amin had given the impression of willingness to meet Ben-Gurion. A Palestinian leader, Musa al-Alami, a man of rare refinement whom I had met several times since my arrival in Jerusalem, explored this prospect, but without success. Ben-Gurion had asked Musa al-Alami to convey the idea of large-scale economic and development aid to the Arabs in return for their abandonment of extremism. Alami had replied in his own behalf that he would prefer starvation for the Palestine Arabs rather than renounce their hope of national freedom. Ben-Gurion regarded this response as so important that he renounced any realistic hope of securing an agreement with the Arabs until the Jewish position in Palestine became too powerful to be ignored. He sometimes gave the impression that he respected Musa al-Alami's reply. It was typical of Ben-Gurion's attitude to diplomacy that he always preferred to meet radical, abrasive leaders on the Arab side rather than those who had a reputation as "moderates." Ben-Gurion's view was that diplomacy had nothing to do with amiability. The test of contacts with enemy spokesmen was whether they were representative, not whether they were virtuous.

My own contacts with Arabs in Palestine were courteous but without intimacy. We did not fool each other. We knew that we were enlisted in opposing causes and that our destinies would soon clash. This did not, in my view, justify a contemptuous Zionist attitude toward them. When I gave a lecture to a group of intellectuals in Jerusalem on "The Modern Literary Movement In the Arab World," my audience seemed to resent the implication that our allegedly uncouth neighbors were capable of literary expression. I always felt that even in the absence of political understanding a degree of respect for the glories of Arab and Muslim culture in past epochs would alleviate their bitterness. Meanwhile, the relative passivity of Arab nationalism in the war years was understandable. They had little incentive for compromise. They assumed that the end of hostilities would bring an increased perception of the range and scope of their territories, and that their opportunity for defeating Zionism would soon be at hand.

How far they and we were apart in every aspect of emotion and allegiance was illustrated by the posture of their leaders. Haj Amin, who had once reflected seriously on the possibility of meeting Ben-Gurion, had since tied himself and his movement to the Nazi cause. It was in 1937 when the revolt against British rule reached its climax that Haj Amin had fled Palestine, never to return. He spent the entire war years in Arab lands of exile, except for his visit to Berlin, where he was ceremoniously received by Hitler on November 30, 1941. The British administration had responded to Arab violence with harsh suppression. Britain had achieved an acrobatic success in alienating the Jews without winning the hearts of the Arabs. The British authorities had executed over a hundred Palestine Arabs in the years 1937 to 1939 and had imprisoned or expelled thousands of Arab nationalists.

From his safe and distant outpost in Damascus, Haj Amin had imposed his domination on all other Palestinians, hundreds of whom were assassinated by his emissaries. It seemed on the surface that the main conflict was between the British and the Arabs, with the Jews in a subsidiary role. But everything in Palestine was tentative in the first years of the war. Only when Allied forces became patently and unreservedly victorious would it become apparent that the volcano of regional conflict would soon erupt.

Early in April 1943 I flew to Cairo to receive my new assignment. This was the first time that I had taken to the air, and nobody could wish for less congenial circumstances in which to live that experience. The plane of Misr (Egyptian) Airlines seemed to be held in relative cohesion with string and plaster and it gave disturbing evidence of having only one sputtering engine. Moreover, the Egyptian pilot chose to land at Port Said ahead of Cairo and he refused to explain the deviation. Among the five other passengers the consensus was that he simply wished to visit his family. Despite this adventure, it was difficult to withhold admiration for the very presumption of Egypt to have a national airline at all when this was usually regarded as a monopoly of a few big countries. My posting was to the office of the Minister of State in the Middle East. This function had been created by Churchill to enable the Cabinet to be represented at its own level during the periods when communication with London had been difficult. I still retained my military status as a major on the General Staff, but the atmosphere was now civilian and diplomatic. The incumbent minister was Richard Casey, who later became foreign minister and governor general of Australia. He was not the stereotype of an Australian. His accent was redolent of Oxford and his sartorial tastes bespoke Bond Street and Savile Row. His moustache and general bearing gave the impression that the Creator had fashioned a special mold for elegantly attired foreign ministers of which Eden, Acheson and Casey were the standard models. If Casey admired Zionism at all, he certainly kept that impulse under close restraint. He was succeeded at Cairo during my service in that ministry by Lord Moyne, who was a close friend of Churchill but not a subscriber to Churchill's Zionist sympathies.

My immediate superior was Brigadier Iltwyd Clayton, a renowned Arabist with a love of books and a philosophical temperament. He wished me to study movements of policy among Arab governments and peoples. Rumor had it that the study of Zionism was in the hands of an Arab scholar, Albert Hourani, who later composed works on Arab nationalism that were marked by incisive analysis and immaculate prose. But my substantive task was to help prepare the agenda and syllabus for a new institution to be set up by the Foreign Office under the title "Middle East Center of Arab Studies." The logic was that diplomats, military officers and business executives, such as heads of oil companies, who intended to serve in the Middle East after the war should be versed in the language and history of the region. This revolutionary insight indicated an unusually innovative spirit in Whitehall, where it had traditionally been held that it was the business of the population to understand its masters, not the other way around. A historian, George Kirk, of virulently hostile attitude toward Zionism would be the other chief instructor at the proposed center. My own task apparently was to give an image of "balance." The center would be established, to my pleasure and good fortune, in Jerusalem, and would be housed in the Austrian Hospice within the walls of the Old City. Some twenty-five officers or diplomats would attend each annual course. The director would be Colonel Bertram Thomas, a renowned explorer who had been the first to cross the forbidding desert in Saudi Arabia known as "The Empty Quarter" (Rub' al Khali). Colonel Thomas had considered that his admittedly intrepid exploit exhausted his mission in life and for the subsequent decades he had lived comfortably on the fame and fortune that derived from his sensational venture. It was evident that he would give the new Center little except the radiation of his rank and renown.

My tasks at the ministry were interesting but not excessively laborious, and with enemy danger repelled the pace of activity was less frenzied than in my first sojourn in Cairo. I was free for other pursuits, the most important of which was the pursuit of Suzy Ambache with the proposition that she should become my wife. I eventually succeeded in this quest to my lifelong pride and emotional enrichment, and we became officially engaged the day before my departure for Jerusalem to take up my post at the Middle East Center of Arab Studies. Suzy was the eldest of three Ambache daughters whose home was in a massive residence in the Zamalek quarter of Cairo. Her parents had both been born in Jewish Palestine, the father in the Neveh Tsedek quarter of Jaffa and the mother in Jerusalem. Simcha Ambache had graduated in engineering in France, but his qualifications went far beyond any function that would be available in a Palestine that was almost innocent of industrial concerns. Like the Hebrew patriarchs he had "gone down" to Egypt in quest of sustenance and livelihood and he had prospered as an industrialist in the Suez Canal region, before moving from Ismailiya to Cairo. The Ambache son and the three daughters, one of whom, Aura, is the wife of the president of Israel, Chaim Herzog, had been brought up in French schools in Ismailiya, where their education was provided by a governess imported for that purpose from Jerusalem. Ismailiya was far more intensively and passionately French than was any town or city in France itself, and Suzy crowned her Hebrew and French schooling by graduating from the American University in Cairo.

Cairo was greatly enhanced in my estimation by Suzy's proximity, and unlike my first arrival there I was not obsessed by an urgent longing to leave it behind. I became more attuned to its amenities, which for me included an opportunity to study the Arab literary movement of which Cairo was—and still is—the recognized center. I developed a friendship with the novelist Taufiq al-Hakim, whose most renowned work, *The Diary of a District Officer in the Provinces*, I later translated and published in English. As I now write these recollections I have before me copies of the Egyptian magazines *Al Megalla* and *Al Katib*, containing my lectures and articles published in Cairo in 1944. On one occasion the chairman at my lecture was the great Taha Hussein, the brightest star in the galaxy of modern Arabic literature. The audience included Taufiq al-Hakim and Mahmoud Taimour and the heads of the Egyptian Academy. There was now a different atmosphere in Cairo from what I had known on my first arrival there two years previously.

The hostilities on the battlefields were nearing their end, but this knowledge brought us no relief. We knew that the end of the war would be the beginning of renewed regional tension. The portents were ominous for the Jewish people. It was in 1943–1944 that the news from Europe confirmed that our people had been assailed by the most violent tragedy that had ever befallen any family of the human race. The full dimensions of the Holocaust would assail our consciousness only when the war against Hitler was won and the death camps and the ravaged Jewish communities were wrested from the darkness of the war and exposed visually to our horrified gaze. In Cairo, of course, there was no preoccupation with the fate of European Jewry. My own consciousness of the systematic annihilation of Jews came from Palestinian Jewish friends who came to Cairo, which was fully open to Palestinian Jewish visitors. One of the most terrifying and authentic reports had been received by the Geneva representative of the World Jewish Congress, Dr. Gerhard Riegner. The Jerusalem and Tel Aviv newspapers in 1943 had reports that were laconic and sometimes vaguely skeptical. Some things in Jewish history are too terrible to be believed, but nothing in Jewish history is too terrible to have happened.

While Cairo was calm and tranquil and Palestine felt physically remote from tragedy, a veritable inferno of horror and savagery was raging in Nazi-occupied Europe. At first the ears refused to hear and the mind to believe the stupendous nature of the tragedy. But there were too many witnesses and survivors coming out of Europe to allow comforting illusions. Millions of Jews—men, women and children—in the Jewish communities of occupied Europe, all the way from Norway to Greece and especially in the densely populated Jewish centers in Poland, Romania, Hungary and conquered territories in the Soviet Union, were being herded like cattle into railway cars, shipped off to special concentration areas and there simply destroyed like useless rubbish.

In those days, to be a Jew in Nazi-occupied Europe meant that a man would be dragged from his home, put into a train with thousands of others, deported to a distant camp with or without his wife and children, beaten, starved and humiliated for a few days or weeks of forced labor, after which his emaciated, wrecked and shambling body would be dispatched into a gas chamber, where he would be scientifically asphyxiated, his hair shaven off to make mattresses, his bones crushed and melted down to make soap. The gold fillings from his teeth would be assembled to sustain the declining German war effort. His wife and children would be submitted to similar agonies, tortures and murders in specially constructed camps.

Particularly unbelievable but patently true was the fact that a million Jewish children were being flung into furnaces and burned to death. Years after, I would visit Auschwitz and come across a "museum" where mountains of small shoes would mutely testify that the inhumanity of man has no fixed or finite limits.

The idea that hundreds of thousands of Germans of all ages were "employed" in these grisly factories for the production of death gave point and substance to the anti-Hitler war and to the pathos and meaning of the Jewish homeland, which, but for the British victory at El Alamein, might have been destroyed. It was hard to deal with such matters at a Center of Arab Studies, or to experience the simultaneous intersection of normal pursuits with unspeakable horrors that is characteristic of wartime life, as the unheeding city of Cairo did not even offer an environment of empathy with the Jewish condition.

On the day after New Year 1945 I ended my tour of duty at the Ministry of State, became formally betrothed to Suzy and was soon speeding in a military vehicle across the black, undulating, sand-fringed road that seems to have no purpose except to link Palestine to Egypt. We planned our marriage for the spring recess in the work of the Center, when I would return to Cairo.

Back in Jerusalem I was startled to find that not even the convulsive and revolutionary events afflicting the Jews in Europe were having any effect on the British bureaucrats in Palestine. They continued, vainly, to woo the favor of an Arab world that had, for the most part, taken sides with those who had been the enemies of Britain and of the Jews. The Zionists and the British were fighting a common enemy, but there was no real solidarity between them. The Jewish plight aroused intense sympathy in London, where the British House of Commons, in an unprecedented parliamentary tribute, had risen for a minute of silence to mourn the tragedy of the Jews in Europe. This gesture might in other conditions have impressed some Jews, but it now vanished from consciousness against the stark gap between words and realities.

On March 1, 1943, Weizmann addressed a hushed assembly of Jews in Madison Square Garden, New York:

Two million Jews have already been exterminated. The world can no longer plead that the ghastly facts are unknown or unconfirmed. . . . At this moment, expressions of sympathy, without accompanying attempts to launch acts of rescue, become a hollow mockery in the ears of the dying.

Side by side with the news of Jewish disaster in Europe came the crowded events in and about Palestine in 1944–1945. Churchill had been virulently opposed by his generals and by his foreign secretary, Anthony Eden, whenever he made a proposal to alleviate the grief and humiliation of the Jews, but in 1944 he broke through with two consoling initiatives: In the spring of 1944 he had informed Weizmann of the decision to establish a Jewish Brigade Group in the British army. His argument with his ministers and generals had lasted for over four years. Churchill said in a Cabinet minute dated July 26, 1944:

It seems to me indeed appropriate that a special Jewish unit of that race which has suffered indescribable torment from the Nazis should be represented as a distinct formation among the forces gathered for their final overthrow. I have no doubt that they will not only take part in the struggle but also in the occupation that will follow.

This was almost the only gain for Zionism during the war. It was too late for the Jewish Brigade Group to take part in the epic battles of the war, but its 3,500 men served creditably on the Italian front under General Mark Clark and subsequently gave afflicted Jewish communities a feeling of pride as well as logistic support in transferring displaced persons across Europe to the Land of Israel. The training, experience and disciplines accumulated in the Brigade were undoubtedly an asset when the Israeli Defense Forces came to be established in 1948.

In 1944 Zionism came poignantly close to a more substantive gain. Churchill had vigorously opposed the 1939 White Paper of the Chamberlain administration, castigating it as a breach of trust, and he wished to undermine the status of that document as the official expression of British Middle Eastern policy. He had appointed a Cabinet committee under the chairmanship of Herbert Morrison to make recommendations on a Palestine settlement. The committee had worked for over a year and had produced a proposal for the partition of Palestine and the establishment of a Jewish state in a larger area than that envisaged by the Royal Commission in 1937. If this initiative had been adopted by the British Cabinet, World War II would have ended for Zionism as triumphantly as had World War I. Anthony Eden and his Foreign Office mandarins had opposed the plan, but it was adopted by the cabinet committee, which included the minister of state in the Middle East, Lord Moyne. Churchill was so jubilant at this success that he called Weizmann to a meeting on November 4, 1944, and said triumphantly that "our Zionist cause is going well. Moyne is now on our side." Two days later, the colonial secretary, Oliver Stanley, sent a car urgently to Weizmann's residence at the Dorchester Hotel saying that he had grievous news to impart. Lord Moyne had been murdered in a Cairo street by two young Jews acting on the orders of the Lochamei Herut Israel (Lechi) organization. Lechi was a small resistance organization of a few hundred men and women that had broken away from a larger resistance group, the Irgun Zvai Leumi (IZL). The Irgun had a few thousand fighters, led and inspired by Menachem Begin, who represented the main opposition in the Zionist movement and, later, in the Israeli Parliament (Knesset). The Lechi leaders followed an anti-British policy so extreme that it "did not recoil during the war from contacts with Otto von Hentig, the Nazi representative in Turkey."[2]

The Lechi leaders who planned and executed the murder of Lord Moyne and the innocent young men who followed their orders undoubtedly believed that they were serving a Jewish national interest. But the results were uniformly and darkly negative. These included: the callous abandonment of the two young men to an Egyptian gallows; and the angry reaction of Churchill, who disbanded the Morrison Committee and dropped all discussion of the Jewish state proposal that had been scheduled for promulgation on December 20, 1944.

Churchill embarked on a long process of sulky indignation that lasted throughout all the remaining part of the war, thus aggravating the unfavorable situation of Israel in the international system. His disengagement from the Palestine issue lasted until the Potsdam Conference, when he received a

[2]Howard M. Sachar, *A History of Israel* (New York: Knopf, 1979), p. 247.

note from the newly inaugurated President Truman advocating the admission of Jews to Palestine beyond the provisions of the 1939 White Paper. Before he could respond positively to this suggestion, as he would certainly have wished, Churchill had been defeated in the post-war election and was succeeded by Attlee and Bevin.

It is historically certain that a crass operation by the Lechi group had a disastrous effect on the national interest of the Jewish people. In the ensuing years, many Israelis became so hypnotized by the heroic dignity of the resistance fighters that they tended to avoid selective discussion of their assignments, not all of which were useful or well guided. As recently as 1988 we find Prime Minister Yitshak Shamir, who had been a Lechi resistance leader, speaking with candor of his own support of the assassination of Lord Moyne.

When the murder took place, Ben-Gurion's fury knew no limits. He now saw the dissident rightist groups as the adversaries of the national interest. Their acts of violence, planned and executed without any knowledge of the surrounding regional and international background, had disrupted an important prospect for a new surge of Zionist progress. Ben-Gurion saw no possibility of a coherent national policy so long as the central Jewish authority had no monopoly of armed action. His rhetoric was fierce: "We must spew forth from our midst all the men of this destructive gang . . . deny these terrorists all protection and refuge, and extend all aid necessary to the authorities to prevent acts of terror and to wipe out this organization, for our lives depend on it. . . ."

Ben-Gurion's phrase about "extending all aid necessary to the authorities" was to have dramatic results. The intention was to denounce members of the dissident resistance groups to the British authorities. This policy, known in Israeli jargon as "the season," was carried out for over a year. It poisoned the relationships between parties and movements in Israel so sharply that many of the wounds have not healed to this day. It was a deviant idea in the generally accepted terms of underground nationalism, but Ben-Gurion thought that the alternative was to expose the nation to superfluous injury and that it was therefore a patriotic imperative to curb policies that violated our central interests. My own feeling then and since has been that the Jewish national struggle would have been a better national event without the "season," but that Ben-Gurion was basically correct in his tenacious struggle to eliminate the independent and irresponsible action of resistance groups.

In March 1945 I returned to Cairo from Jerusalem to celebrate my marriage at an impressive ceremony in the home of Suzy's parents. It was the first time that I was attending a big wedding from a proximity that enabled me to see exactly how such ceremonies are conducted. The diversity of my interests was illustrated by an unusual convergence of guests. David Ben-Gurion and his wife, Paula, attended together with Teddy Kollek, Brigadier

Clayton, some Egyptian business associates of my father-in-law, two Jewish chaplains of the British forces, leaders of the Egyptian Jewish community and some of the younger Zionists from London serving in the forces. My first cousin, Captain Neville Halper of the Army Medical Corps, whom I had casually encountered in a Cairo bookshop, acted as best man and the venerable chief rabbi of Egypt, Nahum Effendi, pronounced the priestly blessing with imposing Sephardic resonance. The Ben-Gurions and Teddy were in Cairo on Zionist business. (It would soon become impossible to draft this last sentence, for Cairo, three hundred miles from Jerusalem, would be hermetically sealed from Palestinian Jews in 1948 for the next thirty years.)

After a brief honeymoon in Aswan and Luxor, Suzy and I traveled to Jerusalem, where we established our first home in the American School of Oriental Research.

I had developed a close friendship with the school's director, Nelson Glueck, who later became the leading figure in American Reform Judaism. His previous claim to fame was that he was the only man in Jerusalem whom I thought I could beat at tennis. Alas, this proved to be an illusion, but its collapse did not ruin our relationship. A more lasting motive for admiring Nelson Glueck was his love for Jerusalem, which transcended his allegiance to Cincinnati, where Reform Judaism had its central sanctuaries. This merit was crowned by the fact that the world owes its precise and appreciative understanding of Nabatean civilization to Nelson's assiduous research in the Negev and Jordan. A few months later Suzy and I moved to North Talpiot. Our house was small, but everything in North Talpiot is redeemed by the view. There was a panorama of rolling hills, some of them dotted with the buildings of South Jerusalem, others farther down cradling the Old City with the Dome of the Rock and the ancient wall. Far beyond, the Moab mountains were visible, suffused in the evenings by a mauve light in which the waters of the Dead Sea could be observed on clear days. In front lay the Valley of Hinnom, very far in its gracious aspect from the "hell" with which Gehinnom is associated by tradition. Far to the right, surrounded by dark green cypress trees, was the white palace of the British high commissioner, one of the few successful architectural enterprises of British Mandatory Palestine. (The other less agreeable architectural relics of the British period were the brownstone police stations of uniform color and shape.)

It was in North Talpiot that we followed and experienced the tumult of the year 1945, which is a landmark in every biographical recollection.

The memory lingers first on May 1945 with Churchill's exultant growl on the radio: "The war with Germany is ended, we can allow ourselves a brief hour of celebration." This was a reasonable thing to say about most of mankind, but not about the Jews, for whom the end of the war was only the beginning of a sharper agony. The notion of "when the war comes to an end" had been a sustaining myth for the Jews, immunizing them against black despair, and now when the end had come there was a shamefaced confession that the myth had not really been credible even when we had clung to it.

It had been bad enough to live for six years on a diet of suspended hope. It was even more painful when the suspense ended with the thin flame of hope extinguished.

It was the lowest ebb in the fortunes of the Jews throughout all their millennial history. The effects of the Holocaust were now starkly visible and the spectacle went beyond our worst terror-stricken apprehensions. In addition, we were being assailed in the promised homeland by regional hostility and international alienation. The world community began to take shape at the first conference of the United Nations in San Francisco: Every nation behind its name and flag except the one that had suffered most from the assault of barbarism! It was hard to find a redeeming gleam of hope beyond the self-consoling thought expressed in the dictum that "the eternity of Israel shall not fail." It is a paradox of history that so much of the vocabulary of hope comes from the people whose experience logically invites despair.

We had long known that the end of the war would release the suppressive tensions of the previous six years, but few of us imagined that the explosion would be so rapid and intense. The darkness that came to surround us was so heavy that we could not even regard the Holocaust as our only and ultimate disaster. It was seriously possible that the Jewish destiny would be betrayed in the post-war settlement.

Churchill had necessarily postponed the Palestine settlement until the end of the war, if only because the involvement of the United States was the centerpiece of his program. It offered him his only chance of breaking the stranglehold of his own British Arabists. He had been vigilant during the war in keeping his post-war options open. We now know from the documents that he had even warned Roosevelt not to interpret the Atlantic Charter's support of self-government too specifically, since "here in the Middle East the Arabs might claim by majority they could expel the Jews from Palestine or at any time forbid all further immigration . . ."

It had been expected that Churchill's electoral defeat would have disconcerted us, but an optimistic expectation of a pro-Zionist Labour leadership sustained our hope. It was only necessary for the Labour Party to honor a tenth of its promises for the Jews to emerge from darkness to something similar to light. Most of the Labour leaders had abandoned all restraint in their passionate support of Zionism in their 1945 conference. "Let the Arabs move out and the Jews move in," declaimed Hugh Dalton, whom everybody, including himself, believed to be the natural candidate for the foreign secretary's position in a Labour government. Zionists were united about the Jews' moving in, but hardly any of them in their senses believed that it would be possible or morally justified to have the Arabs move out. Here we encountered a phenomenon that has characterized Zionists and Israel ever since. Our adversaries are excessive in their censure and our friends are often overzealous in our support. Churchill promised Weizmann, in what was almost a ceremonial oath-taking, that he would "see Zionism through after the end of the hostilities." Unfortunately, he had not taken effective steps to see himself through. In Palestine itself the dissident resistance movements were straining to break out. They were longing to activate the anti-British assaults that they had been formulating during the spring and the early summer. The chief constraint, which was evident even to their hardened view, was the need to avoid prematurely irritating the new British Labour government before it had time to bring its well-known Zionism to the fore. This naive caution was to no avail. When the Labour government was presented to Parliament we noticed that the foreign secretary was not the compliant Dalton, but the enigmatic Ernest Bevin whom nobody believed to have given any thought to foreign countries and peoples at any stage of his life.

It immediately became evident that the conferences of the ruling party had no effective weight. Labour leaders had never studied the Middle East and were unaware of the interests and passions that swept across the Arab East. In office they found themselves faced with a problem much more intricate than that of placating the Jewish Labor groups.

Great Britain was on the verge of bankruptcy. It could not afford to threaten the stability of its oil reserves in Mosul, Kirkuk and other parts of the Muslim world. The economic problem was compounded by a strategic dilemma. The Soviet Union was threatening basic Western interests. The United States was looking to Britain with selfish complacency to hold the fort for Western interests. Here, then, were two reasons, the one strategic and the other economic, that seemed to forbid Britain from following the romantic traditions of the Balfour Declaration. Weizmann, whom they still respected, now seemed to be asking Britain to accomplish wonders that had been feasible in 1917–1922, but that were now objectively beyond its powers. It would not be overdramatic to say that throughout most of 1945 and the whole of 1946 Great Britain and the Zionist community in Israel were in something that could be described as a state of war. It is hard to think of anybody in those times who could be more emotionally affected by this unnatural belligerence than myself. Still clothed in a British uniform, I was in my heart the unreserved and devoted servant of the Zionist ideal. It was obvious that this conflict of allegiances would make the continuation of my ambiguous condition impossible.

By the middle of 1945 I was anonymously writing vehement articles in *The Palestine Post* under the pseudonym "Politicus" against the repressive policies of the British Mandatory regime. Very often after formulating such a tirade I would go back to the officers' quarters in the Middle East Center of Arab Studies to find an irascible officer reading his morning newspaper. "If I could get my hands around the throat of the bastard who wrote this article, I would strangle him to death," said one of them amiably while pouring me a helpful glass of port or claret.

There were now savage exchanges of fire between Irgun warriors and the British Army. In one of these an Irgun bullet killed one of my officer pupils in the Center, Captain Dickie Clark. As we gathered around the table to mourn an innocent colleague, fallen in a conflict in which he had no role and in which his emotion was never engaged, I could feel accusing looks from the British officers directed at me.

The crisis had come on November 13, 1945. It is a date that I have never lost from memory. Bevin's speech made it evident beyond doubt that the Jewish people, plunged in grief, was now going to be assailed without pity by the very British administration that owed its Mandate to Jewish support three decades before.

Bevin's rhetoric now became increasingly vulgar and confrontational. It was disquietingly evident that there was more prejudice than pragmatic thought in the determination of his attitude. It was not objectively unreasonable for a British foreign secretary to believe that Britain should give deep thought to its interests in the Arab world. There was no early sign that Britain was about to abandon its oil resources and strategic assets in the area. British responsibilities were still diverse and heavy. Jordan was virtually a British dependency. Egypt was theoretically sovereign, but had to accommodate a large British force in the Suez Canal under an Anglo-Egyptian treaty. The Iraqi monarchy was under strong British influence and the Habbaniyah air base was a symbol of British regional dominance. Bevin would not have been eccentric in deciding that the weight of these interests required more cooperation between the Arab states and London. But no calculation of geopolitical reality or of objective interest can explain all Bevin's decisions and statements. He was not obliged to declare that "Truman wants the Jews to go to Palestine because he doesn't want them in New York"; or to speak with derision of the attempt of Jewish Holocaust survivors "to push to the front of the queue," thereby "encouraging anti-Semitism[!]" He did not have to reject President Truman's appeal for 100,000 death camp survivors to be admitted to Palestine, when compliance would have defused the intensity of Zionist pressure. It is ludicrous to imagine that this measure would have set the Muslim world aflame. Nor would a man of ordinary sensitivity have urged Jews to look for salvation to the very continent of Europe which they remembered as their graveyard and their torture chamber. All this when Jewish fortunes were at their lowest ebb. Zionism had often been subjected to reasoned criticism, but could anyone consider a more frivolous and offensive "analysis" than that which Bevin formulated on February 25, 1947?

> If it were only a question of relieving Europe of 100,000 Jews, I believe that a settlement could be found. . . . Unfortunately . . . from the Zionist point of view the 100,000 is only a beginning. . . . Why should an external agency, largely financed from America, determine how many people should come into Palestine, and interfere with the economy of the Arabs, who have been there for 2,000 years?

In its long journey across history the Jewish people has encountered serious adversaries who have become symbols of their misfortunes. No historian could have expected that a British foreign secretary, a leading figure in a social democratic party, would fulfill that role. Coming on the scene in the aftermath of the Jewish people's cosmic agony, he passes into history without a single word of respect for the legacy, the sufferings, the aspirations or the international rights of a martyred nation. Bevin was such a decisive figure in Israel's story between 1945 and 1949 that a scrutiny of his motives must figure large in any historical recollection. Historians, respectful of his achievements in other fields of policy, go to tormented lengths to explain his excesses. Bevin's most important biographer, Alan Bullock, draws attention to the fact that the original British decision was to send the *Exodus,* with its 4,500 Jewish refugees, back to France where they would have been free to make their lives anew. The French government had in fact offered the *Exodus* passengers the opportunity to go ashore to settle in France or to go on elsewhere as they chose. But only 130 passengers took advantage of the offer, while the rest refused to go anywhere but Palestine. Not once was Bevin capable of understanding that what the Jews were seeking was not individual salvation or the opportunity to "relieve" Europe of their presence, but a collective solution of their homelessness in the spirit of existing international commitments in whose acceptance his own nation had taken a leading role. Even Lord Bullock loses sympathetic contact with his subject when he writes:

For experienced politicians like Attlee and Bevin and other senior ministers to make a mistake which played so completely into the hands of those whose purpose was to rouse world opinion against the British shows how far their judgement had been clouded by anger and frustration with the situation in which they found themselves placed in the summer of 1947.

A strictly self-interested appraisal would surely have made Bevin give no less weight to the United States than to the governments in Baghdad and Cairo or to the Indian Muslim populations. After all, it was President Truman, and not Prime Minister Nuri Said of Iraq, or King Abdullah of Jordan, or King Farouk of Egypt, who would be needed to solve Britain's most critical dilemmas. As Bullock has written: "Nothing else so much threatened Anglo-U.S. relations as Palestine. Other statesmen, such as Winston Churchill, who could hardly be regarded as less patriotically concerned with basic British interests saw nothing to admire and very much to condemn, in Bevin's approach. . . ."

It was Churchill who coined the words "squalid war" to describe the events of 1945 to 1947. All the hated restrictions on Jewish immigration, whether "legal" or "illegal," were Draconically applied. The smaller Jewish resistance groups, the Irgun and Lechi, eagerly carried out murderous assaults on British soldiery in their military posts and in their clubs. The British replied with emergency regulations under which it was a capital offense to possess arms, let alone to use them. The British resorted to the gallows in which young Jewish resistance warriors displayed their heroism, fortitude and contempt for their foreign rulers. On one occasion the Irgun retaliated by taking two young British officers, innocent of any anti-Jewish action, one of them indeed being Jewish, and hanging them and leaving their bodies booby-trapped. This horrifying action, for which Menachem Begin took personal responsibility, did deter the British general from carrying out a scheduled execution. But it also enraged Israel's friends in London and other West European capitals. In November 1945 the Haganah, under Ben-Gurion's direction, made a formal decision to go beyond diplomacy and rhetoric into active resistance. Bevin's statements made it inevitable that Palestine Jewry would take this course. Haganah operations were more carefully chosen than those of the Irgun, being concentrated on military targets such as bridges and railway lines. The main weapon of the Haganah, with potent effects on world opinion, was still "aliya bet"—immigrant ships landed on Palestinian coasts in defiance of the British blockade. This policy produced a large, crowded camp full of Holocaust refugees in Cyprus. All this time the realities of Nazi savagery in Europe were coming home to Palestinian Jews, creating an aggravated sense not only of grief, but also—strangely—of guilt. Jews in Palestine felt it necessary to atone for the tranquillity and prosperity of the war years. It required the agonizing cry of the American correspondent Edward R. Murrow to make many people in the West believe in the reality of Nazi barbarity. "I pray you to believe what I have said about Buchenwald," cried Murrow in a voice choked with tears. "I have reported only what I saw and heard and yet only part of it, for most of it I have no words. If I have offended you by this rather mild account of Buchenwald I am not in the least sorry." Jews now divided their resentment between the Germans who had murdered their kinsmen and the Western countries who had not prevented them from doing so. Of more than 800,000 Jewish refugees absorbed between 1933 and 1943, some 200,000 went to the United States. These included Albert Einstein, Arnold Schönberg and other men of great talent without whom contemporary culture is hardly conceivable. Nevertheless, the number of refugees accepted by the United States during the Holocaust period pales by comparison with the millions of Jews who had been welcomed at Ellis Island in earlier, less dangerous, eras. Another 65,000 Jews found refuge in England and, in spite of everything, 120,000 in Palestine. But it was toward the British that Jewish anger was felt most sharply, for at the very time when the conditions of European Jewry were most desperate Britain had shut the gates of the Promised Land.

This atmosphere inevitably reacted strongly on me in my own small private world. It goes far to explain the choice of career of which the rest of this book will describe the consequences. That story begins with my sitting on the terrace of the King David Hotel with a brother officer, Captain Francis Noel Baker, the son of a distinguished Labour statesman who became a Nobel

Laureate for his passionate but fruitless advocacy of disarmament. It was the summer of 1945. We were not unreasonably discussing our future now that the war was coming to an end. I had unwisely contracted for a further year of service to the Middle East Center on Arab Studies reaching into 1946, but I had received three communications from Britain. One was from the master of my college at Cambridge, Sir Montagu Butler, whose other claim to fame was that he was the father of R. A. Butler, later to become a pillar of Conservative cabinets. Sir Montagu had been the governor of Bengal in India. To judge from the walls of his master's lodge he had been an implacable adversary of Indian tigers, which seemed to have been saved from extinction only by his reassignment to Britain. Sir Montagu regarded the six war years as nothing but an irrelevant interruption of academic routine, and offered me a return to my research and teaching at Pembroke College from which I would quite easily rise to professorial rank. At the same time the Foreign Ministry, satisfied with my performance in the Minister of State's office and in the Middle East Center of Arab Studies, made what could only be understood as the offer of tenure in that eminent elitist abode. The greatest temptation came from Professor Harold Laski, who was then the chairman of the British Labour Party. After many years of academic penury he could now dispense patronage. He offered me the opportunity to represent a constituency in the July elections. It is true that this was at a village chiefly populated by retired colonels with bristly white moustaches and red faces, where there would be no prospect of a Labour victory. But the professor amiably explained that a self-sacrificial defeat in a hopeless constituency would entitle me to larger consideration when more realistic prospects became available. The Labour Party theoretically saw itself as the champion of the hungry poor, but its election campaigners were actively looking for young men with academic and military titles to adorn their list.

My first reaction was to test Laski's offer for veracity. He had been known to me in my Cambridge days when I used to attend his salons in Hammersmith, where he would hold court in glittering but adenoidal prose to students from distant Asian countries. Now and again he would break off the conversation, answer a telephone in the neighboring room and come back to greet us with a casual "Do forgive me, that was President Roosevelt asking me for advice."

Laski kept up a lengthy correspondence with Justice Holmes in which he continually dropped eminent names of statesmen who were purported to hang on his every word. There would also be accounts of Laski announcing triumphantly that he had just bought the first edition of a valuable autographed book for a sensationally low price. Unfortunately, a subsequent letter to the great justice would announce this bibliophiliac miracle to have taken place with exactly the same book many years later. I duly made inquiries through a university colleague who discovered that the professor had been in one of his rare encounters with accuracy when he made his offer.

So I really had something to consider. Francis Noel Baker did go back to England to cultivate what seemed to be a hopelessly unattainable constituency in Lancashire. For one thing this entitled him, and would have entitled me, to immediate demobilization. He departed for England and was swept into parliamentary office by the unexpected landslide.

Unlike him, I passed up the available liberation in 1945. I was already caught up in a conflict of allegiances to which, surprisingly, most Diaspora Jews have always managed to be apathetically indifferent. I failed to see how I could continue to have an active foot in each of two opposing worlds. Meanwhile, Britain was moving to outright war with Zionism. On May 31, 1946, Bevin rejected a report by an Anglo-American commission recommending the early admission of 100,000 Jewish displaced persons to Palestine. He had previously reacted with anger and contempt to President Truman's own insistence on this matter. In the eyes of Attlee and Bevin, Arab and Muslim sentiments were more important than the Atlantic alliance. Violence escalated. On June 17 it took a crucial turn when the Haganah launched attacks on railways and bridges in various parts of the country. This gave the British-Jewish confrontation a much more important dimension than sporadic Irgun and Lechi operations could possibly signify. It meant that Palestine Jewry was now in full and open revolt. The British response was drastic. On June 29, 1946, Suzy and I were preparing a luncheon in our North Talpiot home for Moshe Sharett, who, to our certain knowledge, was again going to insist on my taking a Zionist career. He was due to come at 12:30 for a preliminary conversation. As we approached 1:00 it was obvious that something had gone seriously wrong. Sharett was so punctilious that if he were more than fifteen minutes late for an appointment it would be natural to start making inquiries at hospitals and police stations. I naturally opened the radio set where I heard that he and other Zionist leaders had been arrested and that aggressive arms searches and curfews were now being carried out in Jewish settlements, especially at Yagur, which I knew to be a major center for the concentration of Haganah weapons. The war of Britain, still a great power, against the Jews was now in full force. Sharett had never relaxed in his appeals for my permanent enlistment. He had tried to entice me with an appropriate promise of "blood, toil, sweat and tears." These in fact were the only commodities in the gift of Zionist leaders at that time. Sharett had even carried out his threat to mobilize Zionist President Chaim Weizmann, in order to make my choice inevitable. This was an ultimate resort for any attempt to get a Zionist to act against his own better interest. I reflected that a man who in 1917 to 1920 had persuaded the world's governments that it would be in their interest and cause no trouble for them to establish a Jewish National Home in Palestine must be capable of persuading anybody of anything. I had pledged my acceptance to the great Weizmann in his study at Rehovot and was therefore effectively trapped.

While Sharett and his colleagues were under arrest at Latrun, Ben-Gurion was by happy chance in Paris where he remained for the next seven months, sharing a hotel with Ho Chi Minh, the Vietnam nationalist leader, and other destroyers of empires. Weizmann was in Rehovot. Even Bevin recoiled from challenging such a legendary figure. A British general had called on Weizmann at Rehovot and had been blasted with such a vast wind of anger that he retired as quickly as possible. Golda Meir was spared arrest either because the British authorities deduced wrongly from her accent that she was an American citizen, or out of male chauvinistic attitudes to womanhood. Golda fiercely resented her exclusion from arrest. For the rest of her eventful life she considered this to be an unsuccessful plot to reduce her subsequent eligibility for prime ministerial office in a decolonized Land of Israel. The sharp break between two peoples whose common purpose had created the very mandate under which Britain held its rule was a grotesque anomaly.

A few weeks later, I received a crumpled piece of paper in an envelope from the Zionist Office. It seemed that Sharett and the other Latrun detainees had established a secret courier service for smuggling papers from Latrun to the outside world. Sharett was not famous for brevity of discourse, but now, in an inspired choice of words, he had drafted his message in a single word: "NOO?" I wrote one word of reply: YES! The die was cast.

It should have been cast earlier. I realized this one day in July 1946 when I was late for an appointment with Suzy in the King David Hotel, where I was due to have a haircut. On this occasion I found unpunctuality to have a life-saving consequence and I have been recommending it ever since. As I came down the Bethlehem Road toward the hotel I heard a vast explosion. By the time that I got near the King David I could see a flaming mass of dust and ruins. The Irgun, in its most daring act of resistance, had blown up the hotel that was the headquarters of the British military and civil administrations.

Even from the distance of 100 yards at which spectators were being held back, it was possible to see harrowing scenes of carnage. My thought was for two British Jews who had been persuaded by the Zionist Organization to volunteer for membership in the Civil Service of the British Mandatory regime, Montagu Brown and Norman Jacobs. It was only the next day that I found that they had both been killed, as were many stenographers and office workers, Jewish, British and Arab, but none of the real architects of the policy against which the Irgun had directed its violence.

Suzy was just as unpunctual as I was and had been the same distance away from the hotel, but on the western side of the city.

Those who had carried out the project had shown great subtlety and tactical purpose. They had entered the hotel disguised as milkmen, bringing their cans into the basement of the hotel. The Irgun claimed, and the British denied, that a telephonic warning had been received in British headquarters and had been ignored by Chief Secretary Sir John Shaw. It is possible that both were right. There had been so many freak calls in those days that few of them were ever believed or acted upon.

My own discomfort as a British officer was becoming intense. My anonymous articles in *The Palestine Post* attacking the excesses of the Mandatory administration have a retrospectively amusing tone, but at the time, my moral anguish was intense. I was, after all, undermining an authority to which I still owed a formal loyalty.

Later in 1946, the ambiguity of my position became even more blatant. After the explosion in the King David Hotel, the commander of the British forces in Palestine, General Evelyn Barker, placed Jerusalem and Tel Aviv under curfew for four days and circulated an order declaring Jewish shops and homes off-limits to British troops. This extraordinary document was impregnated with a vicious racism:

No British soldier is to have any social intercourse with any Jew and any intercourse in the way of duty should be as brief as possible and kept strictly to business in hand. I appreciate that these measures will inflict some hardship on the troops but I am certain that if my reasons are fully explained to them they will understand their propriety and will be punishing the Jews in a way that the race dislikes as any by striking at their pockets and showing our contempt for them.

Seeing this scurrilous document on the notice board of the Middle East Center of Arab Studies, I was filled with hot rage. It seemed to me that the general's fellow citizens should have a chance of seeing what was said in their name. I memorized the short text, line by line, put it all together and took it off to the Eden Hotel where I handed it to my friend Jon Kimche, who then represented *The Sunday Observer* and Reuters.

The remarkable tirade exploded with full force in the British and European press the next day, and was mercilessly attacked in the House of Commons. A few weeks later, Barker was replaced. This must have been inconvenient for the general, for he was then conducting an exchange of affectionate letters with Katie Antonius, the leading Arab political hostess in Jerusalem. When Barker's letters to Katie Antonius, full of ethnic prejudice and sensual insinuations, were published years later in a London Sunday newspaper, any remorse that I might have felt about his removal was allayed. Objectivity was clearly not his long suit. The Barker letter was not classified, since it was intended for the "education" of hundreds of thousand of troops, but it was clearly not intended for parliamentary discussion.

In one of my anonymous articles in *The Palestine Post* in 1946 I had described British Prime Minister Clement Attlee as he hesitated whether to spare 100,000 immigration permits for the victims of the death camps. I wrote:

Nine months have passed since the President of the United States proposed the admission of 100,000 Jews into the National Home. For many tedious weeks Mr. Attlee has lingered beside the still waters of moral duty, reluctant to plunge and adamant against being pushed. He has appointed a committee to take the temperature of the water and estimated the relative consequences of courage and timidity.

It was satisfying emotionally for me to bombard Clement Attlee with sarcasm, but I was after all an enlisted officer and he was the prime minister. It was becoming evident to me that Zionist enthusiasm had become such an obsessive part of my emotion that I ought to regularize my position by putting my loyalties and my arena of action in the same place. As soon as I could be released from my contract I informed my commander in the Middle East Center of Arab Studies of my intention to take service in the Jewish Agency!

My choice was between full participation in the life of a liberal, democratic society and a voluntary removal from my familiar scene with its memories of boyhood and early youth—a withdrawal that entailed the adoption of something remote and precarious. A biographer, Robert St. John, has written:

It was a duality which many Jews in Western countries no doubt also felt. But with Eban it was especially intense because of the unusual balance between his relationships in the two worlds. Men like Herzl, Nordau and many of the German Jewish Zionists had been remote from all Jewish loyalties until some shock, some spiritual or physical experience, some humiliation had brought them back to their roots. In a sense they had gone out of the Jewish fold and then returned. But in Eban's case there had been no going out. Since the age of seven he had lived part of his life in the normal British world and the other part, beyond any geographical context, in a world of historic pride and cultural fascination.

The idea that I would make my life and home in the Land of Israel and in the Zionist service had been prevalent in my mind in my Cambridge days. Perhaps I would have delayed this transition if the war had not sharpened all personal urgencies. But it is also possible that every year in England with bright and fruitful prospects exercising their seductions, I would have yielded to one of the many other options. I was amused to discover that the Zionist leaders, observing the disquieting tendency of youthful Zionists to make for the Land of Israel, had plaintively wondered what would become of Zionism in Britain if all the Zionists made a habit of rushing off to Palestine. Chaim Herzog and Walter Eytan were only two of the most prominent young Jews who were addicted to the heresy that Zionism had something to do with living in the Land of Israel. This was by no means the general view.

I did not adopt sanctimonious doctrines such as "the negation of the Diaspora," which was one of the canons of Zionist faith. The crux of this idea was that remaining in a non-Jewish environment under a non-Zionist flag was a form of desertion since "it is only in Israel that a Jew can live a Jewish life." My study of Jewry in dispersion provided many examples of enviable creativity and I was attuned to the idea that Jewish history would move in two channels. There is the ingathering tendency that causes Jews to seek their own patrimony, legacy and environment and to express themselves in their own identity. But this sense of particularity is offset by a contrary impulse of Jews to throw themselves into all the oceans of history and to seek fulfillment in their interaction with other cultures and civilizations. Since this duality had persisted for so many centuries, I saw little point in rebelling against it in useless rancor. I admired the great poet who sat by the waters of Babylon and wept with timeless eloquence when he remembered Zion, but the fact was that he had wept in Babylon and none will ever know if he returned with the very small minority that answered the call of the Persian king who offered him and his fellow Jews the arduous option of reconstructing the Temple in Jerusalem.

My decision for a Zionist career, if it could thus be described, had a stunning effect on my family and friends. Some of them compared the prospects that I had renounced with the one that I had embraced, and wondered if I had lost my senses. My answer was that we were living a tragic hour that demanded an assertion of conscience. So I bade farewell to the horizons of Cambridge donhood, diplomatic status and parliamentary struggle and took my journey into what then seemed to be a life of embattled obscurity. I had the full support of Suzy, my parents and hers. I thought that for a young man with a sustaining vision, the hardest decision could turn out to be the best. I remembered the great phrase of the Cambridge philosopher Alfred North Whitehead: "Adventure and decadence are the only choices offered to mankind."

In a letter to my family I wrote: "The other possibilities were more tranquil and serene. It is a poetic rather than a prosaic decision, romantic rather than pragmatic. It is a decision I know I shall never regret. . . ."

3

LONDON 1946–1947: THE YEAR OF DISCONTENT

AFTER A MUTED farewell from some of the officers at the Middle East School of Arab Studies in the old Austrian Hospice near the Damascus Gate, I went to a British military base near the Talpiot area of Jerusalem and handed in my military identity papers. I then crossed a few roads to the Jewish Agency building and formally concluded agreements as a Zionist official. I wondered whether anyone else in Jerusalem had ever before made such a transition between three such disparate institutions as a Center of Arab Studies, a British military base and a Zionist Headquarters.

The major Zionist leaders, Sharett and his deputy Dov Joseph, were in detention at Latrun. In true Bevin style, the British government had decided that if it could not lay hands on the underground Zionists who had constantly used force, it should at least imprison the moderate leaders who generally opposed the use of force.

At the Jewish Agency office I arranged my enlistment, undramatically, with the treasurer, Eliezer Kaplan, who assured me that my monthly wage would be above the starvation level, but not far above. The other Zionist officials were in a disgruntled mood, partly because they were obliged to accept the work load of the imprisoned leaders, but even more because they had not themselves "qualified" for detention in Latrun. This indicated that the British authorities deemed them to be unworthy of serious attention.

The next day, Suzy and I went to the Jerusalem railway station, which then, as now, was like a small village station in a sparsely populated British countryside where any arrival of a train would be a source of local surprise and satisfaction. We were seen off by Walter Eytan, previously an Oxford don, now a Jewish Agency officer, who had preceded me in the kind of journey that I was making. After what seemed an endless voyage across Sinai sands we reached Cairo. The Ambache family house was without its owners, who according to the habit of well-to-do Cairenes were vacationing in Europe.

Suzy picked up a few articles evoking youthful memories in her parents' house. We had some intuition that amid the growing tensions between Zionism and Arab nationalism, we might not see that house again. This prediction has, so far, been fulfilled. (In 1978 Suzy and I returned to the street where she had lived and stood outside the gate. Her father's house had become the embassy of Saudi Arabia. We did not seek entry. It was something of a compliment on the part of the new tenants to have chosen this house when they could have had any other that they desired.)

We flew by Air France, in the habit of those days, through Tunis, Malta and Nice, to London, where I took up my duties in the Information Department of the Jewish Agency. I worked in the room that had been the abode of the great writer and Zionist leader Nahum Sokolow, until his sudden death in 1936. From that august desk I called up my mother and pointed out with filial irony that it was "all her fault" for abandoning me one night in November 1917, in order to translate the Balfour Declaration in Sokolow's office in London.

If I had to condemn an adversary to cruel and unusual punishment, I would sentence him to be an official of the Jewish Agency in London in the winter of 1946. Jewish Agency officials were being treated, for the first time since the Balfour Declaration, not as the emissaries of a legitimate national movement in alliance with Great Britain, but as the unwanted agents of a hostile power. In Palestine, Jewish resistance fighters were engaged in murderous combat with British soldiers. Immigrants were arriving in Palestine "illegally" and being apprehended and sent away. Exasperated British troops, longing to get home with the war at an end, were bogged down in a conflict in which their virulent commander, General Barker, had adviscd them "to regard the Jews with hatred and contempt." Public opinion in London was fully alive to the expense, humiliation and sterility of the British task in Palestine. Most people in Britain reacted with hostility to their own government and even more to the Zionist cause.

The pall of gloom in the Zionist office was in no way relieved by the general environment. London was weary and drab, its people underfed and ill dressed during a winter of unparalleled severity. Food was not only scarce; the very procedures for obtaining it required an exhausting effort that was mocked by the poverty of result. With shortage of fuel, English houses were colder even than English houses had always been throughout history. The hulks of shattered buildings were no longer regarded as scars of courage and glory. By this time they signified little but shabby neglect. A people, once renowned for its relaxed humor, was in an angry mood. The British people felt cheated. No other nation had fought the war for a full six years without having itself been provoked by enemy attack. Yet American troops were going home in their thousands, while their British counterparts languished uselessly in outposts of an empire that would soon have to be relinquished.

The 100,000 soldiers in Palestine were the focus of broad popular resentment, for nobody could convincingly explain to them or their families what compensating benefits the occupation provided. The newspapers brought daily reminders of British troops locked in murderous combat with Jewish resistance fighters, many of whom still bore the signs of Nazi persecution. The soldiers' role in Palestine was abrasive, punitive and bereft of the nobility that had illuminated their struggles against the Nazi hordes.

Behind the British view that support of Zionism was no longer a national interest, there lurked darker ethnic prejudices that Prime Minister Attlee and Foreign Minister Bevin did little to allay. In this unpromising atmosphere there were some rays of light. Some friendly British voices, including the most resonant voice of all, that of Winston Churchill, were beginning to ask why Britain should want to cling to a presence in Palestine that was becoming more abrasive and less advantageous with every passing day.

Suzy and I followed these fluctuations of British mood from a small apartment in Highgate that had been made available by a friend of Weizmann, Sigmund Gestetner, the inventor of the most popular duplication process, whose widow, Henny, is one of our closest friends. In another part of West London my former collaborators, Teddy Kollek and Reuven Shiloah, were established at the Atheneum Court in Piccadilly, which was a haven of relative comfort and style in those austere days. They were exercising their persuasive talents on British officials by a judicious mixture of careful argument and lavish hospitality. Professor Namier was no longer on the scene, but Weizmann was still in residence at the Dorchester Hotel, exchanging letters with Ben-Gurion at his place of exile in the Royal Monceau Hotel in Paris.

Shortly after my arrival in London from Jerusalem, I flew to Paris to present myself to Ben-Gurion. He received the fact that I was now one of his associates with as much satisfaction as his outwardly bashful nature would allow. Ben-Gurion was full of confidence in his public attitudes, but was overcome with awkward reserve in all personal relations. He spoke to me frankly about partition as the only viable formula on which to make our bid for support in public opinion. He showed me an exchange of letters that he was having with Weizmann in which they had established understanding on this point. He had reached the firm conclusion that the British government under its present leadership was so hostile to our cause that any further argument with London was fruitless. Statehood could not be postponed.

I considered this conclusion to be basically true, but premature. With all allowance for Britain's future eclipse of empire, London was still the focus of decision in any matter affecting Zionism and Palestine. Most of us predicted that America would soon become the center in which our diplomacy would be enacted, but it was the British government that decided how many or few immigration certificates were to be granted, where land purchases were permitted or forbidden and how the future government of Palestine was to be fashioned. Although we had some supporters among members of Attlee's

Labour Cabinet, they had little influence or effect. Ernest Bevin was in full control. In view of my own political background, the fact that our adversaries were members of the Labour Party added to my bitterness. My task was to capture some islands of sympathy and understanding in the wide ocean of alienation. So I wrote articles, pamphlets and booklets, lunched with editors, reporters and members of Parliament and occasionally accompanied one of the senior Zionist executive members to an interview with the colonial secretary or a high Foreign Office official.

At the Royal Institute of International Affairs at Chatham House I gave lectures on social and cultural developments in the Arab world and did battle with the defenders of Arabism, Professor Arnold Toynbee and Albert Hourani. One of the Zionist myths was that Chatham House was the real ruler of Britain, with Cabinets and Parliaments in a subordinate role. All this activity was interesting in itself, but there seemed to be no prospect that it could prevail against the rocklike determination of Bevin to make common cause with Zionism's adversaries.

I frankly thought that I had made a mistake in my choice of career. I seemed to have committed myself to a hopeless kind of treadmill with no spark of light at the end of any visible tunnel. For Suzy, who had known nothing all her life but Mediterranean sunshine, the fog and gloom and cold and rain of post-war London were a stark contrast with her previous environments.

One of my first tasks at the Jewish Agency's Information Department was to make a survey of the hundred or so people who could be said to have a formative influence in British Middle Eastern policy. These were to be found in the Cabinet, in Parliament, among newspaper editors, in universities, in institutes of foreign relations and among individuals who had the ear of policymakers. I found that most of them had never come within the orbit of the Zionist information effort that had concentrated, with good results, on the wider public and on parliamentary parties neglecting the experts and Orientalists who formulated the strategic analyses on which governments based their policies. Zionism had its own rationality, but it was unlikely to be embraced by anyone who lacked a historic imagination and at least a modest ounce of romantic eccentricity.

Ben-Gurion arrived in London late in 1946 after his colleagues in Palestine had been released from detention in Latrun and he himself could emerge from Parisian exile. I outlined to him my strategy on information. He commented that if this kind of systematic approach had been made a few years earlier the collapse of British support of Zionism might have been averted or at least postponed. He was convinced that at this point it was all too late. There was no likelihood that the Arab lobby in London would change its views now that Ernest Bevin gave it such powerful support. Moreover, Britain itself seemed to be in the last phase of its career as an imperial power. It would henceforward act out of a sense of decline and weakness, no longer out of confidence or power. Nevertheless it would be my duty to exhaust the British phase in Zionist history with a last attempt to see if some kind of understanding could be ensured.

One of my tasks was surprising. I discovered that across the world the Zionist movement was maintaining what it called "propaganda" offices. There was even a special department of "Zionist propaganda." I found it unthinkable that sensitive people accept the implications of a word that the odious Goebbels had polluted during the Nazi years. Today a book called *Contemporary Aphorisms* published in London contains my definition: "Propaganda is the art of persuading others of what you do not necessarily believe yourself." I had no aphoristic ambition when I formulated that sentence; it was designed to be an assault on the very use of the word in the Zionist context. No nation should admit that its own truth is just an exercise in persuasion of inaccuracy.

One of the troubles with Zionism throughout all its history has been a tendency to claim a total rectitude for its views and to be based on the assumption that nobody else has any case at all. It may be significant that the first Hebrew document now available for perusal is a Dead Sea Scroll entitled "War of the Sons of Light against the Sons of Darkness." This confrontational theory does not make room for such relative ideas as "the lesser injustice." I thought that the Jews and Arabs were behaving more or less as each of them would do if their situations were interchanged. The central theme of the relationship between Jews and Arabs is complexity and not simplicity. Since the decision makers in the world are people of sophisticated temperament, I believed that the rights and claims of Zionism had to be interpreted in terms of broader interests and relative values.

But larger interests and broader values were very hard to sustain even in the great capital city whose citizens were much more concerned with basic problems of food and warmth. The political discourse in general and the Zionist idea in particular were no longer revolved at a high level of sensibility and purpose. Weizmann himself was having more and more recourse to my company and advice. This reflected his own solitude. All his hopes had been invested in Churchill and Roosevelt. Now Roosevelt was dead, leaving behind him the equivocal effects of his promise to King Ibn Saud, about whom he had said, "I learnt more about the Middle East in a single hour with Ibn Saud than in all the previous years." His hour with the Saudi monarch had been devoted to Ibn Saud's tirade against Zionism and the Jews, so that this statement had an element of frivolity. The more we have seen of newly released documents the more it appears that it was always a mistake to regard Roosevelt as a friend of Zionism at any time.

Churchill was a different matter. His Zionist passion was constant but his promise of an adequate partition plan had been frozen by the assassination of Lord Moyne, and now that he was ready to return to the fray he no longer held power. Weizmann was therefore condemned to hold his discussions with men of prosaic and restricted intellect such as Ernest Bevin and his colonial secretary, George Hall, who would have had to rise to higher levels than hitherto to qualify as mediocre. How could Weizmann expect to secure the transforming effects of his persuasive talent as when it had been exercised on the romantic David Lloyd George and the intellectual Arthur James Balfour? Moreover, he had made the error of staying away from Palestine too long. His visit in November 1944, on his seventieth birthday, had shown what a profound emotion he could still stir in Palestine Jewry, but the memory had worn off. Indeed, they had become dimmed by the news of the Holocaust and the desperation created by the hostile policies of the Labour Government. His relations with Ben-Gurion were volatile; sometimes they blossomed into harmony, at other times they degenerated into personal friction. In October 1946 he had received a letter from Ben-Gurion in the following terms: "Whatever your views are on all of this you remain for me the elect of Jewish history representing beyond compare the suffering and glory of the Jews and wherever you go you will be attended by the love and faithful esteem of me and my colleagues." This sounded well, but astute Ben-Gurionologists interpreted it as meaning that the Zionist past belonged to Weizmann, while the future belonged to Ben-Gurion.

Yet, despite the differences of their temperaments they usually tended to come together on the major issues. Now they were both totally resolved to win support for the view that a Jewish state with real sovereignty in a part of Palestine was far preferable to access to the whole of Palestine without sovereignty and freedom. They had carried the partition flag very close to victory in 1939; they were now destined to carry it across with further success before the end of the current decade.

But the real test for Zionism would come at the Congress to be convened in December 1946 at Basle. The central theme of the speech that Weizmann asked me to help him draft was the catastrophic change in the Jewish condition arising from the Holocaust and the betrayal by Britain of its international trust.

While Weizmann and most of the workers at Great Russell Street went to Basle for the Zionist Conference, I stayed behind in the London office to hold the fort and to maintain some link of contact with British government officials. From Switzerland came word of the drama of Weizmann's farewell address to the Congress. The draft that I had helped him write was well received: "The shadow of tragic bereavement is upon us tonight," he said in the opening address, casting a tortured glance over the assembly as if to ask where German, Polish, Hungarian, Dutch and Belgian Jewry had gone. The voice was choked and the eyes tense and painful behind the dark glasses imposed on him by his recent operations for glaucoma. "The greatest hatred in the annals of inhumanity was turned against us and found our people with no hope of defense. European Jewry has been engulfed in a tidal wave. Its centers of life and culture have been ravaged, its habitations laid waste."

He spoke bitterly of the Chamberlain White Paper. "Few documents in history have worse consequences for which to answer." He told of British ministerial promises that had been broken: "It seems incredible that anybody could be playing fast and loose with us when we were so battered and exhausted. If there is antagonism directed against the British government its sole origin is indignation at desertion of her trust." He spoke lucidly of Arab hostility. "How can it be moderate for them to claim seven states and extreme for us to claim a part of one?" In a tense atmosphere he declared that he understood the motives that led many young Jews in Palestine to violence: "It is difficult in such circumstances to retain belief in a victory of peaceful ideals and yet I affirm that we have to retain it. Jews came to Palestine to build, not to destroy." And then the crushing statement: "Massada, for all its heroism, was a disaster in our history. Zionism was to mark the end of our glorious deaths and the beginning of a new path whose watchword is life."

These ideas were capable of unifying the Zionist movement, although Weizmann had too much difficulty reading the text to make much of an oratorical impression. But the tone of the speech brought him much closer to the delegates and to the public following the course of the Congress back in Jerusalem and Tel Aviv.

Yet, the impression of harmony between him and the Zionist Congress was suddenly refuted by a violent burst of his pent-up indignation. In the debate on his address he became enraged when an American Zionist leader said that "Palestine Jewry should revolt against Britain while American Jews would give full political and moral support." Weizmann was outraged by the distinction between what was asked of Palestine Jewry and the "political and moral support" that American Zionists promised. He then uttered the rebuke that may have cost him his presidency: "Moral and political support is very little when you send other people to the barricades to face tanks and guns. The eleven new settlements just established in the Negev have a much greater weight than a hundred speeches about resistance, especially when the speeches are made in New York while the proposed resistance is to be made in Tel Aviv and Jerusalem."

In that single improvised sentence he had summarized the existential dilemma of Diaspora Zionism. This lay in its tendency to demand too much of Palestine Jews and too little of their supporters abroad. He had always had this gift for one-line summaries, which made one wonder why all the literature around them was really necessary. It was in the same spirit as his words to the Royal Commission in 1937: "For the Jews of Europe the world is divided between countries where they cannot live and countries where they cannot enter."

The Palestinians at the Congress, and especially Ben-Gurion, seemed rather delighted with Weizmann's rebuke of American Zionists. Ben-Gurion always enjoyed rebuking Diaspora Zionists for their tendency to determine Palestinian events without sharing Palestinian hazards. However, he and other delegates were horrified when a delegate from New York called out "demagogue." Weizmann stopped his speech and stood in stunned silence. Nothing like this had ever happened to him before. His patient toil, sacrifice, leadership, age and infirmity had been violated by a moment of rancor. The Congress sat in shocked tension as he pondered his reply. The Congress Protocol quotes him as follows:

> Somebody has called me a demagogue. I do not know who. I hope that I never learn the man's name. I a demagogue. I who have borne all the ills and travail of this movement [loud applause]. The person who flung that word in my face should know that in every house and stable in Nahalal, in every little workshop in Tel-Aviv or Haifa, there is a drop of my blood [tempestuous applause. The delegates rise to their feet except the Revisionists and Mizrachi]. You know that I am telling you the truth. If you think of bringing the redemption nearer by non-Jewish methods, if you lose faith in hard work and better days, then you commit avodah zarah [idolatry] and endanger what we have built. Would that I had a tongue of flame to warn you against the paths of Babylon and Egypt. Zion shall be redeemed in judgment and not by any other means.

No dramatist could have conceived a more overpowering climax. He left the hall never again to make a controversial address to a Zionist assembly. Between the rows of applauding delegates, standing in awe and contrition, he made his way painfully, gropingly into the street. A few days later he appeared to make a short farewell. Chaim Weizmann had left the Zionist Congress arena for ever.

He had made his presidency dependent on freedom for the Zionist Executive if it saw fit to attend discussions with the British government in London in a last attempt to reach an agreement that would enable the British Mandate to continue. The Zionist Congress, by a small majority, rejected a Labor Zionist resolution proposed by Golda Meir urging support of Weizmann's proposal. It then voted "categorically" against attending the London conference in present circumstances. This was tantamount to Weizmann's non-election.

The words "in present circumstances" were clearly a somewhat sly ladder of escape. "Circumstances" were more likely to change than to remain static. "Everything flows onward," as the Greek writer Heraclitus said. "And nobody dips his hand in the same river twice." Ben-Gurion, in awkward alliance with the American Zionists under Abba Hillel Silver's resonant leadership, wanted to elevate Weizmann to an innocuous emeritus status, while he himself took command of the arena. Everyone knew that if Ben-Gurion could get the leadership he would attend the conference in London and, in his own style, would present the exact cause that Weizmann would have presented had his leadership been prolonged.

I went to see Weizmann the day after his return from Basle. He was in an exceptionally blithe mood. He said to me smilingly, "You wrote me such a wonderful speech that they threw me out." This was good humored but not strictly true. The speech that I drafted would have kept him well within the congressional consensus, his own fiery outburst was noble and prophetic, but nobility and prophecy do not go down well in the political infighting of a Congress.

In any case, his non-election was soon to become irrelevant. No president was elected in his place and there awaited him in the future at least two exploits that were worthy to stand side by side with his successes in the Balfour Declaration period. He would develop an intimate friendship with President Truman, to whom no other Zionist friendships were acceptable, and when the issues to be decided were nothing less than the retention of the Negev in the Jewish state and the recognition of that state by the United States eleven hours after its birth, it was Weizmann who carried the Zionist interest to victory.

There was nothing in the beginning of 1947 that would give augury of its end. It was, at that time, the most sensational diplomatic year in Zionist history since 1917. It was remarkable for two British decisions, although not dictated by any benevolent motive, that were to contribute decisively to the establishment of Israel. The first decision was to abandon the Mandate over Palestine. The second was to seek the active intervention of the United Nations. These two British decisions had as much influence on Israel's birth as did those of George III and Lord North in the emancipation of the American colonies.

It is a paradox of history that intention and consequence are often sharply discordant so that nations owe as much to their opponents as to their supporters. The emergence of Israel between 1945 and 1948 is a trenchant example. The retirement of Britain from its Mandate and its recourse to the United Nations did not proceed from any compelling necessity. British authority in Palestine was suffering many grievous blows and British troops and government officials were taking casualties. In the two years between August 1945 and September 17, 1947, the number of those killed in Palestine under British occupation totaled 347. Of these the highest proportion consisted of the 169 British killed in conflict with Jewish resistance movements. Jewish deaths numbered eighty-eight and Arab eighty-five, while five were unidentified. Most of the Jewish deaths were caused by Arab action. British police and army personnel were heavily restrained in their liberty to open fire on civilian demonstrators, and this exposed them to many of their casualties. But it cannot seriously be said that casualties determined the decision to abandon the Mandate. Whenever Britain regarded a certain interest as vital to its own security and prestige it was not deterred by greater losses than these. They certainly bore no comparison to those that were accepted with docility and courage even during the most murderous periods of World War II. Nor was there any deterministic compulsion on Britain to entrust the construction of a new Middle Eastern order to an international forum over which it would have very little control.

I had diagnosed a British mood of disengagement in early 1946 when the British government accepted the appointment of an Anglo-American commission to make a recommendation on the problem of the Jews in Europe and of the conditions for a Palestine settlement. Bevin's hope was to involve the United States so intimately that it would be possible to share influence if not jurisdiction with America. Churchill had alluded to this repeatedly in complaining of the tendency of the United States to avoid taking responsibility in Palestine while being generous with advice. The Anglo-American commission, however, turned out to be a pallid and uninfluential body. In response to President Truman's pressure, it urged the admission of 100,000 Jewish refugees without proposing the release of Britain from its sole responsibility for administering the country. Subsequent proposals for a cantonized or federated Palestine under virtual Arab rule were anti-Zionist to such an extreme degree that Britain would have needed more force to impose them than the force needed to maintain the status quo.

British casualties and the physical pressure imposed by the Jewish rebellion, especially after the adherence of the Haganah to occasional armed resistance, certainly reinforced the motivation for British withdrawal. But the deeper central reasons lie in events not in Palestine or the Arab world but in Britain itself.

For what rational cause should Britain have wished to maintain 100,000 troops in distant Palestine when its own social fabric and economy were close to disintegration? The years 1947 and 1948 in Britain were a period of drastic food rationing, fuel shortage, depletion of foreign currency assets and above all exhaustion and injured pride. The only nation that had voluntarily resisted Nazism, the only nation that had sustained the burden of that resistance for six whole years, found its military victory receding into memory.

Moreover, the decision to withdraw from Palestine was not an isolated symptom of disengagement. There had already been much more momentous British decisions in favor of unraveling the imperial structure. The Indian subcontinent was to be abandoned. The string of British bases in the Mediterranean passing through Malta, Cyprus and Palestine had originally been envisaged as part of a naval route into the Indian Empire. It was because they were "on the way to India" that these bases had once been deemed indispensable. But now that India was to be relinquished the two small islands and Palestine itself were not "on the way" to anywhere at all. They were links in a chain that moved from nowhere to nowhere. The later epoch-making decision to abandon British responsibilities in Greece and Turkey was the centerpiece in the new strategy of retrenchment. This would open the way to a bipolarized world with only the United States and the Soviet Union being able to present themselves as superpowers. These considerations were not sufficiently understood by the Zionist leadership in February 1947 when the

Attlee-Bevin government, after a fruitless negotiation at the London conference, referred the Palestine question to the United Nations. One defeat of Zionist thinking has been a tendency to look at its own problems in detachment from the general movement of world forces. While it is true that Jewish history has its own particularity, it is also true that it is part of a wider historic design. Why should anyone have believed in the early part of 1947 that a Britain that was disposed to renounce much more lucrative assets would stand its ground on what had become the inhospitable soil of Palestine?

But Jewish skepticism about the prospect of British withdrawal continued unabated, especially among American Zionists. Even after the announcement of Britain's intention to end its rule, there was always a tendency outside Britain to assume that Britain's diplomacy was so sophisticated that its intentions were always the diametrical opposite of its declarations.

Yet it was wrong not to plan for that contingency. If Britain really meant to withdraw its administration and army from Palestine within a few months, the implications for Zionism would be momentous and not exclusively positive. The full responsibility for self-defense and survival would fall upon Jewish shoulders, which at that time carried a limited burden of responsibility for local defense. It was one thing to assert with justification that British protection of the Palestine Jewry had been inadequate and sometimes reluctant. It was quite another thing to deny that the presence of British forces in the Middle East, including Palestine, had saved Palestine Jewry from the horrors of Nazi conquest.

My own view that the departure of Britain was not only a possibility but something very close to a certainty became deeply rooted in my mind from February 1947 onward. The Zionist reaction to this prospect was ambiguous. On the one hand we welcomed the chance of being relieved from domination by a regime that had cut all the ties of mutual interest that had brought our two nations together. But the fact that the British Mandatory regime was bad did not change the central law of Jewish history, which tells us that no situation is so bad as to be incapable of becoming worse.

My only personal glimpse of Bevin at close hand was in the February 1947 talks in which I was a new member of a delegation under the leadership of Ben-Gurion, Sharett and the American Zionist leader Emanuel Neumann. Its task was to make a last attempt to explore the possibility of maintaining a British-Zionist relationship within the terms of the existing Mandate. There were a few original moments in the discussion itself, but what interested me was Bevin's personality. I had never seen a man so able to radiate hostility, not only with every word but with every movement of face and eyes. Not for one single moment did he show us any human respect, let alone diplomatic deference. Even his humor was too heavy to be admired. The sudden extinction of electric light was a common situation during the fuel shortage, and not even the offices of government were exempt. When this happened in our conversation in the Colonial Office, Bevin reacted: "All the lights have gone out except the Israelites." Even Bevin's own associates in the Foreign and Colonial Offices had to make a special effort to greet this humor with a polite snigger. In expressing contempt for partition Bevin observed that it would mean the subordination of 400,000 Arabs to Jewish rule. This led me, despite my juniority in the delegation, to ask him whether this was any worse than subordinating 650,000 Jews to Arab rule when the Arab minority would after all be a small part of the Arab world while the Jews would lose any chance of majority status anywhere. This simply invited a malevolent glare.

When Bevin announced the intention of his government to withdraw from Palestine and place the future of the country before the United Nations, it might have been expected that the Zionist movement would express a sense of relief. This was only one part of our reaction. The other part was the knowledge that Bevin did not believe that he was making us a promise or doing us a favor. He was, in his own mind, uttering a threat. One of his officials later said to me that after we had experienced treatment by the United Nations we might look backward to the British Mandatory Administration with nostalgic regret. His meaning was that we would be exposed to the full fury of Arab hostility without any intervening protective shield.

British policy had lost the old imperial dignity without yet adapting itself to the liberalism of the post-war age. I found it incredible that the very Cabinet that stood paralyzed before the Palestine issue was carrying out the Indian partition with such audacity and sweep.

While Bevin's decision had been motivated by hostility, many of our friends had long believed that the end of the Mandate should be welcomed. Churchill had for several months been advocating this cause: "I cannot recede from the advice which I have ventured to give, namely that if we cannot fulfill our promise to the Zionists we should without delay place our Mandate for Palestine at the feet of the United Nations and give due notice of our impending evacuation of that country."

It is a compulsion of Jewish history that our people should react to every condition in terms of its dangers rather than of its opportunities. The reaction to Bevin's decision emphasized solitude rather than exhilaration. I remembered what a small part the League of Nations had played in the administration of the Mandate of which it was theoretically the master. The United Nations seemed to be a different and more robust international organization. Unlike the League, it was fortified by membership of all the great powers and had American membership and support. Yet I feared that the special pathos of Zionism would be submerged in the cruder calculations of global politics. After all, the charter principle of "self-determination" was admirable in itself, but how could it be applied to a people, in the process of "ingathering," that did not constitute a majority on its soil? And yet I believed that along with the danger went an opportunity. The Jewish claim would now be weighed on the scales of international justice and would not be dependent on the strategic interests of a single power. In the technical sense our diplomacy would have to liberate itself from an exclusive, obsessive concentration on Britain and would have to set sail on the wider ocean of a multilateral system.

My first reaction was to go to Foyles bookshop in Charing Cross Road and buy six books about the United Nations, its Charter and its procedures. Having adjusted itself to the new situation, the Zionist leadership sat long into the night analyzing the possible reactions of countries large and small, which until then had seemed remote from any operative relevance to our future. As a result of my book purchases I displayed greater learning than did any of my colleagues, who looked aggrieved when I rattled off some allusions to various Articles of the Charter of which none of them had ever heard. All of us knew about the dangers. The Soviet Union would surely express its anti-Zionist tradition. The states of Latin America and some in Western Europe would surely be influenced by the Vatican, which had never adjusted itself theologically to the idea of Jewish statehood. Surely the wishes of their mother country would have a strong influence on the four British Commonwealth members of the United Nations. We were painfully aware that the Arabs had six votes in the General Assembly of fifty-seven members, whereas we had none. In addition there were countries whose attitude would be determined by their Muslim solidarities. All in all, the UN prospect did not arouse buoyant optimism in Zionist hearts.

One of our acute problems was that we did not have a free hand even in defining our own positions. The official platform of Zionism had been formulated in the 1942 Biltmore program, named after a midtown New York hotel that has no claim to special renown except that a Zionist conference was convened there. The Biltmore resolution called for the transformation of an undivided Palestine into a "Jewish Commonwealth." In theory, therefore, we had no authorization to accept a partition compromise. But in reality we knew that a Jewish state in a part of Palestine was our maximal prospect. Ben-Gurion and Weizmann had agreed on this in their exchange of letters late in 1946. The Jewish Agency Executive, meeting under Ben-Gurion's leadership in Paris, had authorized Dr. Nahum Goldmann, a senior member of the Zionist Executive, to explore this idea in Washington with Assistant Secretary of State Dean Acheson. Goldmann had come back with a generally affirmative reply based, however, on the assumption that the British government would cooperate with this solution, which after all had its origin in British thinking before and after World War II. Acheson's statement meant that the United States would acquiesce in a partition solution but would not necessarily crusade for it or help us to overcome obstacles.

Ben-Gurion's letter to Weizmann of October 28, 1946, had included the following sentence: "We should in my opinion be ready for an enlightened compromise even if it gives us less in practise than we have a right to in theory but only so long as what is granted to us is really in our hands. That is why I was in favor of the principle of the Peel Report in 1937 and would even now accept a Jewish State in an adequate part of the country rather than a British

Mandate with a White Paper in all of the country." Weizmann had replied briefly on November 6: "I am in cordial agreement with the main lines of your policy. I can't help feeling that the inexorable logic of facts will drive America and Britain toward partition."

The agreement of Weizmann and Ben-Gurion was of greater importance than their divisions on smaller matters. By early 1947 Weizmann no longer had any official position in the Zionist leadership, and yet it was obvious that before the committees of the United Nations his voice would have an enormous resonance. Whenever Weizmann heard about a commission he sniffed the air like a war-horse looking for a new arena of triumph. His credit lay in his willingness, despite age and a sense of grievance, to enter the fray. Ben-Gurion and Silver should be praised for encouraging his participation. I have not known of many governments, let alone organizations, in which newly elected leaders have accepted an active and sometimes a decisive role for their deposed predecessors.

At the Zionist Office in London we began our operations by enlisting two newcomers who were to be my colleagues in great ordeals. One of them was Jacob Robinson, an international lawyer of high repute, who had been a member of the Lithuanian Parliament and who had all the facts and assumptions about the UN Charter at his fingertips. The other was Moshe Tov, an Argentinian Jew, who was to be our effective voice in Latin America. More than one-third of the membership of the United Nations were delegates from Latin America. They would therefore have a decisive influence on the vote. Most of those countries were unknown territory for the Zionist leadership. My own acquaintance with such names as Paraguay, Chile and Peru arose from the beauty of their postage stamps.

The Zionist Office in London studied a map of the United Nations and began portioning out areas of responsibility to each of its members. For various reasons, including my command of French, I was asked to visit France, Belgium, the Netherlands and Luxembourg.

Modern Israelis, pampered by nearly five decades of sovereignty, should remember that in those days we were a non-governmental organization with no automatic right of access. Accordingly when I arrived in Paris, Brussels and The Hague in April 1947, I had to struggle hard to get audience with prime ministers and foreign secretaries. My first stop was Paris. With the aid of the veteran Zionist Socialist leader Marc Jarblum, I obtained an interview with Prime Minister Paul Ramadier. The bearded Ramadier, looking like a goat seeking pasture, sat at a desk that he had never seen until a few days before and that he had every prospect of losing a few days hence in a ministerial reshuffle. He offered me a cigarette, pulled a lighter from his pocket and snapped it several times. Nothing was ignited. As I took a packet of matches from my own pocket, the prime minister laughed and said, "Well, that's France, nothing works but it's charming, isn't it?" He then began to look for some documents on the Palestine question. Unfortunately he didn't have the keys to his own closets. Zionism had a strong public echo in France. It had always been a source of French enjoyment to benefit from Britain's troubles, and here were we Zionists, providing that sensual satisfaction in full degree. Britain had exploited France's weakness in the recent war to undermine the French positions in Syria and Lebanon. This had rankled the politicians of the Third Republic and had also irritated Charles de Gaulle. At the same time France was still a Muslim power, as a result of its large areas of rule in North and West Africa. Understandably Ramadier's promises of support were very carefully reserved. In my cables from Paris, I warned Silver and Sharett not to take French support for granted at that stage.

My next stop was in neighboring Brussels, where I encountered a personality far more powerful than Ramadier, although he represented a much smaller country than France. Paul Henri Spaak was both prime minister and foreign minister. He was vigorous, ebullient, rhetorical and strangely similar in appearance to Churchill. The resemblance was intensified when he began to speak. Although there was nobody in the room but the two of us, he addressed me as though I were a mass audience in a vast public hall. Spaak said, "Partition is certainly the logical conclusion. If we see any possibility of supporting you, we will." Once again I warned the Zionist leaders against receiving this statement with excessive enthusiasm. I was beginning to learn about the little "escape ladders" that sophisticated statesmen attached to their promises. Spaak's belief in the "logicality" of partition did not mean that he would support it. Logic, after all, is not everything, and the statement that his support would be given "if there is a possibility" seemed to refer to the natural solidarity that linked the Belgium Socialists to the British Labour Party. I reported cautiously that we had made some dent in the West European position without yet having achieved anything like a breakthrough.

A few hours later I was in The Hague, where my interlocutors, in addition to members of the Foreign Ministry, included ex-colonial rulers who had served in Indonesia. One of them, Nicholas Blom, would later be the Dutch representative on the UN Special Committee on Palestine (UNSCOP). I had the uneasy feeling that British withdrawal would be regarded by the Dutch colonialists as an ominous precedent for their own withdrawal from Indonesia. I hoped, therefore, that our future contacts would be with Socialist and Liberal politicians sensitive to the recent Holocaust rather than to colonial rulers.

I looked forward with some zest to the prospect of making an official visit to Luxembourg. I have always had a particular affection for states that have had the good grace to be smaller than Israel not only in numbers but in territorial size. I remain to this day the only Israeli foreign minister who has ever paid an official visit to Reykjavík, the capital of Iceland. This would come to pass in 1966. I felt that Luxembourg proved the capacity of a small society to reach a high level of political and cultural cohesion while avoiding the domination by bigger neighbors.

Before I could realize this prospect, however, I received an urgent cable from Moshe Sharett, who had gone to New York, where a special session of the United Nations had convened on the motion of the United Kingdom. Having made its decision in favor of accepting a United Nations debate, Mr. Bevin wanted to illustrate his sincerity by giving a sense of urgency to what he had decided. Now that the withdrawal of British forces and the formulation of a United Nations recommendation were tangible prospects, it was an obvious British interest to get on with the proceedings as early as possible.

A special session of the General Assembly was considering the proposal of Secretary-General Trygve Lie to conduct the exploration of the Palestine problem not in the bulky General Assembly but in a smaller committee of eleven UN delegates representing medium-sized states. It was understood that the proposed committee would reflect the diversity of the international system both in geographical and in ideological terms. Although the terms of reference were modestly restrictive the fact remained that this would be Israel's first contact with the United Nations. The Jewish Agency had been recognized as the spokesman of the Jewish people without any reservation or objection largely because of Weizmann's achievement in integrating the Jewish Agency status into the League of Nations Mandate. Not all national movements have subsequently been accepted in their representative capacity with so little challenge or complication. Sharett's cable requested me to end my tour of West European capitals and to come immediately to New York in order to join the Israeli delegation there. He told me that the Jewish Agency had invited a distinguished group of lawyers to prepare a brief for the Zionist case. This document was scholarly, precise and authoritative, yet it seemed to Sharett to lack the tang and flavor of the Middle East and Palestine. It dealt with this region more as a "problem" than as a physical reality. Zionism was treated as a learned argument rather than as a human drama.

Sharett believed that there was importance to the legal aspect of our case but that this by no means exhausted the full meaning and significance of the Israeli claim to statehood. The fact that a certain course of action was legally valid did not necessarily prove that it was politically wise. Moreover, Sharett believed that the Israeli document should be somehow more impassioned and polemical than the distinguished jurists tended to be. Accordingly, I returned to London and prepared to cross the Atlantic for the first time. It was April 1947.

It was typical of the Zionist way of life during most of 1947 that if I was asked where I lived I would be unable to answer. I did not know or ask if I was being invited to New York for a week, a month, a year or a decade. I decided to take no risks and to travel with Suzy at my expense. There thus opened for me an epoch that was to make America central in my consciousness. I had little preparation for this. My education in school and university had been rigidly centered on Europe. I probably had inherited the complexes and prejudices that educated Europeans bear about a supposedly vigorous but immature America.

There was apprehension in my mood and step when I reached New York after a long flight through Ireland and Newfoundland. Twenty four hours after my arrival I was in the committee rooms of the United Nations at Lake Success. I had entered an arena that was destined to dominate my life and to set me on hitherto unanticipated roads of action. I had no idea that international organization was destined to figure so prominently in my future career. Like many young students and graduates of universities in the 1930s, I had been a supporter of the League of Nations. I attended conferences of the League of Nations Union. I regarded the idea of collective security as the only valid concept capable of challenging the fearsome progress of Fascist and Nazi power. The idea of a family of nations united in a covenant of law and peace is, in its origins, a Hebrew idea. The longing for an age when "all nations shall flow" to Zion to inaugurate a Utopian era in which "nation shall not lift up the sword against nation" shone radiantly upon the world as a revolutionary Jewish aspiration.

The uneasy thought that dimmed my enthusiasm was the stark fact that the great experiment had been tried and failed. It had been demonstrated that an international organization is not immune to the imperfections, compromises, evasions, rivalries, antagonisms and subterfuges that are traditionally associated with the politics of nation states. Human nature is not necessarily perfected by institutions. Nonetheless, it was difficult to ignore the hope and deference that the idea of international organization evoked in world opinion.

By the time that the international agencies took up their bleak abodes in Lake Success and Flushing Meadow it had become evident that the first post-war decade would be a less Utopian epoch than the idealists hoped. The frigid Cold War atmosphere would not permit great-power cooperation or the enforcement of peace by collective action. The idea of American and Soviet troops side by side, resisting what they would both agree to define as aggression, seemed naively absurd in the late 1940s. The central actors in world politics would be nation states claiming full sovereignty and giving international institutions a subsidiary role. Balance of power and spheres of influence had not lost their dominant influence. Governments would vote in accordance with national interests, alliances, friendships and prejudices—not in equal justice toward friend or foe in conformity with objective law as defined in a prestigious document. The Charter of the United Nations has its own innocent charm, but it presupposed that states would act as states had never yet acted in all of history.

And yet, with all my skepticism, my knowledge that Jewish destiny would be potently affected by what would transpire in the United Nations imparted a sense of relief. We had reached a deadlock so tight and relentless with the British government that it would be challenging for our cause to be tested in a new arena. The British era was ending. Even in the formal diplomatic sense, all the world was now our stage.

4

THE FIRST
BREAKTHROUGH: 1947

OUR FIRST IMPRESSION of New York was not inspiring. The housing and hotel shortage of the post-war period still affected American cities, and Zionist headquarters in New York were not disposed to be very lavish in the treatment of a young Jewish Agency officer joining it from the London office. Suzy and I spent our first night on American soil at the Paramount Hotel near Broadway. This was a strident and unrefined place. Its chief renown lay in the circumstance that it housed a nightclub called Billy Rose's Diamond Horseshoe in which young ladies of exceptional height and harmonious configuration walked around in what, in those austere days, was regarded as the minimal covering compatible with the law. This meant that sleep was available to the hotel's inhabitants from 3:00 A.M. onward, when the noise subsided.

A few days later we were at another hotel near West 63rd Street and Broadway where the atmosphere was no more "diplomatic" than at our first abode. It was clear to me that Zionist service was not going to be a passport to gracious living. The shortages of apartments and hotels figured in conversations with New Yorkers as "war hardships," as if they stood on an equal level with the bombardment of Coventry or Rotterdam or even with the "two-eggs-a-month" ration for Londoners. Indeed, my first impression of the United States was of the gap of reaction and experience between those who had seen a war theater and the tens of millions who had not.

First reactions to America in the minds of Europeans usually reflect a cautious reluctance to commit oneself until the immensity of the experience is absorbed, although few such recorded impressions are as evasive as that of Churchill after his first visit to the United States ("the newspapers are too thick and the toilet paper too thin"). In any case, being at the United Nations is not the same as being in America. The United Nations was already creating its extraterritorial world in the gyroscope factory at Lake Success, Long Island.

The General Assembly agenda for the session beginning on April 28, 1947, consisted exclusively of the "Palestine Question" and was supposed to end with nothing more eventful than the appointment of a committee that would go to the Middle East and formulate recommendations to the Mandatory power and members of the UN.

The eleven countries chosen by the General Assembly to form UNSCOP were assumed to be objective and totally immune to the strategic interests of the major powers. None of them appointed a man of international renown.[1]

We now had an arena quite different from the British governments and administrations with which Zionists had worked in the past. The eleven representatives had no capacity of coercion, could not open or close doors, or wield military power, or put anyone in detention. All that we wanted from each of them was his vote. For me and my colleagues in the Jewish Agency delegation, the Special Assembly gave useful practice at diplomatic lobbying, and Zionist leaders would have their baptisms of fire as orators before international tribunals.

Internal relations within our delegation were not excessively cordial. One of our delegation's heads was Abba Hillel Silver, the unchallenged leader of American Zionism, whose dominant character and resonant eloquence had made him a favorite among the Jewish masses. Silver had many qualities, and in later months, especially when I was the leader both of our embassy and of our UN mission, he and I developed relations of mutual confidence, but not even Silver's most fervent admirers ever described him as an easy or tolerant character. He had a tendency to regard any divergence from his views as evidence either of imbecility or subversion. The idea that there could be more than one side to any question never seemed to have entered his consciousness. He was an eloquent exponent of democratic values and principles, but he could not be said to have a democratic temperament. In both these respects he was similar to Ben-Gurion and, as is usual with leaders of similar characteristics, the relations between them were devoid of warmth.

The other head was Moshe Sharett, who represented the Jews of Palestine whose lives and future were at hazard. He was the head of the political department of the Jewish Agency in Jerusalem—the equivalent of a foreign minister, outranked only by Weizmann and Ben-Gurion. It was reasonable, therefore, that he should share the leadership of our delegation with Silver. We tended to split into two camps: Those like me, who were deputed from headquarters in Jerusalem or London and accepted Sharett as our chief, and Silver and his American Jewish associates, who regarded us as a regiment of Trojan horses whose presence had to be tolerated in the name of a unifying cause. The talent of living and working together has never been cited by historians as a salient Jewish attribute.

---

[1]The eleven countries chosen for the committee were Sweden, Canada, Australia, Holland, Czechoslovakia, Yugoslavia, Peru, Guatemala, Uruguay, India and Iran.

While there was some importance in the precise choice of nations entitled to send delegates to the eleven-country committee, this subject had a dull, procedural aspect, and it seemed unlikely that many headlines would come out of the special session. Yet it was here, beyond any expectation, that Zionism reached one of its revolutionary turning points.

Instead of making the expected ritual assault on Zionism as an imperialist conspiracy, the Soviet ambassador, Andrei Gromyko, spoke with subtle understanding about the aspiration of the Jewish people to a state of its own. Ignoring the limited parameters that UN Secretary-General Trygve Lie had laid down for the discussion, he showed only a passing interest in the appointment of Committee members, and plunged straight into the issue of national identities and structures. He insisted, as was expected, on the end of the British Mandate, and then projected two alternative solutions of approximately equal weight. One option was the establishment of a single federal state with self-government for Jews and Arabs within their own provinces. But if the relations between the two communities made agreement impossible, the Soviet Union would support the establishment in Palestine of two states, one Jewish and one Arab, in the area of the Palestine Mandate. Gromyko illuminated his proposal with references to the historic roots of the Jewish people in its ancient home and its sufferings in the recent war. His formulation was unforgettable:

Both Arabs and Jews have historical roots in Palestine and it would be unjust to deny the rights of the Jewish people to realize their aspirations to establish their own state.

Nothing had prepared us for this windfall. Both Eliahu Epstein, who headed our office in Washington, and Sharett were fluent in Russian and had conducted many conversations with Gromyko and with his deputy, Semyon Tsarapkin, without receiving any intimation of Soviet support. It was only from Gromyko's speech that they heard for the first time that Moscow was reversing its traditional posture by proposing the option of a Jewish state. I had come to the United Nations with pessimistic assumptions about its balance of forces; I now revised my predictions. If we could get American consent to the partition idea, we would be celebrating the first American-Soviet agreement in the post-war era. And since partition had, after all, been a British invention, it did not seem hopeless, despite Bevin's acrimony, to imagine the United Kingdom cooperating in a policy with which two of the great powers were already associated.

For the first time in many months, our political sky was lit up with a gleam of hope. It was no longer necessary to be a romantic optimist in order to foresee a Zionist success. Gromyko had become a Zionist hero. On the other hand, as we listened to the Arab and Muslim delegates, it became increasingly clear that we would have to fight hard for any advance, and there was always the possibility that Bevin, if he became unpleasantly surprised by the United Nations, would renege on his promise to accept its recommendation as he had done previously with the Anglo-American committee on Palestine.

Together with this first premonition of success, we received from the Special Assembly in May 1947 a valuable acknowledgment of our national identity. The Jewish Agency and the Arab Higher Committee were requested to appoint liaison officers to the UN Committee. This sounded like a mere administrative convenience, but for a Zionist movement working in an arena in which its adversaries were sovereign states, the prospect of a defined status in the UN context was an important gain. The Zionist leadership selected David Horowitz and me for this task. It was understood that he would explain the economic and social viability of a small Jewish state while I would expound the problems arising from Israel's relations with the Arab world. In the event, he and I worked together across the whole field in an atmosphere of complete collegiality. Horowitz later became governor of the Israel State Bank.

This was my first approach to the international scene. By accepting liaison officers from the Jewish Agency, the United Nations was virtually acknowledging the legitimate national identity of the Jewish people in relation to its homeland. No questions were raised about the Jewish Agency's competence. For what must have been the first time in Jewish history, no other organizations asserted their candidacies for Jewish representation. We were inheriting Chaim Weizmann's success in securing a provision in the League of Nations Mandate under which the Mandatory power was obliged to cooperate with a "Jewish Agency" in all matters relating to the working of the Mandate itself.

To make our success complete, the Arab Higher Committee contemptuously refused to nominate its liaison officers. It resented the implications of equality with representatives of a Zionist movement whose very existence affronted Arab pride. We benefited greatly from Arab errors in those days and on many occasions thereafter. My own experience tells me that nations benefit far more from the errors of their enemies than from their own wisdom or the goodwill of their friends. The Arabs were committed to the doctrine that the end of the British Mandate could be followed by nothing except the establishment of an Arab Palestine. The idea that their rights and claims were equal to that of the Zionist establishment was an affront.

In mid-June UNSCOP set out together with the two Jewish liaison officers in an ancient, decrepit and excessively noisy aircraft from New York to Jerusalem. The eleven committee members and their alternates were accompanied by a United Nations secretariat headed by Victor Hoo of China, Ralph Bunche of the United States and Garcia Robles of Mexico.

David Horowitz and I were instructed by the Zionist leadership to win the support of a majority of the eleven within the next few weeks. The noise of rusty engines bearing us to Jerusalem was so intense that we had no opportunity of beginning our persuasion during the flight. There was time for me to reflect that our national struggle had reached a decisive stage. If UNSCOP refused to recommend Jewish independence I did not believe that we could hope for remedy in the General Assembly or anywhere else. On the other hand, even if the committee were to make a positive recommendation, this would still not guarantee a favorable UN vote, but it would create a positive momentum and keep our prospects alive.

The task that confronted us was to eliminate the skepticism that had grown around the partition idea since it had first flourished in Britain in 1937. There were some who thought that the Palestine area was too small and poor to contain two sovereign states in any kind of stability. Others asked themselves what the effect on the Arab world would be of establishing a Jewish state against vehement Arab resistance. Might this not kindle a permanent war? Or, on the other hand, as I was to urge, might a firm insistence of the international community on Jewish sovereignty amid so many Arab lands create an atmosphere of acquiescence? Could we prove that the Jews of Palestine, without being a formidable power, were still strong enough and obdurate enough to reject a minority status?

It was difficult at the time to analyze the background of the eleven members on whose vote so much of our future history would depend. My own feeling, which I hoped was not excessively pessimistic, was that the eleven governments had not decided to send us their luminaries. They were men of competence rather than of inspiration. Not one of them had ever been involved in any decision as momentous as that in which he would now have to participate. The chairman, Emil Sandström, was a Swedish supreme court justice near the end of his career, slow in thought and speech but shrewd, solid and deeply rooted in humanitarian values.

Nicholas Blom of the Netherlands was a former colonial governor in the Dutch East Indies. His experienced eye would surely detect whether the British colonial regime in Palestine had any chance of survival.

John D. L. Hood of Australia was a professional diplomat whose sharp mind was concealed by an easygoing disposition and a very marked taste for conviviality.

A key figure would be Justice Ivan Rand of Canada, an old-fashioned man of refinement, probity and independent temperament. He was the kind of man who would not be easily moved from any positions that he would take and on whom there would be no prospect of influence by intimidation. His judicial career was assured and he had no political ambitions.

The three Latin Americans were as different from one another as could be imagined. Salazar of Peru was like a movie stereotype of an ambassador—white haired, taciturn, austere and charged with an air of reticent mystery that he must have picked up at the Vatican, to which he was accredited. The other two were boisterous, mercurial and fervently sympathetic to Zionism. Rodriguez Fabregat of Uruguay, bald, passionate, loquacious and wildly

sentimental, worked closely with the Guatemalan delegate, García Grana
dos, short, stocky and experienced. His country had a territorial conflict with
Britain about a small enclave called Belize, and however marginal this dispute might be to his colleagues in the United Nations, it played a very large
role in his emotions. He was prepared to believe the worst of Britain and the
best of anybody seeking to remove British power from anywhere. A few
decades later Belize became a member state in the United Nations, but its
very existence was a new reality to me and my Zionist colleagues in 1947.

Karl Lisicky of Czechoslovakia, a friend of Czech Foreign Minister Jan
Masaryk, was a large, shambling, rather awkward man caught up in the
psychological torment of many Czech patriots who saw their country lurch-
ing, under fragile leadership, from social democracy toward communism.

The Yugoslav, Vladimir Simic, was a placid veteran diplomat, but we
attached more interest to his deputy, Josef Brilej, one of Tito's younger
supporters.

Although the Arabs decided not to be represented as liaison officers, they
must have been consoled by the presence of two representatives of Islam. One
of them was an Indian judge, Sir Abdul Rahman. His mannerisms and accent
were far more British than those of any British diplomat that I had ever met,
and he was disarmingly candid in confessing that he felt more affinity with
Arabs than Jews.

More subtle was the Iranian statesman, Nasrollah Entezam, who was later
to be my friend and colleague for many years. He fluctuated between the
positions of Iranian foreign minister and his country's ambassador to the
United States and the United Nations. He would never have survived a
Khomeini regime.

It was a strange gallery. As we talked casually on the plane I found little
evidence that any of them had ever made any study of Jewish history or of
the Palestine problem. They were making a voyage into undiscovered countries of thought and seemed nervous with their authority.

When we reached Malta we became aware that Bevin's animosity toward
Zionists and Jews now infected his government's attitude to the United
Nations as well. The treatment of the committee by the British authorities in
Malta fell short of elementary courtesy. They allowed a distinguished international committee, including many elderly men, to be housed in stark
barracks and huts, fed on rough army food and offered no opportunity to see
the beauties of the island. Later, on arriving in Jerusalem, the committee
found a country torn by violence and unwilling to stop shooting for its
benefit. Perhaps this was just as well for our cause. I thought it salutary for
them to see the problem in its inflamed condition, without a cosmetic disguise. If Palestine was a success story, we could find ourselves saddled with
the British Mandate.

The British administration naturally had a large share in planning the
itinerary. The committee and its liaison officers were treated to an encyclope-

dic sightseeing tour carefully balanced between Jewish and Arab farms and factories. The emphasis on balance was so stringent that the Indian member of the committee asked me at Degania: "All right, we have seen a Jewish kibbutz; I assume that we shall be seeing an Arab kibbutz tomorrow." Between tours, conversations and hearings we liaison officers were required to fill the minds of the committee members with some ideas on the permanent solution. The public hearings were held in the YMCA hall, with the committee on the platform and what were called "Arab and Jewish notables" in the auditorium. I was charged by Sharett with the effort to make the best use of Weizmann's prestige and experience. We helped draft a careful and emotional speech that Weizmann read to the committee, until his eyes failed him, whereupon he put the papers aside and went into a reverie out of which he produced a poignantly moving and extraordinarily systematic account of the hopes and ideals that had illuminated Zionism in the past three decades. He still saw a vision of Arab-Jewish coexistence, but only on a basis of sovereign equality. He said that this could only be achieved by the plan of partition. Once again he surpassed all the Jewish speakers in the depth of his impact on his hearers.

In one respect, however, this address by Weizmann had a much greater operative effect than was implied in its rhetoric. The official Jewish Agency leaders were desperately anxious for the committee to reach a verdict for partition. It was inconceivable that the committee would advocate a Jewish state in the whole of the Land of Israel. But the members of the committee had decided not to adopt any proposal that might provoke total rejection by all the parties. They knew that the Arabs were going to reject any compromise proposal. Partition had a prospect of Jewish and international support. It was therefore necessary for us to find a way in which the partition proposal could be tabled without the Jewish Agency leaders being accused at the next Zionist Congress of having exceeded their mandate, which required them to demand a hundred percent of Palestine as defined in the British Mandate. Ben-Gurion proposed that we should use the fact that Weizmann was not formally a member of the Zionist Executive and therefore not bound by its limitations. The passage in Weizmann's speech proposing partition was drafted in close conjunction with Ben-Gurion and Sharett.

It was obvious that, with their conservative frame of mind, the committee members would first want to examine carefully whether they needed to make a drastic proposal at all. Was surgery really essential? Could the British Mandate still be kneaded and shaped by effective international persuasion into a viable system? Was it true the British did not really wish to rule? Could they be trusted to continue their administration effectively if Bevin's attitude were to prevail?

It was providential that at the moment when the committee's mind was torn between the continuation of the Mandate and its cessation, Bevin decided the issue himself.

An immigrant ship, *Exodus*, arrived at Haifa port bearing 4,500 Jews from the displaced persons camps in Germany. They were crowded on deck in terrible squalor, but burst into tearful rapture when the green pine trees and white houses on the slopes of Mount Carmel came into view. In consultation with Horowitz, and later with Sharett, I decided to try to get some of the committee to see the ship with its human cargo. It seemed to embody the whole Palestine predicament in visible form. We made the proposal to Sandström, who went to Haifa himself accompanied by Bunche and the Yugoslav Simic. The Jewish refugees had decided not to accept their banishment from the shores of their homeland with docility. If anyone had ever wanted to know what Churchill meant by "a squalid war" he would have found out by watching British soldiers using rifle butts, hose pipes and tear gas against the survivors of the death camps. Men, women and children were forcibly taken off to other ships, locked in cages, and sent out of Palestine waters. The sight of the cages had a specially traumatic effect on the UN observers. It must have aroused in the refugees themselves a shockingly acute recollection of the agony from which they thought they had escaped.

Bevin decreed that they should be dispatched to a French port. A few days later the French government, inspired by one of its younger ministers, François Mitterrand, refused to receive the refugees except on their voluntary request. Then Bevin had the obtuseness to order the ship back to Hamburg. While Sandström and Simic watched this gruesome operation I awaited their return to Jerusalem with tension. When they came back they were pale and shocked. I could see that they had come to one conclusion: If this was the only way that the British Mandate could continue, it would be better not to continue it at all.

Sandström invited Horowitz and me to accompany the committee in Geneva as well as in all its subsequent deliberations.

The consciousness that the British Mandate was collapsing in moral ruin was further strengthened in the committee members' minds as soon as they left Palestine. On July 29 the British administration executed three members of the Irgun Zvai Leumi (IZL), and two days later two British sergeants, one of whom turned out to be Jewish, were held hostage by the Irgun and were hanged in a ghastly and macabre fashion by personal order of the Irgun chief, Menachem Begin. Ben-Gurion's fury knew no bounds. His resolve to put the Irgun and Lechi out of business became obsessive. He was convinced that if actions of far-reaching moral and political effect could be undertaken by any small Zionist group, the authority of the central Zionist establishment would be corroded and Zionism would become involved in internecine gang warfare and lose the image of statehood.

Before the committee left for Geneva, however, much of its work was already accomplished. The members had the courage to meet representatives of the underground resistance organizations, including Begin himself. This was a specially delicate operation, since there was a heavy price on Begin's head if the British police ever found him. The UNSCOP members may not have learned more than they would have deduced from books and writings, but the very symbolism of their meeting with Begin illustrated that they were an independent United Nations committee owing no allegiance to anyone but their parent organization.

Even more decisive in the early history of UNSCOP was a meeting to which Ben-Gurion invited members of the committee at Sharett's home in Ben-Maimon Street in Jerusalem. He had decided to destroy the possibility that the committee would reject partition on the grounds that nobody had officially proposed it. I knew from Bunche that UNSCOP would not initiate a partition proposal. It would, however, be willing to react to the idea if it was seriously proposed in any quarter. To my astonishment and admiration, as soon as the committee members were seated, Ben-Gurion took out a pencil and a large piece of paper and drew a partition map indicating what he thought would be the basic minimum for a Jewish state. When one of his Jewish Agency secretaries in an apprehensive whisper said something to Ben-Gurion about the Biltmore Program, Ben-Gurion said sotto voce in Hebrew: "Biltmore, shmiltmore, we must have a Jewish state."

A journey from the turmoil of Jerusalem to the tranquillity of Geneva was the emotional equivalent of a Turkish bath. It was hard to conceive a sharper contrast of mood within so short a time. In that respect, if in no other, the transition from Jerusalem to Geneva has not changed very much since those days. On arrival at the airport, Suzy and I immediately purchased the local newspaper, *Journal de Genève,* whose main headline announced in very large type: "Cyclist collides with pedestrian." I did not know if I should feel envy or compassion for a nation whose range of tensions was fixed at that phlegmatic level. There was a Zionist mythology, proclaimed with special constancy by Weizmann, that held Switzerland up as a model of what the renascent Jewish state would be. The intention, of course, was to emulate the Swiss in their cleanliness, precision and technological virtuosity, not in their temperament. That a Jewish state would ever know the serenity of the Swiss lakes and mountains was improbable.

Nevertheless, our very arrival for the work of the UNSCOP introduced to Geneva something of the frenzied atmosphere of Zionist life. For the next five weeks Horowitz and I, with our chief colleagues, Gideon Rafael and Moshe Tov, would be working at a Zionist, not a Swiss pace, seizing the ears and attention of the eleven members, their alternates and their secretariat, pacing the corridors of the Palais des Nations where the ghosts of the League of Nations lurked in the spacious corridors. We also frequented the restaurants and cafés, which were at once the sensual delight and the dietetic danger of the city. If Calvinism has any connection with austerity, the link was surely suspended at the gastronomic level.

We took up our residence in the Hotel d'Angleterre, oblivious of the ironic

symbolism of the name. I remarked to Horowitz and Sharett that our ambi
tion was surely to sunder the roots of Zionism in its British context, yet here
we were back to the familiar flag.

Sharett had preceded us to Geneva by a few days. This meant that he had
chalked up about seventy-two hours of anxiety. Our men in Washington,
London and Paris had reported in almost identical mood that there would
not be a single country among members of the United Nations ready to
support the establishment of a Jewish state unless the UNSCOP Report
called for the repeal of the British Mandate and the creation of a Jewish state.
This meant that our mission was far more crucial for Jewish destiny than we
could ever have anticipated. We were not attending a learned seminar; we
were fighting for the life and soul of our movement and for the only faint
hope of salvation that Jews had nourished since the terrible decade of the
1930s.

The committee's chairman, Emil Sandström, had been so overwhelmed by
the spectacle of the *Exodus* in Haifa that he asked Horowitz and me for a
long discussion about what had transpired since then. The British authorities
had refrained from sending the *Exodus* refugees to Cyprus because Bevin
regarded Cyprus as a stepping-stone to the Land of Israel. By dispatching
them to France and thereafter Germany, Mr. Bevin had clearly expressed the
hope that they would never see the shores of Palestine again. The three
British prison ships to which the refugees had been transferred had put in at
a small French port, but the majority of the 4,500 passengers refused to go
ashore despite their hunger, thirst and suffering. Sandström expressed what
seemed to me sincere regret that he had no power to intervene. In an unexpected decision the committee had decided to visit the displaced persons
camps in Europe as part of their aspiration to understand the motivation of
Zionism. We knew that they would discern that Palestine, and no other
destination, was their sustaining dream.

Meanwhile we had learned that Yugoslavia, which was represented in
UNSCOP, was much attracted by the idea of a federal state with Jewish and
Arab provinces but without any of the capacities or emblems of Jewish
sovereignty. This anxiety sent Moshe Sharett to Belgrade to see the Yugoslav
foreign minister. While he was gone the UNSCOP mission to the camps came
back from their tour. They had found not a single camp inmate who was not
passionately eager to reach Palestine.

We saw little virtue in peering over the shoulders of the committee members while they conducted their deliberations. If Sharett was worried about
Yugoslavia, I worried with even greater intensity about Britain. We had been
so shocked by Bevin's virulence that we had never made a detailed analysis
of the impulses that had brought about Britain's desertion of its Zionist trust.
The question that none of us could answer was why Britain was willing to
evacuate India, Egypt and Greece and yet seemed reluctant to extricate itself
from Palestine, where it was carrying an almost intolerable burden. Was it all
because of Bevin's prejudices? Was he the only one who counted in London?

Sharett and Horowitz suggested that I should go to London on a fact-finding mission.

I went to London for four days in an effort to discover whether, even if the UN would pass a partition resolution, Britain would accept it. The answer would greatly influence our tactics. Amongst the spokesmen whom I interviewed were Harold Beeley, who had been Bevin's adviser in the 1946 Anglo-American Commission; Harold Laski, the Labour leader who had tried to tempt me into a British parliamentary career; and Richard Crossman, the Labour Party maverick who, as a member of the Anglo-American Committee in 1946, had startled Attlee and Bevin with his support of the Zionist cause. Dick Crossman had always appeared to me as a man who would never allow emotion or sentiment to affect his austere pragmatism. He was not interested in what was right or wrong but only in what was possible or impossible, logical or offensive to reason. His Zionism was the exception to all his rules.

Harold Beeley began with a sincere attempt to give Bevin's policy a rational interpretation. He did this by probing the roots of Ernest Bevin in his impoverished childhood, his gallant struggle for minimal livelihood and his leadership of the Trade Union Movement. Beeley said that I should understand that Bevin was a self-made man. I thought that this definition relieved God of an awesome responsibility.

Beyond the psychological analysis of his minister, Beeley allowed himself a frank prediction: "There is no prospect that a two-thirds majority will vote for a solution satisfactory to Zionism. The split between the two great powers will prevent this and any motion involving partition would fail." I thought that he was not ascribing due weight to Gromyko's UN speech of May 15.

The current view among Zionists was that an imperial power rarely moves out of anywhere voluntarily, and that even if the United Nations adopted a partition resolution, Britain would cling to Palestine tooth and nail. Laski and Crossman, however, gave me a different impression. With their ears to the ground they heard rumblings of protest in the British public against the commitment to continue ruling Palestine. The economic crisis in Britain had made the Palestine burden unpopular, and if one added the violence that assailed the British forces and the abrasive relations with the United States, there was good reason on national British grounds to feel that the Mandate might well be renounced. On the other hand, the editors of the *Times* told me of a background briefing by Prime Minister Attlee, who had said: "Britain will carry out any reasonable decision reached by the United Nations to the best of its ability." This was one of the longest statements ever attributed to Clement Attlee, who was not generous in the use of words. (Attlee would later write an essay on "The Art of Chairmanship," which began with the statement that "the central purpose of a chairman should be to ensure that the shortest possible time should elapse between the beginning of any meeting and its end.")

The other impression that I had picked up in London was that British military experts estimated that Britain would require fewer battalions to cope with Jewish opposition to a pro-Arab solution than it would need to cope with Arab revolt against a pro-Zionist recommendation.

The upshot of my mission was to strengthen the conviction that there was no use in spending time or effort in an attempt to change British policy. That policy would continue to be antagonistic to us.

As I went back to my liaison duties in Geneva with Horowitz, Gideon Rafael, Moshe Tov, Jacob Robinson and others, I felt the full benefit of the reckless Arab decision to refuse the appointment of Arab liaison officers. It illustrated an attribute that I was to encounter very often in my close observation of Arab leadership. Passion had a higher place in their hierarchy than reason and utility. Words and phrases were of overriding importance and once a slogan was officially canonized it would command unswerving and rigorous allegiance. In this respect Arab nationalism operated in the intellectual domain in a somewhat Marxist spirit.

I concluded that the Arab leaders would not be able to make proposals that the eleven members of UNSCOP could accept. The eleven were pragmatic men whose minds never soared into the realm of vision and rarely descended below the level of concrete practicality. I felt that they would insist on recommending ideas that would have a good chance of acceptance. Whatever could be said against our partitionist doctrine, it would sound more balanced and practical than the Arab ambition to maintain one hundred percent control in a unitary state or any British idea about continuing the restless, anguished life of the Mandate.

Much of our lobbying had to be conducted at hurried luncheons in restaurants between the formal meetings of the committee. This fact caused great concern to Horowitz, who had come to Israel in the austere mood of a kibbutz settler and held ascetic self-denial as one of the purposes of life. He told me that he looked forward to the day when nourishment could be ensured by swallowing a pill once a day, thus liberating us from the tyranny of protracted lunches and animated table talk. I confessed that I was fully prepared to live the whole of my life without that seductive prospect being fulfilled.

We decided to use one of the intervals in the committee's deliberations to visit Weizmann, who was vacationing in a Swiss village near the Austro-Italian frontier. While we were briefing him on the status of the committee's deliberations, Horowitz received a call from Sharett in Geneva. He wanted us to communicate to Weizmann, and to understand ourselves, the significance of a conversation that he had conducted that day with the French political adviser to the committee, Henri Vigier, who had told him bluntly: "You will have to choose between complete independence in a limited area or limited sovereignty in a larger area."

This formulation, characteristically French in its conciseness and its emotional detachment, went to the heart of our problem. I found Vigier's formulation encouraging, because it indicated that the committee was faithful to pragmatic criteria.

I had heard from members of UNSCOP that Chairman Sandström intended to ask a vote on four questions: One: Who favors a continuation of the present British Mandate? Two: Who favors an Arab state in all of Palestine? Three: Who favors a Jewish state in all of Palestine? Four: Who favors the partition of Palestine into an Arab and a Jewish state?

The committee had given itself a deadline of September 1 to complete its work. This was a prudent calculation, since the habit of international organizations is that they touch nothing that they do not adjourn. Secretary-General Trygve Lie in New York was badgering the committee on the need to have a dignified document on the General Assembly's table in mid-September. Having made an inquiry in the late afternoon of August 31, I learned that the committee members were still sharply divided and were holding a debate that had become passionate for the first time.

I was told to be at the Palais des Nations at 9:00 to receive copies of the report. When that hour came there were still no reports. Apart from Horowitz and me, the British liaison officer, Arthur McGillivray, was in attendance, pretending that he was as ignorant of the committee's outcome as were we ourselves. I paced the hallways of the Palais like a lion in a cage or, perhaps more accurately, as an expectant father in a hospital corridor. I wandered into the Assembly Hall in which Haile Selassie had pleaded vainly before the League of Nations for help in the face of the Italian invasion.

Just before midnight, the door opened and the eleven members and deputies filed out. Bunche whispered to us, "It's a boy." (I doubt if he had known that this was the phrase that Prime Minister Lloyd George had used to apprise Weizmann of the Balfour Declaration on November 2, 1917.)

Several committee members seemed to have tears in their eyes. Minutes later, at 12:05 A.M. on September 1, the Report was officially handed to me. Seven members of the committee—Sweden, Canada, Czechoslovakia, Guatemala, Uruguay, Peru, and the Netherlands—favored an independent Jewish state, an independent Arab state, and a separate status for the City of Jerusalem. A minority report signed by Yugoslavia, India and Iran favored a form of cantonization with Jewish immigration ultimately to be determined by the Arab majority of the new Palestinian state. Australia abstained from the vote.

The report, with all its geographical and administrative limitations, surpassed any rational expectation that Zionism had nourished since the end of the war. The UN had given us its first sign of understanding and compassion. Back in the Hotel d'Angleterre Sharett proposed that we open a bottle of champagne. This rare non-Zionist indulgence was unanimously adopted. I will never forget those who were present with me: Sharett, Horowitz, Moshe Tov, Gideon Rafael, Mordecai Kahane, Eliahu Sasson and Leo Kohn. We were all tired from the plethora of last-minute rumors, false reports and fears. We could allow ourselves a moment of satisfaction.

Early the next morning, the Zionist Actions Committee, led by Ben-Gurion, was meeting, for obscure reasons, in Zurich. Horowitz and I enjoyed the comfort and precision of a Swiss train as we made our journey on September 2 among the lakes and lawns. We found Ben-Gurion in a deep reverie, sitting at an empty desk. I briefly outlined the content of the report that we had received. It seemed uncertain whether he was listening or not. Finally he looked up and said crisply: "We must get rid of the dissident armies."

It was clear that the problem of authority in Zionism had continued to obsess him. He said to us, with what we both felt to be monumental irrelevance: "There cannot be any progress unless underground forces are eliminated." I interrupted his reflections to say: "We have come to tell you that the UN Commission has recommended a Jewish state."

Ben-Gurion replied, "We can't go on the way we are. We must eliminate the Etzel."

I said, "The Negev is included in the Jewish state."

Ben-Gurion replied, "We must finish with the Stern group as well."

Horowitz and I exchanged glances. In total despair of getting Ben-Gurion's attention, we started to move to the door. Ben-Gurion's voice pursued us while my hand was on the handle: "A Jewish state with the *whole* of the Negev? Why didn't you tell me that earlier?"

5

SUCCESS AT LAKE SUCCESS

ON SEPTEMBER 1, the day after the UNSCOP Report, the Zionist Actions Committee meeting in Zurich had a moment to celebrate. A Jewish state had never before been proposed by an international organization. But some Zionist leaders were frightened by the tortuous partition map as well as by the painful exclusion of some areas of Jewish settlement and, above all, of Jerusalem, destined by UNSCOP for an international status.

"The partition report is a nightmare," said the veteran leader of the center party, Peretz Bernstein. His anguish was visibly sincere.

To which Ben-Gurion replied: "This is the only time that I've wanted a nightmare to come true."

The Zionist Executive congratulated our Geneva team on our success with UNSCOP. I was asked to go to London to explore the British reaction to the UNSCOP Report, and then to New York with Horowitz for the General Assembly meeting on September 22. Bevin had maneuvered his own country into a collision with an international body, and we were frankly eager to witness his frustration. The idea of a visit to London attracted me for a reason that could best be described in the German word *Schadenfreude*. Roughly translated, this means "joy in the discomfiture of others." There are times when it seems that is about the only kind of joy that politics allows, and I wanted to see Bevin's frustration firsthand.

We found British political leaders in a rancorous mood. Ernest Bevin had expressed his frustration by declining to receive Weizmann. This was a break with an established tradition. Readiness to receive Weizmann, in or out of office, had become a ritual obligation for British statesmen for over thirty years. Refusing to see him had never been considered as an available option. Bevin was clearly out to smash the Zionist tradition in British policy.

The opposition leader, Churchill, on the other hand, was emerging out of the sulky mood that had afflicted him since the murder of Lord Moyne. He was now reminding Weizmann how close the UNSCOP Report was to the proposals that the Cabinet committee would have published but for Moyne's assassination in November 1944.

The Foreign Office reaction to UNSCOP was muted. Harold Beeley told me that the UNSCOP Report was now of secondary importance; the future of Palestine was obviously going to be decided by war, not by the text of reports. It was clear to him and his colleagues that whether or not the General Assembly adopted the Report, the Arabs would fight.

Before leaving London for New York I went to Oxford to introduce my colleague, David Horowitz, to Professor Sir Reginald Coupland, who, as a member of the Royal (Peel) Commission in 1937, had been the pioneer of the partition idea. It is incongruous that no street in Israel carries his name: men of far lesser impact on our history are "immortalized" on our signposts.

There had been little serious talk of partition in Zionist or international literature before 1937. It was known that Weizmann had been probing the idea in a surreptitious way with a few of his closest colleagues. He had become convinced that independence would have to come to Palestine before the Jews could achieve a majority. In the mid-1920s he had issued his despairing cry: "Jews, where are you?" This was a rebuke to Diaspora Zionists who were willing to sacrifice everything for Zionism except their passports and their comfortable Western homes. The consequence would be that if independence came to Palestine prematurely, it would find a country with an Arab majority. Weizmann examined the question whether a Jewish state of adequate size could be carved out of an area in which a Jewish majority existed. Nothing came of these explorations. It was the 1937 Peel Report, followed by UNSCOP, that made partition a serious option.

It had erupted suddenly from the individual mind of its originator. Coupland was an Oxford professor whose specialized interest was focused on the structure of states and the conditions of nationhood. What are the minimal affinities that enable diverse peoples to build and hold a society together? Is there any coherent principle that explains how they make the choice between union and separation? In 1943 Coupland, as a member of Attlee's Indian Commission, was destined to discuss these themes in relation to the partition between India and Pakistan. But six years earlier, in his capacity as a leading member of the Peel Commission, he had explored this predicament in relation to Palestine. He had put his conclusions in words of great lucidity, unsurpassed as a description of the Arab-Israeli problem then and ever since:

An irrepressible conflict has arisen within the narrow confines of one small country. There is no common ground between them. They differ in religion and language. Their cultural and social life, their ways of thought and conduct, are as incompatible as their national aspirations. Arabs and Jews could possibly learn to live and work together in Palestine if they would make a genuine effort to reconcile their national ideals and build up in time a joint or dual nationality. But this they cannot do. National assimilation between Arabs and Jews is ruled out. The national home cannot cease to be national. In these circumstances to maintain that Palestinian nationality has any meaning is a mischievous pretence. Neither Arab or Jew has any sense of service to a single state. Peace and order and good government can only be maintained in a unitary Palestine for any length of time by a rigorous system of suppression. The answer to the question which of them will in the end govern all Palestine surely must be neither. But while neither race can justly rule all Palestine we see no reason why each should not rule part of it. There is little value in maintaining the political unity of Palestine at the cost of perpetual hatred, strife and bloodshed.

Anyone who now pursues the illusion that all of Palestine can be governed as a single country, whether on behalf of Arabs or Jews, should be intellectually obliged to comb through these sentences one by one and explain exactly where and why they are inapplicable today.

The British government accepted the partition provisions of the Peel Report in 1937, but discarded it temporarily in the post-Munich period. Appeasement of Hitler and the Arabs was not compatible with the idea of a Jewish state, and the 1939 White Paper was based on the prevention of Jewish independence, not on its promotion. The partition idea had been reborn briefly in the recommendations of the Morrison-Moyne Cabinet Committee in 1944. Those who murdered Lord Moyne were effectively murdering the prospect of a Jewish state coming to the international agenda before the end of the war. Churchill reacted to the death of his friend by fleeing from the Palestine problem, and the partition option receded.

The UNSCOP Report had now restored partition as the central theme of Middle Eastern politics. I was not surprised to find Sir Reginald Coupland elated by the delayed success of his idea. He thought that our victory had been achieved in the nick of time. Anti-Semitism, he said, was growing in the world. Now that Hitler had punctured the myth of Jewish omnipotence, whatever the Jewish people did not achieve while the world's conscience was still wounded would become unattainable in the more cynical atmosphere that would soon prevail. Coupland reminded us of what he had told Weizmann and me before: We should beware of the "unitary illusion"—the illusion that two peoples who hold none of the purposes of life in common can be forced to maintain a single statehood. In the case of Palestine, he said, partition was even more compelling than in India. There might have to be argument about boundaries, but we should never let the partition principle drop from our minds. It was the only concept that reflected historic reality. "Palestine" as a single entity, said Coupland, was a fiction, "a mischievous pretense."

I now wished to explore whether the partition report had made any impact on Arab thinking. An occasion that made an indelible impression on me came in the late summer of 1947. Together with Horowitz, I took part in a meeting with Abdul Rahman Azzam Pasha, secretary-general of the Arab League. We were accompanied by Jon Kimche, who had successively been editor of Reuters agency and correspondent of *The Observer*. His journalistic eminence had enabled him to persuade Azzam to see us. It was a daring thing for an Arab leader to do.

In those days, the Arab League had a more central position in Arab diplomacy than now. It had been established in Cairo under strong British pressure to coordinate the policies of the Arab governments in World War II. While the British had envisaged it as an instrument of their will, it had developed into an independent expression of Arab unity and cooperation. Azzam could accurately be regarded as the central spokesman of Arab nationalism.

We met in the Savoy Hotel with London traffic booming a few yards away. Horowitz and I sat on each side of Azzam while Kimche, who had initiated the meeting, introduced us with glowing tribute to our qualities. Horowitz and I spoke proudly but cautiously of our success with UNSCOP, predicting, with more confidence than we felt, that the General Assembly would ratify its conclusions and that Jewish statehood was now an inseparable part of the international landscape. Azzam kept muttering something about war. I said that I had a simple suggestion. If there is a war, there will have to be a negotiation after it. Why not negotiate before and instead of the war?

Azzam's reply was indignant but shatteringly candid. "If you win the war, you will get your state. If you do not win the war, then you will not get it. We Arabs once ruled Iran and once ruled Spain. We no longer have Iran or Spain. If you establish your state the Arabs might one day have to accept it, although even that is not certain. But do you really think that we have the option of not trying to prevent you from achieving something that violates our emotion and our interest? It is a question of historic pride. There is no shame in being compelled by force to accept an unjust and unwanted situation. What would be shameful would be to accept this without attempting to prevent it. No, there will have to be a decision, and the decision will have to be by force."

This conversation with Azzam has never been canonized as one of the major signposts in Jewish and Zionist history. In the more modest domain of my personal life, however, it had an indelible effect. I came away with a conviction that Azzam, unfortunately, was realistic. Both Arabs and Jews were acting under the compulsions of their respective histories. It was unrealistic to believe that we Jews could give up our urgent claim to a state. It was equally unrealistic to imagine that the Arabs would accept a Jewish state with docility just because an untried international organization was about to authorize its establishment. There was no need for sentimentality or passion. Each of these two peoples was moved by elements in its own nature. Neither would yield to the other in advance. There would have to be adjudication either through international pressure, or more probably through the result of physical conflict and the Jewish resistance.

Azzam was saying words of grave portent. He was appealing to traditions that had given Islam its original impetus in world history. He was placid and confident, and could afford to be personally polite. Being still young to the contradictions of diplomacy, I was disconcerted by the contrasting atmosphere ("We shall have to try to destroy you. Won't you have another cup of tea?"). We had told UNSCOP, as we would now tell the delegates to the General Assembly, that if the international decision was firm, there was a good chance of compliance. We could hardly say anything else. But I realized after the talk with Azzam that the greater likelihood was that we would have to fashion our independence in the hot crucible of war.

The immediate task was to win international legitimacy for our impending struggle. As the time for the General Assembly vote approached, it was by no means certain that we would be able to muster the two-thirds majority necessary for approval. British opposition was not our only obstacle. The political establishment in Washington was sharply divided. Most of the State Department's leaders were in favor of prolonging British rule under United Nations trusteeship. The hostility to Zionism in the upper echelons of the American diplomatic establishment was no less virulent than that of the British Foreign Office. All attempts to persuade Secretary of State Marshall to make an early statement in favor of the UNSCOP Report had failed. There would be weeks of agonizing suspense. Flushed with our victory at Geneva, we were forced to tell ourselves that an early goal at halftime is no assurance of ultimate victory. Whatever had been achieved in Geneva would become irrelevant if we could not overcome one hurdle after another at Lake Success.

The political environment was unfavorable. In Palestine the British authorities were intercepting and turning back all European Jews who approached Palestine's shores. The Jewish resistance was escalating its armed revolt. The Arabs were serving notice that we Jews, as Azzam had told me, would have to win our state not by a show of hands but by force of arms. Our first task was to make sure of great power support.

On October 9, after a few weeks of hesitation, the United States, on Truman's instructions, made its long-awaited statement in the General Assembly in favor of partition. Washington had expressed no views about partition during the Special Assembly in April. It had sedulously avoided contact with UNSCOP during its deliberations in Palestine and Geneva. The State Department was reluctant throughout the summer to criticize British policy in case Britain retorted with an invitation to the United States to inherit or share the British responsibility.

The UNSCOP Report broke down U.S. reserve. The United States representative, Hershel Johnson, compared the positions of the Arab and Jewish peoples in the world. The former, he said, enjoyed independence symbolized by the presence of six Arab representatives in the Assembly. The Jewish aspiration for independence, first recognized in the Mandate, had not yet been fulfilled.

Our next apprehension was that Gromyko's speech might turn out to have been an impulsive expression of opinion without foundation in Kremlin policy. Our characteristically Jewish anxieties were swiftly allayed. Gromyko's deputy, Semyon Tsarapkin, declared: "Every people, and that includes the Jewish people, has a full right to demand that their fate should not depend on the mercy or goodwill of a particular state. The members of the United Nations can help the Jewish people by acting in accordance with the principles of the Charter which call for the guaranteeing to every people of their right to independence and self-determination."

It is hard to describe the elation with which we received these bold words. Tsarapkin continued:

> The minority plan has its merits and advantages since it is based on the idea of creating a single Arab-Jewish state in Palestine. However, the relations between Arabs and Jews have reached such a state of tension that it has become impossible to reconcile their points of view on the solution of the problem. The minority plan appears impracticable. In these circumstances, therefore, the partition plan proposed by the majority offers more hope of realization.

Against the Cold War atmosphere which prevailed in every other sector of the international arena, there was something almost messianic in this convergence of American and Soviet ideas. None of us had any illusions about the motivation of Soviet policy. Stalin's Soviet Union after World War II was obsessed by the danger of what it called "encirclement." Having lost twenty million of its citizens in the war, the Soviet nation could not be expected to recover swiftly from the trauma. Its fears of attack by neighbors had their roots in a long experience. Soviet policy sought to create a belt of surrounding states whom the Kremlin euphemistically described as "friendly to the Soviet Union." The phrase "friendly to the Soviet Union" in Moscow's interpretation meant total subservience to the Soviet Union. This explains the struggle for ensuring the subordination of Poland to Moscow, as well as the subsequent incursions into Czechoslovakia and later Hungary. In areas such as ours, where no such enticing possibility existed, the Soviet Union would insist, at the very least, on the absence of foreign bases.

The Western position in the Middle East in 1947 was still based predominantly on Great Britain. The independence of Arab states was theoretical and fragile. There was a strong British military presence in Egypt. The monarchy in Iraq was closely tied to London, especially during the premiership of Nuri Said. Syria and Lebanon, although independent sovereign states, had acknowledged a vague but pervasive French domination. The Jordanian kingdom had a British officer in command of its army and was under authoritative British diplomatic control. It must have appeared to the Soviet Union at that time that the Palestine Jews, in the heat of their conflict with Ernest Bevin, would be much more effective in banishing the British presence than Arab states, which were willing to accommodate the reality of British power side by side with a facade of Arab independence.

The Soviet Union's suspicions were focused principally on the Negev, where it was well known that Britain hoped to retain a military base bridging Egypt and Jordan and giving London a continuing role in the manipulation of Arab policies.

The fact that Soviet support of our cause was based on self-interest rather than on benevolence was a positive factor in my eyes. My experience has told me that all nations determine their policies in the light of self-interest and then explain their policies in terms of self-sacrificial altruistic morality. Even the Soviet Union feels a need to idealize its self-interest by reference to liberal, Enlightenment values. Its objectives in 1947 were pragmatic, concrete, tactical and strategic, but its justifications were formulated in terms of self-determination and equal national rights.

Perhaps we should have seen more clearly that, once the British were removed from Palestine, the Soviet interest in a Jewish state would swiftly evaporate. But in the fall of 1947, as we lobbied for support in the United Nations, our minds were set on a short-term objective. If we failed to win the General Assembly vote, our previous successes would be reduced to ashes. On the other hand, if we could win the vote, we would have made a breach in the wall. And nothing could be won without Soviet support.

The weeks between September and late November 1947 are vivid in my memory. I can still recall my daily hour-long automobile trips between the Barbizon Plaza Hotel, where I subsisted on a Jewish Agency allowance of twenty dollars a day, and the temporary UN building at Lake Success on Long Island. Occasionally we would stop near La Guardia Airport, where the General Assembly held its plenary sessions at what had been a skating rink at Flushing Meadow. Many of the recognized leaders of Palestine Jewry were in our delegation. They were something of a burden to those of us who had operative tasks. At times when I should have been talking to delegates from Uruguay, Luxembourg, the Netherlands and Iceland, or conferring with the Soviet delegation in its Park Avenue headquarters, I would instead have to soothe venerable leaders of Palestine Jewry or ensure that they had tickets for meetings or that their hotel accommodation was satisfactory. The mood of our Founding Fathers was hypochondriac. They could not possibly believe that a gathering composed of such a distressing preponderance of non-Jews would defend the Zionist cause against Muslim, Catholic and British opposition. But in the long run, their participation in the work of our UN delegation was beneficial. No one who had attended a UN session could believe thereafter that victories could be won without effort and compromise.

It is implicit in the Jewish condition that dangers should be more credible than opportunities. We have no need to apologize for this. There have been many more dangers than opportunities in the Jewish experience. To regard worst-case contingencies as more real than successful outcomes is our legacy from generations of suffering. It was not easy, however, in international struggles during the late 1940s to be surrounded by so many apprehensive Jewish faces. On the other hand, we took comfort from the militant and efficient way in which American Jewry was organizing itself under the somber but dynamic leadership of Abba Hillel Silver. The subterranean rivalries between him and Weizmann's followers, as well as the more overt jostling for credit between Silver's American Zionists and the Palestine leaders led by Sharett, threatened to mar our sense of occasion. It was obvious that if we were successful there would be a struggle about how the publicity and credit should be divided. But if there were no victory there would be no spoils to argue about.

Under the influence of this sober reflection, the Jewish Agency delegations under Silver and Sharett settled down into a fairly workable rhythm. Those like myself who were employed by the Jewish Agency had no specified ranks, positions or hierarchical priorities. Was I senior or junior to Eliahu Elath, Moshe Sasson, Michael Comay and others? Nobody took any interest in this. Looking back, I am struck by how little these things seemed to matter. We knew that Silver and Sharett were in command, and that a few of us had access to the peak of the Waldorf Towers where Weizmann sat in dark, brooding splendor.

He was gratified to feel that he was still indispensable in the struggle. Despite his lack of office, many heads of delegation and foreign ministers were accessible to nobody but him. Foreign statesmen faced him with a curious mixture of apprehension and awe.

The United Nations seemed to matter very much to the world in those days. Its early years, from 1946 to the Korean War in 1950, were its era of promise. As a result of Truman's militant approach, the UN Security Council had been the arena in which the Soviet Union had been forced to evacuate Azerbaijan, a province of Iran which the Soviet Union had held when that country was partitioned between Britain and Russia during World War II. The British and Arab efforts to pry France loose from Syria and Lebanon had been sustained by United Nations action. While the Jewish struggle for independence was going forward, the Security Council was developing a muscular influence in favor of the liberation of Indonesia from Dutch rule. The Foreign Offices of major powers regarded the UN sessions as the landmarks in their diplomatic calendars. In the days before the existence of NATO, the Warsaw Pact and the European Community, the UN was the only convincing expression of the multinational idea. In addition to wide coverage by the American and international press, the major organs of the United Nations seemed to evoke a deference in world public opinion that made even the most cynical statesman responsive to their voice.

If I were asked who were the most helpful delegations to Israel in the 1947 struggle I would put the Arab states at the top of the list. Their feet seemed to attract banana skins for the purpose of slipping on them. Having refused cooperation with UNSCOP, to our Zionist advantage, they now went on to reject both parts of the UNSCOP Report. While their revulsion from partition was understandable in their terms, there was something eccentric in their rejection of the minority UNSCOP Report in favor of a federal state in which the Arab province would have a veto over immigration to the Jewish province. The only solution that they would consider would be the establishment of an Arab state in which the existence of a separate Jewish nationality would be ignored.

It should have been obvious to them that any idea of disregarding the existence of a Jewish nationhood was now internationally unacceptable. By the extremism of their demands the Arabs strengthened the impression that Jews would need powerful safeguards not only to defend their national existence, but even to protect their very lives.

One of the procedural results of Arab extremism was the way in which the General Assembly organized its work. Since the Arab states would refuse even to sit down with the pro-partitionists, it was decided to work in detail through two subcommittees, one of which would discuss the partition plan. The composition of this committee gave us strong hope that partition would win the day. It consisted of the United States, the Soviet Union, Canada, South Africa, Poland, Czechoslovakia, Venezuela, Uruguay and Guatemala. The chairman would be Lester "Mike" Pearson of Canada, who was putting his emollient diplomacy to work for the first time in a major international issue. All the members of the subcommittee were ardent supporters of the partition principle. The absence of any Arab or Muslim representation was a gift from Arab nationalism to the Zionist cause.

We had other good allies. The president of the General Assembly, Brazil's Oswaldo Aranha, was a man of passionate and romantic disposition who was religiously exalted by the idea of Jewish statehood. At his side stood the rotund and solid figure of Secretary-General Trygve Lie, who had a dual interest in Zionist success: He needed an achievement for the United Nations that would give it a resonance in world opinion, and as a Norwegian Socialist he had seen the horrors of Nazi persecution at close hand. The idea that the organization of which he was the central spokesman should reflect every nationhood and culture except that of the Jews was repellent to his libertarian nature. It was only later that I learned that Norwegian was one of the languages in which the Palestine area had never ceased to be called "Jewland."

The subcommittee under Lester Pearson would have to report to the Special Political Committee, of which the chairman was the foreign minister of Australia, Herbert Evatt. His self-confidence was absolute. He never allowed his resolution to be blunted by any confession of fallibility. He was quite tolerant toward people who agreed with all his ideas. The Australian people for whom he spoke had a traditionally chivalrous attitude to the Jewish people, and many of them had a close acquaintance with the Palestinian landscapes in which Australian soldiers had found repose from the heat of desert conflict during both World Wars. Evatt was a contentious man. He did not suffer fools gladly. In fact, I found it hard to think of anyone, foolish or wise, whom Evatt would gladly suffer. He expected deference and was seldom inclined to regard any praise of himself as excessive. There was always a danger that some injury to his vanity or sense of hierarchy might provoke a vindictive reaction. On the other hand, he was the kind of man who would give full play to any authority with which he was charged.

One of our acute problems was to prove that the kind of Jewish state envisaged by UNSCOP would have coherence and viability. Here my fellow liaison officer, David Horowitz, a trained economist, put his immense dynamism into play. Horowitz deployed his talents on a high level of intensity. His discourse was quick, his devotion undivided, and his belief in the rationality of Zionism so strong that it was likely to overpower any except the most determined resistance.

I had two assignments in the Zionist delegation to the General Assembly in the fall of 1947. In the division of the world into what we called "spheres of influence" I was allotted four Scandinavian countries along with France and the three Benelux countries. I was to work with Nahum Goldmann. His attributes were stark realism, personal charm and responsiveness to the amenities and pleasures of life. None of these was a strong point among his contemporary colleagues. My trouble with him was that when I wished him to hold a dialogue with a Swedish representative, Nahum would find it hard to renounce a night at the opera or a concert or the superior allurements of gracious company. These characteristics were well known in the Zionist leadership and were accepted as an engaging eccentricity.

Nahum Goldmann's career knew many fluctuations. After the establishment of the State of Israel he could have taken a leading part in Israeli politics, but he recoiled from the idea of sundering his roots in the outside world. Even these roots were somewhat diffuse. His citizenship was American, although he looked and sounded less American than anybody could ever conceive. There was a time during World War II when he traveled with four or five passports, including one from Honduras, in order to facilitate his entries and exits at airports. He needed to express himself in a wider world and a broader range of interests than were available to him within the small parameters of Israel. He was undoubtedly the primary agent in securing massive aid from the German Federal Republic under the Compensation Agreement (shilumim), which facilitated Israel's economic and industrial development and also paved the way for our integration into the European Community. Toward the end of his life, however, he developed such a passion for peace with the Arabs that he tended to be one-sided in his denunciations of Israeli policy. Nothing, however, was less becoming to the State of Israel than the tendency of Israeli leaders to pursue their grievances against one of Zionism's greatest leaders up to and beyond his death.

In addition to my allocation of eight countries, whose votes I was supposed to obtain, I had an additional function that probably nobody else could have fulfilled. Both Silver and Ben-Gurion wanted me to elicit a maximal contribution from Weizmann. Few political leaders like to have their predecessors too near, especially if they cast as formidable a shadow as Weizmann. It must therefore be recorded in praise of Ben-Gurion and Silver that they had no hesitation in harnessing Weizmann's influence in the common cause. Their own relations with him were awkward, and I was given the task of deploying his prestige in the most effective way. My work was especially delicate since Weizmann had quarreled violently even with Moshe Sharett, despite the affinity of their political views. Weizmann believed, I thought with little justice, that Sharett could have done more to save him from being deposed at the 1946 Zionist Congress in Basle. Weizmann never had much taste for compromise in personal relations. He was always a hundred percent for or against, and Sharett was now definitely in the against column. Thus, the hope of keeping Weizmann in contact with the general operation of the delegation depended largely on me.

The work of Lester Pearson's subcommittee demanded a detailed knowledge of Palestinian geography and economics, and here Moshe Sharett's meticulous talent for accuracy was of enormous value. When I made my own survey of prospects in the early phases of the debate, I reached the conclusion that our main obstacle would be a natural reluctance to divide what had been an integral country. Most people regard a unitary state as preferable to a divided one. The authority and eloquence of the UNSCOP Report and of Reginald Coupland's previous formulations in 1937 stood us in good stead, but the idea that the political unity of Palestine, in Coupland's words, was an "idle pretense," was not easy for delegates to absorb.

Contrary to conventional illusion, the General Assembly debate was not merely a tug-of-war between pressure groups, the one relying on the weight of oil and the other on the weight of Jewish electoral strength in the United States. These, of course, were important elements in the contest, but, in addition, there was a serious inquiry, marked by intellectual rigor, into the structure of states and the conditions of coexistence between communities. Thus the Canadian representative declared, "The representative of Pakistan has said that partition should not take place without consent, but my question is whether it is any better to try to maintain the unity of Palestine without consent?" He was speaking, of course, in French and reflecting the dilemma of a country in which two nations were maintaining a single sovereignty. Even more cogent was the European experience. The Netherlands representative recalled the time after the Napoleonic wars when Belgium and Holland were brought together in one unitary state.

Although our two peoples had very close ties, relations and interests of a cultural, historical, ethnological and economic nature, this unitary state ended rapidly and unsuccessfully. The differences between Arabs and Jews are much greater than those between Belgium and the Netherlands. Now, together with Luxembourg, our countries are united, not politically but economically, and what counts now is not our political separation but our union for economic purposes. History has taught our countries this valuable lesson of independence combined with unity for certain important but limited purposes.

This was international debate at its highest level. In later years when the number of member states rose from fifty-eight to one hundred sixty it was difficult to create the kind of deliberative atmosphere in which the 1947 debate was conducted.

I saw no reason to underestimate the intellectual and moral quality of our Arab adversaries. The most effective delegates were from Lebanon, in the persons of Camille Chamoun (who later became President of Lebanon) and Charles Malik (who was the leading political thinker among Arab scholars). Their weakness lay in the fact that their personal stature transcended their political base. They represented only Lebanon and, within Lebanon, only the Christian community that was steadily losing its majority status. They had heavy reinforcement from the Pakistani representative, Mohammed Zafrullah Khan, an eloquent jurist who later became a judge at the International Court of Justice in The Hague. He was less fanatical than the Arab representatives in recoiling from Jewish and Zionist contacts. He had been a friend of one of my own closest British acquaintances, Sigmund Gestetner, and had developed a respectful relationship with Weizmann. On the floor of the Assembly, his advocacy of the Arab cause was fervent, articulate and indignant. However, when I met him in the Delegates' Lounge he praised my speech with the words "You made a good defense of a bad cause," and then added, "So did I."

Weizmann's appearance was scheduled for October 24. It was now plain that American and Soviet support could be expected, but even so, the two-thirds majority was not yet assured. Weizmann's task was to make an impact on the uncommitted delegates who had been shaken by the strong blasts of Arab pressure. He was listened to in suspense. He was more personal than usual and he made light of Arab spokesmen's aspersions that the Jews were the descendants of the Khazars of Southern Russia. He said, "It is very strange. All my life I've been a Jew, felt like a Jew, been talked about as a Jew, and yet I now learn in my old age that I am, what was it, oh yes, a Khazar. I'm not a Jew."

He said this with a very Jewish shrug. The idea that Weizmann was not a Jew evoked a hilarious reaction, and the Khazar myth was hastily dropped. The effect of his words was strong. At the time I thought, wrongly, that this would be his last act in the Zionist drama. It became evident that even if Jewish statehood were proposed in the General Assembly our adversaries, especially in the British delegation, would move away from direct anti-partitionism toward the aim of truncating the Jewish territory so as to make it unacceptable to us. Early in November the United States, influenced by British pressure, requested us to yield the Southern Negev to the Arabs. American representatives were even hinting that without this concession they would abandon support of the partition plan. Our problem was that the doors of the White House were closed to us. President Truman was so offended by what he called "the intensity of Zionist pressure" that he refused to receive any of the accredited representatives of the Zionist movement. This refusal could have been fatal to our cause. Although Truman had created the momentum that had led us through the UNSCOP Report and was in head-long conflict with Ernest Bevin, it was obvious that he could not follow all the vicissitudes of the General Assembly discussion. It was doubtful if the question of excluding the Negev from the proposed Jewish state would mean anything to him. I even asked myself whether Truman had any obligation to know where the Negev was.

On November 19, Weizmann rose from his sickbed and went to Washington for a talk with the president. He took our advice to concentrate entirely on the importance of the Southern Negev. He was warmly received at the White House and plunged immediately into that theme. As a student and teacher of science, Weizmann was temperamentally impatient with anything that diverted him from a well-defined theme. Whenever Truman wandered, in his own way and temperament, to other subjects, Weizmann brought him back with a sharp professorial statement: "Mr. President, we have come here to talk about the Negev." It is doubtful if Truman would have accepted this peremptory remark from anyone else, but he meekly accepted the hint. Weizmann then expounded a memorandum prepared by Eliahu Elath, the Jewish Agency representative in Washington, in which Elath pointed out that the Arab states already had an outlet to the Red Sea on the Gulf of 'Aqaba through Transjordan, Egypt and Saudi Arabia. For the Jewish state, however, a gateway to Africa and Asia would be an indispensable enlargement of its place in the international system, and this was feasible only through the Southern Negev. Weizmann managed to keep Truman's mind riveted on this point alone.

The president seemed to have become fascinated by the excursion into a phase of remote political geography. Grasping the simplicity and force of the argument, he gave his assent. But there was a race against time. The Jewish Agency representatives, Sharett and Horowitz, had been invited to meet the American delegate, Hershel Johnson, at 3:00 the next day in the United Nations Delegates' Lounge to hear the State Department's decisions against retaining the Negev in the Jewish state. Ambassador Johnson began to pronounce judgment of execution. His intention was to tell us frankly that if we wanted a Jewish state we could not have the Negev. In midsentence a messenger from his delegation tried to call him to the telephone. He told the messenger that he could not be disturbed and sent his deputy, General Hildring, to take the call. The general returned to whisper to him that the president himself was holding on at the Washington end and that Ambassador Johnson's career was unlikely to prosper if he did not take the call.

The ambassador leapt to the telephone booth like a startled and portly reindeer. Twenty minutes later he returned. Seating himself opposite Sharett and Horowitz, he blurted out an embarrassed retraction. "What I really wanted to say to you, gentlemen, was that we have no change to make in the UNSCOP map."

Horowitz has recorded the Jewish reaction with quiet understatement. "We sighed with relief. Weizmann's talk had been successful. The struggle for the southern boundary had ended in victory."

Eventually the Partition Committee adopted the draft of Lester Pearson of Canada, which was acceptable both to the United States and to the Soviet Union. This was the stage at which "Mike" Pearson's career as an international conciliator had its takeoff point. Some changes were made to the UNSCOP proposal with the object of reducing the Arab population of the Jewish state. Sharett rose to meticulous statesmanship in the detailed account that he gave on the map of the Jewish state. Together with Horowitz and an Israeli water expert, Aharon Wiener, he fought hard to make everyone see that the proposed state, in spite of its tortuous boundaries, would have a relatively high degree of economic viability.

By mid-November we were ready for the decision. All arguments had been exhausted. All influences had been put to work. It was now a question of counting heads. For a whole week we were to live in continued and increased suspense. The committee adopted the majority report in favor of partition by a vote of twenty-two to thirteen with about twenty abstentions. Since we would need a two-thirds majority, this vote meant that the partition proposal was neither dead nor fully alive. We would have to change an unpromising voting pattern. For the next few days Arabs and Jews summoned every resource of influence and persuasion to secure the victory of their cause. My own personal anxieties were great, for the abstainers in the committee included France and Belgium, whose support in the final vote was my own responsibility. In particular the prospect of French abstention threatened to disrupt the entire West European front. I went to see Weizmann, and we drafted a telegram to Léon Blum, the Socialist statesman, who would have a strong influence on the French Socialist Cabinet. "Does France wish to be absent from a moment unfading in the memory of man?" We subsequently learned that this searing question, penetrating Blum's tragic experience in a German concentration camp, had an irresistible effect.

Our difficulties were compounded by the complex American position. Although Truman had put himself formally behind the partition proposal, many of his representatives at the United Nations, long familiar with Arab causes, were creating an atmosphere of skepticism around their own government's policy. General Hildring had been appointed as a special presidential representative acting as a watchdog to ensure that the State Department's prejudices did not get the better of the president's policies. This was comforting in itself. On the other hand, I reflected that if there had been no cause for disquiet, there would have been no need for such an appointment. Doubts about the United States' position were creating a difficult situation in Latin America and in countries, such as the Philippines and Liberia, that were accustomed to follow the American lead on international issues. At Jewish Agency headquarters, and in our hotels, we worked around the clock telegraphing, telephoning, writing, cajoling, pleading all over the world. Did anybody in Manila or Monrovia have access to the presidents of those countries? Who were the friends in the United States who could influence Liberia? What were the motivations and impulses that had caused Haiti to abstain? What was needed, above all, to bring France and Belgium into the column?

Here was the Jewish people at the threshold of its greatest transition, and yet there was a danger that everything could be lost through marginal circumstances in countries ostensibly external to the issue. It is a weakness of the United Nations' system that countries that have no particular stake in a problem can outvote nations whose very survival is at hazard.

When the General Assembly came together on November 27 we were in desperate tension. There was good reason to fear that if the vote was taken that day we would fall short of the two-thirds majority. The day before, the odds had seemed in our favor, but at precisely that moment the French delegate, Alexandre Parodi, had called for a postponement of the session. It seemed that we had lost ground. Our only hope lay in a postponement in the course of which we would try to strengthen our ranks. I turned to some of our Latin American delegates and expressed the hope that they would embark on long filibustering speeches. I made this request in particular to Professor Rodriguez Fabregat, an ardently pro-Zionist member of the UNSCOP team. I said to him, "Professor, do you think that you could make a filibustering speech for about an hour?" He replied, "For me an hour-long speech is not a filibuster. It is a brief observation."

When the speech-makers and their audience were exhausted, the General Assembly president, Ambassador Aranha of Brazil, revived our hopes. He said, irrelevantly, that the following day was an American national holiday, Thanksgiving Day. Is it really courteous, he asked, to employ American staff on one of their national holidays when, after all, we could easily come together to vote on November 29? Before any protests could be uttered he had dispersed the General Assembly. Aranha had the swiftest wrist action with a gavel of anybody that I have ever known.

When our delegation convened on the morning of November 29 we knew that the day's proceedings would be decisive. There was no further possibility of delay. We hoped, and yet could not fully believe, that the intensive lobbying by ourselves and by the White House had brought us the prospect of a majority. There was, however, a procedural obstacle. A committee of three rapporteurs had been appointed to present a report of the Palestine Committee's findings to the Plenary General Assembly. There was danger that they might report to the Assembly that "an agreed solution" between Arabs and Jews might still be possible. This, of course, would merely be a device for sidetracking the partition vote. The chairman of the Rapporteur Committee was Ambassador Thor Thors of Iceland, the smallest country in the United Nations, whose population then was about 175,000. On that day I rose much earlier than usual and went to a midtown hotel to call on Thor Thors. My aim was to persuade him to report to the General Assembly that nothing would be gained by postponement; that there was no chance for an Arab-Jewish agreement; that the General Assembly, therefore, would have to make its adjudication.

It was a strange encounter. On reaching the Icelandic ambassador's suite, I said, "History is very strange in its manifestations. Here is your country, Iceland, the smallest nation in the international community, able to have a decisive effect on whether or not the Jewish people shall achieve its independence. By any slip of the tongue or the pen you could banish the Jewish people and put an end, perhaps forever, to its most cherished hopes and dreams."

Thor Thors, like most of his countrymen, was profoundly religious. He kept repeating, as though in a state of shock, "How did it ever come about that our little island should have such a profound influence on the history of such a great people?" He would do whatever was necessary to make November 29 a turning point in what he called "the spiritual story of mankind."

A few hours later the General Assembly opened in an atmosphere of excitement. Millions of New Yorkers, whose business or domestic affairs made it possible, had their radios tuned to the stations that carried the UN proceedings in full. The UN building seethed with excited crowds: delegates, correspondents, photographers, Jewish Agency officials, UN staff, lobbyists of every kind, and officials of national Jewish organizations. Arab delegates and ordinary citizens were eager to be eyewitnesses to what the newspapers said would be a sensational day. The large General Assembly hall was filled to overflowing. Thousands of people were lined up outside, refusing to leave even when told that no places were available. When I reached the building I heard of many last-minute developments. General Carlos Romulo, who had spoken so brilliantly against partition in the Palestine Committee, had left New York and there was a good chance that the Philippine delegation would vote "yes." Because of a revolution in Thailand, the Thai prince, Prince Wan, who had voted against partition in the Palestine Committee, but whose authority was now in question, had quietly left the country on the excuse that he had reservations on the SS *Queen Mary* and if he stayed over now he would not be able to get home. American oilmen and their lobbyists were making desperate last-minute efforts to gather anti-partition votes. There were, however, indications that Liberia and Haiti had yielded to the joint influence of the Israeli delegation and the White House and might now favor partition.

The session opened with Dr. Oswaldo Aranha of Brazil, sitting at the podium beside Trygve Lie. Thor Thors made his report. I heard it with a sense of relief. He said that there was no reason at all for the Assembly to shirk its responsibilities. The majority had voted for the establishment of a Jewish and an Arab state. It would be untrue to its mission if it did not take a stand. Making a last frantic effort to postpone the voting, Camille Chamoun of Lebanon proposed a compromise full of pitfalls. Hershel Johnson for the United States and Andrei Gromyko for the Soviet Union exposed his suggestion as a trick. Aranha kept the meeting in a state of urgency by his insistence that a vote be completed by the end of the day.

Finally the dramatic moment arrived. There was a hush as the representative of each country responded with a "yes," "no" or "abstention." France, on the previous day, had succeeded in postponing the vote for twenty-four hours in the hope of a last-minute compromise. Now, as its name was called, a clear "oui" rang out.

Further balloting was interrupted by a storm of cheering. When the last country's name had been heard, President Aranha rapped his gavel and announced: "Thirty-three in favor, thirteen against, ten abstentions, one absence. I declare that the motion has been accepted by the requisite two-thirds." It was clear that the French vote had broken the ice.

France still had a powerful stake in Muslim North Africa and took a protective interest in a number of French Catholic institutions scattered throughout the Middle East. On the other hand, it had close ties with the Maronite Christians in Lebanon, whose hand might actually be strengthened by the emergence of a Jewish state. In a memorandum submitted in January 1948 to the Jewish Agency Executive, Eliahu Elath had indicated that in conversations with high-ranking members of the French Embassy in Washington he had learned that the head of the French government's Africa-Levant department had privately promised the Arab states that France would not support the creation of a Jewish state.

There is little doubt that Léon Blum's intervention was decisive.

When the vote was announced, the Arab delegates, led by Azzam Pasha and Prince Feisal of Saudi Arabia, stalked out of the Assembly hall in rage. On reaching the press room, Azzam said that "any line of partition drawn in Palestine will be a line of fire and blood." I went out into the lobby where the Jewish delegation was caught up in the embrace of an enthusiastic throng. There were Jews in tears and many non-Jews moved by the nobility of the occasion. No one who lived that moment will ever lose its memory from his heart. Suzy and I entered one of our delegation's cars, together with Moshe Sharett and Moshe Tov. Strangely, yet perhaps understandably, we made the journey into Manhattan in silence. A natural deference made us go to the Plaza Hotel to greet Chaim Weizmann, who had been waiting on tenterhooks. We persuaded him, against his first indignant reaction, to attend a Labor Zionist rally in Madison Square Garden, where he was later given a rapturous homage.

It was evening in Jerusalem. Crowds had gathered near the Jewish Agency building in Rehavia to hear the recitation of the vote. They burst into song and began dancing in the streets. Ben-Gurion was silent in the Galei Kinneret Hotel in Tiberias where he took his occasional periods of rest. He understood the greatness of the moment, but when he heard that there was dancing in the streets of Jerusalem, he found it necessary to express detachment. He, more than anyone, knew that the charter of Jewish freedom would also be the signal for a savage war. He believed that Azzam Pasha's ominous warning about blood and fire was authentic.

These apprehensions were fully shared by those of us who took part in the celebrations in New York. We understood, no less than our fellow Jews in Palestine, that the Assembly resolution would be a mere scrap of paper unless it was confirmed by sacrifice and toil. And yet we had the strong intuition that this date would never lose its meaning.

We had come a very long distance in a single year. At the beginning of 1947 the Jewish people's hope of statehood had been nowhere recognized. It was being crushed by the convergence of British hostility and Arab guns. The "displaced persons" were still pining away in their camps. Now, eleven months later, everything had changed. The Jewish people in Palestine was in danger, but it was now recognized as a nation fighting for its patrimony. The glow of international legitimacy illuminated its path. A war for independence was obviously inevitable, but it would be fought in conditions different from anything that could have been predicted a few months before. It was a genuine watershed. The Jewish state was no longer a hopeless dream.

Those who danced in the streets of Jerusalem were less aware than I of the fragile thread on which our victory hung. If Iceland had not made a decisive report; if Liberia, Haiti and the Philippines had resisted White House pressure; if France had abstained, a historic opportunity would have slipped away beyond recall. Above all I was disturbed by the weakness of American support. As late as mid-summer 1947, the State Department officials, supported by Secretary Marshall, had argued strongly for a unitary state under a United Nations trusteeship. In July Secretary Marshall had been assuring Bevin of American cooperation to help suppress "illegal" Jewish immigration to Palestine. When the General Assembly convened on September 22, its delegation was still under Marshall's instructions to avoid supporting the UNSCOP majority report. It was only President Truman's intervention on October 9, 1947, that compelled Secretary Marshall to obey presidential instructions and support the partition plan. Even then, U.S. support had been more lukewarm than that of the Soviet representative, Tsarapkin, who went so far as to suggest that the British should immediately give up their authority and enable the Security Council to administer Palestine in the months that would elapse until the establishment of Jewish and Arab states. The inhibitions of the State Department, unlike those of Bevin, were not inspired by heat and passion. They were dangerous precisely because they rested on a certain logic. Three hesitations were at work. First, many American leaders believed that the Jewish population of Palestine would be massacred as a result of an action for which the United States was largely responsible. Second, there was a feeling in the State Department and in *The New York Times* that if immigrants poured into Palestine from Eastern and Central Europe they would bring the Communist virus into the Middle East. Third, it was feared that America's interests in the Arab world, although not as vital as they later became, would be subjected to threat and pressure. The oil weapon was already being brandished.

The events of December 1947 proved that the UN vote had been dramatic but was not irreversible. Although the defense of Jewish settlements by the Haganah was generally successful, the Arabs were able to sunder communications between the scattered parts of the area designed for the Jewish state. They had decided to avoid a frontal assault and to fight a war of communications. They would cut Jerusalem off at the Latrun salient; they would interpose themselves between the northern and southern Negev; they would send "volunteer" armies from Lebanon and Syria into Galilee. Thus the map of the Jewish state would lack coherence so that no Jewish government authority would be able to establish its writ in any consecutive area.

As if the difficulties from the Arabs were not enough, it soon became evident that Bevin had not renounced the hope of frustrating the partition plan. The British government announced bluntly that it would do nothing "to facilitate the fulfillment of the partition recommendation." This meant that public order would collapse and that the country would fall into chaos. It must have been one of the least creditable decisions ever made by a British government. Britain's allies in America and Europe were visibly ashamed. The nation that had taken the lead in resisting Hitler seemed determined to prevent redress for Hitler's victims.

Three days after the historic international vote an impression began to spread throughout the world that the November 29, 1947, resolution would be crushed by the weight of opposing pressures. The period between December 1947 and April 1948 would be among the most perilous in the Jewish story.

6

THE END OF EXILE

IT WAS HISTORICALLY and emotionally correct for Jews to celebrate the 1947 Partition Resolution with relief. We shuddered when we looked back on the chasm into which we would have fallen but for that victory. In later years, David Ben-Gurion allowed himself to underestimate the effect of the 1947 Resolution. Having wisely and fervently devoted himself to the preparation of Israel's armed strength, he had taken little part in the diplomatic struggle of 1947–1948. It was natural for him to describe our military victory as the exclusive source of Israel's birth. A favorite utterance by him was that "Israel did not arise through the 1947 Resolution."

This was not Ben-Gurion at his best. It was only partly true, and therefore not true in any real sense. The UN Resolution would admittedly have remained a mere scrap of paper unless it was made effective by sacrifice on the battlefield and by subsequent diplomatic perseverance, and yet I had the conviction that the November 29 date would never lose its resonance. It is significant that in the Declaration of Independence that Ben-Gurion himself brought for approval on May 14, 1948, the 1947 Resolution was quoted as one of the elements by virtue of which the state arose.

If the United Nations debate had ended in deadlock, it is unlikely that the British, with their massive armies, would have walked out and left us with a vacuum of authority. The strongest probability is that the country would have continued to live under international tutelage, with a joint American-British administration. And if the United Nations had asserted its sovereignty by proclaiming a UN trusteeship, it is unlikely that even President Truman and the Soviet Union would have extended recognition to a Jewish state established in revolt against an international jurisdiction. History, after all, is the story of opportunities; once they are lost they are unlikely to recur. In that sense the claim of the 1947 Resolution to be recognized as a watershed is unassailable.

I cannot construct any scenario for 1947–1948 in which a Jewish state, recognized by the major powers, could have emerged if there had not been Zionist victories at UNSCOP and in the UN General Assembly. Nevertheless, within a few days of the Partition Resolution scores of Jews had been killed, and it was brutally clear that Jews would not have their state "awarded" them or "established" by international decree. The UN resolution had stark limitations. It had contributed decisively to the British departure. It had exalted Jewish morale. It had given advance legitimacy to a Jewish state that would arise by force of its own responsibility and sacrifice. But it did not assure survival.

This reality has its positive side. Israel does not owe the debt of its very existence to the sacrifice of others. This truth has had an immense effect on the national mentality. The memory of having won birth and survival by a lonely decision has worked on Israel's life and policy in many ways. It has served both as a summons to national unity and as a warning against giving inflated importance to outside pressures. After its brief moment of grace, the United Nations appeared to Israelis very much like the alligator that, according to the legend, gives birth to its young with great tenderness and then devours them with cold apathy. This is an exaggeration; UN bodies have adopted more significant resolutions in support of Israel's sovereignty than in violation of it. Yet it is true that the major powers, especially the United States, who supported the resolutions on Israeli independence did very little to follow up their parliamentary action with concrete assistance.

Self-reliance would become the natural posture for a people for whom nobody in the outside world had risked any blood even when destruction stared it in the face.

The Jewish leadership, represented by our UN delegation, reacted somewhat naively to its own success in November 1947. The delegation calmly began to disperse. Silver went back for a time to his post as a rabbi and spiritual leader of a large congregation. He returned to the center of the fray some weeks later in fiery mood when the United States reneged on its support of partition. Sharett, Horowitz and I made plans to return whence we had come. This meant Jerusalem for them and the London Zionist Office for me.

Here, however, I raised a question. Were we not acting in an absurdly routine way? Did London really matter now? Surely the political battle would have to be fought at Lake Success and the physical battle in Jerusalem. Therefore, Jerusalem and New York were the only two places for any of us to be. Sharett recognized this logic and asked Horowitz and me to remain within sight and sound of UN headquarters. Horowitz, weighed down by anxiety about his family and alarmed unduly about his own health, insisted on returning home. The upshot was that the "captains and the kings" departed and I stayed on in a capacity of vigilance in New York. It was a heavy responsibility for a young man living in a third-rank hotel on a minimal per diem with no sense of the future.

Within a few days it emerged that we had advanced to the threshold of national freedom with a good chance of being thrown back into tutelage and subjection. The first months of 1948 were darkened by two developments. Our military prospects were poor, and there was a stunning American retreat from the support of Jewish statehood. I felt that all the fruits of our November victory were slipping away.

Arab governments had naturally gone into high gear after their defeat in November 1947. It would soon be apparent that the Arab prediction that "any line of partition would be a line of fire and blood" was not mere rhetoric. On December 2 there were violent attacks on Jews in Jerusalem, Haifa and Jaffa. At the same time, the Arab-Jewish confrontation spread throughout the Middle East. Murderous assaults on Jews took place in the north and south of the Arab periphery—in Aleppo and in Aden. On the outskirts of Damascus a headquarters was established for enlisting Arab "volunteers" under the command of the guerrilla leader Fawzi Qawukji, whose forces would grow to 7,000 by the end of March 1948.

The Arabs were showing resilience in recovering from their diplomatic defeat, and the Jewish military posture was defensive. The protection of Jewish settlements by the Haganah was heroic and generally successful, but the Arabs, showing unusual sophistication, had decided to abstain from head-on confrontation: They continued their war of sundered communications. Within a few weeks Jewish rural settlements were isolated and roads between urban centers were cut. Three of the roads leading to Jerusalem had fallen into the power of Arab warriors, and the Jewish convoy system was throttled, facing the city with the prospect of starvation. Arab forces had interposed themselves between the northern and the southern Negev. They had sent "volunteer" armies from Lebanon and Syria into Galilee. The bright prospect that had glowed in November was being extinguished in March. Thus, the map of the future Jewish state lacked coherence. A Jewish authority would find it hard to establish control over any consecutive area.

Worst of all, casualties were multiplying and the brunt of sacrifice was being borne not by soldiers, but by civilians. In Ben-Yehuda Street, Jerusalem, the very heart and center of Palestine Jewry, scores of men, women and children were killed or maimed when Arab assailants exploded a bomb in the crowded city center. Determined assaults from Jaffa were endangering the civilian population of Tel Aviv. It is true that Jewish forces were inflicting casualties as well as suffering them, but the more savage the fighting the more doubtful world opinion became about the possibility of implementing partition.

It was at this stage that we came face-to-face in the cold light of morning with a reality that Jews had been reluctant to confront. The November 29 Resolution was historically dramatic, but juridically weak. During the first part of 1948 Zionists would speak of "the UN decision." The Arabs called it "a recommendation." Here they were on stronger ground than we were. The UN structure is based on a hierarchy in which five members—the

United States, the United Kingdom, the Soviet Union, France and China—are awarded a right of veto and are described in the UN Charter as having "primary responsibility for the maintenance of international peace and security." The only matter in which the General Assembly uses the word "decision" is in the admission of states. This is a very powerful capacity. The world community has consistently agreed that the United Nations can determine the structure of the international community by its own membership. A state thus admitted acquires automatic recognition of its legitimacy. For the rest, however, the Founding Fathers of the Organization, aware of the disparity of real power among member states, had envisaged the General Assembly as a forum or a stage. It was to be not an instrument for solving disputes but an arena for waging them. Thus when the Egyptian delegate declared, "We do not intend to carry out the recommendations of the General Assembly. This is our right under the charter," he was on strong legal ground.

The optional character of the 1947 Resolution had first been emphasized by the British government, but the tendency to deprive Assembly Resolutions of compelling force began to infect American policy as well. While they placed their main hopes on success in the field of battle, the Arabs tried to reverse the Partition Resolution by appeals to the Security Council, which had taken the question on its agenda in mid-December. I was in a curious personal position. My senior colleagues had left the arena and I could only sit helplessly among visitors and tourists while the oratorical contest in the Security Council was reopened. At the end of December I was sending warnings to Jerusalem about the decline in our political fortunes. At the Security Council table the United Kingdom, represented by Sir Alexander Cadogan, seemed to carry much more weight than it ever did among fifty-seven members of the General Assembly.

Cadogan had all the qualities of an iceberg except its ultimate capacity to melt. Diplomacy is popularly associated, in professional literature, with amiability and refined courtesy. It would appear that Cadogan had ignored all the traditional texts that laid down how a diplomat ought to behave. He exuded a lack of charm from every pore.

The Security Council was theoretically a colleague of the General Assembly in the hierarchy of international institutions. The chairman by rotation of the Security Council was Ambassador Alfonso Lopez of Colombia, a former president of his country, who, without approaching Cadogan's frigidity, was himself without warmth. So was the Belgian delegate, Ambassador Fernand Van Langenhove, who seemed to have an obsequious fixation on the British government. No comfort was to be found from Dr. Tingfu Tsiang, the representative of China, which was then still under Chiang Kai-shek's regime. The Arab assault was developed intensely by a veteran Syrian statesman, Faris al-Khoury. When he presided the meetings were constantly interrupted by his adjournments "for consultation." It later transpired that the motive for this frequency was not diplomatic but urological.

I was so concerned about the deteriorating situation and my own responsibility at Lake Success that I went to Washington to take soundings in the State Department. I was accompanied by Eliahu Elath, the head of our Washington office who later became Israel's first ambassador to Washington. American officials, led by Dean Rusk, were perfunctory in support of partition and deeply skeptical about the possibility of putting it into effect. The legalists were making full play with the juridical optionality of General Assembly resolutions. On February 24, 1948, the five permanent members of the Security Council, who constituted the engine that drove the United Nations train forward, ruled that the Security Council had no automatic duty to implement recommendations of the General Assembly. They could carry out such recommendations if they wished. They could also reverse them and, with greater possibility, allow them to subside in benevolent neglect. The Big Five expressed the view that General Assembly resolutions had "moral weight," which in international tradition is as near to weightlessness as it is possible to conceive.

Symbolic of our worsening diplomatic situation was what came to be called "the case of the five lonely pilgrims." They were members of what was technically called the "Palestine Committee of the UN." Its purpose was to see that the partition plan was put into operation as effectively as possible. The members were Czechoslovakia, Denmark, Bolivia, Panama and the Philippines. It is not disrespectful of that composition to say that if the United Nations had wished to illustrate its impotence it could not have chosen that team more deliberately. The British government treated it with contempt and refused to admit it to Palestine until the last British official had left the country. And so the five sat in New York, frustrated and inert, while Palestine was bleeding. One of the committee members, Per Federspiel of Denmark, who was more articulate than his four colleagues, said to me: "The British want to create a vacuum in Palestine but they refuse to hand the vacuum over to us." The Arabs were finding the Security Council more responsive to their pressures than the more sentimental General Assembly had been. My first fear was that the five lonely pilgrims might write an anti-partition report of their own. I realized the importance of getting into the record a UN statement that would ascribe responsibility to the Arab forces who were defying the General Assembly's Resolution by force. I concentrated my efforts on the Bolivian delegate, Ambassador Raoul Mendoza. Federspiel was too British, and the Panamanian and Filipino were men whose goodwill exceeded their capacities. By mid-March Mendoza and I had developed a text that was subsequently embodied in an official report by the commission to the General Assembly:

Arab opposition to the plan of the Assembly of 1947 has taken the form of organized efforts by strong Arab elements, both inside and outside Palestine, to prevent its implementation and to thwart its objectives by threats and acts of violence including repeated armed incursion into Palestine territory. The Commission has had to report to the Security Council that powerful Arab interests, both inside and outside Palestine, are defying the Resolution of the General Assembly and are engaged in a deliberate effort to alter by force the settlement envisaged therein.

I saw the adoption of this text as a modest personal success. It signifies that the Arab-Israeli war is one of the few conflicts in modern history for which culpability has been clearly defined by a competent international authority. It was not even contested by the Arabs themselves. They had taken responsibility for the war and therefore for all its consequences. The Syrian representative said, quite accurately,

The recommendations of the General Assembly are not imperative on those to whom they are addressed. I fail to find in this Charter any text which implies, directly or indirectly, that the General Assembly has the authority to enforce its own recommendations by military force. The General Assembly only gives advice and the parties to whom advice is addressed accept it when it is rightful and just and when it does not impair their fundamental rights.

In subsequent years the Arab governments would ascribe sanctity to General Assembly recommendations, which by then had become uniformly supportive of their cause. All that I and my colleagues could do at the time was to defend the principle that while it was legally permissible to refuse acceptance of General Assembly resolutions, it was not legally permissible to use armed force to prevent others from implementing them. UN members had agreed that force could not be used except "in the common interest" of the United Nations or in self-defense.

While our political gains were being eroded in the international arena, our fighting men and women were having a hard time in the field of battle. Arrayed against the "volunteers" of Fawzi Qawukji were Jewish units consisting mainly of the Haganah, whose striking force was the four battalions of the Palmach commando units with about 2,100 members and 1,000 reservists. In addition, there was the field army, consisting of about 1,800 full-time members and 10,000 reservists. The Haganah could also count on the reserve army with 32,000 members, many of whom were tied down to defending the areas of their abode in villages and cities. Finally there was a youth unit (Gadna) made up of youngsters being trained for auxiliary tasks with the ambition of joining the Palmach. Apart from the Haganah, and not always acting in concert with it, were two much smaller resistance groups, the IZL, composed of 4–5,000 men, and the Lechi with a few hundred men. The IZL and Lechi were functioning as independent military organizations.

The Labor movement was predominant in the sacrifices and responsibilities of the battle. Jewish weaponry was pathotically inadequate. It consisted at first of rifles and light and medium machine guns with no artillery or air support. In the beginning there was a primitive structure of command and organization that evolved into an orderly pattern only toward the end of May.

When Jewish casualties mounted in December, it seemed that the threshold of statehood would never be crossed. The Jews were everywhere at bay. Arab forces surged around them with impressive vigor, attacking isolated Jewish settlements and the Jewish sectors of the cities with mixed populations. By now the Arabs controlled most of the high ground. The war was certainly not going to respect the boundaries recommended by the General Assembly. Indeed, it was in the area allotted to the Jewish state that the Arab assault was most fierce.

The first effort of Jewish forces was to retain thirty-three settlements, which under the partition map would have been included in the Arab state. A major target of the Arab attack was the Etzion block southeast of Jerusalem. The assault was repelled but the population of Etzion, cut off from any sustaining proximity of fellow Jews, was in constant need of arms and supplies. On January 17, 1948, 35 young Palmach fighters, on their way to reinforce the Etzion settlements, were ambushed and killed by Arab forces in the area. By the end of March the Arab military strategy seemed to be successful. The Negev was cut off from the center of the country, Jerusalem was now isolated from the coast, and the villages of western Galilee had little contact with other areas of Jewish population.

Across the world, military strategists and political observers began to regard a Jewish state as a dead issue. Their appraisal found immediate reflection in the political climate. Field Marshal Montgomery, the victor of El Alamein, reported to Attlee and Bevin that "the Jews have made a colossal mistake and have lost their cause." What concerned me more directly was that in my conversations at UN headquarters I found that the original supporters of partition were now wavering and were inclined to seek "alternative solutions." All these proposed solutions would have involved indefinite postponement of Jewish statehood.

I became so worried about the outlook that I took a personal initiative. Without consulting anybody, I sent Weizmann a cable to the Dorchester Hotel, London:

> In view worsening situation urge you to reconsider decision to go to Palestine in January. Everything depends upon outcome of negotiations here Lake Success Washington. Most crucial phase of all now approaches here in which we sorely miss your presence advice activity and influence.
> Affectionately,
> EBAN

I received an irascible response of which the substance was that if the Zionist Executive, having dismissed Weizmann from office, nevertheless needed his services, they could at least have the grace to say so. Accordingly I sought and obtained a message of endorsement both from Sharett and from Arthur Lourie, the secretary of the Zionist Emergency Council. Six days later Weizmann, accompanied by his wife, sailed from England on the *Queen Mary*, arriving in New York on February 4. That night I dined with them at the Waldorf Towers. He began the conversation belligerently: "Why in heaven's name did you drag me to this frozen waste when I might have been in Rehovot?" I explained that there was a serious danger that the United Nations might reverse itself. Also, the situation in Washington was worse than ever. Truman was the only person alive who could stop the State Department from sabotaging the partition plan, and yet for more than a month Truman had been furious with American Zionist leaders, even refusing to see any of them. Truman had said that they were wanting in moderation and in respect for his person and office. I explained to Weizmann that the only hope was for him to talk to the president.

Truman's resentment at what he called "immoderate Zionist pressure" had not subsided nine years later when he published his autobiography, *Years of Trial and Hope.* He then wrote:

> I do not think I ever had so much pressure and propaganda at the White House as I had in this instance. The persistence of a few of the extreme Zionist leaders actuated by political motives and engaged in political threats disturbed and annoyed me. The Jewish pressure on the White House did not diminish in the days following the partition vote. Individuals and groups asked me, usually in rather quarrelsome and emotional ways, to stop the Arabs, to keep the British from supporting the Arabs, to furnish American soldiers, to do this, that and the other. As the pressure mounted I found it necessary to give instructions that I did not want to be approached by any more spokesmen for the extreme Zionist cause.

In objective terms Truman's attitude was preposterous. His government was at the center of an explosive international crisis and here he was refusing even to have discourse with one of the parties in the dispute on the trivial grounds that he found them personally abrasive. His attitude was that if you are a president of the United States you can decide for yourself with whom you will and will not speak.

The pivotal event in our political drama was a bizarre episode that took place in late March. Nothing like it could ever have been conceived anywhere but in the United States. While Truman had refused to meet the official Zionists, he had a warm memory of his encounter with Weizmann about the Negev in 1947. We speculated that this might give Weizmann access to the

White House again. One day Truman was talking in the White House with his previous business partner, Eddie Jacobson from Kansas City. In a later recorded statement Truman would say, "Eddie was the best buyer we had in the store and I was the best seller." In this case, however, what we needed was Eddie's ability to sell an idea, not to buy shirts.

Truman has recorded how he saw that Eddie Jacobson appeared to be dejected. Truman had asked, "Eddie, why are you going around looking like you've heard about the destruction of the Temple for the first time?"

Jacobson replied, "Well, Mr. President, it's because you will not agree to meet any of my Zionist friends, not even Chaim Weizmann. You really must meet him. He, after all, has taken this cause through forty years of wilderness. He is the Andrew Jackson of the Jewish people."

Eddie Jacobson would probably have been hard-pressed to explain why Truman hero-worshiped Andrew Jackson, even to the extent of having a sculptured portrayal of the great Southern president on his desk. After this talk and Truman's reserved response, Jacobson called me in New York. He said that our only hope of getting Truman to receive a Zionist spokesman lay in Weizmann, and even this only if we could convince Truman that Weizmann was, in effect, a reincarnation of Andrew Jackson. I told Eddie that I, myself, believed that no two human beings had ever walked on the face of the earth with fewer common attributes than Chaim Weizmann and Andrew Jackson. On the other hand, the establishment of a Jewish state was in my view a superior interest to historical accuracy. I told Eddie to go ahead and to tell Truman whatever he thought would induce him to open his ears to an exposition of Zionism by its most eminent standard bearer.

Jacobson went back to Truman and told him that he had studied the situation and concluded that Andrew Jackson and Chaim Weizmann were so similar in every respect that it was difficult to tell them apart.

On March 18, six weeks after Weizmann's arrival, his meeting with the president took place and only then on condition that the venerable Zionist leader would enter by a side door in order to avoid inviting what Truman called "immoderate pressure." To Weizmann himself Truman was humbly apologetic about the delay. "I told him as plainly as I could," Truman wrote later, "why I had at first put off seeing him. He understood. I explained to him what the basis of my interest in the Jewish problem was and that my primary concern was to see justice done without bloodshed. And when he left my office I felt that he had received a full understanding of my policy and that I knew what it was he wanted. . . ."

In reality there was a full misunderstanding. The State Department had been given no prior knowledge of Weizmann's visit to the White House and was relentlessly pursuing its efforts to undermine the American commitment to partition. Almost before we heard Weizmann reporting on Truman's assurances of his support of partition, Ambassador Warren Austin made a sensational speech in the Security Council recommending that partition be suspended. He suggested that the General Assembly be convened in a special session to consider the establishment of "a temporary trusteeship over Palestine." Although Austin said that this proposal was "without prejudice to the eventual settlement," it was plain that the United States had totally reneged on its support of Jewish statehood as embodied in the November 29, 1947, Resolution.

It was fully in accord with Truman's disposition to personalize international events. In this spirit he ordered his senior political adviser, Clark Clifford,

> to find out how this could have happened. I assured Chaim Weizmann that we were for partition and would stick to it. He must think I am a plain liar.

All the evidence points to the fact that the State Department had in fact sent a copy of Austin's speech to Truman for approval. Truman quite clearly had not grasped the full import of what he was approving, but his assertion that he was "double-crossed" does not hold water. The fact that Truman distrusted both his own State Department and the official Zionist leaders did not make for coherent procedures of decision. Moreover, the draft of Warren Austin's speech had been sent to him while he was aboard the presidential yacht *Williamsburg*. The nautical atmosphere and the card games with close friends may not have been congenial to meticulous documentary scrutiny, which in any case was not Truman's strongest point. His reliance on sporadic meetings with Weizmann was providential for the Zionist cause, but it was not an efficient way to develop a consistent policy.

Our cause was strengthened by the circumstance that the trusteeship idea appeared to be as unattractive to others as it was to us. The thirty-odd governments who had supported the partition resolution felt insulted by the American repudiation. The UN secretary-general, Trygve Lie, believed that the United States had struck a blow at the foundations of the United Nations.

More unexpected was the attitude of the British government. In spite of its anti-Zionist policies, the United Kingdom strongly opposed the American initiative. Ernest Bevin feared that the United States was trying to jog Britain into a prolongation of the Mandate. By mid-March all the actors in the British political establishment were sincerely resolved to end their Palestine commitment. This was not surprising. There was bloodshed and chaos on the ground. The smaller Jewish resistance organizations were attacking British installations and the Haganah was in open rebellion. Nor could Britain elicit from the United States how Washington believed that a trusteeship could be enacted and still less implemented. Defense Secretary James Forrestal, who had been one of the instigators of retreat from partition, sheepishly confessed that the Pentagon would not send any forces to Palestine to implement a different policy. Subsequently published documents tell us that the British Cabinet, after hearing an appeal from Washington for Britain to extend its rule in Palestine, decided on March 22 that it would not in any circumstances cooperate with the new United States trusteeship plan. The State Department, facing humiliation, increased its pressure on London. Seven times during April, Secretary Marshall sent Ambassador Lewis Douglas to Bevin, pressing him to change his mind on this matter. Douglas even threatened Bevin that if Britain insisted on ending its Mandate on May 15 "American cooperation in the rest of the Middle East, as agreed in the Pentagon talks, would become impossible."

There can be no doubt that for the few weeks between March 24 and Truman's recognition of Israel on May 14, the United States was a more virulent adversary of Jewish interests than was Britain under Bevin. By early May, Britain was "only" attempting to diminish the size of the Jewish state, whereas the United States was still attempting to prevent the state from even coming into existence. The British Cabinet decision of March 22, 1948, stated:

There should be no change in the date fixed for the surrender of the Mandate and the British civil and military authorities should make no effort to oppose the setting up of a Jewish state or a move into Palestine from Transjordan.

In these conditions the only sane policy open to the Zionist leadership was to go ahead with preparations for the Declaration of Independence and to ensure that no legal situation incompatible with Jewish statehood would meanwhile be created at the United Nations.

Amid the diplomatic disarray, it was evident that our political fortunes would remain bleak unless our forces could reverse the military tide. April was the month of counterattack. It was Ben-Gurion's finest hour. On April 1 he heard an anxious report from the Haganah commander, Yigael Yadin. "At this time," said Yadin, "we are being assaulted only by a paramilitary force with simple weaponry. What will our position be when the Egyptian, Jordanian, Syrian and other Arab armies, march, as they were preparing to do?"

Ben-Gurion now made swift and brave decisions. "We will reject all attempts to postpone statehood or to impose trusteeship. We shall go on the offensive. We must not merely defend existing Jewish populations and settlements. We shall move out into the open field and capture cities and villages. We shall smash through to Jerusalem. We must accelerate arms supplies. We shall uncompromisingly reject any pressure for delaying the Declaration of Independence by a single day."

These expressions of resolve and the actions for implementing them turned the tide. The first Czech planes landed at a deserted airfield late on

April 1. Thousands of rifles and hundreds of machine guns came by the same route a few days later. We were reaping the fruits of Soviet support. Its crucial value was enhanced by the fact that the United States, despite Truman's friendly purpose, was maintaining a strict arms embargo on all the countries of the Middle East. This was not as evenhanded as it sounds. The Arabs could count on British armaments, whereas our so-called "underground" forces had no such recourse.

There were tragedies in early April that affected innocent civilians without changing the military balance. Later on December 9 combined Irgun and Lechi forces captured the village of Deir Yassin and killed over 250 Arabs, mostly women and children. The official Zionist bodies expressed their execration of this act, which in their view went even beyond the intrinsic savagery of war. The Haganah officer who arrived later on the scene reported, "It was a massacre. There was no doubt about it. . . . Deir Yassin became a slogan, a derogative one. Whenever the Arabs henceforward had something against the Jews the banner was raised 'Deir Yassin.' "

World opinion tended to forget that Arab violence had preceded, and would also follow, the Deir Yassin incident. A few days later, Arab forces attacked a convoy of doctors and nurses of the Hadassah Medical Center. The director of Hadassah and his seventy-five dedicated colleagues were burned alive. For me the pain was excruciating. Dr. Yassky, the Hadassah director, was a vivid presence in my memory, and the Hadassah organization represented the Zionist idea in its purest form.

Our military aim was not to inflict casualties but to capture and unfreeze points of communication. At Castel, on the road to Jerusalem, 1,500 Haganah fighters in 250 vehicles broke the blockade, giving the city a few weeks of continued supply. The British Army left Haifa, except for the Port area. On April 13, Haganah took command. Acre, Tiberias and Galilee were almost all under Jewish control. The position of the Negev was less solid, but a line of communication was opened. Under Yigal Allon's inspired military leadership Safed was taken in mid-May. On May 14 Jaffa was captured and its 70,000 Arabs fled. But the main accent was placed heavily on Jerusalem. It was vital to open the road joining the city to the coast. To this end "Operation Nachshon" was conceived. The aim was to secure a corridor to Jerusalem that would enable free movement in and out of the city. This, in turn, necessitated the capture of several Arab villages lined along the corridor. Some of those battles, such as that at Castel, had taken a heavy toll of blood. To this day the traveler on the road between Jerusalem and Tel Aviv can see the charred remains of half-tracks and armored vehicles lying along the roadside in mute but eloquent testimony to the cost of Jerusalem's lifeline. Young men by the scores were shriveled and lacerated to death within those burning tombs.

The important fact was that the Haganah had emerged from its fortress mentality. It had learned to do more than merely rebuff Arab attacks. The

Jews no longer waited for the enemy to come and put his fingers on their throat. Operations using complex technical methods and sweeping waves of movement were now attempted in areas outside Jerusalem. After the capture of Haifa on April 24, most of the city's 70,000 Arabs fled to Lebanon. It was incontestable that Jewish leaders in Haifa made efforts to preserve the hope of coexistence by keeping the Arab population intact. This, however, was not the universal attitude. It is tendentious and unnecessary to claim that the Jews longed for the Arabs to remain or that our military forces did not, at times, stimulate and encourage their departure.

A controversy has been raging for over four decades about the reasons for the exit of the Palestinian Arabs in 1947–1948. Is it true that they fled with the encouragement of their own leaders? Did the Israeli authorities at any time deter them from going? Was it the policy of the Israeli High Command to secure the evacuation by Arab populations of areas into which the Israeli army entered? Did Israeli security forces believe that security would be more easily maintained without large Arab populations at crucial points? Was it a fact that the Arabs, unlike the Jews, had somewhere to go if they wanted to avoid the terrors of war? Did the very possibility of escape become a source of their weakness? After all, those who have nowhere to flee cling most tenaciously to their existing ground. This was the Jewish strength.

The real answer is that each one of these motives and incentives forms a part of the picture. None of them is exclusively true. Every one of them was true in some context, in some place and at some time. There were some voluntary panic-stricken flights, there were some encouragements of flight by demoralized Palestinian leaders and there were also some expulsions and intimidations by Israeli military forces. It would be more seemly for Israel not to assert unremitting tactical altruism at every stage, but to draw attention to the overriding fact that the flight was the consequence of war, that it would not have taken place without the war and that those who decide on war are responsible for the ensuing chain of consequence.

On the question of who was responsible for the decision to make war, we have the accord of Israelis, Arabs and the international agencies alike. Israel in later years would have been well advised to rest its case on the general premise that the refugee problem was caused by the war and not to claim rectitude for each and every phase in the evolving human tragedy.

By the day designated for the Declaration of Independence the Jewish condition, though still fragile, was more robust than could have been imagined six weeks before. Jewish Jerusalem had survived and was not completely severed from neighboring settlements. The Arab Liberation Army and Qawukji's forces had been routed in the north. All Galilee, both East and West, was under Jewish control. The Jewish position was less stable in the Negev, but at least the roads were open and the Jewish forces everywhere had been strengthened by the mobilization of manpower and shipments of Czech rifles. There were now 50,000 armed Jews in the field, with the Irgun and

Lechi under Haganah control everywhere except in Jerusalem, where they still maintained an explosive independence of action. A rough and ready artillery unit had been built around veterans of World War II. Palestinian Jewish manpower was being replenished and encouraged by the arrival of Jewish volunteers (Machal)[1] from abroad. These were especially crucial in training pilots for the minuscule air force. Even a tiny navy had been put together and manned mostly by Jewish volunteers from abroad. Thus the Jewish leaders could celebrate their wisdom in not having been tempted to cut losses by defeatist solutions when military fortunes had temporarily been at a low point in March.

If the issue were now to be drawn between Israel and Palestinian Arabs with their "liberation armies," the prospects of Jewish victory would have seemed high. But of course everybody knew that this was not the issue. The context of the war was now going to change. Compared with the improvised Jewish forces and Arab bands in Palestine, the Arab armies poised to sweep down on us had a professional look. If only they had not marched off the parade ground and onto the battlefield they would have preserved an impressive military reputation. I recall the Roman historian Tacitus's reflection on a celebrated Roman emperor: "If only he had not become the emperor, everyone would have said what an excellent emperor he would have made."

So during April our disquiet gradually returned from the military to the diplomatic front. I remember a lunch in which I participated with the French head of delegation, Alexandre Parodi, in Weizmann's apartment in the Waldorf Towers. Parodi, a renowned Resistance leader, was telling us, with evident pain, that the proposed Jewish state had no prospect of survival and that if we persisted we would face a massacre. At that moment the door opened and Weizmann's devoted secretary, Joseph Cohn, brought a copy of the *New York Post*. It announced in large front-page headlines "Jewish Victory" in the north. The story was of a military success for Haganah at Mishmar Ha'emek. Parodi had warned us with sincere concern that our condition would become desperate when the Egyptian Army entered the fray. Weizmann replied, "The trouble with the Egyptian Army is that their officers are too fat and their soldiers too thin." Brave words. In reality neither Weizmann nor any of us knew how the Egyptian army would perform, but such victories as at Mishmar Ha'emek made our self-confidence seem more well-founded than it was.

May 1948 was destined to be Israel's golden month, and something of this scent of reviving fortunes impinged personally on many of us as well. A turn of the wheel came to my notice on April 25. Two days earlier, on Passover eve, one of Truman's White House staff, Judge Samuel Rosenman, called Weizmann urgently for a conversation in Manhattan. Rosenman had a

[1]Mitnadvei Lechuts Laarets: "Volunteers from abroad."

remarkable story to tell on behalf of the president. Truman had not ceased to be embarrassed by the fact that in his talk with Weizmann on March 18, he must have presented an absurd picture to the Zionist leader and to many people beyond; he had reiterated his continued fidelity to a policy that his own ambassador had repudiated the next day.

As I was later to discover in my own subsequent contacts with him, Truman was chronically suspicious that the mandarins in the higher reaches of the bureaucracy did not take him seriously. This was substantially true. He had not been elected and his nomination as vice president had been accomplished with casual negligence by party functionaries who did not really believe that he was fit for the highest office. The self-revealing phrase "these people forget who is president of the United States" was often on his lips, even in conversations with foreigners. The March 18 episode seemed to bear out the image of a man whom his own subordinates could affront with impunity. Rosenman told the Kramarskys that Truman had said "I've got the old doctor on my conscience." Rosenman was instructed to let Weizmann know that if the Jews were to proclaim their state on their own responsibility, without laying obligation on the United States, he would be ready to extend recognition. Rosenman added that in the light of this assurance it would be important for Weizmann and nobody else to write a requesting letter to Truman a few days before independence was declared. This was another example of the irregularity that Truman imposed upon our procedures. The normal course would have been for recognition to be sought in a communication from representatives of the community that would form the new government.

Weizmann reacted soberly to this prospect. He had captivated Truman by his dignity and magnanimity. When all the Jewish organizations had understandably accused Truman of trickery after Austin's trusteeship speech, Weizmann had said, not very convincingly, that the president could not have known about the Austin speech. Moreover, there was always the possibility that Rosenman was reading too much into what he had heard, and Weizmann had long been the victim of his own tendency to believe reassuring words. Many people and some governments were so respectful of his prestige that they tended to understate their reservations. Had not Anthony Eden once conveyed to him the official decision of the British government to establish a Jewish division in the British army, only for Weizmann to hear the repudiation of this intention a short time afterward?

So this chink of light flickered hesitantly in the consciousness of the few among us who knew of Rosenman's initiative, while our work went on as though it had never existed.

For me and my colleagues in the UN delegation the message of President Truman to Weizmann was urgent. It told us that we could not afford to lose our fight against the American trusteeship proposal. The British Mandate would expire on May 14 at 6:00 P.M. New York time. It was vital that an

Israeli sovereignty should step into the vacuum and immediately campaign for the recognition by other states. I did not believe that the president of the United States would "compete" with the United Nations in determining the legal status of a previously mandated territory.

Sharett, having returned to New York, found himself immersed in a Security Council discussion on proposals for a cease-fire or truce. Yet at the same time, the more crucial debate on the U.S. trusteeship project was in full spate in the General Assembly.

Suzy and I, who hardly knew from one day to the next where our work would take us, were residing in the home of Meyer and Shirley Weisgal in West End Avenue. Weisgal was the sort of character in whose existence nobody would believe even after hearing a detailed description. He was the product of a typical American Jewish upbringing—the son of immigrants reared in an atmosphere of piety in which non-Jewish influences played little part. Through self-education and an intensely energetic spirit he had developed a formidable journalistic talent and a love of drama. He had produced a Zionist pageant of startling dimensions and reverberation. He loved big occasions with the drums and trumpets in full sound, and his mordant tongue made him a strident and much-feared polemist. His Zionist fervor was unlimited, although he shunned anything that was remote from reality and moderation. The contrast between the extremism of his style and demeanor and the refinement of his cultural perceptions and enthusiasms made him a byword for paradox. His conversation would erupt in such shattering vulgarities that no listener would fail to be shaken by paroxysms of surprise and disbelief. Two things seemed impossible: that he would become an intimate friend and follower of the dignified and fastidious Chaim Weizmann, and that he would create, sustain and ultimately lead a great Institute of Science in Weizmann's name in Israel. Each of these developments came to pass.

In his personal relationships he was capable of brutal denunciation and of bursts of generosity and comradeship. Seeing Suzy and me carrying out difficult missions in excessively straitened personal circumstances, he had offered us his apartment while he went to Palestine to keep watch over Weizmann's interests there.

Weizmann bore Weisgal's turbulent character with amused and affectionate tolerance. Everything about Weisgal was loud—especially his booming voice. I recall a day in London in the late 1940s when I was in Weizmann's Dorchester Hotel suite in quiet discussion with "the Chief," as we called him, when Weisgal's stentorian voice from an adjoining room made the cups on Weizmann's tea table quiver.

Weizmann: "What's that noise?"

Eban: "It's Meyer talking to someone in Jerusalem."

Weizmann: "Why doesn't he use a telephone?"

But all was quiet in the Weisgal apartment in the owner's absence on the night of April 30 while I was drafting a speech for Sharett to deliver in the

General Assembly the next morning, explaining why the defeat of the U.S. trusteeship proposal was important and urgent. The telephone rang, and Sharett was on the line in an embarrassed tone. He said: "Since you are writing the speech it is only fair that you should deliver it."

In the austere ethic of the Labor Movement, the idea of hiring somebody to put words into one's own mouth had never taken root. The prevalent morality was that everyone, equal under Providence, should appear in his own colors. Sharett was moved by conscience more frequently than any of his political colleagues. By his action he was opening broader horizons for me than I could ever have reached in a normal climb up a bureaucratic ladder.

Within a few hours, I was seated at the table with the "Jewish Agency" nameplate, while Sharett and other members of our delegation sat behind me. When I spoke there was both curiosity at the sound of a new voice and a basic willingness to frustrate the ill-considered American proposal for a new period of colonialism for the peoples of Palestine.

The theme of my speech was that Jewish statehood was already a reality in everything but name. The vacuum of power created by the British administration had been filled by solid, coherent institutions, developed, by ironic chance, in the very atmosphere of autonomy and decentralization that had been characteristic of the British Mandatory power. We had our schools, our language, our Zionist civil service, our parliament represented by an elected "National Council," our trade unions, our free press, even our flag and our "diplomatic representation." The existence of our "underground army" was no secret to those overground. And we had a certificate of legitimacy from the very international organization that was now debating the wisdom of its own recent judgment.

My peroration affirmed that to prevent Jewish statehood would not only be a grotesque exercise for an international organization pledged to the advancement of dependent territories; it would also be unprofitable. More force would now be needed to prevent Jewish statehood than to let it take its course. It was a rare case of principle and expediency pointing toward the same horizon. How absurd it would be to ask a nation that had advanced to the threshold of independence to retreat back to tutelage! In addition and above all, the flight from partition would be a blatant acceptance of illicit force as the arbiter of international policy, and the United Nations at a formative stage in its career would be covered in universal derision.

The speech was heard in an atmosphere of sympathetic tension. More smiles than frowns. Interest in a youthful debut merged with an authentic sentiment that the United States was on a mistaken course and should be guided back toward a line of reason more characteristic of its power and fame. Sharett followed my discourse with audible murmurs of pride and accord. I was therefore disconcerted and surprised when after a brief handshake he had slipped away from his seat behind me toward the Delegates' Lounge. I later discovered that he had made for the telephone, where he sent a cable to my family in London extolling my speech. He showed me his longhand notes:

Happy be able congratulate on your son's striking maiden speech in appearing as official spokesman Jewish people in international councils. His extraordinary brilliance in thought and expression and powerful cogency and reasoning dignity of presentation did outstanding credit to our cause and made us immeasurably proud. Friend and foe listened with rapt attention many characterizing it as one of the highest water marks of entire session stop warmest regards Moshe

I do not know of any other Israeli leader who would have given a young colleague such a massive push from the obscurity of back-room draftsmanship to the place where the floodlights cast their deferential beams. In a single moment of Sharett's generosity and my response, I had passed from the margin to the center of a unique and compelling drama.

This was one of the turning points in my life. The first result was an emergence into the arena of publicity. And the effect was immediate. That very afternoon I went with Sharett to a luncheon at the home of Secretary-General Trygve Lie in Forest Hills. Among the guests were Gromyko and Bevin. Gromyko bore down upon me with the nearest that he could come to a smile and said in English, "Congratulations, you have killed American trusteeship." (I was already inured to the absence of the definite article in Russian syntax.) From that day onward his personal attitude toward me began to approach equality. He would later forgive me for depriving him of his title as the youngest UN ambassador. He had a booming bass voice, and his words evidently carried across the room. I looked toward Bevin. He had given me the ritual handshake, limp and flabby, when I entered, without hearing or caring who I was. He now directed toward me what novelists call "a withering look"—a phrase that I had never really understood until then. Mrs. Bevin tried to shrivel me with the kind of look that deters any idea of conversation. The concentrated rancor and vengefulness in her eyes defy description. The Bevins were here violating the parliamentary routine that dictates a pretense of cordiality even in adversarial situations. Until that moment I had presumed that it was in the British parliament that this tradition was most sacrosanct.

I now moved with quickening pulse toward the most extraordinary day in Jewish history. As May 15 came closer, all the actors in the drama made their final bids. The United States tried with extraordinary tenacity to prevent the Jewish people from celebrating its version of July 4. The State Department again sent the American ambassador Lewis Douglas to Bevin incessantly and in vain to persuade Britain to prolong its tenure. Dean Rusk, the head of the United Nations division in the State Department, intimidated the Zionist leader, Nahum Goldmann, into frightened reluctance to support the Declaration of Independence, Rusk painted a gruesome picture of the slaughter that would be the only tangible result of such a declaration. Goldmann succumbed and entered history, sadly, as a man who had wanted to postpone Israel's greatest hour. Goldmann sought support from Weizmann and Sharett. Weizmann rebuffed him sternly and sent a message through his loyal flag-bearer, Meyer Weisgal, urging Ben-Gurion not to miss the opportunity of a Declaration of Independence. Weisgal had traveled to Switzerland from Tel Aviv for the express purpose of receiving the call.

Sharett was perturbed by the pressures on him to delay the independence declaration, but he was steadfast in his response, despite his inner turmoil after his visit to Washington. Secretary Marshall had warned him on May 12 that if the Jews went ahead, proclaimed their state and got into serious trouble against Arab armies, they should not rely on the United States for rescue. Sharett saw the gravity of this intimidating remark, but on the issue itself, he was now firm as a rock. He said that the impending hour of the Mandate's expiration was "a moment of opportunity which, if missed, might be irrevocably lost." Marshall had relented to some degree. "If you make your decision, it will be on your own responsibility. If you then succeed, I shall wish you well, but I warn you not to accept military people's advice too easily." Sharett proceeded to the New York International Airport, where Weizmann reached him with the message: "Don't let them weaken, Moshe, it may be now or never!"

In accordance with our plan a letter from Weizmann to Truman had been sent on May 13 asking him to recognize the new state. The expected infant was still nameless, since the Zionist leaders were still, characteristically, arguing over the name (should it be "Judea," "Zion," what about "Israel"?). Weizmann, for the first time in history, was asking for a nameless state to be recognized:

I deeply hope that the United States . . . will promptly recognize the Provisional Government of the new Jewish State. The world, I think, will regard it as especially appropriate that the greatest living democracy should be the first to welcome the newest into the family of nations.

If the Mandate was to end before May 15, the decisive events would have to unroll on May 14. The day dawned bright and clear. Nothing in its beginning gave augury of its end.

Would the British forces really depart? In the mythology of many parties and especially of the Jews, British diplomacy had built a reputation for intense subtlety. Many Jews suspected that the intensive preparation to depart concealed a latent determination to remain.

Another mark of interrogation was poised over the Jewish reaction. Would the Jewish leaders really proclaim the state? There were known to be cautious voices advising postponement. At a meeting of the Zionist leadership body on May 6 the decision to go ahead had been adopted by forty to sixteen, and in the meantime American pressures and military complications had intensified.

Would the Arab armies really invade? It was known that there were hesitations in Cairo although no longer in Amman. Golda Meir in Arab disguise had crossed the Jordan on May 11 to renew her dialogue with Emir Abdullah, the ruler of Transjordan. At a meeting near Naharayim in November 1947 he had secretly promised to occupy only the areas of Palestine that were not designated as part of the Jewish state. He now told Golda that this promise had lapsed. He was no longer the master of his own fate. He was an instrument of a collective Arab will. He would have to make a special bid for Jerusalem, east and west. Golda had rejected Abdullah's suggestion that Israel postpone the Declaration of Independence, and we had no reason to believe that Jordan, with its 5,000 trained Arab legionnaires, would stay out of the war. Yet nothing is certain in Arab politics except uncertainty, and nothing that day was either possible or impossible.

A fourth question: If independence was proclaimed, would anyone recognize or acknowledge it? Against Truman's vague message, bereft of official commitment on April 23, all we knew was that the State Department's pressure was immense. There was even a bizarre proposal that Jewish and Arab leaders should fly in President Truman's aircraft "The Sacred Cow" to Jerusalem to discuss an "agreed solution." What further threats and blandishments would or would not come next?

The truth was that at dawn on May 14 British, Jewish, Arab and American intentions were still in abeyance. There were tendencies, but not decisions. Many things that were tentative and doubtful in the morning would be answered for good or ill by the fall of dusk.

The first unraveling of the puzzle came in Jerusalem. The last high commissioner for Palestine, General Sir Alan Cunningham, was on his way to Haifa port. His flag had been lowered that morning on the mast of Government House. At midnight he was to set sail on board the cruiser HMS *Euryalus* with the last units of his civil government.

Twenty-six years had passed since Britain had been entrusted by a Mandate from the League of Nations "to ensure the peace and security of the Holy Land" and to promote the establishment of a National Home for the Jewish people. It was a high vision, and there is no evidence that any other government would have risked such an imaginative and complex enterprise. Nor had any country other than Britain shown any signs of defying and challenging Hitler for six years. When we add the circumstance that British victories and sacrifices at El Alamein had saved the Palestine Jews from extermination by Nazi conquerors, it would have been logical to assume that there would develop a strong affinity between Britain and the new Jewish state. But Ernest Bevin had squandered this potentiality by what Churchill later called his "bias and prejudice against the Jews of Palestine." Bevin had pursued his vendetta beyond any objective need dictated by his country's national interest. In the end Britain was ruling with iron fist and gallows with the aim of preventing the very thing that it had been charged to promote. And all this in an hour of Jewish agony such as no family of the human race had ever known. Some time would pass before a sovereign state of Israel would see the Anglo-Israeli relationship in the broader and deeper perspective of three decades. The Mandate, despite all disappointments, had left behind a solid, articulated, coherent national Jewish society mature enough to make its own way without contentious argument with its previous rulers.

Sir Alan Cunningham parted from Palestine in military uniform with medals ablaze. His much-photographed salute was charged with silent dignity. He was a tranquil man who had not impressed any particular attitude on the discharge of his mission. He surprised us in 1973 in his ninetieth year when he sent Golda Meir a letter just after the Yom Kippur war congratulating Israel on its successful quarter of a decade as a sovereign state. Nobody who has ever made his home in our fascinating and infuriating land has ever forgotten the experience.

So now we knew the British decision and its fulfillment. What about the Arab answer to the challenge of the day?

There is a popular colonialist myth that ascribes deviousness to the "Arab mind" and even to the Arab language, which is alleged always to impel Arabs to say something other than they mean. Arabic is, in fact, a well-honed precision instrument in which a speaker can be as clear or as obscure as he wishes to be, and there was no gap between rhetoric and policy when Israel's greatest ordeal began. By midday Egyptian forces had advanced deep into the southern Negev. An Iraqi column moved in strength toward the Jordan river. The Transjordanian Arab Legion was arrayed along the river with its main encampment at Zerka. On the upper reaches of the Jordan, a Syrian brigade was ready to attack the Jewish farming villages in the hot, green valley. Apart from the impetuous Egyptians who had already printed stamps to commemorate their "imminent victory," the Arab governments were awaiting the Mandate's last official hour before launching their armies in attack. The states of the Arab League had concerted their policy at a meeting in Damascus late in April. Their aim was to occupy Palestine, subjugate its population and strangle Israel's statehood at its birth.

Most pressing of all was the need to take a Jewish decision. As Jewish leaders in Palestine and abroad surveyed the scene, their decision seemed almost to be compelled by events. Dark in their recent memory were the ashes of millions of their kinsmen; the uncomprehending screams of Jewish children in the Nazi slaughterhouse; the knowledge that Jews without number had been killed with a brutality that, in most civilized countries, would not have been shown toward the lowest animals. And on another plane of recollections was Palestine Jewry's own ordeal and the knowledge that the toil and dreams and sacrifices that had gone into its making must now either be lost from history or ratified by larger dangers and higher dreams. The cold fear that a declaration of Jewish statehood would set off a massacre that might otherwise be avoided had gripped some men and governments otherwise favorable to the Jewish cause. But the majority, led by Ben-Gurion and spurred on from afar by the aging but indomitable Weizmann, was convinced that if the sun set on May 15 without the renewal of Jewish statehood, it would never rise again. And so as crowds gathered quietly outside the Tel Aviv Museum, thirty-seven Founding Fathers with David Ben-Gurion as their spokesman came face-to-face with their collective immortality. Ben-Gurion, in a declamatory, high-pitched voice, brought Israel into modern history. Despite a gloomy report from the Haganah leader, Yigael Yadin, about the danger to the Jewish population and especially to Jerusalem, the Zionist inner cabinet had rejected American truce proposals by six votes to four. All that was needed was the final act . . .

What a long, weary and blood-drenched journey it had been across the infinities of space and time since the nation had first been born under those very skies! There had been the generations in which kings and prophets flourished and then the seemingly final end, when Jerusalem crumbled before the legions of Titus. And across all the intervening centuries the beat of Jewish hearts had everywhere been quickened by the prospect of return. Now the choice had come, imminent and implacable. Something of great moment would be enacted of which future Jewish generations would never cease to speak and dream.

The State Council had been convened on the afternoon of May 14. A silent, thoughtful crowd was clustered outside the Museum Hall. The atmosphere was tense, with opportunity shimmering in the springtime sun. No wonder that a silence, full of awe, sat heavy on the room until the last words of the proclamation died away:

By virtue of the natural and historic right of the Jewish people and of the Resolution of the General Assembly of the United Nations, we hereby proclaim the establishment of the Jewish State in Palestine—to be called Israel . . . With faith in Almighty God, we set our hands to this Declaration, on this Sabbath Eve, the Fifth Day of Iyar, Five Thousand Seven Hundred and Eight, the Fourteenth Day of May, One Thousand Nine hundred and Forty Eight . . .

The oldest signatory arose spontaneously and, in quavering voice, uttered a more ancient benediction:

Blessed art Thou, O God, King of the Universe, who hast kept us in life and sustained us and enabled us to reach this Day . . .

The astonishing day had not yet done its course. Those of us who knew of the Weizmann-Truman contacts focused our expectancy on Washington.

American recognition, which seemed dubious amid the frenetic attempts of the State Department to prevent our statehood, was itself dependent on the defeat of the competing trusteeship proposal.

Abba Hillel Silver was in the committee at Lake Success when the news of the Declaration of Independence came over the radio. He interrupted the desultory proceedings with a brief, dignified announcement that the state now existed, so that "what was envisaged in the General Assembly six months ago had come to pass."

The idea that its own resolution had produced a result seemed to petrify the other delegates to the General Assembly. What would happen, they seemed to say, if people went around implementing UN resolutions? Whither would this explosive precedent lead?

The ceremony in the Tel Aviv museum that had sent a nation's history rocketing into an uncharted future made no immediate impression on the UN General Assembly. On and on they went, discussing a tutelary system that nobody required and nobody would enforce. It might have been expected that a proposal so sharply offensive to Jewish hopes would in simple logic enjoy Arab support. But logic has had little effect on human history, and no effect at all on the life of the Middle East. The Jews opposed trusteeship because we believed that the alternative would be a Jewish state in a part of Palestine. The Arabs opposed trusteeship because they believed that the alternative would be an Arab state in the whole of Palestine. The sensation of the day was that the U.S. trusteeship proposal was going to be defeated by a combination of pro-Jewish and pro-Arab votes!

I found this strange parliamentary convergence congenial. Whenever an Arab speaker seemed to be driving a nail into the coffin of the American trusteeship, I could not abstain from applauding the result, while condemning the motive. As on November 29, 1947, I called on our faithful friends to prolong their discourse without result until after 6:00 P.M. Lengthy speeches in which a minimum of thought is compressed into a maximum number of words are not beyond the capacity of diplomats in the multilateral arena.

The audience could not grasp the abstruse significance of the clock. The issue was plain: The United States had pointed out that its proposal for a trusteeship in the entire Palestine area, or of a trustee commissioner for the Jerusalem area alone, would have to be determined by 6:00 P.M., when British rule would lapse. Failing this, there would be a juridical vacuum that a declaration of Israel's independence would fill. When the clock's large hand moved to the stroke of 6:00 P.M., the British mandate had expired. This thought so delighted the Iraqi representative that he arose triumphantly and proclaimed in messianic voice that "the game is up, trusteeship is void." The Assembly now passed no resolution of substance and contented itself with the appointment of Count Folke Bernadotte as a mediator to promote peace in the Palestine area.

But meanwhile, there was a rustle in the hall as rumors spread through the gossip-saturated air. "What," asked the Cuban delegate, "is all this that we hear about President Truman recognizing the Zionist state?" The head of the U.S. delegation was an international lawyer of towering eminence, Philip C. Jessup. He was a man who liked straight facts and rational conditions. Neither of these commodities was available in the General Assembly that day.

Jessup rushed into Trygve Lie's room to seek guidance about what his own government was up to. The secretary-general had an addiction to regular and substantial meals, which became available to him at different hours of the day. He was out to lunch. Jessup saw a paper on Lie's desk that, by its form and texture, he knew was a draft for a UN press release and therefore open for the knowledge of all delegates. When Jessup scrutinized the document, it turned out to be a draft statement from Washington, telling the UN secretary-general that the president would shortly recognize the Provisional Government of Israel. Having confirmed this by telephone to Washington, Jessup, much chastened, went to the Assembly Hall and, in a voice choked with embarrassment, read out the text of President Truman's statement saying that the United States recognized the Provisional Government of the State of Israel. If the word "pandemonium" had not existed, it would have been necessary to invent it in order to describe the General Assembly of the United Nations on May 14, 1948.

It was not long before I received a detailed report of the "recognition meeting" in the White House on May 14. It had been called to consider Weizmann's letter of May 13 in which he had briefly called for recognition of the "new Jewish state." When we heard in New York that the founders had decided on the name "Israel," we dispatched Weizmann's faithful secretary, Joseph Cohn, to Washington to have Truman insert that name in his letter of recognition!

The White House meeting developed into a bitter duel between Truman and his own secretary of state. Marshall had opposed recognition of Israel in the most vehement terms. The other main participants in the meeting were Robert H. Lovett, the Under Secretary of State, and Clark M. Clifford, Truman's political adviser (who later became secretary of defense in the Johnson administration). Clifford has described Marshall's language as virulent: "They don't deserve a state, they have stolen that country. If you give this recognition, Mr. President, I may not vote for you in the next election . . ."

It required courage and tenacity on Truman's part to have resisted this assault, which reinforced the existing opposition to Jewish statehood expressed by Defense Secretary Forrestal and the entire American diplomatic establishment. The rancor was so great that Lovett believed that the Truman administration was in danger of disintegration. He had moved to induce Marshall—and to persuade himself—to accept the president's verdict with a maximum show of loyalty. We must remember that Marshall at that time had a larger credibility in the American nation than Truman, whose accession to the White House had been regarded in the world as an illustration of the casualness with which Americans choose their vice presidents. The kind of self-confidence that enabled Truman later to defy the other heroic military commander, Douglas MacArthur, would come to expression if and when Truman won election in his own right. We were receiving advance payment on this prospect at a most decisive hour.

The General Assembly broke up in confusion, leaving us in possession of the field. Sharett had been absent from the last few sensational days. He had taken the wise precaution to be in Tel Aviv when the Cabinet was formed and the portfolios distributed. This was a prudent thought, for Israel's competitive instincts in domestic politics were as fully developed at birth as were those of older countries whose traditions of manipulation had been refined by centuries of experience.

Before leaving the deserted General Assembly meeting, I went to the UN post office and sent a message to Sharett: "What do I do now?" I felt as if I had climbed with a few companions up to a towering peak and that there could never be a higher or more glorious mountain to scale.

That evening a triumphal meeting was held at Madison Square Garden at which Silver and Neumann revealed how their efforts had produced a Jewish state. Tribute to other participants was minimal. I was to learn that mankind's political nature is not human nature in its most refined state.

Weizmann, ill and exhausted, lay in the darkness of his hotel suite. The Zionist Executive had prevented his presence in Rehovot by laying crucial tasks upon him, and yet had not left space for him on the list of signatories of the Declaration of Independence. It was a vulgar omission. He had lived some extraordinary months. Without office or formal status he had carried two missions to success, one to keep the Negev in the international map of Israel and one to break through the White House blockade against Zionists and to negotiate recognition by the United States. He was listening to the radio, which was broadcasting the formation of the provisional government, with well-known Zionist names now adorned with resounding ministerial titles. He had reason to feel abandoned and alone. Was he to be King Lear on the windswept heath?

Suddenly, a bellboy arrived with a Western Union cable. It was a warm greeting to Weizmann from Ben-Gurion and his principal colleagues expressing their tribute:

Greetings to you on the establishment of the Jewish State. Of all those living no one contributed as much as you to its creation. Your position and help at this stage in our struggle encouraged us. Looking to the day when we shall be privileged to see you at the head of the State.

Weizmann was particularly moved by the reference to his "position and help at this stage in our struggle." He had played the Negev and recognition phases very close to his chest. He had even been suspicious of whether his decisive breakthrough with Truman had been conveyed to Jerusalem. It was a fantastic ending for his active political career to have been able to conduct two such crucial operations on the strength of his personal prestige and talent.

A few hours later the radio published his election to the presidency of the Provisional Council of State. I came into his suite in the Waldorf Towers with Arthur Lourie and Ivor Linton, one of Weizmann's longtime aides, and we opened a bottle of champagne. Cables began to pour in. The first of them, from Felix Frankfurter, was more brief than his communications usually were: "Dear Chaim, mine eyes have seen the glory of the coming of the Lord!!"

So between one dawn and another, all the obscurities of the day before had been resolved. British rule had ended; Israel had proclaimed its birth; America had moved to Israel's side; the Arabs had launched their invasion; and the United Nations by its own default had enabled these streams of history to rush together in a single torrent.

And yet amid the popular joy there was still a sensation that nothing was yet fully secure. That night the settlers of the Etzion block near Hebron were captured by the Transjordanian Arab Legion. Two Egyptian planes were brought down and their crews captured. Newspapers across the world were divided between emotion at Israel's birth and speculation about its ability to survive. Most foreign commentators were not optimistic on the second score. In the British press the declaration was treated as a moving but futile gesture, soon to be shattered by military defeat.

The emotion of the world on the morrow of the declaration was partly clouded by the tensions of the war. But it was also enlarged by vistas of memory. Nothing in history was similar to the resurgence of a people in a land from which so many centuries had kept it apart. For many millions in the world this was a unique and noble mystery. Israel's independence resembled neither of the conventional forms of national liberation. Here was neither an indigenous uprising against an occupying power nor a colonial migration to an unfamiliar land, but a reunion between a people and a land that had once lived together and had been separated for nineteen centuries. Yet for all the length of the separation, the restored nation still uttered the speech and upheld the faith that that same land had nourished three thousand years before. A world that had seen the death and birth of many nations now, for the first time, beheld something like a resurrection. We went to our rest that night feeling larger and prouder than we had been at dawn.

The Jewish communities across the world were in a tormented alternation between ecstasy and fear. They knew our peril, but they also understood that the conditions in which the danger would be faced had been transformed. For all the centuries of exile, the central fact of Jewish life had been passivity. Jewish history had consisted of what Jews had suffered, endured, resisted or survived, not of what they themselves had initiated or resolved. The point of reference had always been the attitudes and policies of others. Now, for a change, the world had been waiting many days to see what Palestine Jewry would say or do. There was an exhilarating sense of control over the flow of events. Within a territory, however small, Jewish decisions could now open the doors to kinsmen, move armies, create institutions, levy taxes, reanimate a culture and compel reactions near and far.

It was a day that would linger and shine in the national memory forever—a moment of truth that would move Israel to its ultimate generations. . . .

At dawn the next day Egyptian aircraft bombed Tel Aviv and Arab armies moved ever closer to our centers of population.

Israel held the joy of birth and the fear of death in a single taste.

7

THE MORNING AFTER
MAY 15

THE ALTERNATION OF joy and fear was unceasing for Jews throughout the rest of 1948. The fear came from news of the battlefield. The joy came from the symbols and panoply of statehood that suddenly confronted an incredulous Jewish world. The words "State of Israel" were rolled around our lips like some enchanting nectar—a taste the like of which Jews had not known for nineteen centuries.

On the first day of Israeli independence, our small team at the United Nations, aglow with recent diplomatic victories, worked in an atmosphere of egalitarian anarchy; we had no idea which of us was the leader of the squad! Israeli sovereignty required each of us to make an individual choice of allegiance. It was clear that no American who intended to avoid Israel's citizenship could convincingly represent what would now be a "foreign" state. I was even told that this would be illegal in American terms.

Abba Hillel Silver and Emanuel Neumann opted for continued American identity. After a short twilight period they folded their tents at our UN delegation, gathered up their papers and stole silently away.

Silver's appearances at the Security Council were already becoming awkward, when he argued against his own American government and once nearly used the phrase "our government."

British citizenship is theoretically adhesive beyond recall and there is no procedure for disengagement. Presumably, nobody in the British legislature ever envisaged that anyone in his right mind would seek an alternative distinction. It is, however, possible to renounce all the privileges, duties and symbols of that citizenship on the grounds of having taken a foreign allegiance. This I did immediately, and so, with far more significance, did the great Weizmann. Thus ended the journey that he had begun in 1906 when he left a Russian home and German and Swiss exile for England. At the age of eleven he had written a letter in Hebrew to his teacher in Motele predicting that England would redeem the Jewish people from servitude. He had seen that promise initially fulfilled only to see Bevin bring the fulfillment to a screeching halt.

The Security Council of the United Nations was still our central arena. The United States had made a bizarre exhibition of itself by trying to prevent the Israeli Declaration of Independence for several anguished weeks—and then endorsing it by presidential recognition eleven minutes after its promulgation. Emissaries from the State Department flew from Washington to New York to dissuade the red-faced members of the U.S. mission from resigning. They had been defending a policy that their own president had already decided to repudiate. But the United States had swiftly relegated the trusteeship proposal to the spilt milk department, and was now making much more sense at Lake Success by concentrating on a cease-fire. In this aim it had the support of the Soviet Union, which had been our most steadfast champion in the last phases of the expiring British regime.

During most of April, I had spent more time in the Soviet Mission at 680 Park Avenue than in that of the United States. Andrei Gromyko and, later, Yacov Malik, like ghosts in Shakespearean drama, preferred to walk forth at night. I would often be invited to confer with them at 11:40 P.M. and when midnight struck they would leave the room with Cinderella-like promptitude and would return after ten minutes. Several weeks later I learned the reason for this unexpected habit. Midnight in New York is 8:00 A.M. in Moscow, and at that kindly hour the Kremlin's emissaries at Lake Success could divine the will of their masters, all the way up to Stalin, without risky guesswork. Random conjecture was not a rewarding pursuit for Soviet diplomats.

At the first meeting of the Security Council on the morrow of our independence, we asked our legal adviser, Mordechai Eliash, to occupy the chief delegate's seat for no particular reason except that he had a pleasant voice and a photogenic bearded aspect reminiscent of Charles I. But the impression that we were appointing Eliash to be the permanent head of our delegation elicited a stern telegraphic reaction from Ben-Gurion and Sharett, who demanded that I and nobody else should speak for Israel in the spirit of my maiden speech in the General Assembly of May 1. So now from May 16 onward I was Israel's chief spokesman at the highest and most public international agency, defending our new state in its desperate struggle to prevent its independence from being extinguished at birth. By mid-April I held responsibilities beyond anything that I could have anticipated three weeks before.

On May 20 Sharett informed Secretary-General Trygve Lie that I was the representative of the Israeli government at the United Nations. The following morning I appointed Arthur Lourie, Jacob Robinson, Moshe Tov, Michael Comay and Gideon Rafael as my alternates and advisers, and I. L. Kenen as the delegation's spokesman.

Our labors in the Security Council were only one part of the national struggle of which the main theater lay in the Middle Eastern battlefield. Our forces were fighting no longer against unskilled volunteers, but against the armies of sovereign Arab states, lavishly equipped by the major arms-supplying countries. Despite our military success during April and early May, there was no doubt that we would need help from the UN and its leading members in order to achieve a respite through a truce or cease-fire. The news from Tel Aviv and Jerusalem proved that our very national survival might hang on this prospect.

The hasty departure of the American Zionist leaders from the United Nations delegation meant that we "backroom boys" were now out front. The stately Zionist leaders who had been in the spotlight became, at best, our advisers, while we, previously in the backroom, carried the flags. These changes intrigued the public, which was hearing the names of Israeli diplomats for the first time.

While I was appointed to head our UN delegation, Eliahu Elath became the official representative no longer of the Jewish Agency but of the "provisional government of Israel." Nobody in the world community had asked us to parade this provisionality, which simply confessed that our government had not yet been elected. But most of the members of the UN have governments for whom election is not even a serious ambition, so our humility was ennobling but excessive. In the course of time, humility would not emerge as the most spectacular of all the Israeli virtues.

We organized our mission in a many-storied brownstone house at 16 East 66th Street but soon moved to our new building at 11 East 70th Street. Two plaques now went up on the door. One read, "Consulate General of the State of Israel"; the other, "Permanent Delegation of Israel to the United Nations." Whenever I went out of my room into the street I would see clusters of Jews assembled there, sometimes standing in silence at these unprecedented evidences of sovereignty, at other times clicking away with cameras in an effort to absorb and perpetuate the new wonder of statehood. The Consulate General under Arthur Lourie's leadership was now frequented by many prospective immigrants and tourists, but I suspected that many dozens came in and out for no purpose except to see what an Israeli passport looked like and how an Israeli consulate functioned.

The first Israeli passports were printed in Hebrew and French in an effort to "punish" the English language for the crime of being the vernacular of Ernest Bevin. I thought that this was somewhat farfetched since Bevin's attachment to the glories of that tongue had always been restricted to the simplest usages. This was but one of the many anglophobic gestures that the newborn state had conceived with the motive of putting distance between ourselves and our former rulers. It was by no means the most eccentric among them. That particular championship was revealed to me a few months later when I traveled to Tiberias. As my car slowly climbed the curvaceous road hugging the exquisite edge of the Sea of Galilee, I saw a sign announcing: NIVEAU DE LA MER. Thus had renascent Israel delivered its anti-imperialist message to the language of the transgressor. When a British ambassador later presented his credentials, the English language was forgiven, and a signboard inscribed with the words SEA LEVEL now informs travelers about their location and altitude above Lake Tiberias.

An Israeli consulate held messianic associations for New York Jews, but the idea that there was such a person as an Israeli delegate to the United Nations took most of them even higher up the ladder of ecstasy. Those whose immediate forebears had immigrated from Russia would not have admitted that mortal man can aspire to anything more splendid than a consulate. Jews had encountered British consuls in the Czarist empire who carried the key for their salvation in the form of visas for the West. Some consuls had used this compassionate power with zeal and had earned renown far and wide. In the summer of 1948 when I went back to Israel I had visited Suzy's very aged grandfather in the village of Motza on the hill opposite Jerusalem. He had settled in a desolate Israel in 1880 in a spirit of Jewish piety and in advance of Zionism, and was among the pioneer founders of Motza, where he had become the first captain of industry by virtue of the factory for red bricks that he and his family owned and operated. He uttered a pious greeting from his bed, inspected me with interest and asked what I had been doing since he had known me as a uniformed bridegroom in 1945. I answered with suppressed pride that I had just been appointed to the rank of ambassador. He nodded consolingly and said in a tone of warm encouragement "Don't worry! Please God you'll be a consul some day . . . !"

On the day after our Declaration of Independence the Israeli flag went up on the central pole of the Waldorf Towers in New York, in testimony to the presence of a head of state. On May 25 Weizmann went to the White House at President Truman's invitation. This time he did not enter the presidential residence by a back door, as on March 18. He and his wife and retinue traveled to Washington with all the ceremonial honors due to the head of a sovereign state. Flags of Israel greeted them on both sides of Pennsylvania Avenue as their limousine slowly drove up toward the White House. They stayed at the official residence of the president's guests at Blair House. The visit was not devoted to ceremonial gestures alone. Weizmann never had any taste or time for protocol, and felt most at home when expounding some concrete issue. The points which he impressed on Truman with his usual brevity and precision were the need for a development loan for Israel, a relaxation of the arms embargo and some indication that full recognition with an exchange of embassies would be granted as soon as an election in Israel converted the provisional government into a full-fledged parliamentary democracy. Weizmann's "magic touch" accompanied him even here and he received firm commitments on most of those points, but not on ending the embargo. There was also some anomaly in the fact that even after the establishment of the state that he had recognized with such moving promptness, Truman still found it unnecessary to make the acquaintance of any Israeli or Zionist leader except Weizmann.

Apart from the grave business to be transacted, the Weizmann-Truman meeting in Washington was the scene of a memorable episode in the history of protocol. Someone in our Washington mission had naturally considered it appropriate for our president to bring a gift to President Truman. It was decided in the mission (not yet an embassy) that a Scroll of the Law (Sefer Torah) would be the most spiritually effective present. Unfortunately nobody in the White House had troubled to explain to Truman what this strange-looking article was. All who were present could see the perplexity on the president's face as this article with tinkling bells, silver breastplates and blue velvet with golden thread was brought into his presence. President Truman was visibly attempting to conjecture what this unfamiliar device could be. He must have assumed that the Israeli president would not give the president of the United States a gift that had no functional purpose. When Weizmann put the Sefer Torah with all its glittering trappings into President Truman's hands, there was a tense moment when the president of the United States realized that he would be called upon to make some response. After moments of anguished suspense, he gave voice to an immortal utterance: "Thank you, Mr. President. I've always wanted one of these!"

Although I bore the title of permanent representative to the United Nations, we were not yet members of that body or of any important international agency. This battle still lay ahead. I was six years younger than the thirty-nine-year-old Gromyko, who was then the baby of the diplomats accredited to the United Nations. I could not, however, threaten his juniority since I had only observer status as the envoy of a non-member. Over the years, he would often make reference to this rivalry with a show of jocularity. On those occasions, something like a a smile would brighten his countenance like the blue light in a refrigerator. Despite our lack of membership, we were a part of the UN landscape and the press was following my encounters and speeches with constancy.

While our friends in the United States were celebrating the symbols of our statehood, my own thoughts turned back more and more frequently to events on the battlefield.

A few days after the Declaration of Independence, David Ben-Gurion had unified the Jewish fighting forces to create the Israeli Defense Forces (IDF). The Haganah, affiliated to the Israeli Labor Movement, furnished the bulk of our official army. The dissident Irgun (Etzel) and Lechi were curtly ordered to disband and were gradually absorbed in regular battalions. The Palmach, led brilliantly by our most dynamic and successful commander, Yigal Allon, was officially integrated into the IDF, but with permission for the time being to maintain a separate command. All the officers and troops now had to take an oath of allegiance to the State of Israel. An official uniform was introduced and ranks were created for officers and noncommissioned officers. The former Haganah commander, Ya'akov Dori, became the first chief of staff of the IDF with the rank of major general. Soon after, he retired through illness and was succeeded by the more charismatic Yigael Yadin. Our forces received invaluable aid from Jews and others abroad. Foreign volunteers under the name of "Machal" flocked to us from all over the world. Many of them had seen service in World War II. Some of the most cherished volunteers had flying experience in the British Royal Air Force. A former American pilot, named George Barling, was known to have downed thirty-two German aircraft. He was killed in Rome while taking off in a fighter aircraft for Israel.

Yigael Yadin had frequently warned us that the real test for Israel's capacity of survival would come when the "volunteer" Arab bands were succeeded by the regular forces of Arab states. This proved to be true. In the first weeks of our independence the Arab forces had great advantage in their equipment and manpower. The Jewish forces at that time were fewer than fifty thousand. There was a heavy casualty rate amongst officers as a result of an Israeli tradition under which officers went forward at the head of their men with the slogan "Acharay—after me!"

The Israeli forces had naturally expected to face greater resistance after May 15 than before the entry of Arab armies. There were three major points of danger. Syrian, Lebanese and Transjordanian forces on Israel's second port made a strong bid for the capture of Haifa. In the course of this attempt they laid siege to Kibbutz Degania, the flagship of the kibbutz movement. Syrian tanks broke through the fences and were set on fire by fire bottles thrown by the kibbutzniks at close range.

The second point of danger was in the south, where the Egyptian army began with a swift advance along the coast. Proximity to Tel Aviv and other areas with dense Jewish population made the Egyptian advance particularly perilous. Heroic resistance was offered to the Egyptians from Kibbutz Yad Mordechai, which however was evacuated on May 24 with heavy loss in men and material. The Egyptians actually reached Ashdod, which is now Israel's southern port, and were only halted at a bridge twenty miles south of Tel Aviv, where they were subjected to fierce attack by Israeli fighter planes.

As if the need to fight on two fronts in the north and in the south was not a sufficiently hazardous ordeal, our forces were constantly preoccupied with the defense of Jerusalem. The Jewish quarter of the Old City was encircled and the defenders were no longer able to resist. I remember exactly how I was sitting in the Delegates' Lounge of the United Nations when the news that the Old City had been captured came to me by telephone from our delegation office. There were 2,500 inhabitants, all of whom were taken prisoner. Outside the Old City, Israeli forces were recording victories, but these, however impressive, could not compensate for the morale effects of losing that part of Jerusalem that commemorated Israel's links with a royal and prophetic past. Nearly two decades would elapse before any Jew would be able to visit the holiest of all Jewish shrines.

A personal saga second in resonance and pathos only to that of Orde

Wingate was celebrated in the person of Colonel Mickey Marcus, a West Point graduate who was given command of our Jerusalem front, despite the competitive murmurings of ambitious Israeli commanders. His heroism was clouded by the grotesque triviality that brought about his death. He left his tent to relieve himself and was challenged by a sentry in Hebrew. He was asked for the password and when he replied in English was precipitately shot.

I had met Marcus in New York before his departure for Israel. He had spoken to me with hope but without certainty about Israel's future victory. He told me that apart from his military plans he intended to rely on intangible and sentimental memories that would help to defend Jerusalem. I confess that whenever I hear a general promising us victory with the aid of Providence or a Divine Being, I feel a secret wish that he would leave messianic concerns to the rabbis and concentrate on getting some rifles, artillery and aircraft into place. But Marcus had shining courage and a brilliant strategic competence that, alas, he never had time to bring to expression.

The paradox that weighed heavily upon me during those anxious weeks in New York was related to the sources of our arms supplies. These were flown in great abundance from Czechoslovakia at the instigation of the Soviet Union, while the friendly President Truman, who had granted us his official recognition, continued to embargo weapons destined for the Middle East. Truman never explained this paradox, and our reliance on Soviet aid was poignant. None of us was fooled about the Soviet motives. The Soviet support of Israel arose out of an obsessive concern for pushing the ring of Western bases farther away from the Russian homeland. No nation has ever had better cause than the Russians to be suspicious of foreigners. The motive for Soviet aid was strictly egotistical, and for that very reason I believed it to be authentic.

Meanwhile in the Security Council, where I was trying to generate pressure for an effective truce, the Arabs were showing a rhetorical defiance that was out of accord with their attainments in the battlefield. Thus on May 26 they indicated a willingness to stop the fighting on condition that we would regard the proclamation of our statehood as null and void and that no further Jewish immigration would be accepted. I felt that these preposterous demands required a more vehement response than was normal in the welter of legalisms that typified United Nations discussions. I took the floor for no more than a few minutes, and referred to the Arab rejection of the Security Council's resolution. I added:

If the Arab states want peace with Israel, they can have it. If they want war, they can have that, too. But whether they want peace or war, they could have it only with the sovereign independent state of Israel.

This was dramatic stuff with a flamboyant touch about it. I did not think it was disproportionate to the occasion. Jewish states had not been proclaimed in every decade, and the idea of abolishing our sovereignty was not something to be discussed defensively. My short sentences with their monosyllabic words reverberated strongly, and I was henceforward what is called "a television celebrity." A New York paper gave a vivid portrayal of my physical appearance, attributes and style.

In the last week of May I discovered that our work among the delegates to the Security Council was bearing fruit. The brooding, thunderous atmosphere of mid-March had been banished by the tenacity of our defenders. On May 28 the Security Council discussed the third or fourth Arab refusal to cease fire. This time, however, the United States came out in our support, not with a still small voice, but with a loud roar. Ambassador Austin positively thundered with Yankee indignation that reflected the puritan rectitude of his native Vermont:

> Their statements are the best evidence we have of the international character of this aggression. They are saying, "We are there only for the purpose of overwhelming the government of Israel. We are going to overwhelm it by power and we are going to determine this international question ourselves." An existing independent government cannot be blotted out in that way. The Arab states are taking the only course that can be taken by them and that is marching in with their armies and blotting this state out. This is a matter of international concern, a matter of so great importance that we cannot sit here and say oh, we wash our hands of it. We shall not do anything about it that will be effective. We know, of course, that this is a violation of the Charter.

Austin ended in a great rhetorical flourish:

> This is equivalent in its absurdity to a legend that these five armies are there to maintain peace and at the same time are conducting a bloody war.

The Soviet representatives were not to be outdone. Thus, in the Security Council on May 29, Gromyko said:

> The Soviet Delegation cannot but express surprise at the position adopted by the Arab states, and particularly the fact that these states or some of them at least have resorted to such actions as sending their troops to Palestine and carrying out military operations aimed at the suppression of the National Liberation Movement in Palestine. We can only wonder at the course taken by the Arab states which have not yet achieved their own full liberation from foreign influence and some of which have not even real national independence.

□   □   □

This debate ebbed and flowed, surged and receded for over three weeks while the clash of arms went on in the field. The declarations of the United States and the Soviet Union on May 28 are historically important. I attached more weight than did most of my harassed colleagues to the need for documenting responsibility for the war and therefore for the consequences of the war, including the refugee problem. Whatever may be said in criticism of Israel in later years, the fact that the first links in the chain of violence were fashioned by Arab decisions remains a potent element in the unceasing litigation and debate.

A month after the war Israel could feel that it had held its ground without making decisive progress. The larger cities captured in March and April—Haifa, Acre, Safed—were still in our hands. But there was danger that after the fall of the Old City, the modern, Western part of Jerusalem would be captured by the Arabs as well. Here the battle was joined for the Jerusalem road. Many assaults on the Latrun fortress were driven back with heavy losses. Some of the Israeli fighters had come straight from immigrant ships and had been thrown into the battle without due training or preparation. Arrayed against them were the regular Arab armies that proved to be more formidable than the ragged bands that had confronted Israel before May 14. By mid-June, although the Arab advance had been stopped, Israel had had to pay a staggering price. Nearly twelve hundred Jews had been killed, of whom three hundred were civilians. Our troops were becoming exhausted by the diversity of the fronts on which they had to fight. Some generals, especially Yigal Allon, were transferred from one center of danger to another in order that their inspired dynamism could be put to work at points of crisis.

The Security Council debates provoked much commentary in Israel itself. After a few biographical sketches about my career had been published, opposition newspapers, faithful to the Herut Party, the precursor of Likud, managed to hint darkly that I had a record in what they ominously called "British Intelligence." Since this referred to my role in training Palmach fighters in World War II, I thought that the irony was extreme and the chutzpah beyond belief. On the other hand, I could understand the Israeli public asking day by day who in heaven's name is the man speaking in their name?

What had given Sharett and Ben-Gurion the courage to produce me out of obscurity with jack-in-the-box suddenness? These things were gravely revolved on countless Tel Aviv terraces amid the starker and more important news of the ebb and flow of battle.

The denunciation of Arab aggression by the American and Soviet representatives in the Security Council on May 29 had given Israel an injection of self-confidence. I was fascinated by the contrast between the American attempt to prevent Israel's statehood up to May 14 and the resounding U.S. denunciations of what the U.S. representative in the Security Council called

"Arab aggression" two weeks later. This swift change proved that we had been right to make a solitary decision in declaring our independence. It was one thing for American leaders to accept advance responsibility for a daring revolutionary act. It was much easier for them to accept an action successfully accomplished by others. This change of posture was not conspicuously heroic, but it was convenient to our cause. Yet as the battle raged from one day to the other it was clear that consoling speeches in the Security Council would not affect our condition on the ground.

It was evident that the United Nations could be impotent even when its resolutions were sustained by the two superpowers. The United States and the Soviet Union had been unable to prevent the war or even to influence its course. The Arab governments were fighting in blatant defiance of a joint American-Soviet position. The notion that small nations would always throw up their hands when Washington and Moscow stood together now proved to be an innocent delusion. But as the war took its toll, the possibility that both Arabs and Israelis would have an interest in calling a halt to the fighting stimulated the Security Council to a new assertiveness.

Israel needed the truce of mid-June more acutely than the Arabs. We were stretching both our manpower and weaponry beyond the limits of their capacity. The Arab reserves were massively more abundant than ours.

In the second week of June, I was receiving desperately urgent messages from Jerusalem to work more rapidly for an early truce. Our chief danger was, as always, in Jerusalem. The future of the city would be decided not so much by the fighting within it as by the attempt to cut it off from outside. The advantages gained by the breakthrough in April had by now been annulled by the entry of the Arab Legion into the arena. The Arab Legion commanded the coastal road, cutting Jerusalem off from the rest of the Jewish population and preventing our convoys from bringing supplies and ammunition to the city. By the end of May, it became seriously possible that even the western part of Jerusalem, with its Jewish majority, would not be able to hold out unless ways were found of opening a lifeline.

While maintaining full pressure on the main coastal route, Jewish forces attempted to open an alternative line. Working in secrecy, the Haganah transformed a sandy path winding around the south of Latrun into what was to be known as "the Burma Road" and later "the Road of Heroism." Jerusalem was almost down to its last gallons of water and loaves of bread when the first convoys, circumventing the main route, burst triumphantly into the city. On the advance trucks of the convoys were inscribed in large letters the words "If I Forget Thee O Jerusalem May My Right Hand Forget Its Cunning." The Jews of Jerusalem were not forgotten or alone.

Nevertheless, the Israeli forces were hard-pressed. There were successful operations that had checked the enemy at Yad Mordechai in the south and at Degania in the north. But with the the Egyptians within twenty-five miles of Tel Aviv and the Negev cut off from the rest of the state, we could not claim to be in a victorious position. And Ben-Gurion knew better than anyone else that it was only in late June and early July that we could expect more shipments of Soviet arms. In one message Ben-Gurion told me that an immediate cease-fire was "existentially urgent." A terrible anguish reverberated in his words. He sent an emissary to tell me to suggest that the UN Security Council should meet daily and nightly. He seemed to be under the impression that I controlled the UN Security Council's agenda.

Few Israelis today understand that we nearly lost our first war and that without UN pressure for a truce our cause might have perished.

Thanks to Secretary-General Trygve Lie, whose Norwegian heart now burned with biblical ardor, it was possible to ensure that the Security Council would in fact be convened in almost continuous session, lasting from day to day. In the end a truce and cease-fire were adopted by the Security Council that ordered a cessation of all acts of armed force for a period of four weeks. Nobody seemed perturbed by the paradox that the UN was giving an implied green light for more battles after July 13.

All the reputable military historians agree that the first truce (mid-June to mid-July) was crucial. I am content with the most authoritative of these judgments. It comes from Chaim Herzog in his book *The Arab-Israel Wars:*

> The first truce came as a welcome respite for the hard-pressed Israeli forces but above all, it was most welcome in Jerusalem. When the truce began, no more than three days supply of food remained in the city. The United Nations organized convoys and Arab legion inspection which allowed only a certain amount of supplies to move up into the city, but the "Burma Road," bypassing Latrun, was meanwhile improved and civilian supplies, military equipment and reinforcements moved along it freely and without inspection to the city. . . . The Army was reorganized and underwent intensive training as more material arrived from Europe, particularly from Czechoslovakia. Artillery units were being added and a hodge-podge of tanks and armored vehicles acquired from various countries throughout the world was gathered together to create the Eighth Armored Brigade. Even the Air Force was receiving air craft and had shot down some Egyptians which were sent to bomb Tel Aviv.

But the improvement in our military condition was tragically interrupted. The IZL brought in a ship named *Altalena,* which had sailed from Europe with some nine hundred men and large stocks of arms and ammunition. Menachem Begin was the commander of this enterprise. Ben-Gurion now faced a hard decision. When the leaders of the *Altalena* refused to give an undertaking that they would hand their arms over to the Israeli army, which had been constituted legally on May 28, he understood that Israel's statehood was at issue. How could Israel claim the recognition of our own citizens, still less of the outside world, if our army was only one of several militias, each one serving its own political ideology and program? Ben-Gurion ordered fire to be opened on the *Altalena*. Fifteen men were killed and the *Altalena* was eventually sunk by gunfire. Ben-Gurion would later say that Israeli sovereignty was established not, as had been hoped, on May 15 but on June 28 when an oath of allegiance was taken by all the armed forces and the Irgun ceased to function as a separate force.

The UN mediator, Count Bernadotte, had convinced himself, or perhaps been convinced by some of the Western powers, that the truce period would be congenial for the promotion of a permanent settlement. There was no good reason for believing this. It was obvious that a boundary agreement would be largely influenced by military conditions on the ground. In this respect the Israeli "map" was so fragmented and fragile that it could not possibly contribute to a favorable demarcation. On the other hand, the Arabs, although they had been disappointed by their small progress since the entry of their regular armies into the fray, had not despaired of inflicting greater loss on the defending Israeli forces. When the four weeks prescribed by the Security Council truce resolution expired, we had not yet made the fullest use of the short time made available by the June truce. The directive that I received from Ben-Gurion was to secure a prolongation of the truce so that our consolidation could go forward to a more advanced stage.

I have already remarked on the chronic tendency of the Palestine Arabs to make decisions against their own interests. They certainly made a mistake from their point of view in accepting the June 11 truce. They now went on to crown this error with the more crucial mistake of resuming the hostilities on July 4.

The first two weeks of July were a golden period for Israel and a time of deep dejection for the Arab world. Their first misfortune was in the Security Council, where the United States and the Soviet Union pressed them hard to avoid renewed hostilities. Instead of concentrating its resources and preoccupation on victory and war, the Israeli government now had to enter a new phase in its diplomatic struggle. One day in mid-June I received a copy of the mediator's report. He had gone far beyond any reasonable interpretation of his mandate. Instead of discussing how the State of Israel should be reconciled with the Palestine Arabs, Bernadotte began to dictate to both parties not only how they should behave but also how they should define their own boundaries. He proposed that the areas originally allotted to an Arab state in Palestine be joined instead to Transjordan together with the whole of Jerusalem and the Negev. Haifa and Lod were to be free ports and the "Jewish state," as he still called it, could have western Galilee. The Jewish state and the expanded Transjordan would have a unified fiscal military and foreign policy so that neither would be completely independent. Jewish immigration after two years would be subject to approval by the Economic and Social Council of the United Nations, and Arab refugees would be repatriated and have their property restored.

The plan was espoused with suspicious speed and enthusiasm by Britain and less fervently by the United States Department of State. What Israelis resented was not only Bernadotte's actual proposals but his implication that Israeli sovereignty was still optional and subject to a greater measure of external interference than has ever been suggested for other states. Perhaps if the United Nations had done something effective to save Jewish lives and protect Jewish interests after November 1947, its advice might have been more respectfully received. As things were, the United Nations was bound to appear in the intolerable posture of claiming jurisdiction without accepting either responsibility or risk.

There was something suicidal in the Arab decision to renew the fighting against an Israeli army refreshed and replenished by the truce. Israel responded reluctantly but dynamically. The Arabs were now to suffer resounding defeats in what was to be known in Israeli history as "the ten-day offensive." The Arabs had put themselves in the wrong with world opinion. They had managed to maneuver themselves acrobatically into the unusual position of an unpopular underdog. Bernadotte himself had said that

a decision to resume fighting would be universally condemned and a party taking such a decision will be assuming a responsibility which will be viewed by the world with the utmost gravity.

Bernadotte had no power, but he now tended to speak as if he were a world conqueror dispensing stern edicts to the entire world.

In the next ten days the Egyptian assault was decisively shattered. Egypt lost over seven hundred killed, one thousand wounded and hundreds of prisoners. Israeli forces swept forward to capture Lod and Ramle on July 11–12 and to repel a Transjordanian counterattack inflicting six hundred fatalities. In the north the Israeli commanders, now freed from any pressure on Haifa, drove Arab forces back across the Lebanese frontier and captured Nazareth. Near Jerusalem Israel dislodged Egyptian forces south of the city and took Ein Karem in the west. We had by now even acquired some offensive air strength in the form of venerable and slow-moving Flying Fortresses that attacked Cairo and Damascus with more damage to Arab morale than to the bombed cities themselves. So when I came to the Security Council for a meeting on July 15, the Arab cause was at its lowest ebb. Both the American and the Soviet delegates turned their fury on the Arab governments. A resolution was adopted that not only "ordered" a cease-fire but determined the existence of "a threat to the peace" and menaced the Arab governments with sanctions under Chapter Seven of the Charter if they declined to cease fire. Moreover, the truce was no longer to be limited by a new date of expiry. It was to continue until "a peaceful adjustment was reached."

This was strong language. It was the first time that the coercive provisions of Chapter Seven of the United Nations Charter had ever been used. It would be easy for the United Nations to say that its pressure was effective, for the Arabs accepted the truce, but I felt that their response was dictated more by the disintegration of their military resistance than by the strength of international pressure.

The second truce in Israel's war of independence took effect on July 18, 1948. That was the point at which Israel's mind began to shift from mere survival toward the tasks for which it had survived. The Arab states had laid down their arms in exhaustion and defeat, but there was no disarmament of their spirit or emotion. There would still be more fighting in the fall and winter months of 1948 and in January 1949, when Israel would strike out to break an Egyptian blockade of their settlements in the Negev and to banish some pockets of Arab forces in Galilee. The first of these operations would bring Beersheva under control and enable Israeli forces under Yigal Allon to take over the Negev and eventually to occupy Eilat peacefully in March 1949.

Nevertheless, mid-July was a convenient signpost for me to reflect upon Israel's war of independence. There had been some sixty days of fighting in three separate spurts between December 1947 and January 1949. Israel's losses—four thousand soldiers and two thousand civilians killed—sound limited in comparison with the enormity of the change that had come about in the nature and direction of Jewish history. But we should recall that the Jewish community that paid this price had only six hundred and fifty thousand Jews. It was as if the United States in 1947 to 1949 had lost a million and a half killed. We had other burdens and anxieties. There was a salient cutting into Israeli's farming area in upper Galilee. Mount Scopus was still cut off. Jerusalem was still divided. The Latrun wedge was still in Arab hands. At a rough estimate Israel, whose annual export earnings then amounted to less than fifty million dollars, had spent five hundred million dollars on the prosecution of the war.

But all these defects were little more than blemishes on the glowing countenance of our triumph. Our state was solidly entrenched. Our rule now extended over the whole of Galilee, the entire coastal strip, except for the twenty-seven-mile Gaza salient in Egyptian hands. West Jerusalem, with a sizable corridor to the coast, was no longer in hazard. The area of our effective jurisdiction was over eight thousand square miles. The Arabs had prevented the establishment of a separate Arab state west of the Jordan and had also obstructed the internationalization of Jerusalem. Their capacity for acting in diametric opposition to their interests was now a permanent feature of their policy. The parts of western Palestine outside Israel's jurisdiction were under Transjordanian or Egyptian control. Most important of all, the gates were open and masses of Jewish immigrants were flowing in. We were free to build our future. We had carved our freedom out of adversity, for the most part unaided and alone.

My letters and diary entries in that period reflect a deep national and personal exhilaration. I was in the center of a great enterprise and my voice resounded in the world. Even as late as the end of June, I do not recall believing that the stability of our state was assured. After the Arab defeats in the ten-day offensive I was certain that something irreversible had occurred.

Whatever would happen thereafter, the image of this war would live on unfading in our recollection. It had told us some unexpected things about ourselves. It had brought to the surface a whole range of qualities that would have further tests in other ordeals. Clearly there was an underlying coherence beneath the diversities that marked the Israeli population. There was a capacity for organized action, a talent for making the most of small resources and a unifying energy that could be invoked in times of stress. Above all, there was a conviction that the central national aims were worthy of sacrifice and that individual advantage must, if necessary, be qualified by the general need. All these attributes had been enlarged by a sense of history. For the most part our defenders knew the dark background out of which Israel had emerged and to which it would again recede if its courage or resolution faltered. Without victory there would be no survival.

So when the clang of arms was silenced our nation looked back with pride and rectitude on what it had accomplished in those sixty days. The graves that had been dug, the tears that had been shed because of them, the griefs that had been suffered, the perils that had been surmounted, the inexpressible hopes that had been kindled would all live on deep in the mind and heart of Israel so long as any memory of the past endured. Some citizens had won particular renown amid sharp ordeals, but in the deeper truth it was a people's victory won by countless men and women caught up together in poignant alternation of suffering and hope, of courage and despair. When the war ended it was everyone's possession, and from its dust and havoc a new tomorrow was waiting to be born.

8

WHEN IS A STATE NOT A STATE? JULY TO DECEMBER 1948

ISRAEL WAS SOVEREIGN, but still besieged. It had shown a great capacity to overcome obstacles, but our adversaries had equal capacity to create new ones. Some of our opponents were still ready for rearguard actions. Ernest Bevin, in particular, still declined to recognize the new reality. For the first time, Jewish leaders encountered a British statesman with whom it was not even profitable to hold mutual discourse. His personal rancor was intense. Behind his abrasive exterior there lurked an abrasive interior. Even his protective biographer, Lord Bullock, has written:

> He still believed that events would justify his warnings but this did not alter the fact that the Zionist triumph, although he had for some time accepted it as the most likely outcome, represented a defeat and a damaging one. He had been proved wrong in a belief on which he had staked his reputation, that it would be possible to find a compromise settlement. There had also been errors of judgment and timing as well as faults of temper on his part. Ernest Bevin's masterful temperament made his failure more conspicuous.

This reference to Bevin's "failure" by a friendly biographer highlights the paradox of his career. In general terms, he was a successful foreign secretary. During years of national decline he gave Britain an influence that was greater than its power. He was liked by Acheson and respected by Gromyko. In a foreign ministry dominated by an elitist atmosphere, his down-to-earth style and his strong position in the Cabinet and Parliament compensated for his lack of diplomatic experience and won him the loyalty, if not the affection, of the permanent officials. His anti-Zionist prejudice was a deviation from his own standards. It is as if he had concentrated all his defects of mind and

168

character into a single compartment of conduct and experience. It seemed incredible to me that a statesman of his caliber, who was one of the leaders of the Western alliance in its containment of the Soviet Union, could have shown such little pragmatic intuition in this case.

We find him as late as May 25 informing the American ambassador in London that there were

> two points on which he believed the Jews would have to make concessions. One, the inclusion of Gaza and the Negev in the Jewish state, had been a mistake as there were no Jews there and this must be righted; two, Jaffa and Acre, which were purely Arab towns, should be given back to the Arabs.

Bevin's point about the Negev was particularly absurd. It was precisely because the Negev was empty that Ben-Gurion saw it as indispensable to a Jewish state. He wanted to build a society without constantly shoving and pushing against Arab neighbors. The Negev's emptiness was also the main argument on which Weizmann had built his successful conversation with Truman in November 1947.

Bevin had by now reached the position that the existence of a Jewish state could, "unfortunately," not be prevented, but it might be possible to make it a truncated dwarf of a country with no possibility of development.

Lord Bullock admits that Bevin's obduracy on the Palestine question was often attributed to anti-Jewish bias. Bullock believes that this charge was unfounded.

Was it really? The strongest evidence comes not from Bevin's adversaries but from his faithful supporters. One of them, Christopher Mayhew, made an entry into his own diary on May 16, 1948:

> I must make a note about Ernest's anti-Semitism, which has come out increasingly sharply these past few weeks with the appalling crisis in Palestine. There is no doubt to my mind that Ernest detests Jews. He makes the odd wise-crack about the "chosen people," explains Shinwell[1] away as a Jew, declares that the Old Testament is the most immoral book ever written and declares publicly: "We must also remember the Arabs' side of the case. There are, after all, no Arabs in this House (loud cheers)." I tell him afterwards that this remark is going too far and we have a general talk about the Jews. He says they taught Hitler the technique of terror and were even now paralleling the Nazis in Palestine. They were preachers of violence and war. "What could you expect when people are brought up from the cradle on the Old

---

[1] Emmanuel Shinwell was a Jew and minister of fuel, later of defense.

Testament?" I starkly deny most of it and tell him that anyway, true or false, what he says in public on this subject only gives his enemies a handle against him. He smiles sardonically. I allow him only one point, that in giving voice to his irrational and indefensible prejudices, he is speaking for millions of British people.

Lord Mayhew's testimony is of particular relevance because it comes from one who shared Bevin's anti-Zionist views. This diary entry leaves us with no doubt about the convulsed mood in which his chief approached the Palestine question. It is significant that in all other relinquishments of empire, the British attitude had been conspicuously serene.

But by mid-May 1948 Ernest Bevin's hostility had long become irrelevant. Our friends in London were telling us with confidence that it would be only a matter of months before a more traditional British attitude asserted itself: Bevin would not be able to maintain a policy of non-recognition without support from the United States or Europe or from his own public opinion.

Meanwhile, we still faced obstacles in the very UN organization that had witnessed and promoted our birth. The UN General Assembly must have been afflicted with a fit of absentmindedness on May 14, 1948, when it appointed Count Bernadotte to make urgent proposals for a full peace settlement. It was fantasy to believe that a conflict so deeply rooted in the emotions, passions and experiences of two nations could be usefully explored in a document drawn up by an inexperienced envoy in a few weeks, yet this is what Bernadotte attempted. He had changed some features of his report during the summer, but it was still marked by illusion. It was not only that he had virtually asked Israel to renounce its independence in order to promote a "union" with Transjordan. His most preposterous proposal had been that

> immigration within its borders should be within the competence of each member provided that following a period of two years from the establishment of the union either member would be entitled to request the Council of the Union to review the immigration policy of the other member and to render a ruling thereof. If they did not agree to this "ruling" the matter would be "referred to the Economic and Social Council of the United Nations whose decisions, taking into account the principle of economic absorptive capacity, would be binding on the member whose policy was at issue."

This provision was so insulting that I had little indignation left with which to say what I thought of Bernadotte's idea about Jerusalem, which, like the Negev, was to be included in Arab territory. There was also to be a free port at Haifa and a free airport at Lod. Israel was to be virtually dismembered.

Bernadotte seemed unaware that Jerusalem was the only city in the Middle

East and, indeed, in the whole world in which Jews had been a majority for a whole century. His effrontery in believing that everyone except Israel had rights in the city left me breathless.

In sessions of the Security Council in July, I developed a strong criticism of the Bernadotte report. In one speech I said that "it is very much as though the surgeon went away with most of the patient's vital organs." However, the report was not substantively discussed, partly because most Security Council members felt in the depths of their heart that it was an unworthy document, and partly because the Council's time and preoccupation were totally absorbed by the necessity to bring about the second truce. But the report hovered over us in the near horizon as an ominous cloud. Nevertheless, I was confident that the Bernadotte report had no chance of endorsement. It would be opposed by the Jews because it gave us too little, and by the Arabs because it gave us too much. Whatever its other defects, it did accept the principle of a Jewish state, while the Arabs were still living in the illusion that even our statehood was still open for appeal and reversal.

More attention was now being devoted to the domestic scene. It was an inspiring era. Immigration had been the sharpest issue of contention with the British government. Indeed, had Bevin been prepared to show flexibility on this matter, it is possible that the pressure for the establishment of a Jewish state would not have arisen when it did. With some of the immediate political and military aims secured, the nation's main business could now begin. The task was to open the gates and thus to heal the wounds of homelessness that had afflicted European Jewry and had denied them any refuge from the Holocaust. Beyond Europe, Israel could respond to a surge of exaltation in other parts of the Jewish world where the rise of a Jewish state was like the sound of a trumpet calling Jews to change the direction of their lives and help Israel to write new chapters in a long and ancient saga.

In the first four months of Israel's independence, when the country's fate was still in the balance of the war, fifty thousand immigrants reached our shores. By September 1948 the stream became a torrent. Between May 1948 and December 1951, 687,000 newcomers had landed in Israel. It had taken thirty years under British rule for the Jewish population to increase by 600,000. This was now accomplished and even surpassed by the State of Israel in less than four years. There was a frenzied ingenuity in the search for roofs to put over the newcomers' heads. Former British military camps in various stages of disintegration and neglect, barracks, huts, prefabricated dwellings, Arab homes abandoned during the war—every device was put together in an astonishing enterprise of human rescue.

The black tents in which thousands of immigrants were lodged looked alarmingly thin and fragile. They aroused anxiety and compassion even then, but individual suffering was offset by a large and spacious vision of national interest. It was a prodigious achievement. For the forty months of mass immigration, Israel was a vast, noisy workshop filled with the clatter of countless tools knocking houses, roads and schools together at headlong pace. One hundred and forty-five new villages, kibbutzim and moshavim were established between 1948 and 1951, more than in the seventy previous years. The map of Jewish habitation, which had seemed disappointingly full of gaps in my first sight of it in the 1940s, was now dotted with new and living place names. Only in the Negev, in Galilee and in the Judean hills did the population pattern remain sparse.

The tide was bound to end sooner or later under the weight of economic crisis, but when it did the decline was shockingly abrupt. In 1953 there were only 10,000 new immigrants and only a total of 50,000 in the three years 1952–1954. The Israeli economy and society had undertaken tasks beyond its own unaided power.

Meanwhile, I could not have regarded our international position as satisfactory. We lacked the kind of diplomatic status that would be needed for effective resistance to hostile pressures. In a dramatic Security Council meeting I had declared that "Israel is an immutable part of the international landscape; whoever plans without it is building delusions on sand." This sounded well, especially in my own ears, but not everyone agreed that we were all that "immutable." Our foot was barely in the door of the world community. Every time that I came to the Security Council table I was made aware that our diplomatic business was unfinished. Before me stood the nameplate describing me as the representative of "the Jewish Agency." I found it intolerable that Israel's name should be forbidden for use in the international forum. How could we expect Arabs to get used to the idea of "Israel" if the highest international bodies still saw us as a vague, indeterminate entity? The United Kingdom delegate, Sir Alexander Cadogan, had even taken to addressing us as "the Jewish authorities in Palestine."

To remove this insult we would have to get seven of the eleven members of the Security Council to agree to call us "Israel" at the Security Council table. Unfortunately, we were not sure of having seven votes. At this point I hit upon an alternative device. If the rotating chairman would routinely invite the "representative of Israel" to take his seat at the table, the opponents of this action would need seven votes to override his ruling. Ambassador Philip Jessup, conspiring with me against his legalistic habit, informed me that our adversaries did not have seven votes to overrule the chairman, any more than I had seven votes to make a successful positive motion.

Accordingly I laid ambush to our adversaries by suggesting to Gromyko that his colleague Dmitri Manuilsky of the Ukraine, as the next president of the Security Council, should invite "Israel" to the table at the next Council meeting and then challenge members of the Council to overrule him. Gromyko, in a humorous flight, informed Gideon Rafael and me that he thought that he had "some influence over the Ukrainian delegate."

Our stratagem worked. The Security Council met. The Ukrainian president called upon the "representative of Israel" to take his seat at the table. I almost ran to the table as if I expected to be physically obstructed. An official of the secretariat promptly affixed the plaque ISRAEL before me and retired. Cadogan led a chorus of dissent, stating that the president had acted prematurely and irresponsibly. Other Council members took up the cry. Manuilsky asked in a show of presidential indignation, "Does the Council challenge my ruling?" He asked the question in an incredulous voice, as if he were a pope asking if anyone objected to the doctrine of immaculate conception. The vote was taken. There were only six votes for the challenge.

Argentina had caused me a tremor of apprehension. Its delegate, being certain that we would carry the day, had "invested" his vote harmlessly in friendship for the Arabs. We were now irreversibly "Israel" in the Security Council discussions.

The Palestinian representative, Jamal al-Husseini, proved that his movement had not exhausted its repertoire of folly. He arose and walked out of the chamber, proclaiming that he would not return so long as a representative called "Israel" sat where I sat. Thus, for the next twenty-five years, until the PLO became recognized by the UN, the Palestine Arabs were unrepresented in the highest international agency, while Israel was present in full sovereignty.

While I was pleased with this procedural victory, I was depressed by the indignity to which we had been subjected. We had been forced into an ingenious stratagem in order to obtain what was, after all, our absolute and natural right, to be addressed in our own name and title. I concluded that this experience made it imperative for our status to be regularized by full membership in the United Nations. I resolved to make this the priority issue in our delegation's work after the summer recess of the General Assembly.

Since there was reason to expect a brief respite in the Security Council's work during the summer heat, I asked for permission to come home to Israel. Suzy and I accordingly embarked on the British Cunard liner *Queen Elizabeth* for the first stage of our journey. I look back with almost sensual nostalgia to the time when a normal way to cross the Atlantic was by sea. One Sunday morning I saw Sir Alexander Cadogan emerge from the ship's chapel amid the sound of organ music. I asked him if he had been "praying to the God of Abraham, Isaac and the Jewish authorities in Palestine. . . ." He looked around furtively as if to be assured that Bevin was not lurking in the neighborhood and said, "Isn't our policy a bit absurd?"

Although the aim of my visit was to consult with the Cabinet on our prospects in the forthcoming September session of the General Assembly, another motive was to create relations of mutual acquaintance between the government of Israel and myself as its spokesman in the international arena.

We arrived by air from London at the small Haifa Airport in August. I was warmly received. The defiant tone that I had adopted in the Security

Council corresponded to the emotional needs of the Israeli people. No television yet existed in Israel, but thousands of Israelis had shortwave radio sets. This meant that my voice was much better known than my face.

Sharett felt that it would be appropriate for me to be inspected by a large and selective audience. Accordingly, a meeting was convened in the very Tel Aviv museum in which our Declaration of Independence had been signed. Although I wished to interest the audience in what I was saying, I could see that most of them were both perplexed and astounded by the fact that I gave my lecture fluently in Hebrew without using notes. Later I was told that Suzy heard a whispered conversation between two Israelis who sat behind her. One of them said to the other: "You see, I told you that if one tried hard one could learn Hebrew in a few months."

A few days after my baptism of eulogy in the museum, I was invited by Prime Minister Ben-Gurion to attend a meeting of the Cabinet. This became a practice during all the years of my service in the United Nations and Washington.

This contact with my Israeli home base was immensely encouraging. I had my first proof that whatever one might say about the limitations of UN debates, they had great resonance in world opinion. Having received detailed instructions for our work in the imminent UN session, I decided with Suzy to spend a few days in Geneva, where her parents were resting from the summer heat. At that stage in her life Suzy had never known what the burning heat of the Middle East was, since from earliest childhood her parents used to leave Egypt in June and not return until autumn.

We found Weizmann installed in his customary hotel in Geneva. His temper was not good. It was only on arrival in Switzerland that he had heard what the prerogatives of an Israeli president were. They were certainly not those with which he was familiar from his contacts with Roosevelt and Truman in Washington. They were even less than the attributes wielded in the Third Republic by the president of France, who used to attend Cabinet meetings and receive all government minutes. Rumors had it that Weizmann was going to reject the office without ever assuming it. I naturally joined in dissuading him from that course, pointing out that it would do injury to the State of Israel, whose sovereignty, in the minds of millions of people across the world, was expressed in Chaim Weizmann. I added, without much conviction, that his personal prestige would give him more real influence than could be adduced from the restrictive terms in which Ben-Gurion had cast the presidency.

There was no doubt in my mind what the motive for this constitutional gambit was. Ben-Gurion was determined that the executive powers should be almost unlimited. His view of democracy was that there should be a decent amount of discussion, after which the prime minister's will should be done. There was also a personal consideration. Ben-Gurion knew that Weizmann was accustomed to wield any authority that he had up to and somewhat beyond its full potential limit. If one wanted to restrict his powers, this intention would have to be specifically enacted.

Geneva is not a city where a visitor usually expects drastic surprises. I could not help comparing the public atmosphere with the turbulence of Jerusalem and New York. I assumed that in a country in which the central theme of life was the pursuit of tranquillity, I would be safe from excessive tension. It was not to be. A few minutes before going to lunch with Weizmann at the Richemond, I received a cable from Sharett: "Please don't forget to apply for membership in the United Nations." I found this formulation somewhat eccentric. It is true that I had a reputation for forgetfulness, but this referred to such things as pipes, handkerchiefs, glasses, scarves and other portable articles. The idea that applying for membership in the United Nations would require a reminder had never occurred to me before.

On returning to my hotel, I found another cable from Sharett, saying that Count Bernadotte had been assassinated, presumably by young men of Lechi. I stuffed the two cables into my pocket. I was being asked to get ourselves admitted to the organization whose representative had been killed by one of our political parties.

This action by Lechi could well compete with the murder of Lord Moyne in 1944 for unadulterated folly. It illustrated how easily zealots, who live outside the field of national discipline, can inflict injury on the cause which they claim to cherish. The murder of Moyne in Cairo had prevented the idea of a Jewish state from arising on the international agenda in 1944, before the war had ended and at a time when the Hungarian Jewish community was still intact. It went far to explain why the Zionist cause emerged from World War II in disarray and despair. And now, the assassination of Count Bernadotte, quite apart from its moral callousness, could not but lead to results dangerous to our fragile statehood.

I had come to Geneva without the slightest doubt in my mind about our capacity to defeat the Bernadotte proposals, since they were rejected both by Israelis and Arabs as well as by loyalists of the November 29, 1947, Resolution. Now all that had changed. There is nothing like martyrdom to bring posthumous success to a public figure. I was afraid that the rituals of burial and the human sympathy for an innocent but foolish man would generate a UN majority for the support of his legacy.

Suzy and I bade farewell to her parents and, after packing our suitcases with exceptional haste, boarded the night train for Paris where the General Assembly was to convene at the Palais de Chaillot. In the Security Council over which Alexander Cadogan presided, looking very much like a professional undertaker, sincere tributes to Bernadotte's memory were uttered by each of the eleven members in turn.

I had met Bernadotte in New York at an early stage of his mission. He did not have deep political convictions, but he gave me an impression of fundamental integrity. His main defect was a weakness of resolve that seemed almost natural for a man brought up in an atmosphere of affluence and deferential servility on the part of those who surrounded him in his own country. The Swedish Royal Family were his relatives, and he had moved all his life in an atmosphere free of personal hardships. Nevertheless, like many aristocrats, he felt an obligation to contribute to the society that had pampered him for so long. A Jewish leader in Stockholm, Hillel Storch, had spoken to me movingly of Bernadotte's attempts to promote the rescue of Jews during the Nazi decade.

His later fault was to have accepted British and Arab pressures too uncritically. At the beginning of August he had modified the proposals that he had made at Lake Success in July. His proposal was now to make Jerusalem an international city in conformity with the 1947 Resolution, and not an Arab city, but the main weight of his report was to advocate with total lack of realism that the Negev be annexed to Transjordan.

I was told in Paris that all the members of the Security Council and many other heads of delegation would proceed to Stockholm for Bernadotte's funeral. This would take place ten days after his death. I spoke to Secretary-General Trygve Lie, who expressed paternal sympathy with my personal plight in becoming the unwitting target of so many black looks. In order to alleviate my solitude he offered me a place in the aircraft that would carry him from Paris to Sweden.

When I left Paris the Swedish UN delegation had appeared in the General Assembly in somber black. When I reached Stockholm, however, it appeared to me that the Swedes have a unique approach to funeral occasions. The guests in the cathedral were dressed in white ties and tails, which I had always associated since my Cambridge days with festivity. A great deal of alcohol was being consumed, and as time went on, many heads of state and foreign ministers found opportunities for useful consultation. A few years later, having Bernadotte's funeral in mind, I went to the burial ceremony of the German Chancellor Adenauer in company with Ben-Gurion. On that occasion the interchange of ideas and commitments amongst heads of state—Lyndon B. Johnson, de Gaulle, MacMillan, Gromyko and others—was so intense that I coined the phrase "a working funeral," which was later introduced by my nephew Jonathan Lynn into the script of his memorable TV series "Yes, Prime Minister."

When it first became known that I would go to Stockholm for Count Bernadotte's funeral, Eliahu Sasson, Israel's leading expert on the Middle East, who had a rich experience of funerals in Arab countries, had urged me not to attend the burial ceremony since I would surely be "stoned to death by an enraged throng." Although I had never been to Sweden before, I found it hard to believe that the phlegmatic Swedes would react with Mediterranean passion against a foreign guest. I patiently informed Sasson that as far as I could judge, there would be very few stones to be found in Stockholm's meticulously tidy streets.

In Stockholm I was received with tact and personal sympathy. I had a moving conversation with Countess Bernadotte, who asked me to keep contact with her in the future. Swedes were saddened by the sacrifice of one of their citizens but proud of their service to the international cause. Nevertheless, some months later when the vote was taken on Israel's admission to the United Nations, Sweden abstained on the grounds that the Israeli government had never fully explored the responsibility for the assassination. In Israel itself it has long been well-known and even admitted that the perpetrators were a group of Lechi adherents who had also carried out the murder of Lord Moyne.

I returned from Stockholm to Paris to resume the struggle against the Bernadotte Report in an atmosphere sharpened by the sense of international bereavement. It was clear that if we were to lose the Negev as Bernadotte had proposed, it would cut the size of our state in half and leave no room for future economic development. My task was to ensure that the United Nations would not approve the plan, but would also refrain from confirming the boundaries defined by the General Assembly Resolution of November 1947.

I thought that Israel should be free to delineate its frontiers in negotiation with its Arab neighbors, and that it would be a defeat if the aggression of Arab armies were to leave them in continued occupation of the territory into which they had moved without any international justification. The best result would be a defeat for the Bernadotte plan without a reiteration of the November 1947 demarcation lines.

The difficulties that I faced were enhanced by the fact that Secretary of State George C. Marshall had already committed the United States to support the Bernadotte plan. Our only hope was to cut the ground from under Marshall's feet. First, President Truman must be persuaded to oppose the plan, and thereafter a serious attempt should be made to create a split in the American delegation.

At this moment I had a stroke of good fortune. Secretary Marshall was called by Truman to return to Paris because of the escalating Berlin crisis, leaving John Foster Dulles, the deputy head of the U.S. delegation, in charge.

I arranged for Sharett and myself to see Dulles at the Crillon Hotel, where the United States delegation had its headquarters. Our meeting was amiable, and this may have had something to do with the frankness with which Dulles explained his predicament. Here he was in the ambivalent position of having been appointed by Truman to the UN delegation while at the same time being foreign policy adviser to Thomas E. Dewey, who was running for the presidency against Truman. I thought that this situation suited his ambiguous nature. Despite or because of his talents, he had a reputation for deviousness that he was to earn handsomely in the forthcoming years. But when Sharett and I visited him, he surprised us by stating that although he had been appointed by Truman to the UN delegation, he felt himself free to serve the interests of Governor Thomas Dewey, who—he added—"as you both must know, will shortly be the president of the United States."

I had anticipated that Dulles, because of his exaggerated pragmatism, would side with the Arabs in this controversy. Nothing of the kind. He was not even ambivalent about the Bernadotte plan. He was dead set against it. He told us that Israel's military victory had proved something about the character of the Jewish people and therefore had strong moral and spiritual implications. He disagreed with Secretary Marshall so vehemently on this and other questions that he had stopped attending delegation meetings. He had felt himself sustained in his support of Israel by other members of the U.S. delegation, including Eleanor Roosevelt and the distinguished jurist Benjamin V. Cohen. Marshall's allies included Dean Rusk, in whom Israel had never aroused a visible measure of enthusiasm.

My anticipation that the Bernadotte report would fail was borne out by events. The strange coalition of pro-Israeli and pro-Arab representatives ensured its collapse in the political committee of the General Assembly. It was not even brought to a vote in the plenum. The Paris session ended with the appointment of a "Palestine Conciliation Commission" composed of the United States, France and Turkey, with a mandate to explore the possibility of a peace agreement between Israel and its neighbors.

Another General Assembly resolution recommended that Arab refugees who had fled the territory of Israel during the fighting should either be able to return or be offered compensation. In the initial text, this was drafted in mandatory language as though Israel would have no say in the matter. In concert with Dulles, I managed to moderate this text in an important respect. In its final wording the resolution adopted by the General Assembly in December 1948 recommended that refugees should be "permitted" to return, and that those not receiving this permission or unwilling to return could claim compensation for their abandoned property. Dulles and I considered that the word "permitted" effectively put the determination in the hands of the ruling territorial power, which by then was Israel and no other. "Permission" is an acknowledgment of power and authority. The result is that there is no such thing in the General Assembly Resolution of December 11, 1948, as "a right" of Arab refugees to return irrespective of Israel's permission.

All the Americans whom I met in Paris in October 1948 were convinced that President Truman's tenure was virtually over and that Governor Thomas E. Dewey of New York would win the upcoming election. In that case, Dulles would become secretary of state. There was a constant round of dinners, luncheons and other social events at which Dulles met with delegates to discuss the future relationship between their governments and the forthcoming "Dewey administration." My own invitation in this series of social events was for the day after the election. Had Dewey really won the election, it would have been a gala party. Dulles still made his hospitality available, but it had all the gaiety of a funeral service. I had been unable to work out what the appropriate greeting is to a host who had invited you to dinner on the assumption that he was going to be secretary of state.

While I was involved in the proceedings of the General Assembly, Moshe Sharett fought a rearguard battle in the Security Council, where strong efforts were being made to defend the Arab invaders against Israeli military successes. Our own forces under Yigal Allon had broken through the bottlenecks that prevented continuity of access between the Negev and the more northerly parts of Israel. The Arab and British delegations attempted to secure our withdrawal. It was plain that the Israeli hold on the Negev was still being challenged. Our soldiers had responded heavily and had broken through, banishing Egyptian forces from nearly every strongpoint except Faluja, where they were surrounded and besieged. There was one agonizing week in which I tried to delay a cease-fire resolution until such time as Faluja would fall. I kept receiving reports from our chief of staff, General Yigael Yadin, saying that this might take place within a few hours. The hours turned to days. The siege continued, but so did the tenacious presence of the besieged Egyptians at Faluja. One of the besieged officers was a young officer named Gamal Abdel Nasser.

During 1948 while news was reaching us of General Allon's successful thrust in the south, fighting had also broken out again in Galilee where Qawukji's forces were renewing their assault. In the Security Council I renewed my traditional duel with the United Kingdom delegation. The world press regarded these occasions as very good theater. Bevin was by now in poor health and constantly going back to London, but Cadogan was reinforced by a minister of state in the foreign office, Hector McNeil, a soft-spoken Scottish socialist. At a UN Committee Session he took the floor to explain eloquently how useless and unpromising the southern Negev was. I replied that since the area in question was so repellent, I assumed that Britain would not wish to deprive Israel of the burden of its possession. I added, "I have never heard of anything so undesirable being coveted by the United Kingdom with such intensity."

Our only setback in the 1948 General Assembly at its regular session was that the Security Council did not provide the necessary seven votes for our admission to the United Nations. The United States and the Soviet Union both voted in favor, as did Ukraine, Argentina and Colombia. Syria voted against, but Belgium, Canada, Great Britain, China and France abstained. Although privately disappointed, I was publicly cheerful in reporting that there would be some changes in the Security Council early in 1949 and that I would try again in the spring, with hope of a better result.

The Assembly Session gave me the opportunity for the first time in my life to live for three consecutive months in Paris. I could not forbear from comparing my new amenities with those of my student days, when I stayed at a squalid hotel on the Left Bank, optimistically called Hotel de la Sorbonne, with the smell of decaying cabbage and a constant noise of creaking floors as hotel guests changed their residence with what I should have understood to be suspicious speed. I had chosen it because of the deceptive academic name. This time my residence when in Paris was at the Hotel Raphael in the Avenue Kleber, and it so remained for many years. Many leading UN figures were there, including Lester Pearson, by now Foreign Minister of Canada, who was destined to play a central role in our affairs. Sharett himself had rented a villa in the area of Port St. Cloud in an effort to distance himself from the turbulence of Parisian life.

The Latin American countries were unknown territory, hardly ever charted by Zionism until the late 1940s. Here our links were cherished and developed by Moshe Tov, an Argentinian Jew who had providentially joined our ranks at a time when we were in desperate need of deeper emotional contact with a continent that then commanded one-third of the United Nations' votes. Moshe Tov was known throughout Latin America as a consummate orator. He had an almost hypnotic effect on the delegates of Spanish-speaking countries. Nevertheless, I felt that I needed to have my own contact with so large a proportion of the United Nations family. I accordingly decided on Moshe Tov's advice to learn Spanish myself. When I looked around for methods of achieving this ambition, it seemed to me that the easiest would be to attend all the speeches by Victor Belaunde, a prominent diplomat and jurist from Peru. Belaunde's speeches had the pedagogic virtue of being long, exquisitely eloquent and sufficiently repetitive to make provision for a didactic effect.

Some years later I was to have a haunting experience. Between the years 1960 and 1964, I had no part in the United Nations' proceedings, since my work in Israel was confined to the parliamentary arena and to my own ministry of education and culture. My last memory of the General Assembly before laying down my embassy there in late 1959 was of going into the assembly chamber to say my farewells. When I left the hall, Belaunde was speaking with thunderous passion on the roster. When I returned to that same hall five years later, there was Belaunde on the same platform, a little grayer than before. For me this coincidence symbolized the unchanging continuity of the UN process. I turned to my alphabetical neighbor from Ireland, the distinguished writer Conor Cruise O'Brien, and asked him how long Belaunde had been speaking. "Only for two hours," was his reply.

I pursued the matter further. "What is the subject of his speech?" I asked. "He hasn't yet decided," replied O'Brien.

I intended to return from Paris to New York in order to continue with the consolidation of the delegation of which I was the head. While I was engaged in my UN work during December, dramatic events occurred in America. Secretary Marshall had precipitately pledged American support to the Bernadotte plan and I feared that he would continue his fidelity to the plan's territorial provisions, even after its defeat in the General Assembly. A week before the election, Truman's Republican adversary, Governor Thomas

Dewey, made a speech strongly attacking Truman for betraying Israel by allowing his secretary of state, George Marshall, to advocate the excision of the Negev from Israel's territory. At that time our boundaries were not recognized formally by any state or international authority. Dewey's speech left Truman himself no other course but to go before the public at Madison Square Garden and swear devoutly that he would never be a party to such a painful operation at Israel's expense. The Negev, said Truman, must remain in Israel and Galilee did not have to be taken away.

Truman's greatest moment of satisfaction came on election day, when he was able to brandish a headline from *The Chicago Tribune* prematurely announcing in the largest possible letters "Dewey Elected!!"

I had to go back to Tel Aviv to report on the results of our work at the General Assembly session. This was not strictly necessary, since the results were well known and generally greeted with relief. Sharett, however, had been persuaded to go to an agreeable Mediterranean resort in the south of France. He called me up agitatedly to say that he found the process of taking a vacation completely intolerable. Resting in a quiet place was to him a grave affliction that brought him very close to a breakdown of his nervous system. He asked me innocently what there was to be done in the south of France. Knowing something about his temperament, I hesitated to recommend such joys as golf and fishing. He replied that he would only agree to rest in the French Riviera if I would go home to Tel Aviv on his behalf in a kind of exploratory mission to tell Ben-Gurion and his colleagues exactly what we had achieved and what we had thwarted.

Sharett's total inability to come to terms with leisure reflected the characteristic single-mindedness of Zionist leaders. Chaim Weizmann's thousands of letters preserved in his Rehovot archives deal with only two themes: Zionism and science in relation to Zionism. He was impatient with fundamental, theoretical speculation. He put his formidable scientific talent to work exclusively in applied technologies that could be turned to account for immediate use, either to serve the economy or security of the nascent Jewish state or to furnish an incentive for governments to seek his favor. One of his letters bears a date that coincides with an earthquake in an Italian town that he was visiting. In his letter to his wife Weizmann makes no mention of any such small detail, while his contacts with Zionist leaders and Italian statesmen are exhaustively reviewed.

At the height of his fame as a statesman in London, where he behaved as though he was already the head of a sovereign state, Weizmann often caused problems when he attended dinners in which there was political conversation. If the subject of conversation departed from the theme of Zionism for any length of time, he would sink into a sulky petulance that usually had an intimidating effect on the other guests. He would revive and enrich the table only when the talk came back to a Zionist theme.

Ben-Gurion was no less single-minded. He was married to his wife, Paula

Mabovitch, on December 5, 1917, in a New York Registry Office. He wrote in his diary: "11.30 I got married." As soon as the brief ceremony was completed, he said with relief: "Now I can go back to the meeting" (of the Zionist Action Committee). The idea of anything that could be called a honeymoon was utterly alien to Zionist nature. It was the kind of cause that demanded obsessive and unreserved devotion. Sharett was more open than most of his colleagues to general themes of intellectual and cultural experience, but the idea of awakening to a day free of Zionist action violated the austerities to which he had consecrated his life and career.

When I arrived back in Tel Aviv, I discovered as I expected that my journey was not really essential, for the air was tranquil and serene. Nevertheless, the military situation in the Negev was still tense. The major domestic development had been the total elimination of all the dissident military organizations. Ben-Gurion had reacted fiercely to the murder of Bernadotte. Not for the first time an armed action with far-reaching political consequences had been taken outside the range of constituted authority. Ben-Gurion feared that if this kind of thing went on, there might be an impression that the Jewish people was constitutionally incapable of maintaining a recognized authority. He felt that Israeli sovereignty was involved here just as surely as it had been in the *Altalena* incident and the murder of Lord Moyne. He now understood that the voluntarist era of Zionism was at an end and that his office as minister of defense authorized him to insist on the total disbandment of all military forces other than the Israeli Army.

Menachem Begin, the Irgun leader, had understood the implications for Israel's sovereignty and had cooperated in the merger of the dissident forces with the main body of the Israeli Defense Forces. This marked the end of separatist actions by the dissident organizations until the storm over the German Compensation Agreement in 1952.

Historians will long dispute the precise weight of the small resistance organizations in the process that had led to Israel's independence. Their claim to primary credit is exaggerated. If the main body of Palestine Jews with the Haganah at their head had not pursued a policy of resistance, together with a patient diplomacy, the military effort of the Irgun and Lechi would have been marginal and, in the case of Lechi, negative. All the resistance groups separately and together did help to create the conditions of intolerability in which Britain decided to surrender its role. The dissidents certainly inculcated in their followers an authentic resistant spirit, including readiness for ultimate sacrifice on behalf of a national cause. On the other hand, their indiscipline weakened the political cause and raised seeds of internal conflict that would harass Israel for many decades to come.

9

OUR FLAG WAS NOW
THERE

ON JANUARY 7, 1949, Israeli fighters shot down five British planes—four Spitfires and one Mosquito—which had been carrying out flights over Israeli positions near the Egyptian-Israeli boundary. A powerfully equipped British base had been established by the conquest of the Suez Canal area in 1875. I had no doubt that the Egyptian government, concerned at the consolidation of Israeli positions in the Negev, had sought reconnaissance assistance from the British forces in the Canal. The British were long accustomed to doing as they liked in the Middle East and had not imagined that they would suffer interception at the Israeli border by an air force to which they attributed no power.

We seemed to be approaching great-power status. We were taking on not only the Arab world but also what was then the major military power in the Middle East, guided by a foreign secretary of exceptional malevolence toward us. Our air force must surely have been the most modest entity to which the phrase "air force" had ever been applied. Yet here it was inflicting humiliation on the prestigious air force of the few to whom the many had owed so much.

After obtaining intelligence about the relative size of the British and Israeli air strengths, I thought it imprudent to gloat. It was urgent to bring this David-Goliath spectacle to a decent end before it dawned on Goliath that David did not even possess an effective sling.

Foreign Minister Sharett had renounced his unsuccessful attempt to celebrate a leisurely vacation in the south of France and had returned to the welcome congenialities of a busy ministerial routine in Israel. At his request I left Jerusalem and flew back to the UN, where I found that the British deputy delegate, Sir Terence Shone, had called on my deputy, Arthur Lourie, with a protest. But his letter was addressed, absurdly, to "The Jewish Authorities in Palestine" and I had instructed Lourie to accept diplomatic representations only if they were properly addressed. The British protest was returned unopened. It could not have happened to a British government many times before.

Many people, even among our friends, had not yet awakened to the fact of Israel's sovereignty. Even so staunch a supporter as Justice Felix Frankfurter believed that we had exceeded our station in life. Frankfurter had developed a very strong Anglophilia. He kept in close touch with British politics and constantly evoked his two years as visiting professor at Oxford. I assured him that a U.K.-Israeli air battle would be such a bizarre development in the eyes of the British public that it might inspire saner counsels than Bevin had been displaying over the three years of his anti-Zionist vendetta.

It now turned out, as so often in our history, that "sweetness cometh out of strength." It was incredible to most people in Israel and even in Britain that Bevin should still be fighting against Israeli sovereignty eight months after the issue had been decided against him.

Some of us feared that the loss of its aircraft would spur the British people to a vengeful assertion of defiance and to violent reactions with anti-Jewish overtones. Exactly the opposite occurred. The greatest British voice made this the occasion for a triumphant vindication of Zionism. In a stormy debate in the House of Commons, Winston Churchill rose to his highest flights of oratory, leaving Bevin gasping for breath in the throes of parliamentary defeat. Churchill spoke in the familiar growl:

> I am quite sure that the Right Honorable Gentleman will have to recognize the Israeli government and that this cannot be long delayed. I regret that he has not had the manliness to tell us that tonight and that he preferred to retire under a cloud of inky water, like a cuttlefish, to some obscure retreat.

Churchill then answered what he called the "imaginary objections" to recognizing Israel as a state: These had included Bevin's own passionate assertion that states with unsettled boundaries are rarely recognized in international bodies.

> There are half a dozen countries in Europe which are recognized today whose territorial frontiers are not finally settled. Surely Poland is one. It is only with the General Peace Treaty that a final settlement could be made. How absurd it is to compare the so-called Republic of Indonesia with the setting up in Tel Aviv of a government of the State of Israel with an effective organization and a victorious army.

In a final rhetorical flight the great voice boomed across history:

> Whether the Right Honorable Gentleman likes it or not, and whether we like it or not, the coming into being of a Jewish state in Palestine is

an event in world history to be viewed in the perspective not of a generation or a century, but in the perspective of a thousand, two thousand or even three thousand years. That is a standard of temporal values or time values which seems very much out of accord with a perpetual click-clack of our rapidly changing moods and of the age in which we live. This is an event in world history. How vain it is to compare it with the recognition or the claims to recognition by certain other countries.

He added:

Many in the Conservative Party, including myself, have always had in mind that the Jewish National Home in Palestine might some day develop into a Jewish state.

Churchill was not prepared to leave his condemnation of Bevin at this point. He uttered a charge that was unusual in House of Commons history.

All this is due not only to mental inertia or lack of grip on the part of the ministers concerned, but also, I am afraid, to the very strong and direct streak of bias and prejudice on the part of the Foreign Secretary.

Churchill said that he was sure that Britain could have obtained both Arab and Jewish support for a partition scheme whereby two separate states, one Jewish and the other Arab, would have been set up in Palestine. When the prime minister, Clement Attlee, interrupted him to say, "May I ask you if you thought that could have been done, why did you not do it immediately after the war? You were in power." Mr. Churchill replied, "No, the world and the nation had the inestimable blessing of the Right Honorable Gentleman's guidance." Attlee seemed to have forgotten that he had taken office in the summer of 1945, before the war had even ended!

In an unexpected part of his speech, Churchill attacked the notion that an Israeli state would be too small to absorb a great population. He said:

The idea that only a limited number of people can live in a country is a profound illusion. It all depends on their cooperative and inventive power. There are more people today living twenty stories above the ground in New York than were living on the ground in New York a hundred years ago. There is no limit to the ingenuity of man if it is properly and vigorously applied under conditions of peace and justice.

Who else in our generation could have packed all this experience, authority and good humor into a twenty-minute speech? No historian can doubt that this address spelled the collapse of Bevin's policy and would lead inevitably to British recognition of Israel. This came in nine days.

Recognition of Israel by Britain was not the only historic development of importance in January 1949. The Egyptian government had drawn prudent conclusions from the fighting in the Negev. The Security Council had opened a window when in November 1948, during the sessions in Paris, it adopted a Canadian proposal to initiate a more stable juridical and security relationship between Israel and its neighbors. This took the form of a proposal for General Armistice Agreements to be concerted between Israel and each neighboring Arab state.

While in Paris I had sounded out Security Council delegates on the need for a better framework than that provided by repetitive truces and cease-fires. My chief interlocutors were Lester Pearson of Canada and Philip Jessup, who had taken over the leadership of the United States delegation in the Security Council. The outcome was a Canadian proposal submitted in November 1948, calling upon Israel and the Arab states, then referred to as "the governments and authorities in the Middle East," to enter into negotiations under the auspices of the acting mediator, Ralph Bunche, in order to conclude armistice agreements, including the establishment of agreed armistice demarcation lines. I had spoken strongly for that proposal in the Security Council during the second and third weeks of November. Despite strong Arab opposition, the Canadian resolution was eventually adopted on November 16.

It was a turning point. It virtually made the establishment of provisional boundaries dependent on the realities of the battlefield to which, after all, the Arab governments had confided the outcome of the conflict. If we could achieve an armistice of this nature without any time limitation, we would be liberated from a constant feeling of volcanic suspense between one fragile truce and another.

By the turn of the year, the Egyptian government had decided to regard exchanges of fire as unproductive. The Canadian proposal for "General Armistice Agreements" had been adopted by the Security Council at its Paris meeting on November 16, 1948. In the perspectives of those days, it was the first act of conciliation ever concluded between an Arab country and a Jewish state, and the reverberation was very strong in the international community.

The negotiations had been conducted in the serenity of the beautiful Greek island of Rhodes. Although in theory it was concluded between military officers, the head of our delegation was Walter Eytan, the director general of the Foreign Ministry, with the participation of Reuven Shiloah, the permanent gray eminence of our Intelligence services. The army was represented at its highest level by General Yigael Yadin, who had been the supreme commander of our forces for the greater part of the war of independence.

The signature of an armistice agreement with Egypt on February 24, 1949, must be added to the glittering chain of diplomatic achievements that had begun in May 1948 and that were evidently not at an end. The initial Arab reaction to the idea of an armistice had been hostile, but by early 1949, the Egyptian hold on the Israeli Negev was broken and Israeli forces bent on opening the road in the Negev had entered northeastern Sinai and advanced toward Rafiah. In that atmosphere, the episode of the five British aircraft brought down by Israeli guns stimulated Egypt to review its position and to abandon its militancy. It used the Canadian resolution of November 16 as a face-saving bridge toward the negotiating table. Thus, all in all, the year between May 1948 and May 1949 had been Israel's wondrous year. We would never know the like of it again.

The negotiations at Rhodes began separately between Bunche and each delegation, but the absurdity of this separation became so manifest that after a few days the delegations were facing each other across a single table, under Bunche's inspired leadership.

When the text was agreed on February 24 and was studied in the world capitals, it became clear that the system of relations that it described went far beyond the normal concept of an armistice. There was, of course, the provision for a cessation of fire; but this was accompanied by a rigorous undertaking that the cease-fire would be permanent and would last until a final peace settlement had been achieved. Thus the agreement had none of the permissive indulgence to renewed belligerency, which was always implicit in the classic concept of armistice. On the contrary, the object of the agreement was defined as the promotion of "a return of permanent peace to Palestine." It was described as "an indispensable step toward the liquidation of armed conflict and the restoration of peace."

It is true that the demarcation lines were not described as permanent, but since they could only be changed by agreement, they were similar in every practical sense to permanent boundaries, which are also subject to change by agreement. Speaking as chairman of the conference, Bunche added a sentence that was to reverberate in future crises in 1956 and 1967:

There should be free movement for legitimate shipping and no vestige of the wartime blockade should be allowed to remain, as they are inconsistent with both the letter and the spirit of the armistice agreements.

This provision was to be central in my mind when in September 1951 I successfully appealed to the Security Council to rule that the blockade of Israeli ships and goods in the Suez Canal was illegal.

It is no reflection on the memory of Bernadotte in human terms to say that the advent of Ralph Bunche to the role of UN mediator reinforced the cause of conciliation in the Middle East. When he received the Nobel Peace Prize for his achievement, he was the most eminent black American in the international arena. His achievement is reflected in the fact that the life of Israel still flows, for the greater part, in the channels of authority and legitimacy that Bunche had conjured out of the turmoil of 1949.

Bunche had a depressed childhood in New York, when black Americans saw nothing but bleak horizons before them. By solid academic effort, he had become renowned in the black community as a respected leader without being a strident or militant activist. The US State Department, more sensitive than usual to the special ethnic makeup of an international organization, deputed him to the upper reaches of the UN Secretariat. He had a quiet, slow manner of speech and carried unobtrusiveness to great lengths. He seemed to be obsessed by a decision not to be conspicuous. But his patent integrity and capacity for mastering his assignments enabled him to enter slowly into the confidence of those with whom he had business to transact. His first connection with Jewish affairs came after Horowitz and I were appointed as liaison officers with UNSCOP: Secretary-General Trygve Lie had told us that Bunche, rather than his nominal senior, Victor Hoo of Nationalist China, would be our main contact with the UN Special Committee.

Without the least evidence of demonstrativeness, Bunche had revealed a sudden and drastic surge of emotion when the extent of the Jewish tragedy entered deeply into his consciousness. He was therefore emotionally balanced in his attitude to the two peoples contending for position in Palestine. The Arabs, in his eyes, were the victims of imperialistic and colonialist domination since medieval times; and the Jews were the victims of totalitarianism and blatant racism. Bunche could not detach himself from either of the two parties, nor could he give himself wholly to either of them. He was not above traditional stratagems of diplomatic virtuosity. To the Arabs he gave the impression that the borders that he was crystallizing in the maps attached to the agreements were open to their hope of improvement. To us Israelis he stressed the solidly entrenched nature of the armistice lines and the practical difficulty that anyone seeking modification would inevitably encounter. This was not duplicity: Both of these elements were justifiable in terms of the actual texts of the General Armistice Agreements.

The UN structure excluded charismatic pretensions for Bunche, even if he ever harbored them. It is traditional practice for the UN to avoid appointing a citizen of any of the permanent members for the role of secretary-general. After his triumph at Rhodes and the sequel in the agreements with Lebanon, Jordan and Syria, Bunche reverted to his subordinate status and served Trygve Lie, Hammarskjöld and U Thant loyally. He worked sedulously with Hammarskjöld and Lester Pearson to create and maintain the peacekeeping forces of the United Nations that served devotedly, and sometimes sacrificially, in areas of conflict.

The Egyptian-Israeli armistice set up a strong momentum. On March 23 a similar agreement was signed between Israel and Lebanon after negotiations at the international boundary at Ras el Nakoura. As water flows into a canal, so did Israeli life grow and develop within the armistice lines until their quaint contours were to become the familiar shape of Israel.

In telegrams and memoranda that I sent to the Israeli government in Jerusalem in March 1949, I appealed to its members and especially to the Foreign Ministry to present the armistice agreements with our four contiguous neighbors as the foundation of our policy. I suggested that we call them boundaries and not demarcation lines. I explained that in fact they superseded the far more parsimonious territorial provisions of the November 29, 1947, Resolution. This, after all, had been only a recommendation to the Mandatory government that that government had, in accordance with its Charter rights, refused to accept. The armistice agreements, on the other hand, had contractual force that constitutes the highest expression of international law. As we look back from our present vantage point in time, it becomes evident that the armistice system was a remarkable success. Bunche fully deserved his Nobel Prize.

The armistice agreement with Egypt and the consequent release of the Egyptians encircled at Faluja liberated a young officer, Gamal Abdel Nasser, for the continuation of his revolutionary struggle.

He had fought several battles in Palestine, apparently with valor. Six years later he wrote that he detested war. He said to himself that "humanity does not deserve to live if it does not work with all its strength for peace." In his recollection of the 1948 war with Israel, Nasser added: "When I learned that one of my friends had been killed, I swore that if one day I found myself in a responsible position, I should think a thousand times before sending our soldiers to war. I should only do it if it were absolutely necessary, if the fatherland were threatened and if nothing else could save it but the fire of battle."

The Arab governments, had they been wise, would have accepted Israel's assurances that these marked the end of our territorial ambition. If they had done so, they could have obtained the strongest and most universal international guarantees. The West Bank and Gaza would now be under Palestinian rule. The Arab governments assumed that any subsequent change could only be to their benefit, and they refused to acknowledge the permanence of the armistice map. In their rhetoric and jurisprudence they constantly stressed its provisional character. They kept alive the hope and dream that one day the armistice lines and the State of Israel would be swept away by successful force. From 1967 onward they were to regret their tenacious struggle to deny permanent validity to the armistice lines.

Apart from their stabilizing regional effects, the armistice agreements gave a sharp stimulus to our campaign for international recognition. In the summer of 1948, American and Soviet embassies were established in Tel Aviv. Israel did not claim Jerusalem as its capital when independence was proclaimed. On one messianic occasion, the flags of the two superpowers flew in unison over a modest hotel on the Tel Aviv shoreline in which both ambassadors happened to be staying at the same time. There was in fact nowhere else for them to stay. The American ambassador, James G. McDonald, and his Soviet colleague, Pavel Yershov, became conspicuous figures in Israeli society. They were stared at with the faintly incredulous awe whereby Israeli citizens registered the fact that great nations of the world now recognized their statehood, and had to present their credentials to our eminent president, Chaim Weizmann. So the wave of recognition swept over most European countries, the Commonwealth and all of Latin America.

This led me to feel that the time was propitious for us to try our luck again on the crucial question of membership in the United Nations. I made application for admission.

France and Canada had joined the five states that had voted for our admission at the 1948 Paris session of the General Assembly. They were joined by Norway and China, with Egypt as the only negative vote and the United Kingdom in embarrassed abstention. The Arabs considered this abstention to be an insult to them, since they had become accustomed to Bevin's unqualified identification with their cause. To me and to most Israelis the abstention seemed somewhat parsimonious and grudging since Britain had, after all, given full recognition to Israel two months before under the impact of Churchill's verbal bombardment. It is curious that Bevin had no desire to end his career with a graceful gesture, for his health and consequently his political condition was in sharp decline, and within a year and two months he would be dead.

It seemed on the surface that the Arab attempt to challenge Israel's legitimacy as a state had collapsed. Yet in large parts of the Arab world no such logic was yet accepted. Israel's non-membership in the United Nations seemed to symbolize the unfinished nature of our enterprise. I felt that it was urgent to correct this anomaly, since it had a great bearing on our relations with a world that still had difficulty in getting used to the idea of a sovereign Israel. The question that I was determined to put to the General Assembly was: "How do you expect the Arab world to recognize Israel if you yourselves do not give it your own recognition?"

When the General Assembly met in special session in April 1949 to take up the unfinished business left over from Paris, I hoped that our request for membership would be ratified quickly in the preliminary session, as had been done in all previous membership decisions. The massive nine-to-one vote in the Security Council encouraged this optimism. I should have known better. Israel, after all, is the exception to every rule. When the secretary-general proposed that Israel's application for membership should be considered and voted upon according to the normal procedure, in a plenary session of the General Assembly, the Arabs mustered support for the motion that the matter be referred to an ad hoc committee consisting of all the members. The only difference between a plenary meeting of the General Assembly and a meeting of one of the committees is that in the former the speakers address the Assembly standing at a rostrum, whereas in the committee they are seated around a table. A resolution with a heavy majority in the committee can count on adoption in the plenum a day or two later.

The motive for submission to the committee was substantive and ominous. At best, our adversaries would stretch out the debate across large vistas of time and thus secure postponement until the September 1950 session. At worst, they would sell their acquiescence dearly and attempt to extort language from me, which would amount to an erosion of our national interests. It was clear that I would be faced with a detailed scrutiny in the political committee.

Sharett regarded the submission to a committee as a very hard blow. He no longer believed that we would succeed in our application. At best we would be required to give such undertakings in return for membership as would seriously prejudice our sovereignty and security. He decided, despite my more optimistic protestations, to leave New York for Israel and to entrust the entire membership struggle to my hands. I accompanied him to the airport in New York, where a newspaperman asked him about Israel and the United Nations. He said with extreme irascibility, "I'm much more confident about the survival of Israel than I am about the survival of the United Nations."

I thought to myself that if this was going to be his mood and style, it would perhaps be better for him to stay away. Sharett had been exhausted by the asperities of our domestic politics. He was not showing the exemplary patience that he had tried to inculcate into all of us and that would have to be our most essential commodity for the coming months. The domestic political honeymoon that Sharett had enjoyed during our international successes was fast wearing off. He was a statesman of high quality, but he would also have to be a politician fighting hard on his home ground. The Herut party (the precursor of the Likud) had made Ben-Gurion and, still more, Sharett the targets of vehement rhetoric. Moreover, in spite of their general reverence for all the external symbols of statehood, Herut was opposing the very idea of Israel's seeking admission into the United Nations. Its official organ, *Hamashkif,* openly opposed our membership application in its issue of April 27, 1949. That newspaper wrote: "Greater, older, stronger states than us are standing outside the organization and do not even attempt to enter it. No harm has come to them from this." I considered this to be nonsense. The truth is that "the greater, older, stronger states" were unchallenged in their statehood and all of them, with the exception of Switzerland, were either members or were passionately attempting to achieve membership. I presumed that the real reason for Begin's resistance to our membership was twofold. First, as the opposition leader he naturally wished to arrest the momentum of the Labor Party's international successes. Second, more substantively, he feared that entering the United Nations would imply satisfaction with our existing territorial configuration. When he left the Cabinet on August 4, we felt that our councils had one of two plans.

As if this unexpected opposition were not sufficiently disconcerting, I suddenly found myself exposed to the opposition of Dr. Nahum Goldmann, who was diametrically opposed to Begin across the political spectrum. The adversaries of these two distinguished leaders used to say that there was no Israeli territory that Begin would ever give up and none that Goldmann would ever insist on keeping. Neither of these assertions was true, as subsequent history would prove. Goldmann thought that Israel would have a better chance of maintaining a neutral attitude if it was not called on to pronounce on controversial international issues. My own conviction was that nothing could be more disastrous to our hope of peace with the Arab nations than to leave an unnecessary mark of interrogation over our status. I failed to understand how we could possibly claim the benefits of sovereignty without paying a price in burden and responsibility. Moreover, countries such as Sweden and, at a later stage, Austria and Finland, had no difficulty whatever in reaping the advantages of membership without prejudice to their neutrality.

When Sharett's airliner disappeared into the distant horizon, I turned back to my car and reflected with shock that I now had to direct a political operation that had no precedent in international history. No other state had ever been called upon to vindicate its membership by being submitted to cross-examination, advocacy and rebuttals as though it were a defendant in a criminal trial. The UN Political Committee had fifty-eight members, and my modest wish was to make them fifty-nine. The chairman of that committee, elected by the General Assembly, was the Philippine statesman General Carlos Romulo.

I regarded him as a friend of our cause. However, he was a man for whom the flow of rhetoric was a staple diet. He would dearly have liked to make the most of his opportunity, not least because he aspired to higher rank than that of ambassador to the United Nations, and that of political committee chairmanship. He wanted the office of foreign minister at home and that of the president of the General Assembly abroad.

He proposed to invite me to the table to make a statement in support of our admission, then to listen to questions and observations by member states, and thereafter to explain how, if we were elected, we would shape our policies on refugees, boundaries, Jerusalem and responsibility for the assassination of Count Bernadotte.

Romulo was a man for large occasions and spectacular performances. It was evident that I would be the defendant in a noisy trial in a biased court and that I would certainly be asked whether Israel still regarded itself as bound by all the provisions of the 1947 partition resolution against which our neighbors had violently fought.

I now began to reflect that Sharett had not been all that improvident in taking a swift homeward flight. Romulo told me that I would have unlimited time for my speech. It was his religious belief that speech was the greatest endowment of man and that all speakers should have unlimited time for everything. Arriving at the table with blinding television klieg lights upon me, I decided to begin with the kind of offensive that is usually regarded as the best form of defense. Pointing to the Arab delegates, I said:

> We are as one who, having been attacked in a dark street by seven men with heavy bludgeons, finds himself dragged into court, only to see his assailants sitting on the bench with an air of solemn virtue, delivering homilies on the duties of a peaceful citizen. Here sit representatives of the only states which have deliberately used force against the General Assembly Resolution—the only states which have ever been determined by the Security Council to have caused a threat of the peace, posing as the disinterested judges of their own intended victim in his efforts to secure a modest equality in the family of nations.

This was far closer to an explanation of why the Arab states should not be members of the United Nations than an explanation of why Israel should be such a member. I could see, however, that accusing and reproachful eyes were turned upon the Arab countries.

I felt that this was much more effective than making perilous definitions of our position on boundaries, refugees, Jerusalem and responsibility for the death of Count Bernadotte. On the boundary question, I said somewhat daringly that Israel and the Arab states had a perfect right to agree on such changes in the 1947 boundary proposals that seemed essential to them. They should negotiate on this subject at the Lausanne Conference called by the Palestine Conciliation Commission.

My proposal on Jerusalem was that international authority should be applied, not to the city as a whole but to that which was truly universal and international, namely the Holy Places and the rights of religious communities. It was essential to separate the secular from the spiritual aspects of Jerusalem.

In my opening speech, the questions by members, the attacks by Arab states and the ebb and flow of reply, caused me to sit at the Security Council's table for nine hours. Nothing of the sort has happened to any applicant state, either before or since. I concluded:

> Whatever intellectual or spiritual forces Israel evokes are at the service of the United Nations as a reinforcement of its activity and prestige. You will certainly lose nothing and you may perhaps gain some modest asset if you join our banner to your honored company. A great wheel of history comes full circle today as Israel, renewed and established, offers itself, with all its imperfections, but perhaps with

some virtues, to the defense of the human spirit, against nihilism, conflict and despair.

It was now important not to lose ground when the preliminary session came to ratify the committee's decision. We had gained more than a two-thirds majority in the committee, and if that voting endured or was even enhanced, we would be safely home. Before the vote was taken, however, obstacles suddenly appeared in Washington. The assistant secretary for UN affairs, Dean Rusk, telephoned our ambassador, Eliahu Elath, and complained that I had not gone far enough in my address to explain the concessions that Israel was willing to make about refugees, Jerusalem and boundaries. He said further that the vote on Israel's admission to the UN might go against us unless we complied with the State Department's wishes on these matters.

It was a not very subtle attempt at political extortion. It was obviously Rusk's duty to attempt this gambit, as it was my duty to ignore it. We had taken a head count and we were miles ahead of the support that we had on November 29, 1947. I told Elath that if we stood firm, I was sure that we would get our membership without any unnecessary complications. I was willing to make concessions in a peace negotiation, but not to gain a status that the Arabs had already achieved without any price.

It was now certain that the substantive decision for our membership had been taken in the committee and that the plenary session would have little but protocolar and image-making importance. I knew, however, that it was customary for newly elected members to make a very brief speech of thanks. As I began to prepare this, I suddenly thought of Sharett, not of Moshe Sharett the foreign minister, but Moshe Sharett the friend. I remembered how the opportunity that he had given me in the small hours of May 1 had projected me large distances forward to a pinnacle in my career. Although I had fought the admission battle alone, in spite of his skepticism, and would certainly enjoy being in the spotlight, I felt that I was bound historically and morally to send Sharett an urgent cable: "You must, repeat, you must come make speech of acceptance. We shall hold up the voting if necessary." Back came a quick reply: "What happens if I set out from Tel Aviv to come to the General Assembly and the plenary session does not give us the required two-thirds? Won't I look foolish?"

I did not think that this was the right approach. In fact, his whole mood and attitude on the struggle for our admission continues to puzzle me to this day. I could only reply that I could almost guarantee a favorable vote, but if he wanted to be overly cautious he could have a plane ready and as soon as the actual vote started and I could be positive of the outcome, he could start for New York. I would try to delay the speech-making. Back in Tel Aviv, Sharett at last allowed himself to be convinced and boarded a plane at once without waiting for the certainties of the ratifying vote.

THE CAMBRIDGE UNION was my first arena of oratory. Here are the Committee members, along with guest speakers George Strauss, MP, and Kenneth Lindsay, MP (front row left, first and second), both of whom became Cabinet ministers. Of our own group, one became Finance Minister of India and I (far right) became Foreign Minister of Israel.

THE ZIONIST CONGRESS, Geneva, August 24, 1939. This was the moment when the Zionist leaders learned that Ribbentrop and Molotov had signed the Soviet-German pact. We understood that war was now inevitable. [From left to right: Moshe Shertok (Sharett), David Ben-Gurion, Chaim Weizmann, Eliezer Kaplan.] Weizmann rose to disperse the Congress saying, "There is darkness all around us and we cannot see through the clouds . . ."

THE ZIONIST FLAG in Cairo in April 1942. Cairo was a tolerant place then. Here I am with Moshe Sharett, later Israel's foreign minister, the chief chaplain to the British Forces Rabbi Israel Brodie (later Chief Rabbi of Britain), and Reuven Shiloah in the foreground.

MAJOR EBAN, 1945.

JERUSALEM, 1946. MAJOR Eban with the officers of the Middle East Center on Arab Studies. I was the vice principal and senior tutor in Arabic. I wore civilian clothes since I was now a foreign office official.

WITH CHAIM WEIZMANN as he gave evidence to UNSCOP, Jerusalem, 1947.

AN IMPORTANT MOMENT. At a press conference in Geneva, at midnight on August 31/September 1, 1942, I announced, "I have just received the report of the UN Committee (UNSCOP) which contains a proposal to establish a Jewish state."

MY FIRST APPEARANCE at the Security Council, May 1948. Seated next to me, from right to left are: Warren Austin, U.S.; Sir Alexander Cadogan, UK; Andrei Gromyko, USSR; and Vassil Tarasenko, Ukraine. (United Nations)

IN MY NINE y
1951. Here he
be seen, beam

WITH SECRET
aid, which h

WITH RALPH BUNCHE.

ON SEVERAL OCCASIONS I made great—and not unsuccessful—efforts to win the trust of American Jews, as at this "Salute to Israel" at Yankee Stadium in 1956.

AFTER ELEVEN YEARS as chief delegate to the UN, Suzy and I were given a farewell party in 1959 by the UN elder statesmen. Here we are with Eleanor Roosevelt and the president of the Security Council, Sir Pierson Dixon. (Courtesy of Israeli Office of Information)

MY FIRST
Office of I

IN MY NINE years as ambassador, Prime Minister Ben-Gurion came to America only once, in 1951. Here he is arriving in Washington, D.C., with his wife, Paula. A young Teddy Kollek can be seen, beaming, behind her.

WITH SECRETARY OF State Acheson. At this moment, Israel became eligible for American foreign aid, which has brought in tens of billions of dollars over the ensuing years.

WITH SOVIET FOREIGN Minister Andrei Vyshinski, 1953. We were both vice presidents of the UN General Assembly. (Courtesy of Israeli Office of Information)

THE DRAMA OF Ethiopian Jews began in the reign of Emperor Haile Selassie, whom I met at the United Nations and again in Addis Ababa. (Courtesy of Israeli Office of Information)

AT THE UN, with a friend in a moment of crisis: the Canadian foreign minister (Mike) Lester Pearson, in 1956 during the Suez debate.

FOR SIX YEARS of my embassy in Washington, the secretary of state was John Foster Dulles. Here he is at the height of the 1956 Suez Crisis.

PLAYERS IN THE Suez Crisis included: Harold Macmillan, UK; John Foster Dulles, U.S.; Maurice Couve de Murville, France; President Eisenhower; and Paul-Henri Spaak, Belgium. (Courtesy of Dwight D. Eisenhower Library)

THIS WAS THE night of high tension between the U.S. (Dulles and Lodge) and Israel (Eban with legal adviser Jacob Robinson and Mordecai "Reggie" Kidron.) (United Nations)

WITH PRESIDENT HARRY Truman, Governor Herbert Lehman of New York and Chief Justice Warren (back to camera) at the Liberty Bell in Philadelphia, commemorating the tenth anniversary of the State of Israel, 1958.

I OFTEN SHARED platforms with John F. Kennedy before he became president in 1961.

I SERVED THROUGH most of the Eisen-hower regime.

ON SEVERAL OCCASIONS I made great—and not unsuccessful—efforts to win the trust of American Jews, as at this "Salute to Israel" at Yankee Stadium in 1956.

AFTER ELEVEN YEARS as chief delegate to the UN, Suzy and I were given a farewell party in 1959 by the UN elder statesmen. Here we are with Eleanor Roosevelt and the president of the Security Council, Sir Pierson Dixon. (Courtesy of Israeli Office of Information)

AT HOME IN Rehovot, with Suzy, Eli, Gila and our dog, Ringo, 1960.

THE NEPALESE AMBASSADOR presents his credentials to Israel's President Zalman Shazar.

ADDRESSING ARABS IN Arabic. Nazareth, April 1966.

As PRESIDENT OF the Weizmann Institute in Rehovot, I confer an honorary degree on Dr. Konrad Adenauer (center). Beside him, from left, are Professor Yigal Talmi, Meyer Weisgal and Nahum Goldmann.

The speech of the representative of the Dominican Republic advocating our membership had already begun when word was flashed from the New York international airport that Sharett's plane had landed and he was on his way to Flushing Meadow by police-escorted car.

After the presentation speech, the president of the General Assembly, Herbert V. Evatt, the foreign minister of Australia, announced in his sharp, cockney-like twang that Israel had been elected in accordance with the provisions of the Charter, and that the two-thirds majority had been duly recorded. Sharett, who had very recently entered the hall, was in time to hear the vociferous applause. He made his speech, ending with a solemn Hebrew declamation of the words of the great prophet of Jerusalem, Isaiah: "Nation shall not lift up the sword against nation, neither shall they learn war anymore."

The next morning we went out into the summer sun and I raised the Israeli flag on the flagpole with a sharp and emotional tug of the rope. We had come a long way since the days of solitude and adversity.

It was already clear to me that the decision we had just obtained had a far more compelling force than anything that had occurred in 1947. The November 1947 Resolution created no legal obligations. It was a recommendation that those addressed by it could either accept or reject. On November 30, 1947, Israel's status in the international community was just as it had been on November 28. Not a single act of recognition flowed from the 1947 Resolution. But regardless of the nature of General Assembly or Security Council resolutions, membership in the UN would always be a symbol of national equality and dignity. It was the most visible outward sign of Israel's return to full sovereignty after so many centuries in the political wilderness.

The provision of the Charter discussing membership in the UN speaks of "the sovereign equality of all its members." This meant that Israel's juridical and international status was now and thereafter equivalent to that of the United States, the Soviet Union, Britain and each of the Arab states whose own membership had only recently been confirmed. The resolution endorsing our admission contained the word "decides." On all other matters, the General Assembly can only recommend. It does, however, have the acknowledged and universally accepted right to define the structure of the international community through its membership. Thus, UN General Assembly Resolution 273 is by far the most crucial document in Israel's international armory.

Suzy and I got into a cab and, as I remember, kept almost total silence as we drove back to Manhattan. Quite apart from the transition that had taken place in our nation's status, from the depths of despair to high peaks of exaltation in a period of less than three years, it would have been difficult to find words proportionate to the event.

When I entered the political committee room the next morning to take Israel's place at the table, I could see that the Iraqi and the Lebanese delegates were leaning across the empty space in which the Israeli chair was situated. They were conversing in some agitation. Several times during the morning, whenever there was a pause in the proceedings, the Iraqi and Lebanese delegates would lean toward each other behind my back and engage in whispered conversations, sometimes in a very confidential nature, about the procedures with which they hoped to confound me. This went on for several days, to my delight, until someone warned the two Arab delegates that I understood every Arabic word that they were saying. Immediately the whispering stopped and was superseded by the passage of written chits back and forth behind my back.

The next morning the first evidence of our new stature became evident. Instead of haunting the halls and lounges of the General Assembly, seeking votes for Israel, I suddenly found myself in the position of being solicited for votes in the service of other interests. One group of delegates, led by Latin American members, urgently requested me to vote for the annulment of a previous resolution against the admission of the Franco regime in Spain, which was remembered by many countries as an ally of Hitler and Mussolini. The trouble was that all the states, most of them with social-democratic governments, that had fought against the Fascist powers in the recent war had initiated the continuation of the anti-Franco ban. Norway, Denmark, Holland, Belgium and France composed the camp from which I was asked to dissociate Israel, and the representatives of Republican Spain were vigilantly lobbying us. It was psychologically impossible for us to forget the devastated regions across which Hitler had marched and to turn our back on memories that would, one day, have to be transcended, but that still defined our Jewish identity. It was a complex issue, for although Franco had taken his nation into the Nazi-Fascist camp, his role in helping to salvage some thousand Jews from catastrophe was bright in our recollection.

At the same time I was lobbied frantically by the supporters and opponents of plans for the former Italian colonies. Somalia was subjected to a further period of Italian trusteeship, but a corresponding proposal for a British trusteeship over Libya was defeated by a single vote. The Libyan regime at that time, headed by an amiable monarch, King Idrisi, was not an area of particular concern to us. There may have been a vengeful anti-British element in our delegation's decision to vote against trusteeship for Libya. It seemed to me, however, that we would make ourselves quite incomprehensible if, after our own passionate revolt against proposals for imposing a trusteeship on our country, and after so many reverberating speeches in favor of self-determination and independence, we were to be the agent for imposing on another state the very servitude that we had shaken off our own shoulders.

The Arab governments were now in disarray. One blow after another had fallen on their heads. Despite their superior numbers in the international system and their vast resources of territorial, mineral and monetary wealth, they had lost every phase of the game. They had not prevented the adoption of a partition plan. They had not succeeded in stemming the tide of our military victory. They had been coerced into accepting a truce that was hostile to their military interests. They had been threatened with condemnation and sanctions by the Security Council. They had looked on in astonishment as the United States and the Soviet Union accorded their recognition with lightning speed. They had seen the prospect of Israel's truncation through the Bernadotte report wither away. The fortunes of battle had swung so sharply against them that they had been forced on the defensive to the point of having to accept an armistice regime that virtually legitimized Israel's existing boundaries on the basis of our military victories in the war of independence. What they had vowed to prevent had come to pass.

Surely this was the hour when they would have to think of making peace as an alternative to sterile and ineffective hostility?

This was not the way in which they saw their condition. The Arabs were in a crisis of wounded pride. They had gone to war in confidence of swift and easy victory. They regarded themselves as inherently superior to their despised enemy. However the outside world might regard them, they saw themselves as authoritative governments performing a respectable task of "restoring order" in a neighboring territory suffering from turbulence created by "Zionist gangs." Once they had committed themselves to the doctrine that the Jewish nation in Palestine was little more than a well-organized crime syndicate, the rest of their logic became consistent. They had portrayed their Israeli adversary as subhuman creatures devoid of valor, nobility or authentic national feeling. In caricatures, Israel was drawn in the stereotyped figure of a hook-nosed bearded oily creature, sometimes with horns sprouting from the hairy forehead. The impression was of something that fell outside the human context, worthy only of extermination. It followed that defeat by so contemptible a creature dealt a traumatic blow to Arab self-esteem. It was only in order to avoid greater humiliation that they had accepted the armistice agreements.

They now refused to abandon the fight. They believed that the arithmetic of territorial, demographic and economic power was on their side. The Arab leader whom I had met in London in 1947, Azzam Pasha, the secretary-general of the Arab League, said, "We have a secret weapon which we can use better than guns, and this is time. As long as we don't make peace with the Zionists, the war is not over and as long as the war is not over, there is neither victor nor vanquished. As soon as we recognize the existence of Israel, we shall have admitted by this very act that we are vanquished."

The internal politics of Arab states also worked against peace. Here the dominant theme was the tension between two impulses in Arab history. Arab unity was a slogan that was recited with reverence but that had never been expressed in real habits of cooperation. There was much more rivalry than fraternity in the relations between Arab capitals. Nothing has ever divided the Arab world more than the attempt to unite it. The unification of the Arab world would raise the problem of hegemony. Who would be the leader of the family? I had early reached the conclusion that the Arab states have united emotions but separate interests. There is a manner of speaking, feeling, loving, hating that is common to all men and women of Arab speech. They might frequently come together on the plane of rhetoric and ideology, but not on the level of affirmative cooperation. Above everything else, the Arab mind was haunted after the failures of 1948 and 1949 by an irrational but authentic fear of Israel's alleged power.

There has always been a sharp ambivalence in the Arab vision of Israel. Sometimes the tendency is to portray us as beneath any standards of honor or respect, a figure to be derided and contemptuously liquidated. At other times, Israel's qualities are magnified until they come close to omnipotence. Israelis and Zionists, according to this portrayal, are unlimited in their capacity, cleverness, strength, skill, malevolence and international influence. They are believed to have a lordly imperial dimension, according to which their existing state is only a stepping-stone to a domain that would ultimately extend from the Nile to the Euphrates. Intelligent and responsible Arabs, including Nasser himself, as well as even the most pragmatic of Palestinian leaders, have spoken as if they really believe that a map showing this Israeli empire is suspended on the Knesset walls. Seen in this light, Israel's very existence is deemed a threat to Arab security. The best that can be done in their terms is to refuse to make peace with an entity that one hopes will one day disappear.

By mid-1949 Israel had won decisive military and diplomatic victories. Henceforward the hope of peace would depend on a readiness of all parties to despair of war. The Arabs had not yet reached that point. They would probe Israel's points of political vulnerability. These were Jerusalem and the Arab refugees.

These two issues would long cloud our horizon. It was, however, immensely consoling to face them in full international stature. To have had a central role in establishing our flag in its own name and pride filled me with a satisfaction beyond any other that could lie ahead.

10

A JERUSALEM INTERLUDE:
1949–1950

ISRAEL LIVED THE first twenty months of its turbulent life with Tel Aviv as its capital. On the seashore at a busy Tel Aviv corner, the former opera house was being converted into a permanent Knesset building. The Israeli opera was not of a level at which masses of Tel Aviv citizens would be broken-hearted if it ceased to perform. There were many who thought that the Knesset proceedings would offer better drama and more interesting vocal activity.

During the eighteen months in which the Knesset and the ministries were in Tel Aviv, not one single Cabinet minister ever informed the Cabinet secretary that he wished to raise the question of moving them to Jerusalem.

The Tel Aviv buildings in which the ministries and the Cabinet office were housed lacked any hint of architectural dignity. They were crowded together in what had once been a German-Christian settlement at Sarona composed of small cottages that were confiscated by the Palestine British administration during the war when no trace of German ownership could be tolerated. When the British left in May 1948, the new Israeli administration moved in.

The armistice system was completed in August 1949, when the Security Council ratified the Israeli-Syrian Armistice Agreement. We now had a contractual basis for Israel's relations with all four of its contiguous neighbors. The negotiations with Syria had at times seemed likely to break down owing to rival interests near the Sea of Galilee and the Huleh marshes. In the end, a demilitarized zone of ambiguous sovereignty was established near Lake Tiberias. From New York, I made one contribution when I suggested that there should be a belt of ten meters on the western side of Lake Tiberias in order that no part of the lake should have a Syrian shore. This was accepted and is embodied in the Armistice Agreement.

When the Syrian-Israeli negotiations were completed, Ralph Bunche duly received the eulogies of members of the Security Council at a meeting that I addressed on August 4. Events were to prove that it was a prodigious achievement. The boundaries were so drawn and the agreement so formulated as to give our relations with the four Arab countries most of the attributes of a permanent territorial settlement. They were clearly demarcated, no movement across them was permitted without authorization of the country concerned and they could not be changed except by mutual agreement. I repeated to my government that the distinction between permanent boundaries and armistice lines of this kind was very small. Bunche was the first of the world statesmen to receive the Nobel Prize for work on the Arab-Israeli conflict. When Lester Pearson, Menachem Begin and Anwar Sadat were similarly honored in later years, the conflict had generated more Nobel laurels than permanent solutions.

Suzy and I were seeking greater stability for our lives. Since leaving the London Zionist Office in 1947, we had been leading a nomadic existence between one hotel and another, living out of suitcases without pause. Through the friendship of Jack Weiler, a loyal Zionist prominent in the real estate business, we rented a small penthouse apartment at 241 Central Park West, with a view over the reservoir and the Fifth Avenue towers beyond. Suzy was in an advanced stage of pregnancy and we moved into this residence none too soon.

I was involved in preparation for the regular session of the UN General Assembly to be convened at Lake Success in September 1949. To my astonishment, an item was inscribed on the General Assembly agenda by the Australian delegation asking for a discussion on the internationalization of Jerusalem. Nothing was happening in Jerusalem itself that seemed to call for this initiative. The city was settling down in its admittedly tense partition between the Israeli area based on the modern districts in the west of the city and the Jordanian part based on the Old City. Divided sovereignty is no prescription for development, and from the Jewish point of view, there was the harsh fact that the most sacred Holy Place of Judaism, the Temple Mount near the Western Wall in Jerusalem, was under Jordanian control with every sign of permanence. It would soon appear that this control was being exercised in a vandalistic spirit, which did not in any way harmonize with the urbane, civilized demeanor that King Hussein presented to the outside world. Jews were barred from access and venerable gravestones were used as latrines. Another complication was that the buildings of the Hebrew University and the Hadassah Medical Center on Mount Scopus were a small island cut off from the main body of the Jewish population and accessible only by a complicated system of convoys under United Nations protection. Nevertheless, it was obvious to us that if the only way to change the situation was by war initiated by Israel, the division of Jerusalem would remain as it was.

The founding fathers of Zionism and Israel had always been somewhat intimidated by the idea of Jerusalem as a wholly Jewish city. Theodor Herzl, the founder of the Zionist Organization, had been repelled by the squalor, poverty and ecclesiastical rivalries in Jerusalem and had uttered a solemn prayer that the capital of the Jewish state would be somewhere else. Chaim Weizmann understood the mystical and spiritual lineage of Jerusalem and had brandished it with memorable rhetoric in the ears of Balfour ("we had Jerusalem when London was a swamp . . ."), but he personally preferred the intimately Jewish atmosphere of the coastal plane. He once expressed to me his skepticism whether the concentration of priests, rabbis and muftis in Jerusalem would ever allow it to assume the kind of Jewish character in which "a Jew could take off his coat, sit back and feel at home." Ben-Gurion had visited the Land of Israel for the first time in 1906, and left behind profusely descriptive diaries with hardly any allusion to Jerusalem. Golda Meir had proposed during the UN discussion on partition that the capital of Israel should be situated in Haifa close to Jewish populations and territory. On the other hand, there was no question that all Israelis, deeply affronted by the negligent and irresponsible way in which the General Assembly had left Jerusalem to its fate during 1947, were resolved never to put their faith in the international organization as the protector of the city. The Jewish consensus was that West Jerusalem must be unequivocally within the State of Israel, but not necessarily as the capital.

When the General Assembly opened its September 1949 session, I highlighted the question of Jerusalem in my speech in the general debate, emphasizing that the present division between Israel and Jordan was perhaps the least offensive of all of the options and was in any case juridically based on the armistice agreements. There was therefore a kind of Arab-Israeli accord on avoiding the illusion and chaos of what was called "internationalization." I myself and some of my colleagues, especially the energetic and resourceful Gideon Rafael, had often met Jordanian representatives whenever the danger of international sovereignty loomed. Since the international interest arose from the Holy Places, nearly all of which were in the Old City, it was clear that an international regime would encroach on Jordan more than on Israel. I was much more "altruistic" than the Jordanian delegates in offering international supervision of all the Holy Places to an international agency on condition that there would be no encroachment on the secular domain. The Arab reply was that "Eban is generously offering to internationalize a part of Jordanian territory."

None of this, however, deterred the Australian delegation, under the direction of Foreign Minister Herbert Evatt, from inscribing the item and demanding that it be debated.

My speech to the General Assembly, in which I made the customary general review of the international situation, was well received. *The Jerusalem Post* wrote in mid-September that "the great respect which the Israeli representative, Abba Eban, had gained at the United Nations will be enhanced by the speech which he made at the closing of the general debate." Toward the end of the 1949 session, however, the assault on Israel's status in Jerusalem was launched in full fury. We expected to be challenged by the

Arab states and by many in Latin America who were under the influence of the Catholic Church, but we were never able to diagnose the cause for Herbert Evatt's strange obduracy in this matter. He had never struck any of his friends as a man of obsessive religious piety. It was known that the elections in Australia would be tightly fought, and that the Catholic vote was of some importance, but I found it embarrassing to be in conflict with a delegation that had given us such strong support, especially when its foreign minister had presided over the General Assembly in the debate on our admission.

Although we achieved the support of the United States and Britain, as well as the Protestant European countries such as Sweden, Denmark, Norway and Holland, the vote went against us. The Christian Protestant states would have been well satisfied with an extraterritorial status for the Holy Places without attempting to establish UN control over the secular aspects of the city.

Moshe Sharett, who had taken no part in the UN admission debate, had led our delegation during the struggle against the reinstatement of the internationalization principle. He took his defeat very hard and even offered Ben-Gurion his resignation. There was no justification for this. He was a victim, not of his own failure, but of the statistics of UN membership. I always regarded the United Nations as a business enterprise in which the Arabs had many more shares than Israel. Back in Israel, however, Prime Minister Ben-Gurion reacted vigorously by deciding to ignore the UN resolution and to move the Knesset and government agencies from Tel Aviv to Jerusalem. Sharett believed that this was an unnecessary defiance of the international forum. I found it difficult to share his concern. I did not believe that our transfer of the ministries to Jerusalem would have any effect on our basic international position. I was convinced that the UN resolution for internationalization would not be implemented one way or the other, and that there would not be any attempt to carry it out. For one thing, the United Nations was not so equipped as to be able to govern a turbulent and rebellious population. Second, the internationalization idea was opposed by the United States and Britain, who were, after all, the dominant powers in the Middle East. I thought that the 1949 Resolution would have no effect whatever.

In order to put my optimism to the test, I went to Washington, where Dean Rusk, on behalf of Secretary Acheson, told me that the United States intended to ignore the resolution and advised us to do the same. However, the United Nations' organs have their own dynamism, and the General Assembly, having reasserted the principle of an international regime, called upon the Trusteeship Council to elaborate a statute. This meant that I would have to take an Israeli delegation to Geneva to thwart the new political assault. The bizarre element in this situation was well exemplified by the choice of the Trusteeship Council. This had been and would remain the most inactive of the principal organs of the UN. Its objective had been to guide subject areas toward independence. In the case of Jerusalem, as I pointed out, it was attempting to guide an independent area toward unwanted tutelage.

Ben-Gurion's "seizure" of the capital reverberated strongly in the press, despite the fact that there was no concrete measure for carrying it into fulfillment. A Yiddish newspaper reported in New York: "Ben-Gurion made a vehement and enthusiastic speech, stating that Jerusalem would be the eternal capital of the state of Israel. In his peroration he said, 'We have come here forever. We shall never part from Jerusalem again.' " The effect of this headline, however, was somewhat reduced by the concluding sentence, which was "Having delivered his address, Ben-Gurion returned to his home and office in Tel Aviv." Some years would elapse before ministers and their staffs would deign to live in their own capital.

In my speeches in the debate I spoke on several occasions about Jerusalem, stressing how the Jewish population had been subjected to siege and famine while the international community, which had promised it peace, security and development, had stood idly by while its people and buildings were being destroyed. I flatly claimed that Israel aspired to "full international recognition of the political status of the government of Israel in Jerusalem."

The need to spend a harsh winter in Geneva was unattractive to me for many reasons. My son Eli was born in New York on January 17. I barely had time to attend his circumcision and to install ourselves in our new home before going abroad ten days later. On the day of that ceremony, I was making a UJA fund-raising talk, but I rushed from the meeting, driving my own car to the hospital, arriving just in time. It was heartrending to bring Suzy and Eli home to our Central Park West apartment on the afternoon of January 27 and a few hours later to rush off to catch the plane. We faced our longest separation since our marriage. Suzy wrote to me from New York to Geneva:

I don't know if you are a subject of public interest, but your son Eli is. I never thought a baby could arouse so much curiosity and excitement among strangers. I am spending all my time acknowledging gifts and congratulatory messages. The apartment seems dead without you. Our living room now has an air of quiet elegance and invites one to relax and take a peaceful view of the world.

There was no "peaceful view of the world" in Geneva. For one thing, it was the first of my birthdays since our marriage on which Suzy and I had been apart. In the war I had no contact with my family for five years between 1941 and 1946, and the continuation of such separations was one of the negative aspects of the diplomatic life. A few days later Suzy wrote:

I presume that you will spend the weekend preparing your speech, marching up and down your room looking very thoughtful and very offensive and very single-minded and very detached from the world.

Monday night I shall be glued to the radio and will try to be satisfied with one of those frustrating UN broadcasts from Geneva. But I know it will surely be nothing but another wonderful presentation of our point of view on Israel and its problems.

Life in Geneva is afflicted by a phenomenon called "la bise," an icy wind that cuts through the most protective of garments with a message of frigidity from the lake. This asperity is counterbalanced by the wondrous profusion of excellent restaurants in Geneva. Accompanied usually by my deputy, colleague and friend, Gideon Rafael, I would make the rounds of these excellent eating houses. On one occasion, however, entering a particularly famous gastronomic sanctuary, I saw the Iraqi representative, Dr. Fadhil al-Jamali, about to partake of the repast. At my side at the table of the United Nations he had no choice but to suffer my presence. Here, however, he had a nationalist option. He arose without even paying his bill and left with many signs of wrath and revulsion.

Suzy was writing from New York:

I shall never forget the lonely days and nights alone, just watching tenderly and sadly over little Eli. When I lecture myself and tell myself that this will probably have to happen again and again in our lives, my courage fails me at the mere thought.

My addresses to the Trusteeship Council were encapsuled in a major speech on March 15:

The spiritual ideals conceived in Jerusalem are the moral basis on which modern democracy rests. Would it not be incongruous if the United Nations were to advance the course of democratic liberty everywhere and yet prevent self-government from taking root in the very city where the democratic ideal was born? Our vision is of a Jerusalem wherein free people develop their reviving institutions while a United Nations representative, in all tranquility and dignity, fulfills the universal responsibility for the accessibility of the Holy Places. This is a vision worthy of the United Nations. Perhaps in this, as in other critical periods of history, a free Jerusalem may proclaim redemption to mankind.

Although in a rare gesture the Israeli Cabinet, at Ben-Gurion's prompting, instructed the foreign minister to send me a cable of appreciation "of your magnificent effort on behalf of Jerusalem," international interest in the Jerusalem problem was meager. My task was to ensure, however, that no legal situation would occur that might weaken our status in what had now become the capital of our state.

The Trusteeship Council embarked on long and unbelievably fantasy-ridden discussions about the exact prerogatives of "the Governor of Jerusalem" who would never arrive, and the size of his staff and the nature of his rule, as well as of such details as whether the television system should be public or private. When the statute had been formulated in the third week in March 1950 and was ready to be voted into adoption for later ratification by the General Assembly, we had to devise a parliamentary strategy. In consultation with Gideon Rafael and Moshe Tov, I concluded that the ideal solution would be to allow the statute for Jerusalem to rest in peace in UN files without, however, being formally adopted. We were fortunate in securing the cooperation of a distinguished statesman who then presided over the Trusteeship Council, Roger Garreau of France. We had expected the French government, with its traditional status as the "protector of the Holy Places," to be rigorously hostile to Israeli policy in Jerusalem. Either this was not so or M. Garreau had managed to evade the notice of his own government in nearby Paris.

At a dinner that Rafael and I had with him, we secured his agreement that we should leave Geneva with the statute unratified. In a statement to the Trusteeship Council, Garreau said vaguely that he thought that members had done an excellent job and should now leave the matter to higher international authority, such as the General Assembly.

There the statute for an International Jerusalem rests until this day without any implementation. The Geneva meeting in 1950 marked the demise of the idea of an internationalized Jerusalem.

While the Trusteeship Council pursued its abortive debates, the Palestine Conciliation Commission, established by the UN General Assembly in December 1948, pursued a similarly unproductive course. Its members were the United States, France and Turkey. The Egyptian government maintained a representative in Lausanne for the purpose of liaison with the UN Committee. Abdul Mun'im Rifa'i was a diplomat of refined and courteous disposition, and Gideon Rafael and I held many talks with him in a café in Lausanne with the aim of clarifying the prospect of an understanding between Egypt and Israel. It was clear that Egypt's relations with more militant Arab governments made this impossible at that stage. The habit of encounter, however, was a positive symptom and the fact that this was more feasible with Egyptians than with other Arabs was the augury of a subsequent breakthrough many years later.

On the Jerusalem issue, we found Jordanian representatives only too willing to cooperate with us against the internationalization proposals. This proved that Arab policy is not closed in on rhetorical flourishes when concrete issues are at stake.

Shortly after my lengthy stay in Geneva in defense of Jerusalem, I received a request from Sharett to come to report to the Cabinet. On this occasion, I rebelled. It would not be fair to me or to Suzy to prolong my absence any further merely to receive plaudits on the repulse of the UN assault. Sharett accepted this protest and I returned to New York.

The Soviet Union delegate, Yakov Malik, announced that his government no longer felt committed to the internationalization of Jerusalem and called for the strict observance of the armistice agreement that divided Jerusalem between an Israeli and a Jordanian sector. This was an unexpected windfall. It proved that an international sentiment for Jerusalem is more legend than fact. All that the United Nations achieved in 1949 and 1950 was to "compel" Israel to do what it had not intended to do, namely to establish its capital in Jerusalem in defiance of the Australian-Catholic-Soviet resolution.

The United Nations had elicited a defiance that would be characteristic of Israel's historic career. Just as Ernest Bevin's virulent hostility compelled us to make a radical claim for statehood instead of a lesser demand for free immigration, so did the General Assembly's actions in December 1949 remind Israelis that history would not allow them to underestimate the centrality of Jerusalem in Jewish history and destiny.

The idea of a separate international regime for Jerusalem has always been a fantasy, and its bizarre anomalies have been exposed in every attempt to put it into effect. It rests on a false picture both of Jerusalem and of the United Nations. Jerusalem is not an ethereal abstraction revolving in a vacuum of history. It is a city of living men and women with sharply defined national allegiances and identities. It cannot be anything that the majority of its citizens do not want it to be. While its spiritual and universal interests can be isolated for symbolic expression, its secular interests can never be detached from a normal political, social and municipal context. The Holy Places and the churches, mosques and synagogues are only a part of its life, and these are intensely oriented toward national devotions. Moreover, nobody believed in the United Nations as a provider of physical security after the neglect and apathy that it showed toward Jerusalem's inhabitants during the siege and blockade of 1947 and 1948. Many people have spoken about their love of Jerusalem, but none except its Jewish residents have been willing to stay and die in it as did the besieged Jews in 1947–1948 and as they did again under totally unprovoked attack in 1967. The United Nations can do many things, but administering and protecting a city is a task for which it was never constructed and for which it has no resources or capacities.

The Geneva discussion in 1950 had an almost farcical aspect when it began to debate the functions of a "governor" coming from outside and imposing himself on the Jewish and Arab populations. The conduct of the UN's activities on the East River in New York and in the Palais des Nations in Geneva is its maximal administrative vocation.

Without deluding ourselves to believe that we could play a dominant role in affairs beyond our region, I thought that we should adopt a conciliatory posture in the discussion of other international tensions.

I had hoped that our government would develop a relationship with mainland China. However, Sharett's decision to consult the United States before sending an embassy to Beijing dealt a death blow to this idea. The consultation took place with Under Secretary of State Walter Bedell Smith, who predictably urged us to wait until United States public and congressional opinion became less inflamed on this issue. It was clear that having initiated the consultation, we could not defy the advice without causing damage that would have been avoided if we had abstained from the consultation. By the time that Israel was ready to move forward, it was too late. China had more interest in dozens of Arab votes than in Israel's lonely suffrage.

While I pursued my career as an ambassador to the UN I had no premonition of an approaching change in my responsibilities. My surprise was great when, during a visit to Atlanta, Georgia, to make a speech to a Jewish audience, I received a cable from Sharett. The text was brief. "Can you do both?" Sharett did not find it necessary to say both of what. It was very enigmatic, but from previous soundings I knew what he meant. Would I be willing to retain my UN post in New York and at the same time accept appointment as Israeli ambassador to Washington? Having telephoned Suzy in New York and noting that her response was instantaneous, I sent an uncoded Western Union cable from Atlanta accepting the appointment.

Sharett explained that I was clearly making a public impression through speeches at the United Nations and articles in the media, and that this energy would be more fruitfully applied to Washington, to which our prime minister attached much greater importance than to the United Nations. At the same time, both Ben-Gurion and Sharett wished me to retain the UN platform since their intuition told them—correctly—that we would still face many tempests in that arena.

I was again reminded of the degree to which the speed of Israel's development had determined the pace of my own progress. Only four years had passed since Moshe Sharett, incarcerated at Latrun, had sent me his clandestine message with one word: "NOO?"

11

FIRST STEPS IN
WASHINGTON

UNTIL I RECEIVED the unexpected telegram from Sharett at my hotel in Atlanta, the prospect of being ambassador to Washington had never entered my head. I was prepared to continue an exclusively UN career during years when the exciting challenges of 1947–1948 seemed unlikely to recur in that forum. This was not a tragic fate for a thirty-five-year-old diplomat. If I feared being swamped by torrents of legalistic UN rhetoric, I would be consoled by having a platform for political dialogue and large access to the media. My policy in the UN had always been to forget the immediate, specialized audience and to address my language and emotion to the wider world beyond. The UN was then a more resonant platform than it became in the 1960s and 1970s. I was even seduced by the idea that Israel would not be the permanent victim appealing for support or compassion. We might perhaps earn a role in international issues outside the Arab-Israeli conflict.

This latter hope was short-lived. An incident in the UN General Assembly illustrated the degree to which regional hostility would inhibit our international role. In the discussion of a cease-fire in Korea I managed to find a formulation that won wide acceptance among delegates, since it did not contain Cold War language. *The New York Times* of January 13, 1952, had a front-page headline announcing "an Israeli initative" to end the Korean war. This eruption of Israel into the central international arena seemed eccentric. The underlying logic was that any cease-fire to be taken seriously by China and North Korea would have to be sponsored by a country that was not fighting in Korea.

The British delegate, Sir Gladwyn Jebb, asked the Indian delegate, Benegal Rau, to suggest that I file my proposal on Israel's behalf before the Communist countries could seize the procedural deadline.

The rest of the story and its conclusion is narrated in the memoirs of the foreign minister (who later became the prime minister) of Canada, Lester Pearson:

Everything should have gone smoothly today, but the contrary was the case. The difficulty arose over the fact that the resolution sponsoring the statement and referring it to Peking "for their observation" had been sponsored by Israel. This was enough to arouse the ire and opposition of the Arabs, who, one after the other this morning, recanted their earlier decision of approval. . . . I then got hold of Eban, Jebb and Padilla Nervo of Mexico, went to the Hidden House Restaurant (an appropriate place) for lunch and discussion. Nervo promised to persuade the chairman and Eban agreed that if the statement of principles was carried, he would withdraw his resolution.

Pearson went on to record that Norway later proposed the identical text that I had formulated and that "Eban therefore withdrew his own resolution completely. Now we can sit back and see what happens in Peking during the next few days. And I can go to Ottawa."

In later years, statesmen like Pearson, Jebb and Benegal Rau would not even trouble to seek Israel's aid to resolve crises, knowing that this would automatically lose available Arab votes. I reconciled myself to the idea that our work in the United Nations would have to be limited to our own national concerns.

A break in this tradition came a few months later when Secretary of State John Foster Dulles insisted on my membership in the Peace Observation Committee established after the Korean armistice, and again when Dag Hammarskjöld as UN secretary-general in 1963 supported my election as vice president of the UN Conference on Science and Technology and as a member of the UN committee that continued the work of the conference. These latter two appointments, however, were personal gestures that acknowledged a special role that I had played when I brought eminent scientists and leaders of developing countries together in the Rehovot Conference of 1960.

Before that, Israel's only success in a UN electoral contest was in 1953 when I was unexpectedly elected to the higher dignity of a vice president of the UN General Assembly, paradoxically at a time when Israel was being condemned in the Security Council for reprisal actions.

The Korean experience convinced me that, apart from intermittent crises, the center of gravity of my work would be in Washington.

I had been told that Justice Felix Frankfurter, having heard that Eliahu Elath was going to be replaced but without having heard who his successor was to be, said either to Ben-Gurion or to Sharett: "Please don't send us a too clever Jew." Nobody was ever able to obtain confirmation of this remark. My own instinct at the time was to wonder why Frankfurter upon his appointment to the Supreme Court was regarded by all his brethren on the Supreme Court as "a much too clever Jew," should want the Israeli Embassy to be headed by a foolish Jew. I already knew Felix Frankfurter very well. He was a man of effervescent intellectual activity, but he also emitted a constant stream of froth and foam. In later years, our friendship was based on an agreement to listen carefully to each other, although listening to others was not a quality for which either of us was uniquely celebrated.

Many of my friends, and others who could not be so defined, predicted that I would find it hard to keep my two embassies in harness. In the event, that difficulty would come to expression only during the three months in which the General Assembly was in session. Each autumn my life was a tale of two cities. Washington and New York are two separate realms of experience, so that movement between them is very much like foreign travel.

My inauguration into the life of the Washington diplomatic service was gradual. I could not cut loose from the UN delegation, although it was comforting to know that Arthur Lourie, a man of cultivated mind and shining integrity, would be my deputy at UN headquarters while simultaneously holding his function as the consul general in New York. He was succeeded later in his UN function by Mordechai (Reggie) Kidron, whose candor and realism often embroiled him in tensions with Golda Meir.

I found that I was not alone in bearing the double load. On airliners and trains bearing their distinguished diplomatic cargo between the two cities I often used to encounter Sir Carl Berendsen, a New Zealander of gravelly voice and a "no nonsense" demeanor, who was one of our most ardent supporters in the crucial debates of 1947–1948. Another shuttle diplomat was Charles Malik, a Lebanese Christian statesman and scholar. Malik was our most formidable adversary on the parliamentary floor, but he was caught up in a tormenting conflict between his Arab patriotism and his Christian and humanistic values. In his heart he probably had a stronger affinity with me than with his Muslim fellow-Arabs. Most of them applauded his rhetorical skills but doubted the authenticity of his anti-Zionist credentials.

Malik, who later became a president of the UN General Assembly, held all the records for the frequency with which he invoked the Creator in his political discourse. He seemed oblivious of the fact that, after the admission of many new members in the fifties, the Christian God no longer commanded a two-thirds majority in the United Nations. Countries inspired by the biblical culture would soon be a small minority. I doubt if Israel could have won admission to membership of any international agency in the atmosphere and composition of the UN in the sixties and seventies.

Malik sat immediately to my right in the days before Ireland and Italy acceded to membership in the United Nations and separated us by alphabetical chance from Iraq and Lebanon to our right and our left. Charles Malik and I could feel a constrained and stifled "reaching out" toward each other that neither of us was free to express.

It would be different in 1957 when the Lebanese Christian leadership, threatened with subversion by the hegemonistic ambitions of the Egyptian leader Gamal Abdul Nasser, would call for American marines and expect

Israel to support their arrival. Malik was then the second man in the Christian government headed by Camille Chamoun, and he and I would exchange surreptitious notes at the UN committee table like schoolboys evading a schoolmaster's vigilant gaze. He reached out for a meeting with me in 1982 when Beirut was aflame after successive Syrian, Palestinian and Israeli bombardments and implored me to come to Beirut. By then he was crippled with gangrene and saddened by the eclipse of his particular vision, at the center of which was the image of a Christian Lebanon mediating across the Mediterranean between Christianity and Islam, between Europe and Asia-Africa, between the rationalism of the West and the resurgent faiths of the East. All I have from him now are a few scribbled chits and a letter that he wrote when I congratulated him on the birth of his son: "Dear Ambassador Eban, it was most kind of you to have sent us your personal congratulatory note for which we sincerely thank you. We too wish you and Mrs. Eban the true and abiding happiness that can in truth come only from God."

It is typical of the rancor of those times that such a normal, human courtesy would have been a sensation if it had become known in the Arab countries.

The ambassadors who served simultaneously at the United Nations and in Washington developed a club-like solidarity. The motive of my double appointment was Ben-Gurion's indication to Sharett that the American sector of Israel's international relations interested him far more than the United Nations. The embassy in Washington should, therefore, be headed by somebody with whom he, as prime minister, could have a confident relationship. This was not true of the relations between Ben-Gurion and Eliahu Elath. Elath was a man of handsome appearance with an ardent talent for exposition. This, however, came to expression in individual conversations, less so, or hardly at all, in his public appearances. Moreover, he had not learned that Ben-Gurion's quickness of mind was such that it was seldom necessary to make a point with him in identical terms in more than one sentence. Above everything else, however, Ben-Gurion had the feeling that relations with the State Department and other ministries in Washington should not be the only field of activity for an Israeli ambassador. As one Israeli newspaper editor said:

There was a general feeling in Jerusalem and Tel Aviv that we ought not to measure an Israeli Ambassador by any general standard. Washington was growing in importance to us and we realized we must have as Ambassador a man who could attain a public position so that when he came into the State Department, they would not look at him in relation to a few hundred thousand Jews in Israel but as somebody whose word would carry weight in the world and especially throughout the United States.

When Ben Gurion raised this point with Sharett, the foreign minister pointed out that at that time I was the only Israeli diplomat who already had that qualification.

Eliahu Elath was not being discarded. He was going to be Israel's first full ambassador at the Court of St. James's at a period when Britain's position in the Middle East was hardly less influential than that of the United States. Indeed, in terms of physical presence and day-to-day operational activity, Britain was still the senior partner. It had a large force in Egypt as the guardian of the Suez Canal. Its resident envoys were virtually the rulers of Jordan, and it had a very strong hold on the policies of the pro-Western monarchy in Iraq.

I made a few journeys to Washington in advance of my presentation of credentials in order to test the lay of the land. I came away with a feeling that my task would not be easy. It was true that after a period of frigidity toward the idea of an independent Israel, the United States had come to our international rescue on several occasions. It had abandoned support of the Bernadotte report. It had resisted attempts to excise the Negev from the Israeli map, and after the appalling tensions and confrontations with us on its trusteeship proposal, in which it had frankly attempted to prevent us from becoming an independent state, it had reversed its position by recognizing Israel and fiercely denouncing the Arab assaults on us with memorable speeches in the Security Council.

I could not, however, ignore the fact that all of these had been cliff-hanger occasions. We had been on the verge of failure until Harry Truman, like a knight on a white steed, arrived when all seemed lost and personally imposed his policy on the Washington Establishment. In most of these cases, a unique personal rapport had developed between Truman and Weizmann and brought us a desired result. I did not believe that this situation could endure. These special procedures were no sort of basis on which an embassy could conduct its work or create a tradition. I was inheriting a relationship that had no fixed institutional framework.

I knew in my heart that Weizmann, whose health had deteriorated sharply, would never come to the United States again. Letters over his signature did not have the same effect as his style and presence. Moreover, there was no evidence that Truman's warm sentiment and astute sense of political expediency were at work on the mind of Dean Acheson and other departmental heads in the capital.

Eliahu and Zahava Elath had lived in a hotel. Suzy and I therefore had to concern ourselves with the establishment of an ambassadorial residence. In addition, we were crowded into narrow quarters of the chancery at 2210 Massachusetts Avenue. Our nearest neighbor was the Embassy of Luxembourg, which seemed to be incongruously larger and more spacious than our own. They had much more space for far fewer problems.

My feeling that the relationship between the United States and Israel would need more precise frameworks was strengthened by the fact that we were not even eligible as beneficiaries of the United States foreign aid program. These had begun in the context of the European Recovery Program and the Marshall Plan without much relevance to nations outside Europe. The secretary of state himself, Dean Acheson, had never concealed his belief that Europe was the main arena in which American diplomacy had to operate. Until the end of his tenure in 1953, he never showed effusive interest in countries of the Third World.

An exception to his European emphasis lay in Korea, where large American forces were involved. Dean Acheson had taken a leading part in the decision by the United States to make this a test of the confrontation between the West and an expansionist Communist empire. This was the least that he could do to atone for an unfortunate statement in which he had enumerated the security commitments of the United States and omitted South Korea from his list. This was not a triumph for the principle of deterrence.

Truman was at the height of his power and self-confidence in 1950. His sympathies with Israel had been tested under pressure, but he was also capable of irascible reactions. His friendship had to be carefully tended and was largely dependent on the creation of personal chemistry between himself and his interlocutors. It was clear that we could not come to him for every small decision.

Acheson's view of Truman's Zionism was more complex. He was later to write:

> Both Prime Minister Attlee and Ernest Bevin, in the heat of their annoyance with Truman, charged that his support of Jewish immigration into Palestine was inspired by domestic political opportunism. This was not true, despite the confirming observations of some of his associates. Mr. Truman held deep-seated convictions on many subjects. From many years of talk with Truman, I know that the Balfour Declaration had always seemed to him to go hand in hand with the noble policies of Woodrow Wilson, especially the principle of self-determination. I did not share the President's view on the Palestine solution to the pressing and desperate plight of great numbers of displaced Jews in Eastern Europe. The number that could be absorbed by Arab Palestine without creating a grave political problem would be inadequate and to transform the country into a Jewish state capable of receiving a million or more immigrants could vastly exacerbate the political western interests in the near East. From Justice Brandeis, whom I revered, and from Felix Frankfurter, my intimate friend, I have learned to understand but not to share the mystical emotion of the Jews to return to Palestine and end the diaspora. In urging Zionism as an American governmental policy, they had allowed, so I thought, their emotion to obscure the totality of American interests.

Zionism was the only topic that Felix and I had by mutual consent excluded from our far-ranging daily talks.

Acheson, with his usual trenchant phraseology, has described how the war between Israel and the Arabs was almost a mild affair compared with the internecine fighting between pro-Israelis and anti-Israelis in Washington.

It was indeed a stricken field. Attlee had deftly exchanged the United States for Britain as the most disliked power in the Middle East. The center of battle was moving from Israelis and British fighting in Palestine to civil war along the Potomac.

Acheson's coolness toward Zionism was, however, counterbalanced by a much stronger element in his outlook: He insisted on meticulous obedience to the president's will. When one considers the divergent temperaments of Truman and Acheson and the fact that Secretary of State George Marshall had never hesitated to grapple with President Truman to a degree that approached insubordination, and when one also takes into account Acheson's superior intellect, his fidelity to Truman appears profoundly moving. Thus, Acheson made no demur when on October 4, 1948, at a meeting in Madison Square Garden, Truman, shrewdly anticipating a pro-Zionist statement by his rival, Governor Dewey, announced that he would oppose any tampering with the UN partition resolution, would continue his efforts for the immigration of Jews into Israel and that some solution based upon partition "would command the support of public opinion in the United States."

The fact that we were constantly rescued from defeat by Truman's personal interventions gave me reason to predict a hard struggle in Washington. Our successes all seemed to hang on a single slender thread. Another weakness was that in the Congress, Israel was supported mainly by senators and representatives from states with large Jewish populations. Moreover, Eliahu Elath, despite his diplomatic skills, was not an eloquent man and had made little use of the radio and the public platforms as a means of enlisting public support to counteract the coolness of official Washington.

It was with those cautious estimates of my prospects that I got up on the morning of September 17 in the totally inadequate home in Myrtle Street provided by a fiscally cautious Israeli government and set out to present credentials to President Truman.

Having seen photographs of other ambassadors presenting their credentials to presidents, I was aware that this is normally one of the most pompous ceremonies in American democratic procedure, although not quite as fanciful as the horses and carriages and plumed hats of ambassadors presenting themselves at Buckingham Palace. I was routinely attired in a dark suit, silver tie and homburg hat, which in those days was an identity card of a diplomat.

A White House aide escorted me into the president's office. It was hot, the air conditioner was not working, and President Truman was at his desk with his coat off and his bright red suspenders in full view.

It occurred to me that I was sitting a few yards away from the most powerful leader in the history of mankind. More powerful than the emperors of antiquity, than Alexander the Great, Julius Caesar, Napoleon, the rulers of the British Empire at its zenith, or the Russian and German dictators of the twentieth century.

There had never been a time when one nation held such predominance of military and economic power as that wielded by the United States in the years immediately after World War II. America had attained this primacy during a conflict in which all the other participants had suffered defeat or devastation or exhaustion or all of them together. The United States had a monopoly of nuclear weapons, created half of the world's product, and dominated the voting systems in the new international agencies. The United States was not just a superpower, it was a monopower.

As I looked at Truman I wondered if power had ever been expressed with such total absence of pretention and pomp. He was no more than five feet nine inches tall, with square shoulders, a long sharply edged nose, steel-rimmed spectacles and gray-white hair cut with care and precision and smoothly brushed. If you passed him in the street of a small town, you would imagine that he was on the way to a small office in the central part of a moderately sized building. If there was such a thing as an "imperial presidency" no one seemed to have broken the news to Harry Truman of Independence, Missouri.

I was carrying with me documents wrapped in leather, containing the letters of credence that would assure President Truman that I really was what I purported to be, namely the ambassador extraordinary and envoy plenipotentiary of the State of Israel to the United States of America. Credentials are formulated almost entirely in capital letters and are rarely noted for literary grace or innovation. It was evident that the president feared that I might follow tradition and actually declaim the text. In order to preempt this danger, he moved with vigor and precision. He snatched the documents from my hands and said, "Let's cut out the crap and have a good talk." He then cast a triumphant glare at the disconcerted chief of protocol, who had rehearsed me for a much more eloquent ritual. It was soon to emerge that Truman regarded his own State Department as a hostile foreign power.

Our conversation, without the forbidden "crap," took its course for forty minutes. This caused further disquiet to the chief of protocol, who knew that the Dutch ambassador, Hermann Van Roijen, was waiting for the privilege of being my junior by half an hour. Truman's sentences flowed without any expectation that his voice or formulations would rise even spasmodically above the solid flat farming earth in which he had been nurtured. Yet there was no difficulty in grasping the core of his thought. He praised the Israeli government for speaking in favor of his action in Korea. "If a small country out there can be swallowed up, it's going to be tough for other small countries like yours." He told me twice that his decision to drop the atomic bomb on Japan had caused him no anguish or discomfort. From this I deduced that his anguish and discomfort must have been intense. If it were not, why should he bring this up in a conversation with no applicable context? He warned me to beware of the "striped pants boys in the State Department," staring reproachfully at the striped pants of the hapless chief of protocol. From this charge he exempted Secretary of State Dean G. Acheson ("He does what he knows I want and even seems to like doing it. In addition, he has more brains than a dozen ordinary men").

His language was lean but without obscurity. Whatever might have been the limitation of his powers of expression, his courage and independence of decision were unique. I was to have more meetings with him than are usual between a president and an ambassador from a small country. I knew, however, that since his chief talent was decision, it would be a mistake to involve him in abstract discussion or generalized conversation. It would be fruitful to do what Chaim Weizmann had the genius to do—to take one subject requiring a yes or no decision, to focus briefly upon it, and to allow no other issue to intrude. Weizmann had applied this technique in the case of the Negev in 1947 and of partition and the recognition of Israeli statehood in 1948. The results were spectacular.

From this memorable White House encounter, I went back to our chancery. The staff that I inherited was small for a full embassy. The counselor, Moshe Keren, a German-Jewish immigrant of centrist views and a love of precision, would shortly leave to be succeeded by the formidable Teddy Kollek. There were two first secretaries, a second secretary, a press attaché, an agricultural attaché and an economic counselor. More by coincidence than plan, my first military attaché was Suzy's brother-in-law, Chaim Herzog, who had completed his assignment as head of Intelligence of the Israeli Army. Neither he nor I predicted that he would become Israel's sixth president.

I now discovered the difference between life in New York and in Washington. At the United Nations there had been few social obligations, but in the capital much of the business of diplomacy seemed to be conducted at receptions, dinners, balls and cocktail parties. The latter institution disquieted me considerably, since I have never believed that the most rational method of discourse is to stand up with a cold glass conversing amid a deafening hubbub of conflicting voices. I once wrote and said that the cocktail party is the only human institution that does not even have a theoretical justification. It involves proximity without communication. Yet as a method of creating a contact, or of watching over its continuation, there was no substitute for the occasions when deals and promises were discussed with cocktail glasses in hand or between the dinner courses. In Washington, if one does not want to lay constant siege to a departmental head's office, processes of discussion and decision sometimes have to be spasmodic and to include informal stages.

On the number plates of my automobile, I was now number fifty-nine with the Dutch Van Roijen as number sixty. That was the number of embassies in Washington, which today exceeds 150. I could see that it would not be wise to ignore the social imperatives. To avoid "calling" or to "regret" an invitation might be taken as a diplomatic affront. The only "free" people in society are those who can decline a dinner invitation without giving a reason or excuse, and an ambassador is closer to slavery than to freedom. There had to be reciprocity, and here Suzy's ideal qualifications as a hostess and the bearer of unlimited personal charm would be a dividend for Israel's diplomacy.

I made an early decision that 1951 must become a breakthrough year in American-Israeli relations. When I surveyed the situation at the end of December, I could feel that this intention had been fulfilled. After patient work in Washington, with some offshoots in the United Nations, I could take satisfaction in several achievements. There is a memorable photograph of me signing a document with Secretary of State Acheson. This accord created legal eligibility for Israel in two fields. It confirmed that we were an acceptable candidate for the receipt of aid from the American foreign aid programs, and it laid the basis, carefully prepared by Herzog, for Israeli eligibility to acquire arms in the United States. In neither case did eligibility itself create a certainty of concrete allocations, but I could see that the United States is an obsessively legalist nation. The secretaries of state with whom I had to deal were all lawyers. So were many of their Cabinet colleagues and a preponderant number of senators and representatives. As a pioneer in this relationship, I thought it essential to create the necessary legal frameworks.

At a time when Israel's major anxieties were in the economic field, I had developed relationships in the Congress of the United States that resulted in what were in those days regarded as relatively vast funds for the Israeli economy. A congressional appropriation of seventy million dollars and export-import bank loans totaling $135 million all sound like small change in relation to the inflationary heights of 1992. It must be remembered, however, that in those days, Israel's total earnings of foreign currency from exports were $50 million and the revenues to Israel from the United Jewish Appeal were just over $60 million. The millions of the 1950s are proportionally nearly equal to the tens of millions of the 1990s.

Moreover, in pursuit of a far-ranging program for Israel's economy sponsored by Prime Minister Ben-Gurion, my colleagues and I had successfully negotiated Israel's eligibility for the sale of its bonds in the United States. In the light of Israel's meager productivity and exports at that time, this denoted an act of friendship and not merely a certificate of commercial correctness. Our learned economic adviser, Oscar Gass, had told me that the experts whom he had consulted had been astounded by this success. They had predicted that we would not be able to sell our securities in the American market and if we sold them we would not be able to repay. Four decades and four billion dollars of repaid bond sales later, I was able to observe that an expert is someone who understands everything—but nothing else.

Another achievement in September 1951 was a favorable response to the complaint that I had made to the UN Security Council against Egypt's blockade of Israel's approaches to the Red Sea via the Suez Canal. Here I had an important ally in Sir Gladwyn Jebb, the chief delegate of the United Kingdom. Our relations with London had substantially improved since the departure of Ernest Bevin, who was succeeded by Herbert Morrison in April 1950.

Sir Gladwyn had competed in frequency with my appearances in the televised broadcasts from the United Nations. The American public admired his tranquil style of speech in defense of the Western action in Korea. He had to make a considerable effort to adjust his Foreign Office manner to the realities of the American media. On one occasion, he and I were interviewed on a local station about the international situation as seen from the UN. After our interchange of jocularities, he was more startled than I was to hear the moderator announce: "Sir Gladwyn Jebb and Ambassador Eban have come to you by courtesy of Manischewitz Matzoh Balls and Kreplach."

Our admission to the U.S. foreign aid club, the loans and grants from U.S. banking agencies, the condemnation of the Egyptian maritime blockade and American support for our compensation claims from the West German government all converged in the fall and winter of 1951. At the end of the year an appreciative telegram came from Ben-Gurion.

I was also able to plant what then appeared to be small seeds in the American Jewish community: They were later to grow into luxuriant foliage. The fraternal support of Israel by American Jews through their organizations was obviously an important element in Israel's strength. The fact that an Israeli ambassador appearing at the White House or the State Department was known, however discreetly, to have a large backing behind him gave particular weight to our representations and elevated the level at which American-Israeli affairs were transacted. Here, however, there was a difficulty: American Jewry has a dispersed structure. It is recalcitrant to centralization. In this respect, American Jewry reflects the federalist tradition of the United States as a whole. My standard of comparison was with Britain. Since British society is organized as a pyramid, with authority flowing from the broad popular base upward through Parliament, individual ministries, the Cabinet and theoretically toward the Crown, it is natural to find British Jewry organized on the basis of a similar model. There is a single chief rabbi recognized as the spiritual authority. There is one Board of Deputies regarded, for obscure reasons, as representative of the Jewish community. There is even a single journal, *The Jewish Chronicle,* which justifiably calls itself "the organ of Anglo-Jewry." In the United States there is no chief rabbi, no single centralized representative institution, and not a single Jewish periodical that can claim to speak for the Jewish community as a whole.

One prosaic result of this fragmentation was that my colleagues, and especially I myself, had to have separate communion with the Zionist Organization of America, Hadassah, the Pioneer Women, the B'nai B'rith, the Anti-Defamation League, the Orthodox, Reform and Conservative branches of religious Jewry, and the leaders of the United Jewish Appeal and the Bonds Organization. The exhaustion and repetitiveness of these occasions was becoming especially burdensome in the light of the fact that I was the head of two very busy embassies. After a Security Council meeting in May 1951 to discuss fighting near the Huleh Marshes, I fainted in the Security Council through nothing more organic than a recent lack both of food and of sleep. Ben-Gurion, who was on his only visit to the United States during the nine years of my stewardship, sent an anxious letter saying, "People like you are not all that plentiful. Look after yourself."

I therefore turned to Dr. Nahum Goldmann, who was in effect what medieval Jewish writers called the "Leader of the Exile," with an appeal that he convene the major Jewish organizations periodically for consultation with me in order to exchange views and impressions about the American-Israeli relationship.

Most organizations responded favorably to Goldmann's appeal on my behalf. The exception was the American Jewish Committee, which under its revered leaders, Judge Joseph Proskauer and Jacob Blaustein, worked in solitary devotion for American-Israeli relations while being unwilling to join with other organizations of less aristocratic lineage. A handwritten letter from me proposing collective consultation bears the date of May 25, 1951, from the now extinct Savoy Plaza Hotel. It is the constitutive document of the Conference of Presidents of Major Jewish Organizations. From that time on, the work of the Conference of Presidents of Major Jewish Organizations has expanded into a recognized forum of American Jewry, acknowledged as such by the White House, State Department and Congress of the United States. At the same time, I invited Isaiah (Si) L. Kenen, a Canadian Jew, to come to Washington and, as a non-Israeli, to work on Capitol Hill to secure understanding of Israel's need for economic support. In my naïveté, I said and wrote to him that this might mean that he would have to stay in Washington for three months. Over thirty years later, Kenen was still in Washington, at the head of a modest but efficient organization—the American-Israel Public Affairs Committee (AIPAC)—producing the Near East Report and creating a mass of links with leading members of both Houses of the Congress, supported by willing volunteers in individual cities.

Forty years later, I find it hard to imagine that we could ever have been effective in Washington without the active support of the Jewish Organizations and AIPAC. In my contacts with these organizations, I advised them to look for the common factor in the American and Israeli legacies, and to with their points by mutual sympathy, not by abrasive confrontation. I stipulated that my support of AIPAC would be conditional on their avoidance of threats to individual senators and representatives. They and I also avoided the frequent use of the word "lobby." This is not a popular word in the United States, even though it is an accepted part of the democratic system. The idea of "lobby" implies an effort for a special interest to obtain more aid and consideration than those to which it is objectively entitled. The consequent atmosphere of incentives and pressures creates delicate situations, which must be handled with care on the underlying assumption that those who operate them have a parallel and equal concern for American and Israeli interests and are not the uncritical standard bearers of every Israeli position, including those most at variance with American consensus.

During the years when I guided these relationships as ambassador and foreign minister, we were not always able to avoid tensions between Israel and the United States. But there was not a single case in which we had been unable to bring these under restraint and to restore a routine of intimate cooperation.

Henry Kissinger has written that I regarded "objectivity" as the blind acceptance of all Israeli positions. I don't know how he would have described my more militant colleagues and supporters.

Here I had to fight a tendency, both in Israeli and in American Jewish opinion, to generalize every single collision of policies into a theory of "crisis" and sometimes of "betrayal." I once told an American ambassador who had been designated for service in Israel that he would find us very easy to get on with. "All you have to do is to agree with everything that we say." On the other hand, I added, even this was not a viable option since we do not say the same thing.

Israel does not reach its decisions by blind adherence to governmental dogma but rather by the interaction of alternative and contradictory choices. I took it for granted that while Israeli and American interests are nearly always parallel, that does not mean that they are always identical. Nor have I ever believed that an American Jew who takes a different view from that of the Israeli establishment is necessarily a violator of Jewish solidarity or a deserter from the struggle for Israeli security. He is very often simply a Jew who cares very much about Israeli values and who has a more incisive vision of damage that would result from extremist and strident self-assertion.

The test case during my tenure of office would of course be the Suez-Sinai War, in which there was something close to a rupture in American-Israeli relations. We had opposing strategies and interests. The basic strength of the relationship, however, was such that the tension lasted no more than a few weeks, after which Secretary Dulles and I were taking counsel on the common aim of curbing President Nasser's expansionist ambitions.

I was haunted by a traumatic recollection of a period before I became ambassador in which President Truman had been so offended by what he called "immoderate pressure" that he shut himself hermetically against dialogue with the American Jewish community. The fact that we had been able to overcome that crisis by the intervention of the Truman-Weizmann friendship was something that I regarded as fortuitous. It held no assurance for the future.

On the face of it, the need to combine my ambassadorship in the United Nations with that in Washington appeared to be a burden. In the deeper sense it was helpful. Although it forced me to spend much time commuting between Washington and New York, my UN status was an advantage in Washington, where few ambassadors were in the public eye or had much national recognition. Our embassy residence was physically one of the most inaccessible and least splendid in the city. But it was a place to which other diplomats valued invitations.

My aim was to build a structure that would be resilient enough to absorb the divergences between American and Israeli attitudes that were bound to occur, and one that would not depend exclusively on presidential rescue operations that could no longer be counted upon. The key lay in American public opinion, at the center of which stood our Jewish solidarities. Israel, without the American Jews, is a small island of territory in an ocean of hostility. It lacks geopolitical weight. Israel plus the Jewish people is an eternal nation, striding across unlimited expanses of space and time. My task was to make Israel so acceptable to the American public that an administration would be reluctant to take confrontations to extreme lengths. But our need of American support was so intense that I could not afford the conventional routines. This explains my constant rush from Washington to college campuses to Jewish meetings to state houses to lecture platforms, to foreign policy councils and associations, and above all, to the electronic media. I did not observe any other ambassador in Washington leading such a frenzied existence.

This emphasis on Israel's place in public opinion helped me to succeed in the first two objectives that I sought: the acceptance of Israel for eligibility in the American aid programs when we were in danger of being crushed by the weight of immigration, and the attainment of American support for our claims on the Federal Republic of Germany.

These two objectives required different techniques. In the case of German compensation I needed a favorable nod from Dean Acheson, representing one of the occupation powers, in order that Adenauer, Nahum Goldmann and Ben-Gurion could pursue their negotiations in a framework of legality. This was the most burdensome task ever assigned to me, because I had to try to impress the cold, pragmatic Acheson with the horror of the Nazi crimes against the Jewish people. I was accompanied by David Horowitz, who had been my colleague as a liaison officer with the UN Special Committee and later became the first governor of the the Bank of Israel. Mindful of our successful experience in the UN, we made a combined assault that for the first twenty minutes appeared to be having no result. There sat the secretary, a distinguished statesman and graduate of Yale, giving off an air of mahogany-paneled law offices, seemingly impervious to emotion, and stubborn in his belief that reason, not passion, should govern human destiny. For a time I had the feeling that it was more important for him to refrain from wrinkling his impeccable clothes than to listen to what we were saying.

There came a moment, however, when Horowitz and I were describing the brutality of the Nazi oppressor. Suddenly I saw Acheson wrinkle up his face as though he was about to collapse in deep emotion. He came very close to tears. Thereafter he became a constant supporter of our claim for compensation. He gave firm instructions to John J. McCloy, the high commissioner in Germany, to support our case. It was clear to me from then onward that Acheson's habit of staring into space uncomprehendingly whenever he heard emotional language was simply a veil under which he maintained a sensitive conscience and a passion for rectitude. He lived intimately by the ethic of the European Enlightenment and the American Founding Fathers.

My campaign in the Congress, however, illustrated the permanent eccentricity of Israel's diplomacy. My first soundings in the White House and in the State Department led me to believe that the Truman administration would include our country in the foreign aid package, at a rate roughly proportionate to our physical size. But Israel's physical size is of no use whatever to Israeli emissaries seeking inclusion in international programs. When an American Treasury secretary assured me that we could expect justice from his department, I replied, "I don't need justice, I need mercy."

Moreover, many professionals in the State Department and some congressional leaders found something eccentric in our application. The American foreign aid program was not universal in its scope. It was strictly focused on the rehabilitation of the European countries from the havoc of war and from the danger of inundation by Communist influence. This was not a fictitious danger: In France and Italy, Communist parties achieved electoral results that must have inspired disquiet for the future of democracy in Europe. In addition, the United States owed special consideration to Britain, which had held Hitler at bay during years when the United States was exasperatingly evasive in its responses to Hitlerist aggression.

It was obvious that there would have to be a special expression of "favoritism" in the Congress if Israel were to receive aid well beyond its political and geopolitical size. Accordingly, I began our soundings on Capitol Hill. In short time I reached the enviable position of having four members of the Congress willing to sponsor a bill irrespective of the views of the Executive Branch. The quartet had the power of long-range howitzer guns. My senatorial friends were Paul Douglas of Illinois and Robert Taft of Ohio. The support of Taft was a surprise to many of my friends, for in principle the austere, aloof senator was no friend of foreign countries. In his conversation with me, however, he confessed that there were two exceptions to his instinct for restraint. One was Israel and the other India. I never managed or even attempted to elicit from him an explanation for his unexpected support of India, whose leaders were not beloved in the world of market economies, free enterprise and conservative statesmanship. In the House of Representatives the majority leader, John McCormack, and the minority leader, Joseph Martin, were willing to head the list of sponsors of the Israeli Aid bill.

There was an embarrassing moment when Joseph McCarthy of Wisconsin invited me to his office in the Senate Building and asked me to include him in the list of sponsors of the Resolution urging Israel's inclusion in the foreign aid legislation. I knew that this would lead to the self-exclusion of the sponsors and others. I took refuge in the formal truth that I was merely a spectator of the exercise and that he would have to address his request to Senators Douglas and Taft. I never heard from him again. I must recall, however, that Israel and the Jews never became a target of McCarthy's denunciations.

Armed with my imposing quartet of sponsors and assisted at a later stage by Si Kenen and Teddy Kollek, I reached a point at which the majority of members of the Senate and a large number of representatives were willing to face the Truman-Acheson administration with the news that they expected a more generous approach to Israel's needs than to those of countries of similar size. This approach was so successful that by the time that I reached Secretary Acheson to make a formal application, I found him reacting with benevolent irony. He told me that it was very good of me to inform him of what we wanted. He knew very well that I had already secured the support of congressional leaders, both in the Senate and in the House of Representatives, as well as the ear of the White House through the instrumentality of David Niles, who was the president's unofficial representative for contact with minorities, including Jews. It was extremely courteous on my part, said Acheson, to keep him in touch with these developments.

Acheson made this statement to me without any hint of indignation. What I was doing was unusual in the traditional sense, but knowing his president well, Acheson decided to accept the idea that Israel was a special case.

Since those early days, all American administrations have been willing to understand that Israeli embassies do not confine their efforts or concerns to the straight furrow of the executive branch. This particularity of Israeli diplomacy has not only survived but has developed in the ensuing decades. I saw no reason to be apologetic about this. Professional diplomats took for granted that the Arabs could parade their advantage in mineral and monetary wealth as well as in space and population. Why should Israel not deploy its compensating advantage by using its access to friendly public opinion? This did not seem invidious or illegitimate except to hidebound diplomatic traditionalists. Why should we alone be prudish about our chief asset?

There were two further innovations that I introduced into our embassy practice. It was normal for ambassadors to convene press meetings only when they had something new to seek or to expound. I instituted regular meetings for general press briefings and discussions. I retain verbatim records of these meetings, which were attended by such revered pundits as the brothers Joe and Stewart Alsop, Arthur Krock, James Reston, Martin Agronsky, Marquis Childs, Cyrus Sulzberger and others.

I also made a pilgrimage to Georgetown to see Walter Lippmann, with whom it was necessary for ambassadors to deal on the same basis as with senior Cabinet members. Acceptance of his invitations was mandatory and to be able to invite him back was a sign of relaxed prestige. I recall his presence at an embassy function where Daniel Barenboim, a young musical prodigy from Israel, was exposed for the first time to an expectant audience. My only discomfort with Lippmann lay in his tortured relationship to his Jewishness. He, the son of Jacob and Sarah Lippmann, never discussed his origins and when the Holocaust was mentioned he reacted with due revulsion but always with an addendum that it would be salutary for Jews to be more discreet and reticent. He once expressed himself in a way that could be interpreted as insinuating that the habit of Jewish ladies in Miami to wear mink coats could be a contributory factor in leading Jews to persecution.

Another reinforcement that I sought in my effort to surround the embassy with friendly and vigilant American eyes was among what came to be called the "Wise Men" of Washington. The United States has an enviable talent for using the accumulated prestige of its statesmen and for putting them to work in disinterested counsel or in special missions. I made early contact with Arthur Dean, Dulles's law partner; John J. McCloy, who had been a U.S. high commissioner in Germany; Lucius Clay, the hero of the Berlin blockade; and with General Bedell Smith, a senior associate of Eisenhower in the world war. Bedell Smith had a close relationship with Secretary of State Dulles, under whom he subsequently served in the State Department mission to Cairo in 1955, which convinced the administration in Washington that Nasser was an incorrigible expansionist.

In my first visit to San Francisco, the citadel of the anti-Zionist Council for Judaism, the local Jewish grandees were so relieved to find that the Israeli ambassador did not have a beard and a Yiddish accent or wear a Hasidic hat, that they embraced me with obsequious warmth. Former anti-Zionists such as Fred Lazarus of Columbus, Ohio, and John Zellerbach and Philip Ehrlich of San Francisco became valued intermediaries between my embassy and the White House.

The eclipse of Jewish anti-Zionism was in full momentum. Even the most timorous and apprehensive American Jews who were in constant fear of being regarded as second-class Americans could not deny that their own government, parties and fellow citizens regarded Israel as a valued thread in the American tapestry. I could never decode the paradox according to which those Jews whose unreservedly American image seemed most unassailable were those who were most apprehensive of its erosion. They had benefited immensely from an American pluralism, which respected coexisting loyalties, and yet they sometimes doubted their own right to acknowledge their diverse legacies. I took a mischievous pleasure in enlisting former members of the Council for Judaism in the Zionist purpose of cementing American-Israeli relations.

As the 1952 presidential election campaign drew near, there was a general fear among Israelis and American Jews that Truman's successive interventions had been a one-time act of grace that could not be relied upon when his successor would come to office.

In truth, there was nothing that American Jews did not fear. Support for Israel was regarded in many circles as a peculiarity of the Democratic Party and an individual part of Truman's world.

I was obsessed with the need to ensure continuity. I therefore suggested to Foreign Minister Sharett that we should use the General Assembly in Paris in 1952 to inaugurate a relationship with General Dwight D. Eisenhower, who had taken up his duties as Commander for the North Atlantic Treaty Organization. We visited him at his office outside Paris where NATO headquarters had been established. He spoke to us with amiability and fluency. On the other hand, when we came away we found it difficult to remember a single commitment that he might have made. He had the strange gift of being articulate without always being specific. This was because his thoughts were always well ahead of his capacity of expression. He frankly revealed to us his lack of roots in the understanding of Jewish problems. Taking us into his confidence, he said that having been brought up in Abilene, Kansas, he had not suspected the existence of Jews during much of his childhood and early youth. It is true that Jews were described in the Bible, but the Bible also spoke of cherubim and seraphim and other creatures who, to the best of his knowledge, no longer existed. He thought that Jews were in this category of extinct species, until, he said, "I came to New York and I found out how wrong I was."

While we were in his singularly stark and unattractive office, we had a good illustration of his self-controlled character. An officer came in and handed him a note. Having finished reading it, he said, "I'll have to leave you and prepare to go to London. King George VI has just died." I noticed that although he had been an intimate acquaintance of the monarch during the days of the war, he showed no emotion at this news. With impressive tranquillity he watched the flags at NATO headquarters come down to half-mast and continued his conversation from the middle of the sentence at which he had been interrupted.

While a Republican success was generally predicted, there was no reason to take for granted the idea that the Democratic Party had ceased to exist. At a large gathering in support of Israel Bonds, in the Opera House in Chicago, Adlai E. Stevenson, the governor of Illinois, listened carefully to my address. He had introduced me with eloquent phrases in which he expressed what I felt to be an authentic historic emotion at the spectacle of Israel's renewal. I developed a friendship with him that lasted for the dozen crowded years in which he developed his remarkable political career. Much of his discourse and all his humor had a self-deprecatory tone, as if he was doubtful of his special worth. I once tried to test the general theory that "the average man" in America could not understand his speeches. I traveled in a cab in Manhattan in which the radio was blaring out Stevenson's most recent speech. The cabdriver was a man of uncouth aspect, unshaven, slovenly in dress and afflicted with the disagreeable habit of spitting through the open window and assailing other cabdrivers with four-letter words. I said, "Did you hear Stevenson's last speech?"

"Sure . . ."

I asked, "Did you understand it?"

The reply was swift: "Yeah, but the average man wouldn't understand it . . ."

Thus began a friendship that flourished while Stevenson deployed his astonishing talent for reconciling immense public respect with electoral failure. His diffidence was sustained even in conditions that should have assured him that his quality was understood in the world. Meeting him in New York during his 1952 campaign, I heard him say that he intended to "talk sense to the American people." I asked him why he had decided to end his political career at such an early stage. His laughter filled the room. His face had a peculiar capacity to pass from implacable gloom to sudden flashes of joy that lit up the human world around him.

While my mission pursued its course, Washington was beginning to awaken out of provincialism to a sense of its growing centrality. America lived intensely with its own paradox. It had come into existence as a nation in rebellion against the Old World with a strong impulse for detachment. In its heart, it wanted nothing more than, in Jefferson's words, to be "separated by Nature and a wide ocean from the exterminating havoc of one quarter of the globe," yet here it was, entangled more and more with all the international rivalries. It was developing a sophisticated political tradition. A powerful realist school was hard at work teaching Americans that a nation must respond exclusively to its self-interest. But there was always a rhapsodic element in the American character, and it was in this part of America's spiritual soil that Israel's cause could flourish.

I had come to America skeptical of its style and values and full of European prejudices. I said, half jokingly, to a Boston audience: "If your tea was what I drank out of a tea bag this morning, I'm not surprised that you threw it into the sea." More substantively I reacted against a tendency for Americans to pontificate against "appeasement." By this they meant quite correctly that Britain and France had decided to resist Hitler too late. But the United States had never intended to resist Hitler at all, and but for Germany's declaration of war in December 1941, Britain would have followed France into subjugation. In that case, there would have been no base on which the United States could have built the immense coalition that later swept Hitlerism into defeat and disgrace.

In short time, I was captivated by the endless variety and spaciousness of America's scenes and the vivid interchange of its moods. This was the greatest union of strength with freedom that had ever lived on earth, and to become the personal recipient of American hospitality and respect was the central experience of my diplomatic years.

The changes in the leadership of the United States and in the policies of the Soviet Union after the end of Truman's presidency were a watershed for Israel. One after the other of those who had written the history of our dramatic half decade began to fade from our scene. Those who had been the architects of Israel's early structure abandoned the stage and left marks of interrogation behind.

Weizmann died in November 1952. Truman left the White House three months later, and in 1953, to general shock and surprise, David Ben-Gurion resigned his historic premiership and settled in the Negev desert at Sdeh Boker.

The lesson for me was plain. I felt that American-Israeli friendship was not yet a tradition and that it would be necessary to reconstruct the solidarities that had illuminated our early years.

Weizmann's passing was the least unexpected of these changes in the human landscape. His health, never robust, had been in rapid decline from the first moment of his presidency. Indeed, he never fully activated that office. Even the blazing successes that he recorded in his two major encounters with Truman were achieved before he assumed the presidency. The first of these kept the Negev incontestably within the Israeli map and the other enabled Truman to recover from the "trusteeship" fiasco and to recognize Israel as soon as its independence was proclaimed. The wonder of Weizmann's career, dating from the Balfour Declaration and the Palestine mandate, lay in the fact that lack of official status never prevented him, or permitted anyone else, to be regarded as the foremost spokesman of Zionism.

When the news of Weizmann's death reached Flushing Meadow, the president of the General Assembly, Foreign Minister Lester Pearson of Canada, convened the General Assembly in a session of tribute. This is not the usual habit of the United Nations. Pearson understood that Weizmann represented the Founding Fathers generation in Israel and that his passing was a special landmark. Responding to Pearson's tribute to President Weizmann, I took the rostrum for a very short speech of thanks:

> He led Israel for thirty years through a wilderness of martyrdom and anguish, of savage oppression and frustrated hope, across the sharpest

agony which has ever beset any family of the human race; and at the end of his days he entered into his due inheritance of honor as the first president of Israel, the embodiment in modern times of the kingly tradition which once flourished in Israel and became an abiding source of light and redemption for succeeding generations of mankind.

When I came down from the podium, Anthony Eden, who had come to the UN to take part in the Korea debate, approached me and said: "That was very eloquent. You know he was a great friend of mine."

I knew nothing of the kind. More than any other British statesman, Eden had put sharp brakes on Churchill's desire during World War II to give evidence of sympathy for Zionism. In 1944, when most ministers were attuned to the idea of partition with a Jewish state, Eden's foreign ministry had been the only focus of opposition. Neither Eden nor I in our brief exchange could have predicted how sharply and ironically our respective interests would bring our countries together in a strange, tense ordeal about the Suez Canal within four years.

On the day after Weizmann's death I received a coded message from Prime Minister Ben-Gurion instructing me to talk to Professor Albert Einstein in Princeton and to find out what his reaction would be if he were offered the presidency of Israel. I was astounded by the originality and audacity of this approach, although I knew in my heart that it would fail.

Before I could plan any action, I received an agitated phone call from Professor Einstein himself. He said that the press was already discussing the possibility of his appointment. He wished me to note that it was quite unthinkable, and he wanted me to make every effort to see that the press ceased dealing with it. There was a tone of panic in his voice. Einstein said, "I am moved by the audacity of the thought, but my rejection is firm and implacable." He added, "I know a little about nature, but hardly anything about human beings. Please, Mr. Ambassador, do whatever you can to lift the siege of journalists around my house."

I told Einstein that I fully understood and respected his position. He should, however, in return understand my inability to accept a rejection of the offer to be president of Israel in the course of a telephone conversation. "I must ask you to receive a spokesman who would seek your reaction in a more formal and dignified way." He agreed. In my letter to Einstein I wrote: "The prime minister assures me that in such circumstances, complete facility and freedom to pursue your great scientific work would be afforded by the government and people who are fully conscious of the supreme significance of your labors."

I dispatched my deputy, David Goitein, to Princeton and he returned with Einstein's written reply. Goitein was soon to become a justice in the Israeli Supreme Court, and this was almost his last diplomatic function. Einstein's reply to me made Goitein's mission worthwhile:

I am deeply moved by the offer from our state of Israel, and at once saddened and ashamed because I cannot accept it. All my life I have dealt with objective matters. Hence, I lack both a natural aptitude and the experience to deal properly with people and to exercise official functions. For these reasons alone, I should be unsuited to fulfill the duties of that high office, even if advancing age was not making increasing inroads on my strength. I am the more distressed over these circumstances because my relationship to the Jewish people has become my strongest human bond since I became fully aware of our precarious situation among the nations of the world.

I have always cherished this letter and have thought that it was worthwhile for me to elicit it from him. For Zionists, the most impressive word is *"our* state of Israel" and *"our* precarious situations among the nations of the world."* Surely, the apologetic, self-effacing doctrine of Jewish assimilation has never been given a more decisive body blow than in the spectacle of the greatest Jew of this century speaking of Israel and of the Jewish people in such intimate identification.

Suzy and I were unable to attend the ceremony of Eisenhower's inauguration or to witness Truman's departure from office, since we were plunged in a personal bereavement through the death of our infant daughter, Meira, in one of those cradle asphyxiations for which no explanation has been found to this day. On the television, however, we followed the drama of Truman's departure.

There is a moving and simple dignity in the process whereby power is assumed and relinquished in the American system. As I watched the black-and-white television screen, I reflected on Truman's glittering record of influential decisions. He had decided to devastate Hiroshima and Nagasaki with nuclear weapons, to force Soviet troops out of Iran, to assume the responsibilities that Britain had abandoned in Turkey and Greece, to offer Marshall aid to Western and Eastern Europe, to accept the Soviet Union's rejection with serenity, to establish the North Atlantic Treaty Organization, to contain Soviet expansion, to resist the North Korean invasion of South Korea, to dismiss General MacArthur for insubordination, to despise Senator McCarthy in strident terms, to recognize Israel and thus fix the parameters of the post-war Middle East, and to fight a successful election campaign that he seemed to have no chance of winning. He had many hard edges, but it is hard to withhold respect for his unexpectedly assertive use of the presidential power and for his success in securing consensus in its behalf.

I had been in the United States for five years, all of them dominated by the Truman administration. I felt that he had influenced the direction of his nation's life more profoundly than any of his predecessors. The Truman presidency is the constitutive period in the modern international system. Most of the vocabulary and conceptual habits of American thinking on international politics became firmly embedded in the national consciousness in those years. Truman had wielded his last office without ever being obsessed by the grandeur of his status. It was precisely this lack of pretension that helped him keep his feet on the ground and his hand in touch with the common stream of his nation's life.

After listening to Eisenhower's unmemorable inauguration address with a subtle hint of skepticism on his expressive face, Truman went to Union Station, boarded a train and chugged his way back to Independence, Missouri. He didn't feel that anything was very different from when he had gone to Washington seven years before. He gathered his friends around him and played cards as he used to do in the past, and probably with the same neighbors. Nothing much had happened to him. Except that he had changed the world . . .

We had known for some time that we would have to pursue our national tasks without Weizmann and Truman. Ben-Gurion's abrupt departure was a different matter. This was an affair of choice. Ben-Gurion had every right to be tired. He was a buoyant, vigorous man who sent out sparks of energy in all directions. But since 1933, he had borne heavy responsibilities. Although he was sixty-six years old, physical strain did not seem to be the main factor in his exhaustion. His capacities and opportunities of leadership reached their highest point relatively late in life, as was the case with Churchill, Konrad Adenauer, Charles de Gaulle, and others before and after him, including our own Eshkol, Golda Meir, Menachem Begin and Shamir. Behind his ritual words of parting one could sense his dissatisfaction with some elements in Israeli life. The intensity of parliamentary warfare, the fragmentation arising from the electoral system, the need to be perpetually conciliating small groups in order to maintain a coalition—all these were repellent to his dynamic nature.

The idea of Israel without Ben-Gurion's leadership had never yet dawned on Israeli minds, not even on those of his opponents. But there was no sense of permanent parting. Ben-Gurion did not actually hang a message "I Shall Return" on the doorknob, but I could not forbear, perhaps with some irreverence, to remind my friends of Metternich's reaction when he heard of the death of a famous Russian ambassador whose skill he had admired: "You say he's died? What was his motive?"

Happily, the analogy is not complete, for Ben-Gurion had many years of activity ahead, but the search for the motive of his resignation in 1953 is still alive. He will always keep posterity intrigued. One thing is certain. Nothing in him was ever exactly what it seemed. . . .

12

NEW REGIMES: 1953–1956

FOR FIVE YEARS, since 1947, nothing important had gone wrong. There were now four years, from 1953 to 1956, in which nothing at home or abroad seemed to go right.

Weizmann, Truman and Ben-Gurion had been the central figures in the partition breakthrough. By early 1953 their places had been filled by Yitshak Ben-Zvi, Eisenhower and Sharett. This was disconcertingly unfamiliar. Before we could grow accustomed to the new faces the clouds grew thick on our horizon. On the adversarial side of the barricade, well-known faces vanished. King Abdullah of Transjordan had been assassinated in the Jerusalem mosque in July 1951, King Farouk of Egypt was removed from office by the revolutionary officers headed by Muhammad Naguib and Gamal Abdel Nasser in 1952, and Stalin died in 1953.

The entire gallery of leaders who had dominated the Middle East since the end of the world war was swept away by the hand of time or by the characteristic turbulence of our region. The Middle Eastern story would be written by different hands.

It was an ominous story. The Soviet Union abandoned its support of Israel in 1953. The first indication of this change came to my anxious attention in 1952, when the Soviet Union joined the Arab states in defeating a proposal for a negotiated settlement for which I had mustered majority support in the UN Political Committee. I had called this proposal a Blueprint for Peace, and it won approval in the world press. It recommended free negotiation not to be tightly bound to the November 1947 provisions that had been morally and politically weakened by Arab rejection, as well as by the war and the armistice agreements.

The negative Soviet vote was only the first vague hint of a departure from Moscow's previous support, which had been consistent during our early years. But the clouds continued to accumulate. In November 1952 the Communist government in Czechoslovakia executed party leaders, including Rudolf Slansky, the secretary of the Communist Party who was a Jew but a rabid anti-Zionist. The former Czech foreign minister, Walter Clementls, with whom I had worked in the UN, also went to the gallows. An Israeli left-wing leader, Mordechai Oren, was implausibly accused of subverting Czechoslovak security. He was later released. His trial had served as an occasion for vicious propaganda against Zionism and Israel.

In January 1953, a worse blow fell. The Soviet Union arrested several Jewish doctors and accused them of diabolically seeking to murder Soviet leaders. The ugliest forms of anti-Semitic agitation accompanied this judicial farce, which turned out to be one of the death throes of Stalinism.

In response to these provocations, demonstrations took place against Soviet policies in all countries with Jewish communities. A foolish Israeli set off a bomb in the Soviet Mission in Tel Aviv. Israel's official apology was swift and patently sincere: Nothing could have served our interest less. But our expression of regret was contemptuously rejected, and the Soviet Union broke diplomatic relations with Israel. In other countries where demonstrators had caused damage to Soviet missions, the U.S.S.R. response had been much less extreme.

Some experts who professed to understand Soviet motives conjectured that the Kremlin's new hostility toward Israel was a response to our support of the U.S. action in Korea. I am convinced that this is inaccurate. Israel was one of dozens of countries that were far more influential than Israel in endorsing the UN role in Korea. The greater likelihood is that the change of Soviet policy reflected an intensified desire to pursue the Cold War. The Arabs were candidates for an anti-Western coalition and Israel was not. The motive for Soviet support of Israel had been the elimination of the British base in Palestine. This was achieved. It is not a Soviet habit to go on paying for a service already obtained.

I experienced no personal change in the attitude of Soviet diplomats toward me. One of them, the virulent Andrei Vyshinski, even invited me for a talk in which he explained with pedagogic care the "objective" compulsions that stood in the way of anything more than a formal Soviet relationship with Israel. The Soviet Union, he explained, was the target of United States hostility, which found particular expression in international agencies. Moscow had a prospect of winning understanding from Arab states, and no such prospect from Israel. This was because Israel depended economically on the Western powers, and economic interests, "as is well known" to students of Leninism, defined political attitudes. Therefore, added Vyshinski, "even if you wanted to give the U.S.S.R. equal weight with the United States in your calculations, it would be objectively impossible."

My contacts with Vyshinski increased in those years despite tensions between our governments. By some strange quirk of fortune I was elected as one of the vice presidents of the UN General Assembly. This seemed a strange result, since Israel at that time was being mercilessly castigated by the Security Council and the major powers for its retaliation to *fedayeen* raids.

A vice presidency of the General Assembly of the United Nations is not an onerous function, but it did bring me into frequent proximity with the heads of the major powers at dinner parties and consultations. At one of these functions, having watched Vyshinski's lavish absorption of vodka, I decided to take advantage of his amiability to pose a question: "Tell me, Andrei Andreyevitch, why don't you let the Soviet Jews emigrate? What does it really matter to the Soviet Union?"

His reply: "What are you talking about? If the Jews leave, everybody will want to leave!"

The next morning, in the cold light of sobriety, he sought contact with me very early and said anxiously: "I hope you understood that yesterday was joke." Then with great formality, "Since was only joke I assume Your Excellency did not send telegram . . ." I left him in suspense for a castigatory moment and assured him that My Excellency had not cabled his heretical words. Siberia receded from his horizon.

Egypt was no exception to the wind of change that was blowing many a leadership away in the early months of 1953. The Egyptian monarchy was overthrown and a "revolutionary" regime under General Naguib, and later Colonel Nasser, had been instituted. There would now be a competition between the superpowers for the favors of the new regime. My own inclination had been to look with a measure of hope on the young revolutionaries. During my years in Cairo I had not developed any sympathy for the decadent regime of the repulsive monarch, King Farouk, and his courtiers. It was soon apparent, however, that Nasser would give priority to an Arab constituency and that militant anti-Zionism would be the main component of his Arab and domestic strategy.

The winds that blew on Israel from the West were less harsh, but far from consoling. The Eisenhower administration, which had taken over from Truman in January 1953, did not drastically change anything in American-Israeli relations. The economic support that was then the main element of United States–Israel cooperation continued to flow. But Washington announced a "New Look," thus equating the Middle East with the lengthened hemlines featured in the fashion industry. In an effort to win Arab smiles, the administration avoided the traditional rhetoric of friendship with Israel. In October 1953, when we were agonizingly harassed by Arab assaults on frontier villages and by interference with Israel's irrigation projects in the north, the United States joined in heavy condemnation of Israel's reprisals, especially after a raid at Kibya, which most of Israeli opinion also regarded as excessive. Over sixty Arabs, many of them women and children, were killed. Reprisal raids at that time were assigned to a special formation called "Unit 101," under the command of Colonel Arik Sharon.[1] The army had never

---

[1]Chaim Herzog, *The Arab-Israeli Wars* (New York: Random House), 1982, p. 120.

concealed its responsibility for these actions, which were taken in response to attacks by *fedayeen* terrorists. On this occasion, however, Ben-Gurion had instructed me to explain that the raid was undertaken not by the Israeli army but by enraged settlers. Nobody could possibly believe this preposterous story, nor would it have brought any credit to Israel if it were believed. I solved the problem by taking the telegram and saying at the Security Council, "I have received the following telegram from my government," and then declaiming the text.

In the same month, when Israel refused to halt its development work at B'not Ya'akov in the northern demilitarized zone, the United States suspended its grants in aid—only to renew them a few weeks later under indignant public pressure in America.

I experienced an unusual hour of satisfaction when an emissary of Secretary Dulles's, Assistant Secretary Henry Byroade, came to New York, where I was attending a meeting of the UN General Assembly, to ask me urgently to accept the renewal of the suspended aid and to announce this before the mayoral election in New York City. I overcame a mischievous instinct to reply with a lordly refusal to accept the proffered millions. This, however, would not have served my cause with our Finance Ministry. If one wants to be excessively dignified, it is advisable not to be insolvent.

Secretary of State John Foster Dulles visited Israel and Arab states in the summer of 1953. He called me to the State Department soon after his confirmation to tell me that he would give priority of attention to the Arab-Jewish conflict. He began with Cairo, where he distinguished himself by offering a silver revolver to President Naguib on behalf of President Eisenhower. He did not indicate the direction in which he wanted Egypt to point this weapon and the symbolism did not sit well with the Israeli leaders whom he met the next day—and to whom he offered no gift except an abundant quantity of advice. On his return to Washington he apprised me of his conclusions. These were not all adverse to Israel, but he hinted that Israel should offer boundary concessions to Egypt and Jordan as the price of a peace settlement, which these two Arab governments showed no signs of desiring. He did not seem to understand that Egypt and Jordan wanted slices of our territory without wanting peace.

Although the new rulers in Moscow made some impressive gestures of conciliation, such as the acceptance of the Austrian State Treaty, the conclusion of an armistice in Korea and the resumption of relations with Israel, Eisenhower and Dulles saw nothing but an intensification of danger to the United States from what they called "world communism." They attached high priority to thwarting the aged Winston Churchill's ambition to probe the real intentions of the post-Stalin leadership in the Kremlin. Like most of my colleagues in the Washington diplomatic corps, I could not understand what harm could arise from such an exploration by the world's senior statesman. My impression was not that the Eisenhower administration feared that a Churchill initiative would reveal a negative trend in the Soviet Union. They feared that the Soviet leadership might reveal a more pragmatic face and thus undermine the faith of the American people in the theology of the Cold War. This had implications for Israel. I believed then, and continually thereafter, that Israel had nothing to gain from American-Soviet rivalry and that an intense Cold War environment would always make Israel's position precarious.

After the tremors in Washington and Moscow in 1953, Israelis had less confidence than before about their place in the world. Israelis have always been prone to interpret any sign of coolness from its friends as abandonment or even betrayal, and Jewish history explains, if it does not justify, an excessive sensitivity about what non-Jews think of us.

The domestic situation augmented our gloom. Immigration had dwindled to 11,000 in 1953. More Jews were leaving the country than were entering it. Israel seemed to be evoking a diminished resonance in the world.

All in all, it could not be said that Ben-Gurion was handing the country over to his successor in a prosperous condition. Sharett was inheriting what I called "a beehive without honey." His difficulties were compounded by a visible lack of authority. Ben-Gurion had spoken of retirement "for a year or two," but it was not much of a "retirement." During his residence in the Negev at Sdeh Boker, Ben-Gurion exercised strong influence on his party, on many ministers and on leading army officers. And, in the manner of strong leaders, he generated a subtle atmosphere of skepticism around his successor. Thus an air of transience pervaded the Sharett government from the first day to the last. For the first time, the prime minister was not also the minister of defense. Both positions had previously been held by Ben-Gurion. Sharett, as prime minister, now was the foreign minister, while defense went to Pinchas Lavon.

Lavon was energetic and strong minded, but of bitter, contentious disposition. He came to his office with a pacifist reputation, which he strove to live down by proposing ferocious reprisals after every Arab provocation and by defiant attitudes to the outside world. I found it impossible to establish anything except a cold, formal relationship with him. He gave no deference to Prime Minister Sharett and lived in permanent tension with the army commanders and officials of his ministry. A frosty air flowed among Ben-Gurion, Sharett and Lavon. None of the three had any respect for the other two. The country incurred all the defects of a prime minister's resignation without the balancing advantages of a new, stable leadership.

The year 1954 opened ominously with a Soviet veto in the Security Council on a plan enabling Israel to carry out a development project at B'not Ya'akov on the Syrian-Israeli boundary. There was no objective reason for this. No harm to Syria's interests was involved in the compromise worked out by an ingenious UN representative. My own efforts to win Andrei Vyshinski's understanding of our position had ended with his genial exhortation to me to "settle it all with Syria directly."

This first Soviet veto had a significance far beyond its particular context.

From that day on, the UN Security Council would be closed to Israel as a court of appeal or redress. Arabs could kill Israeli citizens across the border, blockade Israel's Red Sea port of Eilat, close the Suez Canal to Israeli shipping, send armed groups into Israel for murder and havoc, and decline to carry out crucial clauses of the armistice agreements in the certainty that the Security Council would not adopt even the mildest resolution of criticism. Sometimes the veto was actually used by the Soviet Union against majority resolutions. At other times, the very anticipation of it prevented the majority from submitting texts that would give any support to Israel's interests. The jurisprudence of the United Nations thus came to imply that Arab governments could conduct warfare against Israel, while Israel could offer no legitimate response.

On September 1, 1951, I had won a diplomatic victory for Israel by persuading the Security Council to condemn all maritime interference or claims of active belligerency against Israel as "inconsistent with the letter and spirit of the Egyptian-Israeli armistice agreement." The Soviet Union had not obstructed that judgment; its abstention was almost its last gesture of relative goodwill toward Israel. But the blockade continued. Egypt refused to take any notice of the Security Council's Resolution of 1951. Now, in 1954, the Soviet Union vetoed our complaint that the Arabs were winning recognition for the doctrine that all resolutions of international agencies were binding on Israel, but not on themselves.

It was not only a question of political discrimination. There were practical effects of the most tragic kind. The Arab governments had resolved, without risking total war, to drive Israel out of its mind by a constant torment of piecemeal violence. The crisis over the B'not Ya'akov project had arisen only because Syria opened fire to stop Israeli development work. It was easier for the United Nations to order the suspension of the Israeli work than to order the cessation of the Arab fire.

In his report to the Security Council on September 7, 1954, the Canadian General E. L. M. Burns, who had become the UN chief of staff, predicted that incidents on the Jordan-Israel border could spread "like brush fire." He added that "marauding into Israel by armed gangs is serious," but "Israeli retaliation by armed raids is a dangerous remedy." The United States was using a similar formula: Infiltration from Jordan constituted a serious problem, but Israel's "apparent policy of armed retaliation had increased rather than diminished tension along the armistice lines."

Whether there would really have been less tension if Israel had sat back and let its citizens be killed without "armed retaliation" is moot. Since no such bizarre experiment in national masochism has ever been tried in any country, we shall never know the answer. The crux of the matter was that an urgent problem existed and no solution was at hand.

After our disastrous Kibya raid in October 1953, I had obtained the Israeli Cabinet's support for proposing a review of the Armistice Agreement with

Jordan in accordance with Article XII, which stipulated that if after a year (from March 1949) either signatory asked the secretary-general to convene a conference with the other party to review or revise the agreement, attendance was mandatory. Secretary-General Dag Hammarskjöld turned to Amman, received a refusal to attend the "mandatory" conference—and there the matter ended.

So the Security Council was blocked by veto, the Mixed Armistice Commissions condemned reprisals and provocations with equal voice, and a review of the agreement was illegally refused. It was at this stage that many of us began to wonder if we had any deterrence except armed response.

This was tried on a local level with no good effect. The most drastic Israeli action was at Gaza in February 1955. There had been incursions into Egyptian territory, and Egypt had been condemned by the Mixed Armistice Commission twenty-six times. The Israeli riposte at Gaza left thirty-eight Egyptian and eight Israeli dead. Sharett, who had approved this operation, said that this was a larger number of Egyptian casualties "than had been intended." I never considered that it would be possible to maintain a credible quota system in estimating the human consequences of a military operation.

The armistice system was approaching a dead end. It had been founded on a basic contradiction between the intentions of its signatories. Israel had regarded it as the end of the war and as a virtual peace settlement in embryo. It therefore stressed those provisions in the agreement that gave a hint of stabilization and finality. The Arab governments saw the armistice as a temporary phase in a continuing war that had never been renounced. They therefore placed their accent on the provisional and noncommittal spirit of some formulations, especially on the boundary question. The major powers and the United Nations began with strong support of the Israeli interpretation of the armistice agreements as stable international contracts; but as a result of Arab pressure Eden, Dulles and even Hammarskjöld began to speak of the 1949 lines as though they had no durable legitimacy. Thus the political force of the armistice agreements was undermined at the very time that their security provisions were being disrupted by daily violence.

From his voluntary "exile" in Sdeh Boker, Ben-Gurion was urging young Israelis to abandon the cities and even the kibbutzim in order to settle the Negev. Suzy and I visited him on several occasions at his desert home. It was a somewhat surrealistic experience. His residence was a small wooden hut, crowded with books and papers, and nearly always frequented by politicians or foreign visitors. The politicians were in quest of directives about how to conduct the country while evading any subordination to the will of the incumbent prime minister. The foreign visitors were attracted both by the idea of an interview with the real center of power and by the paradox of Ben-Gurion's ostensibly austere circumstances. He rejected air-conditioning for some time in order to establish his status as an "equal" member of the kibbutz. He himself was totally immune to the seductions of personal comfort, but he was shielded from real austerity by the protective ministrations of his wife, Paula, who fed him on Tel Aviv delicacies while offering his and her guests the barely edible but plentiful fare of the kibbutzniks. Paula regarded her husband's movement to Sdeh Boker as an offense to her central human interests and she filled the air with expressions of outrage formulated in Brooklynese English, with an admixture of Yiddish imprecations describing her illustrious husband as "meshugge" for coming to "this place." She would then embark on nostalgic descriptions of the family home in Tel Aviv, which she painted in poignantly palatial terms as if it were an immense distance away, like Jerusalem in the memory of the exiles in Babylon. Having listened in emotional sympathy to these tirades we would find Paula the following day in Tel Aviv, quite often with Ben-Gurion himself in residence for the purpose of plunging into the opulent riches of his immense library.

If Ben-Gurion's intention had been to attract masses of young Israelis away from urban indulgence toward the asperities and challenges of the Wild South, his gesture could not be adjudged as a great success. The demographic relationship between the populous Tel Aviv area and the open spaces of the Negev remained depressingly constant, despite the encouraging growth of Beersheva, which Ben-Gurion did not regard as sufficiently southern to be graded as genuinely pioneering country. But the didactic influence of his "flight" to the Negev was not negligible. He was illustrating the theme that Israel was still a half-empty country, with no real need of annexing Arab-populated areas. He also stressed the theme that the ennobling devotions of Zionism were giving way prematurely to a measure of hedonism. His message to Israeli youth was "if you insist on living in cities, at least feel guilty about it."

Ben-Gurion's awkward self-imposed exile came to a close in February 1955 when Lavon ended his uneasy reign at the Ministry of Defense. Lavon had reacted almost hysterically to the aggravation of Israel's solitude. He interpreted the agreement for the evacuation of British forces from the Suez Canal area, under a new treaty with Egypt, as a dangerous body blow to Israel. There was now no non-Arab force between Israel and its most powerful and hostile neighbor. This was an exaggerated reaction. While the British forces were in the Canal Zone their presence had brought little comfort to Israel. I recalled the incident in December 1949 when British aircraft had actually intervened against Israel in an air clash in which five British planes had been shot down. The British occupier had not managed to secure Israel's right of free passage in the Suez Canal. We had no complaint on this matter since the British force was severely limited in its function by the dictates of Egyptian sovereignty. Moreover, I felt the paradox in our position. Here was Israel, who had fought arduously against British occupation of Palestine, weeping bitterly because neighboring Egypt had decided by peaceful contract to do what we had done by armed struggle! It looked as if we were in favor of all countries being occupied by foreign forces except our own. It had been because of my sensitivity on this point that I had voted against a continuation of British tutelage in Libya in the General Assembly vote of 1948.

Lavon's nervousness was reflected in the organization of a complex Intelligence network in Egypt, involving both Israelis and Egyptian Jews. In an ill-conceived operation known in Israeli folklore as "The Mishap," these agents had blown up British and American civilian buildings, including cinemas and restaurants in Cairo, in the hope that these assaults would be regarded by the U.S. and Britain as symptoms of Egyptian hostility to the West. The "logic" was that in that case the West would decide not to leave the Canal Zone and would act punitively against Egypt. The tragic consequence was that some Egyptian Jews were executed in Cairo and others were imprisoned for agonizingly long periods.

The question whether Lavon had given the order for this folly or whether, as he alleged, the order had been given without authorization by Intelligence chiefs, acting under the inspiration of Lavon's enemies, was to agitate the Israeli political system for many years and would in the course of time bring about Ben-Gurion's final resignation in 1963. It was evident that against this background and in the light of the distrust with which Lavon was seen both by Ben-Gurion and Sharett, there was no course except for Lavon to resign from the Cabinet. Ben-Gurion was back, if not at the helm, at least in an influential position as defense minister.

I was able to escape from my struggles in Washington for a week in April when I went to San Francisco for the celebration of the tenth anniversary of the United Nations. The associations of the place were very moving. I recalled the day in Jerusalem when I saw a picture in the newspapers of the 1945 meeting and observed that every nation sat behind its name and flag except the one nation that had suffered most from the assaults of Nazi barbarism. There was a stir in the hall when I opened my speech with the words: "Ten years ago we were not here. Our absence revealed the deep chasm of weakness and disaster into which we had fallen."

Amid the intersecting encounters I used the gathering to explore some new contacts. A great deal goes on in international assemblies behind the scenes. Indeed, the chief value of scenes lies in what can be done behind them.

I visited British Foreign Secretary Harold Macmillan, who invited me for what he called "a drink," which turned out to be several drinks for him and one tepid, weak whisky and soda for me. He ruminated in a rich Edwardian accent as though he were doing an exaggerated imitation of himself. Everything about him was easy, languid and self-confident. He had the disconcerting habit of appearing as if he could only avoid going to sleep with great difficulty by keeping his eyes open with intense ocular effort, but when I left him and weighed up what he had said, everything was coherent and in place. The general trend of his utterance was in praise of Zionism. Had not Winston Churchill and Leopold Amery been among his mentors and friends? It was only later that I came to discern the deep strain of social compassion that hid behind the conservative facade.

More exacting was a luncheon party that Foreign Minister Vyacheslav Molotov of the Soviet Union gave in honor of our delegation. Before the convivial part of our meeting, I had a talk with him for an hour and a half. There was a legend that nobody had ever seen him smile, and I was curious to know if this was true. I left him a few hours later with the legend intact. He had given notice to me that he did not speak or understand English and that I should bring an English-language interpreter. I decided that if I was to talk a language that he did not understand, it might just as well be Hebrew. Accompanied by our erudite legal counselor, Dr. Jacob Robinson, I arrived at Molotov's headquarters and began my Hebrew remarks. I had not gone very far when he interrupted me: "What exactly is the language you are talking? I've listened carefully and it sounds nothing like Yiddish. I know, because my wife speaks Yiddish."

After the necessary philological clarification we went on to our business. He was plain and blunt. His information was that the United States was going to get Israel to sign a defense treaty. This would be a tragic development; the central aim of Soviet policy was to avoid being encircled by American and other imperialist bases. The Soviet Union had helped Israel come into existence in the hope that it would never lend itself as a base for the hostile actions of one power against the other.

The idea that Eisenhower and Dulles were ardently pursuing Israel as a partner for their defense pacts was too painful an irony for me to sustain. I could see, however, that Soviet policymakers were in earnest. They cared little how Israel voted and not much about what Israel would do in the UN. They would maintain a correct, if not a cordial, official relationship. They believed that Israel's statehood was immutable. They had a quarrel with our policies, not with our existence. The only serious thing they asked of us was that we should resist the blandishments of American policymakers, who were trying hard to conclude a military alliance with us.

When we sat down to the table, Molotov and the other Soviet diplomats with him seemed to be concentrating their most suspicious gaze upon me, as if to probe whether I had been negotiating defense alliances with the United States between drinks and the first course. It was decided that at the dinner there would only be toasts, no speeches and no political remarks. Molotov's toast was "to the government and people and delegation of Israel, health and prosperity—and please do not sign defense pacts with the United States."

In a year in which there were few consolations, we had to draw some comfort from the fact that we had access to all the Great Powers and could hold discourse with them. France had spent two years almost totally concentrated on its predicaments in Tunisia and Morocco. This created both a sense of detachment and an atmosphere of sympathy. French prime ministers had come twice to Washington and stayed at Blair House, where they received me for discussions in which they revealed their distaste for U.S. policies. By coincidence, they were both Jews: Pierre Mendès-France at the height of his prestige after the Indochina conference and the Tunisian settlements, and later René Mayer, who had agreed to attend a seder in our residence but had been recalled to Paris for one of his parliament's recurrent crises.

Until 1955 the American "New Look" had been expressed mainly in reluctance to articulate the importance of the U.S.-Israeli relationship. It was possible for Israel to live with this somewhat ungracious posture. But it never occurred to me that a massive infusion of Soviet arms into Arab states at levels and quantities that would shatter the balance of forces in the Middle East would be greeted by Washington with nothing but a friendly warning to us "not to worry." Yet this was precisely the reaction of the United States and Britain to the announcement of an arms transaction agreed upon between Egypt and Czechoslovakia, under Soviet inspiration. Aircraft, tanks and guns of a destructive capacity hitherto unknown in the region would now pour into Egypt at a rate beyond all previous experience. We saw ourselves faced with strategic dangers far greater than those involved in the daily border attacks.

The bottom had clearly been knocked out of our security balance. It was the Jewish New Year when a messenger brought me the news of the Egyptian-Czech arms deal to the Adas Israel Synagogue in Washington. My thoughts strayed away from prayers for the distant future toward concern for the immediate present.

The criticism of Western policy that I now developed was not that it failed to prevent Soviet penetration, but that it neglected the measures by which the effects of that penetration might have been counteracted. What was now needed was a show of Western strength to demonstrate that the Middle East was not going to become a Soviet preserve. And in relation to Israel, there was a need to maintain stability by a modest reinforcement of Israel's armaments and a stronger support of the armistice lines as internationally recognized boundaries that must be carefully safeguarded until they were replaced by a new agreement. Neither of these courses was taken.

The first link in the chain leading toward explosion was the Baghdad Pact of February 24, 1955. This was a "pact of mutual cooperation" between Iraq and Turkey, linked to an earlier treaty between Turkey and Pakistan. Britain and Iran joined in 1955. The United States did not formally adhere to the Pact, but its spiritual father was John Foster Dulles and the main support in arms and money came from the United States. This was part of Dulles's policy of containing Soviet expansion by contractual deterrents that would prevent Soviet penetration of the Middle East.

Nasser was violently offended by what he interpreted as an effort by Washington and London to divide the Arab world into rival blocs corresponding to the East-West division. His position as the leader of the Arab world was being challenged. He responded by a vehement anti-Westernism.

He pressed for the overthrow of pro-Western regimes in Baghdad, Amman and elsewhere and strengthened his links with Moscow.

All that eventually remained of the Baghdad Pact was its negative effect on Israel. Dulles explained to me that by involving Arab states in a "northern tier" defense against Soviet expansion together with non-Arab states, like Iran and Turkey, he would be substituting communism for Zionism as the major foe of the Arabs and would divert Arab preoccupation from the Israeli issue. It was hard to listen to such talk without violation of courtesy. The idea that Arab emotional priorities could be changed by signing documents and creating institutions revealed an obsessive legalism and a lack of understanding of Middle Eastern history and culture.

Israel had an acute sense of exclusion and solitude. Arab states were being rearmed under defense pacts with the major powers, while Israel had neither an assured source of arms nor any international support of its security and integrity. All I could do was to stimulate the growth of American public opinion against this folly. On a CBS "Face the Nation" program at the end of February, I tried to put the matter in simple terms:

> British tanks to Egypt; American tanks to Saudi Arabia; British planes and tanks to Iraq; British planes and tanks to Jordan; American arms to Iraq; Soviet bombers, fighters, tanks and submarines to Egypt; and no arms for Israel. Bombers to Egypt to terrorize our cities? Yes. Fighters to Israel to help ward off those perils? No.
> What kind of policy is this . . . ?

There was a strong resonance to this interview, and the Eisenhower administration took it seriously. Deputy Secretary of State Robert Murphy, a genial man, said to me: "The secretary thinks that this was a pretty strong criticism from an ambassador—against the government to which he is accredited . . ." It was the only occasion on which I ever received even a low-key warning about my appeals to American public opinion.

The fear that Israel's security was being compromised to a horrifying degree was not merely a subjective "complex" of Israelis. Anxious support for Israel came from an unexpected source. One day in April 1955 our information officer in the consulate in New York, Reuven Dafni, called me to say that Albert Einstein had written to express deep consternation at Israel's plight. He suggested that we meet to discuss how he might help. I made my way to Mercer Street in Princeton with Dafni. Einstein opened the door to us himself. He was dressed in a rumpled beige sweater and equally disheveled slacks.

He came straight to the issue. He said that the radio and television networks were always asking him for interviews, which he always refused. He now thought that if he had some "publicity interest," he might as well use it. Did I think that the media would be interested to record a talk by him to the

American people and the world? I exchanged glances with Dafni, as if to say that this was the newspaperman's dream. Einstein took out a pen, dipped it in an old-fashioned inkwell and began to scratch some sentences on a writing block. We soon decided that he needed more time and arranged for Dafni and me to come and help him with the formulation of the text another day. Einstein courteously asked if we would like some coffee. Assuming that he would get a housekeeper or maid to produce the beverage, I politely accepted. To my horror Einstein trotted into the kitchen, from which we soon heard the clatter of cups and pots, with an occasional piece of crockery falling to earth, as if to honor the gravity theory of our host's great predecessor, Newton.

Arrangements went forward in Dafni's energetic hands for Einstein's planned television address, which was to be nationwide. But when Dafni and I were to meet him we were told that the professor had been taken to the hospital. A few days later he died. Among his papers were found the handwritten pages that he had prepared for the opening of his address. It began:

I speak to you tonight as an American citizen and also as a Jew and as a human being who has always striven to consider matters objectively.

His unspoken text went on:

What I am trying to do is simply to serve truth and justice with my modest strength. You may think that the conflict between Israel and Egypt is a small and unimportant problem. "We have more important concerns," you might say. That is not the case. When it comes to truth and justice there is no difference between small and great problems. Whosoever fails to take small matters seriously in a spirit of truth, cannot be trusted in greater affairs. . . .

The extract breaks off after a few reflections on the Cold War, which made it plain that Einstein held Soviet and U.S. policy in equal criticism.

We shall never know how Einstein proposed to end his appeal on Israel's behalf. At a crowded memorial to Einstein in Carnegie Hall on May 14, 1955, the seventh anniversary of Israel's independence, I said:

He saw the rebirth of Israel as one of the few political acts in his lifetime which were of an essentially moral quality. . . . When he felt the cold wind of Israel's insecurity, he apprehended that something very precious was being endangered, and at that moment he fell into a deep, responsible and active preoccupation with Israel's future which brought me to him in the final days of his life, in encounters which I shall always cherish, recalling the warm and proud Jewish solidarity which enriched his discourse and endowed it with undying grace.

By this time the pressure on Eisenhower and Dulles to do something effective about Israel's declining balance of power was coming loudly from the American public, and not only from the Israeli embassy. Dulles's resistance to our arms request was beginning slowly to erode. At a dinner in Washington he had said cautiously that the United States had an obligation to prevent Israel suffering from "an imbalance" of arms. Later that month he confessed his dilemma to me with candor. He said that he was now convinced that the needs of equilibrium required Israel to receive some modern jet fighters and other arms. On the other hand, if the United States supplied them directly, it would be under irresistible pressure to open a supply relationship with Arab states. The question was whether Israel could get what she wanted from somewhere else. I replied that this was not possible, since the fighters that we sought were manufactured only in the United States and Canada.

On hearing the word "Canada," which I had mentioned only in routine pursuit of accuracy, Dulles seemed to spring to attention, as if he had suddenly stumbled on an unexpected treasure. The doodling on a yellow pad and the nervous twitch of eyes and mouth abruptly ceased. He said with contrived casualness that Lester Pearson, the foreign minister of Canada, was in Washington that very day. I could not understand why he was telling me about his schedule. After all, foreign ministers were coming in and out of Washington almost every hour. Dulles said that some American F-86s were manufactured on license in Canada but were nevertheless at the disposition of the United States.

A few hours later I called the Canadian embassy, where Ambassador Arnold Heeney informed me that Dulles had asked Lester Pearson to make twenty-four F-86 jet fighters available to Israel out of the American quota production line!

There now began an extraordinary period of equivocation in which the United States pressed Canada and France to do that which it wanted to avoid doing itself. From my point of view, this was better than nothing at all, but I could well understand the resentment in Paris and Ottawa. I also thought there was something rather childish in the exercise. It would not be beyond the wit or resource of the Arab governments to learn the active role of the United States in producing this equipment for Israel. In fact, as we expected, the Canadian government, when it decided to give its authorization in September 1955, stipulated that the United States should let it be known publicly that this was being done at America's behest.

As if this situation were not enough of a burden on Israel's jangled nerves, there now came another element in the nation's discomfiture: a resolute attempt by two of the Western powers to press Israel for territorial concessions.

The United States' move came in August 1955, when Secretary Dulles made a major policy speech in New York. It later became evident that he was trying to forestall the Soviet arms transaction by sending out signals to Egypt of American support for territorial concessions by Israel. Dulles's speech did not ignore Israel's security problem. He even held out the possibility of the United States entering into formal treaty engagements guaranteeing the boundaries of Middle Eastern states. Ben-Gurion said that the very fact that Dulles had mentioned the words "a security treaty with Israel" was historic. But Dulles had added:

> If there is to be a guarantee of borders there should be prior agreement upon what the borders are. The existing lines . . . were fixed by the Armistice Agreements of 1949. They were not designed to be permanent frontiers in every respect.

He went on to advocate the fixing of permanent boundaries, and in a clear allusion to the Negev Desert, he added: "The difficulty is increased by the fact that even territory which is barren has acquired a sentimental significance."

Nothing could have irritated Israelis more than the reference to the Negev as having "only" sentimental significance. For Ben-Gurion in particular, the Negev, more than any other area, symbolized the Zionist vision of conquering the wasteland and avoiding encroachment on Arab-populated areas. The general tendency to associate diplomacy with the idea of tact had never been communicated to Foster Dulles, despite his diplomatic lineage.

If Israel had been disturbed by American "hints" on the status of its frontiers, it was even more shocked by the speech of British Prime Minister Anthony Eden at the Guildhall on November 9, 1955. In more forthright language than that used by Dulles, Eden called for "a compromise between the boundaries of the 1947 UN Resolution and the 1949 armistice lines." In simple terms, it became evident that London and Washington favored Israeli concessions in the Negev to Egypt and Jordan, to enable them to establish a "land-bridge" to each other without passing through non-Arab territory. For Israel this was tantamount to the loss of its exclusive control of the Negev, which had been the main benefit secured in the political struggles of 1947–1949. In the Knesset on November 15, Ben-Gurion firmly rejected Eden's offer to mediate on this basis, since it was designed "to truncate the territory of Israel for the benefit of her neighbors" and therefore had "no legal, moral or logical foundation."

The Dulles-Eden relationship was abrasive, and the diminution of Israel's territory was almost their only common purpose. Our tenacity prevailed. The negotiation was delegated from the foreign ministers to a team of officials headed by Francis Russell, a member of the American foreign service, and Evelyn Shuckburgh, the senior Middle Eastern expert in the British Foreign Office. In Shuckburgh's mind the Middle East included Israel only as the result of unmitigated folly going back to Lloyd George, Churchill and Balfour and pursued against all reason by subsequent American and British governments. The bureaucratic Russell-Shuckburgh duo produced a bizarre scheme in which Israel would yield some triangles of territory in the Negev in a geographic pattern that would maintain Israeli communication to the Negev at one point and create Egyptian-Jordanian contiguity at the same point, presumably by an overpass highway. Neither Eden nor Dulles was distinguished by a sense of humor, but they speedily discarded this plan and pretended for some years that it had never happened. It lives on in the archives under the name Alpha. Neither government ever explained why the United States and Britain should wish to create contiguity between Egypt and Jordan, the effect of which would be to establish Nasser's domination of the entire Arab world, beginning with Cairo's control of Jordan.

I have never discovered what Operation Beta was, if it ever existed, but from early January, I was much occupied with Gamma. This was an operation conceived by President Eisenhower for exploring the possibility of an understanding between Nasser and Ben-Gurion. It was a far more rational and, at one stage, hopeful project than the ludicrous Alpha. The idea was to send a presidential envoy to Cairo and Tel Aviv in an effort to induce Nasser to meet Ben-Gurion in secret with no formal agenda except to seek a convergence of interests. The chosen emissary was Robert B. Anderson, a Texas businessman who had served as secretary of the Navy and would eventually become secretary of the Treasury.

Eisenhower sent identical letters to Nasser and Ben-Gurion introducing Anderson as "my good and trusted friend" and requesting the two leaders to "go over with you and others some of the various serious problems of the area which concern you, your neighbors and the free world generally."

I met Anderson together with Reuven Shiloah and Teddy Kollek, who was Ben-Gurion's most intimate and trusted adviser. I recall wondering whether Nasser would enjoy being associated with Eisenhower and Ben-Gurion as members of the "free world," but I felt that this was not my problem. I reacted approvingly to one particular aspect of this initiative: the emissary was not charged with any documentary definition of his assignment. For years before and since, there has been a tendency, unique to this dispute, to haggle about UN resolutions or declarations of principle without which the parties would not come together. Pre-negotiation has taken so much time that little negotiation has taken place.

I found Anderson to be an easygoing, reticent man capable of reaching personal contact with people at first meeting. He traveled between Cairo, Jerusalem and Washington from January to March 1956. He had two aims. One of them was to achieve a Ben-Gurion–Nasser meeting. The other was to persuade the two leaders to accept U.S. mediation if a direct meeting turned out to be impractical. Ben-Gurion flatly rejected mediation because the ground had been spoiled in advance by American and British efforts to secure specific territorial modifications at Israel's expense. He was affronted by the idea that any part of the territory within the 1949 armistice boundaries was in the nature of occupied territory of undefined status. Another reason for our opposition to a prolonged Anderson mission was that the U.S. made it plain that the ban on arms sales to Israel would be frozen as long as the mission was active.

Our rejection of American mediation seemed likely for a time to provoke a crisis in our relations with the United States. The opposite occurred, and once again Israel was released from trouble by its adversary. During the three months of the Anderson mission, Nasser was cultivating an image of hostility to American interests all over the world and was undermining regimes in Iraq, Jordan and Lebanon, which sought cooperation with the West. He reached the conclusion that Nasser could not be relied on for any compromise with Israel, with or without a direct meeting. In his diaries, President Eisenhower summed up the Anderson mission in cogent words:

Nasser proved to be a complete stumbling block. He is apparently seeking to be acknowledged as the political leader of the Arab world . . . The result is that he finally concludes he should take no action whatever . . . rather he should just make speeches, all of which must breathe defiance of Israel—

Eisenhower, in the same entry, described Israel as being unwilling to make any concession and as obsessed only with arms requests.

Toward the end of 1955 we decided to make a desperate attempt to project Israel's plight into the dialogue of the "Big Four" foreign ministers at their meeting in Geneva. Our targets would be Dulles (U.S.), Molotov (U.S.S.R.), Eden (U.K.) and Pinay (France). The suggestion came from Gideon Rafael, whose qualities have always included a capacity for innovation and a reluctance to allow Israeli policy to be bogged down in routine. Sharett was still the prime minister at that time, and this might be the last occasion on which he would be able to use the aura that came with the highest rank. He was linguistically equipped to talk to all four ministers without translation.

He was too realistic to expect success from his visit to Geneva, but he believed in historic duty. Even if we did not achieve anything by talking to the Great Powers at high levels, he felt that it was his obligation to exhaust every remedy.

I joined Sharett in Paris, where we had a preliminary talk with Dulles before proceeding to Geneva. Dulles was the most nomadic and mobile statesman at that time. He was unjustly accused of measuring the value of diplomatic activity in terms of air mileage, and it is only right that the Washington, D.C., airport bears his name.

In Geneva, Israel's ambassadors to the U.S., Britain, France and the Soviet Union were assembled, together with Eliahu Sasson, our Arab expert, Reuven Shiloah and Gideon Rafael. While I maintained contact with Dulles,

Sharett's meetings with Macmillan, Pinay and Molotov were held with the accompaniment of Ambassadors Elath, Yaacov Tsur and Yosef Avidar. Macmillan was bland, amiable and totally noncommittal. Molotov was unresponsive to the point of rudeness and with none of the conviviality that he had shown me in San Francisco. He recited to Sharett the same text as that which I had heard from him in April.

The Paris-Geneva foray was not a success, but it was the occasion for the first break in Israel's battle against enforced military weakness. On his way from Paris to Geneva, Sharett had obtained the promise of French Prime Minister Edgar Faure to supply Mystère aircraft to Israel without reference to the United States and Britain. The main activity in this field was being conducted with dynamic intensity and growing success by Deputy Defense Minister Shimon Peres, but there is no doubt that the Sharett-Faure meeting was the first stage in our emergence from the tunnel of frustration. Ben-Gurion's graceless refusal to acknowledge this achievement by Sharett would later be one of the indications that the cooperation between Ben-Gurion and Sharett was at an end.

An election was held in 1955, with Ben-Gurion in his traditional place at the head of the Labor list. He formed a government with Sharett as foreign minister. Sharett had enjoyed his status as prime minister, and the country was impressed with his efficiency. He had involved himself in a wider range of problems than the political and security issues that almost monopolized Ben-Gurion's time and attention.

But Sharett's tenure even as foreign minister was by now becoming fragile. A short time before the election, I had received a vivid illustration of the lack of human contact between the two leaders. Hearing that I was going down to Sdeh Boker to see Ben-Gurion, Sharett had asked me to discover if Ben-Gurion really intended to return to his leadership of the party and the government. I came back and said: "Yes, he is!" Sharett said "Oy!" On the rare occasions when Sharett attempted brevity, he went the whole way.

Ben-Gurion was not slow in making his resumed leadership effective. While the Egyptians were trying to make the Negev uninhabitable, the Syrians directed their fire from the eastern bank of Lake Galilee against a fishing boat in midlake. The incident took place in early December 1955. Although there were no Israeli casualties and little damage, Ben-Gurion ordered a massive attack on Syrian positions, leaving seventy-three Syrians and six Israelis dead. The scenes of carnage were horrific. This disproportionate action was criticized in Israel itself because of the unexpectedly heavy toll of Syrian casualties, and also because Foreign Minister Moshe Sharett was working with me in Washington, where we awaited a response to our request for permission to buy jet aircraft. James Reston of *The New York Times* had informed me that the response was not going to be negative. Our attack at Kinneret was inevitably followed by a deferment of the American response on our arms request.

Apart from the international consequences, which were severe but transient, this decision by Ben-Gurion was fiercely resented by Sharett. "Only the devil could have conceived such an outrage," he cried. He expressed his views to me and others in a form that could only be interpreted as a suspicion that Ben-Gurion had sanctioned or initiated the Kinneret attack for the purpose of denying Sharett a personal victory in the quest for arms.

I ignored these evidences of domestic turmoil and wrote indignantly to Ben-Gurion protesting the decision to embark on a sensational military assault in response to a minor provocation at the very moment when the United States seemed about to accept Israel's case on the arms balance.

His reply was breathtaking. "I myself thought," he wrote, "that we had made a grave mistake, but when I read your great speech in the Security Council defending my decision I concluded that we had acted correctly. I have nothing more to add . . ."

This mischievous response was the nearest that Ben-Gurion would ever come in the direction of either humor or penitence. He derived immense pleasure from narrating his response to anyone who crossed his threshold. My argument with him was about priorities. There was a conflict between the very short aim of punishing Syria and the longer-term aim of achieving a better arms balance. Ben-Gurion this time had chosen the short term.

By now the tormenting pressure of raids by Egyptian and Jordanian forces and *fedayeen* groups had taken heavy toll of our nervous energy. It also provoked deep divisions within the Israeli leadership about the scope, range and intensity of armed retaliation. Ben-Gurion and Sharett were often at variance on this issue. Even more serious was the development of independent initiatives in international policy by Defense Ministry officials, without the coordination with the Foreign Ministry that would have been natural if personal tensions between the two ministers had not become extreme.

Ben-Gurion had been encouraging his Defense Ministry to go full speed ahead with the development of Shimon Peres's remarkable links with the French Defense Ministry. In doing this without consulting Sharett he was clearly undermining the authority of the Foreign Ministry. On the other hand, Peres's cultivation of friendships in Paris may have been jurisdictionally subversive, but it was of immense value for the nation's security. The French connection was soon to flourish into two of Israel's most spectacular achievements: the development of an important armaments-manufacturing capacity that has lifted the country to hitherto unanticipated heights in technology; and the introduction of Israel into the world of nuclear research through the establishment of the Dimona reactor with French cooperation. Neighboring countries ascribe great importance to Israel's achievements in these fields, and our deterrent power has been vastly enhanced.

But the difficulties between Ben-Gurion and Sharett went far beyond quarrels over "turf." In theory, they should have constituted a balanced harmony. Each possessed some virtues and had some faults that the other lacked: Ben-Gurion was impulsive, imaginative, daring, dynamic; Sharett was prudent, rational, analytical, realistic. Had they been able to work in close harness, an ideal equilibrium might have been achieved. But the contradictions that divided their characters also created an incompatibility of emotion. They had gone together through many of the most testing ordeals of Jewish history, each with his own temperament and character as his guide. Far from moving toward a sense of partnership, they had become unable to bear the sight of each other. Ben-Gurion thought that Sharett was talented, but pedantic, excessively meticulous, and inclined to confuse the vital with the incidental. Sharett, with all his admiration for Ben-Gurion, considered him demagogic, tyrannical, opinionated, devious and, on some occasions, not quite rational. Their complementary virtues should have been harnessed for the national interest, but their antipathies were too strong for these potentialities to be fulfilled.

By this time Ben-Gurion must also have known that he would wish to make decisions in 1956 that Sharett would be certain to contest. Each had his loyal adherents within the Labor Party, but this very fact created the danger that in the absence of a clear-cut adjudication between them, the party itself would become split into rival camps. On June 18, 1956, after many relatively polite maneuvers, Ben-Gurion had directly requested Sharett's resignation. Despite the opposition of forty percent of the party's Central Committee—an unusual scale of revolt against Ben-Gurion—Sharett made his resignation effective at the end of June and was succeeded by Golda Meir. He sent me a touching letter, full of gratitude for the support that I had been able to give him, but also charged with bitter reflections on the circumstances that had brought about his resignation.

This was to be Sharett's last appearance at the center of Israel's stage. Although he was not advanced in years by the standards of Israeli leadership, he never overcame his rancor sufficiently to assume a place in the national leadership under Ben-Gurion's authority. By the time Ben-Gurion left the scene in 1963, Sharett had already been sidetracked into the motionless waters of the Zionist Organization, with Levi Eshkol filling Ben-Gurion's place.

Sharett impressed his personality deeply on the first decades of our political struggle. He had the same zeal and single-mindedness as his distinguished contemporaries in the Israeli and Labor leadership. But what separated him from them was his reverence for correctness and symmetry of thought, his belief that statesmanship is a rational as well as a humane exercise, his disrespect for anything that was shoddy, imprecise, or still worse, morally questionable. He was a man of sharp colors and straight lines, and the very probity of his character and the constancy of his values made it difficult for him to accept the compromises needed for cooperation with a leader whom he mistrusted. He seemed unable to give some of Ben-Gurion's foibles the particular indulgence to which Ben-Gurion was entitled by the compensating weight of his virtues.

Sharett spent the next decade brooding unfruitfully on his fall from power with no serious effort at political recuperation. In view of Ben-Gurion's growing dominance of the domestic arena, Sharett's departure may have been inevitable, but there is no doubt that with his resignation, the Israeli leadership was impoverished and the nation lost one of its ennobling dimensions. In one quality he surpassed all the leaders of Zionism and Israel—in his warm human spirit and his proud and unselfish cultivation of younger talents.

Ben-Gurion was aware that with Sharett's departure he was losing specialized skills that might be hard to replace. He asked me to come home to Jerusalem for consultation and suggested that I leave my Washington embassy to become chief adviser on foreign affairs to himself. I would thus be a kind of watchdog over the new foreign minister, Golda Meir, with a direct line of command to Ben-Gurion.

It seemed clear to me—and even clearer to Golda Meir—that this was an infallible prescription for antagonistic explosions in which Mrs. Meir and I and, perhaps, even Ben-Gurion, would be injured every day by flying splinters of jurisdictional discord. At luncheon in her house, Mrs. Meir and I agreed that we could best cooperate across the ocean, with me pursuing my mission in Washington, which, in any case, had reached such a point of cruciality that it would have been irresponsible to abandon it. Whatever status and resonance I had been able to develop in Washington and throughout America in the past six years would now have to prove their value in great ordeals. Golda and I reached unprecedented harmony by agreeing on one point: that she and I would be happy and creative in proportion to the geographic distance separating us from each other.

The political attempts of the U.S. to draw closer to Egypt had failed because Washington could not compete with Moscow in rearming Egypt without any thought of the effect on Israel's future. There was more hope in the economic field. It was thought in Washington after the Soviet arms transaction that Egypt's economic future could be linked so closely to the United States and other Western powers that Cairo would be precluded from subservience to Soviet policy. For many weeks negotiations had gone forward for the financing by the World Bank of the High Dam at Aswan, on which Egyptian planners relied for the increase of agricultural productivity in the next decades. In the spring and summer of 1956, the United States had given Egypt every reason to assume that the Aswan project depended exclusively on Egypt's readiness to accept it.

But new thoughts had arisen in Washington. Egypt was exercising hostile pressure on Israel; it was also making overt attempts to undermine King Hussein in Jordan. In addition, Nasser, especially since the Bandung Conference[2] of nonaligned states, had been following a Soviet direction in most

---

[2]The Bandung Conference of African and Asian states, held in Indonesia in 1955, spent much of its time and effort in attacking Israel and the United States.

international questions. He had established relations with Communist China, which was then anathema in American eyes. He was showing hostility to nearly all the aims that the United States pursued across the world. The negative remarks about Nasser in Robert Anderson's report on his mission in March 1956 had alienated Eisenhower, whose diaries contain shrewd and lucid appraisals of Nasser's character and ambitions.

Nasser had also generated antagonism to himself in the United States Congress, whose support would be needed for the appropriations that the World Bank project would demand of the American taxpayer. The Egyptian ambassador to the United States, Dr. Ahmed Hussein, had not followed this change of atmosphere; and on July 7, after returning from Cairo, he publicly announced that Egypt had "decided to accept" the help of the United States and British governments in carrying out the Aswan Dam scheme through the World Bank. He added that he intended to see Mr. Dulles in order to speed up negotiations for a financial agreement.

I was coming out of Dulles's room as the Egyptian ambassador went in. He was looking more buoyant than I expected him to be a few minutes later, since Dulles had told me of the decision to annul the Aswan Project a few minutes before the Egyptian ambassador would hear of it. In the ambassador's meeting with the secretary of state on July 19, Dulles stated bluntly that the United States did not regard American and British participation in financing the High Dam as "feasible in present circumstances." The withdrawal automatically prevented the World Bank from addressing itself to the project.

The cancellation of the Aswan Project was Nasser's first serious setback. He was no less affronted by the manner of the annulment than by the act itself. He reacted in a speech of unrestrained virulence: "Choke with rage, but you will never succeed in ordering us about or in exercising your tyranny over us!" He added: "We Egyptians will not allow any colonizer or despot to dominate us politically, economically or militarily. We shall yield neither to force nor to the dollar." He had no objection to yielding to the ruble.

Nasser was not satisfied with rhetoric alone. He looked for ways of dealing a blow at the Western world. In a speech in Alexandria on July 26, 1956, the bombshell burst. Nasser announced that the Egyptian government had nationalized the Suez Canal Company and would use the income from the Canal—about $100 million a year—to build the Aswan Dam. Describing the Suez Canal Company as "an exploiting company" and a "state within a state," Nasser declared that it had now been nationalized "in the name of the nation" and that all its assets and commitments would pass to the Egyptian state.

No special antenna was needed to sense that we were near to war. Britain and France found themselves dependent for their major supplies, especially of oil, not on an international waterway in which they had a controlling interest, but on Egyptian goodwill, which was dubious. Preparation for military action went forward in London and Paris. Dulles announced that Nasser must be "compelled to disgorge" what he had seized, but Eisenhower soon thereafter declared that he would oppose military action, which alone could bring the "disgorging" to fulfillment. The blatant divergence between these two signals caused confusion, and the British and French approached a decision to go it alone—and together. When the French foreign minister, Christian Pineau, declared that France would not accept the unilateral action of Colonel Nasser, the British response was unusually mild.

On July 30, 1956, Guy Mollet, the prime minister, described Nasser as an "apprentice dictator whose methods were similar to those used by Hitler, the policy of blackmail alternating with flagrant violations of international agreements." The notion that the nationalization of an economic project was equal in kind to the first phase of a cataclysmic conquest of all Europe struck me as unconvincing, but the diplomatic stereotypes were becoming deep-rooted.

Stimulated by a farfetched anti-Hitler analogy, the two European powers flexed their muscles. Both the French and British governments seemed resolved to pry the Suez Canal loose from Nasser's hands by military force.

The influence of France on Israel's policy was not solely the result of having a common adversary. In the early months of 1956, France had rescued Israel from the decline of its military strength by an unprecedentedly lavish supply of armaments. In a speech to the Knesset (October 1956), Ben-Gurion felt able to refer cryptically to the fact that Israel would soon have an "ally." When the first arms shipments from France reached Israel, the event was rhapsodically celebrated in verse by the Hebrew poet Nathan Alterman. Intimate cooperation in arms supply and political planning had already developed between the General Staffs and the Ministries of Defense of the two countries. Shimon Peres was the moving spirit in these developments.

By the time Nasser made his dramatic speech on July 26 about the nationalization of the Suez Canal, the idea that France might help Israel to resist Egyptian pressure was already familiar in some echelons of both governments. Israel was so confident of French arms supplies that in the late summer, when Secretary Dulles eventually submitted to what he called "Eban's attrition" and encouraged the release to Israel of twenty-four F-84 jet fighters manufactured in Canada under American license, the Israeli government refused to take advantage of the offer.

I was greatly irritated by this action. My fluctuating relationship with Shimon Peres had begun in a poor atmosphere. Our energetic ambassador in Ottawa, Michael Comay, had worked hard and long to secure the breakthrough enabling us to receive serious arms supplies in North America. It was shortsighted to rely on French goodwill alone. It would take a full decade before this would be confirmed by events.

Freed from Sharett's restraining hand, Israeli policy in 1956 went straight out for short-term physical security. But France did not wish to act alone. It had despaired of any American understanding for the use of force; but it had observed the sharp upheavals in British policy created by Nasser's actions. It would not be easy to bring Britain into harmony with French and Israeli interests. For one thing, most of the pressure on Israel's borders came from Jordan, to which Britain was almost endemically attached. But Paris was confident that London was moving in its direction.

Nasser was so busy goading Israel and France into a paroxysm of hostility that he may not have observed a development in London. On October 3, British disenchantment with United States policy became complete. Secretary Dulles had made a statement in Washington to the effect that the plan to put the Suez Canal under the control of the Canal Users' Association could not be said to have had its teeth drawn, "because it never had any teeth!" Eden's conclusion was that Dulles's previous assurances to him of a determination to make Nasser "disgorge" his gains had been opportunistic and insincere. He developed a burning distrust of his American colleague, together with an urge to prove that Britain could still act independently in defense of its interests.

For the first time, there was a prospect that if Israel struck out in its own defense, it might not be alone. When one reflects on Israel's complex of solitude in the preceding years it is easy to understand the exhilarating effect of the possibility that other powers would regard an Israeli action as legitimate and salutary. This chance had become reality by the early days of October 1956. Only a year before, the Israeli Cabinet had considered a proposal for taking independent action to open the Straits of Tiran. The proposal had been rejected by Ben-Gurion, largely because Israel had no hope of support and would have been exposed to the full fury of Egyptian air attack. Now it seemed that through a strange convergence of opposing interests, the dangers of solitude might have been removed. Israel, long choked by a sense of impotence and encirclement, had a unique chance of tearing the hostile fingers from its throat.

I had no reason to be surprised by the events that reached their climax in October 1956. A full year before, I had sent Prime Minister Ben-Gurion and Foreign Minister Sharett a lengthy dispatch in which I predicted that if we were unsuccessful in gaining reinforcement and international support for our security by the early spring, we would have no rational option except to challenge Nasser militarily as well as politically. I had written:

The Soviet-Egyptian agreement is a revolutionary event in the Middle East. It involves a dangerous erosion of Western influence as well as a danger to the very existence of Israel . . . I recommend that a decision be taken in Israel in favor of a program of action of which the aim should be to weaken the Nasser regime either with our own strength or in cooperation with Western powers. We should spend the next six months strengthening our arms to counterbalance the Arab escalation and also try for a security treaty. If this is not successful . . . and if there is no escape from a trial of force with Egypt, it will be very necessary to acquire allies and partners.

Since I was generally expected to reflect the diplomatic, nonmilitary emphasis in Israeli policy, this cable from me aroused surprise in Jerusalem. Sharett had been far from pleased. I was giving inadvertent reinforcement to currents of thought that were already alive in the Israeli establishment in the direction of a preemptive military action. It was not my intention to strengthen any particular side in a domestic controversy. But I always believed that the avoidance of a drastic change in the balance of power in favor of an expansionist dictatorship was an understandable motive for military action. I was enraged by Dulles's refusal to apply this historic logic to Israel's growing vulnerability. I have never attached any importance to the hawk-dove categorizations that are commonly applied to political leaders. To be invariably in favor of military solutions is just as absurd as to be unrealistically opposed to any use of force in situations of conflict. I have voted for and against military operations in an empirical spirit devoid of ideological or temperamental commitment to any single formula.

The Israeli government did not react to my dispatch, although every development in the region in the first half of 1956 had validated my somber conclusions. On October 14, I was surprised to receive a summons from Prime Minister Ben-Gurion to fly to Jerusalem for a consultation of senior ambassadors. My assumption was that the tensions between Israel and Jordan were coming to a head as a result of the prospect that the Jordanian government would allow Iraqi troops to take up positions on Jordanian territory. This idea was officially endorsed by Britain, whose government was pledged to defend Jordan against possible Israeli attack. The United States was giving qualified acquiescence to the proposal as an insurance against Jordan's disintegration. The Jordanian excuse for the proposal was "the need to ensure stability." The real objective would of course have been to restrain Israel from reacting against infiltrations and penetrations of *fedayeen* into Israel. Ben-Gurion, after some vacillation, had replied that Israel would regard the entry even of a small Iraqi force into Jordan as a violation of the status quo and a serious threat to our security. In a talk with Dulles on the eve of my departure for Jerusalem I had deduced that the secretary was not irrevocably committed to support the plan for the entry of Iraqi forces into Jordan.

The consultation of ambassadors in Jerusalem had a somewhat bizarre quality. In addition to myself, the participants were Eliahu Elath (ambassador in London), Yaakov Tsur (ambassador in Paris) and Yosef Avidar (ambassador in Moscow), with Gideon Rafael representing the Foreign Ministry. The discussion centered on the problems of Iraq and Jordan, with marginal references to navigation in Suez and in the Straits of Tiran. There was also a review of our relations with Secretary-General Hammarskjöld and the UN staff in Israel. The idea of a military initiative against Egypt had no place in these discussions, although it was clear that our relations with the Nasser regime were becoming more and more tense and would soon reach a climax of hostility.

I had the strange feeling that we were participating in a charade. Ben-Gurion's motive was evidently to use the much-publicized ambassadorial meeting to focus world attention upon our eastern rather than on our southern frontier, where our real crisis lay.

During my flight by El Al on October 16, the aircraft had made a stopover in London. As I went into the transit lounge, I noticed great commotion on the tarmac. Amid great flourish of secrecy, Prime Minister Anthony Eden and Foreign Secretary Selwyn Lloyd could be seen furtively entering an official plane, apparently en route to Paris. It was clear that whether or not their preoccupation with Iraq and Jordan was sincere, their main thoughts were focused upon the prospect of an Anglo-French confrontation with Nasser. I had wondered why I should be hurrying to Jerusalem to discuss a problem less urgent than that posed by Egyptian policy.

After the ambassadors' consultation on October 22, when I was preparing to return to Washington I received a message to see Ben-Gurion urgently. He spoke to me in a conspiratorial whisper, which surprised me since I did not assume that he was eavesdropping electronically on himself. He told me that he would travel to France that day to confer with members of the French government. There was a plan under discussion that would have "sensational results" if it came to fulfillment. Ben-Gurion was skeptical and did not really think that anything would come of it, since it involved "very complex understandings." He was convinced, he said, that the French ministers whom he would meet would recoil from the plan of action that had been discussed between Jerusalem and Paris in previous weeks. However, if it did, unexpectedly, become a real prospect I would get a little, though not much, advance notice. Looking at me closely, Ben-Gurion said: "Most of the effects would happen in your area of responsibility, probably in less than a week."

Ben-Gurion spoke only of a visit to Paris and made no allusion at all to a British involvement. Without openly confessing to have organized a charade, he gave me to understand that our meeting about the Iraqi-Jordanian scheme had an element of disinformation.

I was so deeply infected by Ben-Gurion's show of skepticism that I made my way back to Washington without any strong tension of mind or emotion. When I reached New York, my deputy, Reuven Shiloah, seemed to have surreptitious knowledge that something momentous was afoot, but he was, for a change, less up to date on events than I was.

It was a few weeks before I knew what had transpired on October 22 and

23 in Paris. Ben-Gurion, Moshe Dayan and Shimon Peres had gone to a villa in the suburb of Paris called Sèvres, where they had met Prime Minister Guy Mollet, Foreign Minister Christian Pineau and Defense Minister Maurice Bourges-Maunoury. They were joined by British Foreign Secretary Selwyn Lloyd. This was a sensational change of alignment, since only a few days before, British officials had been planning to make war on Israel if Israeli forces attacked Jordan with any degree of intensity. At Sèvres, the three groups of leaders decided on a grotesquely eccentric plan. Israel would attack Egypt and advance swiftly toward the Suez Canal. Britain and France would pretend to be indignant and wrathful and would issue an ultimatum calling on Israeli and Egyptian forces to retire an agreed distance from the Canal. Egypt would naturally refuse, and Britain, France and Israel would fight against Nasser. Israel would invoke the excuse of being threatened by Nasser's aggression, and the French and British governments would take the sanctimonious line that they were defending the Canal against physical danger arising from Israeli assault.

This fantasy was embodied in a written document signed by the British, French and Israeli ministers on October 23. It stipulated the degree of British involvement, since Ben-Gurion, deeply mistrustful of the British, had not credited their intention to bomb the Egyptians along the Canal in order to relieve the pressure on Israel. Anthony Eden was angry with his leading Foreign Office subordinate, Sir Patrick Dean, for having left a copy of the document in Ben-Gurion's hands. He feared that his own deceit would become exposed. It needed no exposure, since it was intrinsically transparent.

None of this was in my mind when I went to the Woodmont Country Club on Saturday, October 27. My fellow golfers were the celebrated journalist Martin Agronsky and Congressman Sidney Yates of Illinois. I had some prospect of avoiding humiliation at the hands of Martin Agronsky, who had the disconcerting habit of addressing the ball in a direction sharply divergent from where he wanted it to go, but no such hope from Sidney Yates, whose professional talent reduced me to jealous despair.

At one of the tees I was pursued by a messenger who brought the tidings that Secretary Dulles would like to consult with me at once. The need to be in close touch with his president had made Secretary Dulles something of an expert on the location of golf courses in and near the District of Columbia. I was reluctant to leave, as I was hitting the ball with greater effectiveness than usual.

Having met Reuven Shiloah at the State Department lobby, I ascended to the familiar floor, where I found Dulles and his senior officials grouped around a large map mounted on an easel. The map had the Israeli-Jordanian area at its center, with only a part of Sinai on the bottom margin. This did not surprise me. I had been receiving instructions on my return from Israel on the need to sharpen our dispute with Britain, Jordan and Iraq, and had spoken in that sense in the Security Council. I assumed that the Paris voyage had expired in the manner predicted by Ben-Gurion, that nothing had come of it and that we were back to our more traditional preoccupations.

By October 27 the U.S. had not yet heard about the Sèvres meeting and was apparently convinced that there were two sources of crisis. One of them was focused on the British and French plan to invade Egypt. The other, in the U.S. view, was a potential operation by Israel against Jordan.

Dulles spoke to me of mobilization in Israel with massive call-ups that the U.S. ambassador in Tel Aviv, Edward B. Lawson, had described as "unprecedented." President Eisenhower wanted Ben-Gurion to know of his deep concern. Dulles swept aside all my comments on Israel's vulnerability. "What have you to worry about? Egypt is living in constant fear of a British and French attack. Jordan is weak. It is now clear that Iraqi troops are not going into Jordan. On the other hand, if your government is planning an attack, you might be thinking that the present time is suitable." ("The present time" was a code word for the U.S. presidential campaign then approaching its final day.)

I temporized with vague assurances, sent a cable to Golda Meir, received a reply that said nothing in a great many words, failed in an attempt to get telephonic connection and became convinced that the Paris voyage had borne fruit after all.

The next morning, Shiloah and I were in the office of William Rountree, the U.S. assistant secretary for Middle Eastern Affairs, emphasizing our defensive posture, when Donald Bergus, the head of the Palestine-Israeli desk, came in with a note that Rountree read aloud. It reported a massive eruption of Israeli forces around the Egyptian boundary and a parachute drop deep into Sinai. Rountree said with justifiable sarcasm: "I expect you'll want to get back to your embassy to find out what is happening in your country."

It was clear that we were at physical war with Egypt, and almost at emotional war with the United States. All contact between the embassy and the State Department was sundered. When my counselor, Yochanan Meroz, made some representation to Bergus, he received the cold reply that "the only matter to be discussed between our two governments is the evacuation of American citizens from Israel . . ."

A wave of high tension ran through Washington. Eisenhower returned from his combined election campaign and golf weekend in the South. He issued a statement to the effect that "the United States under this and prior administrations has pledged itself to assist the victim of any aggression in the Middle East. We shall honor our pledge."

The French ambassador, Hervé Alphand, told me that he knew nothing more than I did and asked where our British colleague was. I made inquiries and learned that Sir Harold Caccia, newly appointed after the departure of Sir Robert Makins, was on his way to America by sea! "Ah! the phlegmatic British . . ." said Alphand enviously. He had a right to be envious. So did I.

Washington was no place for a British (or French or Israeli) ambassador to be. *The Washington Post* thundered:

No amount of provocation can justify Israeli aggression against Egypt. It involves the most frightful risk of larger war, and it may lose for Israel the sympathy of the free world.

The American Zionist leader, Rabbi Abba Hillel Silver, telephoned me from Cleveland and promised solidarity and assistance. But he added his opinion that "an error of judgment has been committed even more serious than in the case of the Kinneret Operation."

Washington was on a diplomatic war footing, with generals, ambassadors and Cabinet officials in full momentum of consultation and the media in happy ferment. There was tumult in the Security Council in New York. I recalled that I was, after all, the UN ambassador in addition to all else. I drove to National Airport and routed myself to New York.

Straight from the frying pan toward the fire.

13

EXPLOSION AT SUEZ:
1956–1957

THE BRITISH AND French operations around the Suez Canal would be over in a few days, leaving nothing behind for military academies to study or admire. On the other hand, Moshe Dayan's achievement in bringing 40,000 Israeli troops deep into Sinai, after a daring parachute landing at the Mitla Pass, exalted Israeli morale, which had been at a very low ebb. The Israeli forces were now liberated from the congested limits of our small land and were able to conduct a campaign of movement and strategic maneuver over a broad expanse. This not only elevated their professional pride; it also sent an infusion of self-confidence into the entire nation of which they were the emissaries. The troops were human enough to contrast the swift thrust of their own advance with the hesitant, tentative, stammering pace of the British-French campaign. But Dayan was probably frank enough to admit to himself, though probably not to anyone else, that if one had to fight an Egyptian army, it would be enviable to do so with massive British and French air forces attacking the Egyptian mainland, and with Egyptian leaders giving priority to the defense of their positions in the Canal zone.

The Suez-Sinai War does not earn its fame as a military exploit. Its importance lies in the widening repercussions that it sent into international history. By mid-November, it had become evident that Britain, which had dominated international diplomacy and strategy for the best part of two centuries, was no longer capable of independent military action on a strategic scale. It would have to abandon unilateral dreams and seek its destiny in cooperation with the United States—or within the European context that both Ernest Bevin and Anthony Eden had unwisely despised. Britannia could no longer rule all the waves, or even most of them.

This reality had been latent long before 1956, but it had been partly concealed by the diversity and scope of Britain's apparent centrality, with American consent, in so many of the focal points of Middle Eastern politics. Anthony Eden's error, the greatest that any statesman can make, was to confuse the impressive form of his nation's power with its declining substance.

France absorbed the Suez failure with greater serenity. It had the most luxurious of all French enjoyments—that of being able to blame Britain for the errors of the joint military command that lay in the responsibility of an unremarkable commander named General Sir Charles Keightly. French policy and emotion turned away from the imperial role and went into an intense, self-searching pursuit of a new constitutional order to be crowned and adorned with the return of the national hero. The de Gaulle presidency, fashioned in the tall dimensions of its incumbent, the withdrawal of France from Algeria, and its advance toward the leadership of a European Community, were the direct offshoot of the Suez drama. In all these respects, France revealed a capacity for resilience and recuperation that would have been a welcome gift to human history if they had been in effect two decades before.

Of the three adversaries that rose up against Nasser, Israel alone had a clear notion of what it was trying to achieve. At a Cabinet meeting on October 28, a minister had asked Ben-Gurion: "What is the ultimate objective of this invasion? Let us assume that it goes off as planned. Do we wish to annex the Sinai Peninsula or any part of it? And what will happen to the Gaza Strip?" Ben-Gurion had replied:

I don't know the outcome of Sinai. We are interested first of all in the Straits of Eilat (Tiran) and the Red Sea. Only through them can we secure direct contact with the nations of Asia and East Africa. The main thing is freedom of navigation in the Straits of Eilat. As far as the Gaza Strip is concerned, I fear that it will be embarrassing for us. If I believed in miracles, I would pray that it would be swallowed into the sea.

Thus, when Israeli forces burst into Sinai and Gaza on October 29, they were acting in the service of coherent and limited aims. No such clarity marked the British and French action. The central idea was to recapture the Suez Canal and establish an international regime for its management. A corollary objective was to bring about Nasser's collapse. But did London and Paris really believe that an Egyptian regime, installed by their military power, would have an effective lease on life? This was only one of the awkward questions that London and Paris chose not to face. The truth is that the British and French peoples were stirred more by emotion than by a lucid vision of their objectives. Nevertheless, in France all parties rallied to support the military resistance to Nasser.

In Britain, things were more complex. In the first flush of indignation, after Nasser's nationalization of the Suez Canal, the Labour Party spokesmen, Hugh Gaitskell and Herbert Morrison, supported a military response. Indeed, Gaitskell was one of the first to draw the parallel between Nasser and the dictators of World War II. Later, he and most of his party were to object vehemently to the British military action and to part company with their Israeli friends.

Eden had played the October preparations very close to his chest. He had cut off most of his ministers, the entire Foreign Office, and the United States Embassy from any normal contact with the flow of events. He was doomed very soon to crumble in failure, not only or chiefly because of American pressure, but mainly because the British Parliament never sustained him in his surreptitious action. All this, however, belonged to an unknown and rancorous future when the tensions exploded on October 29.

On that day everything had been made ready for the forward leap of Israeli forces. It began with a daring movement in which a paratroop battalion was dropped near the Mitla Pass about twenty miles east of the Suez Canal and one hundred miles beyond the Israeli boundary. Egypt's troop concentrations and fortifications were now outflanked from the rear. Israeli power had never been as far from home as this. The next task was for the main body of Israel's airborne brigade to make contact with the paratroop battalion. Our military commanders and their political chiefs were acting on the realistic assumption that international pressure would give little time for military action. Whatever could not be accomplished in a few days would have to be renounced.

The appearance of Israeli forces at Mitla stirred the Egyptians to panic. Here was the enemy at a short distance from the Suez Canal threatening the major Egyptian supply lines in Sinai. There was a fierce Egyptian counterattack that our Mitla contingent was able to resist, but only with heavy losses. Twenty-four hours later, the Israeli offensive branched out into two directions. Southward a brigade equipped with civilian transports made its way along the western shore of the Gulf of 'Aqaba until it overran the Egyptian positions at Sharm el-Sheikh. The Red Sea was now open to Israel. We did not expect it to dry up so as to facilitate our crossing, but we looked at the incredible blue of the glittering waters and were overcome by the sense of having cast off the shackles of confinement. We were in touch with the expanse and commerce of a region from whose life and faith and tongue we had been sundered partly by their virulent resolve to exclude us.

North of Sinai there were heavy battles with casualties on both sides. Once Rafah had been taken, the Gaza Strip was cut off from contact with any Arab forces or territory anywhere. Not surprisingly, the city of Gaza soon fell with little resistance. There were some notable air battles in which Israel's French-made Mysteres came out victorious against the Soviet MIGs, causing extreme satisfaction in Paris. There were even successes at sea. The Israeli navy, such as it was, had captured an Egyptian destroyer that was sailing northward to capture Haifa. By November 5 the Israeli part of the operation— biblically named "Kadesh"—was over. We had lost 180 Israeli soldiers killed and four soldiers taken prisoners of war. We had routed the whole Egyptian

Canal force, leaving a thousand Egyptian dead. We had captured vast amounts of armament and equipment. The Egyptian forces avoided even heavier casualties only by swiftness of flight. Here was Israel, in command of most of Sinai, controlling the entry into the Straits of Tiran and, thereby, into the Red Sea and the Indian Ocean.

To understand the repercussions of these events and my reaction to them we must refer back to the frenzied atmosphere in the United Nations in the last days of October and the first days in November. The knowledge that I would now be personally involved at the center of world-changing events led me to keep a detailed diary, which I submitted to Ben-Gurion and Golda Meir in mid-March 1957 when the new decade of stability had begun.

Diary, October 30

Our Consulate told of a disquieting atmosphere among the Jewish leaders who were meeting in New York. They recommended full solidarity with Israel, but they were clearly embarrassed by the fact that no ground had been prepared, and that a military operation a week before the presidential election seemed somewhat anti-American. Some of them wanted to criticize President Eisenhower, his party, and his administration, thus giving their protest an undesirable political color. Since I could not leave the Security Council I sent Shiloah to a meeting of the President's Conference. From his report, I gathered that he had a difficult hour. For the first time in our history there was reluctance to justify Israel's actions without reserve. Some of them suggested that Jewish reservations about Israel's steps be openly published. In the end, however, the leader of the President's Club, Philip Klutznick, brought all of them together with an expression of solidarity for Israel and an appeal to the United States to strengthen Israel's security and Middle Eastern peace. Phil was diplomatically adept enough to avoid comment on the past and to cement solidarity for the future.

As I walked from the Security Council Chamber into the Delegates' Lounge, I was followed by a blinding flash of cameras which my public relations advisors would have deeply welcomed in previous days. I made for the French representative, Bernard Cornut-Gentille. He was dripping with perspiration, not all or most of which came from the heat. To compound the irony, he was now the president of the Security Council by virtue of alphabetical rotation. He did not seem to enjoy the experience of being both the chief justice and the prisoner in the dock. The U.S. delegate, Henry Cabot Lodge, requested the Council to take immediate measures for Israeli withdrawal to the armistice line. With a significant glare at his British and French colleagues, he asked "all members of the United Nations to abstain from extending any aid which might prolong the hostilities."

Later:

A brief, dry report from Hammarskjöld, looking angry and grim. Endless speeches by Yugoslavia, Iran, Australia, China, Cuba, Peru, the
Soviet Union, and Egypt. Sobolev, with a sly surreptitious grin, quoted
a news item from London about the intention of Britain and France to
take military action against Egypt! Newspapermen scurried in and out
between the telephones and the Council chamber.

So far, not a word had been said by Sir Pierson Dixon or the French
chairman. I noticed, however, that Dixon and Lodge—of the U.S. and
the U.K. whom the alphabet brought together—were ostentatiously
cutting each other like school children celebrating a tiff. I went to the
Chairman's seat and asked Cornut-Gentille if he had any news. He
whispered: "Don't worry, my friend, there is going to be a veto." This
was the first hint that reached me with the assurance that we were not
alone.

4:00 P.M.—the Council resumed. I remembered Sam Goldwyn having said to his MGM executives in Hollywood: "Boys, I want a movie
that begins with an earthquake and works its way up to a climax." That
is what we had this afternoon. Pierson Dixon announced that Prime
Minister Eden had made a statement in his name and in that of the
French Prime Minister Guy Mollet about an ultimatum that had been
handed in London and Paris to Egypt and Israel, calling on them, "to
remove their troops to a distance of ten miles from the Suez Canal."
This created no problem for us since, at no point, were we anywhere
near the Canal from which we were being called upon to "withdraw."

The French delegate made a speech totally identical with that of
Britain. Cabot Lodge, who was never marked by any urgency, now
took off like a rocket. His aristocratic family in Boston had once been
described as being dominated by "a tranquil air of effortless superiority." He seemed to have overcome this in the virulence of his assault on
his NATO allies. He drafted a resolution calling not only for Israel's
withdrawal, but also for "the duty of all member states to withhold all
military, economic, or financial aid from Israel until it complied with
the withdrawal resolution." Sobolev joined Lodge in the verbal castiga-
tion. This lent a bizarre note to the occasion since, in a parallel discussion on the Soviet assault on Hungary, Lodge and Sobolev were at
daggers drawn.

I took the floor to describe the Egyptian threats to Israel's existence,
the savagery of the *fedayeen* raids, the inaction of the United Nations,
and the Egyptian "paradox of unilateral belligerency." I was consciously keeping my main assault for what I knew would be an Assembly meeting in the next few days. Reading from Ben-Gurion's telegram,
I stated that Israel did not intend to acquire new territories, but merely

to eliminate threats to our nation's security arising from the murder gangs and the hostile armies. The U.S. resolution was put to the vote—seven in favor. Abstentions by Australia and Belgium. And, oh, great sensation, Britain and France raising their hands in negative votes which amounted to a double veto. The French chairman announced, with undisguised pleasure, that "the resolution has not been adopted." Australia and Belgium abstaining; and Britain and France against.

Back to the Delegates' Lounge. I found myself enclosed in a strange capsule of apathy. Israel being castigated by the Security Council was a familiar theme. A British and French conflict with the United States and the Soviet Union was great copy. This was "man biting dog." It was well past midnight in Israel, and I received no news of any substance from hurried telephone calls. The wire services, however, were reporting spectacular Israeli advances.

October 31

Security Council convened again. Press reports say that the Israeli government had accepted the Anglo-French "ultimatum," that Egypt had rejected it, whereupon British and French aircraft have begun to bomb Egypt as a preliminary to military landings. Pierson Dixon strongly denies that Britain and France acted in common cause with Israel. Goes on to say that his government "does not support Israeli intentions to capture Egyptian territories." Heavens alive, what cynicism and hypocrisy! Britain, he says "had no doubt that in crossing the Egyptian boundary, Israel had violated the armistice agreement."

I found this sanctimonious tone hard to take—two weeks after the collusion with Selwyn Lloyd at Sèvres for a united assault on Egypt!

The United States and the Soviet Union are preparing for an emergency meeting of the General Assembly under the "Uniting for Peace" resolution. Scheduled for November 1, at 5:30.

October 30. Late evening

More fireworks. We were gathering up our papers to prepare for the November 1 meeting when Hammarskjöld asked quietly for the floor. He usually did everything quietly. Now in a voice shaking with emotion, he read out a "personal declaration" which implied a clear threat to resign in protest against British and French violations of their Charter obligations. He was more eloquent, even, than ever before. He said that the principles of the Charter were much more important than the organization that embodied them. "In order to preserve the efficacy of the UN, the Secretary-General must abstain from taking a public position in relation to a conflict between member states, unless taking such a position would help to remove the conflict. But a Secretary-General cannot fulfill his function except on the assumption that all members of the UN, especially the five permanent members of the Security Council, would carry out their obligations. If they are members who believe that the welfare of the organization requires a different conception of the Secretary-General's role, it is their right to act accordingly . . ."

Hammarskjöld has a refined sense of drama. He knows how to create publicity by an air of conspicuous unobtrusiveness. His passionate speech has had a sharp effect on the news media. World opinion, shattered by the impotence of the Security Council, is looking for an international hero. Hammarskjöld has thrown his hat into the ring. (Not that anyone has ever seen him with a hat.) There was an air of deliberate martyrdom in his bearing. A chorus of loyalty and almost of worship went up loudly around the table.

Looking back to this diary entry, I recall that Dag Hammarskjöld always interpreted the office of secretary-general more distinctively than did anyone who preceded or succeeded him. It is strange to reflect that his chief credential for appointment was his alleged anonymity. Trygve Lie, in his blustering way, had set a precedent for candor and self-assertion. But he had conducted himself so abrasively that his personality was bound to collide with the urbane refinements that the task required. Hammarskjöld moved and spoke and reacted with an extraordinary lightness of touch. Indeed, lightness was the adjective that most corresponded to his personality. He was slight of build and surrounded himself with art and music and, above all, with literature, with the air of one who despised the strident diplomatic arena in which he operated.

Some people thought that he would have made a great actor, but, in my view, the art that most reflected his personality would be that of the ballet. He knew how to glide and pirouette between the obstacles. In his discourse with me as with other UN ambassadors, he cultivated a sharp intellectuality, constantly appealing to logic that alone could save errant mankind from self-inflicted perdition. Yet, there was a metaphysical side to his character. He seemed to be appealing above the dust and heat of the marketplace to visions of beauty and rectitude that seemed incompatible with a vocation whose exponents were men of this world, wearily aware that conflict is endemic to human nature and that it operates in the international domain without any of the consensual restraints that prevent national societies from leaping toward their own doom.

A conversation with him had its aesthetic quality, which was rare in UN discourse. He also brought to his task something of the northern darkness, which broods over so much of Scandinavian literature and art. He was a man who felt very close to what a Roman philosopher called "the tears of things." Yet, often, when one expected elevation and remoteness, he would astonish his listeners with a dry legalism, articulated from memory, with all the texts and dates and details and deductive power that might have been expected from a mathematician.

Many foreign ministers and ambassadors felt betrayed by the degree in which he refuted the legend of his alleged vagueness and self-deprecation. The truth is that the office of UN secretary-general, in the contemporary international context, is not fashioned for idiosyncratic personalities. After Hammarskjöld's mission ended with appropriate drama in the flames of a crashed aircraft in Congo, I closely followed the search for his successor. I remember a distinguished British diplomat approaching me in the Delegates' Lounge with a question about U Thant. He wanted to know if, in view of Israel's close relations with Burma, I had studied his opinions and attitudes. A few days later, I returned and told my colleague that I could not recall a single opinion that Thant had expressed on any question at all. "Ah, that's just the man for us," said my British colleague, rubbing his hands in satisfaction, as though he had seen a sudden gleam of treasure. Hammarskjöld also had been appointed on the assumption that he would be innocuous and subservient to the powers.

Hammarskjöld's outburst in the Suez crisis ran against the grain of his temperament. As a rule, he hated confrontation. My worst moments were when I went to see him with Golda Meir, when she was foreign minister. Her directness clashed excruciatingly with his subtlety. I have never been in a room with two people whose aversion for each other was more intense.

Not that his attitudes in the Suez crisis were congenial to me. His outburst in the Security Council was inspired by the idea that since Britain, France and Israel had acted outside and beyond their Charter rights, it would be vital that none of them should gain benefit or reward. In the ensuing months, I was to develop the theme that it would be grotesque to restore such illegalities as maritime blockades and belligerent raids just because their elimination had been brought about by violence. Yet, this was Hammarskjöld's attitude from beginning to end. Even when statesmen like Lester Pearson and, to some extent, Foster Dulles were inclined to use the explosion in Sinai and Suez in such manner as to give a new direction to Middle Eastern politics, Hammarskjöld rigorously defended a return to the previous status quo. His position was based on the formalistic line that nobody must derive advantage from the Sinai campaign or the Suez invasion. My reaction that this attitude would only build a new bonfire, and even put a match to it, was one that he seemed to absorb intellectually, but from which he recoiled in the passion of his devotion to principle.

Since there would be a full day between the Security Council and the General Assembly, I flew back to Washington on October 31. Sherman Adams, who had been Eisenhower's chief of staff, had conducted a telephone conversation with Abba Hillel Silver. The president asked Silver to tell Ben-Gurion that he would make a broadcast to the nation the next day and would like to abstain from condemning Israel. He, therefore, wanted to receive a promise that Israel would not retain its forces in the area that it had occupied. Could Ben-Gurion announce that since the Israeli forces had completed their mission, namely the liquidation of the *fedayeen* bases, they would return to the previous boundary? If we were to do this, the president would include in his broadcast a statement of deep appreciation and of friendship toward Israel. Eisenhower added that, even though it seemed that there was a convergence of interests between Israel and those of Britain and France, Israel's future was bound up with the United States. Eisenhower, suspected of woolliness, was in fact capable of sharp lucidity in judgment, if not always in expression.

Silver, at my suggestion, telephoned this message personally to Ben-Gurion, who replied, "The enemy is listening, and I can't possibly tell you now if we will withdraw or not."

A few hours later, when the enemy presumably was not listening, I received a coded cable from Ben-Gurion permitting me to meet Eisenhower's request, provided that I could avoid using the word "withdrawal." I sent back a message stating that my speech would include the sentence that "Israel has no desire or intention to wield arms beyond the limit of its legitimate defensive mission. But whatever is demanded of us by way of restoring Egypt's rights and respecting Egypt's security must surely be accompanied by equally binding Egyptian undertakings to respect Israel's security and Israel's rights."

I was rather pleased with this and so, apparently, was Ben-Gurion. His method of expressing enthusiasm about something was to receive it with total silence, which I could interpret at my own peril as acquiescence.

Diary, November 1

My statement on behalf of Ben-Gurion that Israel did not intend to expand its territory reached the White House at 4:00 in the afternoon today. It appears to have had some influence on Eisenhower's speech.

I had begun the day in New York with telephone conversations with Golda Meir and Shimon Peres from Tel Aviv. They told me about the success of our military operations. We were within a dozen miles of the Suez Canal; most of Sinai and the Gaza Strip were in our hands; the crew of an Egyptian warship that had tried to bomb Haifa had surrendered; the Egyptian armies in Sinai had collapsed; thousands of prisoners had been taken; enormous quantities of arms and equipment had come into our hands.

Amid all these good tidings, I was disturbed by a question that Peres asked me on Ben-Gurion's behalf: How can the United Nations be dealing with the problem when Britain and France had vetoed the discussion in the Security Council? It was clear to me from this ostensibly innocent question that I had stumbled upon a grave error in the planning of the operation. In our relations with the French, enormous efforts had been invested in the aim of securing a French veto. It appeared that the Israeli government believed that this would end the UN intervention!

Since the planning had been carefully kept secret, neither our UN delegation nor our Foreign Ministry had any opportunity of informing Jerusalem that a Security Council veto, however satisfying, would not arrest the ongoing momentum of a UN debate. It was clear that two elements in the planning of the operation that would soon prove erroneous had won the day in the pre-war consultations. First, it was believed that a veto would paralyze the United Nations; second, it was taken as axiomatic that a choice of timing, a week or so before the election, would effectively neutralize the activity of the president of the United States. As it predictably turned out, this was the precise opposite of what would happen. The fact that we had acted in conscious awareness of the election date was responsible for a very large proportion of Eisenhower's rage. We were not only disrupting the Atlantic Alliance, we were also seeking to undermine his election campaign.

I expected my talk with Dulles on November 1 to be confined to his declaration about the suspension of our aid program. I already had indications of this in the State Department. The journey of a team of the Export-Import Bank, which was due to recommend a new loan of $75 million, had been held up. So, too, were negotiations on the utilization of the residue of the grant-in-aid, and on the food surplus agreement, which I had negotiated with Secretary of Agriculture Ezra Taft Benson. In spite of these portents, I told my embassy staff that I did not intend to talk about financial aid to Israel. I would use my talk with Dulles to expatiate on the motives for our military action.

Diary, November 2

My talk with Dulles yesterday began with his statement that he was naturally looking at the United States aid programs, but would first like to hear about our intentions. Did we intend to remain in Sinai or go back to the previous boundary after carrying out the mission that we had assumed?

I decided to go on the offensive. I said, rather grandly with an opulent sweep of my hand, that with all the importance of the money, which we appreciate very deeply, my own mind was occupied by fundamental thoughts about the future of our region. "The military power of Nasser," I said, "is in collapse; his prestige is sinking; it is possible to bring him low and thereby to deal a heavy blow to Soviet influence in the Middle East, simultaneously with Soviet troubles in Europe. In this revolutionary situation, a crucial hour has been reached; the aim should be not to restore a situation charged with explosiveness, but rather to make a dramatic leap forward to peace."

As soon as we left the subject of financial aid and began to talk about strategy, Dulles's demeanor changed. The question of the economic aid program was shelved. The secretary said that my conceptions were big and he liked them. "Look," he said, "I'm terribly torn. No one can be happier than I am that Nasser has been defeated. Since Spring, I have had only cause to detest him, but can we accept a good end when it is achieved by means which violate the Charter?" He asked, "Do you think we should have one standard of reaction to our adversaries and another standard for our friends?" To his evident dismay, I replied, "Oh, yes, Mr. Secretary, I do. Isn't that what friendship's about?" The rest of the conversation proceeded in a relaxed tone. This extraordinary man was capable of swift changes of mood and emotion. He was even prepared to try his hand at humor of a sort. He said, "You must confess I was right when I told you that your military situation was not all that bad; why did you have to panic about Egypt receiving Soviet arms?"

This remark appeared to amuse him immensely, and his unaccustomed laughter followed me down the corridor.

November 2

The General Assembly meeting last night opened at 5:00. The hall had never been so crowded. It was estimated that 70 million people were watching the proceedings.

The Arabs requested a strong condemnation and sanctions. Dulles admitted that there were "provocations" and that there had been a certain measure of "neglect by the United States." But all that could not justify recourse to force.

As the debate went on, it became evident that I would have to speak that night. I adjourned to the Westbury Hotel restaurant on East 70th Street, just opposite our delegation building. With me was Dr. Jacob Robinson, our legal advisor. He asked me anxiously whether I intended to defend our action in terms of Article 51 of the UN Charter, which provides for the exercise of the inherent right of self-defense. I replied that, in my UN experience, there was no action that was incapable of being ascribed to Article 51 of the Charter. The important things for me were to separate the Israeli action from the less convincing motives which had inspired the British and French interventions. When Robinson left, I borrowed a pencil from the waiter and a few pieces of paper and hurriedly wrote out a few main headings for my speech.

I had been given a friendly tip by David Sarnoff, president of RCA, the great broadcasting consortium, that if I could arrange to get on the air at about 11:30, I would get complete national coverage, since the regular television programs—especially those devoted to sport—would be over. It was nearly midnight when I rose to make my address.

I had decided that my main task was not to argue about the legalistic justifications of military actions, but to tell the story of a people driven to rage by its solitude and the lack of friendly support.

Stretching back far behind the events of this week lies the unique and somber story of a small people, subjected throughout all the years of its national existence to a furious implacable comprehensive campaign of hatred and siege, for which there is no parallel or precedent in the modern history of nations.

Whatever rights are enjoyed by other members of this organization belong to Israel without addition or diminution. Whatever obligation any member state owes to another, Egypt owes to Israel and Israel to Egypt.

Are we acting legitimately within our inherent right of self-defense, when having found no other remedy for two years, we cross the frontier against those who have no scruples about crossing the frontier against us?

Surrounded by hostile armies on all its land frontiers; subjected to savage and relentless hostility; exposed to penetration, raids, and assaults by day and by night; suffering constant toll of life among its citizenry; bombarded by threats of neighboring governments to accomplish its extinction by armed force; embattled, blockaded, besieged, Israel alone among the nations faces a battle for its security anew with every approaching nightfall and every rising dawn.

I had a feeling that everything was flowing well, with thought and speech in total unison. The hall was hot and tense with listening. I could feel that many of the 70 million beyond were held in similar suspense. The speech approached its end:

Our signpost is not backward to belligerency but forward to peace. Egypt and Israel are two nations whose encounters in history have been memorable for mankind. Surely they must take their journey from this tragic moment toward these horizons of peace . . .

I still remember how the cascades of applause broke out around me, growing in intensity, sometimes accompanied by emotional stamping of feet. It was a moment both of exhaustion and relief. The exhaustion belonged to the tension of recent days and the knowledge that I had been afforded a unique opportunity to affect the direction of world opinion. The relief came from feeling that I had got something off Israel's chest that had badly needed saying. No matter what the political or voting outcome would be, the cathartic liberation from a pent-up grievance would have a healing effect.

It was past 2:00 in the morning when the vote came: sixty-four in favor of the withdrawal resolution, five against—Britain, France, Israel, Australia and New Zealand—with six abstentions. As I walked down to the lobby, Dulles was waiting there with his legal adviser, Herman Phleger, a stereotype of San Franciscan rectitude. I thought that Dulles looked haggard and yellow. He chewed and swallowed nervously, then he began to speak with typically forensic professionalism: "Listen, you didn't seem to be reading. Did you have a manuscript?" I told him that, owing to pressure of time, I had not prepared my speech at all but had formulated it on the basis of a few notes. I took out the piece of paper on which I had written about twenty lines at the Westbury Hotel. He looked at me hard and offered a memorable tribute: "Jesus Christ," he said, as he stalked away. I was later told that this was the only occasion on which that austere churchman had been heard to utter the familiar but irreverent expletive.

This had been a highlight for me. Echoes from my address came streaming in. The radio and television stations kept repeating full transmissions of it. Our delegation, with miraculous speed, produced a verbatim transcript, in thousands of copies. Hundreds of telegrams reached me on that day, and more by the end of a week. Ben Raeburn of Horizon Press approached our consul, Reuven Dafni, with a suggestion that I publish a book of speeches. An enterprising radio company put a record into the stores within a week.

The problem was how to give expression, in concrete terms, to this flood of goodwill. The United Nations, in its usual manner, expressed a sharp dichotomy between its reaction and its conclusion. Having applauded the speech with sustained and vigorous applause, it had gone on to vote against us by a huge majority. Opinion was one thing and policy was another.

If our only aim was to explain our rectitude, we had done as much as was possible. If there was the added ambition of finding a way out of the deadlock, the natural thing for me to do was to invite the assistance of Mike Pearson. I found him at his place at the table greeting me with the wise smile of a man who knows that there is a great amount of hysteria in the world but that it is not mandatory to join it. He was rather like the sane, solid brother in a family whose other members repeatedly get themselves into tangled dilemmas. He evidently thought that the very intricacy of the mess that all the parties were in made it objectively timely to seek a way out. He thought that Nasser had been intolerably provocative. On the other hand, Mike Pearson was a zealot of the United Nations ideal and a firm supporter of its law. It was clear that, despite his devotion to the two countries—Britain and France, out of which Canada had been born—he attached no weight whatever to the British view that Nasser's nationalization of the Canal was anything like the eruption of Hitler in the 1930s; nor did he like the British and French contention that the ignorant Arabs would be unable to bring ships through the Suez Canal. He regarded this as colonialist contempt.

He had spent many weeks trying to explain to the British—both in London and in Ottawa—that the United States, and indeed Canada, would find it impossible to regard the nationalization of the Canal, or even Nasser's previous activity, as an adequate reason for all-out war. In a memorable address explaining his abstention in the vote, he suggested that the General Assembly should use the cease-fire, not simply for perpetuating the deadlock, but for advancing a political solution, not only of the problems of the Suez Canal, but also of the Arab-Israeli relationship. He then threw an idea into the air that was to play a central role in future events: He proposed that the United Nations should establish an international force that would replace the British, French and Israeli troops, and would remain in place to ensure the maintenance of peace on the boundaries.

In later months and years, the UN peacekeeping role developed quickly, and Pearson was justifiably awarded the Nobel Prize.

In my cable home to Ben-Gurion and Golda Meir, I was able to say that the United States resolution that had been adopted did contain some loopholes through which we could maneuver: First, the references in the Security Council text to sanctions against Israel had been omitted. Second, the General Assembly had determined that our neighbors had often "violated the armistice agreement." Most important of all, there was to be a gap of time between the cease-fire and the withdrawal of forces. The cease-fire was to be "immediate," while the withdrawal of forces was to take place "as soon as possible."

I now found myself in a paradoxical situation that would have been amusing if human life had not been at issue. The Israeli forces had accomplished their military aim, while the British and French had not even begun theirs. On November 3, when the cease-fire was to go into effect, we had nearly all of Sinai in our hands. But the Anglo-French landing in the Suez Canal had not begun at all. Britain and France, therefore, rejected the call for a cease-fire. They were theoretically fighting to secure our withdrawal from a place that we had never reached, and in the language of their weird ultimatum, they were to "separate" forces that had already stopped fighting!

When I let it be known at the UN that I saw no objection to a cease-fire, I received an agitated telephone call from our Foreign Ministry in Tel Aviv. I was told that, while we had very little more to do in the field, except to advance to Sharm el-Sheikh, the French and British were embarrassed by the idea that we would cease fire before they had begun. What would now happen to their assertion that they had only entered Egypt in order to prevent Israel from pursuing its campaign?

It was clear that my speech and Pearson's concrete proposal had changed the atmosphere. Ambassador Lodge had no course but to accept priority for the Canadian resolution, asking the secretary-general to establish an international force in the next forty-eight hours. He announced that the United States would meanwhile not press for action on its two resolutions. Extraordinary staff work by Hammarskjöld, Bunche and the UN Secretariat made it possible for a UN Emergency Force (UNEF) to be proposed in the General Assembly on November 5. At 3:30 on the morning of that day, the Assembly adopted the Canadian resolution with sixteen abstentions, including the Soviet Bloc, France, Britain, Australia, New Zealand, South Africa, Israel and Egypt. It also voted again for withdrawal, to which again there were five opposing votes: Israel, France, Britain, New Zealand and Australia.

Moscow was sensitive about a force that would, in all likelihood, be confined to Western and neutral countries, and reflect the power of the pro-American majority in the General Assembly. The Soviet Union was also traumatically affected by the memory of a previous "United Nations force" that had, in fact, been a cover for an American operation under President Truman and General Douglas MacArthur in Korea.

It was only on the morning of November 5 that the airborne assault by Britain and France in the Canal zone began at last. Having been late in its commencement, the operation was now to be ineffective in its execution. There was, naturally, a vast intensification of international pressures. This time, the Soviet Union called for a cease-fire, stipulating that it must come into effect "within twelve hours." The Soviet proposal went on to say that, if this did not happen, the United States and the Soviet Union, as two countries with air and sea power, should help Egypt with weapons, volunteers and "other military means."

The conflict had thus been propelled into the very eye of a global storm. The Arab-Israeli confrontation had developed into a test of strength and nerve for the nuclear superpowers. Eisenhower sternly rebuked the Soviet "offer" to assuage the regional fire by pouring large barrels of global oil upon its embers. But the second week in November was an inferno of overlapping tensions. The United States and the United Kingdom were not on speaking terms. Washington was squeezing Britain at the most sensitive points of its economy. British opinion was flowing swiftly away from support of Anthony Eden's adventure. Great crowds were assembling in Trafalgar Square to protest the war. And the landings in Port Said and the air attacks on Egypt were nothing but the petulant and belated symptoms of a military fiasco. The nervous and physical collapse of Anthony Eden compounded and aggravated his nation's agony.

Many aspects of the Anglo-French action might have been forgiven if the military campaign had been successful. But nothing fails like failure. A Britain divided against itself, humiliated by defeat and subjected to American hostility, had no course but to abandon the field. The French leaders were more robust, but reacted with exaggerated seriousness to the Soviet threats to drop missiles on Paris and London. In the end, Britain and France accepted a farcical procedure; the United Nations took over their positions in a revolving-door movement and then handed the Canal Zone back to Egypt a few days later. The objective was to enable Eden and Mollet to say that they had captured the Canal and transferred it to the world community, not to Egypt. It was the most transparent veil in diplomatic history.

More disquieting for me was the fact that our own Israeli leadership was in disarray. I felt that Ben-Gurion was, for the only time, out of touch with reality and with his own duty.

He was clearly unnerved by Eisenhower's hostility and still more by the brutality of the Soviet pressure. On November 5 he had received a letter from Soviet Prime Minister Nikolai Bulganin declaring that Israel was performing criminal acts at the behest of external imperialist forces. The letter was full of menace:

> The Government of Israel is criminally and irresponsibly playing with the fate of the world, with the fate of its own people. It is sowing hatred of the State of Israel among the Eastern peoples such as cannot but leave its mark on the future of Israel and places in question the very existence of Israel as a state. The Soviet Union is at this moment taking steps to put an end to the war and to restrain the aggressor. The Government of Israel should consider before it is too late. We hope that the Government of Israel will fully understand and appreciate this warning.

The background for this unprecedented tirade was the hint in other Soviet communications that its missiles could easily reach the transgressor states. The Israeli reaction was to pass from excessive exuberance to excessive panic. The exuberance was expressed in triumphant oratory that gripped an ecstatic people when the first news of military success had been heard and reported. This was a natural first reaction to a providential emergence from blockade and embattled solitude. But it continued far beyond the limits of reason and prudence. In the Knesset on the evening of November 7, Ben-Gurion described the campaign as "the greatest and most glorious operation in the annals of our people and one of the most remarkable in world history." He stated, absurdly, that according to a Greek historian Sharm el-Sheikh had been the seat of an ancient Jewish kingdom. And he announced the termination of the Egyptian-Israeli armistice agreement and the refusal of Israel to allow any foreign soldier, even an international force, in any of the areas occupied by Israel. He added that these positions would be maintained by Israel "with full force and unflinching determination."

I saw no chance that Ben-Gurion would be able to maintain his "unflinching determination" for a single week. In a conversation with Lester Pearson the next day I found this friendly and earnest statesman sharply alienated. He said, "This speech must have been as offensive to the British, the French, the Americans and to us Canadians as it was to the Arabs. If you people persist with this, you run the risk of losing all your friends."

Historians and Israelis close to Ben-Gurion have never found a convincing explanation of this speech Yaacov Herzog, Ben-Gurion's principal and most talented adviser at that time, said indulgently that it was a deliberate tactic to shock the world into helping Israel to end its "nightmare" of insecurity. Shimon Peres held the view that Ben-Gurion aimed to capture Sinai only as a bargaining device to secure free passage in the Gulf of 'Aqaba. Golda Meir said more realistically: "I think Ben-Gurion believed that we could stay in Sinai and Gaza. He did not take into consideration, nor did any of us, that the Soviet Union would respond as it did."

Ben-Gurion, however, had a simpler and disarmingly serene explanation, quoted by the historian Michael Brecher:

> I made a few mistakes in that speech. I went too far and it was against the views I had expressed in the Government on October 28 that they would not let us stay in Sinai or Gaza and that our only aim should be to open the Straits . . . But, you see, victory was too quick. I was too drunk with victory.[1]

Eisenhower sent an angry message to Ben-Gurion, protesting his speech. Herbert Hoover, Jr., acting as secretary of state while Dulles was absent for an operation for cancer, predicted to my deputy Shiloah that Ben-Gurion was risking "Israel's eventual expulsion from the United Nations."

I thought that my own duty as the head of our two most important diplomatic missions was not only to register the breakdown of our international position, but to suggest a remedy. I proposed a formula that would enable us to satisfy the United States, which alone could neutralize the Soviet threat, while leaving the door open for us to resume the pursuit of our limited but eminently righteous war aims—free passage through the Straits and tranquillity on our southern border facing Gaza. I cabled Ben-Gurion that he would have to retreat from the refusal to admit the international force. On the contrary, we should use the international force as an instrument for gaining both time and opportunity. My proposal was that we should inform the United States that we would withdraw from Sinai and Gaza "when satisfactory arrangements are made with the international force about to enter the Canal Zone."

Ben-Gurion's first reaction was to suggest a meeting with Eisenhower. This was totally unrealistic. Eisenhower's mood was punitive. He had won reelection by a huge majority against a distinguished opponent in a campaign he thought that Israel had attempted to derail. He had refused to see Anthony Eden, the head of America's principal ally. Eisenhower was asking all over Washington whether Ben-Gurion's reputation for lucidity was justified. I explained to Ben-Gurion that the U.S. was not convinced that the Soviet

---

[1]Michael Brecher, *Decisions in Israel's Foreign Policy* (New Haven: Yale University Press, 1974), p. 283.

threats against Britain, France and Israel were anything more than intimidatory, but it was taking no chances and ships of the Sixth Fleet had been ordered to the high seas in order to avoid a Pearl Harbor kind of attack. My estimate was that the U.S. would not use military force to dislodge us from Sinai but that it would exert all its influence to replace Israeli troops with the international force that Pearson had proposed.

I was now faced with one of the most extraordinary situations that I or, for that matter, any other ambassador had ever confronted. The Israeli Cabinet on November 8 was in constant session, reeling under its international unpopularity and Soviet rocket-rattling. The French defense minister, Maurice Bourges-Maunoury, had told Shimon Peres that he would advise us not to take the Soviet threats lightly. The Cabinet was taking them so seriously that it was almost paralyzed. There were two options: One was to announce complete and unconditional withdrawal; the other was my proposal to make the withdrawal dependent on satisfactory arrangements with the projected international force. In the first case, we would emerge from the war humiliated and with no gain from much effort and sacrifice. In the second case, we could mount an intense diplomatic and public campaign to secure our aims with intermediate partial withdrawals parallel with the diplomatic effort.

The second course was evidently more favorable to our interests, but some of the more nervous ministers, including Pinhas Sapir and Zalman Aranne, feared that anything short of an unconditional capitulation would bring the dreaded Soviet missiles on our undefended heads. "Eban must be out of his mind," said the trembling dissentients. Ben-Gurion's reaction was spectacular in its originality. He had decided to leave a peace-or-war decision to me. In the words of two witnesses—Yaacov Herzog and Gideon Rafael—Ben-Gurion said that "if Eban takes responsibility, then I agree." He then held up the speech that he had planned in a national broadcast for some hours to give time to see if I would still hold to my proposal after taking soundings in Washington.

In two and a half hours, I had made the soundings with Walter Bedell Smith, Allen Dulles (the director of the CIA), and with Senators Lyndon B. Johnson and William F. Knowland, who were the two congressional leaders serving with the U.S. mission to the UN. I even made indirect contact with Foster Dulles, who was in temporary convalescence from his operation.

I advised Ben-Gurion to take version two of the fateful paragraph in his delayed speech, and to make withdrawal conditional on the entry and functioning of the UN Emergency Force. My American interlocutors did not want a victory for Soviet intimidation. My own calculation was that Eisenhower would be firm against Soviet threats and that we would come empty-handed out of the war if we did not have a proviso enabling us to fight politically for free maritime passage and peace in the vicinity of Gaza.

In an age in which heads of government have usurped the negotiating functions of ambassadors in response to the vogue of summitry and the consequent "monarchization of government," the idea that an ambassador can decide between sensitive and potentially explosive courses seems unreal even in retrospect. This situation was achieved in this case as a result of two qualities of Ben-Gurion: his ingenuity in finding eccentric exits from dilemmas, and his tendency to give absolute confidence to a subordinate to whom he had delegated authority.

The unusual character of this procedure has been noted by a historian:

> This summation by Eban reflects the important role of a diplomat in the decision-making process. The strategic decision to withdraw was taken by Ben-Gurion before consulting Israel's envoy in America. Eban's recommendation to retain the (stronger) formula followed approval by the U.S. Secretary of State. At the same time, his role was innovative and the burden of responsibility placed upon him on November 8 was very heavy. He reacted decisively. Finally, the formula permitted phased withdrawal and therefore ample time to secure concessions, the raison d'être of the political struggle to follow.[2]

Conor Cruise O'Brien, who also seems to have had access to much documentation, awarded me Talleyrand's crown in discussing this episode in his review of my book *The New Diplomacy* in the London *Observer* in 1984. The unsolved and unanswerable question is how Ben-Gurion would have reacted and what would have ensued if I had chosen the supposedly "safer" course and left Israel without a right of maritime passage and with a vulnerable southern region after the Sinai War. It is true that ten years later, in 1967, Nasser tried to annul both of our successes, but it was much easier for Israel to defend a maritime passage that already existed than it would have been to resume the fight for a maritime artery that was annulled by a blockade.

By now the British and French landings and air bombings had subsided under the intimidatory pressures of American and Soviet policy. In each of their histories, the Suez fiasco was a turning point. Indeed, it was a watershed in the history of power. The international consequences of the Suez War were more far-reaching than anything that occurred on the regional level. Britian spent some years reflecting on its change of status, vacillating between a hopeless longing for a "special relationship" with the United States and a reluctant acceptance of a European destiny. France accepted the 1956 defeat with better grace and without having to face a hostile domestic opinion. Its response to failure provoked a speedy end of the Algerian occupation, a thorough revision of the anarchic constitutional system, a successful appeal

---

[2]*Ibid.,* p. 290 ff.

to the national hero to return to the helm, the birth and evolution of bomb-ings and the successful bid for leadership in the European Community. Despite the limited contours of the actual battle, the world after Suez was irreversibly changed. It became relentlessly bipolar, with only two nations able to claim superpower status.

Some years later, when I went to see President Johnson before the 1967 Six Day War, he asked me what I had heard in my conversation with General de Gaulle. I said, "He told me that the four Great Powers should concert their action."

Johnson replied: "Who the hell are the other two?" It was the 1956 crisis that made this riposte feasible.

The directives that I now received from Ben-Gurion were to concentrate intensely and exclusively on two aims: to achieve a result in which Israeli and other shipping would be free to navigate the Straits of Tiran and the Red Sea and in which our villages in the Negev would not be exposed to terrorist raids from Gaza. I confess that I felt exhilarated at being able to pursue these difficult but attainable goals without the impediment of attachment to an Anglo-French connection expressed in the ludicrous accord reached at Sèvres.

I had never felt a greater sense of personal excitement or fulfillment than during the four months between November 1956 and March 1957, when I was able to lead two impressive teams—our mission to the United Nations and our embassy in Washington—toward realistic and feasible goals. With the London-Paris collusion out of the way, we found good echoes in American public opinion. No less important was an improved attitude in the State Department, with Dulles, Robert Murphy and Herman Phleger becoming increasingly convinced that Egypt's belligerency was offensive to international law and to world peace. The case that I developed in dozens of encounters with the press, radio and television, foreign policy institutes and all branches of the Washing-ton and UN establishments was now clear and simple. It was based on the doctrine that statesmanship should correct, and not just restore, the conditions out of which the explosion had come. I said that it would be a farfetched legalism to insist that the status quo, including the illegal aspects of it, should be unconditionally revived. I drew up a memorandum in this sense on January 2, 1957, and requested comment and reaction from Dulles.

The diplomatic ice began to melt in our favor in early February, just when the physical snow was thick on the ground. Murphy invited himself to breakfast in my home in Juniper Street and said that there was a disposition to meet our two claims—for free passage in the Straits of Tiran and for a security system in Gaza, both to be implemented through the UN Emergency Force. The point about the Straits was easier than Gaza, since there was no Armistice Agreement relevant to the Straits such as that which gave Egypt a contractual status. I concentrated on the maritime issue. My memorandum went beyond the juridical aspect to touch on a larger vision: a new artery of maritime communication linking the continents of the old and new worlds, depriving Suez of its monopoly and reducing Europe's dependence on a single oil route, which Egypt could open or close at will.

On February 11 I became convinced that we were going to emerge from the war with Ben-Gurion's two objectives achieved. That was the day when Dulles called me to his office and handed me a memorandum on the Straits of Tiran and Gaza. My eyes lit up at the first reading. The United States was promising to support and assert Israel's right to send its own ships and cargoes without impediment through the Straits of Tiran; to acknowledge that if Egypt renewed its blockade Israel would be entitled to exercise its "inherent right of self-defense under Article Fifty-one of the UN Charter"; to encourage other states to exercise their right of free passage; and to maintain UN forces in Sharm el-Sheikh and Gaza until such time as their removal would not lead to a renewal of belligerency.

Dulles accompanied this paper with an uncharacteristic commentary drawing my attention to the excellent quality of the merchandise that he was selling. He said that an American undertaking was far more valuable than a dubious declaration of non-belligerency by Egypt. He added that if we stayed at Sharm el-Sheikh we could build a pipeline but nobody would put any oil in it. He made an eloquent appeal for Israel and the U.S. to build an era of cooperation on the basis of his memorandum. Emphatic calls to us in a similar spirit reached me from our friends in the media and the Congress.

To my consternation, a negative reply came from Ben-Gurion. It said that the solution proposed was not positive; that there was no specific guarantee to protect Israeli shipping and that the concept of free passage was limited(!) to "innocent passage." Ben-Gurion added that "we could not agree to the stationing of UN forces at Nitsana."

We were back to November 7 again. I patiently informed Ben-Gurion that the memorandum had no reference to Nitsana and that the alternative to "innocent passage" is slave and drug traffic, which have never figured prominently among Zionist ideals. Innocent passage does not even forbid warships.

This unexpected rejection set off a whole cascade of pressures and irritations in Washington. Assembling my staff, I said that our government could not take yes for an answer. Dulles came back from consultation with Eisenhower in Georgia and asked me to his home. He said that if we did not see any advantage in the American initiative we were "free to try our luck elsewhere." This was ominous, since the UN General Assembly was discussing a sanctions motion that would certainly not have "encouraged" any state to send its ships through an Israel-dominated Sharm el-Sheikh. Dulles spoke of our being "on the verge of a catastrophe." He added: "If Israel is not interested in taking up the American initiative, the matter will go back to the United Nations, where I doubt that you could get any worthwhile guarantees at all."

Dulles had interrupted our talk twice to speak to Eisenhower on the telephone. Throughout the many years that I served in Washington during the Eisenhower years I never found the least evidence for the media contention that he was a figurehead president.

In order to gain time and postpone a headlong clash with a hundred percent of the world community, I told Dulles that I had been called home for consultation on the February 11 memorandum. In the meantime I arranged for this to become true. I left Dulles's home at the sound of his statement that he presumed Ben-Gurion had weighed all the dangers inherent in this course against the bright prospects available from negotiating on the basis of the U.S. memorandum. "If so," said Dulles, "I am unable to understand how Israel had reached such an eccentric conclusion."

I left for Israel without hearing Eisenhower's broadcast on February 23 in which he spoke emphatically in support of what he had done to allay Israel's concerns. But he had added that if Israel rejected every sincere effort to improve its position "the United States would have to adopt measures that might have far-reaching effects on Israel's relations throughout the world."

By the time that I arrived in Jerusalem Ben-Gurion had evidently been impressed by the gravity of what I had reported about the atmosphere in the U.S. Even Rabbi Silver and Senators Johnson and Knowland, who had assisted me greatly in the struggle for our positions on Gaza and the Gulf of 'Aqaba, had told me that "your chief is carrying his stubbornness too far." In our talk Ben-Gurion was disposed to regard the February 11 memorandum as a great achievement. He spoke vaguely about "internal difficulties" in a way that insinuated that General Dayan was reluctant to abandon his conquests. But he sent me back with pragmatic directives, some of them severe, which in my judgment would enable me to bring the crisis with Dulles and Eisenhower to a successful end. A message from Bedell Smith in Washington in which that good friend of Israel had implored Ben-Gurion "to give Eban something to work with" contributed to the improvement in the prime minister's mood.

In the course of our talk I informed Ben-Gurion that I had heard soundings that some influential Americans close to the "Dulles circles" were indicating that since Egypt took no interest in Gaza, they were exploring the idea of leaving Gaza in Israeli control after the withdrawal from Sinai in the hope that Israel would "break the back of the refugee problem." Golda Meir had asked me to probe Ben-Gurion's reaction. Ben-Gurion went up to heaven in a pillar of fire and a cloud of smoke. In barely suppressed indignation he said: "Gaza is a cancer. A barrel of gunpowder. A cancer can sometimes increase the size of a body, but every sane person tries to get rid of it. How can we take 350,000 Palestinian Arabs against their own will and against the will of the friendly and hostile nations without exploding our state from within? The most important decision that we shall have to take will be to withdraw from Gaza. Do anything! Get your U.N. force in there!"

Ben-Gurion had "awarded" me the UN force but clearly did not want to see Gaza as long as he lived.

I flew back to Washington via London. British weather prevented me from taking an immediate connection, so I checked into a hotel overnight. This innocent necessity not only left the UN General Assembly on tenterhooks with its sanctions resolution hovering over the East River. It also provoked a nervous flutter in Dulles's circles, where it was feared that I was stopping over in order to commit a new collusion with Anthony Eden's successors in Whitehall.

The minister in the U.S. Embassy, Walworth Barbour, was instructed to keep a watchful eye on my flight schedules!

I touched down in New York and used the few available hours to report to Golda Meir. I spoke to Arthur Dean, one of Dulles's close advisers in the same prestigious law office, in the hope that he would soften up the secretary in advance of my afternoon arrival. From National Airport in Washington I went straight to Dulles's residence, which was under virtual siege by news-papermen and TV reporters. The media have a strong nose for imminent blood, and the failure of my mission could mean, if not immediate war, at least a first use of sanctions.

Assembled in the secretary's living room were Dulles, Under Secretary Christian Herter and the five senior officers of the State Department. I recounted Ben-Gurion's position, which amounted to an appreciative accep-tance of Dulles's February 11 memorandum coupled with a demand for a more emphatic statement of American support of Israel's right to forcible reaction if a blockade or raids from Gaza were renewed. When I finished, Dulles said, "Your attitude is constructive." At that moment I knew that Operation Kadesh was over and that we had not lost the struggle.

I went into a Socratic dialogue, while Shiloah made industrious record. Dulles gave the replies in shotgun speed. Yes, the U.S. would send its own flag through the Straits. Yes, the U.S. would support the development of an Israeli oil outlet. Yes, the U.S. would mobilize all the maritime nations to follow its lead in saying this in the United Nations. Yes, the U.S. would work for a UN administration in Gaza to replace the Israeli occupation. Yes, the U.S. would announce that if Israel's rights in the Gulf of 'Aqaba were again violated the U.S. would approve Israeli liberty to react under Article 51. Yes, the U.S. would encourage Hammarskjöld to include a naval patrol in the UN force to be stationed at Sharm el-Sheikh. Yes, the U.S. agreed that the UN force could not move out without that intention being brought to the General Assembly. Yes, President Eisenhower would write to Ben-Gurion setting out the American commitments.

Things were going so well that I whispered in Hebrew to Shiloah that "we ought to get out of here before they change their mind." I said that some of the understandings that we had reached needed Hammarskjöld's approval so I would now set wing for New York.

My relief was slightly premature. In New York Hammarskjöld gave scant deference to Dulles-Eban agreements. He would not sanction a naval patrol for the Straits of Tiran, though he had no complaint against legitimating Israel's maritime rights in the Gulf and the Straits. But on Gaza he was adamant. There would be no UN administration unless Egypt asked for it. Israel had no rights in Gaza, which was as Egyptian as Israel's territory under the 1949 Armistice Agreements was Israeli.

I called Dulles on the phone. He was very impatient with Hammarskjöld, but believed that there would be no majority in the General Assembly to overrule him. Meanwhile, French Prime Minister Guy Mollet and French Foreign Minister Christian Pineau were in Washington on a state visit. They had a proposal about how to strengthen Israel's position in Gaza despite Hammarskjöld's legal fundamentalism. Dulles suggested that I work out a scenario with Pineau.

Diary, February 26, 1957

I reached the French Embassy where I was greeted by Hervé Alphand, the Ambassador. Pineau entered flowing with cordiality. He and his prime minister were strongly in favor of the deal that I had worked out with Dulles. "If you create a real maritime reality in Sharm el-Sheikh and hold it with UN assistance for some years and if you also strengthen yourselves militarily with French and American aid, that will be more important than a quibble over words. Please do this for the sake of the French-Israeli entente.

His contribution was important. Israel should state in the Assembly that just as it could invoke Article 51 to defend itself against a renewal of the blockade in 'Aqaba, so would it defend its right to take action in the event of a recrudescence of raids from Gaza. The U.S. and France would endorse these assumptions, as would some other states. Egypt had promised silence. It did not want to deter Israel from leaving Sinai and Gaza. Pineau also told me that even though the Egyptians would probably not accept their banishment from the administration of Gaza, they had agreed that wherever there would be a UN Force, no other army would be present. This meant that the Egyptian army would not go back to Gaza.[3]

---

[3] The UN force remained in Gaza from 1957 to 1967. During that period the Egyptian army did not return to Gaza, although the Egyptian administration did go back. There were no raids from Gaza into Israel for ten years and the Israeli settlements in the Negev lived in peace. All this time the Straits of Tiran were developed as an Israeli oil and trade route to the East. In May 1967 Egypt under President Nasser occupied both Sharm el-Sheikh and Gaza and suspended the gains that Israel had made in the Sinai campaign. Within three days, however, Israel with American approval restored all the advantages that it had gained in Sharm el-Sheikh and Gaza.

On February 28 Golda Meir joined Dulles and me as we were drafting two speeches, one that Golda Meir would make in the General Assembly the next day and one in which Lodge would endorse the assumptions made in Golda's speech.

At a crowded meeting of the General Assembly on March 1, Golda duly expressed the assumption that we would have free passage in the Straits, that the UN force would remain as long as necessary to achieve that goal, that Israel would repel a resumed blockade in accordance with the inherent right of self-defense specified in the UN Charter and that we would act in a similar sense if the attacks from Gaza were renewed.

This speech was followed by statements of all the maritime powers supporting Israel's right to trade and navigate in the Gulf of 'Aqaba and the Straits of Tiran.

Lodge's speech did not satisfy Ben-Gurion on the Gaza issue, since there was no recommendation for the establishment of a UN administration. After another brief flurry Ben-Gurion was reassured by a letter from Eisenhower that Dulles had dictated to the president for signature from his home in my presence. Eisenhower repeated the American commitments in solemn terms and stated that Israel would not have cause to regret its withdrawal. Ben-Gurion attached overriding importance to the Eisenhower signature. He would not in any conditions try to reassure the Israeli public on the basis of a Dulles signature.

On March 15 Israeli troops withdrew from Sharm el-Sheikh and Gaza. In April the American vessel SS *Kernhills* sailed through the Straits of Tiran to Elath, which began its spectacular expansion and development as a port and tourist city. Except for a few days in May 1967, Israel has been at peace in the waters of the Gulf ever since. Although a UN administration was not established in Gaza, the Egyptian army did not follow the Egyptian administration back to Gaza. There was thus no protection for *fedayeen* raids and the UN forces, thick on the ground, influenced the position by their very presence. Tranquillity reigned in the area bordering Gaza for the next ten years. The UN force was a success story in every respect except in the timing and the manner of its withdrawal by U Thant ten years later in 1967. By then, however, realities and habits had been established that were too solid for Nasser to overcome.

One of the results of this urgent diplomacy was that Israel resumed its rhythm of action and development, sustained by a reinforced friendship with the United States. Ben-Gurion convinced his domestic opinion that the fight had not been in vain; that concrete results had ensued from it; and that the alternative course of standing in embattled defiance of world pressures offered no constructive issue. In the four months during which Israel was developing its battle in the UN, Washington and across the world, the country itself was in sad condition. It was cut off from its commercial links. The Soviet Union and the other Communist countries had withdrawn their ambassadors. Tourism was at a standstill. The rhythm of construction had died down and the country took on a dark, inert and empty aspect alien to its dynamic nature. It became evident that Israel is the kind of organism that can flourish only in close connection with the external realm.

Dulles was now gravely ill, but he persevered in office for the next two years. In all his talks with me he stated that there was a good and a bad Arab nationalism and the Nasser variety was the wrong sort. America became far more sensitive to our dilemmas and more apprehensive of our occasional outbursts of despair.

With their eyes fixed on the Eastern world, now joined to us by an open sea, Israelis would soon be able to explore the effects of their recent ordeals. Would we fall back into isolation and anxiety, or would there be a decade of peace and consolidation?

14

HOMEWARD BOUND: 1959

"HISTORY," WROTE KARL MARX, "would be very mystical if there were no room in it for chance." Surprising comment from that doughty determinist.

Could Israel's 1956 war have been avoided? The question must arise in any war, especially one so complex in its origins. Our military campaign of 1956 was not imposed inexorably upon us as were the wars of 1948, 1967 and 1973. It was not unanimously supported in the Knesset and was strongly criticized by former Foreign Minister Moshe Sharett. The association with Britain and France, whose motives were totally separate from ours, obscured the more realistic concerns of Israel. After all, there was no inferno of insecurity in Sussex or Normandy, as there was in many Israeli areas. Britain and France were not exposed to assaults on their lives and homes. Israel had much greater justification. Once we began to lose our balance of power and were faced by an Egyptian-Jordanian-Syrian alliance with no compensating support from the West in arms or effective guarantees, we were following historic precedent in challenging the adversary before it was too late. Stronger powers have fought "balance of power" wars. Churchill in a memorable speech in the 1930s described the need to curb regional domination by an expansionist power as the justification for his own country's resistance to Philip of Spain, Napoleon, Kaiser Wilhelm and Hitler before any of them had attacked Britain.

If anyone could have prevented Israel's Sinai War, it was the United States, which was the least entitled to self-righteousness. I later called the 1956 Israeli-Egyptian war "the war of the three squadrons." If Eisenhower and Dulles had supplied us with a minimal jet force, there would have been little temptation for us to go to Paris and make common cause with France. When I contemplate the lavish U.S. support of Israel's military power since the late 1970s, I am unable to rationalize the tenacity with which Eisenhower and Dulles refused to apply the "balance of power" principle to a conflict in which that doctrine was most relevant. The amount and quality of the arms that we sought from the U.S. were trivial in comparison with their corresponding dimensions today.

On October 25, the establishment of a joint High Command to control the Egyptian, Syrian and Jordanian armies dispelled any doubt about the gravity of our nation's plight and the need for urgent response. The few writers who have probed the issue of justice in war-making are not unanimous about this one. The best verdict is by Michael Walzer:

> States may use military force in the face of threats of war when the failure to do so would seriously risk their territorial integrity or political independence. Under such circumstances it can fairly be said that they have been forced to fight and that they are the victims of aggression. ... A state under threat is like an individual hunted by an enemy who has announced his intention of killing or injuring him. Surely, such a person may surprise his hunter, if he is able to do so.[1]

Nevertheless, the Israeli campaign in 1956 won little international understanding and few Israelis expected the Sinai campaign to mark an upward swing in Israel's fortunes. The commentators looked wisely at the clouds and predicted unceasing rain. They predicted that Israel would henceforth be identified in world opinion with the colonial powers; that the partnership with France and Britain would permanently mark Israel as an ally of "imperialism" and that Israel would find that it had gravely prejudiced its relationship with the United States.

None of these gloomy forecasts was fulfilled. The first symptom of recovery from our isolation in the Suez-Sinai War came in Washington in 1958. The argument between Israel and the United States was about whether Nasser's expansionist policy justified forceful reaction. In 1956 the United States had given a strongly negative answer. But in the summer of 1958, when Nasser was imposing his domination on other Arab states and attempting to overthrow all Arab regimes uncongenial to his leadership, the United States became as irritated as Israel, France and Britain had been in 1956. Dulles expressed his bitterness in memoranda about the distinction between legitimate Arab nationalism and Nasser's radicalism, which threatened the entire Middle East with instability. He asked me to transmit these dissertations to Ben-Gurion. For Dulles to write these thoughts to Ben-Gurion was rather like a recent convert to Catholicism preaching his new faith to one of the more theologically orthodox popes.

On July 14, 1958, the Iraqi government was overthrown and Iraq's royal family and its veteran prime minister, Nuri Said, were brutally murdered in the kind of bloodbath that has become an Iraqi tradition. At the same time,

---

[1]Michael Walzer, *Just and Unjust Wars* (New York: Basic Books, 1977), p. 85.

Nasserist pressure was exercised both on the Christian government of Lebanon, headed by Camille Chamoun and Charles Malik, and on the Jordanian monarch to accept Nasser's policy of regional domination. A large force of 20,000 U.S. Marines was sent to Beirut, and Dulles asked me to persuade Ben-Gurion to allow British aircraft to overfly Israeli territory on their way to reinforce the Jordanian monarchy in Amman. Neither Eisenhower nor Dulles showed any embarrassment at this new role. Dulles's forensic talent was equal to the task of rejecting any implication of double standards. "You see, Mr. Ambassador," he said, "in 1956 Nasser was the victim and target of an aggressive assault. Today he is himself the primary Middle Eastern aggressor."

In the same conversation he hinted subtly that I might persuade members of the Congress to support the president's decision to send forces into the Middle East. To cap the new atmosphere of intimacy he asked me to come with my deputy, Yaacov Herzog, to follow him to London for a day to continue our conversation on how to thwart Nasser. I duly made the trip and found myself in the dawn's early light in the U.S. ambassador's spacious residence near Regents Park. The ambassador himself, Jock Whitney, took us around the house, showed us a wonderful collection of impressionist masterpieces, but expressed no views about the problems of Iraq, Lebanon and Israel that preoccupied his secretary of state.

On July 15, 1958, when the marines were established in Beirut and a British force took up its position in Jordan, American policy had come full circle toward a new vision of the Middle East and Israel. There was a sense of common purpose. Legislation under which the United States could intervene on behalf of threatened friends, under the name of the Eisenhower Doctrine, had been confirmed by the United States Congress in March 1957. It promised support for any Middle Eastern state threatened by aggression from a state "dominated by international communism."

There was irrelevance in this formulation, since Israel and some Arab states were threatened by a state, namely Egypt, that was dominated by Arab nationalism, not by international communism. However, I had strongly urged the Israeli government to accept inclusion in this quaint doctrine on the principle that if Israel, so long boycotted from Middle Eastern groupings and categories, was unexpectedly asked to join any grouping in our region, we should accept the invitation before it was hastily withdrawn.

The two Western powers were attempting, unrealistically, to dethrone Nasser from his leadership of the Arab world. Nasserism in their eyes had become more than a doctrine of Egyptian revolution. Its central theme was hegemonistic. Cairo saw itself not only as the capital of Egypt, but also as the center in which all Arab policies should be determined. Nasser's policy was one empire, one nation, one leader; and there was no difficulty in diagnosing who the leader should be. Wherever there was a government in the Arab world dedicated to traditional Muslim values, or to cordial relations with the

West, or one that declined to accept Nasser's pretensions to leadership, he and his agents would move for its overthrow. The United States and Britain initiated an Emergency Session of the United Nations in which they interpreted the UN Charter as an endorsement of intervention on behalf of the separate integrity and independence of Middle Eastern states.

Israel felt vindicated by American acceptance of these ideas. Indeed, without the use of our airspace it would have been impossible for the Western powers to supply Jordan. Quite apart from intellectual satisfaction, Israel drew practical relief from this robust American insight into Middle Eastern realities. Economic aid to Israel was renewed and the United States developed a sharper sensitivity than before toward the problems of Israel's defense. The road was open for a more dignified and prosperous period in American-Israeli relations. A note from Dulles told us that the action taken by Eisenhower to defend Lebanese independence should be regarded as an example of what the United States would do if Israel's survival were threatened. I followed my usual course of suggesting that the secretary's note be formatted as a presidential letter. It was a delicate task to indicate to the secretary that his credibility and that of President Eisenhower were not of the same weight.

In the special session of the UN General Assembly in the summer of 1958, I faced a voting dilemma. The Arab delegations, seeking to reunite the Arab world, drafted a resolution calling for respect for "the territorial integrity and political independence of Middle Eastern states." I asked Jerusalem for a directive on the Israeli vote. There was no reply. My political chiefs were otherwise engaged. The president of the General Assembly, Sir Leslie Munroe of New Zealand, left my name on the speaker's list right to the end. When no answer came from Israel, I ascended the podium and announced Israel's positive vote for the Arab resolution. I added that an exhaustive definition of the term "Middle Eastern states" could be found in a little blue booklet containing the names of the members of the United Nations. Golda Meir endorsed my action.

My own appraisal of Arab nationalism had been expressed in a lecture that I delivered in February 1958 at Friends' House in London to mark the tenth anniversary of Israel's independence. The chairman was Lord Samuel, who had been the first British High Commissioner in Palestine in 1920. He was then in his ninetieth year, and he riveted the audience with an introduction of impeccable eloquence and wit, all delivered without the use of notes.

My speech was based on the theme that "nothing divides the Arab world more than the attempt to unite it." I have been bountifully plagiarized on this as on other similar dicta ever since. I did not dispute the fact that the Arab world is a family whose members feel a common emotion, resentment, or pride in whatever moves any part of the family. But this family is fragmented in many of its main characteristics. Its members do not fall into the same economic categories. They cover a wide spectrum, from extravagant oil wealth to acute poverty. Their regimes and orientations are diverse. This pluralism responds to differences of state structure, orientation and geographical positions that are inevitable in a family dispersed over such vast distances and interacting with such varied circumstances. My conclusion is that Arabs are united in their speech and sentiment, but divided in their interests.

Some Arab historians believe that there is only one Arab nation and that the fragmentation of the Arab nation into individual states is "artificial," whatever that means. No fixed criteria of normality have ever been devised for individuals, let alone for corporate entities. Once established with its flags, its place in international agencies, its panoplies and emblems, an Arab state, like any other, evokes allegiances that are not transcended by any larger unit of organization. Normality is an acquired attribute. When it comes down to hard realities it is now the separate, sovereign state that counts.

When one Arab state renounces its name and identity to merge with another Arab state, it is reasonable to be suspicious about whether the resultant "unity" is voluntary. When Syria became part of a "United Arab Republic" together with Egypt, I thought that it would only be a matter of time before Damascus would assert its historic fame as the seat of the first Caliphate. Meanwhile, I expressed my conviction that Syria was "united with Egypt in the manner that our prophet Jonah was united with the whale . . . an uncomfortable, excessively internal kind of union with a resulting sense of confinement."

I have had great difficulty with such sweeping, generic terms as "the Arabs" and even "the Arab world" and have advocated a meticulous study and understanding of each Middle Eastern nation as a distinctive entity in its own form and terms.

The year 1958 saw Arab states bringing harsh accusation against each other to the United Nations, with complaints against Nasser from Jordan, Iraq, Morocco and Lebanon. This was a vindication of my belief that diversity rather than unity is the distinguishing feature of Arab political structures.

For Israel, the recovery of our harmonious relationship with the United States was the most spectacular gain from the 1956 crisis. We were now being treated not as a burden to be chivalrously borne, but as a friend whose cooperation was worthy of respect. In that spirit, Dulles came to my embassy residence in May 1958 on the tenth anniversary of Israel's independence. He made a moving and eloquent speech about our nations' common values and experiences. The other guests around our not very large table in Juniper Street were Senators Symington, Knowland and Javits, Felix Frankfurter and the president of the AFL-CIO, George Meany. The central idea was to have as many couples as possible who never spoke to each other outside the Israeli embassy. In August 1958 I brought Dulles an impressive letter from Ben-Gurion, couched in visionary terms, about Israel's aid programs in newly developing states. Dulles reacted enthusiastically and the U.S. supported the expansion of Israel's development assistance in the Third World.

There were still many ordeals ahead, but it seemed that the nightmare of weakness was over. Before 1956, many in the world still doubted Israel's durability. The country always seemed poised on the brink of bankruptcy. Its international stature had been limited. Nobody in the world made much effort to soothe its apprehensions. But after 1957 the prospect brightened; Israel's sharp reaction to prolonged belligerency had certainly evoked disapproval in many places, but it had also inspired an uneasy respect. It was likely that Israel would at least be taken into serious account and that its reactions to danger or provocation would be more carefully measured.

With every year that passed after the Suez-Sinai crisis, the country seemed to lose something of its fragility. The Jewish population grew rapidly in the next decade. The rate of economic expansion had few parallels. More eloquent than statistics of growth was the visible evidence of a landscape across which a green carpet of cultivation moved like an advancing tide. In the growing cities and suburbs there were signs of relative affluence, with the rise of a mercantile and professional middle class. Israel's agriculture celebrated many triumphs; its talent for profusion stirred the mind and hope of many nations in a famine-stricken world. From a million cultivated acres, Israel was producing eighty-five percent of the food consumed by two and a half million people at a high level of nutrition, while also exporting $130 million worth of agricultural products to the world markets. The industrial infrastructure became more elaborate and diverse. The defense establishment made heavy demands on technical precision and inventiveness, and the challenge was, for the most part, successfully met. The average per capita income moved toward European levels. Israeli research was honored in the scientific world. Much in Israel was still imperfect, lacking outward form and inner harmony; but the country's aspect was becoming less rigorous, its culture less parochial, its energies more robust.

There is an instructive symbolism in the fact that archaeology and science were now the main intellectual enthusiasms of Israeli youth. Here was a people straining to transcend its smallness by an appeal to historic lineage and modern technology. Israel was commonly regarded as a progressive community with a modern scientific outlook; but it was also gripped by a constant search for its roots in a distant past. Much of Israeli life is taken up with reconciliation between past and future; between the old inheritance and the new potentiality; between religious tradition and modern progress; between Western pragmatism and Eastern spirituality; between free enterprise and collective ideals. Contradictions are sharp, and the tang of Israeli life is heightened by them. Above all, there was usually something in the national enterprise that expressed the instinct for innovation. Across the Gulf of 'Aqaba from Eilat, a bridge of commerce and friendship was patiently constructed toward the eastern half of the globe. The National Water Carrier, bringing water from where it was relatively abundant (in Galilee) to where it was disastrously sparse (in the Negev), was impressively completed and Galilee waters flowed southward to irrigate southern fields. For many years the fear of Arab displeasure had prevented the full development of Israel's diplomatic links. But from the late 1950s onward, the country was bountifully visited, inspected, explored, praised and often flattered by the world's intellectual community.

The sources of this fascination were complex. The building of new communities has always appealed to man's creative dreams. But after its first harsh decade Israel had a particular message in the context of its times. In the most advanced countries there was no longer a mystique of struggle. Life had lost its rhapsodical sense. On the other hand, the developing states had let their early exaltation give way to bitterness and despair. Institutional freedom had not been accompanied by any parallel growth in economic resources or social dynamism. The flags were not enough. The emblems of sovereignty were moving, but they could not bridge the humiliating gulf in capacities and resources between the privileged and the disinherited states. Thus the advanced countries admired Israel for its pioneering vitality, while new nations probed the reasons for its accelerated development. Some envied Israel for what it had already accomplished; others for what it still had to do. To Jewish communities, Israel imparted a sentiment of kinship, pride and mutual responsibility.

Israel's struggle against the Arab siege in 1956 had not changed its physical map. The borders were exactly as before. Free navigation in the Red Sea and tranquillity in the settlements near the Gaza Strip were tangible assets, symbolized and monitored by UN forces. But these gains themselves could not explain the new buoyancy in the national temper. The real transformation was in Israel's vision of itself. This had evolved from self-doubt to something like national confidence.

It seemed a good time for me to end my mission and make for home. Since 1947 I had led our delegation to the United Nations throughout the most stormy and tense period of our national struggle. For nine of those twelve years I had simultaneously headed our Washington embassy. In 1958 Ben-Gurion urged me to end my mission in time to take part in the 1959 election campaign. He had promised to include me in his next Cabinet and had added cryptically that Golda Meir announced her decision to resign from Cabinet office. (She eventually carried out this decision fifteen years later.)

In any case I believed that this was a time for me to seek new horizons. Before 1956 I had been known to Americans principally as a voice. We were now moving into an era dominated by television. I was known visually to cab-drivers, hall porters, salesmen in department stores and passersby. My book *Voice of Israel* had been published by the Horizon Press and was well reviewed. The *Times Literary Supplement* in London even compared my speeches to those of Cicero and Burke and reflected on the diplomats of small countries who raised echoes wider than the dimensions of their countries seemed to justify. The American historian whom I most admired, Henry Steele Commager, had written in a review for a monthly publication:

> As Ben-Gurion has been the spirit of Israel, so Abba Eban has been its voice. It is a voice of rare eloquence; indeed, now that Churchill and de Gaulle are off the stage it is the most eloquent of all the leading actors.

Faced with such reactions, it seemed elementary prudence to depart before people had time to change their minds. But in opting for the end of my mission, I was gripped by the challenge of ceasing to be a voice and becoming a hand upraised and a mind occupied in the decision-making process. As an ambassador I had not frequently encountered the ordeal of having to say things that I knew to be untrue, such as the contention that the Kibya raid in 1953 had been carried out by irate settlers, not by the Israeli army; or the statement that we had found a million blankets in Sinai and Gaza, which was adduced as proof that a Russian base was being prepared. (In fact they belonged to UN relief agencies charged with looking after hundreds of thousands of refugees.) I was afraid that the accumulation of such episodes over a long time would erode my personal credibility.

The final argument for separating myself from the allurements of my position in Washington and New York came from the family consideration. Eli had been born in New York and Gila in Washington, and since these were obviously provisional homes, there was need to give both of them the earliest possible chance of absorbing their Israeli heritage. Meyer Weisgal, the formidable creator of the Weizmann Institute of Science, had proposed that I become the second president of the Institute in succession to the great Chaim Weizmann himself, since whose death in 1952 the presidency had been left respectfully vacant.

Weisgal was an astonishing character whose appearance in a Charles Dickens novel would have seemed to carry eccentricity beyond even the most ambitious imagination. A shock of gray hair, a bulbous nose, thick eyeglasses that seemed to glint irascibly and a loud voice uplifted in a constant flood of strident, vituperative speech mostly in Yiddish, all seemed to put the mark of vulgarity upon him. But beneath this facade of overweening self-assertion was a deeply sensitive aesthetic sense, inspired by the urge to make Israel a home of science and the arts and to communicate an Athenian vision of excellence and precision. I never encountered a man whose outer form and inner soul were so discordant with each other. I accepted the presidency at a mammoth meeting headed by Ben-Gurion in the great Plaza of the Weizmann Institute in November 1958. It was understood that this task would not replace or defer the political and parliamentary role that Ben-Gurion had promised. On my forty-fourth birthday, February 2, 1959, shortly after my return to Washington, I announced my intention to resign from both of my embassies with effect from the forthcoming May 15. It was also widely published that I would enter the political arena. The American press reacted with polarized versions: the first that I was obviously going to be the prime minister upon Ben-Gurion's retirement; the second that I was making a mistake to enter the political arena, where I would be devoured in short measure by the wolfish virulence of Israeli politics. It would soon emerge that both of these extremist predictions were off the mark.

The announcement of my resignation set off a moving reaction. A committee of tribute was formed, headed by Chief Justice Warren and Vice President Nixon and including the former presidents Truman and Hoover, the future presidents Lyndon B. Johnson and John F. Kennedy, and all the leaders of both houses of the Congress as well as the democratic leaders Adlai Stevenson and Eleanor Roosevelt. Dozens of editorial articles appeared from coast to coast, not only in *The New York Times* and *The Washington Post* ("he mobilized the English language and sent it into battle on Israel's behalf"), but also in newspapers in San Antonio, Texas, and Sheboygan, Wisconsin, and in Middletown, Connecticut. The significance of this for Israel lay in the fact that few Americans outside Washington could cite the name of the ambassador of a single country or, for that matter, of a head of delegation to the United Nations. Israeli diplomacy, for whatever reason, operated in the United States on an entirely original basis without reference to the general routine. The passage of time and the growth of familiarity have eroded this exceptionality to a large extent, and newspapers in Sheboygan, Wisconsin, no longer record the comings and goings of Israeli ambassadors. But the composers of crossword puzzles still utilize the fact that a name such as mine with two vowels and two consonants within a short word offers a convenient transition between the more challenging questions.

The intensity and range of the farewells compelled reflection on the reasons for the outpouring. It was evident that the idea of a Jewish state continued to fascinate and, sometimes, to baffle the American people. At the root of this emotion lay spiritual mysteries derived from our biblical heritage. The majority of the states represented in the United Nations held the biblical story in reverence and even regarded it as a factor in establishing Israel's right to statehood. In today's international community, the Hebrew bible is regarded by the majority of member nations as nothing but the literature of one small people, while other faiths have a numerical preponderance. I do not believe that we could have obtained membership in international organizations if we had delayed our application for a few years after 1949.

Beyond this mystique lay the spectacle of our recuperation from weakness and disaster. I had expressed this in an address at Notre Dame University, the sanctuary of Catholicism (and of football) in the United States: "Within a few years we have passed from a world in which the existence of a Jewish state of Israel was inconceivable to a world that is inconceivable without its existence."

In all the major cities farewell occasions were organized; it was as if I were running an election campaign in America instead of preparing for one in Israel. In Chicago six thousand people assembled in the Opera House to hear Senator Paul Douglas express regret that I was not running in the United States as the Democratic candidate for the presidency. In New York Eleanor Roosevelt presided over an assembly of permanent delegates and expressed the wistful idea that "it must be wonderful to be young and to be in the service of such a cause." In Madison Square Garden, Abba Hillel Silver was the chairman at a gathering of 18,000 in which the surprise for me was the appearance of Yigael Yadin with a letter from Ben-Gurion, which he read aloud. The prime minister wrote:

> Our international position continues to improve and you have no small part in that achievement. Your appearances in the General Assembly and the Security Council of the United Nations brought honor to your country and pride to all your people. . . . It is in that spirit that I welcome you home . . .

John Foster Dulles had resigned in acknowledgment of the incurability of his cancer, and the news of his death reached me when I was afloat on the liner bearing me across the Atlantic. Israeli readers were surprised by Ben-Gurion's statement that "Israel has lost a friend." Few readers were conscious of the intimacy that had arisen between the two governments during the short period when the United States went over to a policy of containing and even resisting Nasser's disruptive policies.

I derived great satisfaction from my efforts to prove that American sympathy for Israel was a nonpartisan issue. The first Israeli reaction to the Republican victory in the 1952 election was that Truman's support had been a one-time, fortuitous episode sustained by the exceptional circumstance of his respect for Chaim Weizmann and that the geopolitical weight of the Arab world would assert now itself and Israel would be irresistibly pressured to return to the 1947 partition map, to admit a flood of hostile refugees and to abandon its hold on the greater part of Jerusalem. After eight years of the Eisenhower presidency, with all its many storms and occasional frigidities, our territorial situation was unchanged, our hold on West Jerusalem had tightened and we held the keys of our gates in our own hands. The amateurish procedures of the early years had given way to the institutionalization of the Israeli presence in the United States and the United Nations. There was a foundation on which a firm structure could arise.

After a luncheon in my honor at Blair House and a brief farewell to President Eisenhower, who gave me a photograph dedicated in his own hand: "Abba Eban, a distinguished representative of Isreal [sic]," Suzy and I began to pack our possessions. We were sustained by the conviction that future presidents would know how to spell our country's name.

The memories that crowded in upon us were poignant. I had visited forty-two of the fifty states, had traveled two million miles and had fulfilled more than a thousand engagements as well as hundreds of UN meetings. I now found that it had been easier to live that decade than to celebrate it. There had been a transformation in our country's condition, and on the smaller level a change in my own part within the national context. It seemed a far cry from my arrival as a junior member of a Zionist delegation through the stormy UN debates in Geneva and Lake Success and the sudden assumption of a central responsibility for Israel's integration into the family of sovereign states. The storms and stresses of the succeeding years had been almost too swift and intense to be absorbed. What could be more rewarding than to lead two central institutions—the nation's leading embassy and its foremost arena of international contest—during the most formative period of the nation's struggle for independence and recognized legitimacy? I wondered aloud whether the domestic political arena to which I was directing my steps could offer similar emotional and intellectual satisfactions.

I may have idealized the diplomatic function. I had entered it at the summit without ever having been a second or first secretary or attaché or a counselor in a mission where there was no sense of suspense or cruciality and where no great issues hung in the balance. Having a low ceiling of boredom and a distaste for ceremonies and protocol, I doubt if I could have endured the idea of diplomacy as a professional routine. I was sustained in that conviction many years later when the eminent liberal economist and author John Kenneth Galbraith wrote a book that took the lid off the mysterious box in which the secret life of diplomats is enclosed. He must have discomfited many professional diplomats by exposing the inequality of their burdens. He wrote: "In India in my time there were some fifty ambassadors. . . . They were a spectacular example of what economists call 'disguised unemployment.' The ambassadors from Argentina and Brazil could not have had more than a serious day's work once a month. The more deeply engaged diplomats from Scandinavia, Holland, Belgium or Spain could discharge their essential duties in one day a week." The myth of the valuable cocktail party also crumbles before that corrosive pen: "I never learned anything at a cocktail party or dinner that I didn't already know, needed to know or would not soon have learned in the normal course of business. The emphasis that diplomats of all countries in all capitals accord to entertainment is the result of a conspiracy by which function is found in pleasant social intercourse and controlled inebriation."

Allowance must be made here for the humorous talent without which nobody should even begin to envisage a diplomatic career. But I can bear witness that I do not recall a single day in which twenty-four hours were even theoretically sufficient to accomplish the tasks of my two embassies. All my successors would agree that relaxation and ease are not the destiny of Israeli representatives in Washington.

While most Israelis and many American Jews lived the Eisenhower period in a mood of unceasing hypochondria, my own final account was more relaxed. Others were worried by the sharpness of the 1956 crisis, while I was impressed by the rapidity with which it had been overcome. There were not many ambassadors who had watched that period in American history at close hand during the entire course of two administrations. This experience seemed to authorize me to comment on the two leading characters who controlled American foreign policy for eight years.

John Foster Dulles was a man of many gifts, which did not include a capacity to win trust or affection. His policy had its own rationale. His balance-of-power doctrine had respectable roots in diplomatic history and his habit of emphasizing the adversarial nature of Soviet power could be defended on pragmatic grounds. If one wants to mobilize the American people on behalf of a policy of strength and resistance, it is no use telling them that Soviet policy is innocuous. But what disconcerted many Americans in Dulles was his attempt to clothe his defense of American interests in the sanctimonious garb of a moral crusade. His experience and professionalism were widely regarded, but his claim to a particular spirituality was not taken seriously. He always made his principles coincide with his material aims. He often wrestled with his conscience and always won. He also had an irrational belief in the power of contracts to define and systematize the international community. His attempts to organize the "free world" by a series of treaty signatures has dissolved, leaving few traces behind. Who now remembers the Baghdad Pact and SEATO? He was popular in Germany because of his friendship with Konrad Adenauer, but his infidelity to France and Britain led to the crisis in 1956 when he first encouraged London and Paris and then turned his back on them when they resisted too strongly. He had a vision of the world in which the friends and the foes of his country would face each other in neatly defined columns, like the formations of great armies in classical eighteenth- and nineteenth-century battle paintings. He seemed to have no sense of the blurred, gray ambiguities that constitute a great part of international reality. He brought an excessively subtle mind into the service of an excessively simplistic view of the world order.

Eisenhower as a reality was better than his own image. In the light of the Vietnam War, which was mainly the work of the activist school of American diplomacy, many revisionist thinkers in the United States have become fascinated by the idea that success may be achieved not so much by doing great things as by avoiding foolish things. Eisenhower was often vehement in Cold War oratory but careful not to translate that oratory into action. After the eager actions of "the best and the brightest" in the Kennedy and Johnson administrations, one of Ike's biographers was able to write:

He (Eisenhower) ended the Korean war, he refused to intervene militarily in Indo-China, he refrained from involving the United States in the Suez-Sinai crisis, he avoided war with China (over Quemoy and Matsu), he resisted the temptation to force a showdown after Berlin, he stopped exploding nuclear weapons in the atmosphere.

"Refused," "refrained," "avoided," and "resisted the temptation" do not have a heroic sound, but when Americans later came to reflect on what had resulted from the busy, energetic, daring leaders of later years, they had a nostalgic twinge of affection for those statesmen who were capable of constructive inaction. Within a few years of the end of the Eisenhower era, Vietnam would ultimately shatter the illusion of American omnipotence and undermine the consensus underlying the conduct of American foreign policy.

I would follow these events from afar. My Washington mission had to end someday, and it could not have ended on a more felicitous note, but in the end Suzy and I stood in Washington's National Airport bound for Israel via New York. My status was that of one of the 1,600 passengers about to set sail with his wife and two children on the SS *USA*. We had taken a last, lingering look at the home in Juniper Street and at the chancery in Columbia Avenue and had gathered up the mementos of our nine-year journey across personal and national history and had clutched each other's hand in acknowledgment of having seen great visions and dreamed great dreams—together. My dominant thought was that the next day no one would be obliged to report anything to me.

"Tomorrow to fresh fields and pastures new . . ."

15

FIRST MINISTERIAL YEARS

AFTER A SEA voyage from New York to London and a brief sojourn in a Swiss resort we boarded an airliner at Zurich Airport and touched down at Lod in central Israel on a hot July night. I had told Suzy that "a few people from the Weizmann Institute" would probably meet us at the airport. We were astonished to see a variegated and cordial group of about fifty people neatly divided between Weizmann Institute staff and members of the Labor Party top leadership. There were also many newspaper correspondents and radio reporters who assailed me with questions about my political views and plans. None of them asked about relations with the United States or our position in the United Nations. I was clearly being welcomed not as a returning ambassador but as an emerging political candidate.

In the coming days, there would evidently be competition in the coming days for my time and labor. This in itself was a positive fact. Returning ambassadors in Israel are often made to feel superfluous, changing overnight from excellencies with staff cars and drivers to tourist guides for visiting dignitaries. Here was I required to lead the Weizmann Institute into a new phase, marked by its emergence from the "ivory tower" into a complex role as an instrument for enhancing some of the nation's international interests. At the same time, I was to plunge into the dusty, hot arena of party politics.

It was hard to explain why the Labor politicians were so nervous. Ben-Gurion had held office uninterruptedly for a dozen years during which the very idea of anybody else at the helm would have appeared intolerable to some and unrealistic to others. Yet my Labor colleagues genuinely feared that the opposition leader, Menachem Begin, might make inroads on the traditional Labor bulwarks. He and his supporters were registering some progress with the slogan "It's time for a change," as well as with a fiercely aggressive attitude to the Arabs and a populist approach to economic problems.

A few days after my arrival from Washington, I listened surreptitiously from my car to a few minutes of a speech that Begin was making to an open-air meeting in Jerusalem. He listed the accumulated American aid that had flowed to Israel since the early 1950s. He then divided this large dollar accumulation by the total Jewish population of Israel and asked the audience, "Has any one of you received the two thousand one hundred fifty dollars that the Ben-Gurion government received for you from the United States?"

What disturbed me was not the "argument" itself, since I had learned from political campaigns in the United States that all is fair in war and, therefore, in other forms of contest, but it was disquieting that some of the audience seemed impressed by this approach. They reminded me of the volatile crowd that listened, according to Shakespeare, to Marc Antony's speech at Caesar's funeral while changing its attitudes from sentence to sentence. I was listening to the demagogy without the poetry. The listeners were led to suspect that Ben-Gurion had virtually embezzled the meager inheritance of all our citizens and had devoted it to Labor Party funds. It was evident to me that I would be dealing with scientific truth during my mornings at the Weizmann Institute and with a different kind of reality in my evenings on party platforms. On the other hand, I believed that if this was the kind of opposition that faced us, our party's traditional electoral support would not be eroded.

To my surprise and relief, I found little indignation in the public mood about our having liquidated our gains in Sinai. Israelis at that time were accustomed to the idea that we would occasionally spring out of our legitimate confines, strike distant blows, but return to our point of departure. Ben-Gurion's hold on the public imagination in anything to do with national security was strong enough to ensure that a government under his leadership would not be seriously challenged at the polls.

Our home was to be at Rehovot, some fifteen miles south of Tel Aviv, in the grounds of the Weizmann Institute. It was an enchanting setting of date palms, garden walks perfumed by roses and carnations. All in all, a spectacle quite out of tune with the pioneering austerities associated with other parts of the national landscape. The Weizmann Institute was and has still remained an oasis contrasting sharply with the surrounding environment. The neat white houses, the monumental plazas, the laboratories and administration buildings arising copiously year by year, all indicated that this campus was privileged in two senses. It reflected the majestic personality of the founding president who had, after all, been the first scientist ever to be chosen as the head of a sovereign state, and it also reflected Meyer Weisgal's intensive creativity as well as his voracious pursuit of broadening horizons.

In my first conversation with him in my office at the institute he showed me some exchanges of letters that he had conducted with well-endowed Jewish families and foundations in the United States and Britain. To one American Jewish well-wisher who had sent a check of $100,000, Weisgal replied, "Thank you for your symbolic contribution. Please let me know when the rest will follow."

The sights and smells of Rehovot, and especially of the gracious campus, very nearly persuaded me to devote my full time to the development of this exceptional institution. And yet I knew in my heart that at that age on the morrow of an intensive experience in international diplomacy, my activist temperament would not be satisfied with the routines of an academic presidency, with its strong emphasis on fund-raising. For the moment, however, I could taste a sense of relief after the feverish pace of Washington and the United Nations.

While my integration into the campus community was smooth and harmonious, as was to be expected for an expatriate Cambridge tutor, my relationship with party colleagues was more complex. Neither they nor I had any illusions. We were not bound to each other by strong affinities. They had congregated at the airport and would fill all the seats in mass meetings that I was to address for the prosaic reason that they expected me to bring them votes.

I did not accept the idea that Ben-Gurion was "grooming" his younger colleagues for leadership. Only horses are groomed. But he wished to create a new leadership that would leapfrog over his own generation. Most Labor ministers were of authentically pioneering lineage. They had cultivated vineyards, drained swamps, plowed the reluctant earth, rejoiced in the initially sparse harvests and had seen the verdure spread slowly over the dry, brown landscape. They had no time or interest for adornments. They were blunt speaking and rough hewn with a disconcertingly monotonous rhetoric, untidy in outward appearance, and they operated in a political context that was savagely combative. Ben-Gurion wanted younger men, more attuned to the outside world and carrying some cargo of repute from other vocations. He wanted Dayan, Peres, Yigael Yadin and me in his entourage, and all of us except Yadin were available.

There was no democratic process in the selection of Israeli leaders. The structure was pyramidal. Ben-Gurion presided over a strident family, bound together by the incentives of parliamentary and ministerial office. The parties in Israel were more than machines for the garnering of votes. They, and especially the Labor Parties, were considered to be the "homes" of all members, creating the background and context of their worlds of ideas, defining the social proprieties in which they moved, and parading their austerity as indications of a progressive social ambition. Above all, they nearly all originated in Eastern and Central Europe. Israel was one of the few countries where political leaders were expected to make some mistakes in the grammar of their own tongue as proof of "rootedness" and down-to-earth practicality. My own bias for precision in public discourse clearly impressed the larger audience, but within the party command correct Hebrew was regarded as pretentious.

I was therefore entering the political arena without any built-in advantages. Diplomacy had obliged me to take a neutral stance on domestic political affairs, although there was no doubt that my true place was within the social democratic framework. After all, I had spent much of my student years in the confines of the British Labour Party, which stood no nonsense from Marxist ideologies and drew its growing support over three decades from a compassionate view of social responsibility and a relentless accent on expanding welfare and collective effort.

The party chiefs acknowledged my contribution to Israel's interests and respected my capacity to get massive audiences, but they did not hide their feeling that I was not "one of us."

Candidates for parliamentary seats and therefore for ministerial office have no specific constituencies. They have to satisfy small central committees dominated by existing officeholders. With our quaint centralized proportional system of election, Israel is the only democracy in which governments appoint parliaments instead of parliaments appointing governments.

A small group called the Gush (the Block) consulted with Ben-Gurion on the party list, which involved a selection of the fifty to fifty-five candidates who had a realistic chance of being elected. These would be screened and scanned and scrutinized with a view to their ideological rectitude and their geographical and ethnic distribution. The kingmakers asked whether we had enough Sephardim, enough members from development towns and the large urban centers, as few women as one can get away with without causing scandal and a few candidates who would be recognized if one passed them in the street.

One newspaper wrote that my party's attitude to me was very similar to that which existed between Woodrow Wilson and the Tammany Hall that had dominated the New York political machine. The only reason for tolerating me lay in the fact that I evoked a broader public echo than most of them. Those were the days before the domination of electoral contests by television. The old-fashioned meeting, very often in the open air, was still the stereotype for electoral consultation.

I found myself confronted by crowds of five, six, seven, sometimes up to 10,000 people massed together in a public square or on the village lawn listening to my speech, which came to them over somewhat scratchy microphones. Next day the newspapers would report my statistics: 12,000 in Tel Aviv, 10,000 in Ramat Gan, 15,000 in Haifa, 7,000 in Bat Yam, 15,000 in Rehovot, and in the underprivileged quarters of southern Tel Aviv, masses of Jews from Kurdistan, Yemen and Iran, more recently from Morocco. For reasons that I never fully fathomed, I encountered a particular sympathy amongst the Sephardic Jews, who had great respect for language and were impressed by what they believed to be the glamour of international life. Sephardic Jewry has a courtly tradition, rather like that of the American South.

The 1959 election was Ben-Gurion's greatest victory, and it was universally attributed to the new blood that he had introduced into the leadership of Mapai.

I decided very early on not to simplify my own style in order to fit the general stereotype. I even developed a theory that the relative uniformity of our candidates was a drawback that we would have to overcome. It would be much better to present a picture of diversity in origins, actions and temperaments.

Meanwhile, in the Weizmann Institute I was preparing to begin my mission as I had done in Washington, with new initiatives. At the center of my thinking was the need to explore the results of what I called the two great revolutions that had dominated the life of our times. These were the scientific revolution, which had created new potentialities both of disaster and abundance. The other was the national revolution that had multiplied the number of states to such an extent that over ninety percent of mankind lived under sovereign flags. Israel was a rare case of a nation that had an intimate relationship to both revolutions. It had acceded to sovereignty in the late 1940s and had inherited and further developed a scientific tradition and a technological infrastructure. Israel was living proof that nations were no longer imprisoned by their smallness of population and territory. The only greatness that Israel could achieve lay in those fields of thought and action in which matter and quantity could be transcended by spirit and quality. Small communities that created and maintained a relatively large body of research workers, scientists and engineers could be essentially different from societies that did not have such assets. In its scientific manpower and institutions, Israel was amongst the first dozen countries and not amongst the disadvantaged 150.

I believed that science could serve our society in two ways. First, by the increase of security and material welfare and, second, by its capacity to endow Israeli society with qualities derived from the scientific world. The creative skepticism of science, its universal solidarities, its insistence on precision, its challenge to dogmas that cannot be experimentally confirmed, all these, I thought, could ennoble our nation irrespective of their contribution to economic welfare and military defense. I counseled the scientific community to abandon the ivory tower and to recognize that while science deals with the spectacle of nature, the scientist must remain a loyal citizen of the nation that elevated him to his pedestal of prestige and gave him the conditions of his creativity.

There are many elements in Jewish history and experience that stress the emotional, passionate, mystical, metaphysical elements in the social character. The task of the academic community is to contribute the redeeming dimension of rationality.

Within Israel and my own campus I could do little but enunciate these truths. But I saw a possibility of translating them into reality by organizing periodic encounters between leaders in science and technology and those who determine the policies of new states. I drew up a list of eminent figures in both domains and invited them to meet in Rehovot in the summer of 1960. The response to the idea and the invitation was staggering.

The dilemma that I diagnosed was that the leaders of the new nations were not utilizing modern science and technology to accelerate their development, and the scientific community was chiefly engaged in making the strong stronger and the rich richer. I hoped to induce the leaders of the scientific revolution and the leaders of new states to create points of contact and reciprocal advantage.

When I called the "Rehovot Conference on the Role of Science and Technology in Developing States" to order in August 1960, I felt deep satisfaction. The sight of Asian and African statesmen in rich and varied garb and of renowned scientists and heads of United Nations Agencies impressed the Israeli public and was a source of consolation to me in what would otherwise have been a vacuum both of initiative and of public resonance in my personal life after the challenge of the world arena. Despite Israel's consolidation, most of the world's statesmen had managed to evade the chance of visiting Israel. They wished to safeguard their interests in the Arab world. The prime minister of Burma, U Nu, was the only head of government who had visited us during the greater part of our first decade. Now there came prime ministers, foreign ministers, economic ministers, directors of development, and leading educators from thirty countries in Asia, Africa and Latin America, together with heads of UN specialized agencies and representatives of leading United Nations bodies. A group of renowned scientists led by the nuclear physicist Sir John Cockcroft and his fellow Nobel Laureate, Basil Blackett, attended together with biologists, agronomists, nuclear engineers, water experts and the directors of the World Health Organization, the UN Special Fund and Euratom.

My success in convening these spectacular encounters tended to conceal the fact that I had officially ended my diplomatic career. Ben-Gurion in a speech in the Knesset referred in a puzzled way to the fact that as a private citizen I had managed to bring more leaders of states and Nobel Prize men to Israel than had any of our governmental ministries.

The Rehovot Conference helped to take Israel out of diplomatic isolation. In my opening address, which was widely published, I described the speed with which African and Asian countries had broken out of tutelage to liberation.

If institutional freedom could itself guarantee peace and welfare, we should now be celebrating mankind's golden age. But, alas, the flags are not enough. In the awakening continents, freedom has not been attended by a parallel liberation of peoples from their social and economic ills. Behind the new emblems of institutional freedom, millions continue to languish in squalor, exploitation, and disease. Men and women awakened to learn that they may be free in every constitutional sense and yet lose the essence of their freedom in the throes of famine and want.

I pointed out that the business of science is the investigation of nature, but science has a human origin and a human destination. In her autobiography, Golda Meir pays generous tribute to the Rehovot Conference as something of a breakthrough in Israel's international relations.

The Rehovot Conference not only filled the void that arose from my appointment as a "minister without portfolio." It also added a new dimension. Most of my political and diplomatic experience had been in the West. I had now established links with leading statesmen in dozens of developing Third World countries, especially in Africa. There was also a beneficial "fallout" in the psychological effects in Israel. Israel, as a result of regional hostility, is intensely preoccupied with its own affairs. This creates the danger of exclusivism and claustrophobia in the intellectual climate. There has always been an assumption that others owe attention to our problems while we have no particular obligation toward theirs. I felt during that glittering week that I may have helped to focus the nation's interest on something that lay beyond and above its own concerns.

Before this contact with leaders of developing nations, my encounter with the liberation movement in Africa had taken place in the context of the United Nations. When Cameroon applied for membership in the United Nations, its national leader, Ahmadou Ahidjo, had come to lobby at the United Nations. His right to represent his people, however, had been challenged by a rival movement based in Cairo. Ahidjo looked around for someone who could claim to have met and overcome obstacles on the road to membership. It turned out that Israel had been the only country whose right of representation in the UN had been powerfully challenged. As an expert in clearing mine fields, I was able to help Ahidjo through the tortuous procedures of a contested quest for membership. In later years, as president of his country, Ahmadou Ahidjo acknowledged what he called, exaggeratedly but generously, my "support of the liberation of Africa."

At the same time, in 1959, the leader of the national movement of liberation in the Gold Coast (Ghana) arrived in Washington. Israelis had already established strong links with his country in many fields of education and economic development. Kwame Nkrumah's task in Washington was to obtain the inclusion of his country in the foreign aid programs of the United States.

Here again, I could claim to have met more obstacles than most other countries. I therefore guided Mr. Nkrumah through the pitfalls of the Washington bureaucracy, even to the point of suggesting how he should fill in the necessary forms. In reporting to Israel, I paid tribute to Nkrumah's qualities, including what I called his "modesty."

Some years later as foreign minister, I made an official visit to Ghana at the end of which I devoutly wished that I could have laid hands on my original telegram and committed it to the flames. Arriving in Accra, and asking exactly where I should go for my first meetings, I was informed that my driver would take me down Nkrumah Avenue past Nkrumah University, and that on reaching Nkrumah Square, he would take me to my appointment with the nation's leader, whose title was The Redeemer (Osfiego). From this I learned that modesty was a quality that could easily be overcome by a protracted taste of power.

Many of the leaders of new states have suffered from believing their own public relations. But that is true also of the leaders of some long-established sovereignties. A more profound truth is that the tribal tradition out of which the new states have grown always tended to elevate leadership into charismatic worship. When I arrived in Monrovia, the capital of Liberia, in the course of one of my official tours, I asked anxiously whether the glittering marble Presidential Palace in the very center of the city, which Israeli architects and contractors had planned and built, might not provoke resentment against us in view of the depressingly poor areas surrounding it. I was told that the contrary was the case. Many Africans had despaired of achieving a minimal degree of subsistence and economic dignity. It was they who rejoiced vicariously in the fact that their leader was dignified by an environment that paid tribute to all his citizens.

The first Rehovot Conference was followed by others over the next few years that dealt more specifically with agriculture, economic planning and education. The Rehovot movement has played a role in creating a new dimension of international life. Secretary-General Dag Hammarskjöld had followed the conference in a mood of deep personal interest and curiosity. When he himself initiated the creation of institutions that would express the same idea of encounter, he acknowledged the pioneering role of the Rehovot movement and sought my appointment to a vice presidency of the United Nations Conference on Science and Technology (UNSCAT), which convened in Geneva in 1963. It was there that I noted the growth of space technologies with a fascination diluted by concern. Referring to the huge sums that were available to this new enterprise, I asked, "What is our aim? Is it to reach the moon or to liberate this planet from its servitudes and inequalities?"

There may have been something demagogic in my formulation, since I had long found out that even if the nations concerned were to abolish their space programs and their lunar explorations, it was not at all likely that the sums thus released would be devoted to international foreign aid, any more than a reduction of the prodigious armaments bills would automatically create new resources for the development of backward societies.

Nevertheless, the slogan had the effect of accentuating an Israeli interest in that which was concrete, practical and attainable in the slow march of new societies toward minimal standards of welfare.

The Rehovot Conference in August 1960 had been convened a few months after my entry into the Knesset and my appointment as "minister without portfolio." This appointment in itself symbolized one of the more intricate calculations in the mind of David Ben-Gurion. The election campaign of 1959 had highlighted the arrival into the party's hierarchy of several new, young ministers whose names and personalities had a broad appeal. Moshe Dayan, Shimon Peres, Giora Josephtal, leader of the German Jewish Community, and I drew large crowds, but this did not mean that we would be the senior ministers. When it came to forming the cabinet, Ben-Gurion did not wish to alienate his veteran contemporaries. They continued to hold the major portfolios, such as finance, foreign affairs and education. Dayan was called upon to sublimate his martial qualities as the minister of agriculture, a function in which he had to fight against nothing more lethal than the diseases of tomatoes. Shimon Peres was put virtually in charge of the Ministry of Defense, but only in the role of deputy minister. This aroused in his heart a not very successfully concealed resentment at being junior in terms of protocol to Dayan and me, but in substantive issues his post gave him far more capacity to influence the nation's future than did those of Dayan and me in our respective corners of the Cabinet room. The cartoonists had a field day portraying Dayan, Peres and me as having secured the electoral victory without much sharing of its fruits. One of them showed the three of us climbing up a ladder held in place by Ben-Gurion and leading at the top to a vacuum. It was certain that our day would come, but Ben-Gurion thought that it would do none of us any harm if it came later than we wished.

Meanwhile, the vacuous nature of a ministry without specified departmental responsibilities weighed so heavily upon me that I contemplated resignation. A minister without portfolio is a rank without a function. It has its place in the British system, disguised by fanciful titles such as chancellor of the duchy of Lancaster, lord privy seal and lord president of the council. The underlying concept is that there are areas of ministerial dignity and responsibility that do not fall with any precision into the traditional categories and that would respond to an improvised role for ministers free of departmental duties. The trouble was that in Israel, the existence of such vacant areas of responsibility was not acknowledged by any of the departmental ministers, who kept a watchful eye to ensure that the minister without portfolio would have as little as possible to do. I found myself laden with membership in Cabinet committees, including those on foreign affairs, defense, and legislation, but here I felt none of the elation that would have arisen from the actual command of governmental apparatus with an ability to take decisions, to fix budgetary priorities, and to deal with a sector of the manpower resources of the country.

My friends in the Weizmann Institute and beyond argued with my impatience, pointing out that it was no small achievement to have become both a member of Parliament and a Cabinet minister within a few months of my arrival in the country after a long period of diplomatic service. Such a swift elevation had never happened before, and would later occur only in the unusual case of Ambassador Rabin becoming minister of labor and, within a short time, prime minister. I therefore held my peace until the ministry of education and culture became vacant as a result of the resignation of Zalman Aranne, in protest against a lack of support of his position on teachers' strikes.

In July 1960, when the Rehovot Conference was about to convene, I became the minister of education and culture. This was a challenge. After defense, education is the most far-flung and variegated of all the Israeli ministries. It is the second of them in budgetary size. The Israeli school network is highly centralized, rather like the Napoleonic system under which a minister of education in Paris could tell you from his files exactly what subjects are being taught at any given hour in any of the thousands of schools throughout the republic.

In Israel, the Education Ministry has total control of the elementary school system. It was beginning to participate more actively in the secondary school network, which, however, was then somewhat slender in its development. The previous ministers, and especially Aranne, had been inspired more by the social than by the academic challenges of education and placed their main emphasis on the elementary school system. Higher education then consisted entirely of the three veteran institutions, the Hebrew University of Jerusalem, the Haifa Technion and the Weizmann Institute of Science. Yet it was clear that there would be a need for expansion, and newer universities were waiting impatiently for recognition by the Council on Higher Education, over which it would be my duty to preside.

Many of the anomalies in Israeli society came to expression in the ministry of education and culture. The most acute of these riveted my attention in the earliest days. Amidst a mass of paper accumulating on my harassed and overburdened desk was a report from the inspector of education in the southern area, Aryeh Simon. His experience as well as his surveys revealed that there was a disastrous gap in his region between advanced and less advanced bodies of students. There was an abysmal decline of standards, sometimes to the point of illiteracy, that affected a specific sector of our society. In plain language, children of parents who had arrived in Israel from Muslim countries had a vastly lower level of attainment than those whose families had originated in Europe or who had become rooted in pre-state Israeli society.

The children born in Oriental communities had little chance to qualify for post-elementary education. Universities were a distant and unattainable world. This was not due to any intrinsic defect or backwardness. One could see their eyes sparkling with intelligence and curiosity, but their living conditions in large families with overcrowded rooms were not congenial to study. It was therefore likely that many of them would lack productive employment. They could not digest even the modest range of conceptual ideas that the elementary school tried to inculcate.

As I projected this picture across the country as a whole, I could only arrive at a dark forecast. Israel was becoming a country of two nations, one with a capacity of "takeoff" into a swift orbit of intellectual progress, the other hopelessly tied down in a vicious circle of handicap.

What made this situation particularly explosive was the fact that educational backwardness coincided with recognizable ethnic criteria. The prospect, then, was clear but ominous. Israelis of European origin were destined to occupy the top half of the social pyramid, while the broad base of the unskilled and underprivileged would be occupied by citizens whose origins lay in Muslim countries.

When I won the opportunity of having an entire Cabinet meeting devoted to this theme, which had not been an easy task, I could see that Ben-Gurion was shocked and surprised. His personal eminence and remoteness from the prosaic aspects of statehood had removed him from a knowledge of how ordinary people lived. At no stage in his prime ministerial career could he have actually quoted the condition of the balance of payments or the price of milk or bread. His eager mind, however, became obsessed with what I had called "the educational gap." This became a central theme in the public dialogue. I took satisfaction in this. There is no doubt that my predecessors in the ministry had observed this trend and had done their utmost to cope with it. It is, however, one of the main functions of a minister to make his departmental concerns a focus of public interest and attention. It appeared that my appointment to the ministry, which had been warmly welcomed in the intellectual community, was effective in this field.

Thereafter, the ministry devoted special budgetary resources, special textbooks, and other institutional resources in an effort to begin the slow but crucial struggle against the educational gap. I officially inaugurated the long school day in 1962 to ensure that children would spend more time in the atmosphere of school and, more important, less time at home. It was clear that there would have to be a kind of departmental favoritism in an effort to bring the underprivileged sector of the student community onto an upward path.

This, however, had sensitive repercussions. There had to be a great deal of semantic care. It would be fatal in the suspicious atmosphere in which people were alert to discrimination to speak of "the backward schools," or of young populations, or to call any sector of the younger populations "underdeveloped."

I had encountered the same problem on the international level. The word "underdeveloped" was out, and the more positive concept "developing" was in. Under my ministry, we established a category of children "in need of special studies": *teunai tipuach.* And even this appellation became a source of grievance. In later years, under the leadership of my predecessor and successor, Zalman Aranne, the "special education" sector became the main preoccupation of the ministry.

In a report published on the tenth anniversary of the selective educational process, the leading pedagogical authorities were able to report significant advance. Students of Oriental communities were entering the secondary school system in larger numbers. While their percentage in the higher educational network was still lower than it should have been, it had gone beyond the original six percent to something approaching twenty percent.

The grievances of underpaid teachers occupied a great deal of my inexperienced attention. The desire of the teachers was to have their wages and statehood equalized with those of other academics, such as engineers and lawyers, rather than to be in the same category as elementary schoolteachers.

The Israeli wage system is a thing of wonder. A minister's desire to elevate the wages of a sector comprising a few thousand specialists meant that the increase had to be paralleled across the entire range of the professions. If one carriage of a train had to be moved forward, the entire train would have to make that precise percentage of movement all at once, eliciting a cry of despairing pain from the Finance Ministry.

Another problem was the existence of a somewhat snobbish division between humanistic education, which was fashionable, and technical or professional education, which was thought to be the preserve of less-endowed pupils. I felt that the Israeli pioneer economy would have more need of mechanics and engineers than of more lawyers and journalists. Here I was working against the prejudice of my own classical and literary background in trying to see the Israeli reality in its own perspective.

I secured the establishment of an education fund of the United Jewish Appeal in the United States. Generous sponsors helped to build the schools and bring development into towns such as Kiryat Shmona, Beit Shemesh, Hazor, Dimona, Eilat and specific areas in Jerusalem.

In higher education, I found myself in an area of conflict compared with which the savage debates in the United Nations seemed retrospectively tranquil. Some university facilities existed in Tel Aviv as branches of the Jerusalem University, but I thought it to be absurd that an urban concentration so large and central should not have a university independently administered and sustained by civic pride. At the same time, the religious Zionist movement had established the base of a higher educational development in Ramat Gan under the name of the Bar Ilan University. In my capacity as chairman of the Council on Higher Education, I would obviously have an influence on whether this pluralism was checked or developed. I ruled in favor of the recognition of Tel Aviv and Bar Ilan Universities and for the end of Jerusalem's monopoly. Ten years later my Jerusalem friends began to forgive me for this sinful generosity.

What attracted me most in a domestic ministry was a heightened sense of control. Decision was followed by action, and it was possible for a minister to see the work of his hands. In foreign policy, external forces can make all planning vain. What could a minister do if Cuba chose to have a revolution and to transform its intimacy into rupture, or if a leader of monstrous irrationality such as Idi Amin became converted to Islam and led a campaign for Israel's downfall? There is no such sense of fatalism in a domestic ministry. When I added the establishment of a sports authority and the appointment of a new Department of Cultural Affairs to the ministry's expanding empire, I realized that I need be in no hurry to change my responsibilities.

One of my last parliamentary battles in the ministry, however, did much to quench this enthusiasm. I was destined to introduce Israel to the twentieth century through the television age. The British Rothschild family has been our country's most lavish benefactor. It financed the Knesset building, the Caesarea tourist development (including the golf course) and in recent years the Supreme Court building. In pursuit of its educational projects it offered to make an educational-television project available under the direction of the Israeli ministry of education and culture. The building of studios, the purchase of equipment and the training of competent personnel would have been beyond any conceivable power that would ever lie in the hands of an Israeli government.

When I met the teachers' representatives that morning I found them in paroxysms of joy. They had never dreamed of commanding such a potent tool of work. To my astonishment I found that this innocent and valuable offer provoked opposition in many quarters and that I stood a good chance of losing the motion for accepting the Rothschild proposal when it came to the Knesset, in which case I would have to resign!

The objections that were raised seem like a parody. Ben-Gurion had seen television in New York and London and had noticed that everyone on the screen was either shooting or being shot. "Who needs that?" he asked.

My reply: "Nothing comes out of the box that one doesn't put in."

A Religious Party minister asked what would happen if a teacher on television appeared in a classroom of a religious school and was seen not to be wearing a yarmulke. I had no answer for this. One of my young officials suggested that a yarmulke be placed on the top of the TV set. I froze him with a ministerial stare. Rescue suddenly came from France. The minister for culture, the great André Malraux, had said that through television more people had seen the plays of Molière and Racine in a single year than had watched them in the three centuries since they were written. I asked Ben-Gurion: "What is the logic of saying that because murder plays are televised in New York we may not televise physics lessons in Israel?" Teddy Kollek was in great support, wearing down Ben-Gurion's hesitations. Eventually the motion to accept the Rothschild project was adopted by fifty-five votes to forty-three. The Knesset protocol of this extraordinary debate shows a peculiar side of Israel. A talent for modernity and innovation coexists with a curious conservatism and recalcitrance to change.

By the mid-1960s Israel was less cohesive than it had been in its first decade. Israelis stood together for life and death, but in their less extreme ordeals they were conscious of the things that divided them. The word "gap" began to figure endlessly in Israel's constant exploration of itself. There was the gap between the new urban middle class and the old rural elite based on the kibbutz movement. There was the gap between both of these and the struggling disinherited proletariat in the slum areas and shantytowns. There was the gap between the European-educated population and their sabra offspring and the Oriental immigrants with their special pieties, loyalties and family traditions. There was also a generation gap: The young Israeli generation born in the sun and under the open skies was given to a simpler, less tormented, but more superficial intellectual outlook than that which had been common to the pioneering generation. There was also a gap of alienation between young matter-of-fact Israelis and the more sentimental, complicated, introspective but creative Diaspora Jews.

And yet there were common memories that often reminded Israelis that history had dealt with the whole of the Jewish people in a special way, so that in the last resort they were indivisible in their fate. One day in early May 1960 the Cabinet had appointed me to represent the Israeli government at the anniversary celebration of Argentina's independence on May 25. I was told that in order to show honor to Argentina a special El Al aircraft would carry me at the head of a large and distinguished delegation. The next day Ben-Gurion asked me to see him in his office. He told me in a conspiratorial whisper that the real reason for the special aircraft was that Adolf Eichmann had been seized by Israeli Intelligence officers and there would be difficulty in bringing him out of Buenos Aires on a regular Pan American flight. The ministerial plane carrying me would be available for the transportation of Eichmann and his captors to Jerusalem. He would be disguised as a crew member and hustled into the aircraft as soon as it reached the Argentinean capital. I would remain for the week of celebration and would return by civilian American aircraft.

I set out for the journey in a tense mood. The Jewish people was at last in a position to bring its foes to justice. To my consternation, the aircraft reached Recife in Brazil in need of repairs, and the Brazilian authorities offered an alternative aircraft. I saw that matters were becoming complicated. I decided to take one of our delegation members into my confidence. The man chosen was General (Reserve) Meir Zorea, called Zarro by his many friends. Zarro was a war hero who had lost two sons fallen in action in Israel's wars. He was electrified by the news and promised to help me in extricating ourselves from Recife with our aircraft by any and every means. Happily, someone in our crew induced the Brazilian officials to allow us to depart. As we approached the terminal at Buenos Aires and were taxiing, I looked up and saw the small, celebrated figure of Isser Harel, the chief of our Intelligence service, on the balcony, which was crowded with Argentinean Jews shouting my name in joyous celebration of my arrival. A day later I learned that the aircraft with its unusual cargo had departed safely.

Ben-Gurion had promised that there would be no leaking of the news of Eichmann's removal from Argentina until after my own departure from Buenos Aires. Not even Ben-Gurion had sufficient mastery of the press to fulfill such a promise, and the news shouted from the headlines had the full account, including the stratagem with the El Al aircraft. My own terse comment, "I know nothing," hit all the world's media. Nobody believed it.

Eichmann had been in charge of the department appointed by Hitler in 1944 to carry out the extermination of the Jews in Nazi-occupied Europe. He had done his work with horrible competence. After the defeat of Germany in 1945, he had gone into hiding for five years and in 1950 had escaped to Argentina, where he lived under the name Ricardo Klement. Israeli and other Jewish volunteers and organizations had kept up the search. The idea that the murderer of millions of men, women and children was walking the earth in peace and impunity was infuriating to the Jewish conscience. Ben-Gurion put the full weight of his authority behind the worldwide effort to track Eichmann down, and Israeli Intelligence services were decisive in his discovery and capture. One day in May 1960 when "Ricardo Klement" was walking home from a factory in which he worked in Buenos Aires, he was captured by Israelis, who put him on an aircraft for Israel. There were complications in Israel's relations with Argentina, which asked that the Israeli Ambassador be recalled and brought a complaint to the UN Security Council. But the formal irregularity of the capture struck most of the world as subsidiary to the greater drama. Here was an arch-criminal, an assassin of Jewish masses, brought to trial in a Jewish homeland. A free Israel could now offer redress and honor to the afflicted Jewish people.

By the time of the trial in Jerusalem I had become minister of education and I was departmentally as well as personally interested to observe the effects on our Israeli youth for whom the Holocaust had been an item of history, like the Spanish Inquisition and the pogroms in Tsarist Russia. The trial was exemplary in its dignity and judicial precision. The court of three judges, under the presidency of Justice Moshe Landau, heard hundreds of witnesses who unfolded stories so macabre and agonizing that the whole nation was stunned by a new flow of grief. The Israeli attorney general, Gideon Hausner, rose to lofty and somber heights in bringing the indictment in the name of six million accusers, "whose blood cries out but whose voice is not heard."

Sentence of death was passed and upheld in the Court of Appeal, and for the only time in Israel's history, presidential clemency was withheld. At the ministerial meeting to advise President Ben-Zvi on clemency, only Eshkol made a remark that indicated a possibility of mitigation to life imprisonment. I myself abhor capital punishment with all my heart, and I deplore the extraordinary reversion of most American states to this obscene practice, but in this case I felt bound to preserve solidarity with the judges at the Nuremberg War Crimes trial, whom we would have discredited had they taken a different approach. In any case, the Eichmann affair had a sui generis character. Paradoxically, the execution of Eichmann has had the effect of making other death sentences inconceivable. The argument runs: "How can we reduce Eichmann's guilt by creating another category of equal heinousness?"

Of even greater significance than the justice meted out to a single odious monster was the electrifying effect of the trial on world opinion and on Israel's young generation. The mystery of man's infinite degradation was unfolded in gory detail day by day, together with the nobility and despair of Jewish resistance. A sharp light was thrown on the role of the Jewish people as history's most poignant victim. One of the underlying sources of Israel's struggle for freedom and security was brought into view. At one session, Attorney General Hausner recounted the story of sleepy Jewish children being rounded up at dawn and put on buses on the pretense of being sent on picnics, and then being herded into gas chambers for asphyxiation. One could feel the world shudder in a paroxysm of shame. The Eichmann trial had risen above the level of retribution, vengeance and even formal justice.

Despite my irrepressible interest in international politics, I would willingly have continued in the education ministry for a further period. It was a massive remedy for my detachment from the country's domestic scene during my lengthy service in Washington and New York, but the matter was not in my hands. The head of the teachers' union, Shalom Levin, tried to dissuade me from leaving the education ministry, but his persuasion was devoted more to the dislike of Aranne, my successor, than to affection for me. The education and culture ministry had not been a mere waiting room, and I was gratified to note that all the newspapers wrote of my stewardship in respectful terms. I had projected the social gap into the center of the education debate. I had created machinery for its alleviation. I had stimulated the expansion of the higher-education network. I had introduced Israel to the television age and, especially, to educational television. I had initiated the comprehensive school system. I had shown empathy toward the teachers' community that had felt deeply wounded by my predecessor. I had established the sabbatical year for high school teachers. I had founded the sports authority and expanded the council for the development of culture. I had created a link between our scientific community and the developing world. And I had founded the UJA Education Fund, which liberated American Jews from their exclusive preoccupation with "high politics." It would require a sharp degree of churlishness to call this an undistinguished harvest for an incumbency of less than three years.

One day we were meeting in the Cabinet room with President Zalman Shazar, who was reporting on his recent voyage to several foreign countries, when Ben-Gurion said quietly, "Before we go to lunch with the president I want to tell you that I'm resigning today." This time we knew that there would be no return. The Ben-Gurion era had ended.

On June 21, 1963, Levi Eshkol formed a new government with me as deputy prime minister. Ben-Gurion gathered up his papers, said farewell to the assembled ministers and departed for Sdeh Boker.

There was no single cause. Ostensibly the "old man" was protesting against a jurisdictional irregularity in which he saw overriding moral issues. Pinchas Lavon, who had resigned in 1954 for a disastrous intelligence mishap in his Ministry of Defense, had come upon what he alleged to be new evidence that would prove his innocence and demonstrate that he had not given the fatal instruction to activate an Intelligence unit that had been captured with the resultant hanging of two of its members by order of an Egyptian court. A seven-member Cabinet committee had investigated the matter and concluded that Lavon had been blameless. Ben-Gurion argued that the acquittal of Lavon implied that the disastrous order had been given by Colonel Benjamin Gibli, who had been the director of military intelligence at the time of the "Affair." The prime minister refused to accept this method of disposing of the affair.[1] He said that an acquittal of one citizen with a consequent condemnation of another was a matter for legal action, not of political appraisal. If ministers acquitted or accused citizens, the rule of law was at an end.

Ben-Gurion thus presented the action of the Cabinet committee as a major corruption of the democratic process and of juridical integrity. He pursued this theme in writings of unbelievable vehemence and profusion. He also began to express disparaging sentiments about the Committee of Seven, especially his finance minister, Levi Eshkol, and the minister of justice, Pinchas Rosen. Ben-Gurion's critics had a more varied indictment to make: He was exaggerating the importance of a formalistic and debatable issue, upsetting the national priorities and preventing the nation from getting on with its vital work. Leading academic figures entered the fray to allege the existence of charismatic and authoritarian elements in Ben-Gurion's leadership. They raised the question of whether any leader should refuse acceptance of a collective Cabinet, parliamentary and party decision (for the Knesset endorsed the exoneration of Lavon by the "Committee of Seven"). Ben-Gurion found himself beleaguered by public opinion after many years of general adulation.

I was one of the three Labor ministers, the others being Josephtal and Dayan, who believed that Ben-Gurion had a strong case. I refused to vote for

---

[1]Herzog, *ibid.,* p. 129.

the Committee report that exonerated Lavon, thus provoking the anger of Golda Meir and Pinhas Sapir, who were now Ben-Gurion's adversaries. I feel satisfaction at the fact that I was not among those who allowed Ben-Gurion to depart in humiliation and defeat.

There were other points of tension between him and his party, but it was the controversy over his treatment of the "Affair" that tore his mind away from central national issues to brood darkly on something in which most Israelis wanted to lose interest. After the 1961 election in which Mapai retained power but lost seven seats, there was an ardent resolve to have done with the whole issue. The public had a feeling that Israel would lose its sanity unless it abandoned the "Affair," which was eating away at its heart and mind like a curse in medieval demonology.

Ben-Gurion was now estranged from many of his contemporaries, apathetic about many of Israel's parliamentary conflicts, wounded by the rejection of his position on the "Affair" and full of dark fears about the future. In April 1963, when Egypt, Syria and Iraq announced one of their periodic paper "federations" with the usual dire threats of Israel's destruction, Ben-Gurion reacted in an apocalyptic spirit that contrasted with his usual confidence. He sent letters to over a hundred heads of government, sometimes expressing doubt about Israel's ability to exist in the future. He asked President Kennedy, President de Gaulle and Harold Macmillan to conclude binding security guarantees with Israel in view of the "emergency" created by the new Arab "federation." He received frigid replies. The Western leaders did not believe in the "emergency," and I doubted the wisdom of assuming that a letter was the convincing way of bringing about such a revolutionary event.

The Cabinet meeting with President Shazar at the end of which he announced his resignation was a shock, but not a surprise. An era of large and vivid leadership had come to an end.

Professor Ya'akov Talmon, an eminent Israeli historian, has written:

The wonderful gallery of great and colorful personalities thrown up by Zionism will stand comparison with any of the finest and ablest leaders amongst the nations: Herzl with Mazzini, Weizmann with Cavour or Masaryk, Ben-Gurion with Bismarck or Pilsudski, Jabotinsky with Nehru . . . (*Israel Among the Nations,* 1970, p. 133)

Some of these comparisons are more apt than others, and I found the comparison of Jabotinsky with Nehru somewhat hard to absorb. I met Nehru in Washington during one of his visits shortly after the Suez-Sinai War. He received me in his hotel in the presence of his daughter, Indira, who later became prime minister in her own right. He had the disconcerting habit of listening to his guests with his hands clasped and the whole of his face and body registering immobility and reticence, to a point at which I wondered whether he was even listening, but when he did glide into response, it was plain that he had seized every nuance.

Talmon's observation was certainly correct in placing Ben-Gurion's leadership in the most eminent gallery of national leaders. Indeed, he had a more profound impact on his nation's formative years than did the European statesmen with whom he is compared by Talmon. He occupied a larger area of the national consciousness than the premiership strictly required. His squat, short figure, beetling eyebrows, white tufts of hair, staccato form of speech and his quick, jerky manner of moving about gave an infectious impression of energy and purpose. He had a talent for animating the national will. He created a permanent sense of excitement about those objectives, which he deemed central and decisive at any given time. He had a broad, simple vision of Israel's destiny. He saw modern Israel as the descendant of the ancient prophetic Israel, harbinger to the world of the messianic dream. By developing its intellectual and moral resources, Israel could again become a nation of special vitality, able, despite its smallness, to impress itself on history and to ensure its security against heavy material odds.

Ben-Gurion was ubiquitous and all-pervasive in Israeli life. He had something to say about biblical research, science, history, education, religion and, of course, military strategy and organization. His intellect was vigilant and lively, though not formally disciplined. He was perennially open to new interests and enthusiasms. He tended to sharpen his judgments so as to exclude subtleties or ambivalence. He felt that not much could be done about peace with the Arabs until Israel was unbreakably strong; he therefore excluded this problem from his active concern and gave an impression of being unconciliatory.

The impression was inaccurate. His international policy, although sometimes expressed in barks of defiance, was essentially moderate. His immense domestic prestige gave him a wide discretion, which he sometimes used in order to withdraw from untenable positions. He was sometimes more categoric in his definitions than the facts seemed to warrant. He asserted, for example, that the United Nations had played no positive role in Israel's emergence. A more accurate analysis would admit that there is no single line of truth on this issue; the United Nations was extremely important for Israel in some ordeals (as in 1947–1949) and ineffective in others. Similarly, Ben-Gurion's declaration of autarchy ("What matters is not what the nations of the world [goyim] say, but what the Jews do") was probably more extreme than he seriously intended. He knew in his heart that Israel had been more dependent on outside support—and more successful in obtaining it—than any other state faced with similar hazards. But his aim was didactic. He was trying to get Israelis to understand the need for self-reliance and autonomous decision. His method was to concentrate a powerful searchlight on one aspect of a problem, even if it meant creating darkness in surrounding areas.

The issues selected for bright illumination were usually the right ones: military strength; mass immigration; social integration; educational progress. Ben-Gurion had less fortune in domestic conflict. He fully understood the mechanics of power but was limited in his talent for personal relations. He was lonely, introspective, uninterested in outward forms and impatient of small talk. He did not suffer fools gladly. There was no particular reason why he should; after all, the only people who suffer fools gladly are other fools. But in the end, Ben-Gurion placed himself on roads where none but the most uncritical of his devotees were willing to follow him. The public refused to understand his excessive emphasis on the "Affair." Israeli society was emerging from innocence to sophistication and was finding Ben-Gurion's paternalism too stringent and authoritative. It admired his leadership but secretly longed for the experience of breathing for itself. His attacks on Eshkol were ascribed by most Israelis to the human failings that afflict many strong men in their relations with successors. Ben-Gurion had subconsciously come to identify himself with Israel's rebirth to the point where he could not easily admit that the national history would one day have to flow without him. His final months in office and the first two years outside it were unhappy and contentious, but long after they were over his brilliant leadership lived on in Israel's memory and gratitude. He was a leader cast in large dimensions, and he endowed Israel's early years with originality and vital power.

Levi Eshkol, who had been finance minister for a decade, stepped into the vacant place with an air of assurance. He had been the choice of everyone, including Ben-Gurion, who would indeed have preferred him to Moshe Sharett as the custodian premier in 1953. He was Ben-Gurion's loyal disciple and had carried many burdens for his chief, including the distasteful task of settling the Lavon Affair. His serene style and gentle mannerisms were so different from those of his predecessor that there was no danger of imitation. Eshkol was in his late sixties when he took office, and his place in Israel's history had been won not in the heady atmosphere of strategy and international politics, but in the dust and heat of pioneering and economic construction. He was the first authentic kibbutznik to take the supreme office, and the agricultural community and labor movement sustained him with fraternal pride. He had no charismatic pretensions. He sought not to dominate, but to persuade. He could rightly feel that every mile of water pipe, every growing village, every bungalow in Lachish, every factory owed something to his accumulative and constructive zeal. He could look out on the whole landscape of Israel like a man surveying his own handiwork but without any loss of simplicity or balance. He knew exactly what he was and what he was not, and he wielded his responsibilities in strict proportion to his gifts. He had been happiest when his gnarled fingers could dig deep into the soil of concrete affairs; he would now have to test his capacities of supervision and command. He had few gifts of expression. Sometimes, to get at his precise meaning was like trying to grasp a cake of soap in a bath. This handicap was grave and would almost prove fatal to his leadership at moments when the nation expected a trumpet call to action in the service of clearly defined aims. But he believed that solid, concrete facts had an intrinsic eloquence that would make itself heard where it mattered most. His warm humanism was derived from the traditions first of Yiddish-speaking Russian Jewry and later of the Hebrew labor and settlement movement.

As I installed myself in rooms close to Prime Minister Eshkol as deputy prime minister I felt that a period of challenge and fulfillment awaited me. Eshkol made clear that he was not well versed in international affairs and would rely largely on my assistance, especially during the first months of his premiership. He began by requiring Golda Meir, his foreign minister, to meet with him and me every Tuesday. This put me in a relationship with Golda that was different from any that we had known before.

I had left the Ministry of Education with a pang of regret, but my appointment as deputy prime minister had restored me to the arenas in which I was most qualified by experience and training. There was little to indicate that I was moving into an area in which the seeds of war had already been sown. The thunder was muffled, but it was not far away.

16

THE NEW PRIME
MINISTER

THE INTERNATIONAL REACTIONS to my appointment as deputy prime minister
were favorable, but the domestic motives for the appointment were complex.
Since his resignation as minister of education, Zalman Aranne had brooded
sadly in the wilderness, pining for his Promised Land, which for him could
only be his beloved Ministry of Education. Aranne was an interesting personality: an old-guard Laborite with a rich autodidactic Hebrew and Jewish
culture, and almost no contact with the life or experience of the non-Jewish
world. He moved from one stormy gust of emotion to another without any
interval of relaxation. When I took over from him, a high ministry official
said that my predecessor was alarmingly depressed and irascible one day
every week, "but nobody knew which day it was going to be."

His leadership of the Ministry of Education was not just a job. It was a
permanent dedication. So much so that whenever I passed him in the Knesset
library, I felt an acute pang of guilt for having had the effrontery to succeed
him. However, he fully endorsed the line that I followed in the ministry. One
of his eccentricities was to go to western movies very early in the afternoons.
But since he would normally arrive after the show had commenced, he would
complain that a lot of shooting was going on, and that he never got to
understand why. He was a strong ally of Golda Meir and of Finance Minister
Pinhas Sapir in the party alignments. They knew that the permanent denial
of the education ministry would probably have ended his public career. In
agreeing to my appointment as deputy prime minister with inevitable encroachment on her authority, Golda was inspired not by sympathy for me
but by solidarity with Aranne. I was learning the first law of politics: One
should regard the hostility of opponents as normal, and the benevolence of
colleagues as suspicious.

From the first day I felt that Eshkol's premiership was going to be a
success story. He was an accessible and easygoing chief. After a few days in
office he called me in, assured himself that the door was closed and the

telephone shut off, and asked if I could explain to him as clearly as possible what being prime minister really involved. He said that in his post of finance minister, he dealt with concrete and specific matters for which his responsibility was clearly defined. He had now been sitting in his well-furnished rooms for some hours, waiting to know what he ought to do. He had too much leisure, which was an embarrassing condition for a lifelong Zionist.

I explained that the job was like that of the conductor of a symphony orchestra who does not play an instrument, but whose will and personality would decisively determine the sound that would emerge. I added that he could rely on Israeli history to present him with challenging decisions that nobody else could make. Moreover, I said, after a honeymoon period, which in Israeli politics lasts for about twenty-four hours, he would be fully occupied with the task of survival. I assured him that he would not lack opportunities of impact. He replied as usual with a Yiddishism: "Impact, oispact, the chief thing is to make a good impression."

It turned out that my prediction of twenty-four hours of honeymoon was not exaggeratedly pessimistic. Eshkol took over the existing administration with a minimum of reshuffle and we all piously called ourselves a "government of continuity," as if to assure the public that everything would still be decided by consulting Ben-Gurion's conjectured wish. This is not really what the public wanted. It wanted a change. In any case, differences of temperament at the summit of power made a change of style inevitable. I had made what I thought was an innocent remark to the London weekly *The Jewish Chronicle,* to the effect that the new Eshkol administration would undoubtedly review government policies and would see if we could multiply contacts with the Arab world. This provoked a debate in the Knesset in which I was accused by Ben-Gurion's extreme followers of planning to depart from the sacred dogma of Ben-Gurionism. According to the zealots, there was nothing that would ever need review since it was impossible to improve on perfection.

There is a common and recurrent theme in the succession of charismatic leaders by men of lesser initial prestige who unexpectedly demonstrate that national life can proceed in a new era and that nobody is indispensable in the long flow of history. Truman after Roosevelt, Pompidou after de Gaulle, Attlee after Churchill and Erhard after Adenauer, are cases in point. It is significant that without reference to a book I would be unable to recall who became president of Ghana after Kwame Nkrumah. The syndrome usually plays out in two phases. The previous leader feels affronted at the speed with which a transfer of power becomes a transfer of deference. And the nation is pleasantly surprised at the flowering of authority in the new leader once he emerges from the shadows of his previous self-abnegation.

Thus it was with Ben-Gurion and Eshkol. Ben-Gurion's pique was illogical, for he had resigned voluntarily and nobody would have complained if he had chosen to remain in office after 1963. But he chose to ascribe his resignation to Eshkol's refusal to support his position on the Lavon Affair. Eshkol had refused to share Ben-Gurion's indignation on a matter that most Israelis considered marginal and irrelevant to the country's future. In Ben-Gurion's mind, Eshkol was the architect of his dismissal. Moreover, Eshkol followed the normal practice of asserting his arrival by some steps that indicated that he was his own man.

It was apparent that Ben-Gurion would pursue his successor with relentless hostility, which would complicate the position of other members of the administration, including Moshe Dayan and even the deputy defense minister, Shimon Peres, each of whom had only one foot in the Eshkol administration and were under pressure from Ben-Gurion to secede into a new party group.

Eshkol began with domestic conciliation. He saw no reason to inherit Ben-Gurion's quarrels. He authorized the official interment of the remains of Jabotinsky, the Revisionist Zionist leader who had been venerated by the Herut Party and respected by countless others. Jabotinsky had died and been buried in New York, leaving an injunction that he was only to be reinterred in Israel at the behest of a sovereign Jewish government. Ben-Gurion had refused to give this authorization. Eshkol had sought to placate the grievance of his Herut opponents; he also showed more sensitivity than Ben-Gurion for the sentiments and complexes of Zionists in the Diaspora. Jabotinsky's remains were respectfully brought from New York to Jerusalem. In the same ecumenical spirit, Eshkol brought about a union between the mainstream Labor Party and a smaller Labor Party known as Achdut Ha'avodah, whose main strength came from the kibbutz movement. The union of the Labor movement had been an objective for which Ben-Gurion had labored in vain.

Eshkol was setting his own style without departing from established policies. Ben-Gurion responded to Eshkol's gesture toward Jabotinsky with a series of articles in which he conducted a polemic against Jabotinsky's remains as if he were unaware of his rival's demise.

There were fears that Ben-Gurion's departure would weaken the state in its international relations by removing the prestige and historic awe that accompanied him across the world. This danger was surmounted. World opinion and the ruling foreign-policy elites took Eshkol seriously. President Kennedy had opened a narrow but symbolically important window for Israel's purchase of weapons in the United States. The items sold to Israel were Hawk antiaircraft missiles, but anyone who began a procurement program with Israel must have understood that the program was more likely to proliferate than to stand still. Kennedy would now try to induce Nasser to turn his revolutionary fervor inward toward the settlement of his country's chronic economic weaknesses. This attempt failed. Nasser intensified his anti-Israel rhetoric, alienated most of the other Arab states with his expansionist ambitions and plunged his country into a quagmire war in Yemen with the aim of establishing a Nasserist regime in place of traditional rule by a theocratic Imam. Kennedy passed from a hopeful attitude to Nasser to a strong aversion in less time than the same process had taken Foster Dulles.

A short time before Ben-Gurion's resignation in 1963, Kennedy had met Golda Meir in Florida and had referred to Israel as the "ally" of the United States. This was somewhat magnanimous, since Ben-Gurion on meeting Senator Kennedy in New York before his accession to the presidency had asked Kennedy bluntly whether he was really thinking of running for the presidency when "you really are too young, Senator." Ben-Gurion was also doubtful whether the risk taken by Kennedy in the Cuban missile crisis was commensurate with the awful hazards that he incurred.

It was natural for Eshkol and me to plan carefully together with Golda Meir for a meeting with President Kennedy at the summit, but this plan was never put into operation. Golda was out of the country and I was acting both as prime minister and as foreign minister when I sat in my home in Rehovot on a day in November 1963. I opened my radio a little after the hour and I heard the words: "We understand that Catholic priests are with the president now . . ." Before I could continue listening to the broadcast, my telephone rang and the sad voice of Walworth Barbour, the American ambassador, told me officially of the president's death. The shock hit me hard and strong. Suzy and I recalled the evening when we had dined as a foursome in our home—the Kennedys and us during his senatorial days. I had then accepted his invitation to attend the Senate meeting in which he had called for freedom for Algeria from French rule. "It doesn't matter," the French ambassador, Hervé Alphand, had said, "this young man will never go far in politics."

At a memorial meeting in Tel Aviv a few days later I said:

Tragedy is the difference between what is and what might have been. There will, of course, be other eras of zest and vitality when men will feel that it is morning and that it is good to be alive. This, however, belongs to the future. Meanwhile, let us be frank with each other. The world is darker than it was a week ago . . .

John F. Kennedy had not had time to make a substantive contribution to the American-Israeli story, and his passing had little effect on our international relations. The kinship with France was very close. In 1961 de Gaulle had assured Ben-Gurion of French "solidarity and friendship" and had then raised his glass to "Israel, our friend and ally." Israelis had not heard such words since the establishment of their state. De Gaulle repeated this very same phrase in his toast to Eshkol in Paris at their meeting in 1964. Israel's cooperation with the Fourth Republic until 1958 might have been explained as a marriage of convenience, for the two countries had common foes in Cairo and other Arab capitals. But the Algerian war, with the resultant tension between Paris and Cairo, had been over for some years in June 1964, when President de Gaulle gave Israel that reassurance to Eshkol. French arms supplies prevented the collapse of the military balance under the weight of Soviet arms deliveries to the Arab states. France also promised support for Israel's efforts to integrate itself into the new European community. A cultural agreement was in operation, and French and Israeli warships exchanged courtesy visits. At the 1964 meeting in Paris, de Gaulle urged Eshkol neither to provoke the Arab governments by excessive severity nor to tempt them by military weakness. At that time he saw no contradiction between traditional French interests in the Arab world and the cultivation of strong relations with Israel. On the contrary, the very intimacy of France's relations with Israel spurred the Arab states to a competitive quest for France's favor and assured it for the first time since World War II of a central place in the Middle Eastern power balance.

Britain did not maintain the same intimacy as during the few days of common struggle in 1956, but it never reverted to the old frigidity. There was no embargo on the purchase of Centurion tanks and other equipment, and economic ties were close and mutually fruitful. Public opinion in Britain admired Israel's military performance, perhaps with a twinge of envy after the Suez failure, and reacted sharply against Nasser's continued militancy. When in 1964 Harold Wilson formed the first Labour government since the days of Attlee and Bevin, Eshkol was invited to Downing Street and Chequers, where he encountered friendship reinforced by Labourite solidarity.

By the early 1960s, the United States was expressing its support of Israel's independence and integrity more openly. Kennedy had told Golda Meir that the United States was, in effect, Israel's "ally," joined to us in a relationship of special intimacy. With the sale of Hawk missiles and Patton tanks, American components were to become a salient part of Israel's deterrent strength. Surprisingly, Eshkol was to become the first Israeli prime minister to be officially invited by a president of the United States to visit Washington. His intimacy with Lyndon B. Johnson was put to work to ensure the expansion of American arms supplies to Israel. Eshkol was the first prime minister of Israel to make a tour of African capitals.

My own position in the Eshkol administration enabled me to work in the field of the country's international relations without carrying departmental responsibilities. I led the Israeli delegation to the 1964 session of the UN General Assembly and spoke in the general debate, reviving many memories for those who still recalled the historic encounters of the late 1940s and early 1950s. I opened a new avenue of experience by official visits to Colombia, Venezuela and Mexico. I had been impressed by the role of the Latin American group in the UN and other international agencies. My chief aide and counselor had been Moshe Tov, who had helped us carry our banner successfully in the decisive days of our independence struggle, but I did not wish to become entirely dependent on advisers in my relations with the Latin American world. I embarked on a serious and sustained study of the Spanish language by reading the literary classics and listening to the reverberating eloquence of the heads of mission to the United Nations. These speeches were sufficiently long to enable me to study vocabulary and syntax without the time and expense of tutoring, especially as repetition is a pedagogical virtue and UN debaters usually know several ways of saying the same thing. The result was that I was able to address the Mexican Congress and the Committee on Foreign Relations in the Colombian Parliament with a visible absence of text.

The effect of my involvement in the affairs of the developing world was to strengthen my conviction that there is no single principle applicable to the separate dilemmas of what is called the Third World. Each continent needs a different type of revolution. Africa needs an educational revolution—to create cadres of skills and capacities that the colonial powers did little to create. The vastly overpopulated Asian countries need an inverse demographic revolution to bring their resources and their manpower into a less impossible ratio. And the Latin American countries, already graced with sovereignty and educated leaders, need a social revolution to bring about a sane distribution of land and other resources. There is no such thing as a single Third World solution. Israel's foreign aid programs in Africa and Latin America would only be fully effective as part of a general international effort and on the basis of lucid priorities in the planning of Third Word governments.

The Eshkol administration came into office while Nasser was still leading Egypt in confrontational policies. In his assaults in Yemen he was indirectly threatening Saudi Arabia and the Gulf principalities and, consequently, became a source of danger to American interests. The Johnson administration reacted by a more open application of the "balance of power" doctrine. In 1965 it decided to supply Israel with more advanced weapons. American-Egyptian relations declined. The United States cut down its wheat supplies to Egypt. Nasser retaliated with strong verbal attacks on the United States and its president, in terms reminiscent of his assault on Britain and France in 1956. "Let the Americans drink the seawater" was one of his memorable epigrams; he had a liking for schoolboyish expressions of defiance. The seawater remained unconsumed, and Israel's stability became more appreciated in the West.

In its second decade Israel built an impressive structure of relations with the developing states. It had begun in the 1950s with isolated ventures in cooperation with Burma and Ghana; but now it evolved into a vocation of international scale. A state with a population of a little over two million, scarce in resources, was promoting the development of dozens of other countries in three continents of the world. Hundreds of Israeli technologists, scientists, doctors, engineers, teachers, agronomists, irrigation experts and specialists in youth organization were sharing the lessons and experiences of Israeli pioneering with other developing nations. Israel's development role had three expressions. First, there were the Israeli experts working singly or in teams in the developing countries themselves. Then, there were almost

9,000 men and women from some eighty countries who in the years 1957 to 1966 received training in Israel's institutions of higher learning or in special courses related to development. Third, the series of conferences and seminars held in Israel made a contribution to the study and analysis of development problems.

The first Israeli examples in Burma and Ghana were contagious. The arrival of Israeli diplomatic missions and technicians became an almost integral part of the ceremonies marking the independence of new African states. By 1964, Israel was giving assistance of one sort or another to some sixty-five countries in Africa, Asia and Central and South America. This was an imaginative use both of capacities and limitations. Israel had the advantage of being a small country not suspected of domination. But it was also a developing country, so that the relevance of its experience was greater than that of more developed societies. Moreover, Israel had no "master race" attitude. Its people had known suffering and persecution, and it had preceded the other new states in its struggle for recognition and acceptance by the international community. Its work in developing countries helped Israel to transcend the regional "isolation" imposed by the Arab states and to extend its vision beyond its frontiers. It was clear as the years went by that the Arab view of Israel as a dark conspiracy, a rapacious colonial adventure or a regrettable but temporary Crusader occupation, had been rejected by the opinion and emotion of mankind. There were forces at work in the life of the region and the world that outweighed the factors on which Arab nationalism had relied in its dream of Israel's eclipse. Arab leaders could not count, as they had once hoped, on Israel's spontaneous disintegration, or on the help of the world community to bring about Israel's ruin. If they were to succeed in "destroying Israel," they would have to do the job by their own strength and counsel.

Israel's security was seen as a function of her own independent military strength and of her international friendships. Of these, the first loomed largest in our mind. Israel had no automatic commitment from any power to come to its aid if it were attacked or if its vital interests were threatened. Everything depended on its own capacity to deter and contain the regional hostility by maintaining adequate strength. The task was hard but feasible. The commitment of two million Israelis to their own defense was more absolute and far more passionate than the commitment of one hundred million Arabs to Israel's destruction. Indeed, the numerical equation was misleading. Most of the hundred million Arabs, especially those far away, were not aware of any personal obligation to sacrifice themselves for Israel's liquidation. For the Arab nation, with its own survival assured in so many states, Israel's submergence was optional. Thus, Israel's defense was pursued with intense fervor, while the Arab threat to her existence was mainly expressed in rhetoric that offended Israel's pride but left her body and spirit intact. To the advantage of morale we could add the reinforcement of technology. In modern strategy, the value of more numbers tends to decline as scientific skills grow. When technical methods become more sophisticated, the quantitative element loses its decisive importance; the possibility of a small community holding its own against heavy demographic odds becomes more tangible. This is not to say that it is preferable to be small. But it is, at least, a tolerable destiny. In Israel's national memory David's victory over Goliath was a result not of his smallness, but of his compensating agility and talent for improvisation.

I outlined this view of Israel's future in a *Foreign Affairs* article in the spring of 1965 and was surprised to receive a letter from Ben-Gurion saying that this was the best article that he had ever(!) read on the subject. As was usual with Ben-Gurion, there was an immediate national debate about his motive. One version was that his hostility to Eshkol did not carry over to me. A more tortuous explanation was that in a Machiavellian bid to split Eshkol's camp, Ben-Gurion was trying to win me over to Rafi. Few people were prepared to accept my rather simplistic interpretation, which was that the "old man" really liked the article.

In the 1960s Israel's security doctrine was rooted in the idea of an independent deterrent power. I supported this definition. I believed that our strategy toward the Arab world would have to have an attritional stage. First they would have to be driven to despair of causing our downfall and liquidation. At that stage they would perhaps see the advantage and compulsion of "doing a deal." My experience and reading had told me that those who most ardently wanted peace were not always those who obtained it. At the same time, I wrote and said that even if we built a wall against attack or intimidation, we should have a door in the wall in case the attrition was successful and our neighbors came to seek accommodation. Our immediate task was to maintain a sufficient deterrent balance to bring the Arab states, or at least some elements in their leadership, to a realistic preference for compromise.

This policy seemed to respond to broader international realities. Events in Vietnam, Congo, Cyprus, Yemen and Kashmir illustrated the dangers that threatened world peace whenever there was a lack of internal stability in small states or a deficient equilibrium among them. A small nation announcing its resolve to ensure its own defense without falling on the responsibility or conscience of others could expect to hear a sigh of relief go up from harassed and overcommitted powers. For none of Israel's friends wanted to expand its direct strategic commitments. Israel's policy of self-reliance could, therefore, count on support. The embargo atmosphere of the 1950s began to clear away. The Israeli defense establishment under Levi Eshkol's leadership embarked on a program of modernization and intensive procurement. Another aim was to variegate Israel's sources of supply. There was no reason in the early 1960s to be skeptical about French support; but many Israelis thought it wise to avoid the concentration of one's eggs in a single basket. New prospects of armored and air strength were thus pursued in the United

States. The result was that by 1966 the power of Israel in relation to any Arab force likely to be arrayed against her in the coming years was no less effective than it was ten years before.

These were the consoling situations that came to light in the review that the new Israeli government made in its first months of office. The Arab states had not won military superiority; and to make matters worse for them, their pretense of union was collapsing. Rival regimes, contrasting ideologies, competitive bids for hegemony and diverse international orientations tore the Arab world apart. The Yemen war, which had raged since 1961, found the Arab "family" divided into three fronts: the supporters of the Royalist forces, headed by Saudi Arabia; the allies of the 1962 Republican Revolution, led by Egypt; and the uneasy neutrals in between. Jordan was at daggers drawn with Syria and Egypt. Morocco and Tunis were in conflict over Mauritania. Only three Arab states (Libya, Kuwait and Sudan) maintained normal relations with all other members of the Arab League. In 1958 it had been believed that the leftist Kassem regime in Iraq, having overthrown the pro-Western monarchy, would be subservient to Nasser. When it showed an unexpectedly independent spirit, Nasser turned on it with furious invective, thus offending the Soviet Union. Similarly, when Syria, which had formed a union with Egypt in the guise of the United Arab Republic in 1958, broke away from Cairo in 1961, it was met with the full blast of Nasser's disapproval. Nasser was tolerant only of those Arab regimes that accepted his leadership. Whenever an Arab regime sought to go its own way, when regional and particularist tendencies asserted themselves against Cairo's control, he became vituperative. My statement that nothing divided the Arab world more than the attempt to unite it was proving true. Diversity of interests was made more intense by personal rivalries among Arab political leaders. When they embraced each other at airports on official visits, the eyes across each other's backs and shoulders had a cold glint of suspicion.

At first thought it might seem that Israel should have been heartened by the disarray of its adversaries. Things worked the other way. Unable to rally the dispersed and quarrelsome Arab states under his banner, Nasser looked around for a unifying theme. He found it in the vocabulary and idiom of anti-Israel rhetoric.

In later years Nasser and his sympathizers made many efforts to obscure his record of verbal extremism. They cultivated an impression that only firebrands like Ahmed Shukeiry and the radio commentators indulged this vice. But it is Nasser's quiet, silky voice that Israelis remember most acutely when they recall the events that were to lead to the breakdown of the decade of relative stability after the Suez-Sinai War. Nasser had said that "Israel is the greatest crime in history." And again—implausibly—"Ben-Gurion is the greatest war criminal in this century." The fact is that few statesmen across the world had evoked more respect than Ben-Gurion outside their countries. In Nasser's speeches the quarrel was not with Israel's policies, but with Israel's right to live. The very existence of Israel is a "stain," "a shame," "a disgrace," "a bleeding wound." On May 20, 1965, we hear him proclaim that "Israeli aspirations regarding Egypt reach as far as the Al Sharqiyya area because the children of Israel lived in the district before their departure from Egypt."

Far from "aspiring to the Al Sharqiyya district of Egypt," most Israelis would have been hard put to say where that district was. All of them at that time would have been prepared to support a peace treaty with Egypt and Jordan and Syria without territorial changes. Similarly, visitors would have had to look in vain for the "map extending from the Nile to the Euphrates," which Nasser solemnly told foreign dignitaries was carved on a wall in the Knesset building. There is no such map in the Knesset building.

We could not forget that the climax of Nasser's verbal assault came in his endorsement of the anti-Semitic *Protocols of the Elders of Zion,* which has probably caused the murder of more people than any document in history: it is the spiritual basis of European and, especially, of Nazi anti-Semitism. More copies of it were sold in Egypt in the Nasser decades than in all the countries of the world put together since it was forged in the early years of the twentieth century. It is only a short step from this to the communiqué signed jointly by Nasser and Iraqi President Aref in 1963 proclaiming that "The aim of the Arabs is the destruction of Israel."

Nasser's most delicate problems arose when he discovered that the total effect of this ugly stuff was to arouse revulsion but not fear in Israel—and a measure of skepticism in the rest of the world. His response was to call a summit meeting in Cairo in January 1964. It was attended by the heads of thirteen Arab states commanding an area of four million square miles and a population of a hundred million. The motive of their disquiet was their failure to intimidate a small country one fortieth their size in population and one five-hundredth their size in area.

The alarm bell that shook the Arab leaders to a realization of their dilemma was Israel's completion of the National Water Carrier in 1964. This project was of high value to our economy. In scale and technical imagination it would have done credit to a larger state; in human terms it carried the special appeal that belongs to the sudden eruption of verdure in a wilderness. But its implications went deeper. What was ostensibly an engineering enterprise had now become a decisive political issue. For the Arab governments had publicly sworn that the Galilee water would never flow southward. Israel, for its part, had defined the free use of its share of the Jordan water as a vital national interest that, like the integrity of its territory and the freedom of passage in the Gulf of 'Aqaba, would be defended at any cost. Thus the Arab states and Israel faced each other across the ancient river in a test of resolve and deterrent power. If this Arab threat proved hollow, why should any other Arab menace be believed? And if Arab declarations lost their intimidatory force, would not Israel's consolidation go forward in swift and decisive thrust?

Those who look at the river Jordan on the ground are astonished to recall that there was once a likelihood that this would be the focus of a dangerous local war with wide international effects. I received a call from one of the friendliest of American newspaper pundits. Joseph Alsop was declaiming his routine apocalyptic prediction. The familiar voice in its incongruously British accent was telling me that the destruction of the human race would begin with an Arab challenge to Israel's water diversion and would work its way up to a climax of Armageddon involving a nuclear exchange. Alsop's affection for Israel enabled him to forgive my skeptical reaction. My guess was that we would divert the waters, the world would continue to exist and Joe Alsop would write about something else.

Some years later I accompanied Henry Kissinger to the area where the river Jordan begins its flow. He admired the lush, green scenery and said: "Aren't you going to show me the river Jordan?"

I replied, pointing to the modest gush: "This is the river Jordan."

His reply: "This is the greatest achievement of public relations in human history."

The Arab governments could not have chosen less favorable ground than the water project to call world opinion to their cause. The enterprise was radiantly innocent. It caused no harm to anyone, and the threat to oppose it by force was regarded by most of mankind as senseless malice. In January 1964, while waiting for Pope Paul VI at Megiddo, where he was to begin his pilgrimage to the Holy Places, I heard the Soviet ambassador in Israel, of all people, informing Prime Minister Eshkol that "Israel had a right to its share of the Jordan waters."

An allocation of the waters made in the 1950s by a mission headed by Eric Johnston, at the behest of President Eisenhower, gave us thirty-five percent of the total resource. This was disappointing, but in a bid for world support, Israelis preferred the political advantages of third-party arbitration to the unilateral assertion of their own claims.

On June 11, 1964, the water began to flow in the National Carrier. The Arab threat had been quietly but firmly frustrated.

In the absence of Prime Minister Eshkol on a mission abroad, I presided over the ceremony. We had defended our water and had proved that Israel's deterrent reputation was intact.

The Arab Summit Conference in 1964 was followed by another in 1965. It reacted to the Arab dilemma by a doctrine of delayed response. On July 11, 1965, Nasser said: "The final account with Israel will be made within five years if we are patient. The Moslems waited seventy years until they expelled the Crusaders from Palestine." Two years later Nasser was to take a more impatient view of his options; but for the time being he played a waiting game. In reply to Syrian pressure for immediate war, he said with complete veracity: "We cannot use force today because conditions are not ripe."

Evidently the will to make war was strong but the capacity was deficient. Therefore a Palestine Liberation Organization was formed at the Summit

Conference to fight Israel in the undefined future and destroy King Hussein's regime in the more immediate present. A Joint Arab Command was established under the command of the Egyptian General Abdul Hakim Amer to plan the eventual military assault. And instead of preventing the flow of water to the Negev by making war immediately, it was decided to choke off Israel's irrigation channels by a perverse and expensive diversion of the Upper Jordan streams into areas of Lebanon and Syria that had no need of them. The singularity of Arab policy was revealed here in typical form: The aim was not to advance Arab interests, but to harm those of Israel.

Thus the Arab Summit Conferences of 1964 and 1965 sought to postpone the armed conflict in practice, to keep its prospect alive in policy and rhetoric and to stir enough irrigation to prevent any long-term tranquillity. The plan sounded impressive, but its weaknesses were great. It reflected a tendency in Arab politics to prefer the form of things to their substance; for none of the instruments created at the Summit was as formidable as it tried to appear. The Palestine Liberation Organization was ferocious enough in pamphlets and broadcasts, but its martial qualities were dubious. Indeed, the organization derived a comic-opera aspect from the spectacle of its leader. Ahmed Shukeiry's corpulent gait, pompous demeanor and blatant concern for his own vanity and comfort were reassuring to his prospective victims. Israelis reflected that if Shukeiry was their chief danger, they must be tolerably safe.

But for some sections of the Labor movement, the idea of living without Ben-Gurion at the helm was hard to bear. The new prime minister was soon beset by violent criticism and challenge from his predecessor. The immediate cause was again Eshkol's refusal to revive the investigation of the treatment of the "Affair" at Ben-Gurion's request. Ben-Gurion hinted that Eshkol was seeking to cover up discreditable footprints, including his own. For good measure, Ben-Gurion stated darkly that Eshkol had jeopardized unspecified "security matters." By 1965 Ben-Gurion's assaults on Eshkol were unbearably severe. In loyalty to him, some of his strongest supporters, including Moshe Dayan, Shimon Peres and Yosef Almogi, had left Eshkol's administration. In 1965 they formed a separate party (Rafi) under Ben-Gurion. Labor unity had been wrecked, and the nation entered a phase of unprecedented acrimony.

Eshkol met these adversities with outward calm, but they were eating away at his physical and nervous strength. In November 1965, in a massive counterstroke, he took his depleted Labor Alignment into electoral battle.

This was a daring gamble. The party list was no longer graced with the prestigious names and versatile energies of Ben-Gurion, Dayan, Peres, Yitshak Navon. For the first and only time I headed the election campaign in formation committee as well as taking a prominent part in the election meetings. Golda Meir remained loyal to Eshkol at this stage, but her health was no longer as robust as it had been and the burden upon me was heavy, especially as Prime Minister Eshkol was more distinguished in decision than in rhetoric. We scored a triumph, defeating Herut and overwhelming Rafi, which emerged with a meager eight percent of the popular vote, despite the allure of its leading names. Eshkol had reached his highest peak, and with a powerful majority at his command he could speak not as Ben-Gurion's appointed successor, but as the people's choice.

Yet he was still pursued by abuse and derision. There was a wide chasm between his government's real achievements and the negative image which its opponents managed to create. Eshkol had shown courage and resolution in authorizing Israel's controlled military reactions; and the economic measures devised by his finance minister, Pinhas Sapir, though irksome in the short run, were really among the government's most creditable achievements. They were an honest attempt to correct Israel's disturbed balance of payments by a period of thrift and accumulation, in place of easygoing improvidence. Eshkol was calling for immediate sacrifice in the name of ultimate economic strength. The electorate had shown a penetrating understanding of his achievements, even when his opponents were portraying him as a weak and ineffective successor to a giant-size statesman.

The usual practice of prime ministers and foreign ministers is to ensure that deputy prime ministers should have as little as possible to do. This reality was mitigated in my case by health problems that sometimes afflicted both Eshkol and Golda Meir and by the fact that they were often abroad in essential search of friendships. This created an occasional sector of vacant turf for the vice premier, and I carried out a varied schedule of assignments that demanded a certain level of representation. But I was deeply surprised when Eshkol and Golda both approached me in January 1965 with the proposal that I head the negotiating team that would hold a comprehensive negotiation with a mission to be sent by Chancellor Ludwig Erhard of West Germany to negotiate a comprehensive agreement on German-Israeli relations. My two colleagues outlined the talents and prestige that would qualify me for this task. They did this with such generous ardor that I expected them to end by offering me one or both of their jobs.

Without disputing their eulogies, I allowed myself to consider that this offer of a major diplomatic and political opportunity might be touched by a decent ingredient of self-interest. Anything relating to Germany was a kind of hornet's nest, and the complication with which I was to wrestle was severe and full of hazards.

The story began in the late 1950s when the German defense minister and Shimon Peres, our deputy defense minister, concluded a secret agreement for the sale of arms in great quantities and of high quality to Israel. Strauss badly needed evidence of his progressive and humane character, which was not an attribute that many people attributed to him in the light of his hard-line rhetoric and personality. Peres was quite rationally acting under the traumatic memory of the embargo atmosphere with which he had to grapple, especially in the period leading to the Suez-Sinai War when the Arabs were receiving massive arms shipments while we experienced an armament drought in America and Britain. The transaction was approved by Chancellor Adenauer on strict condition of secrecy. Peres, with characteristic ingenuity, had created procedures whereby the weapons would be dispatched from Germany to third countries without mention of their Israeli destination. In October 1964 these transactions appeared in a press leakage in Europe. There was a storm of frenzied repercussions in both countries. In Germany a loud demand for the cessation of this process raged with increasing passion. The conspiratorial nature of the agreement and of its implementation aroused serious constitutional issues. But these were transcended by the diplomatic aspect.

German diplomacy was dominated by the Hallstein Doctrine, which committed the federal government to break relations with any country that dared to establish relations with the East German Communist state. The Arab states thus held West Germany in an iron grip of extortion. They could react against any signs of German rapprochement with Israel by establishing relations with East Germany and "daring" the Federal Republic to cut itself off from its lucrative relations with the Arab world. Moreover, recognition of East Germany by a group of a dozen or more countries would set off a chain reaction that would bring the Hallstein Doctrine crashing to the ground.

After facing considerable agitation the Erhard administration decided on February 10, 1965, to ban further delivery of arms to non-NATO countries. Non-NATO was a euphemism denoting Israel.

There were other points of tension between our two countries. Germany had been unduly permissive and negligent in the prosecution of war criminals. And in 1959 a furor had erupted in Israel and in world Jewry over reports that German scientists were advising the Egyptian government on missile development. The reaction in the Knesset and especially in the Opposition ranks had been regarded by Ben-Gurion and Peres as exaggerated to the point of hysteria, since the missile technologies at issue could have been easily obtained from other sources and could not be compared in importance with the valuable reinforcement that Israel was receiving within the terms of the Strauss-Peres agreement. The trouble was that the German scientists were in the public eye, while the Strauss-Peres agreement was not.

Ben-Gurion had been deeply offended by the fact that some of his own colleagues, including Golda Meir, joined the outcry against the German scientists in close harmony with Opposition speakers and had even accepted a joint text with Begin in the Knesset. In our consultations she had criticized Peres for his allegedly pro-German attitudes and for playing down the threat of the Egyptian missile development. In this matter her priorities were diametrically contrary to those of Ben-Gurion. Some historians have conjectured that Ben-Gurion's 1963 resignation was partly influenced by this rift in the course of which the Intelligence chief, Isser Harel, had resigned.

Both countries were now seriously disconcerted. Israel came away from the drama without arms shipments and without diplomatic relations. Germany appeared in an intolerable posture. It was assailed for insensitivity to the memory of the Jewish tragedy, for disregard of its relations with the Arabs and for a total lack of backbone as exemplified by the arms conspiracy and by the hasty and craven retreat. Not a single positive quality came to light in its furtive, underground treatment of the episode. It was evident that both Jerusalem and Bonn badly needed to bring their relationship into the open and to define their policies toward each other in a detailed negotiation. It was with relief that I heard that Chancellor Erhard was going to send a mission headed by one of his close friends, Dr. Kurt Birrenbach.

Eshkol and Golda each had valid reason to regard this negotiation without enthusiasm. Golda was conscientiously tormented by the German issue. Our diplomats were often excused for rejecting posting to Germany if their emotion or experience made such an assignment difficult. Golda felt conscientiously unable to deal in a cool manner with a German delegation. In a similar emotion she had fallen ill a few months earlier when it had been necessary to receive Pope Paul VI at Megiddo on a visit, which fell short of implying a formal recognition of Israeli sovereignty. The German problem invited far more understandable inhibitions. Eshkol was not in hot pursuit of crises. He and I recalled the occasion in 1952 when the leader of the Opposition, Menachem Begin, had led a riotous demonstration near the Knesset to protest against the German Compensation (Shilumin) Agreement signed by Ben-Gurion and Adenauer. Stones had been thrown at the Knesset building and Begin had been penalized by the Knesset committee with a sentence of five absences from five sessions. It could be assumed that the Knesset debate on the establishment of diplomatic relations would be charged with emotion and that the presentation of credentials to President Shazar with the playing of the German anthem would stir uncontrollable passions.

I saw no reason to reject this responsible and grave assignment. My own outlook on the German problem had been dominated by the principle that there was no atonement for the German crimes and that the only response to the Hitler tragedy was to strengthen Israel as the assurance of Jewish survival. Hitler had decreed the elimination of the Jews from history. History had decreed the survival of the Jews and the end of Hitler's thousand years empire. It was our Jewish duty to see that this legacy was conserved and enhanced.

My negotiations with Birrenbach were conducted with grave dignity. I was accompanied by Felix Shinnar, who had represented us nobly in Bonn as the representative of the German compensation committee, by Ze'ev Shek, a Holocaust survivor who was to become our ambassador in Austria and a member of my delegation to the Geneva Peace Conference, and by Yochanan Meroz, a future ambassador of Israel in Bonn. We reached agreement on what we called a "package settlement." Diplomatic relations would be established and German arms that would be withheld from us under the "No Arms Outside NATO" decision would be obtained from the United States and paid for by the Federal Republic of Germany.

When I rose in the Knesset on March 12, 1965, to seek a vote on the establishment of diplomatic relations with Germany, the atmosphere was surprisingly tranquil. The weather forecast had been wrong. There was no storm. I reiterated my view that to strengthen Israel at the expense of Germany had an intrinsic logic as well as a concrete measure of reinforcement. Moreover, the road to the European Community was now open.

Each of the two countries sent eminently qualified ambassadors, Asher Ben-Natan from Israel and Rolf Pauls from Germany. They laid firm foundations. Konrad Adenauer visited Israel in 1966 and was courteously received. On Adenauer's death, I accompanied Ben-Gurion to his funeral. The most painful sector of our international relations was passing beyond bitterness to a mutual understanding of responsibility and tragedy. Their responsibility and our unfathomable tragedy.

Eshkol's government was not formed until several months after the election. The delay was caused by his heart attack. In January 1966 the Knesset confirmed the establishment of the new government. Levi Eshkol, prime minister. Abba Eban, minister of foreign affairs.

I was back on familiar ground.

17

ONCE MORE UNTO THE
BRINK

THE FIRST OF the many telegrams congratulating Suzy and me on my appointment as foreign minister was signed "Paula." "It should have happened long ago," said the writer. I was surprised by this generosity from Paula Ben-Gurion, the prime minister's wife, who was celebrated for her cantankerous disposition and was keeping a somewhat suspicious eye on me in case I might appear to be usurping even a fraction of Ben-Gurion's publicity. Before Suzy could thank Paula Ben-Gurion for this kindly thought, she went to her hairdresser in Tel Aviv, who said, "Didn't you get my telegram?" Paula the hairdresser had done the noble deed and the former prime minister's wife was acquitted of what would have been an unseemly lapse into generosity. The second message that arrived was from Jacqueline Kennedy, whose friendship with us persists until this day. Thereafter the flow continued and mounted, without surprises.

I had no need of prolonged efforts to get acquainted with the senior officials in the ministry. Most of them had been my colleagues, and they were now quite willing to adapt themselves to the idea that I would be their senior. Simultaneous leadership of our missions in the United States and the United Nations was not a routine diplomatic assignment, and a transition to ministerial status seemed a natural outcome.

I sensed more relief than apprehension in the ministry on my arrival. Golda Meir had never felt fully at home with Foreign Office officials. Her closest personal relationships were with some of her political contemporaries in the Labor movement. She considered the diplomatic professionals to be too polished, excessively inclined to understand diverse points of view and in some regrettable cases afflicted with analytical and intellectual habits that did not facilitate contact between them and her.

Golda's talent lay in the simplification of issues: She went straight to the crux and center of each problem. Foreign policy specialists, on the other hand, are conscious of the intrinsic complexity of international relations.

They perceive the multiple elements that go into most decisions and policies. They react with resignation to the idea that Israel's vital interests are not all that vital to non-Israelis. They are also aware of the volatile atmosphere of a profession in which contingencies can be created overnight by forces alien and external to their own nation. A minister of housing can plan rural and urban developments that are little affected by anything that can occur outside the domestic domain. In my own ministry of education and culture, it was only the interplay of budgetary and syndicalist forces within the country that could have serious influence on my plans. The trouble with foreign policy is that it is foreign, and it is there that a nation's sovereignty has less influence than in any other field of public policy.

Since Golda was a tough character with a domineering streak, the temptation for senior officials to adapt their advice to her prejudices was strong. Habits of consultation in the ministry were few. The very word "analysis" provoked her to irritability. When officials analyzed the contradictory waves of influence that flowed into decision-making, she tended to interrupt them with an abrupt request for the bottom line. The quest for the "simple truth" was not easy when, as often happens, the truth is not simple at all.

In that sense, my appointment gave the Foreign Ministry officials the feeling that they were welcoming one of their own. They expected me to have a compassionate understanding of the dilemmas that faced them. Public opinion at home tends to overestimate the luxury, dignity and ease in which diplomats live, and to underestimate the personal risk and torment of conscience inherent in their task. In most nations, public opinion is in constant revolt against foreign policy precisely because it is a domain in which the national will is not supreme. The constraints imposed by the international systems are blamed on the ministry, which mediates between the nation and its external realm. And, even in their home capitals, Foreign Ministry officials are in danger of living outside their own social reality and becoming enclosed in a special diplomatic world.

What gave me an authentic feeling of legitimate command over the Foreign Office staff was the fact that I, unlike them, was equipped with a dimension beyond their reach: seven years of immersion in the harder realities of political and parliamentary life. There was no embarrassment in being the constitutional chief of those who had long been my equal colleagues. No previous first-name habits were suspended, and team spirit prevailed over hierarchy. The harmony was deep and broad.

Having been uprooted several times since my Zionist career began, Suzy and I now had to leave our home in Rehovot and to install ourselves in a large house of many rooms in the Talbiya area of Jerusalem. The handsome residence was constructed in the early thirties by an Egyptian Jewish merchant of evident affluence, whose ambitions extended even to a swimming pool on the roof. Since there was never any water in the alleged pool, the functional purpose of this structure was obscure. When I ceased to be a

Cabinet minister eight years later, the house became the residence of the prime ministers. The swimming "pool" is still waterless. The small but comfortable house in Rehovot had been our children's first home in their own country, and the parting from its verdant surroundings was not easy.

In our initial discussions in the ministry, we were able to record a condition of stability and consolidation, which had developed after the Suez-Sinai campaign. I could take satisfaction from the speed with which the crisis of 1956 had been transcended. The fruit of the campaign that I had conducted in the United Nations and Washington was visible in the oil traffic through the Straits of Tiran and the nine years of tranquillity in the Northern Negev villages bordering on Gaza.

This was a decade in which immigration would help to increase our Jewish population from 1.8 million to 2.7 million. A bridge of commerce and friendship was patiently constructed through the Straits of Tiran toward the eastern half of the globe. The advanced countries admired Israel for its pioneering vitality, while new nations probed the secret of its accelerated development. I found the friendly nations divided to our advantage between those who envied us for what we had already accomplished and others for what we still had to do.

This was a decade in which our relations with the United States had been repaired. Those with France had been maintained intact. Our ties with Britain and other members of the European community were increasingly built on reciprocal self-interest and not on the characteristic patronizing attitude of established countries toward a nation that had not known a single month of uninterrupted peace in all the years of its national independence.

Our Arab neighbors, wounded by their failure to obstruct the national water plan or to strangle our maritime relations with the southern and eastern worlds, were ferocious enough in broadcast and pamphleteering, but did not seem eager to go beyond sporadic raids and incursions into the risk of all-out war.

Since our security doctrine was based on an intimidating deterrent capacity, it was natural for me to begin my schedule of foreign travel in Paris, which was still the main source of our military equipment. Many of my colleagues in the ministry and among the media were worried by the likelihood that France, now fully recovered from its humiliations in Algeria and Suez, would seek to find its way back to Arab sympathies by underemphasizing its relations with Israel. In my first visit to Paris, I put this ominous scenario frankly before the foreign minister, Couve de Murville. He was an unusual head of the Quai d'Orsay. He did not seem to fit into any appropriate French category. He was a Protestant in an establishment dominated by Catholicism, a pipe smoker in a nation of cigarettes and noxious cigars, and with a temperament sufficiently phlegmatic and free of passion to make one believe that he would have been at home in the Whitehall abode where British diplomacy had its sanctuaries. Couve de Murville represented the two traditions in French diplomacy: the tradition of relentless realism bereft of all emotions, prejudices, and passions—and the tradition of exquisitely elegant skills in expression and formulation. With de Gaulle in the Élysée and Couve de Murville in the Quai d'Orsay, relations with France might be substantively awkward, but they would undoubtedly be a literary delight.

Couve said that there was no real problem in the relationship between France and Israel except what he called an excessive Israeli nervousness about the durability of the French alliance. My long talk with him revealed no major divergences. He pleaded only for understanding if we sometimes heard him express an interest in the Arab aspects of French policy. He said, correctly, that no government, not even the United States, would ever base its Middle Eastern policy on Israel alone.

Couve de Murville's reassuring version of his country's attitudes could have been a sincere reflection of his views. It could also have been motivated by the tactical aim of not wishing to generate Israeli alarm or pressure at a premature stage. This would be quite legitimate. Foreign ministers are dedicated not to scientific truth, but to their own national interests. The instructive point here is that the lenient view of French policy was fully endorsed by our own embassy in Paris. To the disquiet that I had expressed about cold French attitudes in United Nations debates and about the reluctance of French governments to send their ministers to fraternize in Israel, my Israeli interlocutors replied with a polemical question: What is more important— protocol and rhetoric or substantive matters such as the flow of French weaponry, the expansion of trade, cultural and technological cooperation and other indications of normality and friendship?

From Paris, I proceeded to Ottawa, where I renewed a warm acquaintanceship with Prime Minister Lester (Mike) Pearson and External Affairs Minister Paul Martin, who had long been the eloquent spokesmen for Canada in the United Nations. Mike Pearson had entered politics with spectacular results and had emerged as party leader and head of a Liberal government. His temperament and skills enabled him to maintain a sense of proportion in all things and to avoid being swept away by the wonder of his own accession to political power. It was a good opportunity to tell him that one of the happiest decisions that I had ever made in my years as an ambassador was to go to see him on the dark night of November 8, 1956, when our international position was crumbling around us and when I encouraged him in his readiness to seek a way out of the deadlock.

Pearson and Martin did not seem to be unqualified admirers of the Lyndon B. Johnson administration in the United States, which was becoming unduly involved in the Vietnam War. When they asked me how Israel stood in Washington I earned an unanticipated bonus before I had time to reply. One of Pearson's secretaries handed a note to me that had been transmitted from our Washington embassy. It was couched in urgent terms. The text said that President Johnson had heard that I was "somewhere in the region" (which seemed to me a rather personalized way of describing his Canadian neighbor). He wanted me to see him and Defense Secretary Robert McNamara in order to discuss and complete the agreement for the sale of Skyhawk aircraft to Israel. I learned later that the urgency of this summons arose from the familiar reality of congressional pressure. The negotiations had been caught up in a bureaucratic snag. Both the White House and the Defense Department believed that, in a conversation with me, the few remaining difficulties could be overcome.

Mike Pearson was so impressed by this evidence of my presumed influence in Washington that he offered me his official plane to make my way to Washington. Within a few days, the crisis was disentangled, and our delighted air force began to prepare for a new stage in its technological and operative progress.

President Johnson had wanted me to enter the Pentagon by a side door. The sensitivity of the United States about supplying arms to Israel was still in force, though not as acutely as in the Eisenhower-Dulles days. McNamara was amiable and evidently in full and serene control of his vast department. It was a refreshing change from the days when Charles Wilson, who was McNamara's predecessor both as president of General Motors and as secretary of defense, had asked me and my military attaché, Chaim Herzog, whether "Turkey is one of the Arab countries that are not on good terms with you." More memorably, Wilson had coined the unforgettable aphorism announcing that what is good for General Motors is good for the United States. During the Eisenhower era both of them were doing rather well.

When I reached the White House, the president confirmed the Skyhawk transaction and added: "I never want to discuss aircraft with you again as long as I live." He was underestimating both Israeli persistence and his own longevity. I assumed that he was not really serious in what he was saying. I whispered to myself that he could probably count on a year of relief before I would come back for Phantoms.

Even this ostensibly beneficial development had not been easily achieved: A conflict had broken out in the Knesset Committee on Foreign Affairs and Defense when Deputy Defense Minister Shimon Peres had made derogatory references to the Skyhawk aircraft while Ezer Weizman, the virtual architect and founder of Israel's aerial strength, heartily wished me to procure that equipment. This difference of opinion was crystallized at a later stage in an undercurrent of confrontation between the "French school" and "American school" in Israel's foreign policy. I thought it nonsensical to make an ideological issue about a purely pragmatic interest. I believed it equally wrong to ignore the fact that aircraft from the United States, even if they could be obtained elsewhere, would have a psychological and therefore a deterrent influence that would not attach to any other source of weaponry.

I had always believed that a new minister should strive to make a quick mark in the first year of his office. He should strike out in new directions and not merely deepen the exact traces that his predecessor had left in the ground. I decided to apply this principle in two areas: Eastern Europe and Asia.

I felt that the coolness of relations between Israel and Eastern Europe was a source of weakness that ought to be rectified. We gained nothing in the West by this form of isolation. No Israeli Cabinet member had ever been to Eastern Europe in any official capacity. On the other hand, it was very unlikely that I or any other senior member of the Israeli government would be invited officially.

So I approved the idea first broached by my able assistant, Moshe Raviv, of having a conference of all Israeli ambassadors to East Europe countries convene in Warsaw, to symbolize my wish to reach a minimally coherent dialogue with the countries under Soviet domination—a definition that applied to the Soviet Union itself. Until then, my predecessors had convened our ambassadors in Eastern Europe by bringing them to Paris or Vienna. I therefore instructed our ambassador in Warsaw to tell the Polish government that I wished to come to Warsaw for a few days and to meet our ambassadors and heads of mission accredited to the Soviet Union, Poland, Romania, Hungary, Czechoslovakia, Bulgaria and Yugoslavia.

The auspices were not good, since only a year before, Poland had prevented the finance minister of Israel from attending an international trade conference in Warsaw. On this occasion, however, my initiative bore fruit; the Polish government said that it would allow the conference of ambassadors to proceed. It seemed rather flattered that Warsaw had been selected as the site. I heard that they were afraid that if they turned me down I would turn up with my ambassadors in Bucharest or—heaven forbid—in Belgrade.

I had no illusions: It was clear that the Polish government would bug all our discussions and that we would not be able to talk freely. However, I valued the demonstrative effect. And indeed, when the Israeli press announced in large headlines that I would meet in Warsaw with the Israeli ambassadors from the seven Socialist countries, the public reaction was enthusiastic.

So I flew to Warsaw via Paris and met with the converging ambassadors for several successive days, during which we addressed the listening chandeliers with complimentary references to the attitude and policies of the Polish government, and carried out what had been one of my major objectives in going to Poland, which was to visit Auschwitz.

One morning the seven Israeli ambassadors, Moshe Raviv and I flew to Cracow and thence thirty-five miles by bus to the spot where two and a half million Jews had been executed by gas and cremation, and another half million starved to death. I remember finding something offensive in the beauty of the surrounding verdure, in the bells chiming with rich echo from the Cracow cathedrals, in the homely, pungent farming smells from each side of the narrow roads, in the glory of a blue sky untrammeled by any sign of cloud and, above all, in the spectacle of stolid Polish villagers fulfilling simple tasks, as they must have done a quarter of a century before, when they prudently avoided any show of interest or emotion as the trains roared by. Some of the villagers and farmers waved at us as the bus chugged along, giving rise to the tortured question: Did they wave in those days at the passing trains . . . ? Did no sound of agony, no scream of martyred children penetrate those prudent, unhearing ears?

Most of the journey was accompanied in shocked silence. There was an anguished moment when our bus stopped at the railway crossing for a train to go by. I looked at the glint of the steel rails and there came to mind the ghastly vision of the railway trucks that had transported millions of our people at this very place to their final agony and doom.

The Polish government sent its representatives to serve as our guides. They were very professional, almost clinically so, with their "explanations," fluent from constant repetition. We saw the buildings at Auschwitz preserved, as if its inhabitants had moved out only the day before. Everything remained in place as on the day of liberation. Here were the hideous apparatuses of torture: the cells, the dungeons, the furnaces, and the gas chambers. Historic exhibits. Tourist sites.

Everything was exposed. Well, nearly everything. The only anonymous item was the Jewish identity of the victims. I awakened with shock to the idea that Auschwitz was what the Americans call "restricted." Jews were not welcome in their own name even in the places of death and horror in which they had played the central part. Large signs proclaimed that the deportees, who had been tortured and killed there, were citizens of "Norway, Belgium, Holland, France, Greece." There was only one modest sign, hardly visible, that indicated that the slaughtered Frenchmen and Dutchmen and Greeks and Norwegians had been Jews.

I looked at the mountain of hair shaved from the heads of victims. Even more ghastly was the vast pile of children's shoes, reaching almost to the ceiling. They had been taken from their little owners before cremation. I could not tear my eyes away. I have always thought that one of the major horrors of the Holocaust was the union between the satanic "plan" and the calm routines that were essential to its implementation.

In silence I walked with my fellow countrymen through the Auschwitz fields. Behind me at a crawling pace came our official limousine bearing the Israeli flag. I reflected that, for all the millions who lay buried there, this flag would have been not only a symbol of pride, but also a key to deliverance; it would have carried the promise of an open door. It now seemed to whisper to me a consolation so belated as to be unbearable in its poignancy. I was overcome by a sense of desolation. Everything had happened too late.

As we stood by the mass grave, I found it impossible to make a speech. I therefore recited the words of the Kaddish, the prayer of mourning. "He who maketh Peace on His high places will make peace for us and for all Israel. And let us say Amen." There was nothing more to be said.

Before leaving I was shown one of the cells where prisoners were held in solitary confinement. I obeyed an instinct to go in and isolate myself in that corner of living hell. The ambassadors and guides waited outside. I tried to imagine myself in the condition of a Jewish prisoner in that dark solitude. Imagination failed. When I came out my colleagues thought that I was about to faint. In the bus and on the plane carrying us back to Warsaw it was impossible for any of us to utter a single word.

I believe that I must have been vague and distant when I spoke to the Polish foreign minister, Adam Rapacki, later that day. Rapacki, who talked like a French diplomat rather than like a Communist functionary, assured me that his government would continue to maintain steadfast links with Israel "based on memories of a common struggle and a common agony."

I instructed our ambassador in Romania, Eliezer Doron, to examine the possibility of closer cooperation with Bucharest. This was because his report indicated greater signs of sympathy and understanding from the administration of Nicolae Ceauşescu than did the other ambassadors from the governments to which they were accredited.

Golda Meir's travels in Africa had not been followed or accompanied by a corresponding effort in Asia. I had been told that it would not be easy to secure dignified invitations from most Asian countries, but the response was better than we had anticipated. It seemed that my work in the United Nations and in the Rehovot Conferences had made my name familiar to some of them. So in March 1967 Suzy and I, with my assistant Emmanuel Shimoni, set out for a journey that took us to Thailand, the Philippines, Japan, Burma, Singapore, Cambodia, Australia and New Zealand. A few years later, after the 1967 war, many of those countries would have refused to receive an Israeli foreign minister in his official capacity. In many of the countries that I visited, we laid the foundations of increased cooperation projects. I have a moving recollection of our visit to Phnom Penh, the capital of Cambodia, where I conferred with the charismatic leader of that country, Prince Norodom Sihanouk. Perhaps the word "conferred" gives a wrong impression. I heard a magnificent monologue in impeccable French, delivered in such a high voice that it was as if he was addressing a public meeting.

There was a Gaullist pretension, both in his manner and in his literary style. He, more than any other leader that I met in the region, seemed to feel the torment of small nations caught up in the global struggle, trying to find a central place of safety between the allurements of Western aid and the need to conciliate the growing power of China. He spoke to me so sincerely about Israel that I was saddened and surprised by his later decision to turn his back on us. I hold in my memory a day that I spent amid the glories of Angkor Wat with Suzy and with the kibbutznik ambassador, Raphi Norodom, whom I had appointed to Phnom Penh. I also managed to see an Israeli mission at work teaching Cambodian farmers to increase rice production. Strange destiny for a remote country in a corner of the Mediterranean.

In Tokyo, Prime Minister Take Miki explained to me both the potentialities and the limitations of Japanese-Israeli cooperation. The limitations belonged to the immediate present, the potentialities to the distant future. I innocently asked Prime Minister Miki if he could help us break through into relationships with Sony and Hitachi and other electronic giants. His reply subtly indicated that "it is they who tell us what to do and it is not we who tell them." Japanese statesmen and media did not quite know what to make of Israel and the Jewish people. When I told them that Israel's population was less than 2.5 million and that there were some 13 million Jews in the world, they burst into polite laughter and said that it was well known that Abba Eban has a sense of humor, but how many are there really? They reacted with similar incredulity to my revelation that we did not yet have any television except for the schools. They evidently saw us as a technological colossus and wondered why I should be so secretive about our dimensions. We concluded our visit with a brief but enchanting glimpse of Kyoto and a meeting with Emperor Hirohito, whose genial demeanor was in such contrast to the demonic images projected in the West during World War II.

In Bangkok, we found a cordial welcome. Thai statesmen, who had been prominent in the United Nations, greeted me as an old friend, as did Foreign Minister Thanat Khoman, who diplomatically allowed me to defeat him by one stroke at golf. I doubt that this was the trauma that led him soon afterward to abandon diplomacy in favor of the asceticism of a Buddhist monk. King Bhunibol and his staggeringly beautiful wife, Queen Sirikit, explained to us the paradox of Southeast Asian life. Just because nature was so bountiful, said His Majesty, there was no desperate incentive to intense labor, such as existed in the cold lands of the north and the west. Even if you didn't work in Southeast Asia, you simply had to extend a hand to find a banana or to throw a string into a pond to catch a fish. The result was that the stimulus to accelerated development was much less sharp than in Europe. The abundance in Asia was, in a sense, its major handicap.

In the small but intensely vigorous society of Singapore, dominated by the authoritative personality of Lee Kuan Yew, I encountered the strange ambivalence with which Asian governments approached us. (Lee Kuan Yew's published biographies highlighted the double first honors degree that he had won at Cambridge. He had given the impression that this was the highest attainment open to a Cambridge graduate. I duly instructed our press officers to play down my triple first distinction.) On the one hand, they admired Israel's social dynamism and technological inventiveness. They wanted to share it. On the other hand, they wished to keep it under wraps, in order to avoid alienating Muslim opinion in the countries such as Malaysia, with whom Israel has no relations to this day.

In Manila, capital of the Philippines, I was the guest of Foreign Minister Carlos Romulo, who had helped us to surmount the obstacles in the political committee over which he had presided at the United Nations, during our bid for membership in 1949. I came to Manila in the early days of the regime of President Ferdinand Marcos and his wife, Imelda. I made the same mistake as I had with Nkrumah in cabling home to Jerusalem about President Marcos's "quiet modesty." There were no signs of the totalitarian spirit that eventually overcame him, leading to his downfall in the mid-1980s.

I wound up my visit to Asian countries in the more familiar atmosphere of Australia and New Zealand. Here the air was full of United Nations memories, and of other recollections going even further back. The governor general was Richard Casey, who had been my chief as minister of state in Cairo during World War II. In New Zealand, I rejoiced to have a nostalgic encounter with Sir Carl Berendsen, who in the United Nations debates of 1947 and 1949 had thunderously denounced all attempts to abandon the partition scheme or to bar Israel from its rightful place in the United Nations. Another encounter was with Sir Leslie Munroe, who had represented New Zealand in the stormy discussions about Suez and the Gulf of 'Aqaba from 1954 to 1957.

In New Zealand I felt remote from the central core of the world. I had a feeling that if I went a few more miles, I would fall off the globe entirely. I began to understand something of the desperate search for intimacy that had led New Zealanders to cherish their relations with England and Scotland, thousands of miles away. In Wellington, I was told of the American senator who had stood at the seacoast at Sydney, peered into the distance, and asked, "Can I see New Zealand from here?" It was as if he believed that the two English-speaking countries were geographically as close to each other as Hyannis to Nantucket.

When I came to summarize my first year in the Foreign Ministry, I could feel that I had fulfilled the promise of a busy start. My tasks had taken me many tens of thousands of miles from Ottawa and Washington to Rangoon and Singapore, with London, Paris and Warsaw in between. Membership of the UN General Assembly had expanded with the addition of so many Arab, Muslim and Communist members, that I reflected how fortunate we had been in pressing our admission request earlier. There would have been no chance for Israel to enter any international agency if a General Assembly vote had to be taken on the basis of the membership in the mid-1960s. The consoling fact was that the real weight of international relations was no longer in parliamentary debate, but in our bilateral relationships in diplomacy, trade, economics and culture. The UN had remained a forum and a microphone with powerful resonance in world opinion. But the heart and center of the system lay in the pragmatic deliberations of the Security Council. The General Assembly had admitted us to membership when many older states were still waiting at the entry gate. But the actual business of international relations was flowing predominantly in regional organizations, such as the European Economic Community (EEC) and the Organization of American States (OAS). In 1966, the first year of my service as Foreign Minister,

I signed a cooperation agreement with the OAS, and in October of that year, I formally submitted Israel's request for a preferential agreement designed to lead to an association with the EEC.

To all my hosts and interlocutors in the five continents that I had visited in my first year I expressed the mistaken view that in 1967, there would be neither peace nor war. There would not be peace, I said, because, despite occasional tranquillity on three boundaries with Egypt, Jordan, and Lebanon, the rhetoric of hostility was virulent. Nor was physical security on the Jordanian front fully assured, although, paradoxically, Jordan's independence against Egyptian pressure was assured by Israel, largely through our 1955 rejection of the Anglo-American proposal for geographical contiguity between Egypt and Jordan across the Negev. But King Hussein was not in full command. Now and then, a burst of violence would convulse our lives on the boundaries between his kingdom and our land, and he would be unable to absorb the fury of our responses.

However, more ominous than the sporadic violence from Jordan and the saber-rattling from Egypt, was the policy of Syria, whose leaders were determined not to leave us alone for a single week. At the Arab summit conferences of 1964 and 1965, Syria was almost alone in calling for immediate confrontation. In February 1966, a militant Syrian government, inspired by the Baath Party, came into power. In an effort to compete in militancy with Nasser, it sponsored what it called "revolutionary activism." The new leaders, with Nureddin at-Atassi at their head, urged that war against Israel not be confined to declarations and boycotts, but that it be given reality and substance all the time. If the balance of regular armies made the clash of forces unrewarding for Syria, then it must be transcended by guerrilla techniques.

Of course, it was absurd to imagine that terrorist infiltration and attacks could, by themselves, "destroy" anything as solid as the State of Israel. On the other hand, Israeli acquiescence was inconceivable. In the early months of 1967, terrorist units of a few dozen men, operating from Syria, had achieved the following results: The railway between Jerusalem and Tel Aviv had been made unsafe for regular travel. Residences had been blown up within a few hundred yards of the Knesset. Several roads in the north could be traversed only after initial probing by mine-detecting vehicles. And an Israeli youth was blown to pieces while playing football near the Lebanese border where mines had been placed. Four soldiers were blasted to death in Upper Galilee, and six others were killed or wounded in the area opposite the Hebron Hills.

If such results could be achieved by a few dozen infiltrators, what would remain of our tranquillity if the terrorist movement was allowed to deploy its activities over a broader area? I could not think of any country that was more exposed to a form of aggression so cheap in risk and requiring such small investment of valor and skill.

Apart from sabotage techniques, there was another area of confrontation in which Syria had great advantage: The collective farming villages in the Upper Galilee and Jordan Valley are the jewel in Israel's crown. Set in a frame of serene physical beauty, they represent the pioneering values that have given our society so much of its originality. But on the heights looking down upon them with a rancorous vigilance were the Syrian gun emplacements and fortified positions of the Golan Heights.

When Syrian bombardments of our northern settlements were added to terrorist raids, our security predicament became acute. While Nasser, preoccupied with his Yemen adventure, managed to combine his verbal extremism with tactical prudence, Syria was determined to carry threats into acts.

While King Hussein of Jordan was being described by Nasser as "the Hashemite harlot," the "imperialist lackey" and the "treacherous dwarf," he obviously felt no incentive to join a Nasserist expedition against Israel. He managed generally to hold his ground with an independent policy against pressures by Cairo, Damascus and the terrorist groups. Sometimes, however, he lost control over the Palestinian groups, and in November 1966, the village of Samua near Hebron suffered havoc when Israeli forces moved to clean out terrorist bases.

Many uncomfortable questions were asked in the Israeli Knesset about the unanticipated severity of our raid. To me it appeared counterproductive. Our major enemy was Syria, and yet the impact of Israeli reprisals fell upon Jordan.

The advice that we were receiving from Washington and London was to exercise "restraint" and to use the United Nations as the platform for our protests and our quest for remedy. I attempted this on October 19 when I requested the Security Council to discuss murderous Syrian attacks. After many weeks of negotiation, a resolution was drafted criticizing Syria in such moderate terms as to appear almost deferential.

I secured the sponsorship of this resolution by representatives from five continents: Argentina, Japan, the Netherlands, New Zealand and Nigeria. All that it did was to express "regret" at infiltration from Syria and loss of human life caused by the incidents in October and November 1966. I didn't believe that the adoption of this text would have consoled widows or orphans in Israel. It would have saved no lives. At the most, it would have given our harassed nation the minimal comfort that comes from an enlightened human solidarity. But even this was denied: The Soviet Union vetoed the resolution on the grounds that it dared to imply an absence of total virtue among the bellicose colonels in Damascus.

Indeed, Soviet support of Syria was now our major regional preoccupation. I maintained correct personal relations with the Soviet ambassador, Dmitri Chuvakhin, and met at least once a year with Foreign Minister Gromyko. But Soviet-Israeli relations did not depend on what Israel did or said. It was a coldly calculated function of the Soviet policy in the Cold War.

Moscow thought, correctly, that it had more chance of enlisting the Arabs against the West than of mobilizing Israel to that cause.

Yet, at the beginning of May 1967, there was no premonition of war. I had returned from my tour of Southeast Asia in March, to find the country in a tranquil mood. Israelis realized, of course, that there would always be a quota of murderous infiltrations; now and then a flame of aggression would erupt and then subside, leaving some death and wreckage in its wake. This was the familiar rhythm. The special dignity of Israeli life comes from the large place that it gives to sacrifice. Israel lived intimately with danger, so that the very permanence of it had dulled its edge and generated a special adaptability to assault. It would become clear in the third week of May 1967 that we were going to face something radically different from the usual ebb and flow of intermittent violence. All possibilities, including the most unthinkable, would suddenly come into view.

The popular mood at home was favorable to a broad consolidation of Israel's international links. Criticism came only from a few areas of dissent. There were some in the opposition Herut Party who traditionally advocated military retaliation against most acts of Arab provocation. The Eshkol government's responses were more selective. Its object was to keep the Arab attacks within bounds while saving military strength and political sympathy for larger ordeals. Some of the leaders of Rafi (which had split from Mapai) still thought it possible to rely exclusively on France for Israel's air strength and were hesitant about expanding security ties with the United States. They also showed little sympathy for attempts to achieve a thaw in relations with Eastern Europe. The government, for its part, did not delude itself about the prospect, but believed that it was morally imperative to explore it. Setting its face against all restrictive orientations, the government's foreign policy aimed at a universal quest for friendship, commerce and understanding wherever they could be found. The strategy was plain: Instead of allowing Arab hostility to isolate Israel, the government would try to isolate Arab hostility until it choked for lack of sympathetic air.

Nothing in the early months of 1967 seemed to refute this prospect. The argument among Israeli experts and commentators was about whether Israel could count on a continuing respite for five years—or ten. At the beginning of the year, almost every Israeli political and military leader publicly predicted that 1967 would not be a year of out-and-out war. Israel, in this view, must "eventually" be destroyed; but the battle would be joined only when Arab armies were ready and when Arab unity was complete. The second condition seemed so remote that it seemed to convert the threat of Israel's annihilation into a theological idea. Nasser did not give up the dream of war. But while awaiting it, he would bide his time in safety. His fanaticism was sometimes tempered by empirical prudence: He had survived because he sometimes understood the valor of which discretion is the better part. If Syria had been content with a similar passivity, 1967—and the succeeding years— would have rolled on tense and rancorous, but without war.

The Moscow-Damascus equation was the heart of Israel's dilemma. The most violent and aggressive of Israel's adversaries operated against us from the vast shadow of Soviet protection. Syria could thus combine a heroic posture with an unheroic absence of risk. But when the Syrian prime minister declared in October 1966, "We shall set the whole region on fire," events were to prove him right. Israel could never predict at what part of its body the rash of violence would erupt. It could certainly expect no permanent relief from insecurity until Damascus underwent a change either of heart or ideology. Neither contingency seemed probable.

On March 13, 1966, the Syrian newspaper *Al Ba'ath* wrote:

The revolutionary forces of the Arab homeland, the Ba'ath at their head, preach a genuine Arab Palestine liberation on the soil of Palestine; and they have had enough of traditional methods. The Arab people demand armed struggle and day-to-day incessant confrontation through a total war of liberation in which all the Arabs will take part.

This became the central theme of Syrian policy in 1967, and no Arab government was prepared to speak or work against it. Looking back, I find it hard to understand why our Intelligence organizations persisted in predicting an absence of war. Their chief argument flowed from the fact that Syria had no armed forces capable of carrying out its threats and Arab disunity would not favor a convincing assault.

Most of the population lived those years in peace, with no constant sense of being physically threatened. There was, therefore, greater preoccupation with the country's internal problems.

Although most of my own interventions in the Cabinet were about foreign affairs, I participated in a growing concern about the domestic front. New problems had collected, and many of the attitudes on which the national unity had been based were no longer as secure as before. Austerity was no longer an ideal. The nation's resources were growing, but so also was its determination to live beyond them. Standards of consumption were rising faster than the rates of productivity. With the recession came a growth of unemployment. I could claim that the impact of the crisis was softened by two major achievements in Israel's foreign relations. The first was the maintenance of the American aid programs, which brought hundreds of millions of dollars of aid in grants and loans. The other was economic cooperation with the Federal Republic of Germany, based primarily on the investment of $700 million over twelve years, in addition to large sums devoted to the compensation of Holocaust victims. Thus, between 1955 and 1968 $1 billion reached Israel from Germany. The result was a growth of industrial energy and an improved balance of payments; there was also a sharp expansion of exports. But while the statistics looked good on paper, they did not reflect an egalitarian distribution of benefits. Social divisions were beginning to cause concern. The fact that immigrants from

Oriental countries were in the lower reaches of the economy gave a disquieting ethnic aspect to economic inequalities.

I would normally speak in the Cabinet on two themes: the social gap and the religious issue. Israeli society was now more sophisticated than before. The intimate family atmosphere had been transformed by urbanism and economic diversity. Israel was open to winds of opinion from outside, and the impact of years was breaking up the old patterns of thought and custom. The younger citizens of Israel had been raised in an atmosphere of sovereignty, and the heartrending nostalgia of Zionism did not speak to their hearts or their experience. They were sometimes impatient with the old ideological sanctities. Their way of thinking was concrete and pragmatic: They did not share their elders' passion for abstract ideas or social doctrines. Zionism, in their eyes, had fulfilled its aim and should now be left to the appraisal of history. The word even became the target for condescending jokes. Socialism, too, was all very well, but would have to be diluted in order to allow the growth of an industrialized economy, which demanded more freedom for competition and private enterprise. The test of a policy was not whether it conformed to doctrine, but whether it worked in practice. The Utopian vision of becoming a "light of the nations" seemed pretentious and burdensome to young people who thought that they had carried too many burdens already. Many of them would be satisfied with the more modest ambition of making Israel a decent, ordered, agreeable land in which to live.

Even in the kibbutzim, pioneering simplicity was no longer universal. As wealth increased, the buildings and gardens became more lavish. Some of the air-conditioned dining halls, cultural centers and coffee bars would have done credit to the fine hotels and summer resorts, which, incidentally, were also expanding in number and comfort in the hope of attracting and maintaining the tourist trade. The phrase "Espresso Generation" was coined to describe a youth that was prepared for sacrifice if necessary, but was insistent on living in ease and relative affluence if they were possible.

At the same time the new immigrants, especially from Oriental lands, were claiming their inheritance. As in all immigrant societies, there were genuine causes for social tension, but the main complication was psychological. During my stewardship of the education ministry I had explained that the gap between the new immigrants and the established population had been created not by Israel, but by the pre-state history of the Jewish people. History had sent some Jewish masses into countries where the economic and technological rhythm was dynamic and where liberalism provided at least occasional possibilities for Jews to share the general progress of ideas and material wealth. Others had been living for centuries in countries in which the result of the industrial and scientific revolutions had not been felt either by Jews or by anyone else. Thus Jews came to Israel with a gap of standards and capacities already built in. Israel always moved to eliminate the gaps, not to create them. But since the differences in educational standards lay at the heart of the problem, it was plain that the solution would have to be organic, and therefore not immediate. Those of us who described this condition were often portrayed by unscrupulous politicians and historians as snobs and elitists. I have never heard of a problem being solved without first being defined.

The social gap was a reality. It would not go away if we were silent about it. The nation's political and educational leaders drew satisfaction from the thought that it was becoming narrower; the immigrants saw only that it still remained. The special educational programs and institutions designed to elevate children above the conditions of their homes all showed a sensitive urgency for the problem of social integration. Nor was there a failure on the level of consciousness. In the early 1960s, Ben-Gurion and his ministers of finance, education and housing were thinking, planning and doing more about this problem than about any other. For some time it occupied the headlines as the chief item of national concern. But this did not mean that there was no emotional malaise. Social barriers existed. Ashkenazi and Sephardic Jews had derogatory epithets for each other that, at best, were used indulgently, at worst contemptuously. In one meeting I pointed out that "it is sometimes forgotten that Abraham was an Iraqi Jew and Moses an Egyptian Jew."

I took an active part in discussions on the place of religion. Israelis are unanimous in recognizing that their nation could not have been reborn without the persistence of religious memory and practice. Even the most secular nationalists pay tribute to the constancy with which the flame was kept alive against all attempts to extinguish it. To this extent the religious heritage is a unifying force. But the application of religious doctrine, the forms and institutions that expressed it, and the degree of compulsion that the state may properly enlist for its observance are all held in dispute.

The religious controversy was active throughout the period following the Sinai War. Orthodox Jews were in the minority, but their cohesion and zeal gave them a strong tactical position. Few governments or municipalities could form a leadership without them. They did their utmost to impose rabbinical law on the public sector. At the same time a spirit of pragmatism and scientific empiricism was seizing hold of the younger population. Religious disputes were waged in heated arguments and street demonstrations. As public Sabbath observance, transportation on Sabbath (especially in Jerusalem) was debated with a vehemence that surprised many foreign observers. In Jerusalem the discussion between the orthodox and the non-observant was polarized by a fanatical ultra-orthodox group, Neturei Karta, which believed that the State of Israel was conceived in original sin. It had preempted divine revelation by coming into existence through human decision, instead of awaiting the coming of the Messiah. The Neturei Karta treated the state as a hated occupying power and went on praying for the restoration of Zion, which "unfortunately" had already been restored. Sometimes the religious debate invaded the political arena.

Most of the parliamentary crises revolved around the question "who is a Jew?" The controversy arose out of the prosaic problems of registration. The question was whether a Jew, as most Israelis thought, should be defined as somebody who asserted his Jewish consciousness, or whether the condition was more rigid—the circumstance of having been born of a Jewish mother. No other people in the world constantly kept asking itself who it was and in what manner its identity should be defined. The fact is that by the mid-1960s Israel was less cohesive than it had been in its first decade. Israelis stood together for life and death, but in their less extreme ordeals they were conscious of the things that divided them.

In early May, I gave careful study to the reports from our military Intelligence. Their mood was one of complacency. The writers were impressed by the bewildering network of rivalries and antagonisms among Arab states. In my periodic consultations with the chiefs of Intelligence, I was told that our security preoccupation would, for some time, be limited to the need for coping with infiltration and violence from small groups. There was no existential threat.

We now know that this view took insufficient account of Soviet policy. There seemed to be a chain of mutual commitment among the U.S.S.R, Syria and Egypt to keep Israel under murderous harassment while protecting Syria from our reprisals. It was out of this tangled relationship that the war was to grow.

The fatal sequence began in April. The Syrians attacked Israeli farmers in the Galilee area. There was an exchange of fire. In an air engagement, six Syrian MiGs were brought down, two of them in the territory of Jordan, whose government made no attempt to hide its satisfaction. Even in Israel, the scale of the Syrian defeat was unexpected. In the Arab world, the response to Syria's humiliation ranged all the way from open derision in Jordan to embarrassed silence in Egypt. In fact, Nasser made an awkward attempt to point out that his commitment to aid Syria, if attacked, referred only to "sustained warfare" and not to "spasmodic incidents." There was little comfort for Syria here.

The April 7 air encounter had not been expensive in lives; no civilian suffering had been involved. We received congratulations in Paris, where the victory of the Mirage over the MiG had kindled technological pride.

The trouble was that Moscow had been irritated. The leadership in the Kremlin was disturbed by the fact that its "progressive" friends were always getting into trouble. Radical leaders, such as Ben-Bella in Algeria, Nkrumah in Ghana, and Sukarno in Indonesia, had been driven from power. Many countries in the Third World were asking if Soviet protection amounted to anything. In this atmosphere, the Soviet Union seemed to have decided to make the defense of the Syrian regime the foundation stone of a wider strategy.

On the other hand, direct Soviet intervention would have invited confrontation with the United States. It would be better for pressure to be exercised on Israel by somebody else.

In April 1967, the Soviet leadership began a policy of intrigue that would have astonished Iago in his conspiracy against Othello. The Soviet ambassador, observing the elation in Israel after the shooting down of the MiGs, told me, in words to which perhaps we should have given more attention, "You seem to be celebrating your victory of April 7, but I tell you frankly, before long you will regret your success."

Infiltrations and attacks from Syrian territory multiplied. It would be an exaggeration to say that there was a collapse of public order. But Israel is a small and close-knit society. Personal grief afflicting a kibbutz or a suburb invades the whole public mood. I regarded this Syrian terrorism as an early stage of malignancy. It could not be left alone.

We began with defensive remedies by mine fields and barbed wire. We would then interpose a stage of verbal warnings to Syria, before military action was considered. Only if all of this failed, force would be used to punish and deter. Even then, it would be swift and of limited scope, leaving the existing borders intact.

My attempts to enlist the Soviet Union to restrain Syrian violence provoked such bizarre results that it became difficult to take them seriously. Ambassador Chuvakhin had two ways of explaining the Syrian assaults: First, he reflected that the Israeli victims of terrorism were blowing themselves to pieces in a cunning attempt to create an atmosphere of Syrian-Israeli hostility. On one occasion, he came to my office and asked me "to give serious consideration to the possibility that agents of the CIA and of the American oil interests, disguised as Palestinian infiltrators from Syria, were laying mines on Israeli roads in order to provoke Israel into retaliation, which would weaken the regime of Damascus."

In my reply, I invited the ambassador to "give serious consideration" to a less complex idea; namely, that when the Syrians and terrorists said that they were laying the mine fields, they really were. I added, hopefully, "If it were made clear to the Syrians that the Soviet Union opposes terrorist acts, it is quite probable that they would be stopped."

This was about the last thing that the Soviet Union intended to "make clear." Since Israeli responses to Syrian violence weakened the Damascus regime, which the Kremlin wished to protect, Moscow had another bright idea. It would attempt to get Egypt to accept the burden of protecting Syria against the consequences of its own aggression.

On May 12 and 13, in Moscow, an Egyptian parliamentary delegation had been told to expect "an Israeli invasion of Syria immediately after Independence Day, with the aim of overthrowing the Damascus regime." The head of the Egyptian parliamentary group was the president of the national council, Anwar Sadat.

Later in the month of May, when we were visibly on the verge of war, Nasser frankly explained his military actions in terms of Soviet advice. His announcement on May 22 of the decision to blockade the Straits of Tiran included these sentences, which are full of significance for the historian:

On May 13, we received accurate information that Israel was concentrating on the Syrian border huge armed forces of about 11 to 13 brigades. These forces were divided into two fronts; one south of Lake Tiberias and one north of the Lake. The decision made by Israel at the time was to carry out an attack on Syria, starting on May 17. On May 14, we took action, discussed the matter, and contacted our Syrian brothers. The Syrians also had this information.

In discussions with the Soviet ambassador, I decided to rely on my personal impressions of what was happening in the area. On May 11, in the atmosphere of spring and imminent independence celebrations, Suzy and I had toured our northern boundary. The green landscape lay beneath the warm Israeli sun, bathed in total repose. The officer commanding the North, General David Elazar, took us around his area of jurisdiction. I expressed great concern to him about the absence of any visible Israeli military presence. When Chuvakhin was ranting to Eshkol and me about Israeli troop concentrations, Eshkol invited the Soviet ambassador to take his military attaché on an unannounced tour of the northern border in search of "the eleven to thirteen brigades," which Moscow had declared to be concentrated there. The ambassador's genial response was that his function was to communicate Soviet truths, not to put them to a test.

At this stage, Israeli rhetoric entered the picture. On May 14, all our major newspapers carried interviews with General Rabin, the chief of staff, warning "Damascus" of the consequences that would arise from continued terrorist attacks. At Independence Day meetings, most Israeli public figures made the conventional speeches of defiance. I thought at the time, and still more intensely at a later date, that if there had been a little more Israeli silence, the sum of human wisdom would probably have remained intact.

On May 11, our military Intelligence briefed foreign military attachés in terms that they understood to augur a major assault by Syria in the coming days. Rabin had stated that the key to a tranquil frontier lay "in Damascus." His obvious meaning was that only the government of Syria could take the necessary preventive action. The interpretation, disseminated by the Soviet Union, was that Israel meant to capture an Arab capital!

In the heady atmosphere of those times, even the moderate Prime Minister Eshkol could not abstain from shaking a threatening fist. "There will be no immunity for any state which aids or abets Syrian infiltration and sabotage."

There is no room for doubt that the "information" supplied by the Soviet Union on May 13 was the proximate cause of the 1967 war. The nineteenth anniversary of the Declaration of Independence was celebrated on a low key with a modest parade in Jerusalem. It was decided not to display our most effective weaponry. The objective was to avoid increased tension. As the troops marched past, bathed in the affection of the crowd, a messenger went to the podium and to the central part of the stadium. He quietly put a piece of paper in the hands of Prime Minister Eshkol and General Rabin, who were taking the salute. He then came to me and handed me a copy.

The report was brief. Large Egyptian forces were moving into Sinai and advancing westward. Rumors were spreading in Cairo that President Nasser was about to order the removal of the United Nations Emergency Force that had been stationed in Gaza and the entry to the Straits of Tiran since 1957. This would produce the precise situation that we had described ten years before as justifying Israel's exercise of its "inherent right of self-defense."

As I hurried back to my office I knew that the decade of peaceful consolidation had ended. . . .

18

TO LIVE OR PERISH: 1967

THE INDEPENDENCE DAY parade on May 15, 1967, had been a rather subdued occasion. Without the glitter of planes and tanks, there was a lean aspect to our infantry columns. The message about Egyptian movements into Sinai and Nasser's intention to order the withdrawal of the UN force dispelled all celebratory feeling. The press was now giving the public the same hard tidings that Eshkol, Rabin and I had received during the parade. The pattern of stability established in 1957 after the Sinai War was now beginning to collapse.

For a whole decade since 1957, shipping had passed freely through the Straits of Tiran and there had not been a single clash between Egyptian and Israeli forces. *Fedayeen* infiltrations from Gaza had also ceased. The wanton irresponsibility of Nasser's action defies indulgence. It must have been one of the most unprovoked actions in international history. No Egyptian or Arab interest had been injured by the arrangements made at Gaza or Sharm el-Sheikh in 1957.

The Arab press that I studied in my office after the military parade was still claiming that since Israel's main weaponry had not been displayed in the exercise, it must have been concentrated in the North, poised to conquer Damascus. In the unique atmosphere of the Arab-Israeli conflict, it is often impossible to do anything right.

My office in the Foreign Ministry was bleakly empty because of the national holiday, except for security duty officers. I had nobody with whom to share my anxiety. One Intelligence message told me that Mahmud Fawzi, the Egyptian army chief of staff, had flown to Damascus the previous day to coordinate military plans with the Syrian government. One of the most effective false alarms in history was doing its work. Egypt was poised to forestall an Israeli "assault" on Damascus that had never been intended, or even conceived.

The Sinai news was also ominous. Egyptian infantry and armored units had crossed the Suez Canal and were moving into Sinai with ostentatious publicity. Large convoys were deliberately being routed through Cairo's busiest streets on their way to Ismailia, whence they would advance toward Israel. The Egyptian parliamentary delegation led by Anwar Sadat had returned to Cairo from Moscow, fed with Soviet "information" about Israel's imminent "plan to conquer Syria."

And yet the reports from our own military Intelligence were still relatively serene. They stressed that although war had become possible, it was not yet inevitable. In Washington and London, Israeli diplomats were being told that the Egyptian troop movements were only "demonstrative" and without military intent. Officials in both capitals reminded us how in February 1960, after some clashes across the Syrian-Israeli boundary, similar movements had been made by Egyptian armies in Sinai. Yet a few weeks later, they had returned to their bases west of the Suez Canal. The Western consensus was that Israel faced a political maneuver rather than a military threat. Even the skeptical Israeli military staff tended to attach some credence to these appraisals.

My own anxiety was not allayed. What concerned me most was the outburst of emotion that accompanied the military threat. A torrent of invective against Israel poured from all the radio stations in the Arab world. Iraq, Jordan and Lebanon declared states of alert. Martial music was being played on the Egyptian radio. It seemed that Nasser was making a commitment to his nation to challenge Israel in war. This message was also causing delighted reactions among Arab masses far from the scene. With so many hot words in the air, I feared that even a demonstrative intention could pass into active folly.

And so it did. On the morning of May 16, the commander of the United Nations Emergency Force (UNEF), Major General I. J. Rikhye, of the Indian Army, received a message from General Fawzi, the Egyptian chief of staff, asking for the withdrawal of all UN forces along Egypt's borders. The reason given was that the Egyptian armed forces had been ordered "to prepare to go into action against Israel, in case and whenever it launches an act of aggression against any Arab country."

The first UN reaction was formalistic. U Thant had written that a letter from one general to another could not induce the political leadership of the United Nations to act. But he added that if he received a request in proper form, he would order the removal of the force. The pedantic requirement was soon satisfied. The secretary-general received a cable from the Egyptian Foreign Minister Mahmoud Riad, telling him that the Egyptian government had decided to "terminate the presence of the UN emergency force in Egypt and the Gaza Strip."

May 16 and 17 were the most astonishing days in the history of international institutions. U Thant without any serious prior consultation had promised to remove one of the few safety valves that had prevented explosion for ten years. He had added in a note to the Egyptian foreign minister that "a request by Cairo for a temporary withdrawal from the armistice demarcation line and the international front, or from any parts of them, would be considered by the secretary-general as tantamount to a request for the complete withdrawal of UNEF from Gaza and Sinai."

This statement created a dramatic situation for Egypt, Israel and the world. In the unending debate on the origins of the 1967 war, four points concerning U Thant's May 16 letter have received justified criticism.

First, it was a decision of unparalleled speed. It was delivered seventy-five minutes after receipt of the letter to which it made reply. Nothing of the kind had ever happened before. Ironically, the UN had previously built a reputation for excessive bureaucratic delay. That would have been providentially welcome in this case.

Second, U Thant's decision had been taken before consultation with Israel or with the governments that contributed troops to the force. The UN representatives of those countries were not convened formally until the late afternoon.

Third, the determination that a request for partial withdrawal would be "tantamount to a request for complete withdrawal" had never been endorsed by any international organ. Why should the secretary-general have ruled out a face-saving compromise that would have left a smaller force in sensitive areas such as Gaza and Sharm el-Sheikh?

Fourth, the secretary-general's letter contained no appeal to Egypt to reconsider its formal request until all the implications could be reviewed. We shall, of course, never know if President Nasser would have responded to such a request. Nothing could have been lost by making it.

I now felt that all lenient explanations for the Egyptian troop action had been shattered. Nasser may well have been surprised by U Thant's swift acceptance of the removal of UNEF. By the time that he conferred with the Israeli representative, Ambassador Gideon Rafael, and with delegates of the major powers and of his own advisory committee, U Thant had already committed UN action in advance. Two representatives in the advisory committee, those of Canada and Brazil, urged him to temporize without denying the juridical validity of Egypt's request. But it was too late for any maneuver.

No action by the United Nations has ever been more contentiously discussed by governments, the world press and public opinion. The United States, the United Kingdom and Canada, as well as Israel, expressed their disquiet. The secretary-general argued that he had no alternative in law except to accede to a request rooted in Egypt's sovereign rights. He also pointed out that countries that supplied contingents would have acceded to the Egyptian request whatever the secretary-general said or did. This applied especially to Yugoslavia and India, whose soldiers accounted for more than half of the force, and whose governments had decided to accept Egypt's expulsion order irrespective of what the secretary-general chose to do. Later, when Nasser asserted that he had not expected U Thant to act on his request, the secretary-general could attribute this self-serving statement to the retrospective wisdom of a defeated warrior. But it was the speed and indifference to consequence with which he acted that stunned the world.

There was also an element of contractual infidelity on the part of the UN. It was natural for my mind to go back to early February 1957, when the United Nations had discussed the very situation that had now come to pass. I had asked U.S. Secretary of State John Foster Dulles if it was conceivable that the UN force would be withdrawn so suddenly as to create a vulnerable situation for Israel. He had replied that this was theoretically possible but in practical terms "almost inconceivable." In my directive to Ambassador Rafael on May 17, I had asked him to remind U Thant of a specific commitment that his predecessor had given us in 1957, without which it would have been impossible to secure our withdrawal from the Straits of Tiran and Gaza. Hammarskjöld had acknowledged that since the stationing of UNEF had been a factor in inducing Israel to withdraw, there was "in the moral sense, a kind of bilateral agreement between Egypt and Israel." In an August 5, 1958, document Hammarskjöld had said:

> It would be obvious that the procedure in case of a request from Egypt for the withdrawal of U.N.E.F. would be as follows. The matter would at once be brought before the General Assembly. If the General Assembly found that the task of U.N.E.F. was completed, everything would be all right. If they found that the task was not completed, and Egypt all the same, maintained its position, and enforced the withdrawal, Egypt would be breaking the agreement with the United Nations. I showed this text to [Egyptian Foreign Minister] Fawzi at our first talk on November 16, and discussed this issue with Nasser for seven hours, on the evening and night of November 17 [1956].

Hammarskjöld had added that "if a difference should develop, the matter would be brought up for negotiation with the United Nations."

When Ambassador Rafael reported to Jerusalem on his conversations with U Thant on May 17 and 18, it became clear that Hammarskjöld's stipulations had been ignored by his successor. Predictions that had sounded reasonable at the time and had been effective for a full decade had now gone by default. We had never assumed that the UN force could have served permanently. The theory had been that a prolonged situation on the ground would create a de facto reality that no party would have reason to disrupt. Hammarskjöld had said that there would be "an opportunity to turn around and reappraise" a request for withdrawal. No such opportunity was given. The United States, which had inspired the March 1957 settlement for Israeli withdrawal, had said through Ambassador Cabot Lodge in February 1957 that it was "essential" for the UN force to remain at Sharm el-Sheikh and

Gaza until its removal would not give rise to belligerency. It was now going to be removed when its removal would certainly lead to war.

It was in this context that I later said in the Security Council that the United Nations Emergency Force had been treated by the secretary-general "as a fire brigade which would be withdrawn at the first smell of smoke and the first sight of fire."

This metaphor involved me in a bitter running controversy with U Thant over the next few weeks. I have never changed my mind on this question. I had persistently drawn U Thant's attention to the motive that Egypt had invoked for its decision to remove the UNEF. General Fawzi had written, in effect, that he was asking for the withdrawal of the UN forces in order to enable Egypt to wage war, and the UN secretary-general was acceding to the request in the name of international legality. U Thant's exclusive concentration on the legal aspect of the problem showed a false sense of priorities. A more courageous secretary-general could have said that his intention to respect Egypt's legal position was firm, but that he had an equal or even greater and more overriding obligation to ensure that the result would not threaten international peace and security. If the secretary-general had no power to refuse the Egyptian request, he should surely have tried to exact binding undertakings against the resumption of active belligerency. Any time thus gained for discussion could have been crucial. There is evidence that on May 17 Nasser was not irrevocably set on confrontation. A temporary withdrawal of UN forces from most of Sinai, leaving the force in Gaza and Sharm el-Sheikh for international appraisal, did not seem impossible. After all, U Thant himself had reported to the General Assembly in December 1966 that "this force has been an important factor in maintaining relative quiet of the area of its deployment during the past ten years, and its withdrawal may have grave implications for peace." Should not an action "having grave implications for peace" be given time for consideration?

Even after the secretary-general's action I still felt that war might be avoided. After all, no act of war would have actually been committed until Nasser imposed the blockade in the Straits of Tiran. I therefore endorsed a suggestion from Ambassador Rafael at the United Nations that U Thant visit Cairo to explore Nasser's intentions. The visit itself might slow down the dynamism of Egyptian action during the time spent by the secretary-general in Cairo. If U Thant could set out while the UN force was still in its positions at Sharm el-Sheikh, his journey might freeze the situation and give Nasser a last opportunity to stay his hand.

Even this avenue of constructive procrastination was soon blocked. The Egyptian government gave brutal advice to U Thant on May 18 not to go to Cairo until he was invited. By now Nasser's course was set.

Nevertheless, our own government was still indefatigable in its effort to avoid war. It decided not to regard war as inevitable unless or until Nasser actually closed the Straits to Israeli shipping and cargoes. We had received a letter from British Prime Minister Harold Wilson to Prime Minister Eshkol:

I am on public record as saying that the Straits of Tiran constitute an international waterway which should remain open to the ships of all nations. If it appeared that any attempt to interfere with the passage of ships through the waterway was likely to be made, we should promote and support international action through the United Nations to secure free passage. We stand by this statement. We think it important, however, that attention should be concentrated on free passage and not on the shore positions. If we are to give you the international support we wish, it must be based on your undoubted rights.

I instructed Ambassador Remez to say to Harold Wilson: "Our decision is: Unless attacked, we shall not move against the Egyptian forces unless or until they attempt to close the Straits to shipping bound for Israel. They have not done so."

A letter conveying the same attitude was cabled by Prime Minister Eshkol to President de Gaulle. In my accompanying note to Ambassador Eytan in Paris, I wrote that despite this demonstration of patience, Israel's intention not to acquiesce in the blockade was solid and unreserved and Nasser should not have any illusions.

It was necessary, as a matter of routine, to bring the Soviet Union into the process. I therefore invited Ambassador Chuvakhin to see me on May 19. He "informed" me that the crisis had resulted from the aggressive propaganda of the Israeli government and especially the speeches of its leaders against Arab states, notably Syria. He referred in particular to statements by senior Israeli military officers on May 11 and thereafter. He repeated his warning that the entire responsibility for the crisis rested on Israel. When I suggested that he might give his attention to the Egyptian troop concentrations and the acts of sabotage from Syrian territory, he replied that "these matters are not within my competence." As for UNEF, its presence on the territory of any state, said Chuvakhin, depended on the free consent of that state, which had full power to demand its removal at any time.

If any of the major powers addressed strong admonitions to Cairo between May 14 and May 22, their efforts are still unknown. Western policy was correct in substance but lacked incisiveness and urgency. On May 18 President Johnson wrote to Eshkol: "I am sure you will understand that I cannot accept any responsibilities on behalf of the United States for situations which arise as the result of actions on which we are not consulted." Two days later, the United States informed us that they and their friends had done all that they could to "make amply clear both to Cairo and Damascus that there is an urgent need for the cessation of terrorism and the reversal of military movements of the type which we have witnessed during the past week." Assistant Secretary Eugene Rostow found it necessary to inform us that, in strictly legal terms, the Egyptian forces had the right to be anywhere on Egyptian territory that the Egyptian government desired.

On May 21, it was still not easy to calculate what Nasser's precise intentions were. I believed that at that stage, he himself was moving step by step, testing the ground with each advance. He may have been surprised at the lack of restraining obstacles. The ease with which he had sent the United Nations force packing must have led him to believe that it was less dangerous to violate Israel's vital interests than he had ever believed. Actions that he might previously have avoided as fraught with penalty were now reaping uninterrupted success. Above all, they went forward in complete impunity. Might not Western support of Israel's security be more a fiction than a reliable fact? Prospects that but a short time ago had seemed unattainable had now come exhilaratingly within his view.

Events in Israel may have contributed to Nasser's recklessness. Our parliamentary and party relationships were tense. The Rafi Party, led by Dayan and Peres and strongly supported by a disgruntled Ben-Gurion, was engaged in virulent defamation of Levi Eshkol. The Rafi leaders were spreading the idea that Israel, under Levi Eshkol, would not react appropriately to any military threat. Eshkol was accused, satirized and lampooned with uninhibited ferocity. There was an ugly violence in the political dialogue, and the heat of criticism made human relationships shrivel up.

There was now an attempt to depose the prime minister. On May 21 an article appeared in the evening paper, *Yediot Aharonot,* revealing that secret consultations had taken place between Menachem Begin and Shimon Peres about the establishment of a national government to be headed by Ben-Gurion. The two opposition leaders seemed to be under the illusory impression that Ben-Gurion would be more likely to resist Arab aggression than would Eshkol. The truth was that Ben-Gurion was in an uncharacteristically defeatist mood. Menachem Begin, unaware of this new reality, courteously suggested to Eshkol that he vacate the premiership and serve under Ben-Gurion. When Eshkol vehemently refused, Begin reacted calmly and his relations with Eshkol were unaffected.

I knew from our Intelligence reports that the Soviet embassy in Tel Aviv was reporting that the Eshkol government did not have the domestic authority for a decision involving war. If Nasser and his Soviet allies believed sincerely that Israel's support from the Western powers was hesitant and that the Israeli government was not capable of a strong military posture, it becomes easier to explain the audacity with which they now proceeded. Nasser was playing for higher stakes than he had thought possible a short while before. Fortune had been kind to him; why should he not bask in its smile? He may well have passed within a few days from an intention to impose a humiliating blockade to a dream of Israel's total defeat.

My own view was that Begin and Peres would have been better employed in trying to get Nasser out of Sharm el-Sheikh than in trying to get Eshkol out of the prime minister's office. It later became apparent to both of them that Ben-Gurion was in a far less militant mood than Eshkol and was not in favor of immediate response to Nasser's aggressive pressures.

Amid all this confusion, one thing was not in any doubt either in the government or in the opposition parties. If the blockade was actually imposed, we would fight Egypt on every front. The juridical implication of a blockade would be that Nasser did not recoil from an active state of war. Submission by Israel to a blockade of the Straits of Tiran would not only compromise our legal position and our economic interest. It would mean the collapse of Israel's deterrent power, for there was no issue in which Israel had pledged its honor in more irrevocable terms. A nation that could not protect its basic maritime interests would presumably find reasons for not repelling other assaults on its rights. Unless a stand was made here, nobody in the Arab world and few people beyond it would ever again believe in Israel's power to resist.

U Thant now clutched at a straw. He stressed that UNEF operated only on the Egyptian side of the Armistice Line. In the alarm created by the collapse of the UN force in Sinai and Gaza, the UN Secretariat and some friendly powers canvassed the possibility of stationing UNEF on Israeli territory.

There is no validity for the view that this step would have had any bearing at all on the 1967 crisis. The UNEF had always been related to a specific geographical context. It had relevance to Sharm el-Sheikh and Gaza and to nowhere else. The memorandum handed to me by Secretary Dulles on February 11, 1957, had made it plain that the objective was to prevent belligerency in the two places, land and sea, that had a particular international sensitivity. If that presence were liquidated and a blockade were imposed in the Straits, what alleviation could ever be found by having UNEF contingents at Haifa or at Ashdod? Similarly, Gaza had been the breeding ground and springboard for terrorist incursions into Israel. There was no similar area under Israeli rule from which guerrilla fighters had the will or capacity to penetrate Egyptian territory for sabotage and murder. If UNEF were absent from Gaza, no compensation could be found in its presence elsewhere.

If anything, Israel's peril would have been aggravated. Egyptian troops would have concentrated in battle formations in Sinai and terrorists would have assembled in Gaza, while Israel's capacity to resist would have been complicated by the presence of international contingents with no authority or power to act. The idea of hurriedly sending the UN force into Israel was an alibi, not a solution. It was like curing a man's broken leg by putting his arm into a sling.

I was becoming increasingly alarmed by indications of a weak reaction in Washington. On May 22, Ambassador Harman told Assistant Secretary Lucius Battle of my instructions that if Nasser were to believe that the United

States' attitude was as indicated in Mr. Rostow's remark about Egypt's legal rights, he would regard this as an invitation to interfere with shipping in the Straits. When our ambassador pressed for an assurance that the United States had warned Nasser specifically against closing the Straits, he was informed that it was deemed "preferable" to delay any further bilateral action until Secretary-General Thant had reached Cairo.

Yet the door was left open for Nasser's retreat until the very end. On May 22 Prime Minister Eshkol addressed him from the Knesset rostrum. The speech was firm but unprovocative. It said that Israel planned no attack on Arab countries, did not seek to undermine their security or to attack their territory and did not challenge their legitimate international rights. Eshkol added that there was no shred of truth in talk of Israeli concentrations on the Syrian frontier. Israel, he said, was still ready to participate in an effort to reinforce stability and advance peace in our region. But, he added, "Israel's army is ready for any trial and the nation's rights will be defended."

Not that the defense was yet adequately prepared. On May 21 General Rabin, the chief of staff, accompanied by Colonel Efrat, had come to my Jerusalem home to discuss what seemed to be the certainty of an early Egyptian move into Sharm el-Sheikh. Moshe Raviv was with me, taking notes. Rabin was very tense, smoking without interruption. He pointed out that Israel's military preparedness for the past ten years had always been related to the Syrian and Jordanian fronts, with less attention to the South. The Egyptian Army had not come back to Gaza in the wake of the Egyptian administration. The United Nations force had been effective not because of any real military capacity, but simply because the thousands of Norwegians, Canadians and others filled the space and made any surreptitious infiltrations difficult. Moreover, the very act of Egypt in accepting the UN force indicated that it was not looking for trouble with Israel in the near future. Rabin told me frankly that we were very thin on the ground in the South.

When I asked what the diplomatic establishment could do to help the army he said, with a deep sigh, "Time, time, time!" He repeated this word three times. We needed time to reinforce the South.

His analysis was candid and realistic. What disconcerted me was his somber demeanor and the impression of a dark, brooding anxiety that went beyond what citizens would expect of a military leadership that would soon have to face grave ordeals.

In subsequent weeks and months a legend would emerge telling our people and the world that our military commanders were straining at the leash from the very beginning and were held back only by the restraining hands of the prime minister and the minister for foreign affairs. This was certainly untrue about the situation at any time during the month of May. Between the Independence Day parade on May 15 and Nasser's blockade announcement on May 22, the army had been no less insistent than the government on exhausting every rational method of avoiding war. Whether this would have been its attitude if it had anticipated the eventual military result is an open question.

Israel has never worked harder to prevent a war than it did to prevent the war that turned out to be the most victorious of all campaigns.

International apathy now created a vacuum in which the hope of peace could no longer breathe. If the flight of the powers from their commitments was implicit and private, the abdication of the UN was explicit and overt. The Security Council was not disposed to act. The Soviet and Arab delegations did not consider that the body charged with the maintenance of "international peace and security" should occupy itself with such trivialities as the threat of one member state to destroy another state by encirclement, blockade and ultimate military assault.

Meanwhile, the UN action was centered on the secretary-general. Many precious days had gone by since his journey to the Middle East had first been proposed by Ambassador Rafael and endorsed by United States Ambassador Arthur Goldberg. Each day the sand ran swift through the deadly hourglass. By the time that Nasser allowed U Thant to reach Cairo on May 22, the expulsion of UNEF was an accomplished fact. The Egyptian troop concentrations were ominous in scale and all international presence had been banished from what U Thant himself in a report of May 19 had described as "the two sensitive points of Gaza and Sharm el-Sheikh." Above all, Nasser's arrogance was riding high. His ruthless pressure on Israel was evoking strong indignation in public opinion but a careful deference among governments. U Thant's voyage on May 22, as an effort in international restraint, had become too little and too late. By the time his plane reached Paris he heard Nasser's speech confirming the blockade in the Gulf of 'Aqaba. His first thought was to turn back. It was a salutary impulse but was not carried through.

Neither U Thant nor any of his predecessors had ever been treated like this. The careful synchronization between permission for his journey and the cold destruction of its purpose ranks high in modern history among acts of international contempt and treachery. There was a Pearl Harbor aspect about it. All Nasser's attributes were at work here: smiling furtiveness; the slick maneuverability; the innocent face put on mendacity. The United Nations was the victim of a confidence trick pursued with fine perfection on an international scale.

There would be an ironic sequel. In May Nasser was telling the United Nations to keep its nose out of his affairs. By mid-June he would be screaming desperately for the UN's bold and rapid intervention.

I have a vivid memory of the early dawn on May 23 when, a little after 5:00 in the morning, my telephone rang. A minute later I knew that nothing in our country's life and history would ever be the same. There was no audible emotion in the voice from Army Headquarters in Tel Aviv. It reported to me dryly that Nasser had announced the closure of the Gulf of Nastier and the Straits of Tiran to Israeli shipping and to all other vessels bound for Israel with "strategic materials" aboard.

By 6:00 all my senior advisers in the Foreign Ministry were assembled in my downstairs living room. They found me listening to a transistor radio over which Nasser's words were coming in a strident shout. It was clear that he was totally resolved to have his war and to be satisfied with nothing less. He had written years before of "a hero's role searching for an actor to play it." Now the dream would unfold with himself in the central part and with the whole world as a stage. He spoke in a halting voice but in full Arabic literary form:

We are in confrontation with Israel. In contrast to what happened in 1956, when France and Britain were at its side, Israel is not supported today by any European power. It is possible, however, that America might come to its aid. The United States supports Israel politically and provides it with arms and military material. But the world will not accept any repetition of 1956. We are face-to-face with Israel. Henceforward the situation, my gallant soldiers, is in your hands. Our armed forces have occupied Sharm el-Sheikh. We shall on no account allow the Israeli flag to pass through the Gulf of Nastier. The Jews threaten to make war. I reply, "ahlan wasahlan," welcome. We are ready for war: this water is ours.

This speech had been made to officers at the Egyptian air base at Bir Gafgafa in Sinai, one hundred miles from our southwestern border. The commanders of this airfield, and of others, were receiving operation orders listing the targets in Israel that they were to attack. To their valor and efficiency, yet unproved, Nasser had committed the outcome of his most daring gamble. He owed them whatever a leader's authority could do to enlarge and galvanize their powers. But far beyond his fervent audience in the baking desert heat he was appealing to the whole domain of Arabism, calling its sons to such display of union, sacrifice, hate, resilience and selfless passion as they had not shown since the ferocious days of their early history. His declaration of war was unique in one respect. It contained not a single specific charge or grievance against Israel. After all, there had been no collision of forces, no spark of active violence between Egypt and Israel for ten full years. This was beside the point. In Nasser's view Israel's mere existence was an offense that could only be expiated by destruction. The macabre vision of Israel's demise had been nourished in dreams and rhetoric during all the years of his rule. Now, suddenly, the dream seemed ripe for fulfillment.

I noted that what had brought it within reach was Israel's apparent solitude. Nasser had always pretended to believe that Israel's successes were the result of intervention or sustaining influence by external powers. In his logic it was obvious that if Israel were now alone it would not be able to make a drastic decision. Nasser never sought to probe the sources of Israel's autonomous vitality. Once he had scanned the international prospect and found no ally at Israel's side, his course seemed plain. Turning his back on a whole decade of prudence, he now uttered a courtly and exalted welcome to the approaching war: "ahlan wasahlan," welcome, as if he was greeting the unexpected appearance of a beloved and long-absent guest.

Our consultation within the ministry was brief. Messages came from the prime minister's office calling me to the Defense Ministry in Tel Aviv. As I made the familiar journey I looked through the window and saw drivers in passing vehicles giving me gestures of anxiety. Only a few weeks before, the national mood had been as close to normalcy as could be expected of a people born in war and nurtured in siege. As green countryside and white buildings sped past my window I was gripped by a sharp awareness of the fragility of all cherished things.

My car drew up at the Ministry of Defense in Tel Aviv. I saw no cheerful faces around the table. It was not an official Cabinet session. The prime minister had asked for the leaders of major parties and the military commanders to join our councils. General Rabin, Air Force General Ezer Weizmann, and Chief of Military Intelligence General Aharon Yariv were there. Helicopters were swarming all around us bringing ministers and army commanders in their ones and twos. Eshkol solved the emotional problem by a deliberate understatement: "We have news on the political front. I don't know if all of you have heard it. It requires consultation and probably action as well."

In order to achieve a bipartisan atmosphere Prime Minister Eshkol had invited members of Parliament and ex-ministers from opposition parties. Those who attended the talk on May 23 were the following members of Parliament: Golda Meir (then secretary-general of the Labor Party), David Hacohen, Moshe Dayan, Shimon Peres, Menachem Begin, Arieh Ben-Eliezer, Caim Landau, Elimelech Rimalt, Yosef Serlin, Yosef Almogi and, among the non-members of Parliament, Shaul Avigur, a respected Haganah veteran.

The military reports by General Rabin and his Intelligence chief, General Aharon Yariv, did not end with any pressure for immediate military action. Egyptian airfields in Sinai were being made ready but their technical preparedness was still deficient. Nothing yet moved on the Jordan front, where Israel's policy would focus on an attempt to keep Jordanian participation at bay. Strangely the Syrians, who had lit the flames of the impending war with their violent rhetoric, now seemed to be recoiling from their own heat. The most significant reports were those that described the ecstatic mood sweeping over the Arab world. Masses of people, long elated by dreams of vengeance, were now screaming for Israel's blood. There was no doubt that the howling mobs in Cairo, Damascus and Baghdad, and even more ominously from the Old City of Jerusalem, were seeing savage visions of murder and booty. Israel had learned from Jewish history that no outrage against its people was inconceivable. Memories of the European slaughter were taking form and substance in countless Israeli hearts. They flowed into our room like turgid air and sat heavy on all our lives.

Rabin expressed confidence in ultimate victory but warned that there would be "no walk-over." He pointed out how adversely different our situation was compared with that of 1956. Israel had then been flanked by two supporting major powers, Britain and France, and Egypt was the only enemy. This time, Israel would be alone while Egypt might have Syria, Jordan and contingents from other Arab countries at its side and the Soviet Union in full political support. Our military advisers would not make any comforting predictions about the scale of losses that we would have to endure before our victory. Their realistic words left a chilly aftermath. I was asked to speak early. I said that if we did not break the ring of blockade and encirclement, our deterrent power would be destroyed and our international position brought to ruin. There was thus no place for a doctrine of peace at any price. The only alternative to war would be Nasser's retreat. If he could be brought to withdraw, it was doubtful if he could survive. The question was not whether we must resist but whether we should resist alone or seek the support and understanding of others.

I added, "If the Soviet Union has in fact provoked a war, are we sure that it will agree to lose it?" I thought that we had no right to evade this question. Our predicament was international, not regional. If my colleagues believed with me that the Soviet Union had triggered this war and would seek to make it victorious, we must look across the Atlantic toward the only power that could neutralize the Russian danger. Washington must be brought to a less passive mood than that which we had observed in its demeanor so far.

I now turned to an analysis of Western reaction. I pointed out that although France had taken the most vigorous stand of all in defense of our maritime rights in 1957, all my messages to Paris had gone unanswered for several days. Washington, on the other hand, was in movement. The minister in our embassy, Ephraim (Eppie) Evron, had been called to the State Department at midnight on May 22 to 23 to discuss Nasser's speech. He had been told that President Johnson was sending urgent messages to Cairo, Damascus and Moscow urging deescalation of troop movements and respect for free navigation. In the meantime the State Department urged us to abstain from unilateral action—at least for some days. Israel was asked to make no decision for forty-eight hours and during that respite to take counsel with the United States. We were hearing the irritating refrain that the president would take no responsibility for actions on which he had not been consulted.

These were disquieting echoes of 1956. I said that the existing American attitude was not a sound basis on the strength of which we should face the risks of a lonely military action. We needed a better understanding of our predicament than that which had so far been expressed in their statements. I referred to the 1956 experience when we had been victorious in battle but had then faced immense American pressure, which had made it difficult to reap the fruits of victory.

I could feel that this reference to the 1956 Sinai experience carried more weight than any consideration outside the military calculation. Eshkol passed me a note saying "that is the main point."

Not a single voice was raised at the May 23 meeting in favor of immediate military response. Some participants had suggested that although the Straits of Tiran had been the occasion for the outbreak of war, we did not necessarily have to make that area our main priority. One of our advisers proposed an attack on the Egyptians advancing toward Gaza or in Northern Sinai. My own opinion was that any operation, however successful, that left Nasser in command of the Straits of Tiran would be a strategic failure even if it was a tactical success. Any other attack would be absorbed and shrugged off. I thought that if Nasser remained in possession of the southern key to Israel his political triumph could not be offset by any physical blows elsewhere.

The finance minister, Pinhas Sapir, said that the forty-eight hours would probably become seventy-two hours or more. The head of the Religious Party, Interior Minister Moshe Chaim Shapira, made a concrete procedural proposal: namely, that I should make contact with the leaders of the Western powers in their capitals.

The need for deliberation and delay before military action dominated the meeting. Indeed, General Rabin even suggested that we seek a meeting of the Security Council. I opposed this in the strongest terms. It was clear that with the Soviet Union in strong support of our neighbors, the Council would take no action even mildly congenial to us. On the other hand, it would create a diplomatic situation in which we would be unable even to consider a military riposte while the Security Council was seized of our complaint. The fact that our senior military commander was the chief advocate of these delaying tactics at this stage reflects his knowledge that we had not reached full preparedness in the area hastily evacuated by UNEF.

The meeting ended with a formal decision that was accepted without dissent:

1. The blockade is an act of aggression.

2. Any decision on action is postponed for forty-eight hours.

3. The prime minister and foreign minister are empowered to decide, should they see fit, on a journey by the foreign minister to Washington to meet President Johnson.

In my office in Jerusalem I found cables from our ambassador in Paris, Walter Eytan, telling us of an important meeting of the French Council of Ministers to be held the following day, Wednesday. Eytan thought that he might be received by de Gaulle. Eshkol replied that de Gaulle should, if possible, receive a direct impression at ministerial level of the agony and suspense in Israel and that I should seek a meeting with him. Golda Meir strongly emphasized the need to solve the mystery of France's attitude. After all, it was French equipment that stood between us and catastrophe. We would need French understanding if the battle became prolonged. Golda had instantly rejected a suggestion by Zalman Aranne that she should make soundings in Washington since her unofficial status would commit the government less than would a foreign minister's visit.

I arranged with the prime minister that I would set out for Paris in the early hours of the morning, and after conferring with President de Gaulle, go on to Washington. Eshkol's directive was that I should speak frankly of our resolve not to yield to Nasser's aggression but to test, first of all, whether we would be supported and, if possible, even accompanied by any of the Western powers who had promised to stand at our side in conditions that had now ensued. By the time that the Knesset convened on the evening of May 22, Eshkol was able to tell it that Egyptian forces in Sinai had swelled from 35,000 to 80,000 and would probably be further increased. He told our Parliament that the Israeli government would carry out the policy that it had announced to the United Nations General Assembly on March 1, 1957. This was a clear allusion to our decision to interpret a blockade in the Straits of Tiran as an act of war and to respond by force.

There was little sleep for me that evening and probably little for any Israeli who looked our situation in the face. At 3:30 in the morning of May 24 I set out from Lod Airport to Paris with my political secretary, Moshe Raviv, in the huge, otherwise empty Boeing chartered from El Al for the purpose of transporting me to Paris and Washington. At 7:00 in the coolness of a Paris dawn, we touched down at Orly and checked in at the airport hotel.

19

PARIS, LONDON,
WASHINGTON

REGIMENTATION AND UNIFORMITY are more usually associated with Teutonic than with Gallic habits. I was, therefore, impressed to see twenty-four black Citröen automobiles in the courtyard of the French presidential palace, standing in line with meticulous accuracy like soldiers on parade. It told me something of the disciplined habits that the French political system had assumed under its eminent leader. This was clearly a nation with one man in charge.

A meeting of the Council of Ministers under de Gaulle's presidency was still in session. The job of the ministers was not to decide policy but to find out from de Gaulle what French policy was. He had probably decided on his policy before my arrival, and the indications were grave for Israel.

For several months my associates in the Israeli embassy had urged me to attach less importance to external signs of coolness among French leaders, such as their unwillingness to visit Israel and the sudden cessation of the friendly rhetoric that had accompanied our relationship since 1956. The embassy attitude was that the flow of arms, the cooperation in science and technology, the joint work on the Dimona nuclear reactor in the South and the close relationships between French and Israeli ranking officers were more significant than effusive rhetoric.

Nevertheless, I now found it disconcerting to find that France was more reserved toward us even than the United States and Britain. There was disunity in the Western front. I had no illusions that everything would be easy in London and Washington, but both governments there had spoken firmly of their conviction that the blockade of Eilat was provocative and illegal. President Lyndon Johnson and Prime Minister Harold Wilson had undertaken to support the deescalation of the military threat and restoration of free passage in the Straits of Tiran. Nothing of this kind had yet been said in Paris.

As I walked with Ambassador Eytan up the stately staircase to the president's quarters, I was greeted warmly but with disturbingly compassionate glances by ministers dispersing after their meeting. I recall the firm handshakes of André Malraux, the minister of culture, and of my erstwhile opposite number, Louis Joxe, who had been minister of education in the early part of the decade.

I had come to this encounter with a romantic view of de Gaulle. In Cairo I had seen his tall pencil-like figure, with its aggrieved and solemn demeanor, as he passed through the lobby of the Continental Hotel. He aroused little attention among the bustling crowd of British officers who dominated the Cairo scene. He was a marginal figure in those days. He had been even more so a few years before when I listened to the reverberation of his strong, authoritative voice proclaiming, with little tangible evidence, that France "had lost a battle but had not lost the war."

I had made frequent visits to Paris in my student days partly out of affection for the charm and dignity of the city and partly to undertake research in the School for Living Oriental Languages at the Sorbonne University. I spoke and admired the language and made desperate attempts to be worthy of its characteristic lucidity and precision. An innate distaste in the 1930s for everything that was German had sent me on the rebound toward an avowedly francophile devotion. De Gaulle in my vision of him symbolized the very concept of recuperation that had marked our own Jewish history in its darkest hours. At that time, each of our nations in its particular circumstances was vindicating the idea that there is no weakness from which recovery is inconceivable. The French and Jewish minds were inspired by a proud appraisal of themselves and a faith in destiny and ultimate salvation even when the horizon was unrelieved by any glow of light.

The president's office was sparsely but elegantly furnished with not a single piece of paper on any table. I noticed, however, the presence of a telephone. This intrigued me since there had been a legend according to which de Gaulle disapproved of such new-fangled devices. (Later, when I complained to a French newspaperman that one of my cherished myths had been shattered, he had replied with deadpan face, "Oh yes, but it's not like other telephones. That is a telephone in which de Gaulle can speak to other people but on which nobody can get through to him.")

At that moment, however, I was not in a facetious mood. The General rose in a large, shambling, disordered movement of a tall body that, however, showed signs of age. His face was grave. His eyes were constantly blinking as if they had difficulty in coming to terms with the light. The handshake had been brief and perfunctory. Before the foreign minister, Couve de Murville, had time to present me, de Gaulle was already in full spate. "Don't make war," he said, before I had time to sit down. "At any rate," he added, "do not be the first to shoot." The exhortation "ne faites pas la guerre" had a note of hasty rebuke. However, it gave me an opening to say that we could not start the war since Nasser had already started it. His blockade and massive troop movements meant that the choice posed for Israel was clear—resistance or abandonment. Here I was consciously using a Gaullist vocabulary, endeavoring to adapt my emotions to his principles.

The conversation then flowed in what was evidently a Gaullist system. He expected his interlocutors to state briefly and coherently what they thought. After a pause he would make an analytical reaction. There was no atmosphere for brief conversational interruptions. Since I had rehearsed my thoughts during the air journey with a view to conciseness, I put my case into a framework of five minutes. Walter Eytan, a skilled and astonishingly phlegmatic ambassador, was taking notes. This was not a difficult task, since de Gaulle spoke in a slow but fluent cadence. He clearly enjoyed the music of his language.

Before setting out on my journey I had decided to observe a principle that I had ordained for all our embassies. I had insisted that nobody who conducts a conversation should be responsible for recording it. The active participant listens more to himself than to his interlocutor and he has a bias in favor of some themes and against others. His reliance on subsequent memory is a hazard that the note taker does not incur. My conversations with de Gaulle, Harold Wilson and, above all, with President Johnson and his defense chiefs were extensively recorded by Ambassadors Eytan, Remez and Harman with no formulatory input from me except to remind them of some points that had been omitted. This became important in historical and personal terms, since the virulent political motivations of Rafi politicians were soon to generate the legend that I had not given my eminent interlocutors a clear impression of Israel's determination to resist, and additionally or alternatively, that I had exaggerated the original commitment of President Johnson to explore an international attempt to challenge Nasser's blockade.

There was never any such thing as an "Eban Report" to the Israeli government of what the three foreign leaders had said. In each case I put the ambassador's record before the Cabinet and identified myself entirely with its authenticity. In subsequent months and years all my descriptions of these talks were corroborated by the French, British and American participants in their own documents and memoirs.

De Gaulle, having begun with his dramatic plea for Israel not to make war, calmly urged me not to put Israel's trust in "Western naval demonstrations." This was superfluous since neither I nor anyone in the Israeli government had invented what became known as the "armada" project. I now told him that it was natural that we would wish to consult our greatest friend. The crisis had begun with Syrian-based terrorism that had led, under Soviet instigation, to Egyptian troop concentrations in Sinai, the dismissal of the UN force and now to a blockade. "A blockade is an aggressive warlike action that must be rescinded."

I reminded de Gaulle that in 1957, it was France that had given the most energetic and lucid definition of Israel's rights in the Gulf, including Israel's right to defend itself physically against the outrage of blockade. De Gaulle: "That policy was correct but it reflected the heat of the hour. That was 1957. It is now 1967." I said that we had decided to maintain the policy that we had agreed with France in 1957. Israel, without its outlet to the southern and eastern worlds, without its own trade to and from Eilat, would be stunted and humiliated. We would lose the new artery of world communication that we had established a decade ago. At that time we were discussing a prospect. It had now become a reality. And above everything else, we would no longer have any power of deterrence. We were not going to put up with what Nasser had done.

De Gaulle seemed interested in this description and interjected, "What do you think you're going to do?"

I repeated: "If the choice lies between surrender and resistance, then we will resist. That decision has been taken. We have not, however, decided to act today or tomorrow because we are exploring the attitude of those who assumed commitments. We must know whether we are alone or whether we shall act within an international framework. If we are called upon to fight alone, and we do not recoil from this, we will be victorious, although the price in blood may be heavy. If, however, we fight alone, we shall expect that those maritime powers which promised to exercise free passage and which accepted the March 1967 assumptions and hopes, will not interfere with our action. If the maritime powers want to act in accordance with their engagements by defying the blockade, as some of them seem to envisage, then Nasser will have no course but to yield. Especially if the United Nations or the Western maritime powers have a naval force in the area." I said that if Nasser is forced to yield by international action this will be a great victory not only and not so much for Israel as for the idea of international law.

De Gaulle was visibly listening with deep attention. But again, he interjected: "You have a case, yes, but on no account should you shoot the first shell." I countered, "We are not in the position to begin hostilities, since these have already been started by Nasser. The blockade is an act of war. Whatever Israel does from now on will be a reaction, not an initiative. A state can be attacked by many methods apart from gunfire. Civil law recognizes no distinction between assault through strangulation and assault through shooting."

De Gaulle clearly rejected the idea that Nasser had already opened hostilities. He repeated that opening hostilities in the view of France meant literally firing the first shot. "Today there are no Western solutions. The more Israel looks exclusively to the West the less will be the readiness of the Soviet Union to cooperate. It is essential that the four powers should concert their policies."

In commenting on the UN secretary-general's removal of UNEF, de Gaulle said that U Thant had acted correctly in the legal sense, although it would have been much wiser if he had waited for consultation with the four powers.

The theme of "the four powers" was reiterated constantly in the course of our discussion. He spoke as if this were an institutional reality that I ought to know about. For a time he seemed to soften his tone. He said, "What Nasser has done with the blockade and troop concentrations cannot last. Israel must reserve its position. But Israel should not take any action until France has time to concert the action of the four powers to enable ships to pass through the Straits." I said somewhat bluntly that so far France, unlike the two other Western powers, had not raised its voice against Nasser's blockade. I therefore welcomed what he had just said to me. De Gaulle said that he had always upheld the freedom of the seas and that an international agreement on the Straits should be sought, "as in the Dardanelles."

I observed silently that both in his advice "not to fire the first shell" and in his reference to the Dardanelles he was using World War I vocabulary. I said that I was not sanguine that the Soviet Union would play a positive role. De Gaulle said: "Moscow has never questioned the international character of those waters. Israel's enemies are hoping that you will open hostilities, which you must not do."

I said: "I do not believe that Israel will accept the new situation created by Nasser for any serious length of time. I cannot, however, leave you without expressing gratitude for France's help and friendship."

De Gaulle replied: "It is just this very friendship that now moves me to say that Israel is not sufficiently established to be able to solve all its problems itself. Israel should not undertake never to act. But the important thing now is to give a respite for international consultation. You have told me that inaction is sometimes more dangerous than action. That is well said. De Gaulle knows this. But on this occasion there is the alternative of Four Power consultation. I advise you not to be precipitate. Do not make war."

It was a nice classical touch to end the conversation exactly as it had begun. While Couve de Murville and Walter Eytan were receding, I conveyed Eshkol's personal respects, to which de Gaulle replied, "Well I remember exactly what I said to him when he sat in that chair. I said that the essential thing is that Israel should exist and develop."

As I came down the stairs my thoughts were naturally centered on his tenacious refusal to acknowledge that we were already the victims of aggression. I suddenly recalled the saying of the French philosopher Taine: "The aggressor is he who makes war inevitable." That very day Muhammad Hassanein Haykal, the gray eminence of the Egyptian media, had said admiringly that Nasser had now put Israel in a position in which it would have to make war since the other alternatives would be untenable. The French have a subtle expression: "esprit d'escalier." It refers to what a person thinks as he is going down the stairs after a meeting and that he wished he had said in the meeting itself. I did not deem it possible in that particular atmosphere to go back and throw Taine's quotation at President de Gaulle.

The essence of the French position was a repudiation of the 1957 commitment. When de Gaulle said that "1957 is not 1967," I did not have to be oversubtle to understand that in 1957 the tension with Algeria, and therefore the French conflict with Nasser, was at its height, whereas Algeria was no longer a factor in French policy or thinking. De Gaulle had not denied that it was France that had pressed Israel to withdraw from Gaza and Sinai in 1957. France was now quietly but firmly disengaging itself from any responsibility for helping Israel if Israel chose early resistance. In a wider and more surprising context, he was disengaging himself from the West. He had never used that expression except in an adverse sense: "Il n'existe pas de solutions occidentales." I wondered whether I was in Paris or in the Eastern bloc. From some remarks I deduced that he regarded the United States as more responsible than the Soviet Union for the current global tensions. I was also aware of his nervousness. He was doubtful if the war against which he was warning me could be limited in space or time. The need for consultation with Moscow was part of his general fear that mankind was vulnerable to apocalyptic consequences if "the West" (excluding France!) embarked on adventurous courses.

I had been struck by his nervousness. I had thought that I had more reason for anxiety than did de Gaulle. After all, we were under siege and the world seemed divided between those who were seeking our destruction and those who were determined to do nothing to prevent it. Yet anyone who followed the tone of our discourse would have concluded that the security of France was more at hazard than was that of Israel.

De Gaulle often referred to this conversation with me in his meetings with Western governments in later times. He would point to the chair facing him and say: "Monsieur Eban sat there. I told him not to make war—and we [royal plural] were not obeyed." ("Nous n'avons pas été ecoute!").

A year later he made the same accusatory remark to Charles (Chip) Bohlen, the American ambassador in Paris. Bohlen replied, "Perhaps you would have reacted as Mr. Eban did if you were an Israeli." De Gaulle answered: "Oui, mais je ne le suis pas!" ("Yes, but I'm not!")

In his memoirs Couve de Murville has revealed that having taken leave of me he went back to the president's office, where they discussed my conversation with them. The conclusion that they reached was that Israel would not put up with what Nasser had done, and that war was a matter of short time.

This is the time to put other legends to rest. De Gaulle himself and others in his wake have written and spoken as if his conversation with me contained a prediction that Israel would win the impending war with Egypt but that the Palestinian problem would emerge as a burden on Israel's life and future. There was not a single reference to the Palestinians (or to Jordan) in my conversation, which was totally oriented on the Egyptian-Israeli relationship. It would have been incongruous if the Palestine issue had arisen on May 23 when there was no hint of Jordanian or Palestinian interest in the crisis.

Another version includes the assumption that I raised the issue of our arms shipments from France. Again, this is pure imagination. I said in general terms how important French help and support had been to Israel, and de Gaulle had responded that "France will continue to work for a strong Israel." The arms deliveries continued for some weeks until they were suspended when the outbreak of hostilities was imminent. Israel continued to dominate the military balance in the Middle East with French arms for some years.

Representatives of the press with a large Israeli contingent awaited me in the courtyard. I found myself in an embarrassing position. On the one hand, my instincts were to let the press know how I felt. On the other hand, I regarded my country as being already in something like a state of war. Helping the enemy was not part of my mandate. I certainly had no reason to demoralize other countries, especially the United States, by a premature admission that our greatest friend had deserted our cause.

As soon as I left the Élysée our embassy gave me a message saying that Prime Minister Harold Wilson would see me without fixed appointment as soon as I arrived in London. I felt it imperative that Eshkol and his government should learn as quickly as possible about France's attitude. I therefore asked Eytan to summarize for Raviv the main parts of my discussion and instructed Raviv to cable them to Jerusalem while Eytan would prepare a more detailed cable from his verbatim notes.

My intuition that the French government had adopted its decision even before I went to see de Gaulle was confirmed when I left the Élysée and heard the Paris radio broadcasting an authoritative account of the French attitude in terms not much different from what I had heard from de Gaulle.

I had been pleased by Prime Minister Harold Wilson's invitation to come and see him in London as soon as I could arrive. Ambassador Aharon Remez met me at the airport and we went together straight to Downing Street. As we drove up toward Number 10, the Conservative leaders, Edward Heath and Sir Alec Douglas Home, were walking away. They gave me a friendly wave of the hand. There was the usual large crowd in the street carrying out the peculiarly British ritual of staring fixedly at the policeman guarding the door of Number 10 and watching those who came in and out in characteristic silence. It is hard to know what they were achieving by this action. It did, however, denote that there was a national mood of disquiet.

I had known Harold Wilson well since his spectacular election victory in 1964. As a member of an Israeli Labor Cabinet, I felt a special solidarity with him. When I was a deputy prime minister in Eshkol's Cabinet, Wilson once asked me at a dinner which of the two candidates, Dayan and Allon, would become prime minister. I explained why I thought that neither of them would reach that level, since they canceled each other out. He replied, "Well I know that situation. It's exactly as it was in 1945. Since neither Bevin nor Morrison could stand the sight of each other, they had to make way for a compromise candidate, namely, Clement Attlee."

Without making tangential changes in British policies Wilson had found ways of expressing a friendly attitude to Israel. The British approach to arms supplies was to regard them as a commodity to be sold rather than as a political inducement to be conferred or withheld.

Something of the solidarity that bound Israel and Britain together for a brief but dramatic period in the Suez crisis of 1956 still lingered, although in diluted intensity. It was emotionally impossible for British people to have affection for Nasser. I was encouraged and surprised by the fact that the British foreign secretary, George Brown, who had been regarded as a devoted Arabist, had expressed indignation at U Thant's action in withdrawing the UN forces and had called it a "mockery."

Rumor had it that George Brown was personally arranging the loading of weapons for Israel onto air freight planes. Brown was incalculable, abrasive, monumentally tactless, but these very qualities are associated with charismatic personality. The key word is "colorful." Once you attain the reputation of being "colorful" you will be indulged in anything except the more violent crimes.

Wilson was tranquil. He was a man of strong nervous temperament but sharply sensitive to the danger of conspiracy against him. This apprehensiveness was not totally unjustified, since British politics is less "gentlemanly" than is popularly supposed. He was in love with power and like all good leaders did not lack affection for himself. He had begun his office with a Kennedy-like flourish, parading his relative youthfulness and his capacity to live in harmony with the new technological age. He was destined to win three elections, which in Britain is an almost unique achievement, unrivaled until Mrs. Thatcher's decade of rule. He encouraged his family to visit Israel and his son to spend some time on a kibbutz. His friendships with Jews in Britain were numerous but not always rewarding in terms of his own reputation for good judgment.

As I went into the historic Cabinet room I felt the tension flowing out of my mind and body. Wilson in the peculiar British habit sat in the middle of the table with me at his right so that I had to absorb the fumes from a not very savory pipe. It was not a context in which either of us felt it necessary to make a formal speech or statement. Nor would the discourse be stylized as in de Gaulle's Paris. I had the feeling that I was crossing the Channel into the twentieth century. Nobody would talk to me about the Dardanelles.

He asked me first about my conversation with de Gaulle. The French proposal for a four-power consultation had already reached Downing Street. Wilson was skeptical. However, George Brown was about to leave for Moscow, and his meetings there would reveal whether there was any reason to expect the Soviet Union to be helpful either to the United States or to Israel—or even to France.

I told Wilson of our options, of which a well-timed military action seemed the most likely but not the most immediate. The option that was not available was that we would live under threat of Egyptian troop concentrations and a humiliating blockade.

Wilson told me that his Cabinet had met that morning. He said that I would be surprised if I knew who favored and who opposed supporting Israel. (It later emerged that George Brown had supported and Dick Crossman had opposed.) The conclusion had been that Britain would condemn the blockade and would express a willingness to join with others in opening the Straits. He was going to send Minister of State George Thompson to Washington to see if a plan could be worked out for common action. He hoped that the Washington talk would be about "nuts and bolts." He asked if I thought that action on the Straits should be carried out through the UN, to which I replied that so long as the Soviet policy was as it was, the UN would be blocked by veto.

I had expected that I would find more support in Paris than in London, but the opposite had ensued. I found Wilson's attitude realistic and mature. It was also prudent. I noticed that he gave us no advice about what we should do. He must have understood that those who sought either to push us forward or to restrain us would be taking a responsibility that they might not be able to discharge.

Wilson had shown distinguished statesmanship. He was obviously prepared for the maximum degree of commitment compatible with his country's real strength and responsibility. Britain was in full spate of retreat from its obligations east of Suez, although it still had an important naval presence there. Wilson was moving with assurance and precision within the bounds of his own limited possibilities.

In my cable home to Israel on my Downing Street talk, I warned my prime minister and colleagues that although Wilson's views strengthened the chance of international support, their effectiveness would obviously depend on what would be agreed in Washington.

It was too late to get a plane to Washington, so I dined with my family and, overcome with a desperate and sudden exhaustion, I took a cab to my hotel in the hope of getting my first sleep in forty hours. There was a very heavy security guard outside the door of my room. The British press, television and radio were almost unanimously hostile to Nasser. On the other hand, I was concerned with the funereal tone of the sympathy that we were receiving. *The Economist,* for example, had a headline: "Israel's Agony."

I could not get de Gaulle out of my mind. Recalling that Eytan was due to dine with Couve de Murville, I sent him a cable from London asking him to get Couve to convince de Gaulle that "the question is not whether Israel will commit what the General called 'an act of force.' Force has already been committed and, in the shape of the blockade, it is still operating. Please get out of de Gaulle's head any idea that Israel will resign itself to the maintenance of the present situation for any length of time."

□   □   □

I had time on the plane to New York to reflect on the swift turn of our nation's fortune within less than two weeks. We had been taken by surprise. Since we were ultimately victorious in the 1967 war and were only belatedly and partly successful in the later 1973 war, it is often forgotten that the Intelligence failure was equally complete on both occasions. A Military Intelligence document on my desk on May 5, 1967, had greeted the incoming Israeli Independence anniversary with the prediction that any prospect of war was very distant. Nasser, the argument ran, was "bogged down" in Yemen and there was hardly any Arab state that was in good relations with most of the others. After Nasser's surprise moves on May 16, most of us Israelis were too preoccupied to investigate why our Intelligence services had been so complacent. In any case, victories in war do not usually invite stringent investigations about why some parts of the national performance fell short. Israelis were not prone to question the dogmatic certainty that afflicted our military appraisals, although as things turned out, a more searching scrutiny of the surprise in 1967 might have lessened our vulnerability in 1973. Our military leadership was not exactly a sacred cow, but it was certainly far less subject to critical scrutiny than were our Foreign Service personnel.

The swift development of the crisis partly explains the hesitancy with which even the powers most closely involved reacted to a contingency that they had never regarded as probable.

Israeli Intelligence even then had a formidable reputation. Over the years it has performed prodigies in operative assignments, such as the rescue from Entebbe, and has been accurate in describing enemy orders of battle. It has, however, failed in probing Arab motives and intentions. I have always considered that an undeserved reputation is a more impressive achievement than a deserved reputation, since it takes more effort to create and maintain.

I was disturbed by the lack of clarity at home and in the foreign media about the aim of my visit to the three Western capitals. My task, as I defined it with Eshkol before my departure for Paris, was not to persuade other powers to take military action against Nasser. A fallacious version of the Eisenhower undertakings in 1957 had great vogue in Israel, where it was commonly believed that the U.S. had promised to take military action against Egypt if it blockaded our southern maritime approaches. What Eisenhower had promised was to recognize *Israel's* right of military reaction as legitimate in that contingency. It was the international refusal to recognize our own title to take measures in self-defense that had weakened our relations with most of the world community during the fifties. Until it floated the idea of a maritime expedition against the Egyptian blockade, together with Britain, the United States had never offered and Israel had never sought American military action in any context. This fact was a source of Israel's strength in its appeal for the friendship of the United States. What we had requested was that if, despite the arrangements in 1957, Egypt were to resume its blockade of the Straits of Tiran and its encouragement of terrorist action from Gaza, the United States would understand that Israel, not the United States, would take forcible action in accordance with Article 51 of the UN Charter, which included a provision about an "inherent right of self-defense."

The rumors about an international willingness in Washington and London to consider the dispatch of a Western force into the Straits were in some sense a bonus, since they went beyond what Israel had ever requested. On the other hand, the talk of an international expedition had an inhibiting effect on Israel's own action and decision. The idea of sailing or marching with great powers in a common defense of international law was not something that Israel could turn down without serious consideration. But there was yet no evidence that it was really available.

In these conditions I decided not to press Washington for an international armada but to state that Israel was determined to take its own measures and would hold the powers to their 1957 commitment to respect and endorse that right. We would, of course, harmonize our measures with those of other maritime nations if they were in fact ready to act.

All I wanted from the Johnson administration was that it not act like the Eisenhower administration of 1957 if we resorted to what the international lawyers call "self-help" and tore the straitjacket off our backs. To achieve this I would have to lay a burden of conscience on President Lyndon B. Johnson. The 1957 trauma was the main incentive that was driving Eshkol and me on our course of action. The trauma affected me more than anyone else, since I had helped to contrive the arrangements in 1957 that had given us several years of peace on our southern boundary. A decade later, Israelis were less likely to credit me with the decade of stability than to blame me for its termination.

After a seven-hour flight I reached Kennedy Airport on the morning of May 25. I was met by Ambassador Gideon Rafael and the minister in our embassy, Eppie Evron. Again I had to encounter the press and television. Asked whether I was requesting American soldiers to risk their lives for Israel, I stated that we would not ask nor expect that to happen no matter what occurred. I repeated that I had come to seek U.S. respect for Israel's right of self-defense.

Ambassador Harman briefed me in my hotel. That morning, before going to Canada, President Johnson had made a speech condemning Egypt's blockade. The *New York Times* reporter at the White House had been told that on the basis of what I had said in London Israel could be held back "for only a matter of days at the most." Eighty-seven members of the Congress had signed a statement denouncing Nasser and calling on President Johnson to "support" Israel. So far so good. I also learned during my first hour in Washington that Harold Wilson's emissary, George Thompson, had arrived with a high naval officer, Admiral F Henderson, and had received the approval of Dean Rusk for a project under which an international group of ships with naval escort would sail through the Straits of Tiran in defiance of Nasser's blockade. It was evident that approval of this plan would require presidential and congressional sanction. The congressional mood, influenced by Vietnam traumas, was more hesitant than that of the executive branch.

In the light of these movements and attitudes, it is clear that those in Israel and elsewhere who have asserted that there never was a serious plan to break the blockade under international authority are quite mistaken. But the relative simplicity of the logistic aspect could not obscure the gravity of the political decision that could come only from the president himself.

At that point, however, I had one of the severest shocks of my life. Harman produced a cable from Tel Aviv stating that Egyptian troop concentrations in Sinai were dense. Egyptian airfields were on the alert and an Egyptian surprise attack was expected. I was asked to convey all this to the White House in the most drastic and emotional terms and to ask "if the United States would regard an attack on Israel as an attack on itself"!

This cable sticks in my mind as an act of momentous irresponsibility. There had been no new development in the military alignment since I had sat with our advisers on May 22 and listened to their plea for delay in order to get our troops into positions in the South. On the other hand, there were reports of Egyptian forces, strung out across Sinai, becoming entangled in logistic confusions that would greatly increase their vulnerability.

I have always believed in the axiom that it is the duty of soldiers to exaggerate their dangers. Military commanders have a professional commitment to anxiety. But it is the duty of ministers not to take reports of such dangers on trust. Someone, however, had obviously convinced some of our military leaders that it would be tactically wise to give the U.S. an apprehensive picture of our alleged weakness and to ask its government to do what it had no constitutional right even to consider. For the United States to say that an attack on Israel is an attack on the United States, it would have had to undertake a national debate in the Senate and in the public forum for weeks or months. Meanwhile, this eccentric cable meant exchanging an attitude of resolve, such as that which I had expressed in Paris and London, for one of apparent weakness. Instead of being a strong nation announcing its rights to act, we were presenting ourselves as a quivering victim of an imminent attack, the prospect of which had not been proven to anyone.

I later learned that the hypochondriac cables reflected a gust of uncertainty that had come over our establishment. One of the causes was the nervous indisposition of the chief of staff, Yitzhak Rabin, through what was charitably defined as nicotine poisoning. While I was considering my predicament another cable arrived at our embassy asking for the U.S. reaction to the request for an ironclad security treaty! Accordingly, I requested that my talk with Secretary of State Dean Rusk scheduled for 5:30 P.M. be advanced by two hours.

The entire basis of my mission had suddenly been changed. Instead of conveying Israel's real situation I was being called to present a demand that had no justification and that would only invite rejection. I later learned that this cable had been inspired by Chief of Staff Rabin both as a symptom of his own nervousness and in order to defy the United States to expose its own impotence and thereby to make Israel's right of military reply self-evident. The cable lacked wisdom, veracity and tactical understanding. Nothing was right about it.

While I was on my way to meet Secretary Rusk, more telegrams and Intelligence reports were thrust into my hands. One was of importance. It was an account from a friendly government of a meeting of the Egyptian leadership in Cairo on May 21, at which it had been decided to announce the blockade. Nasser had then explained to his military and political leaders why he believed that Israel would not fight: Israel would not fight because it had no allies, because it was afraid of the Soviet Union, because it knew that the United States was too deeply involved in Vietnam to help Israel, and because the majority of UN members favored the Arabs. Also because of domestic division, the reserved attitude of France and the fact that only five percent of Israel's trade had ever gone through Eilat.

It appeared to me that Nasser had been taking into account everything except the Israeli way of thinking and reacting. The obstacles to Israeli action were as he had described them to be. But the idea that Israel would transcend these obstacles in an urgent demonstration of its vitality had escaped his analysis.

Dean Rusk was never numbered among the Americans whose powerful enthusiasms were aroused by Israel's statehood and by our subsequent policies. But his fidelity to the presidents under whom he served was absolute. All three of them—Truman, Kennedy and Johnson—were friends of Israel. Rusk attached little weight to the prospect of an Egyptian attack. It was as obvious to him as it should have been to all Israeli officials that Nasser wanted victory without war. He had put Israel in an intolerable situation and had laid the onus of military reaction upon us. Having given me this appraisal with his customary conciseness, Dean Rusk took the obvious course of referring the request for a defense treaty to the White House. I did not get the impression that the U.S. had ever decided to enter a new and complicated defense alliance between cocktails and the first course of a dinner party.

That evening a working dinner was held on the roof of the State Department. I was accompanied by Harman, Evron and Raviv. Across the table were Lucius Battle, who was in charge of Middle Eastern Affairs in the State Department; Eugene Rostow, an assistant secretary of state; Foy Kohler, an expert on Soviet affairs; Joseph Sisco, director of the UN department; Roy Atherton, subsequently to be ambassador to Egypt; George Meeker, the legal adviser; and Townsend Hoopes, representing the Pentagon. One of that group had seen President Johnson just before he left for Canada. The president had said that he understood the gravity of the situation so well that "he doesn't need to be pushed."

The next morning, Friday, May 26, Dean Rusk telephoned my hotel room to ask if I would still be in Washington on Saturday morning when the report on U Thant's visit to Cairo would be available. I replied that I intended to leave Washington within a few hours because an important Israeli Cabinet meeting had been scheduled for Sunday; it would perhaps be the most crucial Cabinet meeting in our history. Rusk seemed to be disconcerted to hear that the vital Israeli decision was but a short distance away. I then said to Rusk, "I tell you frankly that I think we are in for hostilities next week. This is an act of blockade which must be resisted. I doubt if anything at this stage can change that outlook. The only thing that might have an effect would be an affirmation by your president that he has decided unreservedly to get the Straits open. A public statement of that kind and a letter to the prime minister of Israel on some of the details and logistics might create an international atmosphere that is now lacking."

I knew that I was reacting very sharply to Rusk's assumption that I might be willing to remain in Washington for a further day. That would have had catastrophic psychological effects at home. It sounded like an alibi for procrastination. Rusk, audibly flurried, said: "I get it . . ." and hung up.

I then went with Harman and the Israeli Military Attaché Brig. Yosef Geva to the Pentagon, where I was to meet with Secretary of Defense Robert McNamara, Chairman of the Joint Chiefs of Staff General Earl Wheeler, and others. The Pentagon conversations had scarcely begun when I was handed a cable from Jerusalem reiterating in drastic terms the absurd request for a declaration that "an attack on Israel is an attack on the United States." I felt that I had done my duty in having this "idea" passed to the president and that I need not waste time in hypochondriac frivolities anymore.

Secretary McNamara and the military chiefs seemed to understand my political presentation. They were, however, in vehement disagreement with the military report that I had reluctantly conveyed. Their information was that the positions of Egypt's armed forces did not indicate an early assault, and that Nasser was obviously waiting for Israel to incur the onus of an armed attack that he felt able to repel. Despite the unanimous feeling in the U.S. government that this was the situation, the Egyptian Ambassador Mustafa Kemal had been called in by the State Department the previous evening and had been warned stringently against any reckless act. This had been done not because the United States believed the prediction of an imminent Egyptian attack, but in perfunctory response to the alarmist messages that I had relayed from Jerusalem and that the U.S. did not believe.

Hearing Secretary McNamara and General Wheeler's comments, I felt that the Jerusalem cable had eroded our position. It had resulted in a purely diplomatic gesture from Washington that was probably superfluous and that conveyed a diminished picture of Israeli power.

The American military leaders told me that their studies indicated that Israel would win if there was a war no matter who had the initiative in the air. They believed that if Egypt made the first strike Israel would win in two weeks. If Israel were to make the first strike the war would be over in a week! Their reports from the Middle East indicated logistic confusion in the Egyptian camp. Israel's lines of supply and communications were short and efficient. Egypt's were a nightmare of distance and complexity. Israel's immediate security was in good shape. Egyptian difficulties would grow every hour. Israel's air superiority was great and beyond dispute. None of them thought that Israel was being outmaneuvered in the military domain and therefore would have to act in a mood of "now or never."

I now felt that the crux of Israel's short-term predicament was the divergence between Jerusalem's estimate and that of Washington concerning our security position. If the Pentagon was right and Israel's military success in any confrontation with Egypt was probable in all contingencies of time, it would be irresponsible not to seek political understandings with the U.S. and also to think and plan for our ability to hold on after victory. I found the tone and quality of the U.S. military exposition to be impressive. I did not believe that McNamara and Wheeler would risk their professional reputations by making an appraisal that could easily be refuted by events. I also felt that they wished Israel well and that they had an interest in maintaining American credibility by honoring commitments.

The day before my arrival in Washington there had been a flurry of activity in the U.S. bureaucracy to recall precisely what the U.S. commitment in 1957 had been. Not that this could have been in any serious doubt. The Dulles-Eban memorandum of February 11, 1957, figures in all the official collections of U.S. documents, as do the speeches and letters of Eisenhower, Dulles and Lodge. The administration had also heard from Ambassador Douglas Dillon, who had been ambassador in France in 1957, that the commitment was firm and clear.

Nevertheless, on the day before my arrival, Ambassador Harman had prudently gone to Gettysburg, Pennsylvania, to meet former President Eisenhower. Eisenhower had said that he was not in the habit of making public statements but that if asked, he would say that the Straits of Tiran were an international waterway. This had been determined in 1957. He would repeat the words that he and Secretary Dulles had written and spoken. He would add that a violation of free passage would be illegal. He had told his friends in the Republican Party that this was the position. He strongly objected to the precipitate action taken by U Thant in dismissing the UN force. Nasser had done something illegal in blockading the Straits and there should be no compromise with illegality. Ruminating from the past, Eisenhower said that he still regretted not having been able to take concrete steps to secure free passage in the Suez Canal similar to those successfully applied for ten years in the Straits of Tiran. He said to Ambassador Harman: "When I was president, the Russians tended to believe my statements because I had been a military man."

Eisenhower had added to Harman, "I don't believe that Israel will be left alone."

Before I went back to my embassy, the call came from the White House that the president wanted his talk with me to be serious and balanced. Therefore, he would like to postpone it for a few hours. Moreover, he was concerned with the enormous pressure of the information media in connection with the prospective meeting. Scores of reporters and photographers were swarming around the White House. And there had even been requests to put television cameras in the president's office for the occasion. Mr. Johnson wanted the meeting to be a working session and was displeased with all the theatrical atmosphere that had been created, and also with a stream of telegrams that he had been receiving.

Eppie Evron, the deputy to Abe Harman at the Israeli embassy, was a cherished friend of President Johnson. Sometimes, Johnson would prefer conversation with Eppie to formal encounters with our ambassador, especially when the embassy passed later to Yitzhak Rabin. Johnson now illustrated this affinity by asking Eppie to come to the White House a half hour ahead of my visit to rehearse the imminent discussion. He felt that the very formulation of his views to me could have an effect on the Israeli government's action. More important things than rhetoric were now at stake. I had learned that my statement to Rusk about "a crucial cabinet meeting on Sunday" had lit red lights in the White House. Evron explained that I had no interest in publicity but that I was entitled to a direct exposition of the president's attitude.

President Johnson was known to be playing for time while he waited impatiently for the military appraisal from the Pentagon. He did not want to face me on such a grave matter without all the documentation before him.

As I waited I was being inundated by cables from Jerusalem telling me in one way or another that it would be essential for domestic as well as international reasons that I be back home by Saturday night. It was now almost Saturday morning Israeli time. Important conversations were under way concerning an enlargement of the government coalition. Israeli military circles did not share the Pentagon belief that time was in our favor. They felt that events were rushing toward a climax.

I entered the White House with Raviv by a side door to evade the TV cameras. The president came down the steps of the White House living quarters to greet me and my colleagues and to escort me to his private office. Already present around the conference table were Walt and Eugene Rostow, Secretary McNamara, General Wheeler and George Christian, the president's press secretary.

I felt the weight of history in the room. Our fortunes would be much affected by what would be said in the next hour or two. It would not be anything like the talk with President de Gaulle. I had known the man who was now president of the United States for a dozen years or more as a senator, as a majority leader in the senate, and then as vice president. Johnson's manner now was as courteous as ever, but his demeanor seemed exceptionally grave.

I thought that I could discern a tormented look in his eyes as he sat very close to me, staring intently into my face.

President Johnson and I knew very well that the U.S. was firmly committed to oppose the blockade in the Gulf and to condemn Nasser's military escalation in Sinai. There was no need for a lengthy statement. I knew that he had received the reports of my talks with Secretaries Rusk and McNamara. In addition, the press accounts of my meetings in Paris and London had all ended with the impression that war was a short time away.

I told President Johnson that our country was in acute suspense. Some military circles in Israel thought that Egypt would launch a total assault on Israel in a day or two. The greater probability was that, having placed Israel in an impossible position, Nasser would put the onus of reaction upon us. I had gone to Paris and London in order to explain Israel's position. In Washington my aim was not only to explain our attitudes but to hear what the United States intended to do. A decade ago, the United States had made an explicit commitment at the highest level. President Eisenhower had never promised to put American forces into action on Israel's behalf, and I was not asking for that now. There had, however, been a solemn promise to support Israel's right of self-defense if a blockade were resumed, and if Gaza became a base for terrorist action. Israel at this time had only two options. One was to shake the strangling grip of Nasser off our throat by ourselves. The other was to hold that intention in reserve for a brief time while exploring whether the maritime powers would make common cause with us. If they did, Nasser would retreat, and a victory could be won for international civility without prolonged war.

I said that I was hearing a lot about the "need" to go through the United Nations. But so long as Soviet policy remained what it was, the UN would be a blind alley. It is an important forum, but it has no relevance to operative security problems. "To ask for action from the United Nations with a Soviet veto is like asking for action from the Chicago Council on Foreign Relations."

I said that Israel's maritime communication with East Africa and Asia had been a vague prospect in 1957. Since then, by patient toil it had become a concrete reality, fulfilled by hundreds of sailings under dozens of flags and by a vigorous trade that did no harm to anyone. Our link with the southern and eastern worlds was our new vision. What sort of people did Nasser think we were? Did he imagine that we could be choked and humiliated by a blockade that we had every capacity to resist? What detained us from resisting now was the president's own plea for a respite and his indication that there might be an international effort led by the United States.

I added that my presence in Washington reflected the Israeli government's determination to do everything to avoid the American-Israeli confrontation of 1956. I did not expect that the United States would need any argument about our right to use our outlet to the Red Sea. Would the United States agree to be told by a foreign country that it had the right to trade only in the Pacific and that the Atlantic would be closed to it?

There was a moment of silence as if President Johnson had expected a longer exposition. His response was very emphatic. "You are the victims of aggression. I have made that clear to the American people. The statement that I have made has not yet had the effect that I wanted it to have. But there is no question about our basic position. If, however, you're asking what we can do to help, my answer is that I can help only if my Cabinet, Congress and the people feel that Israel has been wronged. This cannot possibly be achieved before your cabinet meeting on Sunday." (He was confirming that my remark to Dean Rusk about a crucial Sunday Cabinet meeting had seriously jolted the U.S. administration.)

Johnson said, without much sense of proportion, that the Senate was out of town for the Memorial Day weekend. He described in very robust terms exactly what he thought of U Thant's decision to withdraw the UN force at such short notice. Nevertheless, the American people would not allow its president to act unless the UN channel had been tried. Johnson said that he doubted that anything much would come of the UN phase. (He spoke as if he personally did not share the enthusiasm for the UN that he ascribed to the American people.) Israel, in the meantime, should use all its diplomatic efforts to influence countries interested in keeping the waterway open. "The British are with us. Get your embassies moving to build support. I am not going to do any retreating or backtracking. I am aware of what it is costing Israel to be patient. But it is less costly than to precipitate the matter while the jury is still out and to have the world against Israel." He then said with emphasis, "Israel will not be alone unless it decides to go alone."

He spoke of his long personal association with me and his new acquaintanceship with our prime minister and president.[1] "I am not a feeble mouse or a coward. I'm going to do what is right. But if Israel wants the help of the United States it is absolutely necessary for it not to rush into initiating hostilities."

He had listened with care and attention to what I had said about American commitments. "I am well aware of what three past presidents have said, but that will not be worth five cents if the people and the Congress do not support their president now."

---

[1] He had met President Shazar at President Kennedy's funeral in 1963.

He asked me to tell him the gist of what I heard from de Gaulle and Wilson. I told him that the British government seemed to be taking the possibility of an international flotilla seriously. He asked McNamara to give me a summary of the findings of three separate U.S. intelligence groups that had investigated the balance of forces in the Middle East. He himself summed up their reports: "All our intelligence people are unanimous that if the UAR [Egypt] attacks, you will whip the hell out of them."

Although U Thant had not yet reported to the Security Council, Johnson and his associates already knew that the UN secretary-general had been impressed by what Nasser had called a "concession." This was his readiness to allow all shipping through if it did not bear the Israeli flag.

Johnson: "Our duty is to establish your shipping. We're not going to say that it's all right if the rest goes through but Israel can't."

I could see that our positions of principle were not far apart, but our timetables were utterly discordant. The Israeli argument that made the least impression upon him was that of immediate urgency. He said, "My experts could of course be wrong. I remember that MacArthur was wrong about the Chinese intervention in Korea. But on this matter I have told my experts to assume all the facts that the Israelis had given them to be true. They all say that even on that assumption, it is their unanimous view that there is no Egyptian intention to make an imminent attack. And that if there is such an attack, Israel will win."

Knowing that I would have to report to my own Cabinet within twenty-four hours, I said to the president: "Can I tell my Cabinet that you are going to use all measures in your power to get the Gulf and Straits open to all shipping, including that of Israel?" The president stated with great emphasis: "Yes."

He returned to the need for testing the capacity of the United Nations. "If it becomes apparent, without filibuster, that the United Nations cannot do the job of opening the waterway, then it is going to be up to Israel and all of its friends and all those who feel that an injustice has been done, and all those who give some indication of what they are prepared to do, and the United States will do likewise. What is needed in a very short time is Israel's initiative and British help to evolve an international effort with some effectiveness."

The conversation was too intense for me to embark upon reflection before it was over. I remember, however, being almost stunned by the frequency with which he used the rhetoric of impotence. This ostensibly strong leader had become a paralyzed president. The Vietnam trauma had stripped him of his executive powers. "Without the Congress I am just a six-foot-four Texan."

I have often asked myself if there was ever a president who spoke in such defeatist terms about his own competence to act. His temperament made him ambitious for power, not for compromise. But when it came to a possibility of military action—with a risk as trivial, in relation to U.S. power, as the dispatch of an intimidatory naval force to an international waterway—he had to throw up his hands in defeat. Before coming to the White House I had heard that, in conformity with Harold Wilson's promise to me, the British emissary, George Thompson, had come to Washington with Admiral Henderson and had reached an agreement with Dean Rusk on a scheme for sending a group of civilian ships through the Straits with a powerful naval escort. On a purely logistical level, this would have been one of the least hazardous operations in American history—the inhibitions derived entirely from the domestic political context. The senators consulted by Johnson were hesitant and timorous. They thought that the possibility of Soviet intervention, however unlikely, could not be totally ignored.

The revulsion of Americans from the use of their own armed forces had virtually destroyed his presidential function. I was astonished that he was not too proud to avoid these self-deprecatory statements in the presence of so many of his senior associates. I thought that I could see Secretary McNamara and General Wheeler wilt with embarrassment every time that he said how little power of action he had.

I entered the opening created by his plea for "patience" to say that Israel's capacity for patience was limited. What little there was would depend on whether there was an international effort that would be disrupted by an independent Israeli operation.

Dusk was falling over our conversation. As I was about to take my leave the president handed me a document from which he had been reading and which he now communicated with some formality as an aide mémoire. The text was,

> The United States has its own constitutional processes which are basic to its actions on matters involving war and peace. The Secretary General of the United Nations has not yet reported to the Security Council and the Council has not yet demonstrated what it may be able to do or willing to do. Although the United States, for its part, will press for prompt action in the United Nations, I have already publicly stated this week our view on the safety of navigation and on the Straits of Tiran. Regarding the Straits, we plan to pursue vigorously the measures which can be taken by maritime nations to assure that the Straits and the Gulf remain open to free and innocent passage of all nations. I must emphasize the necessity for Israel not to make itself responsible for the initiation of hostilities. Israel will not be alone unless it decides to go it alone. We cannot imagine that Israel will take that decision.

As I rose to leave he accompanied me to the elevator. He asked me to predict how the government of Israel would react to what he had just told me. I said with deliberate evasiveness that this would depend on what I could truthfully report about the president's attitude. I repeated: "Again, Mr. President, can I tell my government that you will take every measure in your power to ensure that the Gulf and Straits will be open for navigation by all nations including Israel?" The president said yes and gripped my hand so strongly that I wondered if I would ever regain the use of it. He waited until I was in the elevator and then turned back toward his office.

20

DAYS OF SALVATION

FROM THE WHITE House I went with Ambassador Harman to National Airport, where we enplaned for New York. There we took rooms in the Kennedy Airport hotel and Ambassador Harman began to work on the notes that he had taken in the White House. We felt it essential that our Cabinet should have the exact wording and flavor of the president's words.

I had more time to reflect on Johnson's definition of his powers, or, rather, the lack of them. I would have found this to be sensational even if Israel had not been affected. What did it amount to? Lyndon Johnson was known to be inspired by a coherent philosophy about America's place in the world. Like his predecessors from Franklin Roosevelt onward, he believed that predominant strength created particular responsibility. He had contempt for the illusion that American peace and prosperity could flourish for long without simultaneous peace and prosperity across much of the world. He rejected isolationism not only because it was ignoble but because, in the final resort, it was ineffective.

He was not widely traveled and did not have a very detailed knowledge of foreign countries. But he had a spacious vision of the world. And in that vision America had the largest role. There may have been something romantic in his notion that the United States, like the knights in the period of chivalry, was compelled by honor and duty to save any weak nation threatened by the dragons of aggression. Like many men who put on a hardheaded front and who speak in vulgar, masculine expletives, Johnson had a soft core.

Nasser's actions, and the role of the Soviet Union in inspiring them, were a clear threat to the aims of international stability and order that are the better side of America's foreign policy. For this reason Johnson was determined not to dishonor the pledge to Israel that he had inherited from Eisenhower ten years before. Here, however, the president came face-to-face with the inhibiting factors at work in American policy. A president who dared to take risks could no longer count on the loyalty of allies or on a national consensus at home.

In Southeast Asia an American commitment had been defended in a most uncongenial arena. As a result, the very principle of international responsibility had been brought into discredit. I therefore believed that the Egyptian-Israeli crisis offered the United States an opportunity of rehabilitation. To act firmly in defense of commitment in the Middle East would be more effective than the Vietnam intervention in restoring respect for engagements.

Here, the American risk was minimal. Israel was strong, resolute and united. It was not a South Vietnam. It represented an asset that had no counterpart in the Far East. The likelihood of Soviet or Chinese intervention was less than in Vietnam. The tactical objective, the cancellation of the Eilat blockade, was limited in scope and entirely feasible. It was everything that the Vietnam War was not.

Lyndon Johnson's perceptions were sharp enough to grasp all these implications. What he lacked was "only" the authority to put them to work. Less than three years after the greatest electoral triumph in American presidential history he was like Samson shorn of his previous strength.

Johnson may have been misguided in his confidence that within a week or two he could overcome these obstacles. I believed that we had an interest in granting him the time. He was ready for leadership, but his country was not. With every passing day the obstacles became greater and the will for action diminished. He inhabited the White House, but the presidency was effectively out of his hands.

I left Harman and Raviv in the unprepossessing atmosphere of the Kennedy Airport hotel and drove into New York for a conversation with Ambassador Arthur Goldberg at his suite in the Waldorf Towers. Gideon Rafael accompanied me.

Goldberg had the most successful public career of any Jew in the United States. Having been a leader of the organized labor movement for many years, he was appointed by President Kennedy as secretary of labor, thereafter as a justice of the Supreme Court, and now later as President Johnson's ambassador to the United Nations. I thought that he had made a personal mistake in allowing President Johnson to persuade him to leave the Supreme Court, with its lifelong tenure and dignity, in favor of the UN mission. Like Adlai Stevenson he had believed, mistakenly, that the UN job would give him a central role in the decision-making process. This was mostly an illusion, but the Arab-Israel conflict was the exception to the rule. In that issue, Johnson and Rusk had delegated the overall diplomatic leadership to Goldberg. He was a man of calm rationality that would always shine forth in a crisis. As the son of an immigrant he had lived the pathos of Jewish history very intimately. And he bore its memories with pride.

He told me that, as he and I had expected, the proceedings of the Security

Council had been farcical. Its meetings had begun on the initiative of Denmark and Canada on May 24. Here was the world caught up in acute suspense as a result of a blockade imposed by Egypt on Israel with an accompanying flood of violent threats. But five members of the Security Council said that they had no idea why the Security Council had even decided to meet!

Its first deliberations were taken up by procrastination that shamelessly served the Egyptian cause.

Goldberg wanted me to understand that nothing now counted in American policy except decisions or statements by the president himself. If Johnson had made clear that Egypt, not Israel, was the author of the crisis, and that Israel had been the object of aggression, that would mean my mission had been a success. Goldberg stressed Johnson's need of congressional backing. It was true that breaking the blockade did not sound venturesome, but many in the U.S. Congress would fear that a small and ostensibly innocuous operation in the Red Sea might escalate into a major American engagement. Johnson's verdict that culpability for the crisis lay with Egypt was, in Goldberg's opinion, the most that was immediately achievable. To have expected an immediate implementation of that judgment would have been unrealistic in the light of Vietnam sensitivities.

Goldberg, familiar with the pluralism and diversity of U.S. diplomatic habits, warned against listening to too many sources. He said that it would be a fatal mistake to rely on statements by the Rostow brothers, whose advice was sometimes rather impetuous. Goldberg and Gideon Rafael (who had joined me at the Waldorf Towers) were in agreement that the UN Security Council would continue to dither and stammer. U Thant had tried his fortune with a proposal to call on Eshkol and Nasser to use restraint: Israel would not send a ship of its own flag through the Straits and Nasser would not actually apply the blockade. The necessary nine votes were not available even for this slender idea.

As I drove with Gideon Rafael toward the airport, we both concluded that Johnson's declaration had some positive aspects. If the United States was willing to "take any or all the measures in America's power to open the Straits," it would hardly be in a position to censure Israel for "taking all measures in Israel's power," if, as now seemed certain, we would have to act alone.

At midnight I took off for Paris and Tel Aviv on an El Al flight. At Orly Airport in Paris I was met by our ambassadors to London, Paris and the Netherlands. I told them that this was not 1956: There was clear recognition by Johnson that Israel had been wronged, that the situation created by Nasser must be reversed and that the United States acknowledged a commitment that could not be allowed simply to languish and die. None of these elements had existed in American policy ten years ago. I felt now that our position could only be improved by giving the United States initiative "a minimal area in which to breathe," and that if we wanted to retain and develop American support, we might have to invest a little time to secure it.

When we landed at Lod on May 27 I had intended to go home to Jerusalem and catch some sleep. This, however, was not feasible. I was met by the prime minister's secretary, Adi Yaffe, who asked me on behalf of Eshkol to join the Cabinet session. He filled me in on events that had transpired during the four days of my absence. The public mood had deteriorated. Our military leaders were sharply divided between those who thought that any further delay would be catastrophic and those who believed that we could give diplomacy as much time as it needed. Those most impatient for action were the air force, which was in total readiness, while the army had the logistic burden of moving its center of gravity from the Syrian and Jordanian fronts down to the Egyptian frontier. The army could therefore use more time for preparation.

From Adi's report I deduced that our Intelligence services, like the Pentagon, did not believe in an early Egyptian attack. They thought that the Egyptians considered that they had put the ball in our court. Nasser's assurances to U Thant that he did not plan an attack on Israel was accurate but meaningless. What he wanted was victory without war. If he could cut Israel off from maritime contact with two-thirds of the world and hold our manpower down in petrified mobilization, he would be prepared to wait and watch while Israel struggled with its own dilemma. Nasser had never been fastidious about the precise manner in which Israel's downfall could be achieved.

On the air journey I had studied Nasser's speech of May 26, in which he declared that Egypt's basic objectives would be "to destroy Israel." In a more subtle mood, Hassanein Haykal had written that a favorable tactical situation had been created for Egypt: if Nasser could humiliate and defeat Israel without war, so much the better. If not, then Egypt would lose nothing, said Haykal, by absorbing the first Israeli reaction and then delivering a knockout blow. He made no provision for the possibility that the first Israeli strike would become the knockout blow, and that it would be Egypt, not Israel, that would be flat on its back. The Egyptian leadership seemed to be in a trance of ecstatic optimism accompanied by a large measure of arrogance. The Greeks called it "hubris," and a Hebrew proverb says that "pride goeth before the fall."

By this time Nasser's momentum of aggression was too swift for anything to overtake it. He was now expressing his resolve "to restore the situation to what it was before 1956." This meant that Israel must lose its maritime outlet to the Red Sea and be exposed to assaults from Gaza. But Nasser also disclosed his ensuing intention—to restore the situation to what it had been before 1948. This was a code phrase signifying that the Middle Eastern map would not contain a State of Israel at all.

There had been times when Arab rhetoric promised more than Arab courage seemed likely to attempt. But in May and early June 1967, the rhetoric sounded very serious indeed. Military detachments from Arab countries were flocking to Cairo to participate in the expected kill. Iraqi troops were arriving to join the assault. Egyptian forces had been recalled from Yemen. The myth of Nasser being "bogged down in Yemen" had been adduced by our Intelligence as the basis for Dayan's conviction that there would be no danger of war for several years. It now seemed that the bog was not very adhesive.

Adi Yaffe told me that the public was suffering the agony of waiting. My own children were noticing that the fathers of many of their schoolfriends were being called up for military service without any clear idea for how long or for what precise national goal. This was new in Israel's military experience. In previous wars, there had never been long periods of suspense or inactivity for soldiers in any front. The national spirit now needed to be rallied by eloquent leadership. Schoolchildren all over the country were digging air-raid shelters. El Al had already conveyed 14,000 tourists and other foreigners out of the country and had brought several thousand Israelis back home to be with their families.

Eshkol had been awakened by the Soviet Ambassador Dmitri Chuvakhin in the middle of the night in order to receive a message from Prime Minister Aleksei Kosygin. This text was not drafted in the menacing style to which we had been accustomed. There was almost a note of entreaty. The Soviet prime minister was imploring Eshkol to understand the hazards that would arise from an outbreak of hostilities. He apparently envisioned it as a danger not only to the Middle East but to world peace.

There had also been a letter from de Gaulle without the patronizing air with which he had addressed me on May 24. De Gaulle, for the first time, affirmed France's devotion to the principle of free navigation in the Straits. On the other hand, he strengthened his detachment from the other Western powers. He wrote with total contempt of the measures being taken by the United States and Britain to explore the prospect of a naval expedition to break the blockade.

I knew by this time that the U.S. and Britain had given de Gaulle his head about the Four Power dream, and had wisely refrained from rejecting it. It was the Soviet Union that had rebuffed de Gaulle with the brusque statement that there was no need for any Four Power consultation; all that was needed, in Moscow's view, was for Israel to accept Nasser's maritime siege and to stop its "warlike preparations."

When I arrived at the Cabinet session I found the atmosphere surprisingly tranquil. There was a heavy representation of military leaders. I recalled that Ben-Gurion had never allowed the chief of staff or his representative to attend a Cabinet at which a vote would be taken on a military operation. He had wished to safeguard ministers from submitting their individual judgments to the intimidating scrutiny of generals. Yet, at the May 27 meeting there was no pressure from the army for immediate action. Eshkol listened to the account of the Johnson conversation that I recited from Harman's report. He then said that the presidential statement declaring we had been and still were the "victims of aggression" was important and that all doubts of the value of my mission were removed from his mind.

Rabin reported recent improvement in our defense posture during the days of waiting. We were now in a high state of readiness, which we had not been a few days before. He spoke in low key, but seemed to have recovered from the nervous condition that had afflicted him for a few days during my absence. No reference was made to the cable in which I was supposed to ask the U.S. to proclaim that "an attack on Israel would be an attack on the United States."

Contrary to the legend, no vote was taken, although the speeches indicated that if it had been taken, the Cabinet would have been split right down the middle. Many ministers had understood that if we acted immediately, the U.S. would be able to say that we had hastily disrupted a promising international plan. Not for a moment was I swimming against any tide. There was no argument between the military participants and myself, and no threats or warnings were exchanged. I proposed that the Cabinet should make its decision within forty-eight hours and should convene frequently in the coming days. Ministers were more impressed than I had expected them to be with Johnson's words sustaining the rectitude of our cause and defining us as the victims of aggression.

I left the meeting to brief the Knesset Committee on Foreign Affairs and Defense in an adjoining room. When I returned, Eshkol had told the Cabinet that a fatigued and divided government should not take grave decisions and that the meeting would resume in the light of morning.

It is almost certain that if a decision had been taken on the morning of May 28, the Cabinet would have decided to give the military command full power to act against Egyptian aggression. But U.S. Ambassador Walworth Barbour had been instructed to deliver an urgent message from his government. He had seen Moshe Bitan, the assistant director general for North American affairs, partly to ensure that there was uniformity in reporting and also because there had been inaccurate newspaper speculation in both countries. Barbour's dispatch said that I had been told of a three-phased operation: First, there would be "proceedings" in the United Nations; second a declaration would be made by the maritime powers and others on the freedom of passage in the Gulf and Straits; and third, a plan would be prepared for "naval presence" that would hopefully deter Egypt from interfering with passage of ships and cargoes. In this scenario, Nasser would have the humiliation of seeing his blockade thwarted and his credibility derided. Barbour's account of my meeting with Johnson continued:

Eban's main source of concern was being bogged down in endless UN proceedings. He thought that the point could be established by a relatively short exercise. He was confident that the U.S. would never be challenged if it announced that it was going to exercise its undeniable right.

Barbour's report from the White House went on: "Eban asked if he could tell his Prime Minister that President Johnson had decided to pursue every measure in his power to ensure that the Gulf and Straits would be open to free and innocent passage. The president had replied 'Yes.' "

I now had the personal satisfaction of knowing that Johnson and I had understood each other perfectly.

The exact wording of Johnson's assurance to me according to which he would use "any and all measures in his power to ensure that the Gulf and Straits are open to Israeli shipping" became an important issue during and after the Six Day War. Those engaged in domestic political intrigue charged that Johnson had never made so far-reaching a promise. The May 28 communication now put this malicious rumor out of court, but it lingered on in some writings by some authors who were infected by the virulence of Israeli politics. In his own memoirs, three years later, President Johnson vindicated my report as recorded by Harman. He wrote: "I said to Eban, 'you can assure the Israeli cabinet that we will pursue vigorously any and all possible measures to keep the strait open.' "[1]

Barbour was instructed to inform the Israeli government that there was a "determination to make the international maritime plan work." The project was no longer described as a British plan but as an enterprise to which the United States had committed its resolve. Barbour's dispatch repeated that the president had expressed "fealty" to the commitments that his predecessors had made. (I was curious enough to speculate where, in the American bureaucracy, the medieval word "fealty" had originated.)

On the heels of this message from Barbour came a dispatch from Secretary Rusk on President Johnson's behalf. Its central theme was that "the British and we are proceeding urgently to prepare the military aspects of the international naval escort plan and other nations are responding vigorously to the idea." The Canadians and the Dutch were said to have offered ships even before the proposed declaration of the maritime powers was formulated for ratification.

As a sequel to the indecisive meeting on the night of Saturday, May 27, the Cabinet assembled the next morning and remained in almost constant session. After the demarche by Barbour and the note from Secretary Rusk came a letter from President Johnson: "I repeat even more strongly what I said yesterday to Mr. Eban. Israel just must not take preemptive military action and thereby make itself responsible for the initiation of hostilities."

□   □   □

---

[1]Lyndon B. Johnson, *Vantage Point* (New York: Holt, Rinehart and Winston, 1971), p. 293.

There was no doubt on May 28 that the United States and Britain had seriously envisaged an international action against Nasser in the Straits. Some ministers who had worried lest I had overestimated this intention now reproached me for not having given it sufficient weight! The cautious accuracy of what I had reported was vindicated on the morning of May 28 when Secretary of State Dean Rusk had sent his urgent dispatch in which he reported what he called "substantial progress" in the organization of an international assault on Nasser's blockade. The reality of a Western plan to break Nasser's blockade had never come to more concrete or precise expression. It would soon emerge that the hour of grace for the armada program would be fleeting. It was our interest to let it take its course.

It was Barbour's message and Rusk's memorandum that induced Eshkol to refrain from drastic decision on May 28. He now asked the Cabinet to give the United States and others a chance for "a few more days" to succeed—or to acknowledge failure—in their efforts. Of the eighteen ministers, only one—transportation minister Moshe Carmel—was prepared to vote for immediate military action.

Later that day when Eshkol informed senior military officers that a further delay period would be necessary, some of them warned him that every hour was working against Israel. I, on the other hand, was hearing from foreign military attachés stories of chaotic dislocation among Egyptian forces in Sinai. I also learned that military equipment previously ordered by us from Europe was reaching us. The French pipeline was yielding abundant material, as if someone in Paris had not heard of de Gaulle's strictures.

While most of our senior officers accepted the prime minister's decision with a disciplined serenity, others created a tempestuous scene. Ezer Weizman had taken off his epaulets and thrown them in disgust on the ground. Eshkol was shaken, but he showed his maturity by believing that a soldier's advice was not necessarily the last national word.

But someone had to tell the Israeli people what its own government's intentions were. Eshkol decided to do it himself. Even his most devoted supporters had never applauded Eshkol for eloquence. He was also suffering from fatigue. The scene with the army officers had undermined his nerves. A dry, legalistic jumble of words had been written for him by Minister Yisrael Galili, who was notorious for his unlimited capacity for platitude. Clichés used to fall from Galili's mouth and pen like autumn leaves, and with the same absence of utility. Never would a visionary idea or an original turn of phrase cast a beam of illumination on his prose.

Galili had introduced into Eshkol's text some semantic ingenuities that nobody but he could ever have understood. Eshkol came to the puzzling word—an unusual transitive verb for "withdrawing." He paused and stammered. His hesitancy was not about his own determination but about Galili's syntax.

It must have been the only occasion in history in which a hesitant stutter resounded throughout the entire world. The Israeli nation would have responded well to a reasoned justification for limited delay to be followed by a clarion call to our people to mobilize its energies and prepare for the eventual confrontation. It would have welcomed a Churchillian promise of blood, sweat and tears. These had always been commodities that an Israeli prime minister could supply. The nation was not prepared for a depressing routine announcement for postponement, recited with what seemed to be a lack of coherence and courage.

It is hard to describe the alarm and despondency that swept through the country. For three wasteful days the theme of the nation's life was not the need for intensified preparation for an ordeal that was bound to come. The issue was whether Eshkol should be the leader of our resistance. As defense minister as well as prime minister, he had two overlapping constituencies: the entire nation and the military establishment. With great numbers of citizens away from home and family, subject to unaccustomed inactivity in military positions, the morale of the troops was an anguished problem that Israelis had never known before. Eshkol's stammer inevitably reinforced the opposition's efforts to challenge the national leadership. Meanwhile, a cascade of disastrous developments in the international domain fell upon us like tropical rain. Arab arrogance increased, the United Nations revealed spectacular ineptitude, and domestic nervousness became extreme.

Whatever it was that had led Johnson and Rusk to proclaim the success of the "maritime effort" vanished from view in a matter of days. The week between May 28 and June 5 was full of crowded, intertwining events criss-crossing each other like a cobweb. It is difficult to place them in any sequential order.

Within a few days of its communications of May 28, which had produced a nearly unanimous Israeli position in favor of a short delay, the Johnson administration was beating a sharp retreat from the maritime plan. By June 1, Johnson was writing to Eshkol:

> We are exploring on an urgent basis the British suggestion of an international naval presence in the area of the Straits of Tiran. As I said to Mr. Eban, there is, however, doubt that a number of other maritime powers will be willing to take steps of this nature unless and until United Nations processes have been exhausted.

In a move toward disengagement, the U.S. was awarding the authorship of the maritime plan to the British. The UN processes mentioned in U.S. statements had not merely been exhausted; they had expired. U.S. hesitancy had caused a corresponding limitation of British resolve. On May 31, the British foreign secretary, George Brown, had given the British commitment a more limited interpretation than had Wilson on May 24. Brown now said,

"We regard the United Nations as primarily responsible for peace keeping." The powers had the habit of describing the United Nations as an entity separate from themselves, as though it were able to deploy energies beyond those with which member states endowed them.

Dean Rusk, who had addressed us on May 28 with blithe news of "substantial progress in the maritime plan," was now saying that the U.S. was "not planning any military effort in the Middle East." Officials in Ottawa hinted, not too delicately, that President Johnson had been in error when he had informed me that "Canada will send a ship or two." Canada was insistent on a UN framework as the condition for its action.

The most serious aggravation of our condition came on May 30, when King Hussein flew to Cairo to sign a defense pact with Nasser. Article VII of the pact placed his troops under Egyptian command. This was a sensational development. Its effects would be no less profound, and even more lasting, than anything that we might face on the Egyptian front. A few days before, Nasser had been calling Hussein "the Hashemite harlot." The Arabs often define themselves as a "family," and the speed of their transitions from mutual abuse to reconciliation conforms with this metaphor. Their rancors are virulent but can be quickly transcended, especially in common resistance to non-Arab adversaries.

The notion of a united Arab world rising to attempt Israel's destruction had sustained Arab dreams and Israeli fears for many years. Now it had begun to take shape and form. I felt that our fortunes were declining and our flame was burning low. I had written a few years before in a much-plagiarized passage that "nothing divides the Arab world more than the attempt to unite it." My view and experience tell me that the overriding reality about the Arab world is fragmentation, diversity and strong rival bids for hegemony. Now and again, however, an atavistic pull and a sudden sense of opportunity create transient attempts at union.

The drama was moving quickly toward its climax. In the last week of May 1967, the Arab world was celebrating a unity of purpose of which Israel was the only possible target. Arabs everywhere were seeing visions of slaughter, vengeance, conquest, and exalted pride that they had never imagined at the beginning of the month. A people that had never lost the recollections of the era when its power and creative genius had dominated a great part of the world had become marginal in history. It had fallen for centuries into humiliating subjection. It now discerned a prospect of sudden recuperation. Arab nationalism in modern times has often been concerned more with pride than with any concrete interest. Utilitarianism was never the theme of Arab collective thought. The Arab masses might hunger for bread, but the self-appointed elites that governed them were far more obsessed with dignity, honor, equality, justice, respect, prestige, status and repute. The Arabic vocabulary is remarkably replete with these terms.

These waves of passion, sustained by a new sense of opportunity, could not have come to expression without a leader to set them in motion and control their course. In the period of conquest under the successors of Muhammad—the caliphs—the Arabs had established a monarchy to ensure a recognized leadership both of their nation and of their faith. This institution had become fragmented when individual caliphs broke away from the center and established their own regimes. For most of history Arab leadership had been exercised in separate arenas of rule, usually in competitive relations with each other. In the summer of 1967, Nasser was emerging as the paramount leader of the entire Arab world.

Arab history is haunted by the fluctuation between unity and particularism. Nasser seemed about to resolve the issue; he would be the quintessential Pan-Arab. It was no accident that he, unlike his Egyptian predecessors, felt able to relinquish the historic name of Egypt ("Misr") in favor of a generic definition of Arabism—the United Arab Republic.

On May 31, our position was so grave that Eshkol asked me to hold a press conference with maximal reverberation. Correspondents now converged from everywhere. I faced dozens of cameras and microphones—a forest of gigantic eyes and ears thirsty for precision and eager, if possible, to pick up a triumphant note. It was in that framework that I told the reporters, first in English, then in French, that Israel was "like a coiled spring" and that the period of waiting should now be measured in days or at most, weeks, certainly not in months. The "coiled spring" became a world headline.

The irony was that while Israelis saw me as the advocate of restraint, Moscow presented me as the chief advocate of an aggressive design. On May 31, the Kremlin delivered a note through our ambassador in Moscow:

> In a declaration by the Israeli foreign minister formulated in a spirit of menace and aggression against Arab countries it was stated explicitly that Israel could wait only for a short time for her demands to be met, that this waiting period would be a question of days or weeks, that inaction was a form of action and that Israel, itself, would if necessary, open the Straits of Tiran if the great powers did not eliminate the blockade. It is a fact, that this statement by Mr. Eban can serve as official confirmation testifying to the reckless activity initiated by warmongering circles in Israel who aspire to dictate a line of action to the government and people of Israel. A line of action that will apparently end in a position which would bring irreparable harm from Israel's point of view.

The two opposition parties—Gahal under Menachem Begin and Rafi of which Shimon Peres was the driving force—were now intensifying their attempt to work for the removal of Eshkol from the premiership. I, on the other hand, had become convinced that we had done all that could be expected of us to give Washington its chance, and that the time was now ripe for military resistance under Eshkol's leadership.

On June 1, while I was planning how to convey this message, Eshkol was making a dignified address to the party secretariat. He explained that his stewardship in the Ministry of Defense had led to an intensive program of modernization and reequipment. He saw no reason to be apologetic about what he had done to prepare the country for the coming ordeal. He remarked, sardonically, that it was Dayan who had repeatedly predicted that there would be no general confrontation with Egypt until the 1970s at the earliest. It was he, Eshkol, who had spurred the high command and the procurement authorities to take graver contingencies into account. When he came to a discussion of recent events he spoke ironically about comrades whose support he had expected in vain.

"If our own party had a little more iron," he said, "we would have maintained our responsibility and avoided the complexities and antagonisms of recent days." He then announced that he proposed to offer the defense ministry to Moshe Dayan and to suggest the inclusion of Begin in the Cabinet as minister without portfolio. He would call for a meeting of the Cabinet later that evening and the coalition government in its enlarged framework would set to work at once.

This brought an end to a farcical attempt to reinstate Ben-Gurion as the nation's leader. The effort to dethrone Eshkol, led by Shimon Peres and the Rafi Party, had nothing but negative effects. It had led the initiators of that process into attitudes that were not easily defensible on the patriotic grounds that they were invoking. It had become apparent that if Ben-Gurion were to take the leadership of our party again, he would use that position not to strengthen our resistance but to fold our tents and avoid confrontation with Nasser. Ben-Gurion did not believe that the nation was ripe for successful war. Shimon Peres was openly suggesting that Israel should "dig in for six months or a year without embarking on any military initiative." He thought that only Ben-Gurion could persuade the Israeli people to follow this course. Begin had been urging Ben-Gurion's return in the hope that it would expedite war, while Peres had been pressing for Ben-Gurion's reappointment in the hope that this would make war avoidable. Their contacts with Ben-Gurion, now well past his eightieth year, convinced both Peres and Begin that his historic hour had passed and his glory could not be renewed. They went over to the more realistic advocacy of a coalition in which both Begin and Dayan could help to strengthen the nation's confused morale. Dayan would not be able to influence the battle plan at this late hour, but the psychological effects of his appointment could be spectacular both for the army leadership and for the nation as a whole.

The streets of Arab capitals were filled with frenzied masses thirsting for Israel's downfall. We had ordered total mobilization. Across the world, demonstrations of solidarity with us were of massive scale with religious leaders, intellectuals, even members of governments marching in our support.

Ambassador Harman had cabled from Washington that President Johnson's mood was now somber: He could not see any coherent direction for the American political establishment to pursue. The maritime plan was in collapse. Hardly any of the eighty countries invited to sign a declaration for free passage in the Gulf and the Straits had given a favorable answer. On June 1, the Egyptian government formally circulated a letter to all governments informing them that a blockade was now in force and that its legal basis was the existence "of a state of war with Israel."

Cairo's theory was that the Arab states were entitled to exercise "rights of war" against Israel, while claiming immunity from any Israeli "acts of war" against themselves. They were not the only ones who seemed to think that the Arabs could behave as though there was war, while Israel must behave as though there was peace. This was the paradox that had ignited the war of 1956 and that brought us to the verge of a new explosion a decade later.

Nasser was now invoking Higher Authority for his ambitions. Addressing members of the National Assembly, he had said:

> God will surely help and urge us to restore the situation to what it was in 1948. It is the aggression which took place in Palestine in 1948. That is the issue.

The adherence of Jordan to Nasser's war plans seemed to give feasibility to Nasser's aims. We were now not only blockaded but also encircled. All the conditions that had induced us to erupt against the siege of 1956 were reconstructed in a more alarming context and without the alleviating affects of alliance with France and Britain. By concluding his alliance with Nasser, King Hussein had made it certain that war would break out and that it would not be limited to the Egyptian-Israeli front.

All the Israeli plans since the expulsion of the UN forces on May 22 had been based on the idea of leaving Jordan outside the range of our military action. Hussein had thoughtlessly destroyed his own immunity. Having thus sealed the Palestinians' fate with a disastrously casual stroke of the pen, Hussein had flown back to Jordan burdened with the embarrassing company of Ahmed Shukeiry, the PLO commander. The Egyptian-Jordanian agreement, together with menacing statements from Syria, made it plain that we would probably have to fight on three fronts.

Arab alliances, pacts, signatures and threats had not always made Israel's flesh crawl. But tens of thousands of Israelis still lived closely with memories of the European Holocaust. Others recalled how in 1948 we had been on the threshold of defeat. Experience had taught our people that a great part of Jewish history was occupied by the simple attempt of Jews to stay alive. Whether they understood it or not, the Arab leaders, with their fiery rhetoric in May–June 1967, were playing on Israel's most sensitive nerve. Even the consoling solidarity of world opinion could not dispel the dark visions that now crowded in upon us. Much of this world sympathy had an ominously valedictory note. Letters came in offering us blood donations and imploring us to send our children for shelter abroad. I remember feeling with characteristic Israeli realism that if our friends were so concerned about us, we must indeed be in great trouble.

We had gained enormously by patiently allowing the United States to test its plan for international action up to its total collapse. As I examined the cables, I observed that we were now being released from the weight of Johnson's pressure. Secretary of State Dean Rusk had been asked by the press whether any efforts were being made to keep Israel from precipitate action.

His reply had been: "I don't think it's our business to restrain anyone." I had a talk with my most loyal adviser and friend, Arthur Lourie, who strongly suggested that I should give the signal for military action. I believed that this would now be received with unspoken relief even in Washington.

One of my reasons for believing this was an unusual communication from our embassy. It had many of the attributes of a Delphic oracle. President Johnson, like many of his predecessors, used to seek counsel outside the formal bureaucratic context. One of his most intimate confidants was Supreme Court Justice Abe Fortas. In theory, Fortas's duties had nothing to do with national security and foreign policy. In practice, Johnson used to confer with him several times a week.

Fortas had sent for the minister in our embassy, Eppie Evron, with a message that was not difficult to decode. He said:

> If Israel had acted alone without exhausting political efforts, it would have made a catastrophic error. It would then have been almost impossible for the United States to help Israel and the ensuing relationship would have been tense. The war might be long and costly for Israel if it breaks out. But Israel should not criticize Eshkol and Eban. The Israelis should realize that their restraint and well-considered procedures would now have a decisive influence when the United States comes to consider the measure of its involvement.

Fortas's message concluded with a prediction that time was running out and that it was now "a matter of days or even hours."

This formulation praised our restraint in the past without any hint that it should continue in the future. Our abstention from direct military confrontation with our foes was described as a matter of history, with no ongoing implication. I now decided to tell my colleagues that if we took military action the United States would not insist on restoring the status quo as it did in 1956.

I picked up the telephone and asked the chief of staff, General Rabin, and the head of military Intelligence, General Aharon Yariv, for an urgent meeting. When we met, I told them that I no longer had any political inhibitions against whatever military resistance was feasible and necessary. I believed that if Israel was successful, the political prospects would be good. This time Israel would not be opposed by a united and angry world.

When I left the two generals and returned to my office I found Eshkol standing silently on the lawn. When I told him what I had just done, his relief was obvious.

Moshe Dayan and Menachem Begin had been co-opted to Eshkol's government on May 31. The nation was living an unusual hour. All the conditions that divide Israelis from each other and give our society a deceptive air of fragmentation, all the deeply rooted Jewish recalcitrance to authority were now transmuted into a new metal that few had ever seen or felt before. It seemed that a great tragedy was sweeping toward us, and in some places in Israel there was talk of Auschwitz and Maidanek. When President Johnson and Prime Minister Wilson met in Washington on June 2 they showed nothing of the buoyant mood that had inspired them a week or two before. If the Western powers had sailed together with Israel through the blockaded Straits, the consequent humiliation of Nasser might have had dynamic results in the Arab world and in Egypt itself. On closer contemplation the prospect grew steadily less real and the future was in our hands.

Our national mood had gone through a sharp transition in the three weeks of suspense. At the beginning of that period neither the military disposition nor the national temper was geared for a decisive struggle. Now, what I had called "the coiled spring" was ready for release. The Israeli people was celebrating a new consciousness of unity and cohesion. Hospital beds by the hundreds were made ready with a quiet and almost macabre efficiency. Trenches and shelters had been dug all over the land. Industrialists, noted in better days for their hardheaded thrift, donated legendary sums for the national defense. The radio was carrying messages from soldiers in the front to wives and families at home recalling stoves left alight and exhortations to be of good courage. The simple pathos was hard to bear.

Hundreds of young men and women were crowding the offices of Israeli consulates asking to be sent to Israel for immediate service. A blind man in Brooklyn offered to send me the money that he had saved over twenty years to buy a house, stating that if Israel went under there would be no point in his life. There was clearly something in Israel's predicament that touched sensitive cores of human feeling. In Israel itself the normal rivalries were softened by acts of mutual tolerance and sympathy, which in other days most citizens would have been too shamefaced to offer or to accept. Synagogues all over the land seemed fuller than usual. The air was quiet with courage and simple rectitude. The nation that was supposed to have lost its youthful idealism and pioneering virtues now celebrated a new solidarity.

June 4, 1967. The Cabinet met for seven hours. My turn to speak came immediately after the military reports. I described an extraordinary tide of solidarity with Israel in every free, civilized community in the world. I believed that if we took military action, goodwill and approval in America would reach into the very highest places.

In France, I reported a wide gap between the official policy and public attitudes. Fifty thousand wildly cheering Frenchmen had demonstrated outside the windows of our Paris embassy. This was a kind of popular revolt against de Gaulle's sudden hostility. Our ambassador, Walter Eytan, had gone to the Élysée to meet one of his friends, and to his surprise, de Gaulle had entered the room. He lectured Eytan on the dark consequences of war, predicted the rise of Palestinian nationalism and said that there would now be an arms embargo that would remain "as long as it is not clear if you will not go to war." So Israel's main supply artery was cut, while Soviet military material continued to pour into Egypt and Syria. Paradoxically, de Gaulle was forcing us to conclude that since the balance of forces would now become less positive for Israel, we would be well advised to strike now!

After the reports, Eshkol called on each minister to give his general view. I said: "Our decision should now be that the government authorizes the security authorities, together with the responsible ministers, to decide on any action necessary to break the enemy's stranglehold, and the time should be determined in accordance with military necessities alone."

Eshkol made a similar proposal and asked for a vote. The room was heavy with a sense of awe. We were deciding on a course of which none of us could predict success. Of the eighteen ministers, sixteen raised their hands in support. The two Labor left ministers were to add their agreement later in the day. We decided to remain in permanent session, and to meet next morning in Tel Aviv.

In order to maintain surprise, I suggested that the Cabinet should transact a little ordinary business for public notice. We drafted a communiqué, announcing that an agreement for cooperation with the Atomic Energy Commission of Peru and a cultural pact with Belgium had been approved by the Cabinet, as well as certain technical legislation concerning State of Israel Development Bonds. A technical agreement with Peru did not sound like a call to battle, and some very capable foreign correspondents went back to their countries believing that they had at least another week or two before anything newsworthy would ensue.

Foreign military experts who took a somber view of Israel's prospects were mainly impressed by our deficiency in attacking aircraft. Except for two squadrons of Vautour light bombers, we were entirely dependent on French-manufactured fighters and fighter bombers, some of them obsolete. We knew that on this slender thread hung the full weight of our history and our sole chance of survival. With the best will in the world, it was difficult to avoid quoting the celebrated Churchillian rhetoric about the many who owed so much to so few. That Syria would participate in the war against us was taken for granted. This meant that we had to reckon with a Syrian army of 50,000 men with at least 200 tanks of operational capacity and 100 Soviet aircraft, including thirty-two modern MiG-21s. This was not a formidable force in itself, but when added to the 100,000 Egyptians and 1,000 Egyptian tanks, it would seriously aggravate our condition.

Political estimates, based on our 1956 experience, were not unanimous about whether Jordan would actively enter the fighting. We were still not fully prepared for that contingency. It had not been taken into account until Hussein's dramatic visit to Cairo on May 30. In the ceremony of signature, Nasser had uttered the last of his boastful predictions:

> Today we tell the Israelis we are facing you in the battle and are burning with the desire for it to begin. This will make the world realize what the Arabs are and what Israel is.

In predicting the dawn of a new "realization," Nasser was more intuitive than ever before. He only misunderstood his own place in the coming dawn.

It is normal in war that air forces begin their bombardment at early dawn. Nothing happened in Israel on June 5 until nearly 8:00 A.M. It was then that the air-raid sirens let out their familiar howl. The roads began to clear as the crowds moved awkwardly and dubiously toward the few existing shelters. The action to which Nasser had been goading us for three weeks had now erupted. Israel was hitting back in the air, and from the very first, there was a glow of victory on our wings. Nasser had gotten the war that he had so insistently sought and passionately welcomed. Haykal's logic was being fulfilled; Israel was doing what he had called "inevitable."

Even before the results of the air strikes were known, I was overcome by a vast sense of relief. Everything that could be done short of war to defend honor and survival had been exhausted. The inevitability of Israel's action would now impress many across the world. The United States could not again question Israel's plight or claim that Israel had not involved it frankly in its dilemma.

I was confirmed in the belief that I later expressed to the Knesset: Wars are most often won by those who have made the greatest effort to prevent them.

Reports arrived of unbelievable successes against Egyptian aircraft on the ground and in the air. All the Egyptian airfields had been attacked, and most of their planes destroyed on the ground. These included the TU-16 jet bombers of Soviet construction that I knew could have wrought havoc on our population centers. When night fell, Israel commanded the skies of the Middle East.

It had been decided that the prime minister and I would work in Tel Aviv on June 5 so as to be close to the map rooms at the Defense Ministry. That very morning, Eshkol had received a short message from Johnson through one of the president's aides, Harry McPherson, who had come to Tel Aviv on his way home from India. McPherson was an improbable name for an American Jew, but nothing is impossible in America. The president's message was brief: "May God give us strength to protect the right." It was as if he had anticipated our decision.

I prepared a draft for a letter from Eshkol to President Johnson, in which the prime minister stressed the need for Johnson to deter Soviet intervention. I drafted the concluding sentence: "The hour of danger could also be the hour of opportunity. It is possible to create conditions for strengthening peace and freedom in the area."

I had asked the British ambassador, Michael Hadow, to tell his government that we were making a great effort to deter Jordanian military intervention. Eshkol reinforced this plea in a cable to Harold Wilson. "Our foreign minister has informed your ambassador of our attempt to avoid any engagement with Jordan unless Jordan makes conflict inevitable. I hope that this can still be avoided."

Could it be avoided? At 9:30 Arthur Lourie, on my instructions, received the chief of the UN staff, General Odd Bull of Norway. The general was to communicate electronically with King Hussein and to say simply that we were engaged in battle with Egypt, but "if you do not intervene, you will suffer no harm."

It seemed to me that in terms of Hussein's self-interest the hope of Jordan's self-exclusion was rational enough; but the Middle East is so constructed that the rational things are the things least likely to occur. Our military authorities ardently supported our political move. Faced by eleven Jordanian brigades on the West Bank of the Jordan, and in the area south and east of the Dead Sea, we needed time for aligning our plans—and our forces.

In the light of what subsequently happened in Jerusalem, the West Bank and Gaza, I bear witness that not a single voice had been raised in the Cabinet for involving Jordan unless Jordan involved itself. There was good military logic, and not only virtue, behind this attitude.

At 10:00 P.M. (Israel time; 11:00 A.M. Jordan time) General Odd Bull telephoned by a special line to King Hussein, who has himself described the outcome of which the tragic consequences are felt to this day. His experience is recounted in his book *My War With Israel:*

It was at this point that we received a telephone call at air force headquarters from the United Nations General, Odd Bull. It was a little after 11:00 A.M. The Norwegian general informed me that the Israeli Prime Minister Eshkol had addressed an appeal to Jordan. Mr. Eshkol had summarily announced that the Israeli offensive had started that morning, Monday, June 5, with operations directed against Egypt. He then added to me, "If you don't intervene, you will suffer no consequences."

However, we were already fighting in Jerusalem and our planes had already taken off to go and bombard Israeli air bases. I answered Odd Bull, "They started the battle; well, they are receiving our reply by air." In three waves our Hawker Hunters attacked the base at Netanya. . . . In addition, our pilots reported having destroyed more enemy aircraft on the ground—the only ones which they found not in the air.

It became evident after the war that the king was not really free to apply his own discretion or to consult his own interest. The Egyptian General Mahmoud Riad had been appointed to command the Jordanian sector, and on the evening of June 4, he had installed himself with an Egyptian staff officer at operational headquarters in Amman. King Hussein has described how the Egyptian general calmly took the Jordanian army and air force under his military command and how Nasser deluded Hussein by false reports of Egyptian successes. In Hussein's account, Jordan is described as having entered the war for two reasons: the first because it was not free to decide otherwise and the second, somewhat less distinguished, because Hussein believed that he was joining a victorious bandwagon. In *My War With Israel,* Hussein has written:

We were the recipients of false information about what had happened in Egypt since the attacks by Israeli air forces on the air bases in Egypt. A new message from Field Marshall Amer informed us that the Israeli offensive was continuing; however, it went on to affirm that the Egyptians had destroyed 75% of the Israeli air force. The same communication told us that the Egyptian bombers had counter-attacked with a crushing assault on Israeli bases.

Amer continued with the information that Egyptian ground forces had penetrated Israel through the Negev. These reports which were fantastic, to say the least, contributed largely in sowing confusion and distorting our appreciation of the situation. At that point, when our radar signalled to us that machines, coming from Egypt, were flying toward Israel, no doubt crossed our minds, we were instantly persuaded that it was true. In fact, they were Israeli bombers returning after carrying out their mission against Egyptian airfields.

I have never had reason to regret the effort that Eshkol and I made to prevent the war with Jordan. When I contemplate both the casualties that we suffered and the consequences of our coercive rule over a large Palestinian population, I sigh with regret that this effort did not succeed.

The Jordanian prime minister, Sa'ad Jum'a, said in his broadcast on June 5: "For many years we have been waiting for this battle which will wipe out the shame of the past." The result of the war makes it almost impossible to remember that Jordan entered the war with such bold determination—and Israel with such strong reluctance.

I now decided that we should take the diplomatic offensive. I requested the Western ambassadors to come to my office to hear our report. It was 3:00 A.M. in New York, and 8:00 A.M. in Tel Aviv, when I instructed Yosef Tekoah, the deputy director general in charge of UN affairs, to make a telephone call to our ambassador at the United Nations, Gideon Rafael. His orders were to ask for an urgent meeting at the Security Council, to which he would unfold the design of Egyptian aggression and Israeli resistance. Rafael contacted the Danish ambassador, Hans Tabor, who was the president of the Security Council by rotation.

We were now at war with three Arab countries, and the gravest immediate threat came not from Egypt but from Jordan, whose forces had captured the Government House building where the UN observers had their headquarters. Jordanian forces encircled Israeli positions on Mount Scopus. Our successes against Egypt were a balancing compensation for our grave situation on the unanticipated Jordanian front.

My work in Tel Aviv on the morning of June 5 had been completed. We would now move to Jerusalem to inform the Knesset and the world of what we had done and why. In the atmosphere of our victory, I assumed that normal routines would continue and that our children could be at school, having spent the weekend, as they often did, with their grandparents in Herzliya. We all took to the road in my official car. As we reached Bab el-Wad, where the coastal road narrows to mark the confluence of the coastal plain with the Judean Hills, there was an absurd and confused bottleneck in which civilian parliamentarians on their way to the Knesset and military formations with tanks and infantry fought for the right of way. The forces under General "Motta" Gur were traveling toward Jerusalem in the convoys of civilian buses that reminded me of organized school picnics. I saw the white mane of Ben-Gurion through the back of his car. He was held up in the traffic but he was reading a book with typical nonchalance.

Generals Gur and Narkis were preparing for the defense of West Jerusalem and the conquest of the eastern city in the most adverse possible conditions. They had to attack heavily fortified positions in the Old City and work their way, street by street, through urban quarters under constant ambush and sniping. In other areas, the Jordanians were in flight. With a brigade in Jerusalem, an armored group of reservists from the coastal plain, a parachute brigade detached from the southern front, and a tank force originally intended for the Syrian front, the Israeli army was confident that it would be able to drive the Jordanians across the river in forty-eight hours.

□　　□　　□

That evening, we held a Cabinet meeting in an air-raid shelter in the Knesset building. Shrapnel was falling on the Hebrew University and the Hadassah Hospital. The Jordanians were using the El-Aqsa mosque as a sniping post. In an Order of the Day, Defense Minister Dayan had announced that Israel had not entered the war for purposes of conquest, but in order to ensure our physical security. While we were conferring in the air-raid shelter in the Knesset, a military officer, Brigadier General Zeevi, had entered the room to tell us the extraordinary story of our victorious battles on every front.

Our Cabinet meeting devoted itself almost entirely to the problem of Jerusalem. It was obvious that, with our overall superiority, we might have been able to capture the eastern part of Jerusalem in a patient siege. However, there was good reason to fear that there would be a Security Council cease-fire order at the United Nations, which would call upon all forces in our area to freeze their positions in place. This consideration, as ministers Begin and Allon pointed out, would argue for a speedy assault. Dayan was the most cautious of the operative ministers in this matter. He recommended encirclement of the Old City and opposed frontal assault. When Jordan became the most dangerous of our adversaries in the war, this debate became academic. Two ministers—Aranne, the minister of education, and the minister of the interior, Moshe Chaim Shapira, who was the leader of the National Religious Party—were hesitant. They pointed out that we would enter a hornet's nest of complexities in relation to Jerusalem's religious status and that we should understand that once we entered the Old City there would be no turning back.

Our Cabinet decided to tell our defense forces that they should act toward Jerusalem on strictly security criteria. If it was necessary to capture the Old City and the Holy Places by head-on assault, they should not recoil. If our security could be ensured by a more patient course, such as encirclement and siege, they should let us know.

It was a strange meeting in the air-raid shelter with the sound of guns a few hundred meters away. With Egypt in total defeat on the first day, Syria maintaining a holding action in the north, and the Jordanians—while inflicting casualties upon us—showing first signs of defeat, our attention turned to the political and diplomatic front. Israelis hardly had time to celebrate the military victory before they began to feel a profound disquiet. Was it not likely that the Security Council, in accordance with normal UN practice, would adopt a unanimous resolution calling for a cease-fire and a return to previous lines? Very rarely had a United Nations body refrained from accompanying a cease-fire with a cancellation of the results already achieved in a war.

This was a nightmare for Israel. To have won a glorious victory and then to be forced back by political pressure without any concrete gain evoked the most painful traumas of 1956. I could not expel from my mind a sense of fatal historic repetition. Here we were again breaking out of the closing circle of

Arab aggression and here again plans would be laid to see that our neck was restored as soon as possible into the encircling noose. Some Israelis, intoxicated with our triumph, were proposing that we now ignore the outside world and take the attitude "what we have we hold and let the world go to hell." I reminded them that on the only occasion when we had faced a unanimous UN call to give up the fruits of victory without obtaining peace, we had withdrawn and had to fight hard for a few remnants of improved security that fell far short of stable peace.

Ambassador Rafael's accounts from the Security Council showed that this prospect was already coming into view. The U.S.S.R., France and India were drafting resolutions calling for a cease-fire and a withdrawal to the previous lines. The Security Council had already heard Rafael's forceful account of our attitudes. The Egyptian ambassador had stated that "for several hours Israeli armed force and the Israeli air force have again committed a cowardly and treacherous aggression against my country." Even hardened cynics and friends of the Arabs in the Security Council chamber and in the press gallery found this hard to take. Only a few days ago Egypt had proclaimed a blockade based on "a state of war" and had asked the UN to keep its nose out of the Middle East! War for one side and passive inertia for the other had never been proposed in the United Nations before.

Eshkol had sent me a note during the Cabinet meeting requesting that I fly to the UN headquarters, where our main challenges and dangers were situated. My task was to inform world opinion of the rectitude of our actions and, above all, to ensure that our military victory would not be frittered away by a call for withdrawal without a negotiated peace. I went back to my residence in Balfour Street to pack and take leave of Suzy and my son and daughter. They would spend the night in the air-raid shelter that, to my relief, my ministerial predecessors had integrated into the house. Suzy came out of the front door. As we drew apart from our embrace we felt a rush of wind. The policeman at our gate drew attention to a piece of shrapnel that had apparently bisected the distance between us. It lies on our living room table as a memento with a few dozen other jagged pieces of steel that Suzy and the children collected later in the few days of fighting in Jerusalem.

My journey to the airport with Moshe Raviv took three hours because of the troop and tank movements on the road. We embarked in a twin-engine aircraft of the Arkia line that was designed for domestic flights. All foreign airlines had suspended their services and El Al planes were in military employment. There were still enemy aircraft and antiaircraft guns not far from our northward flight plan, and the pilot proposed to fly very low to keep out of radar range. It was the lowest altitude compatible with flight, and I thought that it would serve my nervous system best if I abstained from looking out of the window.

When I overcame this inhibition, I saw a poignant flash of scarlet beauty as the dawn broke over the Acropolis. In the Athens airport we negotiated at various counters until we found places on a KLM flight to New York. There was a stop at Amsterdam, where Ambassadors Walter Eytan, Aharon Remez and our ambassador to The Hague, Daniel Levin, awaited me. I gave them good tidings. The pressmen at the airport were confused with fictitious stories from Cairo of Arab victories. There had been a brief statement from General Rabin and General Hod, our air force commander, announcing prodigious losses for the Egyptian air force, but the newspaper and TV world were not yet convinced. My experience was that cease-fire resolutions are adopted very easily in the United Nations if they are designed to stop Israeli advances. I saw no reason to expedite a cease-fire in these conditions, and my countenance was more somber than my mood. I decided to wait to tell the full, authentic story of victory and deliverance at the table of the Security Council the next day.

The Netherlands foreign minister, Josef Luns, later to become the secretary-general of NATO, had been alerted by KLM and sent an officer of his ministry to greet me. This envoy brought Luns's apology for not coming himself. The explanation was that the minister was averting a constitutional crisis provoked by a desire of Queen Juliana to publish a statement criticizing Nasser and praying for Israel's victory. It had been patiently explained to her that this would exceed even the broadest interpretation of prerogatives that the House of Orange had ever accorded to its monarchs.

Indeed, the first prince of that dynasty had been known as William the Silent. His successors could well have borne the same title, since they would have found it hard to get a word in edgewise when faced by Dr. Luns, whose conversation, enlivened by excellent imitations of world statesmen, used to flow like the mightiest of waterfalls. For the moment, the Dutch compromise for expressing solidarity with Israel had been to ring church bells and to ascribe the initiative to the leading clerics.

Some hours later, as our KLM airliner approached the American coast, a stewardess handed me a message from the pilots' cockpit. Our UN embassy informed me that I would be expected to make a speech to the Security Council and to a record world audience as soon as I landed in New York. The KLM crew supplied me with pen and paper and I began to make a few notes. The only sentence that I drafted in full was the proud opening:

I have just come from Jerusalem to tell the Security Council that Israel, by independent effort and sacrifice, has passed from serious danger to successful and glorious resistance . . .

21

THE GOLDEN SUMMER

I DESCENDED FROM the KLM airliner into a world of turmoil. There had been no time for preparation of my speech: a hasty consultation with Ambassador Rafael at the airport; a few minutes at the Plaza Hotel for minimal recovery from jet lag; and then straight to the feverish tensions in the UN building, where the atmosphere recalled the Kennedy-Khrushchev confrontation of 1962. The parallel was not farfetched: The clash between Soviet and American interests had given the outbreak of the 1967 war an international dimension. It also had attributes of poetry and drama. The speed with which fortunes had fluctuated over recent weeks would have challenged Aeschylus or Shakespeare.

All the international TV and radio programs were tuned in on the Security Council chamber. It was clear that I would have one of the largest audiences that any speaker had addressed in all history.

Ambassador Tabor of Denmark, who was the council's president for June, understood where the attention of the world was focused and he brought me to the table as soon as I arrived down. Coming from places of decision in Jerusalem, I was like a traveler from a distant continent where legendary events were known to be unfolding.

My first sentence describing Israel's emergence "from grave danger to successful resistance" elicited a deep sigh of relief in the council chamber. The Arabs had not confessed their defeat, since they feared the domestic consequences, and we had not trumpeted our victory, since we had no interest in inviting pressure for withdrawal. From the beginning of my speech this audience was vibrant with sympathy for Israel and my words were in harmony with their emotions.

I began with a brief reference to the blockade that had throttled our contact with half of the world: "Israel has been and still is breathing with a single lung." But I was reluctant to turn this occasion into a legalistic argument about blockades. It was more important to portray the overpowering

415

sense of approaching doom that hung over our nation during the two weeks of suspense:

> In short, there was peril for Israel wherever it looked. Its manpower had been hastily mobilized, its economy and commerce were beating with feeble pulse, its streets were dark and empty—there was an apocalyptic air of approaching peril, and Israel faced this danger alone. . . .
>
> But not entirely alone! We were buoyed up by an unforgettable surge of public sympathy across the world. Friendly governments expressed the rather ominous hope that Israel would manage "to live." But the dominant theme of our condition was danger and solitude. . . .
>
> The question, widely asked in Israel and across the world, was whether we had not already gone beyond the utmost point of danger. Ours was a most unusual patience! It existed because we had acceded to the suggestion of some of the maritime states that we enable them to concert an international solution which would ensure the maintenance of free passage in the Gulf of 'Aqaba for ships of all nations and of all flags.
>
> As we pursued this avenue, we wished the world to have no doubt about our readiness to exhaust every prospect, however fragile, of a diplomatic solution. And some of the prospects that were suggested were very fragile indeed!

I devoted a few minutes to the events of May 16 when the crisis began.

> The sudden withdrawal of the United Nations Emergency Force was not accompanied as it should have been by due international consultation on the consequences of that withdrawal. Israeli interests were affected. They were not adequately explored. No attempt was made, little time given, to help surmount grave prejudice to our vital interests consequent on the withdrawal.
>
> The United Nations Emergency Force rendered distinguished service for a full decade; nothing became it less than the manner of its departure.
>
> People . . . in many countries ask: "What is the use of a United Nations presence if it is an umbrella which is taken away as soon as it begins to rain?"

I could see how U Thant fidgeted in his chair as these accusations echoed around the chamber. I had the feeling that he himself could have made good use of an umbrella, now that the rain of criticism was beginning to sputter down, and not from Israel alone.

I had previously described the UN force as a fire brigade that had fled at the first whiff of smoke. My transition from the fire brigade to the umbrella metaphor had been spontaneous. So had my reference to blockaded ports:

> To understand how Israel felt, one has merely to look around this table and imagine . . . a foreign power forcibly closing New York or Montreal, Boston or Marseilles, Toulon or Copenhagen, Rio or Tokyo or Bombay Harbor. How would your governments react?
> What would you do?
> How long would you wait?

My choice of the nine ports embraced the Security Council members sitting around the table. The camera played from one to the other. The identification of the audience with Israel—both in its plight and in its salvation—was becoming passionate. I concluded:

> These are grave times, and yet they may have fortunate issue. As he looks around him at the arena of battle, at the wreckage of planes and tanks, at the collapse of intoxicated hopes, might not the Egyptian ruler ponder whether anything was achieved by that disruption? What has it brought him but strife, conflict with other powerful interests, and the stern criticism of freedom-loving men throughout the world?
> Israel in recent days has proved its steadfastness and vigor. It is now willing to demonstrate its instinct for peace. Let us build a new system of relationships from the wreckage of the old!
> Let us discern across the darkness the vision of a brighter and a gentler dawn!

There was an indecipherable muffled noise in the room as if a powerful tension was being released. But I was not addressing myself to that audience alone. The picture of American policy that I had received from our embassy before I came to the table had lingered on President Johnson's concern—not for what our policy was, but for how others thought about it. Our image had become his obsession. He had said to his friends: "Israel will have to make a strong impact on American opinion if I am to act as I want to act."

Nobody would say that this was leadership in its most courageous sense, but what Johnson had said to me on May 25 had given me a realistic picture of his post-Vietnam situation. He could follow public opinion; he could no longer create or influence it. American leaders had lulled themselves into the strange belief that what had been wrong with the Vietnam War was not the war itself, but the failure to explain it.

The impact of the debate became clear next morning. *The New York Times* reported that the audience listening to me had been unprecedented in size and had been glued to television and radio sets all over the world. It commented:

"Abba Eban took honors for mastery of phrase-making and drew applause from the gallery. Last night was one of television's finest moments."

A chain of thirty major newspapers in the Midwest wrote that:

Americans who listened to Israel's Foreign Minister Abba Eban's address at the historic session of the Security Council on Tuesday night heard one of the great diplomatic speeches of all time.

The *Chicago Tribune* wrote tersely: "One of the greatest speeches of modern times." A Washington paper remarked that:

Eban flew out of the bleeding, war-tortured Jerusalem to make a remarkably eloquent defense of his nation's response to Arab provocation. He spoke from a position of strength, but with a magnanimity and wisdom that gives hope for the future.

World opinion had been only one of the fronts on which we deployed our resources and energies. The important aim was to prevent the Security Council from adopting its traditional routine of "cease-fire and withdrawal to previous lines." This had been proposed by the Soviet Union, France and India before my arrival. Ambassador Rafael had mounted a vehement campaign of rebuttal. But there was no doubt that this issue would be revived. In the first round following my speech, the Security Council was willing to accept Ambassador Tabor's draft for a cease-fire in place "as a first step."

There has been a tendency for UN agencies to behave in accordance with the procedure in a soccer football match. You score your goal, accept the plaudits and embraces—and go back to the center of the field. The Arab governments would thus enjoy a position of limited liability. Heads I win— and tails you lose. If they won any territory, they would keep it. If they lost territory, they would regain it. For Israel, the knowledge that not even successful resistance to aggression would leave us any tactical power for the pursuit of peace could well have engendered a desperation in which no moderate counsels would ever prevail.

The Security Council debate dragged on throughout the day, and it was past midnight when I regained my hotel room. All the messages reaching me were of Israeli forces rushing from one victory to another in a war that nobody in Israel had ever expected to erupt.

Our political fortunes were also high. Telegrams and telephone calls were reaching my hotel and our UN Mission throughout the night. The indications were that public opinion rejoiced in Nasser's downfall. It was the simple joy that decent people feel when a boastful bully is unexpectedly thwarted by what had seemed to be a weaker victim.

We turned our minds and hearts to the prosaic issue of parliamentary action. I remembered my experience in the Suez-Sinai debate in 1956. I had

AT AUSCHWITZ IN 1966 with Gideon Rafael and a number of Israeli ambassadors to Eastern European countries. I said, "We and our flag are here too late."

I WAS THE first Israeli foreign minister to visit Germany officially. Here I am with Foreign Minister Willy Brandt. (Courtesy of Israeli Office of Information)

IN 1991, SIHANOUK returned as the leader of Cambodia, where I was received by him in 1947.

THE OVAL OFFICE with President Johnson, May 1967.

JUNE 19, 1967. As foreign minister, I wait to deliver my speech to the UN General Assembly after the Six Day War. With UN Ambassador Gideon Rafael and Golda Meir, then secretary general of the Labor Party. (United Nations)

Symbolically, I am surrounded by Arab states in the Security Council in 1967.

Luncheon at the Knesset Committee of Foreign Affairs and Defense, with Chairman David Hacohen and Chief of Staff Yitzhak Rabin, after the Six Day War.

THE FIRST OFFICIAL Israeli ministerial meeting with a pope. Here I shake hands with Pope Paul VI and Vatican Secretary of State Cardinal Casaroli, in 1969. (Pontificia Fotografia)

I VISITED TWELVE countries in Africa as foreign minister. The first to establish relations with us was Ghana. Here I am greeted by President Kwame Nkrumah in Accra, 1972.

HENRY KISSINGER AND I were negotiating partners at the 1973 Geneva Conference on Peace in the Middle East. Here we are in 1974 celebrating the Disengagement Agreement with Egypt in 1974. (Ekma Ltd.)

PRIME MINISTER BEGIN made his first visit to Egypt on December 25, 1977. He invited Suzy when he learned she'd been born in Ismailiya, the town where the meeting took place. Right to left: President Sadat, Prime Minister Begin, Vice President Hosni Mubarak, Foreign Minister Fahmi and Suzy Eban. Back row, right to left: Brigadier Abrasha Tamir, Ambassador Yehuda Avner and Yechiel Kedashai.

LESS THAN A year later, Sadat greets me while Begin greets Suzy. (*People Weekly* © 1979 Marvin E. Newman)

WITH VICE PRESIDENT George Bush, in 1986. (David Valdez/the White House)

THE GLAMOUR OF television. An interval of rest and refreshment during the production of the series "Israel: A Nation is Born," 1990.

sat down amid sincere applause, but the Assembly had gone on to vote against us by a vast majority. Opinion was one thing and policy was another.

In our desire to avoid a hastily drafted cease-fire decision we received aid from an unexpected source. It was hard to know what the Kremlin and the Soviet embassy in Tel Aviv were up to during those crucial hours. Ambassador Nikolai Fedorenko had been behaving as though Egyptian troops were storming their way to Tel Aviv. He was in no hurry. He had absented himself from the Security Council for some hours and was nowhere to be found. During the whole of June 7, he was taking a delaying action by asking for the "condemnation of Israel," as if a mere cease-fire would not have been enough for him. This was a strange tactic, since Israel, for once, was now basking in the sun of admiring world opinion, and Soviet maximalism was only causing Egypt and Jordan a prolonged exposure to Israeli military power.

The Arab governments were in a real quandary. They were torn in a conflict between dream and reality. According to the official version in Cairo, Amman and Damascus, Arab forces were advancing triumphantly into Israeli territory. If Arab delegations at the UN now acquiesced in a resolution for cease-fire and withdrawal, they would be telling their people a new and unpalatable truth. Victorious armies seldom plea for their own withdrawal, and they are never in a hurry to cease fire. As so often in the policy of the Arab world, rhetoric and pretense overcame concrete interests.

While the Soviet and Egyptian delegates were holding out for "condemnation," Sinai sands were being swallowed up by Israel's advance. In the early afternoon in New York, I knew that the whole of Jerusalem was in our hands. A Jewish nation, stunned by historic emotion, was directing its eyes incredulously toward the Western Wall—the scarred relic of Israel's ancient glory. Curiously, there had been no serious movement for an Israeli conquest of the Old City during the two decades (1947–1967) when this was entirely within our military power. But once Jordan attacked Israeli positions in Jerusalem, the walls and fences that had scarred the city came crashing down and Jerusalem faced a new future. A flood of historic emotion burst the dams of restraint and set minds and hearts in movement far beyond the limits of our land.

June 7, the third day of the war, which saw Jerusalem reunited, was also the day of climax in Sinai, where a brilliant campaign was waged by General Yeshayahu Gavish's forces. His tank-force commander, General Israel Tal, advanced to El Arish, whence the Israeli assault forked out in two directions—one following the coastal road westward toward the Suez Canal and the other moving south to attack the most heavily fortified Egyptian positions.

The Egyptian forces were in full retreat, and Israeli naval forces, steaming up the Gulf of 'Aqaba, were able to seize Sharm el-Sheikh, open the Straits of Tiran, and thus correct the injury that had been the proximate cause of the war. Meanwhile, west of the Jordan, General David Elazar's armored thrust had swept Israeli forces to the river's edge. The defeated Jordanian forces and thousands of terrified refugees were fleeing in disorder across the river. Israel now controlled the entire West Bank area and commanded the whole length of the Jordan from its sources in Dan to the Dead Sea. Before June 8 was out, our parachutists who had landed at Sharm el-Sheikh moved northward to link up with the main body of the advancing Israeli army. The Mitla Pass Ravine was again the scene of sanguinary battles, where a thousand tanks participated. They ended in Israel's total victory. Israel's flag flew everywhere along the Suez Canal. The Straits of Tiran were open. The Egyptian air force was destroyed. Eight hundred Egyptian tanks had been devastated or captured.

The totality of the Egyptian debacle defied belief. Nasser had lost his nerve to such an extent that he spoke to King Hussein on an open telephone suggesting that both the Egyptian and the Jordanian governments should announce that their armies had been attacked by American and British forces! Their "reasoning" was that their populations would be less humiliated by being portrayed as the victims of Great Power aggression than as having suffered defeat by the despised Jews whose "destruction" Nasser had been predicting with a loud voice a few days before. Apart from the mendacity of this stratagem, it was marked by immense irresponsibility: If the charge of American and British aggression were true, it would be hard for the Soviet Union to leave the field open to Western military action alone. Nasser was ready to set the world aflame rather than to accept the results of his adventurism.

President Johnson had been alive to the global implication of the defeat suffered by the friends and clients of the Soviet Union. He had used the hot line to warn Kosygin against any superpower intervention and had set great fleets in motion to demonstrate American power.

I had little time, even in the personal sense, to regale myself by reading the American papers and the cables arriving from other capitals across the world. When I spoke to Suzy and Arthur Lourie by telephone on Wednesday morning, they reported that a determined attempt was being made in Israel to use my absorption in the political struggle to bring about my removal from office! The newspapers were being persuaded to underestimate or ignore the international support generated by my speech on June 7. The leading independent paper, *Ha'aretz,* had shown an astonishing contempt for journalistic integrity by appearing without a single mention of the debate or any report of the echoes that my speech had raised.

Few newspapers at home confessed that there was any significance in the fact that resolutions for withdrawal had been presented and defeated. Two major Israeli newspapers had written that there had been no need for me to occupy myself with such things as Security Council meetings and threats from the Soviet Union and pressure by France and India for withdrawal, since we had won the war and that was that. The most absurd jet of arrogance came from a celebrated scientist, Professor Yuval Neeman, who had said that we should not debate in the United Nations at all; we should tell the world: "We have won the war, and that's all there is to it."

Logic and experience were telling Israelis that unless we showed political vigilance, our military gains could be blown away like cobwebs. But emotion had put logic to flight and set up waves of intolerant rancor. Israel's "finest hour" lasted in its full radiance for about two days. There was still a joyous air surrounding Israel abroad, but at home, the knives were out.

My own inclination was to curtail my stay in New York. On the other hand, I reflected that Israel would look remarkably foolish if, the day after my departure, a resolution on withdrawal to previous lines was adopted.

It was essential to be in close touch with Ambassador Goldberg to find out how American policy was evolving. He intended to present an American draft to the Security Council, looking beyond the cease-fire:

> The Security Council calls for discussions promptly thereafter amongst the parties concerned, using such third party or United Nations assistance they may wish, looking toward the establishment of final arrangements and comprising of the withdrawal and disengagement of armed personnel, the renunciation of force, regardless of its nature, the maintenance of vital international rights, and the establishment of a stable and durable peace in the Middle East.

It was unlikely that a text so congenial to Israel's interest would be adopted, even in a Security Council where sentiment was running strongly in our favor. But this text had gone through a disquieting evolution. In one of its versions, it had called not for the establishment of a stable and durable peace but for "a revitalized armistice."

I have rarely argued with more passion and heat against any proposal than I now used in the attempt to eradicate the "armistice" concepts from the American draft. Here we were at a turning point in Middle Eastern history. The entire balance of forces had been overturned in forty-eight hours. World opinion was alert for a vision of new horizons. I could think of nothing more absurd than for international agencies to waste this golden hour for something as barren and subsidiary as the armistice relationship.

I explained to Goldberg that a nineteen-year-old armistice was already a gross anomaly. I insisted that we should banish all concepts of armistice from our minds, our hearts, our texts, and our vocabulary. Cease-fires, truces and armistices had been tried for two decades. They had all burst into flame. The only thing that had never been tried was peace. It would be illusory to pretend that peace in its full sense was close at hand, but it would be reckless to avoid defining it as the goal toward which all international effort should be directed.

I urged Goldberg to seek approval for a resolution in which the cease-fire would be succeeded, not by an armistice, but by the higher goal of a permanent peace. Goldberg fully grasped the point. By the morning of June 8, I heard to my relief that the United States had approved the idea of calling for a negotiated peace. Armistices, "revitalized" or otherwise, were no longer in vogue. Since June 8, 1967, the Armistice Agreement of 1949, having served a stabilizing purpose for eighteen years, has disappeared from American and United Nations jurisprudence.

While Ambassador Fedorenko was virtually filibustering for no reason that a rational mind could conceive, the Egyptians were becoming aware of their true position. The Egyptian delegate who, a few hours before, had been resisting any cease-fire resolution unless it was accompanied by Israeli withdrawal, was now told by Cairo to get a cease-fire as soon as possible. I confess that even his adversaries were moved by Ambassador El-Kony's humiliation, as he announced hastily to the Security Council that Egypt would accept a cease-fire without conditions, and then retired to the small lounge behind the council chamber, where he was seen unashamedly dissolved in tears.

My immediate mission in New York had been accomplished. The cease-fire had so far been separated from any call for withdrawal. The idea of leaving the armistice behind and moving forward to durable peace had taken root.

While there were strong indications that President Johnson was moving to our side, a cloud still hovered over U.S.-Israeli relations. An American signal ship, the *Liberty,* crowded with distinguished linguists and communications experts, had been attacked and damaged by Israeli aircraft in the east Mediterranean. Thirty-seven of those on board had been killed, and heavy damage sustained. The vessel had entered the fighting area to keep Washington in touch with the course of the war. In view of the global responsibilities of the United States, this was a legitimate purpose, but it seemed inevitable that those who took risks would sometimes incur tragic sacrifice.

Some American leaders—including Secretary of State Rusk—found it difficult to assume that the attack had been inadvertent. They occupied their minds with various scenarios of motivation. All of them were false. Israel had no interest whatever in preventing the United States from knowing what was going on. There was nothing apologetic about our military decisions. In fact, we had the feeling, from the very first takeoff by our aircraft on the morning of June 5, that the United States must have breathed with relief at our assumption of a responsibility that its own president had been unable to fulfill. We had the sense that the United States was now in our camp and that we were marching and sailing together in a single cause.

I categorically assert that the *Liberty* tragedy was not deliberate. I attended all the intimate consultations of the defense and diplomatic leaders in those forty-eight hours, and it is certain that the airmen and soldiers would not have reported falsely to the prime minister, the newly appointed defense minister and to the chief of staff on a matter as grave as the sinking of an American vessel by Israeli forces.

It would have been normal and wise for me to spend a day in Washington to study and, if possible, to influence American policy at first hand. However, I abandoned any such plan in the light of the confused reactions at home. I contented myself with long telephone conversations with leading officials in Washington.

The president's security adviser, McGeorge Bundy, had informed me that President Johnson had watched and heard my speech in the Security Council with appreciation. Bundy said that the president had told him that the speech was "worth several divisions" to Israel. The president was still firmly focused on the question of opinion rather than on the issues of policy. McBundy went on to reflect, in a tentative voice, that it would seem strange that Syria—which had originated the war—might be the only one that seemed to be getting off without injury. Might it not turn out, paradoxically, he said, that less guilty Arab states, such as Jordan, had suffered heavy loss, while Syria would be free to start the whole deadly sequence again?

I had no idea at the time that the question of whether to storm the Golan Heights was being revolved in the Israeli General Staff in an atmosphere of controversy. The Soviets, after all, had lured Syria into provoking the war: How could we know that Moscow would be willing for Syria to lose it?

It was my duty to report to Israel what American officials were telling me about leaving Syria without any penalty for its role in provoking the war. This confirmed a general deduction in Israel that official Washington would not be too aggrieved if Syria suffered some painful effects from the war that it had started, so that Jordan's moderate posture after June 1967 should not seem to be punished selectively.

On the evening of June 8, I set out for home. With me, in addition to Moshe Raviv, were two friends from the newspaper world: Theodore White, the celebrated chronicler of American presidential elections, and Dick Clurman, the head of foreign correspondents at Time-Life. By the time that we reached Lod Airport it was midafternoon on June 9. As we approached the runway, I could see long convoys composed of every kind of vehicle—military and civilian—winding their way up toward the north. The accent of crisis had evidently shifted to the Syrian front.

I had hardly had time to embrace Suzy on her birthday before I found myself in the prime minister's office, where discussions about Golan were in full spate.

After abortive attempts on the second day of the war to invade some northern Israeli settlements with infantry and tanks, the Syrians had returned to their fortifications on the Golan Heights, from which they were bombarding our settlements in the plain. Eshkol explained to me that Dayan was opposing any proposal to storm the Heights. He feared that our forces were becoming overextended, and that the Soviet Union would be more likely to intervene on Syria's behalf than in any other sector.

Unexpectedly, the left-wing Mapam ministers, with their intimate concern fur the kibbutzim in upper Galilee, were urging a reluctant Dayan to storm the Heights.

My own report contained the truthful appraisal that an Israeli military success on the Syrian front would not incur displeasure in Washington. The commander of our forces in the north, General David (Dado) Elazar, had been in suspense while he, his fellow officers, and the representatives of our farming villages in Galilee pleaded their case at army headquarters, and in interviews with ministers. Eventually, Dayan accepted the proposal to force the Heights and went over to a vigorous prosecution of the plan.

The fighting was savage, and our losses of valiant young men tore at the nation's heart. The battle followed the classic pattern of infantry engagements, including hand-to-hand combat, in which all the topographical advantage belonged to the Syrians entrenched on the Heights. Yet, by nightfall on June 9, General Elazar had penetrated the Heights at many points, and the road to Kuneitra lay open to the extreme north of the front.

The message that I had received from the White House included the slogan "Quickest done, soonest mended." While if the United States favored an Israeli victory against Syria, its enthusiasm for that cause was not unbridled. It stopped short at the point at which Soviet intervention could be realistically anticipated.

While our forces rushed forward and upward toward the Heights, I was being bombarded by anguished cables from UN headquarters where the Security Council was in permanent session. At one stage, Soviet threats became so concrete that the United Nations was thrown into a global alarm. Goldberg, through Ambassador Rafael, was conveying President Johnson's urgent request that we cease fire immediately. American representatives were openly hinting that Soviet intervention no longer seemed inconceivable. The hot lines were at work.

The cease-fire became effective at 6:00 P.M. on June 10, and with it, the Six Day War had come to an end. In less than two days, in intense fighting on the Syrian front, we had lost 115 killed and 322 wounded. Syrian casualties were estimated at 1,000 killed, 600 captured, and many thousands more injured.

There was hot rage and deep concern in Moscow. One of the motives for Soviet support for the Syrians was the apprehension that the Soviet Union had been losing credibility as an ally of its friends in the Third World. Nkrumah in Ghana, Sukarno in Indonesia, and Ben-Bella in Algeria had fallen from office and grace without feeling any real support from the Soviet Union. The question for Moscow was whether anybody would take the Soviet Union seriously as an ally in the future. It had, after all, reacted to the Six Day War by heroically watching it through field glasses, with occasional bursts of intimidatory rhetoric.

In the Security Council, at the table and behind the scenes, Fedorenko had warned that Israel's diplomatic relations with the Soviet Union would be broken if we did not halt in our tracks. By the time that Kuneitra had fallen, the Soviet commitment to break diplomatic relations had become too explicit for dignified retreat.

On June 10, Ambassador Chuvakhin, accompanied by his counselor, stormed into my temporary office in Tel Aviv. In a trembling voice, he read out a note in a sonorous Russian, which his associate translated into excellent Hebrew with an even more indignant intonation. The declaration was as follows:

News has just been received that Israeli armed forces, in disregard of the cease-fire resolution of the Security Council, are continuing war-like actions, carrying out the conquest of Syrian territory and moving toward Damascus.

If Israel will not immediately cease war-like acts, the Soviet Union, together with other peace-loving states, will adopt sanctions with all the consequences arising therefrom.

The government of the U.S.S.R. announces that, in the light of the continued aggression by Israel against the Arab states, and the flagrant breach of the Security Council's resolutions, the U.S.S.R. government has adopted a decision to break diplomatic relations with Israel.

I had, after all, been a minister for foreign affairs for just over eighteen months. I had no experience of how to behave when a nuclear power threatens punitive action and announces the rupture of diplomatic relations. I decided to play the scene by ear and by logic. I told the ambassador that he was, in effect, reporting on the well-known fact that there was a deep conflict of interests and opinions between the Soviet Union and Israel. If that was the case, it seemed to me that the logical course would be to strengthen our diplomatic relations, to appoint more people to our embassies, to exchange more documents and appraisals, since diplomacy, after all, was most essential in conditions of conflict. If there was a complete harmony, it would only be a question of cocktail parties.

Chuvakhin appeared confused. He said in a voice much milder than that which he had used in his official announcement: "What Your Excellency is saying is logical, but I haven't been sent here to be logical. I have come here to tell you about the rupture of relations."

I expressed some words of regret, evoking the days when Israel and the Soviet Union had struggled together for common purposes in the Middle East. I then said that I wished him well personally. At this point, to my consternation, he burst into tears. I never discovered whether this was because of his emotion at leaving Israel, or because he had reason to fear that my good wishes for his return to Moscow might not be fulfilled. I had every reason to believe that he had been reporting to his government that the

Eshkol administration was so weak domestically that it would have no ability to take military measures in resisting Nasser.

Within a single day, Poland, Czechoslovakia, Hungary, Bulgaria and even Yugoslavia sundered their relations with us. Romania alone maintained a diplomatic relationship, which it later expanded. Amid the euphoria of our victory and our initial successes in the United Nations, this erosion of our diplomatic network was absorbed more calmly than it would have been in other circumstances. I never imagined that a full quarter of a century would elapse before the formal relationship with East Europe would be renewed. The immediate effect of the Soviet Union's decision to move out of Israel was to exclude itself from any participation in the Middle Eastern dialogue, thus awarding the United States an unearned victory in the competition for influence in an important sector of the international community.

Until the collapse of the Communist empire in 1990 it was the universal habit to believe that Soviet policy was animated by a rigorous interpretation of self-interest and that all its moves were calculated to a utilitarian end. Moscow's rupture of relations with Israel was sheer folly in terms of Soviet interests, especially as there were innocuous options for the expression of dissent, such as the withdrawal of an ambassador in the moment of anger and a surreptitious return when occasion arose. The Soviet government had adopted this tactic twice; first in 1953 and later in response to the Sinai-Suez War in 1956. Chuvakhin's visit to my office on June 10, 1967, with the instruction to break relations shows that the Kremlin is no less prone to fallibility than humble democracies that do not regard their political attitudes as scientific truths. On the issue of relations with Israel, Soviet interests and Soviet emotions collided with each other and Soviet emotions won. The Kremlin is now seeking a way out of the dilemma of interest and prestige that previous regimes had created.

In a book summarizing my experience and study of diplomatic method, I wrote that "it is doubtful if anyone could recount a single instance in which a rupture of diplomatic relations has ever brought any benefit to the government that initiated the break."[1]

By mid-June the Six Day War was over.

What had we gained by victory? Everything that we would have lost without it: life, freedom, security, honor and the hope that had sustained a nation in its long laborious climb from the depths of agony to a sudden glimpse of redemption. The war had been a formative event in Israel's history. We Israelis still divide our experience between what happened before June 5, 1967, and what occurred thereafter. The war itself and the first round in the

---

[1]Abba Eban, *The New Diplomacy* (New York: Random House, 1983), p. 376.

political struggle ended with no certainty about the ultimate outcome. But one consequence was already at work: hereafter, Israel would project a new vision of itself to its own people and to the world beyond. It had given proof of resilience and determination. It had shown the qualities that glow most brightly in adversity, and it had carried its banner forward in an atmosphere of intense world sympathy. Wherever Jews walked the streets anywhere in the world, there was a new confidence in their step.

Israel, after all, was not a great power; it would always be small in size and material strength. Surely then, its victory bore witness to special qualities of spirit. Israel's example had something to say to small, threatened and oppressed countries everywhere. A sense of spiritual vigor went out from its shores, and set imaginations astir in many lands.

Above all, there was a consciousness of having lived a unique and elevating moment. The psychological impact of the victory had been very deep. Not a single Arab soldier or weapon was now in range of Israel's population centers. We held over 26,000 square miles of territory previously in Arab hands. The armies of Egypt, Syria and Jordan were in disarray. Israel's flag flew over the Temple Mount. The contrast between the threats of Arab leaders on the eve of the war and the total disintegration of their power added humiliation to their defeat.

Israeli life was being lived at a pitch of emotion above the reach of diplomatic events. The public joy was clouded by hundreds of private tragedies. The departure of Ambassador Chuvakhin had a curiously trivial dimension amid so many large events. The barbed wire that had stretched like an ugly scar across Jerusalem had been removed and thousands of Arabs and Jews were coming together in a strange mixture of political suspicion and intellectual fascination.

The defense minister, Moshe Dayan, and the mayor of Jerusalem, Teddy Kollek, had opened the city to free movement. They had given the unity of Jerusalem an imaginative expression. Great convoys of buses and cabs were bringing thousands of Israelis up to Jerusalem every day to look with exaltation at the Western Wall. We had come back to the cradle of our nationhood to stay there forever, and the reunion was watched across the world with awed respect.

Beyond Jerusalem, too, we Israelis were feeling our way toward a human contact with the cities and villages of the West Bank and the Gaza Strip. Those of middle age and beyond who had known the undivided Palestine of the mandatory regime recovered their links with Hebron and Ramallah and Nablus, Jericho, Jenin, and Bethlehem. The generation born and bred since 1948 saw a chance to break out of the claustrophobic isolation that had separated us from the Arab world.

I recall that one of the situations that made a strong impression on me was the deference of the conquerors to the vanquished. An Arab world hitherto clothed in mystery was now opening before us, and so Israelis took in the unique sounds and smells of Arab cities and villages with their braying donkeys and bustling markets and the ever-present smell of strong coffee, spices, and home-baked bread. We bargained cheerfully in Arab markets, contemplated landscapes familiar from biblical and pre-Israeli history, and marveled at the new variety and spaciousness of our environment. Those who were capable of objective judgment were bound to admit that there had been some progress under the Jordanian occupation, especially in the Jerusalem area where religious tourism had flourished.

Having satisfied ourselves with these sights, and being assured that they were theoretically available, most Israelis were to show a diminishing interest in the West Bank as the months went by. By the late eighties, at the height of the intifada (the Arab "uprising" in 1989), the average Israeli, unless he was officially involved in the occupation, was as likely to visit Bangkok as to enter Gaza or Nablus.

The Arab population received our scrutiny with phlegmatic calm. Arabs who were politically conscious thought of themselves as passing through a bad dream that would soon end in the usual way, with the major powers or the United Nations sending Israel back to previous borders. It would take many years for any Arabs to believe that they would fail to recapture, by diplomacy, that which they had lost by an unsuccessful war.

Most of my colleagues were so busy celebrating our military victory that little thought was given to the aftermath. I found myself in the position of being the first to express some tentative guidelines. Thus, on June 10, *The Jerusalem Post* carried the following story from its political correspondent, who had met me at the airport on my return:

> The Foreign Minister, Mr. Abba Eban, stated here on his return on Friday evening from the United Nations that the emphasis in Israel's foreign policy now must be on viable agreements, directly arrived at between the governments of our region in order to establish a permanent peace. . . . Mr. Eban, who was spontaneously cheered by a gathering of airport staff, said, "Israel will not squander its opportunities. It will translate them into a new national and regional reality."
>
> In reply to questions, he said that the government now has to sit down and elaborate a policy. Mr. Eban called it "the nation's finest week." It was the predominant belief of world opinion that the Israeli government in recent weeks acted in the right way and in the right places and at the right time. Israel knew when to wait and when to act. Mr. Eban also predicted a boost for Western Aliya. Jewish youth, he said, had been touched by a new pride and vision.

This sanguine view of our situation had been reinforced by experience. It was now clear to everybody of sane mind and balanced judgment that the decision to postpone our military resistance in order to reinforce our political bulwarks had been correct. Reputable surveys of public opinion now showed that the great mass of Israelis considered that the "waiting period" had been a sign of wise statesmanship, while only a small percentage ascribed it to hesitancy or indecision.

Of the many international verdicts in support of the "Hamtana" (waiting) decisions, I select one by a nonpacifist, friendly commentator.[2]

The efforts of Israeli Foreign Minister Abba Eban, although the subject of derision and deprecation by many of his countrymen and even some of his colleagues in the cabinet, have managed to secure for Israel in his two weeks of peregrinations backward and forward to Washington, London, and Paris, a climate of opinion in which it was possible for Israel to take decisive action.

A year later, in a public speech honoring the memory of Prime Minister Eshkol, General Rabin said that but for the "Hamtana" decision and the diplomatic activity between May 23 and June 1, "it is doubtful if Israel would have been able to hold firm at the cease-fire lines and in the political arena two years after the war." In an interview for broadcast in 1990 Rabin pointed out that the military position had improved during the "Hamtana" and that the chances of military success had increased.

It took some time, however, before this kind of sanity prevailed throughout the nation. While the Security Council discussions had been promising from the Israeli point of view, it was clear that the major assault upon us would be made in the General Assembly of the United Nations, where the United States and its Western allies had no veto privilege.

On June 14, Israeli diplomacy celebrated a prodigious triumph when the Security Council rejected a Soviet resolution calling for the withdrawal of Israel to the previous lines. Only four states—Bulgaria, India, Mali and the Soviet Union—supported the operative paragraph "condemning" Israel's "aggressive activities." The second operative paragraph calling for the withdrawal behind the armistice lines obtained only six votes instead of the necessary nine. Many Israelis could hardly believe their eyes or ears. In contrast to 1956, our victory in 1967 was not condemned by any international body, nor was there any pressure to have its results rescinded by a withdrawal to the previous lines.

A few days after the end of the war, the Soviet Union reached the conclusion that it would stand a better chance of success in the broader arena of the General Assembly. Accordingly, it initiated steps as in 1956 for bringing the General Assembly into special session.

I knew that we were in for a hard time in a parliamentary forum weighted

---

[2]Randolph and Winston Churchill, *The Six Day War* (London: Heinemann, 1967), p. 69.

against our cause. To prevent hostile resolutions for condemnation and withdrawal being adopted, we would have to mobilize between forty-five and fifty countries. Any realistic possibility of achieving this would require the closest possible cooperation with the United States. In estimating my chances of success in this struggle, I had innocently believed that my adversaries were limited to the Arab and Soviet worlds. This indicted me for innocence, which is a politician's gravest sin. As I sought to rally our slender forces for the international struggle, I found myself beset by a virulent campaign at home.

On June 13, in Jerusalem, less than a week after my triumphant success in the Security Council, I had worked round the clock at home in a successful attempt to defeat the withdrawal resolution in the Security Council—telephoning, cabling and writing to our United Nations Mission and all the capitals. The payoff for this effort came on June 14, with the sensational defeat of the Soviet resolution. That morning, however, the newspaper *Ha'aretz* helpfully rewarded my efforts by calling for the appointment of a new foreign minister as well as of a new prime minister. This was a strange interpretation of patriotic duty. Nothing but a conspiratorial approach close to subversion could have induced a hitherto reputable newspaper to propose that Israel should enter a domestic political and parliamentary crisis in order to depose a prime minister who had presided over a crushing victory, and a foreign minister who had turned public opinion around in Israel's favor.

The *Ha'aretz* admitted, ludicrously, that everything had turned out very well and the waiting period had been justified, but "things could have turned out otherwise if Israel had waited any longer than it had." But the fact was that we had not waited longer than we had!

Then the punch line: "Since *Ha'aretz* does not have faith in Mr. Eban's ability to carry out this task, a new foreign minister should be appointed."

The article was so clearly partisan that it could not do its intended victims very much harm. The Labor Party newspaper, *Davar,* seized an unusual opportunity to rally opinion in an article that summarized the 1967 war with great lucidity:

Every intelligent and unprejudiced man knows very well that the government's line of action has so far justified itself to a total degree. There was a war in which we won a glorious victory and which evokes enthusiasm across the entire world. The period of waiting has, therefore, justified itself from the military viewpoint as well. We now enjoy a favorable public opinion such as we have never had before. To this day, the United States has not uttered a single vote and word against our military actions, and its representative in the United Nations has struggled with intensity and success against Soviet attempts to get a resolution condemning Israel and calling for the withdrawal of forces. This magnificent achievement is the fruit of the "hesitation" of the government. Let us hope that this achievement will be prolonged.

The justified euphoria generated by the war and by the Security Council meeting was short-lived. The public mood was seized by sudden panic as the General Assembly session approached. Soviet Prime Minister Kosygin had decided to attend the meeting in person, together with the prime ministers of all the Communist states. He made a passionate appeal to the Western powers to be represented at the level of heads of state, or at least prime ministers.

Johnson, Wilson and even de Gaulle rejected this idea. De Gaulle because he had little affection for the United Nations. Johnson and Wilson because they did not wish to inflate the importance of an Assembly, the very convening of which aroused their opposition.

I had no doubt that a Special General Assembly Session attended by heads of state on Soviet initiative would result in a demonstrative "ganging-up" on Israel. This was understood in Washington and London as well, as can be deduced from the following exchange.

Letter from President Lyndon B. Johnson to Prime Minister Harold Wilson, June 16, 1967:

First, at the moment I doubt that anything useful can come from my personal participation in the General Assembly.

Second, from the beginning of this crisis I have not looked with favor on a Four-Power meeting outside the UN Security Council. It is something of an illusion that the Four Powers have the capacity to design and impose successfully a plan on the Near East. The States of the area have made it abundantly clear that they are not subject to effective control from outside.

The Four Power obsession of General de Gaulle had in any case collapsed. It was killed, to de Gaulle's grief, by a Soviet, not an American refusal. Kosygin, who then conducted Soviet policy, was more interested in a direct encounter with Johnson than with diluting his superpower status by participating in a foursome. Moreover, it was plain that the four powers were not capable of consensus. My suspicion that de Gaulle's abrupt withdrawal from his friendship with Israel was a result of his settlement with Algeria was confirmed by Wilson's account of his encounter with de Gaulle on June 19. De Gaulle had said to the British prime minister that the French government of the day (1957) had made a firm public declaration about free passage into the Gulf of 'Aqaba even when the Algerian war was producing bad relations with the Arabs. But the situation had changed. The Algerian war was over. France's relations with the Arabs had improved. She was on reasonably good terms with many of them. Given this, there was no reason for France—"or, I would suggest, the United Kingdom" (said de Gaulle, insidiously)—to ruin its relations with the Arabs, merely because public opinion felt some "superficial sympathy" for Israel because she was a small country with an unhappy history.[3]

It was already clear that our military successes were having an invigorating effect on our position both in Washington and London. Yet, the worst-case scenario for Israel was being seriously debated in every home in Israel. It was feared that the United States would defend Israel's position weakly, if at all, and that a massive UN majority would generate the same pressures as those that had forced our retreat in 1956.

In the week after the end of the war, I had sketched a policy based on using the cease-fire lines as a starting point and working toward the objective of peace settlements with our neighbors. I felt that we should not regard previous armistice lines as valid, but at the same time, it would be wrong for Israel to be swept by such a wave of historic emotion and self-confidence as to regard the new cease-fire lines as our country's permanent boundaries. From my long experience, I was certain that arbitrary and massive annexation would invite international pressure for unconditional retreat to the old lines.

I recalled Moshe Dayan's assurance (which by now he probably regretted) that we had entered the war on June 5 "not for territorial gain but for security and peace."

My strongest emphasis, however, was that we must build a new order of relations between Israel and its contiguous neighbors. "We must not go back to an intermediate situation between war and peace with all its ambivalence and obscurity." Our objective was peace and security, but I added, "These could have a territorial implication."

On Saturday night, June 17, I set off for New York with my head of bureau, Emanuel Shimoni. On arriving in New York, I was informed that the speakers inscribed for the emergency session on Monday were the Soviet prime minister, the permanent representative of the United States and the foreign minister of Israel. That evening, however, the United States decided that President Johnson would state the U.S. position in a public address on Monday morning, and that the UN debate would be left exclusively to Kosygin and Eban. The president had felt that David and Goliath implications would have a strong appeal to the chivalry of the American people and probably of the world at large. The president made it known to his friends at the same time that, while we admired Arthur Goldberg's negotiating skills, he was not excessively impressed by Goldberg's eloquence.

I realized that a duel between Moscow and Jerusalem before so many millions of eyes and ears would be unique in the history of political disputation. Kosygin was coming to New York at the head of a sixty-six-man Soviet delegation. I learned that on Monday all television and radio networks were canceling their entertainment programs and commercials to carry the debate

---

[3]Harold Wilson, *The Chariot of Israel* (London: Weidenfeld and Michael Joseph, 1981), p. 358.

at a cost of millions of dollars in lost revenue. Also, listeners all over the world would hear the debate by shortwave.

Our campaign began with a positive note as a result of a speech made outside the United Nations building. Johnson's "five points" were destined to dominate the parliamentary atmosphere. The president's speech was an exercise in lucidity. He committed the United States to five principles. "First, the recognized right of national life; second, justice for the refugees; third, innocent maritime passage; fourth, limits on the wasteful and destructive arms race; fifth, political independence and territorial integrity for all."

Above all, Johnson's speech described the dispute in terms of a contrast between the past and the future. Everything in the future must be different from what it had been in the past. It would be an exaggeration to say that Johnson's statement brought the United States into full identification with the Israeli position. This would be difficult, since the "Israeli position" had not then been crystallized. But since we were attempting a negative result to prevent a resolution for unconditional withdrawal, the five principles of June 19 gave us an important international opportunity.

Johnson admitted that Israeli troops should be withdrawn from their new positions but not to "fragile and often violated armistice lines." There should be secure borders. He emphasized that the nations that lived together in the Middle East should sit together to work out the conditions of their coexistence. The whole atmosphere of the speech was one of innovation, not reconstruction.

It became evident that the Soviet Union had made a serious miscalculation in convening such a spectacular diplomatic assembly and engaging its prestige in the outcome. Israel's military success had aroused relief around the world, and the attempt to condemn it was an embarrassing failure. Nasser's boasts of victory and his threats to "destroy" Israel were still remembered. To announce an "active state of war" at one moment and then to complain that the intended victim of the war had dared to hit back was to invite derision. Kosygin would find that it is much worse for a statesman to be ridiculed than to be reviled.

When I reached the United Nations building and forced my way through a forest of television cameras to the Israeli desk in the General Assembly, a new phase in Israel's history had begun. At my side was Gideon Rafael, a veteran of all our UN struggles, a man of analytical power and rigorously realistic outlook. Behind me was Golda Meir, at that time a member of the Knesset and secretary-general of the Labor Party. She had tactfully resisted all attempts to project her into the center of the arena, but I found her presence to be symbolically and psychologically powerful. The hall was crowded with ten prime ministers in attendance, and almost every other delegation headed by its foreign minister.

Kosygin, on ascending the tribune to open the debate, must surely have been aware of the enormous public interest focused on him at that moment.

His speech fell totally flat. At the end of it he recited the terms of his draft resolution. The General Assembly was asked to condemn Israel as having acted aggressively, to demand our immediate and unconditional withdrawal to the armistice lines and that we pay compensation for the damage inflicted by "our aggression on Egypt, Syria, and Jordan." My interpretation of this latter provision was that Israel should compensate its assailants for the damage done to their fingers by an attempt to strangle us.

I began on a low key.

This crisis has many consequences but only one cause: Israel's right to peace, security, sovereignty, economic development, and maritime freedom. Indeed, its very right to exist has been forcibly denied and aggressively attacked. This is the true origin of the tension which troubles the Middle East. The threat to Israel's existence has been directed against her in the first instance by the neighboring Arab states. But all the conditions of tension and all the impulses of aggression in the Middle East have been aggravated by the policy of the Soviet Union. The burden of responsibility lies heavy upon it.

At the end of two minutes, I looked up and was encouraged by a feeling that the audience was with me, and that beyond this audience there was a vaster one to which the debate was going out. I spoke in narrative form of our embattled history, of the Holocaust background, of the implacable nature of Arab hostility, and of the period between May 14 and June 5, during which the clouds had gathered fast around us.

On the morning of June 5, our country's choice was plain: the choice was to live or perish; to defend the national existence or to forfeit it for all time. What should be condemned is not Israel's action but the attempt to condemn it. Never have freedom, honor, justice, national interest, and international morality been so righteously protected.

In rebuttal of Kosygin's charge of aggression, I went the whole way in defending our action.

So long as men cherish freedom, so long as small states strive for the dignity of survival, the exploits of Israel's armies will be told from one generation to another with the deepest pride. The Soviet Union has described our resistance as aggression and sought to have it condemned. We reject this accusation with all our might. Here was armed force employed in a just and righteous cause, as righteous as the defense of freedom at Valley Forge; as just as the expulsion of Hitler's bombers from British skies; as noble as the protection of Stalingrad against the

Nazi hordes, so was the defense of Israel's security and existence against those who sought our nation's destruction. Never have freedom, honor, justice, national interest, and international morality been so righteously protected.

In United Nations terms, this was heavy drama. Johnson's David and Goliath metaphor was not exaggerated. Now came an almost unprecedented confrontation.

In a letter to the Israeli government, and in the words of Prime Minister Kosygin, the U.S.S.R. has formulated an obscene comparison between the Israel defense forces and the Hitlerite hordes which overran Europe in the Second World War. There is a flagrant breach of elementary human decency and of international morality in this odious comparison. Israel, with Hitler Germany. Our nation never compromised with Hitler's Germany. We never signed a pact as you did with Hitler in 1939.

In respect to your request for a condemnation, I give a simple answer to the Soviet representative: you come here in our eyes not as a judge or as a prosecutor, but rather as a legitimate object of international criticism for the part that you have played in the somber events which have brought our region to a point of explosive tension. If the Soviet Union had made an equal distribution of its friendship among the peoples of the Middle East, if it had refrained from exploiting regional rancors and tensions for the purposes of its own policy, if it had stood in evenhanded devotion to the legitimate rights of all states, the crisis which now commands our attention and anxiety would never have occurred.

While these words were being uttered, Kosygin, accompanied by Gromyko, arose from the Soviet desk and began to walk slowly out of the hall. It was not a walkout, for at least nine members of the massive Soviet delegation remained in their places. Later, the Soviet delegation apologetically explained that they had been invited to attend a dinner that the senior members of the delegation could not miss. Knowing of the habits of the United Nations members on the stroke of 1:00, I tend to believe this assertion. The drama, however, was a net gain for us.

The majority of member states believed what I was saying about the Soviet role, and the audacity of saying it won many hearts. The spectacle of a very small country pointing its accusing finger at a gigantic adversary sent a wave of surprise through the assembly hall and among the millions outside. It was a few seconds before I could collect my voice for the final sentence, directed this time to our neighbors:

The Arab states can no longer be permitted to recognize Israel's existence only for the purpose of plotting its elimination. They have come face-to-face with us in conflict; let them now come face-to-face with us in peace.

My descent from the rostrum to the Israeli desk, a few meters away, was accompanied with applause no less intense and prolonged than that which had followed my speech in 1956. Back in my hotel, I was awakened by a telephone call from Jerusalem by Eshkol, who had listened this time to the speech on the shortwave radio and wished to convey his emotion. At 11:30 P.M. I anxiously bought the following morning's *New York Times*. It had an article by James Reston:

Mr. Kosygin's request that the United Nations should pretend that two and a half million Israelis were a menace to 80 million Arabs and should be punished like a race of moral monsters, set the stage for the Israeli Foreign Minister Abba Eban, who talked like a Cambridge don and came through like a camp commander. It is easy to understand after listening to this debate between Kosygin and Eban why the Russians are suspicious of free speech. Eban worked through Kosygin's arguments with all the gentility of General Dayan's tanks in the desert.

The next morning, *The New York Post* came on the stands with a comment by James Wechsler:

Kosygin inadvertently set the stage for one of the most impressive rhetorical performances in the annals of the United Nations, or any other major parliament: the speech of Israeli Foreign Minister Abba Eban. All of Israel's heritage seemed blended yesterday in the lyrical Churchillian cadences that Eban brought to the finest hour of his life. The cause of a lonely, encircled nation, born of centuries of travail, achieved new dignity and drama in the UN hall and on millions of TV screens. Listening to him, one had the sense that almost every day of his life had been prepared for this interlude when he would summon all his resources to articulate the anguish and glory of a people so long under siege.

Wechsler was the only American newspaperman to observe the contrast between my position at home and abroad. He wrote:

Perhaps the largest footnote of irony in yesterday's events is that Eban, a prophet less than fully honored in his own country, could not even have the satisfaction of knowing that his historic address was being televised to Israeli homes. Only a limited educational TV network exists in his country at this juncture. But the word one hopes will get around in many places is that few men in our time have spoken with such distinction, under such momentous circumstances, even commanding Mr. Kosygin's recurrent attention for 64 minutes.

It would be absurd for me to say that I was unmoved by these reactions, yet I knew that no nation can live by speech alone. I still faced two questions: We had obviously overwhelmed Kosygin in debate, but could we defeat him in the vote? Second, would the surge of favorable opinion outside the UN break into its walls and save us from losing the chance of peace?

The debate in the General Assembly was not the end of my day on June 19. I had received a telegram from Eshkol summarizing the peace proposals of the government for transmission to Egypt and Syria through the United States. The elaboration of these ideas had begun in Jerusalem on the day of my return from the Security Council on September 9. Strangely, there had been little storm and stress and the main proposals had been decided without much discussion. This is an impressive fact when we recall that in addition to the Labor members, the Cabinet comprised Dayan and Begin.

I had a full opportunity to make my own input to the proposals before leaving Jerusalem on June 16, but I was not prepared for the pleasant surprise that awaited me when it became evident that my general approach was the majority view. The question was whether we should rely for our security on peace treaties, demilitarization, security balances and moderate territorial changes in the thirty-year-old boundaries that had existed on June 4, or whether we should aspire to the maintenance of all our military gains. The Cabinet decided in favor of the former course. It was later epitomized as "territories for peace." If there were real peace the boundaries would not have to be the same as if there were war.

The immediate result of this statesmanship was to create a basis for cooperation between the U.S. and Israel in the General Assembly. With a buoyant step, I therefore made for the Waldorf Towers for my discussion with the U.S. delegation. When I laid the contents of the Jerusalem telegram before the Americans, they responded with sighs of surprise and relief.

The Israeli proposals were: a peace treaty with Egypt on the basis of the international boundary with guaranteed freedom of passage in the waterways; a peace treaty with Syria on the basis of the international boundary with assurances of respect for Israel's water rights; and an indication that we would seek discussion with Jordan by direct channels. The Cabinet was not ready to define its policies for the West Bank and Gaza, since the considerations were not related to purely security considerations as were the proposals for the Egyptian and Syrian boundaries.

The Americans who listened to this exposition were Secretary Rusk, Ambassador Goldberg, Under Secretary Joseph Sisco, Assistant Secretary Eugene Rostow, and Assistant Secretary Lucius Battle. On the Israeli side I was accompanied by Harman, Evron, and Rafael.

Rusk said with monumental understatement that these were "interesting proposals." Goldberg disappeared into an adjoining room, presumably to convey the proposals to the White House. An Israeli government that had not received the least intimation of respect or recognition by any of the Arab belligerents was putting its trust in a large view of regional harmony based on the assumption that the Arabs had deduced salutary lessons from the failure of their aggression. In my speech to the General Assembly, devoted inevitably in large part to polemics, I had sketched a vision of the Middle East in terms of a community of states with mutual accessibility and regional cooperation.

Within a short time, we were to hear the Arab states rejecting these visions in strident abuse. At Khartoum on September 1 they proclaimed their rejectionism in loud tones at the behest of the very Nasser who had plunged the Arab world into humiliating defeat. But I shall never regret that Israel made this response. Nevertheless, I could not ignore Rusk's comment that it would be wise for Israel to think seriously about King Hussein, who was the key to the Palestine settlement.

Before leaving the meeting of the General Assembly, it was clear to me that the U.S. and Israel would be cooperating in the General Assembly to avoid resolutions that would send us back to the previous lines without a fundamental change in Arab policies and attitudes. Our road in the General Assembly debate was still not clear of obstacles, but the prospect of a political victory to crown our military triumph beckoned clear and sharp before our eyes.

But not without many intermediate scares. The Soviet resolutions with their roars of condemnation had been defeated in the Security Council, and we hoped that they would be presented in the General Assembly in a form that would invite rejection. But other events conspired to create a situation in which we were faced with a cluster of anti-Israeli resolutions. And there were other apprehensions.

President Johnson met Kosygin in the unlikely ambience of Glassboro, New Jersey. The U.S. was attempting to achieve cooperation with the U.S.S.R. in many fields, and we felt the usual twinge of Israeli apprehension. This proved to be groundless. Johnson presented Kosygin with his "mosaic of peace" on the lines of the Five Points of his June 19 address. Our American front was holding firm. We had made an error in keeping our June 19 proposals secret in the hope of making it easier for the Arab states to respond. By this somewhat idealistic decision we had lost the possibility of using our moderation as a legitimate weapon of parliamentary struggle.

During the next two weeks I orchestrated the most intense lobbying effort that Israel had undertaken since the 1947 partition debate. Success was by no means assured. On June 27, the Knesset enacted the application of Israeli legislation to Jerusalem. Our delegation at the UN, including the Herut member, Ben-Eliezer, advocated delaying this measure until after the General Assembly, but George Brown's speech with its emphasis on Jerusalem had raised fears that time would work against us in this issue. More seriously, American television began portraying a great flood of Arab refugees moving across the river, probably animated by the fear that an Israeli administration would deal with them as an Arab administration would have dealt with the Israelis in the event of an Arab victory. The Israeli Cabinet responded with a decision to allow a procedure for return, which was only partly implemented.

The greatest danger to our prospect of parliamentary victory lay in an illusory impression of Arab moderation. The frenetic tone of the Soviet proposals with their demand for condemnation of Israel made the acceptance of such a text impossible, but the Yugoslav draft that simply called for peace with "complete withdrawal" seemed likely to pass. King Hussein of Jordan addressed the Assembly in such civilized tones that he increased the prospect of passage for the Yugoslav–Third World text. He appeared as the helpless victim of Nasser's conniving, which was not wholly untrue.

There were days, as the voting approached, when the Yugoslav resolution seemed certain of adoption. This would have been a great defeat. I instructed our delegation members to avoid sitting in the Delegates' Lounge with a look of apocalyptic doom on their faces. I myself led an intense campaign to secure negative votes and abstentions from the French-speaking delegates from West Africa. They had suddenly had the experience of being invited to tea by Foreign Minister Gromyko after being contemptuously ignored for many months, as "the tools of French imperialism." The French delegation, separating itself from the European consensus, was lobbying against us. The most distinguished representative of the francophone states of Africa was President Houphouët-Boigny of the Ivory Coast, and I requested my predecessor, Golda Meir, to find him in Europe. It turned out that he was in Germany, a country in which Golda had never agreed to set foot, but she understood the decisive nature of our struggle and went to Germany to secure his powerful assistance.

I found the tension unbearable when the General Assembly convened for the vote on July 4. What followed stands out in Israel's diplomatic history as miraculous. All the resolutions that contained any criticism of Israel were defeated through lack of votes or withdrawn because of lack of support. So were all the texts that required withdrawal of forces from "all the territories" occupied in the 1967 conflict. Between June and November, condemnation of Israel had been rejected six times and withdrawal to the previous lines had been turned down four times in the two major organs of the United Nations. The Soviet resolution in the Security Council, calling for censure of Israel and the withdrawal of Israeli forces behind the pre-1967 lines, "gathered" four votes (the U.S.S.R., Bulgaria, India and Mali) out of the nine required. The

Yugoslav resolution in the General Assembly, which called, in less virulent terms, for complete Israeli withdrawal received fifty-six positive votes—far short of the two-thirds prescribed by the UN Charter. There is no doubt that this was the greatest Israeli victory in our recent diplomatic career. The stunned look on the faces of Mr. Gromyko and the Arab delegates gave me almost sensual satisfaction. It was a moment that I have never ceased to cherish and whose political effects are still effectively alive.

We had secured an international certificate of legitimacy from the United Nations for our continued presence along the cease-fire lines until such time as the Arab governments were ready for peace.

At 9:00 in the evening I assembled the Israeli delegation in my hotel suite, where we drank enthusiastic toasts to each other. It was 3:00 A.M. in Jerusalem when I aroused the director general of the Foreign Ministry, Aryeh Levavi, from his bed to tell him the news of the vote. He admitted that everyone in Israel had expected the Yugoslav resolution to pass. The skeptical Israeli public was quite unprepared for the victory that we had achieved.

I arrived back in Jerusalem on July 7 to find the country in a mood of political celebration. There was a large and enthusiastic welcoming party at the airport at Lod, including Golda Meir and minister without portfolio Yisrael Galili.

A public opinion poll in Israel published in *Ha'aretz* revealed that eighty-nine percent of those canvassed wanted me to be their foreign minister. The next candidate in line received three percent. Newspapers, which only two weeks before had suggested that I be accompanied to the United Nations by Begin and Dayan, now began to eat their words in varying degrees of pain and relish. *Ha'aretz* published an article expressing "surprise" at the ardent fidelity of the Israeli public to its leaders, but accepting the verdict with belated grace.

In my words at the airport I paid a tribute to the United States for its support. I added: "It was because we involved the United States in the effort to prevent the war that we have secured support for the war's results."

22

UNHAPPY AFTERMATH

JULY 1967 WAS the month of reckoning. Each of the main actors in the drama of the Six Day War experienced a swift change of stature in a single week. Washington and Moscow had passionately wanted to avoid being embroiled in a war that the Soviet Union had provoked and the United States had not been able to prevent. But there was no escape from involvement. The war and its aftermath would pursue them with no respite.

At the first outbreak of hostilities on June 5, 1967, President Johnson had called Prime Minister Kosygin on the hot line and obtained promises of Soviet restraint. But for good measure, he sent impressive fleets into neighboring waters, not with the aim of escalation, but with the contrary objective of localizing the military explosion. His message to the Soviet adversary was plain: "Let's both stay out of this one." Before two days had passed, Johnson had activated all the anti-miscalculation procedures that the two superpowers had elaborated in their arms-control discussions. In my next meeting with him he described these to me as though he was the owner of a new electronic device and had discovered to his surprise that the gadget really worked.

The two superpowers, as they were then called, could only run away from the war. They could not hide. Each of them would end up either a winner or a loser. The proximate causes of the war quickly faded from consciousness. The Egyptian blockade of the Gulf of 'Aqaba and the troop concentrations in Sinai soon receded into subsidiary status, rather like the assassination of the Austro-Hungarian archduke at Sarajevo in 1914, or the German seizure of Danzig in 1939. The spark that kindles a war is rarely its basic cause, or its most significant consequence.

Many nations have suffered travail in their efforts to come to terms with defeat, but Israel's predicaments were those of victory. Our relief was enhanced by the memory of the fear that gripped Israeli hearts in mid-May when numerically superior Arab divisions were moving toward us from north, south, and east. In Israel, Colonel Chaim Herzog had stood almost alone against the rhetoric of despondency, informing his anguished radio-listeners that he felt safer as an Israeli awaiting an Egyptian assault than he would be if he were an Egyptian soldier advancing toward Israel. The popular mood was less confident. We Israelis will never forget the weeks when the prospect of our extinction was taken seriously in Israel and the world.

Throughout the summer of 1967 Israel became accustomed to its new stature. It bestrode the Middle East. Instead of appearing as an apprehensive victim of regional hostility and international isolation, Israel had the image of a superman capable of overcoming perils that would be fatal to normal human beings. A whole literature and folklore based on the idea of Israeli omnipotence was born overnight. Anecdotes proliferated. Diaspora Jews inherited the pride of Israel's triumph without having lived the wrenching pain of personal risk or sacrifice. It was "in" to be Jewish. Children in America played "Jews and Arabs" instead of "cowboys and Indians," and no self-respecting youngster wanted to take the Arab role. I noticed a sudden proliferation of yarmulkes in the streets of New York, London and Paris. Immigration of Jews from the United States and Western Europe to Israel did not become prolific, but it was more abundant than before. Those who thought in religious terms saw a divine hand in the outcome of the war. A more secular view attributed our triumph to our efficient military perform-ance and planning. Eshkol was not a charismatic figure, but he could be relied on to ensure that the gasoline would be close to the tanks and the ammunition would fit the weapons.

A study made by the Institute for Strategic Studies in London summarized our campaign:

> Like the campaigns of the younger Napoleon, the performance of the Israeli Defense Forces provided a textbook illustration of all the classi-cal principles of war: speed, surprise, concentration, security, the of-fensive approach—above all, training and morale.
>
> Military radicals will observe how the Israelis attained this peak of excellence without the aid of drill sergeants and the barrack square. Above all, it will be seen how Israel observed the Clausewitzian princi-ple of political context which the British had ignored so disastrously in 1956. The Israeli high command . . . worked on the assumption that it would have three days to complete its task before outside pressures compelled a cease-fire.

Sometimes the pride went beyond a due sense of proportion. Hastily published albums featuring our victorious generals were snapped up at Is-rael's bookstores. Moshe Dayan, a superb manipulator of his own public image, became a charismatic figure. He could do no wrong in the eyes of the nation, although he made no special effort to appear as of perfect virtue. Part of the general adulation even rubbed off on me, since the TV broadcasts of the UN debates had given me what the jargon of public relations called "a large recognition factor."

If there was excessive self-congratulation in some sectors of Israeli life and opinion, there were symptoms of self-restraint and even of disquiet in others. There was a heavy toll of bereavement—over eight hundred dead and three thousand wounded. The fact that the Arabs had lost twenty thousand dead and a corresponding number of wounded and that a hundred thousand West Bank Arabs had become refugees did not alleviate Israel's grief. A book entitled *The Seventh Day* published the reflections of Israeli soldiers returning from the battlefields. It threw a strong light on the ambivalent mood of Israeli youth. Our soldiers revealed themselves as capable of moral self-analysis. They brooded on the ultimate mysteries of life and death, as well as on the issue of their Jewish identity. They were often tormented by the complexity of their own attitude toward their Arab enemies. Some of them were inflamed with national pride and free of any doubt about the legitimacy and permanence of the new Israeli map. But many of them recoiled from the prospect that Jews would now rule hundreds of thousands of conquered Arabs without granting them either equality in the Israeli system or any expression of a separate national identity.

Our diplomatic successes in the mid-summer of 1967 were more unexpected for the Arabs than our military victory. More unexpected because, in the political arena, the Arabs always begin with greater initial advantage than on the field of battle. Yet the Palestine Arabs reacted to their defeat with a strange fatalism. They discovered that the conquering Israelis did not intend to do to them what they would almost certainly have done to the Jews if the fortunes of battle had gone the other way. Reason and experience supported the conviction of the Arabs that their command of international voting systems and their preponderance in oil, money, and strategic space would force us to relinquish our gains without advantage or compensation.

Their greatest surprise was to have lost the first round in the United Nations, which they hitherto regarded as their home ground. This time everything was different from 1956. The Security Council did not order Israel back to its previous positions. It ordered a cease-fire that froze the advantageous positions the Israeli armies had reached. This time the General Assembly, as well as the Security Council, refused to condemn Israel's preemptive action. They voted down all texts that required the withdrawal of Israeli forces ahead of peace. The Arabs were initially haunted by these reverses, yet they still believed that a more realistic balance of strength would assert itself in their favor. What they had lost in the battlefield, they would regain at the table.

In meetings of our Foreign Ministry staff I presented a picture of the winners and losers. In contrast to the euphoric mood, I said repeatedly that none of the parties had made permanent gains, and none of them had suffered permanent defeat. Nevertheless, I agreed with the Duke of Wellington, the victor against Napoleon at Waterloo, who had said that "nothing except a battle lost can be half so melancholy as a battle won."

First in the line of the losers was the Soviet Union. The 1967 war is the child of Soviet policy. The Arabs, who were meant to be the beneficiaries of the Kremlin's protection, became its victims. Moscow had provoked the Arabs to make war, but did virtually nothing to help them win it. They did not even use their power of intimidatory rhetoric that had worked so well for them against Israel in 1956, when Soviet threats caused panic even among Israeli Cabinet members. The Soviet Union was not sentimental. It believed that the race is to the swift and the battle to the strong, and when the Arab governments and armies proved their ineptitude and even tarnished the reputation of Soviet weaponry, Moscow became detached and cautious, limiting itself to resounding verbiage on behalf of the Arabs. The Soviet attitude toward the vanquished Arab states had an air of disappointed condescension.

Despite their reputation for deliberate calculation, Soviet leaders had committed every conceivable error of judgment. First, they grotesquely overestimated the importance, and underestimated the risk, of protecting the Syrian regime from the consequences of its terrorist activity against Israel. The Kremlin behaved as if a blow inflicted by Israel on Syria would fatally weaken the Soviet position in what was then known as the Third World. This was an exaggerated fear. The Soviet Union was damaged by the Syrian failure, but not to the point of collapse.

Moscow also reaped the bitter fruit of its detachment from Israel. Once the Tiran blockade was imposed, the Soviet leaders showed no ability to probe the consequences. They seriously believed that Israel would swallow the bitter pill. They hoped that a few routine words of rebuke and warning would be sufficient to hold Israel in check, even after the blockade in the Gulf had been imposed. The Soviets were realistic in predicting the failure of American and British efforts to do anything effective against the blockade. But they overlooked the contingency that Israel would break the blockade alone with a high degree of Western acquiescence. Most crucially, the Soviet Union failed to understand the real military relationship between Egypt and Israel. It believed that Israel, without allies, would not dare to break out of siege, and would not win if it tried. There is evidence that Rafi propaganda, portraying Eshkol as incapable of daring military reaction, had made an impression on the U.S.S.R.

Through these accumulated failures of judgment and control, the Soviet Union suffered an erosion of its global interests and prestige. The most massive investment of armaments and diplomatic support ever made by the Soviet Union outside its own Communist sphere was squandered in a single week. Soviet power and realism were thereafter held in lesser awe across the world. Small countries asked themselves what an alliance with the Soviet Union was really worth.

In order to give a reassuring answer, the Soviet Union hastily rebuilt the Arab armies and air forces, and stationed experts on Egyptian and Syrian soil. But the halo of Moscow's power never glowed as brightly in the world as before. No countries in the Arab world or anywhere else have much respect for protectors who do not protect.

Nasser tied with the Soviet Union in the competition for the loser's crown of thorns. The Arabs experienced a defeat of which the sting was sharper because of the anticipation of vengeance, loot, and victory that had gone before. Arabs now began to ask more frankly than usual why everything had gone wrong and who or what was to blame. "A greater disaster than in 1948 has happened," wrote an Egyptian commentator, "and it therefore demands a greater measure of frankness and criticism."

Self-criticism could have had a healing effect, but it was very selectively applied. The old wicked enemies—"Zionism," "imperialism," and "reaction"—were still held mainly responsible for the Arab tragedy. This was familiar stuff. But now, for the first time, the Arab nation focused a searchlight on its own imperfections. We find Arab writers and thinkers castigating their own people as superficial, frivolous, excessively individualistic, prone to illusion, unwilling to recognize facts—in short, deficient in all the qualities by which nations guard themselves against disaster. Arab writers at last confessed that failure had come, not from outward circumstances alone, but to a much greater degree from elements in the nature of Arab society. Every section of Arab opinion had its own answer to the riddle of failure. But nearly all of them came back in the end to the same human issue. "We cannot build a modern army out of a backward community" was a constant theme of Arab rhetoric.

The Israeli image in the Arab world received a more sophisticated and ambivalent treatment. The caricaturists portrayed the Israeli enemy as the oily, curly-headed, hook-nosed monster with horns and tail. But more thoughtful Arabs had a grudging respect for Israel's achievements. Some of their writers implied that only by imitating the qualities that had brought success to Zionism could Arab nationalism ever rise above its own defeats.

This sounds like lucid reasoning, but lucidity came to a screeching halt when it encountered the Egyptian leader. Everyone except Nasser was blamed! He was held innocent of the disaster that he had personally provoked. Our action in June 1967 was portrayed as having nothing to do with Nasser's policies in May 1967. According to this mythology, the Israeli government and army, for no special reason, and under no particular provocation, had decided to make war on the arbitrarily chosen date of June 5, 1967. Nasser explained that he had been defeated not by the Israeli army, but by powerful American and British forces. There is no evidence that anyone else in Egypt believed this, but nobody in Egypt was willing to deny Nasser his face-saving alibi. The Arab defeat was ascribed by the media to defects in education and social development, to excessive devotion to conservative Islam, to inadequate devotion to conservative Islam, to the treachery of imperialists, to the deceit of reactionaries, to Israeli devilry, to anything except the mistakes of Gamal Abdel Nasser. He wore a coat of armor with a thick Teflon covering.

The argument that eliminated Nasser from the causes of his own debacle came to expression in his "resignation." On June 9, Nasser, aware of the true story of his defeat, announced his willingness to step down. There was an organized wave of protest in Cairo; some of it was spontaneous. The Egyptian people had taken Nasser into its possession. It was proud of his prestige. As their world fell about them, Egyptians might have thought that Nasser was the only asset that remained in their hands. Crowds in streets, deputies in Parliament, military leaders, and others joined in urging the great man to reconsider his resignation. He "bowed" to the public opinion that he had created and inspired. He thus won a domestic success at a time of military and international failure. Might this not have set the scene for a similar recuperation by Saddam Hussein in Iraq twenty-four years later?

A new Egyptian leader in 1967–1968 might have been free to criticize Nasser's reckless lurch to war and to set Arab nationalism on a path of conciliation. By clinging to its current leader, the Egyptian people committed itself to its current policies. On September 1, 1967, Nasser orchestrated a unanimous resolution of the Arab League states at a meeting in Khartoum. The decision was no peace with Israel, no recognition of Israel, no negotiation with Israel, no territorial bargaining with Israel. This was a direct answer to the Israeli proposal of June 19 to establish peace on the basis of the international boundaries with Egypt and Syria, and to negotiate a territorial compromise with Jordan, which was then the universally recognized custodian of Palestinian interests. Israeli liberals who fault the Eshkol government with insufficient zeal for peace have a hard time explaining how this accusation stands up against the fact that we had offered the whole of Sinai and Golan and most of the West Bank before any expression of an Arab willingness to negotiate.

The Khartoum resolution proved that Nasser was seeking domestic support for demagogy. He was not seeking regional peace or international admiration. He was not about to end the conflict on the unacceptable basis of the June defeat.

King Hussein of Jordan, like Nasser, was a loser whose only consolation was his own survival. His tragic decision to join Nasser's war or, more accurately, his inability to avoid joining it, generated a crisis greater than any that characterized the Middle East before 1967. But for the involvement of Jordan in the war, there would not now be a problem concerning the West Bank and Gaza. Even after the loss of the West Bank, he had a strong position in the occupied territories where the population believed that he had a better chance than any other Arab authority of restoring the lost lands to Arab possession. He had loyal followers among the West Bank leaders, but it was evident that his prestige would soon dwindle if months were to pass without any progress in the recovery of territories.

There were other subsidiary losers. France, or, to be more specific, Charles de Gaulle, was one of them. De Gaulle and France, in those days, were interchangeable terms. The general had not lost his talent for surprise. Even before May 1967, I had noticed some signs of reticence toward Israel in Paris. But nothing prepared any of us for the jolt that shook our confidence and emotion between my meeting with the general on May 24 and the outbreak of hostilities on June 5.

The 1957 French commitment to support Israel's right to protect its shipping in the Straits of Tiran had never been abrogated. Nor did France criticize the results of Israel's blow to the Syrian air force on April 7, when we brought down six Soviet-built MiGs. The French people gloried in what seemed to be the superiority of French Mirage aircraft over Soviet MiGs. (In reality it was the superiority of Israeli pilots over Syrian pilots.) The flow of French arms to Israel for seven years after the end of the Algerian war convinced many Israelis that the French interest in Israel must be inherently durable. Israelis believed that our two countries went hand in hand, not because they had a common adversary in the past, but because they had common ideals and interests in the present and future. The sudden collapse of this myth was a powerful incentive for Israel to expedite its recourse to military actions.

In November 1990, twenty-three years after the Six Day War, I went to Paris to take part in a colloquium marking the hundredth anniversary of de Gaulle's birth. I fear that my reluctance to join the procession of eulogies must have been abrasive. I could not conceal my view that de Gaulle's policies toward Israel from 1967 until the end of his rule in 1970 were a story of failure. His premature embrace of Nasser and his insensitive observations about Israel in May 1967 ensured that there could be no united Western stand. Most important of all, the embargo that de Gaulle imposed on Israel on June 2 told us grimly that our balance of air strength would soon be eroded. The war that he had genuinely wished to avoid was actually brought nearer by his embargo. We felt that if we did not take the opportunity of resistance at full tide, we would be swept backward into the ebb of a declining military position.

By taking sides so blatantly with Egypt, de Gaulle renounced a potential mediatory role. His insistence on "the concertation of the four great powers" earned him a slap in the face from the Soviet leadership and an expression of gentle contempt from President Johnson. He was an intensely proud man and the option of admitting error and searching new paths never arose in his mind. Within a few years, de Gaulle found himself involved in a dialogue on the Jewish character. On the one hand, he said, there was reason to be gratified that the Jewish people had managed to build its home in the land of its memories. On the other hand, the Jewish people was described in his unforgettable phrase as "an elite nation, domineering and sure of itself."

Generalizations about the nature of Jews are a certain way of getting into trouble, and de Gaulle had jumped with heavy feet into slippery ground. He ingeniously responded that he regarded all three epithets—elite, domineering, and self-confident—as praiseworthy qualities that had often been ascribed to him without evoking any protest on his part. Jews could not accept this interpretation; the very notion of "domination" echoed ironically in the ears of a people whose powerlessness had been tragically illustrated a single generation ago. De Gaulle's observations elicited from David Ben-Gurion one of the longest letters in the history of diplomatic discourse, to which de Gaulle's responses were as laconic as courtesy would allow.

I was convinced that de Gaulle's attitudes from 1967 onward were dictated, not by any Middle Eastern context, but by his determination to detach himself from any appearance of alliance with the West. Once he defined "the Anglo Saxons" or "the Occident" as his adversaries, he was adrift in the international system. It was all very well for him to say that there is no such thing as "Western solutions." The fact remains that, outside the West and the European community, there were no visible parameters within which French diplomatic skills could be deployed. France, as a "loser," was a spectacle that caused me and most Israelis nothing but pain.

The main winner in the 1967 war was the United States, which woke up on the morning of June 6 as a stronger and prouder nation than it had been the day before. There was some irony in this result, for the United States had risked no military action and Israel's victory had been won with French, not American, aircraft. But American foreign policy moved almost exclusively in parameters defined by the Cold War. The essential point in American eyes was that a major international conflict had ended in a manner contrary to the wish and interest of the Soviet Union, and a country friendly to the United States had triumphed against Moscow's clients. After years of frustration at its failure to get its way in Southeast Asia, America found itself on the winning side in the Middle East. Without any of the terrible cost in tears and blood that it had paid in Southeast Asia, the United States had strengthened its strategic position in a more central and sensitive area of the world.

On the face of it Washington's dividend from the 1967 war appeared to have been unearned. On deeper view, luck was not the only component of America's success. Washington had been rhetorically virtuous throughout the crisis. In early June when Nasser threatened to impose the blockade in Tiran, the State Department had addressed the Kremlin in stringent terms:

> The United States will regard any impingement on freedom of navigation in the Strait of Tiran, whether under the Israeli flag or another, as

an act of aggression against which Israel, in the opinion of the United States, is justified in taking defensive measures.

The U.S. representative, Ambassador Arthur Goldberg, had been the only delegate in the meetings of the Security Council to call not only for restraint, but also for the cessation of the Egyptian blockade. On May 26, President Johnson publicly condemned the Egyptian provocations and told me in frank terms that Israel was "the victim of aggression."

All this was well and good. The Johnson administration had built a good record, but the credibility of a superpower is not measured in semantic rectitude alone; it requires tenacious pursuit of harmony between words and deeds. In the days leading up to the war, the United States had been strong in speech but weak in practical recourse. Nevertheless, it had shown courage in departing from the syndrome of 1956: it was now exhorting Israel to stay at its extended cease-fire lines until the Arab states agreed to regard us as a legitimate sovereign neighbor.

The relief with which Washington greeted the results of the war did not mean that the United States was enamored with Israeli policy. American leaders did not regard the Six Day War as a final and providential change in the balance of power. It emerged from the 1967 explosion unscathed in terms of dead and wounded, but it had suffered some erosion of its international position, despite the general rise in its status through the victory of its Israeli ally. Arab states had broken relations with Washington, and the United States would have to spend much effort to reinstate itself in the position that it occupied on June 4, 1967.

Washington even became skeptical about whether there had really been a "Six Day War" at all. On July 1, 1967, a few weeks after the end of the Six Day campaign, violent military actions broke out between Egypt and Israel across the Suez Canal. More than seven hundred Israelis would fall dead between July 1967 and August 1970, and the wounded would number more than two thousand. The new outbreaks of fighting took place in exchanges between Israeli artillery and Egyptian air forces on either side of the Suez Canal, the result was the devastation of Egyptian population centers in the canal zone. The flight of close to a million Egyptians to Cairo and regions around the Suez Canal increased the alarming demographic pressure in the rest of the country. Another consequence was the closure of the Suez Canal, with injury to the European economies whose oil tankers had to take the long route skirting the tip of South Africa. Even Harold Wilson, whose sympathies for Israel were profound, began to grumble to me about the damage to the British economy arising from the closure of the Canal. All I could do was to offer him free advice to build larger tankers and wait hopefully for North Sea oil.

Beyond the fiscal difficulties loomed the danger of global tensions arising from the hostilities in the Canal area. In addition to fire from artillery bases, Israeli forces carried out commando and air penetrations deep into the

Egyptian mainland west of Sinai. While I gloried along with the whole nation in the memory of the famous and imperishable six days, I was at a loss to understand how any responsible Israeli could imagine that our basic national problems had been "solved." I was convinced, in particular, that the territorial structure emanating from the six days of war would collapse under the weight of the untenable regional and international imbalance. I agreed that the enlarged surface of Greater Israel could be a favorable starting-point in a bargaining exercise. I did not believe that it could assure any permanent result. The map showing Israel as a country extending from the Golan to Suez and embracing the length of the Jordan seemed to me to be not a guarantee of peace but an invitation to early war. The new territorial structure would surely become intolerable for all of the involved parties: for Israel because of a constant bleeding of its manpower; for Egypt because of the destruction of entire areas of habitation; for the Palestinians because of the hardship and shame of oppressive foreign rule; and for the world community because of the paralysis of normal intercontinental commerce and the global dangers arising from Soviet-American confrontation. Short-term salvation had come from the battlefield, but long-term stability would depend on diplomacy.

A brief spark of optimism about the possibility of peace was kindled when Israel conveyed its far-reaching peace proposals to Egypt and Syria through the United States on June 19, 1967, and followed up with assurances that we intended to embark on a direct negotiation with Jordan. However, the Khartoum meeting of the League of Arab States in September seemed to leave no room for reconciliation. It was in that context that I told the United Nations that this was the first war in history in which the victor sued for peace and the loser called for unconditional surrender. The United States was unlikely to regard the permanent incorporation of all the captured territories into Israel as an American interest. Our decisive victory was, of course, better in American eyes than our defeat, but the American government and people saw the territorial results of the 1967 war as a problem, not as a solution.

It might have been hoped that the Israeli occupation would eventually lure the Arab states to a peace negotiation. On the other hand, there was the danger that many Israelis would regard the territories not as cards to play at a peace table, which was the ruling Labor Party's official policy, but rather as possessions to be permanently embraced.

For several weeks in the late summer of 1967, I lived in an isolated realm of anxiety while the noise of unconfined joy kept intruding through the window. For me, the Six Day War meant salvation in an hour of peril, an intense elevation of pride, and the possession of territorial assets that could be transacted in a negotiation for peace. For many Israelis, it was a providential dispensation enlarging Israel's areas of jurisdiction beyond anything that had ever been conceived before, inaugurating the renewal of King Solomon's empire, and converting Israel from a beleaguered, tiny state into a central player on the stage of international strategy. The gap between these two conceptions was to dominate Israel's national dialogue and international relations for several decades. Indeed, it has not yet been bridged.

I did not believe then, and I do not imagine now, that it will be possible for Israel to maintain a military occupation over nearly two million Arabs and also to enjoy any lasting peace or social harmony. Yet, the first response of the Arabs in the West Bank and East Jerusalem to Israel's conquest was one of sullen docility. They did not, at any time, resign themselves to the idea of permanent Israeli occupation, but their anxiety was not urgent since they did not believe that the occupation was going to last. Their major interest was to see that international preoccupation with the Middle East would be constant, public and pervasive.

In order to serve that aim, their first recourse was the United Nations, which had long been their favorite arena. They decided to regard their defeat in June as a nightmare too bad to be believed and unlikely to be repeated. They turned to the president of the UN General Assembly, Mr. Abdul Rahman Pazshwak, of Afghanistan, asking him to reconvene the General Assembly for some further days of grace, in the hope that they would get a better result than the astonishing rejection that they had incurred in June. Afghanistan had previously aroused my interest only as a result of its alphabetical priority in the UN roll call. "Afghanistan, no, Albania, no, Australia, yes," was a familiar and ominous litany to our ears whenever anything in Israel's favor was proposed. In the strange causality of international institutions, Afghanistan now became a factor in Israel's destiny.

On July 12, less than a week after my return from the triumphant General Assembly session, I was on my way back to UN headquarters. It had been agreed at the United Nations that unless an accord was reached in a few days, the diplomatic initiative of the Soviet Union, under the inspiration of Kosygin, would expire in deadlock. We would then have a respite from international action until the regular session in mid-September.

Although the Israeli delegation under my leadership had scored a general victory in the June session of the General Assembly, I had to acknowledge a marginal setback. The Security Council and the General Assembly had declared Israel's incorporation of East Jerusalem in the State of Israel to be legally "null and void." It was beyond my understanding why anybody in the world should wish to restore East Jerusalem to a Jordanian regime that had fallen so far short of its minimal thrust toward tolerance and religious freedom. Jews had been barred from the western wall, synagogues had been destroyed, and tombstones had been violated. In a letter to the secretary-general, for universal distribution, on July 10, 1967, I defended the changes that had come about in the city:

> Where there had been an explosive military frontier, there is now tranquility. . . . Where there had previously been strife, there is now peace. Where there had been sacrilege and vandalism, there is now a

decent respect for the rights of all pilgrims to have access and free worship at the shrine which they revere.

On July 10, together with two ministerial colleagues, Menachem Begin and Zerach Warhaftig, I drafted a text that would reconcile Israel's sovereignty in Jerusalem with the spiritual interests of the world community. In this letter, the Israeli Cabinet stated that Israel "does not claim unilateral control or exclusive jurisdiction in the Holy Places of Christianity and Islam, and in the peace settlement, we would be ready to give appropriate expression to this principle."

This was the first time in Jerusalem's history that a government in control of the city had offered the custodianship of the Muslim Holy Places to anyone outside its own jurisdiction. I hoped that by offering to remove the sacred square mile around the El Aqsa mosque from our exclusive control, we would help to create an enclave option that might promote a political settlement with Jordan and the Islamic world at a later stage. The unity of Jerusalem was more popular in the world than its renewed division, and I felt free to indicate this without inhibition.

This is a concept which lies beyond and above, before and after all political and secular considerations. The eternal link between Israel and Jerusalem [is] a link more ancient, more potent, and more passionate than any other link between any people and any place.

Soon after my arrival in New York, however, I saw how fragile our victory in the June 1967 session had been. Early on July 20, when the members of our delegation were assembled in my hotel suite, about to leave for what we thought would be the final session of the emergency General Assembly, a telephone call came from Assistant Secretary of State Joseph Sisco, who was Arthur Goldberg's chief associate in the U.S. Mission.

Gideon Rafael took the call that he and I found disconcerting. Sisco told him that meetings had taken place in Washington on July 18 and 19 between Goldberg and the Soviet ambassador, Anatoly Dobrynin, and on July 19, between Goldberg and Gromyko. Sisco informed Rafael that various tentative drafts had been discussed, and the United States would agree to a twenty-four-hour postponement of the final UN session, in the hope of adopting an international consensus. Meanwhile, Goldberg invited us to come over to the U.S. mission to hear of a new development. After our success in the June Assembly, "new developments" were the last thing that I needed.

When we reached the American mission to the UN I found myself engaged in one of the most embarrassing discussions that ever took place between the United States and Israel. After much talking and meeting, Gromyko and Goldberg had been able to reach an agreement on the wording of a proposal that they would both support in the General Assembly.

When I heard a recitation of the text, my concern leapt up to an astronomical height. Here was Arthur Goldberg, one of Israel's most devoted American friends, asking us to acquiesce in the following text:

The General Assembly affirms the principle that conquest of territory by war is inadmissible under the UN Charter, and calls on all parties to the conflict to withdraw, without delay, their forces from the territories occupied by them after June 4, 1967.

Affirms likewise the principle of acknowledgment, without delay, by all member states in the area, that each of them enjoys the right to maintain an independent national state, and to live in peace and security, as well as to renounce all claims and all acts inconsistent therewith.

As soon as I recovered my breath, I pointed out vehemently to Goldberg that our American friends were giving up all the positive results that we had achieved in the past six weeks of diplomatic struggle. According to this text, the withdrawal of our forces was no longer to be conditioned on peace with secure boundaries. It would be stated explicitly that the June 4 lines would be restored without delay. I said that this was ludicrously inconsistent with the eloquent speech by President Johnson a few weeks before, in which he described a return to the previous situation as "a prescription for the renewal of hostilities."

We would now be asked to withdraw to the old armistice lines without anything like peace. Even the fatal word, "Israel," did not appear in this draft, so that the Arab states would have no difficulty in making a general statement and then claiming its nonapplicability to Israel.

I told Goldberg that I could see no difference between this formulation and Kosygin's call for unconditional withdrawal against which the U.S. and Israel had battled successfully in the United Nations in recent weeks. I found it appalling that after a rare victory in the UN against Soviet mischief, the United States should obsequiously hand the victory back to Moscow and its clients. If this text were to prevail, the United States would have detached itself from Israel and allied itself to the Soviet Union and the militant Arab states without any concern for our most vital interests.

It was clear that the allurement of an accord with the Soviet Union had uprooted American leaders from their own principles, and set them on a course incompatible with our nation's security, and with the interests and dignity of the free world. It was a terrifying moment for me when all the gains of the June and July sessions appeared to be slipping away, not as a result of enemy pressure, but as a consequence of an American ambition to achieve an accord with Moscow.

Just when we were close to an indignant departure, one of Goldberg's subordinates was called out of the room. He returned with a written message that he handed to Goldberg. Goldberg said that Egypt and Libya had rejected the text that he and Gromyko had been discussing. They wanted the full withdrawal of Israel's forces, without making even a meaningless historical gesture "acknowledging the right of all states in the area."

This was not the first or the last occasion on which Arab extremism had saved Israel from international embarrassment. Goldberg now said that the vehemence of my criticism would have required him to seek presidential reconsideration of the guilty text, but, in any case, the Arab rejection of the formula had virtually ended its life. Gromyko had stated that since the new text lacked Arab support, Soviet sponsorship automatically expired. Goldberg said that the United States would now work for a speedy end to the session, without the adoption of any resolution.

Two days later, the General Assembly dispersed, leaving our June victory intact.

The trouble was that Nasser was also intact. Although we were justified by history and conscience in having offered massive territorial renunciations in my meeting with American leaders on June 19, I thought it unlikely that a positive response would come during the presidency of the man who had put his faith in war. Nasser's disruptive initiatives in mid-May 1967 may have resulted from a series of miscalculations. But none of these would have been decisive were it not for the accumulated hostility, which, like a bonfire soaked with gasoline, could burst into flame at any moment. Nasser represented a hatred too violent to be contained. It was nourished by a fallacious version of the Middle East that excluded Israel from the region's past, present, and future. It was ignited and fanned by a charismatic arrogance and a boastful rhetoric that the Arab masses probably took more seriously than did Nasser himself. The Middle East was congested by ideas and emotions that were constantly capable of eruption. The war was "caused," not by its immediate circumstances, but by the Arab denial of Israel's historic personality and sovereign status. So long as Nasser's ideas determined the intellectual and emotional climate of the Middle East, the road to conciliation would be effectively closed. Our task, as I saw it, was to maintain our non-annexationist proposals in the field in the hope that Arab minds, awakening from the trauma of defeat, would understand that opportunities are often the children of disaster.

The scare created by the Goldberg-Gromyko document strengthened my conviction that it would be dangerous to leave a diplomatic vacuum: We should work for an international consensus that would, at the very least, legitimize our positions at the cease-fire lines pending the negotiation of peace. The idea that we could get peace, or even avoid a heavy toll of death while remaining in positions from the Golan and the Jordan River to the Suez Canal, was too preposterous for serious consideration.

The fact that the Egyptian defeat had not paralyzed Nasser's capacity for action was illustrated on October 21 when an Egyptian missile of Soviet manufacture attacked and sank the Israeli destroyer *Eilat*. Our forces responded by shelling the refineries at Port Said. It was becoming difficult to believe that we had secured any prolonged tranquillity from the Six Day War.

On October 24 I called on President Johnson in the White House. I obtained the meeting only two days after requesting it and I found him extraordinarily relaxed in comparison with the tension of our encounter on May 25. He was in a sentimental mood. He said that his mind often went back to our talk on May 25. "You made your position very clear and I had no reason to doubt that your government would fight unless we found a real alternative. But I did feel that you would give me a bit more time. I'm sorry that you didn't but I admit that you put up with the hell of a lot of provocation. When you did fight you showed courage and resolution. Our defense people were sure that you would lick your adversaries. My generals are always right about other people's wars and wrong about our own."

He spoke with solemnity about the attempts of the Soviet Union to recoup its pride in the Middle East after its humiliation in mid-summer. He said plaintively that the United States could cope with this better if it would only snap out of its mood of withdrawal.

As I departed he said emotionally to Ambassador Harman and me that my speeches in the UN in June had moved him more than anything since Churchill's orations in 1940. He was determined to build "an edifice of peace" on the basis of his June 19 speech.

I welcomed this because I did not believe in the stability of our new "greater" map. I was resolved to cooperate with the work that was going forward in the Security Council in an effort to formulate an agreed definition of international policy with which an Israeli government could live. It was in that mood that I worked throughout the fall of 1967 for international policies that were eventually expressed in Security Council Resolution 242. The discussions began in mid-October and ended on November 22, 1967, with the adoption of Resolution 242.

I had hoped that the United States would take the lead in the mediation effort. This hope collapsed when Ambassador Goldberg suggested a formula that was too congenial to Israel to win majority acceptance in the Security Council. On the other side of the barricade, India had drafted a resolution that was totally in the Arab interest. It was evident that neither the United States nor India could have the mediatory role. Thus the United Kingdom, represented by its minister of state, Lord Caradon, emerged as the only government capable of formulating a unanimous Security Council consensus.

Ambassador Goldberg explained to me that this was not a case of the United Kingdom acting as a surrogate for the United States. We should take it for granted that the American delegation would not write the Security Council's resolution. The most that the Johnson administration could do would be to make it clear that the United States would not accept a resolution that did not have Israeli acquiescence. The aim was to secure a unanimous statement of international policy and not a majority statement. Goldberg advised me to satisfy myself that in the British text any Israeli withdrawal of forces would be conditioned by the establishment of peace with secure boundaries. The United States, said Goldberg, would, of course, explore the field in its own interest, but in the deeper sense it would be for me on Israel's behalf to judge if our basic security interests were served by the text that would emerge.

Accordingly, I made a journey to London in the first week of November. My official reason for this voyage was to speak at the celebration of the Balfour Declaration that was scheduled to take place in the majestic ambience of the Royal Opera House at Covent Garden. My other aim was to clarify what Britain, as the prospective author of the Security Council's resolution, meant by the term "withdrawal from territories occupied in the 1967 conflict," which was already being discussed in New York.

I had talks on this question on November 6 with Prime Minister Harold Wilson at 10 Downing Street and with his foreign secretary, George Brown, at Dorneywood, the country residence of British foreign secretaries.

My meeting with George Brown took place at 10:30 in the morning. He explained mischievously that his first objective was to go out and get access to a bottle of Scotch whisky in such manner as to evade the vigilance of his wife, Sophie Brown. After a brief sortie he reentered the room furtively with the bottle gleaming in his hands and tried, unsuccessfully, to get me to join him in his hour of triumph. I would have been unaccustomed to hard liquor even in late evening, let alone at what I regarded as breakfast time.

The outcome of my talks with Wilson and Brown was positive. They made it clear that a British draft, which they showed me in its tentative form, would call for withdrawal from occupied territories without specifying that "all the territories," or even "the territories," would necessarily have to be abandoned. Brown explained that he knew of the American attitude and would, therefore, not waste his country's time in an effort to secure a total withdrawal, which he and Wilson in any case regarded as tactically unwise, since it would release the Arab states from any pressure to moderate their attitudes. Brown said to me clearly that "the omission of the word 'all' and of the word 'the' from the text of 242 was deliberate." The "secure and recognized boundaries" referred to in the draft resolution would have to be negotiated and not imposed. In a later book of memoirs, characteristically entitled *Going My Way,* George Brown repeated this flexible interpretation. This is significant because Brown, unlike Wilson, was not previously or subsequently regarded as an enthusiastic admirer of Israel's policies. The only thing that could confidently be predicted about George Brown was his unpredictability.

Returning to UN headquarters in New York, I felt that we had a rare chance of emerging from a UN discussion with our major interests intact.

This was important because Goldberg had achieved an informal agreement with King Hussein on a moderate text and Nasser had already summoned a meeting of the Security Council in an effort to thwart a possible Jordanian initiative.

Lord Caradon visited me in my hotel on November 15. He was one of the more colorful diplomats that I encountered in my UN experience. At Cambridge where he had been Hugh Foot, his eloquence in Union debates was still remembered when I followed him there. He had made a long career in the colonial service of his country. He became one of the decolonizers of the 1950s and 1960s who wished to end the imperial era with dignity and grace. Lord Mountbatten, the last viceroy of India, was the leading figure in this decolonization process, which contrasted with the bloodshed that accompanied France's attempt to cling to Algeria and Southeast Asia.

Caradon had been a district commissioner in Palestine before the discordant Bevin era and had conceived a passionate love of Jerusalem. He had been the last governor of Cyprus and Jamaica. His father, Isaac Foot, was for a long time a member of Parliament. Hugh Foot's brother Michael became the leader of the Labour Party, while his other brother Dingle Foot, like his father, was a pillar of the small Liberal Party. Michael, Hugh and Dingle were an impressive dynasty. When Isaac Foot was reelected in Cornwall, the Liberal Party leader, Herbert Samuel, had sent him an unforgettable telegram: "My dear Foot, congratulations on your magnificent feat."

Now, ennobled as Lord Caradon, Hugh Foot showed me his proposed draft. It was identical with that which I had seen in London, with one exception: In deference to Latin American pressure, Caradon had inserted a preambular reference to what he called "the principle that there could be no acquisition of territory by war." Since the territories of most states have been decisively influenced by wars, this appeared to be a somewhat insincere proposition. In Latin America, however, the boundaries of that subcontinent's numerous states would be the subject of chaotic controversy if they were not safeguarded against volatile and transient military successes. Since Argentina and Brazil were necessary for the vote, they had to be accommodated. Caradon himself was in favor of strengthening the withdrawal language for his own reasons.

Even in its amended form, the resolution seemed to me to have the following advantages for Israel: First, it gave legitimacy to our presence in the occupied territories, so long as there was no "just and durable peace." Second, it defined peace in rigorous terms to include a total revolution in Arab attitudes. It demanded the end of boycotts and blockades and it sanctified Israel's right, as one of the states in the area, to live in peace, secure from the threat or use of force.

The resolution avoided any reference to any need for returning to "the June 4 lines" or to "the previous armistice lines." Indeed, several resolutions that did call for a return to those lines were defeated in successive votes in the

General Assembly and the Security Council. Caradon's draft gave us a chance of territorial revision.

I reported to my government that acceptance of the Security Council resolution on these terms would be a "tough deal." All the fifteen members of the Security Council were in favor of withdrawal of Israeli forces in each of the four territories that we had occupied: Sinai, the West Bank, Gaza, and the Golan Heights. The resolution would certainly not be compatible with the idea that Israel could abandon Sinai and, in compensation, receive legitimacy for total control of the territories and populations in the West Bank and Gaza.

The United States, which was our potential protector against inequitable resolutions, had made clear through President Johnson that changes in the previous lines should not "reflect the weight of military conquests." (It was only later under the Nixon administration that the U.S. became accustomed to recommending the formula "minor changes.")

I strongly recommended the acceptance of the resolution, not because it was perfect, but because the alternative was much worse. The Latin American delegates, as well as the Soviet Union, India, and the Arabs, would have been quite prepared to call for a peace settlement based on Israeli withdrawal from all the territories at issue.

On November 15, our position was strengthened by a speech made by the head of the American delegation, Arthur Goldberg. It was a breakthrough occasion. Goldberg pointed out that permanent boundaries between Israel and its neighbors had never existed since no agreement had ever been reached. Since the boundaries had never existed, they now had to be negotiated. He added that the resolution neither excluded nor required the restoration of the previous armistice lines.

There now remained two points of contention: First, the British text in its original form implied that the Security Council could impose its consensus on the parties. I made it clear that Israeli acquiescence in the resolution and, therefore, the prospect of the resolution's being adopted, would depend on the inclusion of the phrase "the promotion of agreement." In other words, the United Nations mediator who was to be appointed under the resolution would not have a mandatory power to tell Israel where its borders should be. Ambassador Gunnar Jarring was named as the mediator after the adoption of the text of 242.

The second danger was that, at the last moment, the words "all the" would be inserted to make it clear that we were committing ourselves to a total withdrawal. Ambassador Goldberg revealed to me that the Soviet Union, which had delayed its consent to the resolution, was making a last-ditch effort on behalf of the Arab cause. Prime Minister Kosygin had addressed messages to President Johnson saying that even if the text of the resolution did not require the evacuation of "all the territories," it should be understood by the United States and the Soviet Union that this was their intention. Goldberg told me that President Johnson had instructed him to inform the Soviet Union that the United States would not agree to a single word beyond what was written in the British text. Lyndon Johnson, who had a rich vocabulary of four-letter words, expressed his rejection of Kosygin's proposal in language that I could not reproduce—and that Goldberg probably could not transmit to Moscow without considerable expurgation.

At the table of the Security Council itself, on November 22, the Indian and Arab delegation made further efforts to induce Lord Caradon to state, off the record, that the intention was to demand the evacuation of *all* the territories. Caradon retorted that nothing could be read into the resolution that was not specifically stated therein. When all these clarifications were made and the vote came, the Soviet Union delegate, Vasili Kuznetsov, raised a reluctant hand for its adoption.

I cabled Jerusalem that night to say that since 242 was preferable to any realistic alternative, we should work for its adoption on the basis of the American and British interpretations of its text.

Arriving home in December 1967, I found that the psychological climate was not ripe for the accommodations, flexibilities, and mutual adjustments that are required for a structure of peace. Nor did I feel that the obstacles were on the Arab side alone. The virulent rejectionism embodied in the Khartoum Declaration was, of course, the major roadblock. All the Arab states, as well as the Palestinian organizations, were calling for the kind of gains that usually flow from victory and not from military rout. But the Jewish scene was no less turbulent. A strange amalgam of ecstasy and fear produced an Israeli climate the like of which our country had never conceived before.

The erosion of our positions came just when Israel's situation seemed to be ideal. No one questioned the responsibility of Nasser for the war. Proposals for our ejection from the territories had fallen to the ground in both of the central UN organs. We had transmitted generous compromise proposals to the Arab states. The Knesset had adopted resolutions praising the work of our delegation, even mentioning my name in an unusual departure from its austere traditions. The Khartoum resolutions, which were a negative development in the substantive sense, contributed to the halo of virtue that illuminated our image. I thought that we had a situation in which patient maintenance of these gains would have served our diplomacy and our good name.

It was not to be. By the end of the 1970s the prospect that the fruits of the Six Day War would be peace and security had disappeared. Arab rejectionism was the main cause of this decline, but Israel also was losing an opportunity of maintaining the upper ground of realism. The Six Day War had brought indispensable relief to our short-term security, but it had left all our basic problems unsolved.

23

THE STORM BEFORE THE
STORM: 1967–1970

ON SEPTEMBER 22, 1967, the Israeli newspapers published a declaration, 160
words long, with over fifty signatures, some of them prestigious:

> The victory of the Israeli defense forces in the Six Day War has brought
> the nation and the state into a new and fateful era. Undivided Israel is
> now in the hands of the Jewish people, and just as we had no right to
> renounce the State of Israel, so are we commanded gratefully to receive
> what this era has granted us: namely, the entire Land of Israel.
>
> We owe allegiance to the integrity of our land; to its past and its
> future. And no government in Israel has the right to give up this
> wholeness.

The signatories called themselves the "Movement for a Greater Israel."
The list was unusual. Virulent right-wing extremists, excited advocates of
annexation and veteran Likud standard-bearers appeared side by side with
members of the Labor movement in transferring allegiance from the old
Israeli flag to the new Israeli map. Many of the leading figures in the Hebrew
literary movement gave their names to this document. The list transcended
party barriers and brought together Israeli politicians and writers who had
never before played a political role.

The numerous Labor adherents in the new movement captured my anxious attention. I could not understand how so many people who had accompanied the Labor movement on its great journey culminating in Israel's
independence could have allowed this document to see the light of day.

The most serious element in the text was its assertion that the people of
Israel and its successive governments had no right to decide anything that
contradicted the aims of the Movement for a Greater Israel. This idea was
morally seditious. It was tantamount to the denial of Israeli sovereignty. If
Israeli-elected institutions may not make decisions on matters of national

boundaries and peace terms, it is hard to define what purpose they serve. The new declaration canonized a territorial configuration that arose as the result of the Six Day War. This map did not conform with any historic conception of the country's boundaries. Areas that never formed part of any Jewish kingdom or state, such as the Golan Heights and Sinai, were suddenly made a part of the homeland.

I knew more deeply than most citizens that Israel had entered the international arena in a contractual posture. If we had refused to share sovereignty and territory with the neighboring Palestinian people in 1948, the number of states that would have raised their voice and hand in our behalf would have been zero, and the world community would have organized itself successfully to prevent our statehood.

The partition principle had always been the foundation of Israel's international legitimacy. Turning their back on the historic processes that had brought a Jewish state into existence, the authors of the document sought to commit Israel to a shape that had never existed in history. They had elevated the results of the 1967 war into a kind of sacred text. In so doing, they turned their back contemptuously on the Israeli state as it was conceived in the 1948 Declaration of Independence.

By exalting what they called "the new era," they reduced the "old era" to the status of a shrunken relic to which no allegiance was owed. For nineteen years, the Jewish people, and much of the rest of the world, had been taught to revere and cherish the state that had been forged in the crucible of Jewish martyrdom and won its way arduously into the international community. Now all this was tossed aside in a bizarre consensus carved out of contradictory dreams and fantasies. If no allegiance was owed to the state, as defined by its elected institutions, to whom and to what was allegiance owed?

Beyond this fundamental anomaly, the Movement for a Greater Israel sought to engage the nation in a series of blatant falsehoods. They laid down that within the new boundaries there would be "freedom and equality for all inhabitants." They must have known that this was untrue. A government of Israel inspired by Jewish supremacy and Arab subordination was not going to give Arabs a place in the parliamentary system commensurate with their numbers. The very language of the declaration evoked associations of irredentist movements in Europe that glorified blood and soil, and made military conquests the supreme credential of national identity.

The signatories could not have seriously believed that "the present boundaries of our country are a guarantee of the security of the state and of peace." Unless they were replaced by agreed boundaries they would be a guarantee of future wars. The idea that the peoples of the Middle East and of the world would reconcile themselves "peacefully" to Israeli domination of the entire area, from the Golan Heights and the River Jordan to the Suez Canal, was sheer delusion. There was no prospect that a single country or government or parliament or international institution, or any editorial board of any serious newspaper would regard the dramatic but fortuitous results of six days of fighting as a reason to abolish established international norms and to wipe the political identity of our Palestinian neighbors off the pages of history.

The draftsman and the driving force of the new movement was Nathan Alterman, a stalwart of the Labor movement and hitherto a passionate supporter of David Ben-Gurion. Others, such as the Nobel Laureate Shai Agnon, Chaim Hazaz, Moshe Shamir, Uri Zvi Greenberg, Yaakov Burla, Dov Sadan, and Gershom Shofman, assured a disproportionate representation to the writers' community. After all, Israeli novelists and essayists had not been among the central architects of the Israeli national revolution. The literary and political establishments in Israel have always led separate lives.

Some of the signatories—such as Harel Fish, and above all, Israel Eldad—were well-known ideologists of far rightist movements. Nothing was more incongruous than the name of Rachel Yanait Ben-Zvi, the widow of the second president, in a group, many of whose members had been the sworn adversaries of pioneering labor Zionism.

The Movement for a Greater Israel was a new phenomenon in Israeli domestic politics. The union between theological fundamentalism and territorial ambition was to find expression in such movements as Gush Emunin (Movement of the Faithful), which held their right to settle in occupied territories as superior to the enactments of the state to which they were theoretically subject.

Another symptom of the new era was the domination of Israeli politics by Defense Minister Moshe Dayan. Nothing was more astonishing in Israel after the Six Day War than the subordination of Israeli politics to Dayan's will. His power was undoubtedly greater than that of any other Israeli, even those who were theoretically his equals or seniors. In cold truth, he had not been the architect of Israel's military victory. He came out of the obscurity of parliamentary opposition a few days before the war at a time when the battle plans had been formulated, the commanders appointed, the equipment efficiently accumulated.

Prime Minister Eshkol deeply resented what he regarded as a successful effort to steal the credit of our victory from him. After all, it was Eshkol who had prepared the defense system for its ordeal, and it was he who had fixed the timing of our fight. When the fighting broke out, the commanders in the field, not the political minister of defense, carried the troops forward under merciless fire until their goals were achieved. But when Eshkol said with clear allusion to Dayan, "the boasting and self-praise by one or several people about the military struggle is not dignified," there was hardly any echo to his voice.

Charisma exists when the connection is broken between the reality of a person and his image. Dayan possessed this attribute. There was almost nothing he could do, or say, no matter how outrageous, that the public would find unacceptable. There was always a prior disposition to be admiring, deferential, and indulgent. If Dayan changed his views, he was praised for originality. If he was obdurate, he was praised for stability. He thus got the benefit of every doubt. Not that dissent from Dayan was suppressed; it was simply treated as a harmless eccentricity.

The public indulgence of Dayan was such that he was even placed above the law of the land. In his capacity as an amateur archaeologist, he would buy valuable antiquities from Bedouin Arabs or from dealers who had no possibility of bargaining with him about prices. He knew that this dubious commerce was in articles that were the legal possession of the Israeli government, but it was notorious that the normal legal restraints would not affect him.

In his first reaction to the victories of Israeli armies, Dayan had said publicly that we had not entered the war against Egypt, Jordan, and Syria for purposes of conquest of territory. Within a few days, however, he amended this declaration both in speech and in action. He staked out positions about the future status of the occupied territories before the prime minister and the Cabinet had any opportunity to discuss these matters. As one of his biographers admits:

Long before the other politicians began to debate whether Israel's national interests required her to stay in the occupied lands, Dayan had pushed Israel in the direction of empire building. Whatever wavering he would do later, whatever concerns he felt that Israel's hold on the territories retarded rather than guaranteed peace, Dayan did not waver at the outset. Before the fighting died down, he set Israel on the path of enduring occupation when he alone had the power and authority to move the country along a different path. While senior Israeli figures favored Israel withdrawing from virtually all of the newly occupied lands, Dayan was moving the country through his public remarks in the direction of enduring rule.[1]

The motive for his annexationist ambitions lay in a profound pessimism about the Arabs. He believed that even if any of the Arab countries were to offer negotiation at a diplomatic table, this would merely be a tactical move to secure an interval of tranquillity before renewing the military assault. He said:

It has been decreed that we should live in permanent struggle with the Arabs, and there can be no escape from bloodshed; rest and peace for our nation have always been only a longing, never a reality. And if,

[1]Robert Slater, *The Life of Moshe Dayan* (New York: St. Martin's Press, 1991), pp. 286–7.

from time to time, we Jews did achieve these goals, they were only oases—a breath that gave us the strength and the courage to take up the struggle again. The only answer we can give to the question, what will happen, is "we shall continue to struggle." We must prepare ourselves morally and physically to endure a protracted struggle, not to draw up a timetable for the achievement of rest and peace.

The words "it has been decreed" are instructive; they indicate a bleak determinism that make peacemaking a useless pursuit. I recall one occasion when Dayan predicted that the Palestine Arabs would organize a terrorist movement in and outside of Israel in revolt against Israeli rule. When I asked him on what he based his prediction, he said simply, "Because that is exactly what I would do if I were in their place."

Strangely, the disposition to put himself in the place of our enemies and to understand their attitudes often led him to actions with a semblance of humane liberalism. Since he rejected the idea that we would ever share rule with the neighboring Palestine people, he had no hesitation in keeping the bridges across the Jordan River open and allowing a free influx of Arab workers daily into our country.

On the positive side, this policy created a network of common interests: Jews and Arabs mingling together gave the impression of coexistence on the human level. On the negative side, Dayan's approach to the Palestinians in the West Bank and Gaza was designed to bring about such an intermingling of peoples that it would be virtually impossible to envisage eventual separation. Arab workers from the territories are not citizens of the state that controls their lives. They have no say in the life of the land where they live and where most of them were born. They have no flag to revere, no freedom from arbitrary arrest, and their labor is secured without any principle of equality and with no trade union protection. It was clear that if years passed with these inequalities in force, Israeli society would assume a discriminatory and exploitative aspect, far from the Enlightenment values that had inspired classic Zionism.

Dayan left a hard legacy to his successors by the punitive measures that he took against Palestinian resistance. The blowing up of houses would often leave a dozen members of an Arab family suffering homelessness because one of them was suspected, without formal indictment, of having used violence. Mayors who were not congenial to the Israeli military administration could be removed from office overnight. Free assembly, protest, and peaceful demonstration were forbidden, and leaving the country offered no assurance of a right to return.

Dayan held the belief common to colonial governors that if the Palestinians were given the prospect of minimal economic advancement, they would lose the taste for flags, honor, pride, and independence. He spent most of his time as defense minister, not in perfecting the Israeli forces for the possibility of a future war, but in multiplying his contacts in Arab towns and villages in the West Bank and Gaza, distributing rewards and punishments in characteristic feudal fashion. Like British colonial rulers, he had a genuine affection for the common people, the peasants and farmers in the villages, together with a deep revulsion from urban intellectuals in whose eyes the ambition for national freedom predominated over the daily welfare of individuals.

Dayan's policy was to award the Palestinians individual subsistence without national dignity. Chaim Herzog, who was the first military governor of the Jerusalem area, recalls how he proposed a meeting of Arab notables in an East Jerusalem movie theater, where some kind of Palestinian leadership on the West Bank would emerge. Dayan rejected the idea out of hand.

At that stage, he even rejected a sparse degree of Palestinian autonomy that would reserve the issues of defense, finance, foreign relations, land, and water for the Israeli authority. Dayan was willing to see the Palestinians only as individuals, never as a collective entity. In this vision, bread and schools were for the Arabs, flag and freedom were for Jews alone. In that spirit he and his followers multiplied their annexationist statements in the belief that their very frequency would have an attritional effect.

The annexation theme in Dayan's postwar speeches achieved an effect by multiplication. "There's no Palestine anymore! Perhaps I should say that I'm sorry, but I'm not. . . ." "We should regard ourselves in the administered areas as a permanent government without leaving options for a day of peace, which is nowhere at hand. . . ." "When had we known a situation like this—being able to rule the whole area from Golan, the Jordan River and the area up to the Suez Canal." "The present boundaries will remain as they are for the next ten years and there will not be any serious war." "The present situation is one of virtual peace and one day soon it will be expressed in a diplomatic formula. . . ." "Whoever wants to give up Judea and Samaria has never read the Bible." Then would come his most famous punch line: "I prefer Sharm el-Sheikh without peace to peace without Sharm el-Sheikh."

It is true that many other leaders were also articulating these views, sometimes with even greater degrees of hubris, but there was a great difference between the influence of Dayan in the aftermath of the 1967 war and that of anyone else at that time.

Paradoxically, during all the years in which Dayan was leaving the imprint of his annexationism on Israeli opinion, I was enunciating the official program of the Labor Party calling for a settlement that would involve massive renunciation of territory in the West Bank and almost total renunciation in Sinai and Golan. Dayan was charismatically endowed with the capacity to "educate" the nation in a sense totally opposed to the policy positions of his own party.

As time went forward, he would have to amend these doctrines in deference to the grief and havoc of the Yom Kippur War, against which he had not assured the nation sufficient protection. But the decisive years for appraising the effect of his career are those immediately after the 1967 war, during which he fashioned the national consensus about war or peace, occupation or Palestinian freedom, territory or other forms of security, the hope of Israeli-Arab reconciliation versus the "iron decree" of permanent confrontation. In these issues he made the wrong choices for which he lived long enough to seek absolution.

But was absolution still possible? One device of Dayan's supporters was to ascribe to him the main credit for the peace treaty with Egypt; but the dominant role here was played by Menachem Begin. It was he, not Dayan, who made the decision to restore Sinai to Egyptian sovereignty. Dayan labored skillfully to resolve deadlocks and to prevent ruptures in the negotiating process, but once an authoritative prime minister had agreed to the major concession, it was only a matter of short time before the new era in Egyptian-Israeli relations would unfold.

The Israeli nation, especially its youth, is still laden with the harvest of illusion that Dayan sowed in the years immediately after the Six Day War. His misjudgment of the Palestinian reality set the Israeli mood on what has so far proved to be an irreversible road, dark with false images. His belated revision of his views showed intellectual resilience, but when a teacher repents, his disciples are left high and dry, burdened with obsolete doctrine. The Hebrew prophet teaches: "The fathers eat sour grapes and the teeth of their sons are set on edge." Dayan overestimated the role of war in fashioning national destiny. He never grasped Churchill's poignant phrase: "the fading glare of military success." There is now a Dayan Center for Peace in Tel Aviv, but peace will only be achieved by jettisoning the major perceptions that Dayan planted deep into the Israeli national consciousness in 1967–1973. Individual repentance does not provoke a mass stampede toward rationality.

Until the Six Day War, the religious Zionist parties had been loyal partners of the Labor Movement in Israeli cabinets. The acceptance of a partitioned Land of Israel was not easy for them. The Jewish liturgy and rabbinical statements are based on an almost sensual love of the Land of Israel. Indeed, Judaism is the only religion that is specifically based on a land: "Ten cubits of beauty descended upon the world, nine of them to Jerusalem and one to the whole world." This text makes a similar self-satisfied division—nine against one—in truth, nobility, and other marks of virtue. Throughout the exile Jews constructed an imaginary Land of Israel in their pious imaginations, celebrated its fluctuations of climate and season, and expressed their ardent longing and firm intention to return. In the course of centuries this yearning for the land was sublimated into a vision that did not necessarily commit its followers to concrete action. It was quite possible to long for Zion in synagogues and around the Passover table and yet to maintain a firm intention to remain citizens of other lands. This dichotomy had been familiar from biblical days.

I personally, despite my own choice of citizenship and vocation, have always taken the division of Jewish life between homeland and Diaspora for granted. When a phenomenon has gone on continuously for over two millennia it is unrealistic to call it "artificial." Nor have I ever shared a guilty Zionist view that a new Israel will be constructed on the ruins of Diaspora communities that orthodox Zionism has usually regarded as doomed to eventual decline. I cannot conceive any condition in which weakness and disaster could come upon the Jews of the United States without Israel's very existence being undermined.

Nevertheless, the decision to accept the partition of the land placed religious Zionism in a dilemma in the late 1930s, and again when partition became a concrete political prospect after World War II. At the 1938 Zionist Congress, which I had attended as the youngest of its delegates, Chaim Weizmann had shown his diplomatic resourcefulness in transcending the anguish of overreligious Jews. He had said: "You say that God has promised the whole Land. Well, let us do what we can with our existing modest and constrained circumstances and leave God to accomplish his promise in his own time."

The virtue of this argument was that religious Jews could only reject it by proclaiming that they were not all that convinced that God's promise would be fulfilled. Since it was ideologically impossible for them to do this without falling into heresy, Weizmann's division of the Jewish destiny, between what can now be accomplished and what can remain for divine action, released religious Jews from what would otherwise have been an insoluble spiritual crisis. The result was that both the National Religious Party and the non-Zionist Agudat Yisrael were among the founders of the State and members of its first government.

From the mid-1960s onward, it was my habit on Saturday nights, before the weekly Cabinet meetings on Sundays, to visit the National Religious Party leader Moshe Chaim Shapira at his home on Ahad Ha'am Street, Jerusalem. He was a solid character, with his heart and head dominated by the mysteries of spiritual Judaism but his feet firmly planted on the ground of political and material reality. He himself was not excessively overburdened with rabbinical learning, but a finely bound set of the Talmud formed the background from which he used to speak to me from his desk. He revered other religious Jews who spent their time immersed in rabbinical texts while he gathered the tools and the material resources that would keep organized Judaism in existence. Like all my predecessors and successors in the Israeli ministry of education, I had understood that the allocations to religious schools were sacrosanct and that the competence of the minister of education to distribute them was a benign theory. The real master of this sector of the educational system was the National Religious Party.

For me the central point was that Shapira was moderate in his views. Indeed he recoiled from any optional military action more frequently than I did myself. It was therefore rational for me to give him some idea of the diplomatic and security matters likely to come up in Cabinet and to collude with him in making common cause.

There were many Saturday evenings during which I would make this pilgrimage to the religious Zionist leader before attending the meetings of what was popularly called "Golda's kitchen." It was the habit of Golda Meir, as of her predecessors, and indeed as of all sensible presidents and prime ministers in democratic states, to confer with the few colleagues who were departmentally responsible for international affairs, such as the ministers of defense and foreign affairs, whose opinions were valued irrespective or their positions in the country. A typical Golda kitchen would consist of Moshe Dayan, Abba Eban, Yisrael Galili, the Justice Minister Ya'acov Shimshon Shapira, the spiritual leader of Mapam Ya'acov Hazan, one or more members of the military high command, and Golda's own director general, either Ya'acov Herzog, Simcha Dinitz, or Mordecai (Motke) Gazit, who served in that capacity between their ambassadorial missions. In the kitchen, there was a tendency of the participants to compete with each other in affirmations of militancy to suit Golda's temperament, while in my talks with Shapira in his book-lined study I became assured that I could carry the National Religious Party with me in moderate positions.

The 1967 war revolutionized the mood of religious Zionism. It was no longer pragmatic and empirical, constrained by reality and devoted to compromise. It had been affected traumatically, but also ecstatically, by the war. Its leaders were moved by the actual encounter with the Holy Places in Jerusalem and Hebron, or with the cities whose names evoked biblical recollections, such as Jericho and Shechem (Nablus). They saw our victory not as a result of superior military performance but as a divine miracle.

Inspired by fundamentalist rabbis, many religious Zionists converted solitude from a harsh necessity to a cherished virtue. Here are some of their sayings: "The whole world is against us. Humanity is divided between Jews and Gentiles (Goyim)." "The traditional anxieties of Zionism and the secular camp who are horrified by the prospect of Israel's isolation are not shared by Jews of the Torah," declaimed one influential rabbi. Others pointed out that isolation is not only a burden to be borne but also an opportunity to be exploited because it safeguards Jews from the temptations of assimilation and secularization. In this system of thought, the saying of the Moabite prophet Balaam describing Israel as "a people that dwells alone" is not a biblical curse but a title of spiritual lineage. The conclusion is that Jews should be indifferent to world opinion and should regard the military conquest of 1967 as an irrevocable determination of the Israeli map.

Another leader of Gush Emunim, Rabbi Ya'acov Ariel, wrote that "the religious Jew, despite his higher moral stature, objects to peace because he retains a more developed historical consciousness which does not let him forget the events of his past and induces in him a more suspicious attitude towards the outside world."

These ideologies appeared quaint and unreal until 1967 when the concept of an undivided Land of Israel, comprising the entire area of Palestine between the Jordan River and the Mediterranean Sea, became a reality. The statement published by the Movement for a Greater Israel, issued soon after the June 1967 war, was followed by an intensive reinforcement of the fundamentalist school of thought in Zionism and consequently in Israeli politics. The basic notion was that "every descendant of Esau is in consistent and perpetual ambush against the Sons of Israel so as to hurt and destroy them when the opportunity arises."

After 1967 these sentiments ceased to be somber, meditative reflections on Jewish destiny. They burst upon the scene as slogans with political and diplomatic applications. The Israeli army was exalted by Gush Emunim into a state of sanctity and grace. The founder of the movement, Rabbi Zvi Yehuda Kook, wrote: "The Israel Defense Army is total sanctity. It represents the rule of the people of the Lord over his Land." Rabbi Eliezer Wallenberg, winner of the Israeli 1976 prize for Halachic studies, argues that a non-Jew should be forbidden to live in Jerusalem and that we should have driven all the "goyim" away from Jerusalem and purified it completely.

It was not difficult to find support for these ideas in biblical and even more in rabbinical writings. Thus Rabbi Wolpe, a follower of the Lubavitche Rabbi:

> According to Halacha it is forbidden for a non-Jew to live in Jerusalem and in accordance with the ruling by Maimonides it is forbidden to permit even a resident alien in Jerusalem. Truly this applies when Israel has the upper hand but today, too, although it is not possible to expel them by force this does not mean that we have to encourage them to live there.

Mordecai Nissan, a Canadian immigrant teaching at the Hebrew University of Jerusalem, wrote in an official publication of the World Zionist Organization:

> While it is true that Jews are a particular people they nonetheless are designated as a light unto the nations. This function is imposed on the Jews who strive to be a living aristocracy among the nations. A nation that has deeper historical roots, greater spiritual obligations, higher moral standards and more powerful intellectual capacities than other peoples. According to Maimonides, in return for being permitted to live in the country of sacred history and religious purpose non-Jews must suffer the humiliations of servitude. . . . The sons of the handmaiden may not wield office.

This blatant and ugly racial self-assertion would not have qualified for publication in a mainstream Zionist journal a decade earlier.

Ironically, the religious authority to whom the fundamentalists had most recourse was Maimonides, who is spiritually renowned for moderation and universalism. The secular historian would attribute Maimonides's occasional eruptions of militancy to the fact that he was persecuted both in Egypt and Spain. Moreover, Jews suffering from persecutors in those times had no possibility of fighting back with anything except words, and were therefore entitled to fits of bad-tempered vengefulness. The intellectual crime of the rabbinical fundamentalists was anachronism: They extracted ideas from epochs in which violence and punitive cruelty were prevalent and sought to transport them as binding injunction for a totally different social culture. Anachronism is the basest crime that religious teachers can commit against history.

For many years Israelis were resistant to these ideas and did nothing to put them into effect. But hardly had the cease-fire taken root after the war when small Jewish groups began to create settlements in the occupied territories without reference to the enactments of Israeli governments and parliaments. Once a settlement was established without, or even against, governmental authority, it could usually count on retroactive endorsement. It was natural for Israeli settlement to take place in the Etzion Bloc, which had been a part of the Jewish community right up until 1948. Far more controversial was the arrival of settlers in the Golan Heights. Here the initiative had been voluntary, but governmental approval had been swift.

Dayan, of course, was particularly repetitive and influential in this matter.

We have returned to Hebron, to Shechem, to Bethlehem and Anatot, to Jericho and the fords over the Jordan. Our brothers, we bear your lesson with us, we know that to give life to Jerusalem we must station the soldiers and armor in the Shechem mountains and on the bridges over the Jordan.

These great gusts of theological emotion swept across the land at the very time when, with full governmental authority, I was telling international organizations and friendly governments that we sought face-to-face negotiations with the Arabs in which everything could be discussed, and in which we would be unexpectedly generous in working out peace terms if peace was clearly available.

Despite the ardor of the annexationist rhetoric, the demographic effect on the ground was relatively modest in the years of Labor rule. By 1973, when the Yom Kipper War erupted, there were barely 7,000 Jews living in the West Bank and Gaza. However, these settlements, created either with the initiative or reluctant acquiescence of the Labor Party, became a launching base for the much more intensive Israeli settlement network that arose when the Likud eventually came to power.

□   □   □

Arab intransigence was the ally of the Jewish annexationist school. UN Security Council Resolution 242 was based on the assumption that world opinion urgently required peace in the Middle East, but Arab nationalism drew no such lesson from its failure in war.

The first Arab reaction to defeat was not to assume that the anti-Israeli policy had failed, but rather that it had not been sufficiently applied. The hope of early revenge was expressed with particular virulence by the Palestinian organizations. After some eruptions of military action in 1968 and occasional acts of spectacular piracy against airlines, the PLO shifted its emphasis to the political domain. Their device was to elevate the concept of "Palestine" to the point at which "Israel" would disappear. As long as the struggle seemed to be between Israel and the Arab world, sympathy went to Israel. It was enough to compare our sparse territory with the huge Arab expanse in order to conclude that Arab nationalism did not have much to complain about. But when the context was presented as being not between Israel and the Arabs, but between Israel and the Palestinians, perspectives changed. All the gains of Arab nationalism in nearly two dozen states outside Palestine were taken for granted as though they had no effect on the balance of equity between Arab and Jewish rights to independence. Israel was now portrayed as powerful, sated, established, and recognized, while the Palestinians were by contrast dispossessed, bitter, dissatisfied, and implacable. The current of world opinion flowed away from the embattled victor toward the defeated aggressor. We found ourselves transformed from David to Goliath overnight. Israel had committed the dark sin of survival.

At the Foreign Ministry in Jerusalem my main business was to ensure some diplomatic mobility. The period between 1967 and 1973 is often portrayed as years of deadlock in Israeli policy. This is untrue. It is Arab policy that was deadlocked for the simple reason that the Arabs wanted a solution to be totally formulated by themselves, or one imposed by external pressures or, preferably, a solution to be explored after a military success. In each case, real diplomacy would be evaded. There was never a period in which the Arabs had a greater chance of recovering most of their territories. Yet those of us who wished to explore a compromise did not have an easy task. We were hemmed in on one side by our own political right, and on the other side by an Arab nationalism that did everything possible to frustrate the hopes of Israeli moderates.

For the first two years of this period I was intensely occupied with the mission of Gunnar Jarring, whom Secretary General U Thant had appointed as UN representative for the Middle East under the terms of Resolution 242.

There was an unusually thick fall of snow in Jerusalem on the day of Jarring's first visit to my home. Snow fell again, by chance, ten days later. Jarring commented that Israel and his own country, Sweden, had unexpected climatic affinities. During the first part of his mission he developed the shuttle technique that Henry Kissinger was later to make more famous. Jarring managed to convey an air of tranquil deliberation even in a frenzied schedule of flights among Jerusalem, Amman, Cairo, and Beirut.

His permanent assignment was that of Swedish Ambassador in Moscow, He was a quiet man of scholarly attainments whose greatest virtue may have been his major defect. His mind moved strictly within the rational limits of European humanism. He assumed that nations, like individuals, guided their actions by reason. He later came to learn that, as I have said, logic played a very small part in human history and no part at all in the history of the Middle East. Passions and sensitivities, wounded pride and frustrated hope, together with deeply traumatic memories of persecution, domination, or oppression, had sharpened the intensity of our region's emotional life. Israelis, more than Arabs, could manage to temper emotion with logic. All that Jarring could do was to ask Israel to be less rational and the Arabs less emotional.

For a brief period during February and March 1968, Jarring seemed to be on the verge of achieving a negotiation among Israel, Egypt, and Jordan. I had suggested to him that instead of trying to get agreement on semantics he should convene a conference between the parties under his chairmanship similar to that which had taken place under Ralph Bunche's auspices at Rhodes. Despite a vehement assault on me in the extremist sections of the Israeli press, I told Jarring that Israel would not object to this indirect approach to negotiation and agreement. Eventually Jarring drew up a document that called for agreement on an invitation under which Israel would attend a conference with Egypt and Jordan under Jarring's auspices in Cyprus to discuss the implementation of Resolution 242. To Jarring's disappointment and mine, this text had been rejected by the Egyptian foreign minister on March 7. On March 10 Jarring showed me the document informally. He would not present it to me formally since according to his concept the agreement of all parties was necessary before it would have any official status. I told him that in my view the latter would be fully acceptable to my government if it was also accepted by the other side.

I had suggested that Jarring should go back to New York and invite the parties to meet him without seeking their agreement in advance. After all, Bunche had not asked the parties to the Armistice Conference in 1949 to agree to the terms of his invitation. I wondered whether Egypt would really refuse a UN invitation to come to New York for discussions with the UN special representative and thus incur international opprobrium for obstructing a peace settlement.

Jarring's explorations at least clarified the rival positions. The Arab states wanted full withdrawal without a real peace. They were not prepared to pay any price for the restoration of their lost territory. On the other hand, no Israeli government could be persuaded that Israel should give up bargaining assets without the compensation of a peaceful regional order, which was, after all, not our privilege but our right.

In an effort to win a better world opinion I made a detailed speech to the UN General Assembly on October 8, 1968, containing a nine-point peace plan. In this statement I gave the most moderate possible formulation to Israel's position on peace, boundaries, security, refugees, Jerusalem, and regional cooperation.

For at least a year after the nine-point peace proposal, Israel was immune from charges in the international press about her alleged obduracy and intransigence. Another purpose of my speech was to encourage President Johnson to carry out promises that he had made to Eshkol concerning the supply of Phantom aircraft. This was a crucial matter for our security, since the categories of arms available to our adversaries were escalating under Soviet stimulation.

Yitzhak Rabin, who was now our ambassador in Washington, attacked my speech in a cable to Jerusalem. His "argument" was that talk about peace and an invitation by me to the Egyptian foreign minister to meet me at UN headquarters would give an impression that the arms race was near its end and that the supply of Phantom aircraft had lost its priority. This was the opposite of the truth: President Johnson had indicated that if Israel presented a peaceful countenance, it would be easier for him to approve our arms requests. On the day after my peace plan was expounded in the UN General Assembly, Johnson, by prior arrangement with me, published his decision to make the Phantom available.

A little later in the month I had the last of my meetings with President Johnson during his presidency. It was an impressive experience. The presidential power was beginning to depart Johnson's massive frame, but his dominating air still filled the room. He had helped his nation to absorb the shock and shame of Kennedy's assassination. He had immediately administered a therapeutic dose of harmony. He had then put his vast energy to work to get the Congress to adopt legislation that took America into the age of the welfare state. At the center of his vision was the underprivileged American: youngsters growing up illiterate on southern farms; old people wasting away without dignity through lack of social concern; families of the sick whose resources were being cruelly bled by medical expenses for which no public insurance was available; populations living in areas in which racial discrimination was unrestrained by law.

If he had been able to concentrate on these measures, Lyndon Johnson would have ended his presidency, or even prolonged it, in an atmosphere of domestic and international respect. But across his horizons had come the Vietnam War. The small group of military advisers sent to Saigon by Eisenhower had been expanded by John F. Kennedy in the flush of his imperial presidency. Johnson lacked the courage to break away from the momentum that his martyred predecessor had initiated. By 1968 American involvement had become bulky and untenable and there was no easy way of extraction. With American loss of life growing more alarming, and the American reputation assailed throughout the world, the president had concluded that he could no longer express a national consensus. Moreover, most Americans doubted the morality as well as the utility of the war. In March 1968, Lyndon Johnson announced his intention not to submit himself for reelection.

As we sank into leather armchairs in his office on that October 1968 morning I noticed how his love of gimmickry had affected the interior decoration. There were three television sets that he could work separately or simultaneously without moving from his seat. As he opened a flap in the arm of his chair I noticed a whole system of buttons and switches. Three of them were oriented on the major networks, one of them was anonymous but red in color, and the last button announced "Fresca," a popular diet drink based on grapefruit juice. I recuperated as soon as possible from the apprehension lest a president might confuse the red line, or even the nuclear release button, with the quenching of his thirst.

The president reaffirmed his intention to sign the agreement for the supply of Phantoms. He then told me that both candidates for the presidency, Herbert H. Humphrey and Richard M. Nixon, had agreed to honor that commitment. He wanted me to tell Eshkol that "Lyndon B. Johnson has kept his word." The president went on to speak frankly of his own sentiment on leaving the White House. He had come there with a social purpose, vital to the country's future. The affairs of the world had diverted him into problems of international conflict. What disturbed him now was not so much that the United States would fail, for the first time in its history, to win a military objective. More serious was the fact that the new American attitude to the world would change. Like Roosevelt, Truman, Eisenhower, and Kennedy, he had represented the idea of "American responsibility." But now there was an effort to turn America's back to the world and to retreat into an illusory isolation.

The President seemed to feel that his own party was the focus of this new isolation. He then gave me remarkably frank and somewhat picturesque character sketches of his domestic adversaries. They included Senator J. William Fulbright, Senator Wayne Morse, Walter Lippmann, and in a sad and resigned tone, Frank Church of Idaho. All these had been leading advocates of restricted American commitments. Walter Lippmann wanted the United States to limit American defense engagements to the Pacific, Australia, and New Zealand while maintaining alliances with Western Europe. President Johnson wondered whether it was a coincidence that Lippmann's candidates for U.S. protection "happened to be white." Of Wayne Morse, the senator from Oregon, Johnson recounted to me a story going the rounds in the Senate: it told that Senator Morse had fallen off his horse while riding in his state, whereupon his senatorial colleagues opened a fund to supply oats for the irascible steed until the end of its days.

In a more serious vein the president told me that he had spoken to Nixon and Humphrey not only about the Phantom aircraft but about future American policy toward Israel. He thought that we could be reassured about the future. Either of his possible successors, for different motives, would keep faith with the commitment to Israel's security and independence. He thought that Humphrey had qualities of heart and mind, but lacked potency. Nixon, said LBJ, had mind and potency, but not much heart. Johnson hinted at heart and mind by pointing to his chest and head. He illustrated potency, or the lack of it, by pointing at his own body to the area where virility was popularly considered to reside. He added that if the Congress and public opinion continued to develop an isolationist trend in other contexts, a situation would be created in the United States in which "Israel would go down the drain." He thought, therefore, that Israel and its friends should have an interest in supporting an American policy of commitment. He added wryly, "A bunch of rabbis came here one day in 1967 to tell me that I ought not to send a single screwdriver to Vietnam but on the other hand should push all our aircraft carriers through the Straits of Tiran to help Israel."

I did not feel that I had a special duty to defend American liberals against his charge of isolationism. I was watching the political collapse of a man who was born with all the attributes of command but had lost control of his own vision. I admired his conclusion that it was useless for him to pursue his presidency beyond the point of its relevance. Times were changing and new men would have to meet new opportunities.

Not only in the United States . . .

On February 13, 1969, Moshe Kol, the minister of tourism, was my guest for breakfast in my Balfour Street residence. He was the sole representative in the Cabinet of the liberal party, previously called "the progressives," of which the first representative leader was Pinchas Rosen, the first minister of justice. The liberal progressives had been devoted worshipers of Chaim Weizmann, who appreciated their devotion but attached more importance to the Labor movement that offered him greater protection against right-wing opponents. The tone of the liberal party was emphatically German-Jewish, secular, centrist, humanist, and generally supportive of the line taken by the newspaper *Ha'aretz*. Jews of German origin had created the infrastructure of the liberal machine. They respected order, precision and restraint—qualities not universally admired in the riotous Israeli political arena. Moshe Kol was a man of reason and moderation, although he illustrated his virtues with some loquacity and a tendency to quote biblical sayings in full. The general effect of his influence was, however, enlivening and morally stimulating.

At exactly 8:30 a telephone call caused me to rise from the table to receive a laconic message from Ya'acov Herzog, the director general in the prime minister's office: "Levi Eshkol is dead."

Taking Kol with me, I went to the modest house on Rambam Street that served as the residence of the prime ministers. Eshkol had been ill with heart trouble for a whole year in the course of which Pinhas Sapir had engaged me in an intimate conversation. Sapir had said that it was unlikely that Eshkol would survive another heart attack. As responsible ministers we should think of the succession. Sapir believed that only the appointment of Golda could prevent a suicidal clash in the Labor Party between Dayan and Allon. He had sounded Golda Meir during one of her visits to Switzerland where she was taking an uncharacteristic rest. Sapir had told me that a condition of her acceptance would be that all the other labor ministers remain exactly in their places, thus avoiding the tensions of a reshuffle. He assured me that Golda, whose health was also variable, would take the office only for the year remaining until an election would be necessary. I had given my consent.

Eshkol's death opened a new phase in the country's leadership. Many leaders in Zionism and Israel were more flamboyant and colorful, but none had been called to a responsibility equal to his and none in his lifetime had celebrated so many successes. He had brought unity to the Labor movement, an achievement that had eluded his more eminent predecessor. He had been at the helm during Israel's spectacular military success, and he had seen Jerusalem reunited. After the Six Day War there had been nearly two years of political struggle, that had ended with Israel's positions in the occupied territories intact and the hope of a more secure and stable region more alive than before.

His rivals found it hard to forgive him for his success. He never pretended that he was the sole agent of all these events, but it is certain that if there had been failure, the responsibility would have been laid at his door. His tolerant captaincy was congenial to the free interplay of diverse forces. His revulsion from excessive authoritarianism brought out the latent energies in our community. His temper expanded in an atmosphere of harmony. He had little time or talent for abstract slogans. His gnarled farmer's hands were rooted in the soil of practical achievement. The developing economy that he and Finance Minister Pinhas Sapir had virtually created was the basis on which Israel's military strength and political stability had been erected. When he died suddenly the Jewish world felt that a gentle presence had been borne away, and the appreciation of his qualities would grow stronger as the months rolled on.

It had been widely assumed that the Labor Party would be torn by a contest between the minister of defense, Moshe Dayan, and the minister of labor, later to be Deputy Prime Minister Yigal Allon. Each of them had made his deep mark on Israel's military contests before turning his considerable energies to politics. Yet many doubted whether the issue was really drawn between them alone. The Israeli Labor Party, after all, was a federation with its central bulk in the Mapai Party and with two smaller wings formed by those who had seceded during the past two decades. Allon belonged to the activist Ahdut Ha'Avoda group, which was a minority within the Labor camp, and Dayan represented the Rafi Party, which, despite Ben-Gurion's leadership, had secured only ten out of 120 Knesset seats at the height of its struggle for power in 1964. The main body of the party, the original Mapai, solid, broad-based, cautious, pragmatic, seemed little disposed to bequeath its inheritance to either of the groups that had seceded from it.

Within a few weeks of Eshkol's death the problem of national and party leadership was solved through the election of Golda Meir, who had resigned from the Foreign Ministry for reasons of health a few years before.

This transition had been less smooth than that which Sapir had cautiously planned. There were some weeks during which Yigal Allon, as deputy prime minister, took over the leadership of the cabinet. He did this with such modesty and skill that leading party members asked themselves why he should not continue in the prime minister's office. Dosh, a leading cartoonist in the widely circulated paper *Ma'ariv,* published a cartoon showing Allon, sitting in the prime minister's chair. The caption was: "Why not leave him there?" In one of our intimate party gatherings, two veteran members, Shaul Avigur, the brother-in-law of Moshe Sharett, and Yitzhak Ben-Aharon, the Histadrut leader, had openly supported Allon for the premiership.

I considered that this was good advice. Allon's leadership would balance what I already felt to be the inordinately strong influence of Moshe Dayan, whom Golda both resented and loyally followed. Allon, unlike Dayan, respected Arabic culture and spoke Arabic fluently. His personality was expansive, cheerful, and optimistic. These qualities had inspired his leadership of our armed forces in the war of independence. I asked my trusted political secretary, David Rivlin, to explore directly with Allon whether he would allow his candidacy to be presented. Rivlin visited Allon in the Education Ministry and added on my behalf that I would support him, both in his campaign for leadership of the party and for his premiership if he were to attain that peak.

It later emerged that Allon, while grateful for the support of his friends, was so intimidated by the party veterans supporting Golda, especially Sapir and Galili, that he recoiled from the challenge. Harold Wilson, the British prime minister who knew Yigal and me intimately, said that we both lacked "the killer instinct."

Golda was not slow in discovering that I had been willing to support Allon's candidacy. This meant that both he and I would thereafter incur her suspicious gaze whenever we entered the cabinet room.

The weight of Golda's responsibility seemed to liberate new energies within her. The idea disseminated by Sapir that she would be content to hold office for a year and then pass the burden to younger hands was sheer illusion. Her defiant personality certainly gave the nation's military and political struggle a strong dimension. My own feeling was then, and remains to this day, that the Labor movement and the country would have benefited from the fresh wind that Allon's appointment would have brought to the nation's helm.

Golda, like Eshkol, did not think that Israel's territorial structure was its

only important attribute. She was not a romantic territorialist. The maintenance of Israel's Jewish and democratic character appealed to her more than
anything else. I could not even imagine her making a visit to Nablus, Gaza
or Jenin to find out how her Arab "subjects" were faring in the occupied
territories. She had even written of our settlement in Hebron (Kiryat Arba)
that if Hebron was returned to Jordan, it was right that Jews should be able
to live there. Under her leadership Israel enunciated in clear terms a willingness to accept the principle of withdrawal to secure, recognized and agreed
boundaries. But she was more inclined to articulate this principle than to
"risk" putting it into practice. And she was resolved not to be sold short on
Israeli security.

In December 1969, less than a year after her appointment, we were resolutely opposing a plan conceived by our greatest friend, the United States,
that would have limited us to "unsubstantial" changes in the former lines
with Jordan and to no change at all in the border with Egypt. This proposal,
formulated by Secretary of State Rogers, unjustifiably weakened Israel's
bargaining position by offering Egypt an important concession before Egypt
had accepted the obligation to make peace with Israel.

Golda Meir faced few urgent domestic problems during the first year of
her premiership. On the external front, however, the air was alive with both
opportunities and dangers. Richard M. Nixon had been elected to the presidency in November 1968. His election had been received in American Jewish
circles and in Israel without enthusiasm. We assumed that he would continue
Dwight Eisenhower's reserved attitude to Israel. We all doubted whether
President Johnson's Texan warmth would come to expression in Nixon's
attitude toward us. Nixon had represented the conservative wing in the
Republican Party, which had never had intimacy of contact with American
Jews or with Israel. Nixon's democratic opponent had been Vice President
Hubert Humphrey, who would have brought to the presidency all the eager
warmth that Harry Truman had displayed in his relations with us. Golda
Meir, in her capacity as secretary general of the Labor Party, had indiscreetly
expressed the hope that Humphrey would be elected. Before long we would
discover that Richard Nixon's presidency would be exceedingly fruitful for
Israel's security. Throughout his term of office I rarely heard him say a
sentimental word about our country and its cause, and his utterances about
Jews in America were rarely free from irascibility, but whenever Israel's
security was at issue or in hazard he would supply our needs or lay down rules
for effective cooperation with us.

I had decided to make early contact with the president and his secretary
of state soon after they took office. There was an atmosphere of transition in
every sector of the American-Israeli relationship. Golda Meir instead of Levi
Eshkol, Richard Nixon instead of Lyndon Johnson, and Yitzhak Rabin as
our ambassador in Washington.

The idea of Rabin's appointment had first come to me from Moshe Raviv,
my trusted adviser in the Foreign Ministry. When I broached it with Eshkol

he was not enthusiastic. "Why not one of our Hevra?" he asked, meaning, of course, somebody of impeccably Mapai orientation. Rabin had been "suspected" by Eshkol of being closer to the Achdut Ha'avoda mentality than to the more pragmatic traditions of Mapai. On the other hand, both Eshkol and I were impressed by the allure that the appointment of a celebrated military commander would bring to the central diplomatic post. The fact that Rabin had no experience in diplomacy and very little knowledge of the United States was deemed subsidiary. After Abe Harman's departure there had been a long interregnum with Eppie Evron in charge. This was due in part to the unusual circumstance that in his farewell meeting with me toward the end of 1968 President Johnson had said to me with habitual bluntness: "If you know what's good for you, Mr. Minister, you'll leave Eppie here so long as I'm here." The friendship of a president of the United States for a deputy ambassador of Israel was highly unusual, but then Johnson was an unusual man and Eppie Evron had an unusual capacity to evoke intense loyalties as well as some sharp antagonisms. No one whom I consulted in Washington thought that rejection of Johnson's recommendation would be a rational thing to do for the remainder of his office in the White House.

The atmosphere of change in the White House was expressed in another unexpected event. President Nixon appointed Henry A. Kissinger to the post of national security adviser. Kissinger's appointment attracted more international and domestic attention than did the routine appointment of Rogers as Nixon's secretary of state. Commentators and pundits predicted that the national security adviser's office would become more potent than the State Department under the mild leadership of Rogers. Henry Kissinger did nothing to discourage this prediction. Foreign ministers, like myself, whose countries were involved at the center of American policy, would evidently find ourselves dividing our contacts between two polarized areas of American authority in foreign affairs.

Kissinger had visited Israel once and had been my guest at the Weizmann Institute, of which I was president. He had asked me bluntly if Israel intended to manufacture nuclear weapons. I had given him a negative answer that he totally disbelieved. His friendship for me was illustrated by what he wrote about me in his memoirs:

> The first to be heard from was the eloquent Abba Eban, who arrived in Washington in the middle of March for talks at the White House and State Department. I have never encountered anyone who matched his command of the English language. . . . No American or British personality ever reminded me so acutely that English was for me, after all, an acquired language.

My critics in Israel were surprised to hear that my reputation abroad was for tenacious negotiating positions:

Eban's eloquence—unfortunately for those who had to negotiate with him—was allied to a first-class intelligence and fully professional grasp of diplomacy. He was always well prepared; he knew what he wanted. He practiced to the full his maxim that anything less than one hundred percent agreement with Israel's point of view demonstrated lack of objectivity.

When Kissinger published these words I naturally saw them as proof of his objectivity. He quickly contrived to succeed William Rogers as secretary of state by methods that he engagingly describes in his copious memoirs.

While Kissinger's policies and methods aroused admiration in some of his countrymen and strong reservations in others, he enhanced the rank and influence of his office beyond any level previously or subsequently known. One of his achievements was to convert foreign policy from a narrow, mandarin preoccupation into a theme capable of exciting mass opinion. He was utterly distinctive both in his analytical power and in his language and style. He soon discovered, however, that without control of the State Department bureaucracy, his hold on foreign policy was spasmodic and tenuous, and the main impact of his personality on the international system would come to expression only after his appointment as secretary of state in 1973.

In March 1969 I had set out for Washington with the intention of exploring the attitudes and policies of the Nixon regime. My initial predictions were not optimistic. The first decision of Nixon on the Israeli-Arab conflict had been to make a sharp break from the UN context and to embrace what we thought would be the more dangerous auspices of the four major powers. Nixon had appeared to accept de Gaulle's obsession about the "concert of the four." The first year of Jarring's mission was not productive, but it had also brought us no presentiment of danger. The Israeli tendency is to measure mediators not by the good that they do but by the harm that they avoid. I thought that the replacement of the innocuous Jarring by four powers, two of which—France and the Soviet Union—were sharply pro-Arab, boded ill for us.

During my ambassadorial mission I had taken pains to cultivate the sympathy of Vice-President Nixon. I had once invited him to dine at our residence, to the surprise of some of my more hidebound colleagues in the Labor Party who predicted, wrongly, that right-wing Republicans would be a hostile breed.

I had played a memorable golf match with Nixon at the Woodmont Country Club when he was still languishing in the obscurity of the vice-presidency. His skills and mine fell short of distinction, but were not negligible by amateur criteria. We played a round in which I defeated him by 89–90. This result, comparatively creditable for both of us, was greeted with perplexity when the news broke in Jerusalem. A Foreign Office bureaucrat in Jerusalem sent me a query: "Surely if you scored 89 and he scored 90 he must have won the game, because 90 is a higher number than 89." I was proud to belong to a service whose members were capable of such rigorous arithmetical insight, but I replied with a saying from the Talmud: "Whoever adds subtracts."

In our March 24, 1969, meeting President Nixon was lucid, competent, and authoritative. He greeted me with the words: "We have both gone up in the world since we last met." At the end of our talk he took me alone into the Rose Garden for a few minutes despite the cold March winds. He asked me earnestly why "Israel's friends" did not have more faith in his concern for our interests. He assured me, "I will never let Israel down."

I came to the White House that day with misgivings. Nixon's first visit abroad had been to Paris, where he came under the spell of General de Gaulle's commanding personality. It was Kissinger, the new national security adviser, who had advised the president to accord priority of attention to Paris in the hope that the United States could overcome de Gaulle's reservations about an active role in the Atlantic alliance. De Gaulle had never recovered from the Soviet rebuff to his proposal for a four-power consultation and he still believed that a new concert of Europe based on the "Big Four" was a better policy framework than the despised United Nations or than what de Gaulle called the "hegemonistic pretensions" of an American-Soviet dialogue that would diminish Europe. Golda Meir was justly apprehensive of the four-power consultations. She realized, too, that de Gaulle and the Soviet leadership, could be trusted to indulge a strongly pro-Arab bias while the other two members of the quartet, the United States and the United Kingdom, would at best be "evenhanded."

Israel, in its relationships with the outside world, has never regarded evenhandedness as a favorable attribute.

Israel needed and deserved consideration beyond its physical size and slender resources. Nixon assured me that I should not take the four-power gambit as a serious threat to our interests. The United States would keep close control and would veto any proposal that it thought incompatible with Israel's security. Moreover, he added, the talks would be held by United Nations ambassadors in New York. This was a notoriously weak level of authority in the minds of the Nixon administration, which took a hard-nosed skeptical view about the role of international organizations in a world dominated by nuclear powers. The implication was that he had accepted a four-power approach to placate General de Gaulle but without a real intention to make the quadripartite context decisive.

My first talks with the Nixon administration were reassuring for us. The president, Secretary Rogers, and Security Adviser Kissinger reiterated their obligation to keep Israel strong. They confirmed the American attitude in favor of maintaining the cease-fire lines until they could be replaced by permanent peace. I felt that I had helped to lay the foundations for good relationships in the coming four years. Ambassador Rabin, who accompanied me on these conversations, enthusiastically cabled back to Israel that "the talks of Foreign Minister Eban with the President and Secretary of State have created a basis for positive relations with the Nixon administration."

We would stand in acute need of those relations, for the years 1968 to 1970 proved that the brilliant successes of 1967 had not given birth to any degree of permanent security.

Many otherwise well-informed people, across the world and even in Israel, if asked to enumerate Israel's wars, would give a list beginning with the 1948 War of Independence, continuing with the Suez-Sinai War of 1956, and the Six Day War of 1967, culminating in the Yom Kippur War of 1973. There would then be a pause in declaiming the list until the ill-starred war in Lebanon in 1982 was reached. Somehow the "war of attrition" seems to have got lost in the public consciousness.

This is a strange omission, because what came to be called "the war of attrition" between Israel and Egypt from March 1969 to August 1970 was a momentous event with far greater loss and wider repercussions than are reflected in the research devoted to it. The war was inaugurated by Egypt with the declared intention of changing the adverse military and territorial status that had been inherited from the 1967 war. Nasser's slogan was "what was lost in war must be restored by war."

More than any of Israel's wars, the war of attrition became directly and intimately involved in the relations between the superpowers. It was also the only one of Israel's wars that led to direct military intervention by one of the powers, the Soviet Union, in an effort to vindicate its alliance with a Middle Eastern power, namely Egypt. The levels of casualties and destruction were far heavier than in the wars of 1956 and 1967. It was also of far longer duration.

The war of attrition, as its name indicates, was conducted and brought to an end without anything that could be called victory for one side and defeat for the other. If we make a candid study of the positions of the powers before and after the war, it must be confessed that the psychological and international balance changed to Egypt's advantage.

It was certainly not an Israeli success. By the time that the August 1970 cease-fire came into effect, Egypt was less humiliated and Israel less self-confident than before. Israeli losses became so numerous and poignant that we had to pay a price for the cease-fire by agreeing to concessions that our government had previously resisted. Israel was clearly shaken both by the threat of Soviet intervention and by the intensity of American pressure to end the war. Israel had to return to the negotiations conducted by Ambassador Jarring despite a clear violation of the cease-fire by Egypt, which brought its missiles up to a forbidden area in order to threaten Israel from a shorter distance. Moreover, the dependence of Israel on United States assistance and therefore its need to adjust itself to American demands, all came to public light, as against the heroic posture with which Israel emerged from the Six Day War. We were no longer able to play a lone hand with successful results. For the first time an Israeli military strategy boomeranged. The decision to carry out in-depth raids in Egypt on the false assumption that the United States favored that course had meager military results and brought us to an internationally defensive posture. Egypt benefited from Soviet intervention while at the same time it strengthened its relations with the United States by agreeing to the American peace initiative. It is true that we succeeded in preventing any adverse change in the territorial condition resulting from the Six Day War. On the other hand, there were Israelis whose perceptions were candid and realistic. Primary amongst them was Ezer Weizmann, the architect of Israel's air power and eventually an influential minister in the Likud-Labor coalition. He diagnosed the war as a failure[1] since it solved no problems and produced much grief. He said:

My view was that the War of Attrition in its extended scale was an Israeli mistake; that the government of which I was a member should have given far greater attention to the Jarring mission, to the peace proposals exchanged between Egypt and Israel in 1971, and to the understanding that raids deep into Egypt would inevitably invite greater Soviet involvement and eventually lead to a disastrous military experience within a few years of the 1970 cease-fire.

I shared the view that our hold on Sinai would be a strong factor for bringing Egypt to the negotiating table. (This proved to be accurate in 1977.) I did not, however, believe that the intensification of military pressures in 1969 and 1970 was or would be supported by the United States.

One of the side effects of this debate was a crucial difference between Ambassador Rabin and me about the diagnosis of American policy. I certainly believed that it was the right of an ambassador to recommend exercising Israel's military power in order to achieve political results. On the other hand, I thought it wrong for an ambassador to confuse his appraisal of facts with the exposition of his views, and then to win the day by asserting without sufficient evidence that the U.S. favored the bombardments of Egypt in-depth. On January 2, 1970, I wrote in *Ha'aretz*: "If fate wills it that Nasser should fall . . . I presume that there will be no mourning in Israel. But one should not conclude from this that the U.S. encourages actions taken deliberately in order to overthrow him. That is no sign of a U.S. desire for an energetic increase of activity beyond the cease-fire lines if Egypt does not force us into this."

---

[1]Yaa'cov Bar-Siman-Tov, *The Israeli-Egyptian War of Attrition, Nineteen Sixty-Nine to Nineteen Seventy: A Case Study of Limited Local War* (New York: Columbia University Press, 1980), p. 194.

The discussion about in-depth bombing of Egypt was inseparably linked with the question of whether Israel could bring about the replacement of Nasser by another leader. Most of us believed that there could not be any contingency worse for Israel than the continuation of Nasser's regime. We based this assumption on Nasser's uncontrolled behavior leading to the Six Day War, and his refusal to give any thought to the prospect of restoring his territory by a diplomatic settlement with Israel. Moreover, his constant bombardment of Israel's position east of the Suez Canal indicated that he believed his own rhetoric when he said, "That which was taken by force must be recaptured by force."

I believed that the prospects of peace would only emerge when Nasser ceased to rule Egypt. It was, however, quite possible to embrace this view without accepting the argument that the best way to achieve the replacement of Nasser would be by bombing Egypt in-depth. In my January 2 article in *Ha'aretz*, I wrote, "Our actions are carried out on the basis of calculations of Israel's security and we do not fix any political goal with respect to its effect upon the Egyptian regime." Later that month in a broadcast I stated, "The Egyptian people itself has to decide about the regime as well as the chances of achieving peace." In many later statements I repeated, "I should not weep if Nasser fell but that is not our task nor the purpose we are fighting for . . . the government never adopted a doctrine of overthrowing Nasser by Israeli military pressure and now even less so."

December 21, 1969, Rabin returned to Israel from his post in Washington ostensibly to discuss recent American proposals for a peace settlement with Egypt but in fact to take part in the crucial discussion of the question of in-depth bombing of Egypt. His strong views in favor of this course were already well known from his telegrams, some of which were formulated in terms of sharp rebuke to his government for failing to understand what he termed "an irrevocable opportunity." We in the cabinet had a deep interest in hearing his views on the potential response of the United States to an escalation of our pressure against Egypt. The fact that Rabin had held the highest authority for the nation's physical security would surely enable him to take a balanced view. I found nothing in Rabin's report that would justify the conclusion that the United States had any interest in the escalation of the fighting in or near the Canal area.

Intense Israeli air attacks on targets far west of the Canal zone began on January 7 and continued until April 13, 1970. Early in February, I pointed out that those who believed that the Soviet Union would not intervene should in all honesty revise that belief in the light of the Soviet diplomatic reaction. On February 2, Prime Minister Kosygin sent letters in very grave terms to President Nixon, French President Pompidou, and Prime Minister Wilson. The note contained sharp abuse of the United States and vehement protests against the Israeli raids, which according to Kosygin were made possible by the sale of American Phantom jets to Israel. Kosygin indicated that unless the Western powers agreed to restrain Israel, "the U.S.S.R. will be obliged to supply Egypt with all the arms needed to resist the in-depth air raids." The apologists for the raids consoled themselves by pointing out that the most drastic Kosygin threat was not to order Soviet military intervention but "only" to intensify the supply of arms to Egypt.

I felt that Kosygin's message made it clear that there was no way of pursuing our war of attrition without involving ourselves in an escalating global crisis. I therefore made an attempt at exploring disengagement. At a cabinet meeting in February 1970, to consider its reply to Kosygin's message of February 2, I surprised my colleagues by making a proposal for what later came to be called a "peace offensive." My idea was that we should not only declare our policies but should also give dramatic expression to our readiness for a temporary cease-fire on the Suez Canal as a first step toward military deescalation. At the same time, the minister of the interior and leader of the religious party, Moshe Shapira, suggested that we should declare an unconditional, unilateral cease-fire and a halt to our air raids for forty-eight or seventy-two hours as the United States had done in Vietnam. My proposal was correct: there was nothing to lose by exploring the possibility of ending the war of attrition. Golda Meir had good reason to placate the religious party leader and she was ready for a mild condemnation of Shapira's proposal. She turned her full fury on me. Did I not recall, she said with indignation, that Nasser himself had proposed a temporary cease-fire along the Canal? If this was in Nasser's interest, how could this be in the interest of Israel? Was I not proposing what would turn out in effect to be a dangerous trap for Israel in contradiction of its stated policy? The explorations of the possibility of a cease-fire had been heard in Moscow and in Cairo, as well as in Western capitals. How then was it possible for me to suggest that Israel should initiate what its adversaries had proposed? If Egypt were to agree to a freeze in the fighting along the Canal during a temporary cease-fire, who would guarantee that it would be honored? The Soviet Union? The United States? U Thant?

Golda was joined in her rejection of my proposal by Yisrael Galili and by the police minister, Shlomo Hillel, who rarely abstained from supporting the most militant of the options available to Israel. He said that Nasser was making every effort to relieve himself of the weight of Israel's in-depth bombing in order to rebuild his damaged military potential. A temporary cease-fire would enable him to achieve his military aim. This was a correct analysis, but it did not add up to a justification for an indefinite prolongation of the war of attrition. It was not at all clear who was being the most "attritioned," Israel or Egypt.

I continued to defend my proposal. I asked its opponents what would happen if Nasser were to propose a cease-fire of indefinite length. Would not Israel inevitably give a positive reply? But surely in that case Nasser would be just as free to rebuild his army and to rehabilitate his positions. What greater assurance would Israel have from an allegedly indefinite cease-fire that she would not obtain from a temporary cease-fire? My opponents in the debate replied that we should simply demand that Nasser should unilaterally and humbly renounce the war of attrition and renew a cease-fire of indefinite duration. My feeling was that this would only be possible if we were really winning the war. This, unhappily, was not true.

Noting that there was no majority for my proposal for a peace offensive, I naturally did not wish it to be discredited in a vote. A cabinet rejection would make our international image even worse than it would be if we left my proposal in the air. Golda, however, wanted to give expression to the bitterness that had accumulated in her heart toward me. She insisted on putting my proposal to the vote in order that she should have the pleasure of voting against it. The justice minister, Yaa'cov Shimshon Shapira, and even Yisrael Galili implored Golda to avoid a vote against a peace offensive. The prime minister, however, was insistent, hands were raised. Only the Mapai ministers voted for my peace proposal that was no longer on the table! I declined to take part in a vote for my own proposal in order to illustrate my profound sentiment that it should not have been put to the vote at all.

This episode illustrated the difficulty of being a foreign minister in a cabinet that had an exaggerated vision of the role of war in international politics. The triumph of our forces in 1967 had encouraged a belief in an Israeli invincibility that ceased to operate as soon as the Six Day War came to a halt. It was not Golda at her best. The episode highlighted the centrality of personal rancor in the general system of her thought and emotion.

The U.S. reply to the Soviet warning was sharp. In late February, Nixon sent a warning to Moscow: "The United States would view any effort by the Soviet Union to seek predominance in the Middle East as a matter of grave concern. Any effort by an outside power to exploit local conflicts for its own advantage or to seek special position would be contrary to that goal."

Nixon was at his cool, pragmatic best in handling the American-Soviet dialogue.

The most impressive book on the war of attrition in English is that by Yaa'cov Bar-Siman-Tov.

In the process of reaching the decision to carry out the in-depth raids, what very largely made the decision possible was the Israeli evaluation that the United States was not opposed to them—an evaluation based on the judgment of the Israeli Ambassador to the United States, Yitzhak Rabin. Rabin thought that the United States would not oppose the raids and might even give them silent support. He believed that an identity of interest had been created between the United States and Israel on their attitudes about the Nasser regime and he therefore advocated exploiting this identity of interest in order to utilize the possibility of weakening or overthrowing that regime. Rabin's views on the lack of United States opposition to in-depth raids which he expounded to the government during his visit to the country on December 21, 1969, certainly influenced the decision to carry out the raids.[2]

The operative fact, however, is that Moshe Dayan and Golda Meir bear the major responsibility for Israeli policy during the war of attrition. Rabin could only advise; Golda and Dayan alone could decide.

So far from promoting the "fall of Nasser," as the advocates of the in-depth bombing had predicted, this policy led Nasser to Moscow, where he made a passionate appeal to the Soviet Union for the supply of a modern air-defense system. Brezhnev at first was reluctant to grant this demand. It was not the general habit of the Soviet Union to expose its advanced technologies and its advisers to situations of active hostilities outside the Communist sphere of influence and control.

In the first weeks of 1970 our bombers dropped thousands of bombs on targets in Egypt. The range of Israeli actions became deeper. Bombs falling twelve miles away could be heard in Cairo, adding to the humiliation of Nasser and exposing him as a commander who could not even defend his own capital's airspace. Nasser was in no position to prevent our air actions and yet he was not prepared to work for a cease-fire, still less to enter into peace negotiations with Israel. Nasser's close friend, Muhammad Hassanein Heikal, the editor of Al Ahram, has described the meeting at the Kremlin during a secret visit that Nasser made to Moscow. It is known that Brezhnev was initially reluctant to grant Nasser's request for the dispatch of Soviet antiaircraft missiles with accompanying personnel to carry out the training and disposition of the new antimissile force.

Nevertheless, even Brezhnev, with all his caution and skepticism, could not face the prospect that Nasser might resign, making way for an American-dominated Egypt. If this were to occur, the Soviet Union would lose the centerpiece of its privileged position in the Third World. Moscow began to move its missiles and hundreds of its advisers into Cairo. Egypt's strategic position was strengthened. We would feel the full brunt of this new balance of power and confidence in the new war that was looming on the horizon. The fuse was three years long. It would explode on Yom Kippur 1973.

I obviously had to play my part in preserving our balance of air strength. This was my main concern when on May 24, 1970, I had a discussion with President Nixon in the White House.

Although the war of attrition was having a more devastating effect on Egypt than on us, it was still a fact that we were losing lives and planes.

---

[2]Yaa'cov Bar-Siman-Tov, ibid.

Without the assurance of ongoing supplies of Phantoms and other equipment, our military command would not have enough confidence to take tactical risks with the weapons that it possessed.

Nixon was accompanied by Kissinger and Sisco. With me were Ambassador Rabin and Shlomo Argov, one of our most brilliant diplomats, who later became ambassador in London, where he was savagely wounded in the head by a Palestinian assailant. The main question was whether we could expect a favorable response to our arms requests in the near future.

The president began with a significant question: Was it still Israel's policy that American troops would never be involved in any foreseeable development of the war in the Middle East? When I gave a positive answer, Nixon immediately replied, "Well, in that case, you will get the stuff so long as you don't insist on too much publicity." It was typical Nixon style: no sentimentality or introductory rhetoric. Every word had to be related to an action or decision. He then instructed Kissinger and Sisco to discuss the schedules with us.

Skepticism was so deeply embedded in Israeli minds that even the president's formal announcement to me was not regarded in Jerusalem as final. The public mood about the Phantoms was becoming obsessive. Israelis simply would not believe that they would get the planes until or unless they actually landed on an Israeli airstrip. Some ministers even wondered if the words "You'll get the stuff" could possibly convey a presidential decision. Should not such proclamations be conveyed with more solemnity? My own feeling was that a presidential commitment, such as Nixon had given, was, in fact, irrevocable.

When I reached home, I could feel blasts of doubt flowing toward me across the cabinet table. I had the foresight to send a note to my friend and neighbor Pinhas Sapir: "I predict that the Phantoms will be delivered in September; please keep this chit and open it at the end of that month." Sapir played this game with a straight face. He informed me on October 1, after the Phantoms had arrived, that, "to the surprise of some of our colleagues," I had not been optimistic in vain.

American policy, however, did not concern itself only or chiefly with arms supplies to Israel. In fact, both President Nixon and Secretary Rogers believed, not without justification, that exclusive Israeli preoccupation with its own military strength was exaggerated. The main objective of the U.S. administration was to end the fighting that was increasingly liable to involve the United States in an unwanted confrontation with the Soviet Union. The U.S. did not believe that it would be possible to get a cease-fire without adding a political process of some kind. Indeed, Nixon mumbled a quiet sentence to this effect to Rabin and me in our May 17 meeting, with the addendum that we would get prior information when anything of this sort was planned.

In mid-June, the Egyptians ominously brought their antiaircraft missiles closer to the Canal area. Losses of Israeli planes and air crews increased. It was obvious that we would either have to escalate our attacks on Egyptian territory or move our ground forces into battle in an effort to eliminate the missiles.

On June 24, on my return from West European capitals, I was met at the airport by the director general of our Foreign Ministry, Gideon Rafael, who summoned me to Golda's home for a meeting requested by the United States ambassador, Walworth Barbour. I drove straight to the meeting.

Reading closely from his cabled instructions, Barbour presented us with a proposal in three parts: first, the acceptance of a cease-fire on the Egyptian front for a period of three months. Second, a statement by Israel, Egypt, and Jordan that they accepted the Security Council's Resolution 242, and specifically, the call for "withdrawal from occupied territories." Third, an undertaking from Israel to negotiate with Egypt and Jordan under Dr. Jarring's auspices as soon as the cease-fire came into force. One of the important provisions of the cease-fire was to be a "standstill." Neither Egypt nor Israel would be able to bring missiles or artillery closer to the front than before.

Golda's immediate intuitive reply was an indignant negative. The Americans had interpreted the promise to consult with us in advance as a promise to inform us a few hours before publication. I observed, however, that the phlegmatic American ambassador was by no means disturbed by Golda's rejection. He suffered from a respiratory ailment for which he sought remedy by taking a small vial from his pocket and squeezing a rubber bulb that emitted a firm sputter into his open mouth. He had learned to make operative use of this facility. Whenever Golda would begin a flight of indignant oratory, Barbour would produce his vial and emit the sprits-like squeeze that would break the tension in a single instant.

As he and I left Golda's home I could hear him muttering, "Golda has rejected this. This means that she'll be accepting it in a few weeks."

The ambassador was not wrong. In late July, when we surveyed our situation in all its aspects, we felt that the risks of accepting the American cease-fire proposal were far less than the dangers of rejecting it. Rejection would mean the continuation of savage war with Egypt, the prospect of involvement in military conflict with the Soviet Union, and diminishing American fidelity to Israel. The Egyptian artillery offensive stimulated by the consciousness of Soviet support caused heavy casualties to Israel in the period between March and the end of May. During those few weeks, sixty-four Israeli soldiers were killed and one hundred fifty wounded. It was becoming clear that the task of retaining the territory at Sinai was costing Israel much more blood than the retention was worth.

Menachem Begin and his supporters in the government argued that the United States might be willing to accept the part of the proposal that was congenial to us—namely, the cease-fire—without giving the Arabs the prospect of political negotiation in return. I found this very hard to accept. It was unrealistic to believe that we could get a cease-fire without accepting Resolution 242 and the resumption of the Jarring mission, which would focus on a negotiation with Jordan.

The United States was working not only by the exercise of pressure, but also by the multiplication of incentives. On July 24, Nixon, having received Egypt's acceptance of the cease-fire proposal, sent a presidential message to Israel the like of which we had never known before.

President Nixon promised 1) that there would be a continuation and even a reinforcement of American economic and military aid, even if there were a cease-fire, which might ostensibly justify the diminution of that aid; 2) Israel would not be required to withdraw its forces from the occupied territories until a satisfactory peace treaty had been concluded. Until that time, said President Nixon, Israel would not be called upon by the United States to remove a single Israeli soldier from existing military positions; 3) Israel would not be required to accept a solution of the refugee problem that might alter the Jewish character of the state; and 4) the U.S. would protect us in the UN Security Council against peremptory orders to sacrifice our existing territorial positions without adequate and credible security or political gains.

The mood of Golda and the rest of the Labor contingent in the government now became less militant and defiant than when she had contemptuously rejected my call for a "cease-fire and peace offensive" in February 1970. Moreover, even Yitzhak Rabin, who had led the movement for bombarding Egypt in depth, was now in a far more reflective mood. When Golda had sent an irascible letter to Nixon rejecting the Rogers cease-fire plan, Rabin had courageously taken it upon himself not to deliver the message, thus incurring Golda's rage. He had maintained his position with tenacity. The crisis in his relations with Golda had become so sharp that Yigal Allon had intervened to suggest that he be invited to Israel to explain his apprehensions. He had met me in my room in the Dan Hotel, and we had come to one of our rare agreements to support each other in this matter.

It was becoming clear to me and to many of my colleagues that we would, in fact, have no course except agreement to a temporary cease-fire to be followed by negotiations on withdrawal, not only with Egypt but with Jordan. We knew very well that this might lead to a break with the Gahal ministers led by Menachem Begin. None of us could deny that we were sinking deeper and deeper into a quagmire composed of such unsavory ingredients as erosion of our air strength, tension with the United States, and even direct intervention by the Soviet Union, whose pilots had been heard conversing with each other in Russian during one of our air battles over Egyptian territory.

All these tensions came to a point of explosion in the first week of August 1970. The Israeli government adopted a decision, drafted by of all people Moshe Dayan, announcing our acceptance of the cease-fire and our willingness to negotiate with Egypt and Jordan on withdrawal from occupied territories.

After an impassioned appearance before members of his own group, Begin submitted the resignation of himself and the five other Gahal ministers. In an address to the Knesset on August 4, he had stated that acceptance of 242, in a Jordanian context, meant renunciation of Judea and Samaria—"not all of those territories, but undoubtedly most of them." He described as illusory the views of anyone who believed that 242 meant anything except renunciation of the West Bank and Gaza. Therefore, those who objected to returning the West Bank and Gaza to Arab rule had no right whatever to accept Resolution 242. Begin was absolutely right in his interpretation of 242 and showed great integrity in accepting the consequences of his correct interpretation.

I regretted Begin's departure on personal grounds because his eloquent presence had given zest and interest to the cabinet's debates. On the other hand, it seemed that our hands were now free to express our policy of territorial compromise with less constraint than before.

The cease-fire on August 5, 1970, was received by the Israeli population with profound relief. Events had totally discredited the theory that Sinai, under Israeli rule, constituted "a buffer" between Egypt and ourselves. The contrary was the case. By pushing our armed forces far away from our home base, right up to the Suez Canal, we were, in fact, exposing ourselves to successful Egyptian assaults in which they had the advantage of proximity both to their own bases and to their Israeli target. Most of us had reached the conclusion that Sinai, under Israeli occupation, was not a security asset, but a strangling millstone around our necks.

A security asset should surely achieve two aims: first, the saving of Israeli lives and, second, the deterrence of war. What was happening, in fact, was that Israel was less safe with Sinai in its possession than it would have been with a demilitarized Sinai, which we had advocated in our peace proposals of June 19, 1967. The great value of Sinai lay in the contractual sphere; since Egypt wanted its restoration it would ultimately offer peace, provided that it failed to get it by war.

The intensive military pressure on Egypt had induced the Soviet Union to equip Egypt with a modern air-defense system to deal with the Israeli air raids. The new Egyptian air-defense system was soon spread out across the entire hundred-mile length of the Suez Canal.

If all Israeli policymakers had understood that Egypt now possessed a credible war option, that the adulation of the status quo was shortsighted, and that the occupation of Arab populated territories had become a burden, we would have faced a period of military vigilance and of sustained interest in the doctrine of "territories for peace."

This was not to be. The war of attrition was nothing but the storm before the storm.

24

COULD THERE HAVE BEEN
PEACE?

THE YEARS 1967–1973 ended in war, not in peace. This does not mean that we were inactive in the search for an agreement. Peace is not always obtained by those who seek it most assiduously. Between 1967 and 1973 the Arabs could have recovered all of Sinai, and the Golan, and most of the West Bank and Gaza without war by negotiating boundaries and security arrangements with Israel. The policy of the Israeli government at that time contained no ideological barriers to a territorial agreement, and a parliamentary majority could have been obtained. Emotional obstacles in Israel would have collapsed before the kind of breakthrough that Anwar Sadat later created by alighting from an airplane at Lod Airport.

While I hoped and worked for this outcome, I was skeptical of its feasibility. The results of the Six Day War were objectively uncongenial to peace. There was not enough self-confidence on the Arab side or enough humility on the Israeli side to create a balanced atmosphere. The Arabs were shattered and humiliated, but this did not mean that surrender was their most likely option. They would have been acting out of character if they had regarded the military results of the war as a logical basis for negotiation. They were convinced that those results underestimated their power. They were more likely to try to rehabilitate their honor by a military success. Soviet arms supplies made this feasible. Alternatively, the Arabs could strive in the United Nations for a diplomatic result that would cancel the power gap created by the war. After all, they had tried this successfully before. They regarded their defeat in the June 1967 session of the UN as a temporary setback. In economic, strategic, diplomatic, and even military terms, they have never been as weak as the Six Day War boundaries implied.

Israelis, for their part, were so stunned by the sudden glory of their triumph that many deluded themselves into the belief that we commanded the power balance and could dictate the peace. I was convinced that Israelis who thought that the Arabs were at our mercy were in gross error. None of the Arab capitals had been captured, no Arab regime had been overthrown, and the Arab military systems had been replenished by the U.S.S.R. within a few months of the war's end. We were not—and have never been—in the position of General Douglas MacArthur addressing the Japanese "negotiators" on a battleship and telling them what to sign. Nor were we like Eisenhower, sending emissaries into the historic railway carriage near Paris to tell the Germans that their sovereignty was in abeyance and that they should now await orders from Washington. The Arabs could afford strategy of patience and choice. They also prided themselves on a special national attribute, which they called *sumud,* a capacity for perseverance amid suffering that could outlast all adversaries. They believed that even if they could not avenge themselves in a successful war, they would negotiate one day in a less humiliating atmosphere than that surrounding them in 1967. "God is on the side of those who are patient," says the Koran.

Despite illusions of omnipotence in such circles as the "movement for Greater Israel," acceptance of a peace based on security arrangements, demilitarization, and modest boundary changes could have won through in Israel in the first few years after the 1967 war. When the prospect of real movement in the Jarring Mission seemed to dawn in the summer of 1970, the Labor Party did not hesitate to accept the resignation of the Gahal (Likud) ministers. The Arab world rejected the opportunity, dreamed of vengeance, made an imposing attempt at military recovery, and would have settled for even a minor military or diplomatic success to expunge the shame of their defeat.

While I thought that the emotional condition was not yet ripe for an effective dialogue immediately after the Six Day War, I felt that we should at least test the waters. Peace efforts could possibly secure tactical advantage in the short term and would certainly bring substantive image-making gains later. So I began my soundings with the West Bank and Gaza Arabs, worked hard with the UN emissary, Ambassador Gunnar Jarring, who had been appointed as UN mediator under the terms of UN Resolution 242, met in pseudo-clandestine encounters with Jordanian leaders, took an active stance in the effort to end the war of attrition, and explored what seemed to be new attitudes evinced by Anwar Sadat in 1971. By October 1973, I was discussing with the newly appointed United States secretary of state, Henry Kissinger, the prospect of a negotiation with Egypt under his auspices during the forthcoming UN session. "Since nothing important will happen in October before your elections," said Kissinger, "let us think of a negotiation here in November."

The war broke out on October 6, 1973. . . .

Without ascribing perfection to all aspects of Israeli policy, I have no doubt that the deadlock for most of that time was primarily due to Arab attitudes. On June 19, 1967, and in the ensuing weeks the Arab governments had before them Israeli offers to restore Sinai, the Golan Heights, and most of the West Bank territory to Arab rule. The contemptuous reply in the Khartoum Declaration of September 1, 1967, proved that the Arab priority was not to regain their territory but to reestablish their pride.

The Foreign Ministry official in charge of our Arab relations was Moshe Sasson. His father, Elias Sasson, born in Damascus, had worked under Moshe Sharett, Israel's first foreign minister. Elias Sasson had maintained constant relations with Arab leaders, making good use of his courtly manners and fluent Arabic tongue. The young Moshe had been brought up in an atmosphere in which an Arab-Israeli accord did not seem utopian. When I appointed him as my chief Arab adviser, I hoped to elevate the idea of regional peace into a central priority in the work of the Foreign Ministry.

Sasson offered to bring me into contact with Palestine Arab leaders in the occupied territories. This was not easy. The Palestinian Arab community was sharply fragmented into rival families. The leaders were men whom the British used to call "notables": They exercised authority without electoral process. A sharp sense of regionalism still worked against anything like a Palestinian country-wide representation. Nablus, Hebron, Gaza and Christian Bethlehem, and Ramallah were separate principalities: Their leaders had a common tongue, but this did not commit them to affection for each other, still less to cooperation. Most complicating of all was the fact that they did not regard themselves as entitled to make decisions in their own right and interest. Diplomacy was beyond their scope. Arab decisions, they thought, lay in the historic capitals of the caliphate, in Cairo, Damascus, Baghdad, and the holy cities of the Arabian Peninsula. Many of them looked also to Amman, where King Abdullah and his grandson King Hussein had ruled over the Palestinian territories and populations since the end of British rule in 1948. The Palestinians had no united idea about who their local advocates and spokesmen should be. The voices that resounded most authoritatively in the vacuum were those of the PLO leaders in Beirut, who won astonishing victories in terms of international recognition without sharing the daily fate of Palestinians who spoke from their own soil and homes.

This obscurity about identities and hierarchies came to expression as soon as I began to receive the Palestinians whom Moshe Sasson brought to my home in Jerusalem. The first was Anwar Nuseibeh of Jerusalem, whose name I used to see on the staircase of the building in Queens' College Cambridge where I had my rooms in 1937. Nuseibeh had held distinguished posts under King Hussein, including those of minister of defense and ambassador to Britain. He still considered that the simplest course for Palestinians was to work with Jordan for Israeli withdrawal, leaving the relationship between the Jordanian kingdom and the West Bankers for negotiation in what would then be a purely Arab context. This sounded so sensible that I thought that it had little prospect of acceptance. The other Palestinian option was to link Israeli withdrawal to simultaneous structural changes in the Jordanian-Palestinian relationship. Since this was the most complex and unpractical approach, it was bound to become the official position of a Palestinian movement that seemed to have written failure into its birth certificate. This, however, was for Palestinians to decide, and at that time I assumed fatalistically that they would take the course that was most likely to be against their own interest.

Anwar Nuseibeh was a man of refinement and courtesy, and there was no personal tension in our conversation. At the end of it, he said that he was interested in the outlines of what I had told him about peace with secure boundaries. He would travel to Amman to acquaint the king with our exchange of ideas.

My next visitors were members of the Masri family in Nablus. After our talk they indicated that the conversation was important enough to justify a visit to Cairo, where they would speak with President Nasser.

In their wake came a cleric, magnificently garbed, exuding odors of incense and eau de cologne, and addressing me in fulsome terms of eulogy. He was Bishop Capucci, a Catholic divine who promised that he would take my remarks to Beirut, where he would talk with those whom he tactfully described as leaders of the "organizations" *(munaddamat)*. PLO was still a forbidden term in the Israeli-Arab dialogue. Capucci turned up later as a smuggler of arms and gold, condemned by an Israeli court and later released through papal intervention. In my home in the autumn of 1967 he looked and sounded like a fervent emissary of peace. If anything, he left me with the feeling that his peacefulness was too obsequious to be authentic.

In all my conversations, the Arab interlocutors put less emphasis on the territorial issue than on the question of whether the Arab world was yet ready for a formal peace with Israel. They all stressed that if they were to show audacity and innovation on the ideology of peace they would, at the very least, have to be rigid on their need to recover every inch of the lost territory, including East Jerusalem. This was not surprising in what I thought was an early stage of negotiation. It soon emerged, however, that their opening position was also their final position.

What caused me even more disquiet was their disposition to regard their own political future as an issue beyond their competence. If they were merely carriers of messages to Amman, Beirut, and Cairo, would it not be more fruitful to contact those capitals than to negotiate with men who disclaimed any effective negotiating status?

We were back to the familiar identity problem of the Arab world. Is each Arab people a sovereign entity or is it merely a province in a pan-Arab federation? An eminent Arab scholar, Walid Khalidi, then, as now, a professor at Harvard University, eloquently portrayed pan-Arabism as the principle that defined Arab allegiance. He wrote in the American quarterly *Foreign Affairs:*

> The Arab States system is first and foremost a "pan" system. It postulates the existence of a single Arab nation behind the facade of a

multiplicity of sovereign states . . . From this perspective, the individual Arab states are deviant and transient entities; their frontiers illusory and permeable, their rulers interim caretakers, or obstacles to be removed. . . . Their mandate is from the entire Arab Nation. Before such super legitimacy, the legitimacy of the individual state shrinks into irrelevance.[1]

This would be all very well if the Arab governments believed it. Those of us who had to relate to the Arab world from outside found that the "transient entities" were not all that transient. And the "individual caretakers" were the only people who seemed to control anything. Nasser and Sadat decided whether or not to launch the Egyptian armies against us. King Hussein controlled everything that went on in Jordan, and the governments in Baghdad, Damascus and Riyadh had not delegated any powers to a "super-legitimate" authority. It was the pan-Arab institutions like the Arab League that seemed to be transient entities, unable to transact anything except speeches and conversations. In my experience as a working diplomat, the particularism of individual Arab states was a stronger reality than the theories of "a pan system."

It was therefore to a particular government that I addressed myself in the next stage of my peace exploration. My contacts with King Hussein began in 1968. Prime Minister Eshkol had rejected Dayan's advice to "wait for a telephone call from King Hussein." Of all Israeli prime ministers, Eshkol was the one who attached least awe and deference to Dayan. When one of my colleagues told him that Dayan seemed to have an irresistible charisma, Eshkol replied "watch me resist." Waiting for a telephone call from Hussein was a Dayan slogan, not an Israeli policy.

I have never considered that the contacts I initiated between King Hussein and Israeli leaders were a wasted effort. Although they have "theoretically" never taken place, they are the subject of a fairly detailed bibliography. There are authoritative descriptions in books, articles and memoirs of Israeli leaders. The very existence of those talks gave Israelis a feeling that Arab-Israeli conflicts are not inherently irreconcilable. Here was an Arab statesman, descended from the prophet Muhammad, who held a record for longevity in leadership of an Arab country, expressing his belief, however reluctant, that Israel was an immutable part of the Middle East. Hussein never failed to enunciate a passionately Arab national pride, but he respected the allegiances of his Israeli interlocutors. Meetings with him, and a study of his Arabic rhetoric, which was classically perfect in diction and in range of expression, were for me an antidote to Dayan's bleak theory that struggle had been eternally "decreed" as the law of Arab-Israeli relations.

---

[1] "Thinking the Unthinkable: A Sovereign Palestine State." *Foreign Affairs* (July 1978), p. 695.

Hussein, not Sadat, was the pioneer of realism in the Arab perception of Israel. He was also the only Arab leader who absorbed a large population of Arab refugees into his society instead of letting them languish in squalid camps. But his power base was always inadequate to bring his innovations to effective expression within the larger Arab context.

As King Hussein looked out across the Jordan, either from the riverbank or from his southern vacation place in 'Aqaba, a few kilometers from Eilat, he must have been impressed by the spectacle of an Israeli state, which was no less solid in its aspect than his own kingdom. It was widely rumored that one of our prime ministers, probably Rabin, had escorted him on a ride along Dizengoff Street where our Mediterranean culture was expressed in all its turbulent, strident, neon-lit brashness, but also in the patent civility and deep-rooted peacefulness of the passing crowds. As a fervent Arab nationalist, Hussein would certainly have preferred a Middle East without Israel, but he was quicker than most Arab leaders to understand that this was an impossible vision. He must have been painfully aware that nothing preserved Jordan's survival more than Israel's interest in preserving it. It was known that any conquest of Jordan—either by Iraq or by Syria—would risk Israeli intervention. Thus, Hussein's enemy, Israel, was the guarantor of his nation's independence, while other Arab states, theoretically his brethren, gave that independence very little support.

The impression that I deduced from contacts with King Hussein was that he would give Israeli interlocutors maximum courtesy and minimal commitment. Our encounters took place in the home of a British friend of the king, not far from the Israeli embassy residence in North West London, or in a motor launch swaying from side to side in Red Sea waters off the Jordanian-Israeli coast, or on a coral island near Eilat. It was conventional for us to believe that our London encounters, at least, were concealed from the British authorities by skillful maneuvering, but one day Prime Minister Wilson said to me: "There are rumors that you saw King Hussein today. Absurd, isn't it?" Wilson then winked at me with prodigious emphasis in a gesture of conspiratorial reassurance.

The king himself compensates for exceptional shortness of physical stature by a quiet dignity that flows from a consciousness of his own lineage as a descendant of the family that first claimed and achieved liberation from the Turkish yoke and brought the Arabs into political history. He seemed embarrassed by a feeling that we Israelis were expecting too much of him in proposing that he should take the burden of the first breakthrough to an Arab-Israeli settlement.

I have always believed that the term "Jordanian option" is one of the most unhappy semantic devices in the history of the Middle Eastern conflict. It obscured the limitations of the Jordanian role under the competitive pressure of the Palestinian idea. It also overestimated the stature of Amman within the Arab regional complex. A Jordanian policy of accommodation with Israel could only flourish beyond mere conversation if it were sustained by Palestinian consent and Egyptian, Syrian, and Saudi acquiescence.

Even within those limits, Hussein was consistently rigorous in the formulation of his role. He believes that Israel and the Arabs have no option except eventual coexistence. He has sometimes envisaged the possibility of an individual peace initiative by Jordan, but only if he can succeed in a total restoration of Arab rule in all the occupied territories. He has never been ready to be a pioneer both in the ideology of peace and in the explosive principle of territorial bargaining. His slogan has always been that Israel can have either peace or territory, but not both. This is not far from being a universal international consensus, and King Hussein was the first Arab leader to make it so.

Even within his own Jordanian society, the King's stern but civilized references to Israel have not set a general tone in Jordanian society. The Jordanian media largely dominated by Palestinian radicals have always been relentlessly extreme in their hostility to Israel.

Nevertheless, Jordan does not project a threatening image to Israelis who watch its life and mood on the international television broadcasts that are easily available to Israeli audiences—without paying a licensing fee. The Jordanian government supplies daily Hebrew TV programming directed to Israeli ears though not to many Israeli hearts. It also broadcasts English- and French-language bulletins that enable Israeli TV audiences to escape from parochial self-contemplation and to get images of Arab events that it would not receive otherwise.

Israelis may even be getting an unduly idyllic picture of ordinary Jordanian life by watching the TV programs from Amman. These are focused with attritional frequency on diplomatic ceremonies. One would think that Jordanian life is enacted exclusively at the airport, where the monarch is shown obsessively leaving for a foreign capital or returning therefrom amid detailed and repetitive shaking of hands and selective kissing in strict protocolar regularity. But Israelis also see thriving university campuses, tranquil countrysides, an educated political elite, and other indications of social cohesion that evoke surprise when one reflects on the scanty resources of the kingdom and its vulnerability to the passions that sweep across Jordan's militant neighbors to the north and east.

My encounters with King Hussein convinced me that we were unlikely to celebrate a peace settlement elaborated with Jordan as the central partner, as some of us briefly hoped soon after the Six Day War. This prospect virtually expired in the 1970s when the PLO acquired the dominant influence in the West Bank and Gaza. In 1974 the Arab summit meeting at Rabat in Morocco decided that the PLO was the sole representative of the Palestine people. It was only a relatively short step from that date before King Hussein began to ask himself whether it would not be the wiser course for him to disengage from the Palestine problem. This process of reflection reached its climax in 1989, when the king canceled his juridical link with the West Bankers, and Jordan virtually became "Transjordan" again.

It was correct for us to explore the Jordanian option when it was a realistic prospect. The human connections developed with Jordan since 1968 are an investment in neighborliness that may yield a harvest in better times. Jordan is a potential element in a future peace settlement provided that it is not burdened with the exclusive responsibility.

It remains to examine whether or not there were chances of peace that were lost in 1971 as a result of Israeli obduracy. There is a mythology to this effect that lies deep in the consciousness and remorse of the Israeli Labor Party.

Nasser died in September 1970 and was succeeded by Anwar Sadat, who was an unknown factor surrounded by the derision that often accompanies vice presidents. Even Henry Kissinger has confessed that he initially regarded Sadat as a purely ceremonial figure. Many observers, however, noted that, on his appointment, the new president immediately began a process of de-Nasserization, removing most of the former leader's confidants from access to the levers of decision.

Israel after the war of attrition and the acceptance of the American-sponsored cease-fire seemed to be safe both from war and from the fear of becoming a focus of U.S. tension. But there was so much innovation in the air that few of us were surprised when Anwar Sadat faced us with two proposals in February 1971.

First came a plan for an interim agreement based on the need to open the Suez Canal. The real author of this idea was Moshe Dayan. He had become increasingly apprehensive of an overall settlement that would surely compel Israel to make harsh decisions on the return of abundant slices of territory.

Dayan's plan for an interim agreement would have involved the withdrawal of the Israeli army for a short distance from the Suez Canal. The area evacuated would be demilitarized, as would a corresponding zone on Egyptian territory west of the Canal. Egyptian civilian activity would be restored. The Suez Canal would be open to navigation. The arrangement would be negotiated through the mediation of the United States, not of the United Nations.

When Dayan advocated his proposal, between September 1970 and February 1971, he initially received a cold response. In our own Cabinet, ministers asked why Israel should agree to any withdrawal from existing positions, when even President Nixon had defended Israel's right to remain where it was until or unless there was a fully negotiated, contractual agreement with Egypt. Would it not be strange for us to accept a concession that was more renunciatory than what the United States was advocating?

The United States had initial reservations about a partial settlement limited in its scope to the Canal area. It was far more inclined to favor a comprehensive settlement than to be satisfied with a localized security arrangement. Washington, not unjustifiably, suspected Dayan of desiring an interim agreement in order to evade hard decisions on boundaries and settlements. Dayan tenaciously developed the idea that Israeli forces should withdraw from the Canal and enable it to be opened for international traffic. We would naturally require assurances about the security of our forces at a new line east of the Suez Canal.

President Sadat's first allusion to this project on February 4, 1971, seemed to be promising, but before we could put the idea to an operative test, it was frustrated by an independent initiative of Gunnar Jarring, who, on February 8, 1971, publicly addressed Israel and Egypt on behalf of the UN with a proposal for a comprehensive peace settlement. He was clearly acting with United States support. I thought that it was absurd to address Israel simultaneously with plans for a partial agreement and a plan for a comprehensive settlement. The partial agreement was designed specifically for the contingency that a total "solution," in which all the elements would fall into place, was unrealistic. Thus the United States, in proposing one agreement and supporting another, was effectively working against them both. My impression was that this resulted from the anarchic situation in the Nixon administration where the State Department was indulging its taste for utopian solutions while Kissinger clung to his ideology of gradualism. At one stage I thought of offering myself as a mediator between the two of them.

Jarring suggested that Egypt should give Israel a list of assurances on peace, recognition, and the end of the state of war, while Israel should give Egypt an undertaking on the withdrawal of its forces to the previous armistice lines. In order to correct any impression that the future of Gaza was still open, Jarring added that Gaza should be restored to Arab rule and not left in Israeli hands. He was thus giving full endorsement to all the Arab territorial claims, leaving Israel no opportunity to negotiate even the smallest territorial adjustment. Israel would thus lose the gain that it had made in Security Council Resolution 242, which, according to its sponsors and supporters, allowed for some degree of territorial revision.

The suggested procedure was that Israel and Egypt should accept the Jarring formula as it stood, without any negotiation aimed at clarifying its implications.

On the surface, Egypt seemed to be accepting the very proposal that the Eshkol government had empowered me to offer Egypt on June 19, 1967. Since then, however, Egypt had inspired the Khartoum Resolution, had waged a war of attrition causing hundreds of Israeli deaths, and had violated an agreement by pushing its missiles forward toward Israeli positions despite a specific "standstill" undertaking in the cease-fire of August 1970.

The United States now exercised strong pressure on Israel to accept this proposal as it stood. In our discussions we decided to applaud Sadat's readiness to talk for the first time about a "peace agreement" with Israel, but we added that the terms of the peace agreement, including its territorial terms, must be negotiated between both parties and not dictated by one of them. We expressed willingness to withdraw to secure and recognized boundaries that would be agreed upon in the negotiating process. Some of us, including Allon and me, as well as our skillful ambassador to the United Nations, Yosef Tekoah, wished to be content with this formulation without specific rejection or acceptance of the June 4 boundaries. The Cabinet, however, opted for a categorical refusal to restore the previous line, thus giving our reply a more peremptory tone. Thus, the statement that we would withdraw to secure and recognized boundaries to be determined in a negotiation was followed by a sentence saying that Israel "will not withdraw to the June 4, 1967, lines."

Critics of the Meir government from the Israeli left as well as the United States State Department have argued that the sentence in the Israeli reply rejecting the June 4, 1967, borders spelled the failure of the Jarring Mission and the loss of a peace opportunity. Some commentators have paid me the compliment of saying that if my advice had been taken and this sentence had been omitted, peace would have come without the tragedy of Yom Kippur 1973.

I still regret that my formula was not endorsed. The statement that we would withdraw to secure and agreed boundaries to be fixed in the negotiations was quite adequate to safeguard our right to territorial revision. I find it hard, however, to accept that if Sadat were really ready for a settlement at that stage, the wording of the Israeli reply to Jarring would have induced him to abandon the effort.

The arguments against accepting that severe judgment are numerous and compelling:

ONE: The fact that Israel would seek some territorial revision was well known. It was also clear that the points at issue would be connected with free passage in the Straits. Also, at one stage in 1967, Israel had offered the whole of Sinai for peace. Sadat could have hoped that in vigorous negotiation he could get Israel back to that position.

TWO: While expressing its opening positions, Israel was suggesting a negotiation on the basis of the answers elicited by Jarring. Egypt was rigid in its "take it or leave it" attitude. It was encouraged in rigidity by Jarring and the U.S. If Sadat had really wanted an agreement he would have accepted a negotiation in the course of which Israel's fallback positions could have emerged.

THREE: If Israel's territorial positions were unsatisfactory for Egypt, Egypt's position on peace and security were unsatisfactory for Israel. There is no evidence that Sadat meant a contractual peace treaty of which the provisions would be subject to an exchange of views and interpretations. He was presenting an ultimatum. The idea was that

Israel would put the territories in an envelope and slide them under Egypt's door.

No peace settlement in history has ever been achieved by such a method.

FOUR: Sadat's definition on passage through the Suez Canal and the Straits of Tiran was identical with that on the basis of which Egypt had denied passage to Israel since 1948. In a negotiation, he would have had to be flexible on this vital issue.

FIVE: The Egyptian position on demilitarization was ludicrous. Sadat was asking for equal zones of demilitarization! If Israel wished what it attained in 1979—a demilitarized area adjoining its own vulnerable boundary—the IDF would have had to retire deep into Jordan. No Israeli government before or since 1971 has been willing to reproduce the exact military alignment that existed between Israel and Egypt on the eve of the Six Day War. Yet, apart from the use of the phrase "a peace settlement," that is what Sadat was suggesting.

SIX: The absence of any celebratory or dramatic accompaniment to the Sadat proposal increased Israeli suspicions that his aim was tactical, not substantive. As I said at the time: "In order for peace to be born, its parents must meet at least once."

SEVEN: If Sadat had behaved in 1978–79 as he had behaved in 1971, the Camp David peace treaty would never have come to fruition. None of the processes that made peace possible in 1979 was followed in 1971.

My conclusion is that Sadat's and Israel's replies to Jarring in 1971 would have been reasonable as the opening positions in a detailed negotiation. Jarring and the U.S. representatives, Rogers and Sisco, showed no persistence of the kind displayed by Kissinger in 1974 and Carter in 1977–79. They made a great error in diagnosing deadlock and blaming Israel at a premature stage. The right of Egypt to achieve peace and restore territory without any negotiating process and without setting eyes on an Israeli representative was part of the UN's unique fantasy world.

The success or failure of peace explorations are usually ascribed to the parties at issue. The attitude and skill of third parties are often more determinant. If there was an embryo of peace in the 1971 exchanges, Jarring and the United States are mainly responsible for the miscarriage. Israelis and Egyptians were under the constraints of their domestic opinion and their traumatic experiences. The U.S. and Jarring were free agents. They lacked perseverance and balanced understanding. They did not implement the mediatorial tradition in its rigorous sense.

The Jarring proposal was a windfall for Egyptian diplomacy. It naturally reduced Egypt's incentive to accept a more practical and limited withdrawal at the Suez Canal. A few weeks later, however, it became apparent that the proposal had misfired. Israel had no intention of signing away its right to negotiate on boundary and security arrangements, and her adversary was not prepared to be satisfied with a peace engagement concerning Sinai alone. Egypt insisted on an Israeli undertaking to withdraw from the Gaza Strip and from all other "Arab territories" to the boundaries that existed on June 4, 1967. It also entered a reservation in favor of Palestinian rights. Most important of all, it insisted on a military presence east of the Canal. Such a presence, however small, would have compromised the principle of demilitarization without which no Israeli government has ever agreed to evacuate areas of importance to security.

Nevertheless, the decision of Jarring and of the United States to regard the Israeli reply to the February 8 memorandum as negative was recklessly wrong. In their replies, the Egyptians made more progress toward the idea of a peace agreement, and the Israelis made more progress toward the concept of withdrawal, than at any previous stage. Our reply did not go a single centimeter beyond the 242 as interpreted by its sponsors and supporters, including the United States. The idea that the mediator's duty was to promote agreement and not to dictate his own conceptions was explicit in the language of 242. The wise reaction would have been for Jarring to stress not the gap that still remained, but the distance that had already been bridged. He should have tried to elicit the range and motive of Israel's reservation on full withdrawal. He should also have explored the prospect of bringing Egypt's declaration on peace closer to what Israel would accept. He chose to regard the first replies of each party as final answers and failed to notice our offer to negotiate. The United States was fully behind the erroneous reaction and must share responsibility for it.

To the extent that the idea of an overall settlement receded, the possibility of an interim agreement on the Suez Canal came more vigorously to life. Some ministers had thought that Dayan's readiness to "jump into the icy water" of the Jarring Mission had been premature while we were still attempting to secure the withdrawal of Egyptian missiles as a condition for resuming the Jarring talks. By mid-March, however, this was obviously academic. It was clear by then that the Egyptian missiles would not be withdrawn. We would have to seek compensation through an American agreement to strengthen our defenses so as to meet our new vulnerabilities. We succeeded in this plan and the way was now open for an intensive exploration of a Suez Canal interim agreement.

On March 22 the Israeli government, at the initiative of Moshe Dayan, took another of its important decisions. It virtually renounced the principle (to which American adherence had been obtained) that not a single Israeli soldier would be withdrawn from cease-fire lines except in the context of a contractual peace settlement. Dayan suggested that this far-reaching American assurance be abandoned in favor of a limited withdrawal from the Canal in return for something far less than peace. He proposed that in return for a limited pullback, enabling Egypt to open the Canal, Israel should ask for undertakings that the state of war be ended, that future withdrawals would be subject to negotiation, and that a normal civilian situation would be created in the Canal area. Once the waterway was opened, the cities and villages near the Canal—Suez, El Qantara, Ismailia, and Port Said—should be restored to normality. Another condition was that the United States should make binding engagements on long-term military support of Israel, and should supervise the demilitarized character of the territory we evacuated. Dayan's idea was that Israeli forces be withdrawn some thirty kilometers from the Canal up to the western edge of the Gidi and Mitla passes.

At its meeting on March 22, the Israeli Cabinet accepted the principle of a partial Israeli withdrawal in return for something less than full peace. I was engaged at that time in talks with Secretary Rogers and Dr. Kissinger in Washington. They showed great interest in the Israeli Cabinet's initiative. I suggested that the United States should explore the Egyptian reaction and that we should avoid placing this matter in the hands of Jarring or any other United Nations agency. It would thus be accurate to say that in March 1971 a new era in Middle Eastern diplomacy began. The concept of a partial interim settlement replaced the previous "all or nothing" approach to peace. And the idea of American "good offices" superseded the previous concept of UN mediation.

Unfortunately, our government, although united on the principle of a Canal withdrawal, was in some discord concerning its application. The fact that Dayan had originated the idea may have played some part in creating resistance to it on the part of his political adversaries. Opposition to any substantial withdrawal from the Canal was expressed not only by Galili and Allon, but more surprisingly from the moderate Sapir, who now supported the view of General Barlev that the Israeli withdrawal should not be for more than ten kilometers from the Canal. This limited withdrawal would enable us to ensure that Egypt would not be allowed to cross the Canal in military strength and create a jumping-off ground for assault. It would also enable Israel "to shoot its way back" to the Canal area if Egypt violated the agreement.

On this basis Secretary Rogers and Joseph Sisco set out for an exploration of the interim agreement idea in May 1971.

Our discussions with the United States in Jerusalem opened unpromisingly with a sharp exchange between our prime minister and the American secretary of state. Rogers seemed to have been convinced in Cairo that Sadat was genuinely in search of peace, while Golda felt that the secretary had been unduly credulous. Golda was affronted by the idea that an American secretary of state could discern virtue in an Arab leader. In this somewhat sterile discussion, the practical issue of the interim Canal agreement was lost from sight.

Dayan, who was still the main advocate of the agreement, suggested a private clarification between himself and Sisco the next day. In that talk he explained that there were two possible approaches to the settlement. One was the cautious approach based on a ten-kilometer withdrawal with the option of "shooting our way back to the Canal." Dayan, however, did not disguise that there was another approach which he himself preferred, namely a permanent renunciation of Israeli access to the Canal and a willingness to go back as far as thirty kilometers. Dayan believed that no Egyptian government would open the Canal under the very eyes of an Israeli army and within range of Israeli tactical artillery some ten kilometers away. I had no doubt that he was correct.

When the results of this conversation returned to the broader ministerial group, Dayan came under criticism for what some of his colleagues regarded as excessive flexibility. I sent him a note asking whether he would put his idea to a vote in the Cabinet, in which case not only would I support him but so would other ministers whom I was willing to canvass. Dayan replied curtly that unless the Prime Minister accepted his proposal, he would not even put it up for discussion and would, in fact, deny that the proposal existed. Since there was no Cabinet consensus for a thirty-kilometer withdrawal, Dayan reluctantly let the matter drop.

I have always regretted that he did not show tenacity in support of this imaginative proposal, which could have averted the Yom Kippur War. It would have been a rare case for him and me to carry the burden of a common cause.

There was now a dangerous atmosphere of deadlock. The Jarring Mission was in abeyance, and Israeli initiative for an interim Suez settlement had reached a dead end. Sadat had promised the Egyptian people that 1971 would be "the year of decision." While it was not necessary to take this threat with complete seriousness, it was obvious that total diplomatic immobility would make the cease-fire precarious. There was also the chance that if Sadat had nothing to show in the political sphere, he might be succeeded by a more militant Egyptian leadership. Immobility also had grave disadvantages for our international position. While world opinion respected our aspirations for peace, it was not reconciled to our inflated map. European liberals found it hard to reconcile themselves to a prolonged Israeli control of a million Arab noncitizens of undefined civil status. In Africa our territorial conflict with Egypt, a founding member of the Organization of African Unity (OAU), threatened to create grave tensions. Both in Africa and in Europe, there was a general support of Israel's sovereign rights, but there were sharp reservations about our territorial condition. The absence of any progress toward a settlement worked more against us than against the Arabs, since the disputed territories were in our hands, not theirs.

I therefore recommended that we take the risk of reacting positively to an African move in the early autumn of 1971. The main author of this initiative was one of the most interesting of African statesmen, Leopold Sedar Senghor, president of Senegal. He had brooded long and seriously on the parallel mysteries of Moslem and Jewish history. Senghor had invented the idea of "negritude." Just as negritude had been an inherent condition of suffering, so also was Jewishness. This gave him an initial sympathy for Israel's aspirations. On the other hand, Islam, unlike Judaism, was a solid and integral part of African history. Senghor embodied the paradox of a Muslim state with a Christian leader. His African nation was headed by a man whose cultural roots and style were embedded in the French idiom. It was reasonable for him to think that the special contour of his personality gave him a conciliatory role. He developed the idea of a mission to Israel by four heads of African states with whom we had close relations. They would wear the mantle that Jarring had discarded and that the United States had not yet fully assumed. They would try to see whether a basis could be created on which the Jarring Mission could be resumed.

The four presidents designated by the OAU for this mission were Senghor of Senegal, Josef Mobutu of Zaire, Ahmadou Ahidjo of Cameroon, and Major General Yakubu Gowon of Nigeria. The first three were known to me from my visits to their countries. Each of them was a strong idiosyncratic personality. It would be hard to think of four leaders more sharply divided in temperament and personality. In this they conveyed the richness and variety of African leadership. I had met Mobutu on each of my visits to Kinshasa and had been impressed by his sense of authority in a country whose area and structure seemed recalcitrant to any form of central control. The major link between Israel and Zaire was the training of a mobile Zaire parachute force by Israeli officers. This enabled Mobutu to transfer a unifying power quickly from one part of his huge country to another without maintaining a burdensome standing army. He had a great admiration for Israel's military record and for our robust resistance to Soviet intimidation. One of his prophetic apprehensions was that the weakness of the West, and especially indifference, might open the way to a Communist hegemony in Africa. Leopold Senghor had a deeply analytical mind. His cultural experience was so sharply defined that he found it difficult to react to anything that was not said or written in French. This caused such despair to Golda and her other colleagues that she left Senghor in my care, since I was the only Francophobe member of our team.

With Ahmadou Ahidjo I had an even more intimate personal link. I had first met him in the United Nations in 1959 toward the end of my mission in Washington and at UN headquarters. One of our able diplomats, Aryeh Ilan, later to be ambassador in Burma, had suggested that I take an active role in a discussion on the future independence of Cameroon. The leader of the Cameroon National Movement, Ahidjo was disconsolately pacing the UN corridors in an effort to break through procedural difficulties that impeded his success. He was a small, sad-faced man in a foreign environment giving little sign of the authority that I saw in his demeanor in later years.

Nearly every other African state had achieved independence without any difficulty at the UN. In Cameroon, however, there were disputes about where the legitimate authority of the national movement lay. In particular, there was a claim by a group supported from Cairo that denied Ahidjo's legitimacy, although he was a Muslim. The bilingual character of Cameroon, her complex history of domination first by Germany and then by France, created unusual intricacies. I took an interest in the problem and was able, with the use of our long and turbulent UN experience, to offer some advice on how the Cameroon case might be successfully presented. After all, Israel was one of the few states that had ever needed to fight its way from anonymity to UN membership. Ahidjo remained personally grateful to me for many years and received me warmly when, as Minister of Education and Culture, I made an official visit to his country in 1962.

We had, naturally, been apprehensive about the visit of the African presidents. But during several days of intensive talk we seemed to have made a strong impression on them. In a report to the General Assembly they stated that the Israeli and Egyptian positions, although still separated, were not so incompatible as to make the resumption of Jarring's mission impossible. In this courageous judgment they were virtually criticizing Jarring himself, as well as the United States, which had drawn excessively drastic conclusions from our reply to Jarring's February 8 memorandum. The reports from the African presidents elicited a statement of our views supporting the principle of withdrawal from occupied territories and making clear that in determining our border with Egypt we would be guided not by any expansionist aims, but by considerations of free navigation and security alone.

This favorable report by four African presidents came as a bombshell to the Arab states, and especially to Egypt. Instead of condemning Israel for unilateral intransigence, the African presidents were putting Egypt and Israel on the same footing as having made legitimate reservations to the Jarring memorandum. Mahmoud Riad, the secretary-general of the Arab League, rushed to UN headquarters in December 1971, where he found himself engaged in an extraordinary fight against the acceptance by the General Assembly of an African report favorable to Israel. The Arab steamroller was successful. The General Assembly voted—ridiculously—against Senghor's proposals. Another peacemaking prospect had been frustrated by international irresponsibility.

And yet it had seemed rational enough at the beginning of 1972 to believe that war was not probable. Egypt seemed too weak to undertake either a general or a limited offensive, and her relations with the Soviet Union were becoming tense. Egypt could still count on total diplomatic support from Moscow, but arms deliveries, although still large in quantity, seemed to lack the particular items that would have given her a sense of offensive power. The Soviet military mission, now fifteen thousand strong, was becoming more of a burden than a grace. It gave Sadat's government a dubious image in the eyes of the non Communist nations in the West. It prejudiced Egypt's status in Africa, where a non-African military presence on African soil seemed to violate the entire spirit of the African liberation movement. The spectacle of the Russian officers in the streets and clubs of Egyptian cities evoked memories of the British occupation, against which Egypt's national movement had fought so long. Egyptian pride was injured and there was no adequate compensation in other fields.

All these tensions exploded in the jubilation that seized Egypt in July 1972 when Sadat ordered the withdrawal of all the Soviet military personnel stationed on Egyptian soil. Paradoxically, many Israelis shared the Egyptian relief. The general belief was that Sadat had obtained an emotional satisfaction at the expense of his strategic and political power. The disruption of the military organization in which the Soviet officers had played such an important role would surely weaken the Egyptian order of battle along the Suez Canal. Egypt, deprived of the Soviet presence, also appeared less formidable as a political adversary. Moscow felt humiliated by Sadat's sudden initiative. It even began to show a certain parsimony in the dispatch of spare parts and new equipment. Sadat had made American-Israeli relations more comfortable than before. As long as Soviet personnel were present in the Canal zone, the Egyptian-Israeli conflict was always in danger of erupting into a Soviet-Israeli confrontation. In that contingency, the United States would have to face grave problems about its commitment to Israel's security and to international equilibrium in the Middle East. Along with that, there had been an obsessive fear in Israel that Washington would exercise pressure for a settlement that would relieve it of the menace of global war. From now on, this nightmare seemed to have faded. With the departure of Soviet troops, the powder keg was defused. The United States exercised no pressure on Israel. Administration spokesmen in Washington spoke of an accord between the Arabs and Israel as a long-term aim, demanding slow and prudent progress.

This comfortable view was not universally shared. In interdepartmental meetings, the director-general of the Foreign Ministry, Gideon Rafael, raised the possibility that Sadat's expulsion of Soviet forces might herald his desire to make the war option more concrete. The Soviet Union might have been regarded by Sadat as an inhibiting factor rather than as a potential supporter of military action.

This was the minority view. The general feeling was that a new respite had been won. The Arab states could still win victories in international organizations. By threatening a restriction on the flow of oil, Arab countries could also count on compliance whenever they pressed European or African governments to support the withdrawal of Israeli troops from positions occupied in the 1967 cease-fire. This, however, was small consolation for the Arabs compared with the fact that there was no concrete action likely to lead to early Israeli withdrawal. Thus, the Arabs won their triumphs in the field of rhetoric, while Israeli forces entrenched themselves more firmly in their positions. The Israeli government developed the exploitation of the oil resources in the western Sinai and built apparently impregnable fortifications called the Barlev Line east of the Canal.

All political activity concerning the Middle Eastern conflict was now suspended. The Jarring Mission had ceased to function. The Four Powers had dispersed. Worse still, from the Arab point of view, the summit meeting in 1972 between President Nixon and Brezhnev ended with a vague reaffirmation of Resolution 242. The Arab leaders had reason to fear that their case was not so much rejected as forgotten.

The accent in Israel's national concern shifted from military preparation to antiterrorist activity. There had been violent explosions of terrorism at the airports of Athens and Rome, and hijackings and murders in Cyprus. But the climax of terrorist action came in September 1972 when the civilized world heard with horror about the massacre in cold blood of eleven Israeli athletes under the shelter of the Olympic flag in Munich. The United States and the UN secretary-general made an intensive but brief effort to secure action by the UN General Assembly against terrorism, but the Arabs and the Soviets were able to mobilize enough votes to frustrate any international action against brutality and piracy.

There were times when antiterrorist measures seemed to preoccupy us more than the basic issues of the military balance. Some Israelis might have come to think that the grenades and mortars of the terrorists represented a greater threat to the national existence than the concentration of armies and air forces in Egypt and Syria. In this sense the intensity of antiterrorist preoccupation in Israel may have weakened our security by giving the nation a false idea of its priorities.

At the General Assembly in 1972, I gave full support to Secretary Rogers and Secretary-General Waldheim in their efforts to secure a United Nations convention against terrorism. Another of my preoccupations was with our relations with Europe.

As early as September 1967 I had addressed the Council of Europe in Strasbourg about the relevance of Europe's example to the Middle East predicament. I outlined the prospect of a peace settlement that would give the Middle East a "community" structure. I suggested that Israel and her neighbors to the east and north might develop a relationship similar to the Benelux Agreement, which had been the forerunner of the European community. Could not Israel, Lebanon, and Jordan establish a relationship like Belgium, Holland, and Luxembourg? Europe had discovered a formula for reconciling the separate sovereignty of states with a large measure of integration and of mutual accessibility across open boundaries. At the same time I struggled hard to develop our initial relationship with the European Economic Community into a preferential agreement similar to association.

The chief obstacle to our developing relations with the EEC had been created by France. Paris understood that signature of a preferential agreement between Israel and the EEC would reinforce our international position and thus run counter to France's Arab policy. Surprisingly, the break in the deadlock came from the French foreign minister, Maurice Schumann, whom nobody in Israel had ever regarded as a friend of our cause. I had many conversations with him, and got the impression that his reputation for hostility to Israel might have been exaggerated. In 1971 Schumann had suddenly announced that France would support a global Mediterranean approach by the EEC under which preferential agreements would be simultaneously available to Israel and any Arab state that wished to take advantage of the opportunity. Many people in Israel thought that this was an elegant way of closing the door to us. They assumed that they would withhold their own adherence in order to prevent Israel from strengthening its relations with the EEC. Once again I was in the embarrassing position of suggesting a more optimistic diagnosis than that which was prevalent in the Israeli government. I believed that some Arab countries, especially in North Africa, the eastern littoral of the Mediterranean, would be anxious to use the opportunity whereby Schumann's "parallelism" could solve our own deadlock. Sure enough, as the months went by, it became apparent that Schumann's formula enabled us to enter negotiation for a meaningful agreement that would make us something close to a partner of the EEC, both in trade relations and in technological and financial development.

In June 1970 I had signed our first substantial agreement with the EEC in Luxembourg. The president of the EEC under its system of rotation was Pierre Harmel, the foreign minister of Belgium. It was an impressive experience to sit behind the Israeli sign with all the six representatives of the EEC represented at high levels. The agreement that I signed with Harmel provided for an even more significant stage of negotiation that was to take effect within three years. We were on our way to Europe.

I had been charmed by the special atmosphere of Iceland during my official visit in 1966, and I now succumbed to the appeal of Luxembourg. Here were tiny communities that resolutely maintained their national identity and also expressed a deep solidarity with Israel. Luxembourg, like Iceland, had supported all the international decisions that had helped Israel's integration into the international community. Luxembourg had a Ruritanian quality about it. Verdant scenery, mountains, and ancient buildings give an air of peaceful contentment. This had not saved Luxembourg from a horrifying agony during their Nazi occupation. My partner in the dialogue with Luxembourg was Gaston Thorn, a young statesman (later prime minister and foreign minister) whose capacities went beyond those ordinarily required for so small a country. The European Community and later the United Nations General Assembly, of which he became president, were to be a larger arena of his talents.

Our own Foreign Ministry was at its specialized best in the European question. We had to bring six—and later nine—governments with disparate interests into line on a series of detailed conditions relating to our trade. Some of the difficulties were not political but material. For example, the orange growers of South Italy had reservations about an agreement that would open the European market to Israeli citrus. I established a special European Community Department in the Foreign Ministry under the able direction of Isaac Minervi. I also strengthened our staff in Brussels, where the energetic ambassador, Moshe Allon, was accredited both to the Belgian government and to the European communities. By the beginning of 1973 all the members of the Community, as well as the three new candidates for admission—Britain, Denmark, and Ireland—agreed that Israel would be a constructive partner in the European adventure. In my official visit to Scandinavian countries in the summer of 1972, a further strengthening of our European links took place.

A moving experience for me was the first official visit of an Israeli foreign minister to the Federal Republic of Germany. Both Chancellor Willy Brandt and Foreign Minister Walter Schell greeted me cordially. I had previously been to Bonn only for a ceremonial occasion—the funeral of Konrad Adenauer, which I attended in April 1967 together with David Ben-Gurion. I now trod on soil full of tragic memories for my people. I had obtained the permission of my hosts to begin my visit with a tour of the concentration camp in Dachau. Some of the sharp pangs of emotion that I had undergone at Auschwitz in 1966 came back to me here. Again I found myself reciting an emotional Kaddish for multitudes of Jews who had been the victims of the Holocaust. My visit took place in 1970 despite reservations of ministers of the Gahal party in Israel. It was significant, however, that Gahal was divided on this issue. General Ezer Weizmann and Dr. Elimelech Rimalt supported my decision to undertake the voyage. Brandt, Schell, and other German statesmen did not pretend that the future of German-Israeli relations was already detached from the heritage of the past, but by the exercise of tact and historic imagination they enabled my visit to take place in an atmosphere of truth and candor. Thus, the groundwork was laid for a return visit by the chancellor himself in 1972. The fact that Willy Brandt had been a determined resistance fighter softened the Israeli reaction to his presence. No other German chancellor could have made an official visit with so little abrasive effect on the wounded memory of countless Israeli citizens.

By the end of 1972, there was hardly a country in Europe with which we had not exchanged official visits at prime-minister or foreign-minister level. They included Britain, Germany, Italy, Austria, Switzerland, Belgium, Holland, Luxembourg, and all the Scandinavian countries. And yet it was in Europe that the Palestinian terrorists made their strongest impression. I shall never forget the terrible night of suspense when the members of our Olympic team of athletes were captured in Munich. The German government decided not to yield to terrorist extortion. When the terrorists escorted the Israeli athletes to the Munich airport, ostensibly as part of a deal for the release of Palestinian Arab saboteurs in Israel, the German forces opened fire on them. The operation was conceived in a brave and friendly spirit, but it misfired tragically. Although the German commandos were able to kill most of the terrorists and capture the others, there was a moment of suspense and hesitation in which one of the terrorists brutally killed all eleven Israeli athletes, as they lay bound and gagged in the helicopter.

The most macabre element in our experience that day was a false radio report announcing that all the Israeli athletes were safe. Our experienced ambassador in Bonn, the late Eliashiv Ben-Horin, earnestly exhorted us not to believe the good news unless or until visible evidence was obtained. Ben-Horin, as so often, turned out to be right. When the news came that all eleven had in fact been killed, one by one with shots in the head, a fearful cold silence descended upon us.

The terrible symbolism of this murder of Israelis in the city associated with the Hitler curse cast a pall of indignant fury over Israel and the Jewish world. There ensued a period of coolness in German-Israeli relations. We had been fully in accord with the basic decision of the Brandt government to deal firmly with the terrorists, but we could not fail to be enraged by the clumsy failure in executing the plan.

The Israeli emphasis on antiterrorism as the central theme of our security now became stronger than ever. It is a mistaken emphasis. There is individual tragedy in terrorism and it should be vehemently resisted, but the existential peril to the State of Israel arises from the sovereign Arab states with large and destructive accumulations of weaponry.

Despite some setbacks, 1972 ended with Israel's international position ostensibly strong. Our flag still flew in nearly ninety embassies across the entire world. Although our relations with East European states had not been repaired, the whole of non-Muslim Africa and all of Europe and Latin America were linked to us by strong diplomatic, economic, cultural, and human ties. The Munich massacre, the indecent support given to it by Arab leaders, even including President Sadat, the gloating that ran riot across the Arab world with the honorable exception of King Hussein, all fortified Israelis in the feeling that peace with the Arab world was an Israeli dream with no echo in the Arab heart. At the same time, the Munich attack had reduced the international pressures upon us to make concessions to an adversary who seemed impervious to any human impulse and unreconciled to Israel's identity as a legitimate state.

Yet while it was evident that terrorism would increase, the general feeling in Israel was that the favorable military balance, the strong support of Israel by the United States, and the weakening of Egyptian-Soviet relations, all made the outbreak of war with our neighbors a remote contingency.

25

1973: THE YEAR OF WRATH
AND JUDGMENT

THERE WAS NO drama in the year's beginning. It opened for me, as usual, with a conference of the foreign press in Jerusalem. My theme was that a long political deadlock would drive the Arabs to war and that we should strive "urgently" to make 1973 "a year of negotiation."

This did not sound very sensational at the time, but in terms of the current Israeli temper, it was far-reaching heresy. The idea that anything "urgent" needed attention was not being articulated by other senior ministers. The year of 1973 was one in which the Israeli people lost its balance and ran riot in an orgiastic celebration of complacency.

It seemed perverse to disturb the national serenity, but throughout 1973 I found myself expressing a lonely Cassandra-like vision. My diagnosis was that the main task of Israeli foreign policy now lay not in the foreign capitals, but in Jerusalem: In many speeches and articles I emphasized that the impression of durability was illusory. A security doctrine based on unlimited confidence would degrade the tone and quality of our life: if domestic opinion was ecstatically worshipful of the status quo, the nation would not be prepared for painful choices. Why should we imagine that the Arab governments would permanently abstain from military action to recover what all the nations recognized as their sovereign territories, if they had no hope of resolving anything by diplomacy?

I brought these anxieties to expression many times, and especially in an address at Haifa University on February 26, 1973. I pointed out that "there is much talk of Israel's physical map, but little attention to the problem of her moral frontiers." A note of arrogance in the press and in the public rhetoric had made the Israeli voice abrasive and discordant.

A strong nation does not have to beat the drums every morning in order to illustrate its power. It does not have to be constantly proving its virility. The unsolved question about Israel does not concern its courage or resourcefulness. These are generally taken for granted. The question relates to Israel's human quality. The problem is to emphasize freedom, tolerance, equality, social justice, and humane values as the salient features of a strong and serene society.

I recalled how some Israeli newspapers and broadcasts had been callous in discussing the dead passengers on a Libyan airliner mistakenly shot down by the Israeli air force on the unlikely assumption that the plane was on its way to attack the Dimona research reactor. There had also been many signs of public intolerance toward legitimate dissent. I asked:

Is it just a coincidence that the national style has become strident just when annexationist pronouncements proliferate?

I added:

The problem is not merely to proclaim our own valid historic rights to this land, but to bring those rights into balance with the rights of others—and with our own duty of peace. Since our national experience has sharpened the emotional, passionate, mystical, and metaphysical elements in the Israeli character, the task of the intellectual community is to contribute the balancing dimension of rationality.

I concluded, "Reason without passion is sterile, but passion without reason is hysteria."

Menachem Begin, the opposition leader, was in the Haifa audience. He approached me, characteristically, with a compliment about the quality of my rhetoric and some reservations about my criticisms of the militant trends in society. He could afford to be amiable: the tide of sentiment in Israel was flowing in his direction, although in early 1973 the idea that he would ever preside over Israel's destiny had not entered my head—or his.

The Haifa speech, and others in a similar vein, had a strong resonance, and I received many expressions of support, mainly from the kibbutzim and the universities, and also from officials in many ministries. But it was a disquieting indication of the Israeli political climate that the professors who exhorted me to go on speaking out rarely said a word of encouragement in public when I came under attack from the embattled "hawks."

The Haifa speech and other addresses of similar tone were a personal attempt to break out of a dilemma. As foreign minister, I had to articulate the collective policies of the Cabinet more precisely than anyone else. Nor was there anything intrinsically immoderate in the official formulations that embodied the principle of territories for peace. The trouble was that influential ministers spoke more abrasively than our official platform entitled them to do, so that the more conciliatory definitions of our policy lost credibility.

To restore the balance of the domestic dialogue, I tried to register my individual philosophy. I was in favor of such frontier changes as were essential to ensure our defense and deter a new war. But I emphasized that these should be confined to the minimum required for security. To our party's "Young Leadership" I said later in the year:

> The fact that we cannot give a hundred percent of self-determination to the Palestinian Arabs is no excuse for offering them zero percent.

I urged that "our security should be based on a peace settlement, buttressed by a balance of power, shielded by demilitarization, reinforced by limited territorial change, and supported by a broad international consensus."

All this time, the Israeli defense strategy was frankly attritional. The logic was that if the Arabs were unable to get their territories back by war or by great power pressure, they would have to adapt themselves to Israel's security interests. This view made no provision for a third Arab option—neither docility nor negotiation, but a desperate recourse to war in the hope that even an unsuccessful attack would be more rewarding than passive acceptance of the cease-fire lines.

Meanwhile, Moshe Dayan was spreading the word that Israeli policy should not even present peace as a remote vision. He said that we should at most pursue the idea of dividing Sinai into military spheres of influence, but beyond that there was nothing to be done. "With Lebanon there is nobody to talk to, with Syria there is nothing to talk about, and with Jordan we have already talked without reaching a result." In these conditions it was easy to understand why Dayan put all his mind in the area in which he saw urgent tasks to perform. This was the occupied territories in which he thought that we should be busy delineating "the new map of Israel." He added that this had priority over peace explorations. It would emerge that it had priority in his mind over ensuring the nation's defense against strategic dangers.

By this time preoccupation with antiterrorism had usurped the strategic debate. The chief of staff of the Israeli Armed Forces, General David (Dado) Elazar, made a report to the nation in April 1973 in which the fight against the Palestinian underground figured more prominently than any existential danger from the armies of Arab states.

Americans who heard my description of Israel's concerns in these terms must have been puzzled when they listened to Golda Meir's version of the same theme. Henry Kissinger reports that experience in simple terms:

> At an appointment with Nixon on March 1, [Golda] proclaimed that "we never had it so good" and insisted that a stalemate was safe because the Arabs had no military option. Golda's attitude was simple. She considered Israel militarily impregnable; there was strictly speaking

no need for any change. But given the congenital inability of Americans to leave well enough alone, she was willing to enter talks though not to commit herself to an outcome.[1]

While Golda was in Washington expounding these insights, a high-ranking Egyptian emissary, Hafiz Ismail, was also in town. He was establishing a secret line of contact with Kissinger that was to bring the two of them together in France, in Cairo, and in Washington. We now know that Ismail was exploring American attitudes in an effort to discern whether the United States might help to influence Israel in the direction of compromise. He apparently received jets of cold water from the national security adviser: in several interviews Ismail confessed that he would have got a more flexible response from Golda Meir. The Hafiz Ismail mission and its failure are an important link in the chain of calculations that induced Sadat to prepare the 1973 war.

Sadat himself contributed to this result by maintaining the rupture in the relations between Cairo and Washington. Kissinger has recorded that with all his personal respect for the professionalism of some Egyptian diplomats such as Foreign Minister Mahmud Fawzi and Hafiz Ismail, he had to regard Egypt as a Soviet satellite.

Some mature Israeli minds were moving in what I regarded as the right direction. Amnon Rubinstein, the dean of the law faculty in the Tel Aviv University, had written in 1967:

> Time is working for us . . . because we are in possession of the field. The more that time passes the more will the new reality created by the armed forces become the status quo . . . Time will get the world used to the new Israeli map.[2]

However, less than a year later Rubinstein, now the leader of a liberal party in the Knesset, was firmly and eloquently in the anti-annexationist camp. But in general outline, 1973 was the year in which opinion flowed in the opposite direction. The hawks were winning Pyrrhic victories that were driving us in the opposition direction—toward the precipice.

The 25th Independence Day parade in Jerusalem in April 1973 was conducted in an atmosphere of exuberant national pride. If anything, the self-confidence was too extreme to be attractive. At a meeting of Israeli ambassadors in Europe that I convened in the Van Leer Center in Jerusalem a few months later, I asked our intelligence chiefs to comment on a possibility that

---

[1] Henry A. Kissinger. *Years of Upheaval* (Boston: Little Brown, 1982), pp. 220–21.
[2] *Ha'aretz.* July 21, 1967.

I had heard from an adviser to the British foreign secretary, Sir Alec Douglas Home. The official was Sir Anthony Parsons, who later became his country's ambassador in Tehran and in the United Nations. When I gave Foreign Minister Douglas Home our intelligence estimate that the Egyptians would not attack because they had no hope of real victory, Parsons asked if we had considered the possibility that Sadat might attack without hope of victory but with the motive of forcing international attention to the Middle East. When I brought this possibility to the attention of the ambassadors' meeting in Jerusalem, General Zeira, head of military intelligence, dismissed the conjecture contemptuously. The official doctrine was that an Egyptian assault would be drowned in a sea of blood, that the Arabs had no military option and if they made the attempt they would fail and our deterrent power would be enhanced.

By the summer of 1973 it was expected that two of our former military commanders, Generals Ariel Sharon and Yitzhak Rabin, would soon enter our political struggles. Whatever personal innovation they would bring to our politics, it was clear that they would massively reinforce the prevailing mood of unlimited self-satisfaction.

Rabin published articles and interviews that were designed to relieve Israelis of all serious concern for the future. An article in *Ma'ariv* on July 13 contained a fervent defense of the prevailing concept of Israel's security in the summer of 1973. It reads like an anthology of all the misconceptions that were destined to explode a few weeks later:

> Our present defense lines give us a decisive advantage in the Arab-Israel balance of strength.
>
> There is no need to mobilize our forces whenever we hear Arab threats, or when the enemy concentrates his forces along the cease-fire lines. Before the Six Day War, any movement of Egyptian forces into Sinai would compel Israel to mobilize reserves on a large scale. Today, there is no need for such mobilization so long as Israel's defense line extends along the Suez Canal.
>
> The Arabs have little capacity for coordinating their military and political action. To this day they have not been able to make oil an effective political factor in their struggle against Israel.
>
> Renewal of hostilities is always a possibility, but Israel's military strength is sufficient to prevent the other side from gaining any military objective.[3]

Sharon was urging Israelis to remember that "there is no target between Baghdad and Khartoum, including Libya, that our army is unable to cap-

---

[3] *Ma'ariv*, July 13, 1973.

ture" and that "with our present boundaries we have no security problem."[4]

With this encouragement from charismatic personalities it is not surprising that an atmosphere of "manifest destiny," regarding the neighboring people as "lesser breeds without the law," began to spread into the national discourse. A glance at the headlines reporting speeches by politicians, academics, and articles by columnists would yield the following harvest:

The Status Quo Is Permanent
The Barlev Line Is Impregnable
Israel Must Have Defense in Depth
Arabs Have No Military Capacity
Arabs Flee Whenever There Is War
Our Intelligence Is Never Wrong
Time Is on Our Side
Arabs Only Understand Strength
Golda's Boundaries Better than King Solomon's

A large proportion of these utterances came from senior officers, past and present. A common theme is one of ethnic contempt: Arabs are said to be intrinsically affected by deficiencies of virtue and capacity arising from their inferior culture. Dayan himself said in a lecture to officers that "weaknesses affecting the Arabs will not, in my view, be easily overcome. Defects of educational levels, technology, and integrity . . ."

A scholar who is now in the forefront of the peace movement and who advocates direct negotiation with the PLO was then giving lectures with learned generalizations about inherent defects in Arab character, such as mendacity and a predilection for fantasy.[5] Harkabi later underwent a spectacular conversion that made him the most eloquent critic of the Likud-Revisionist doctrine.

Rabin's favorite theme during the countdown to the war attributed a mystical power to boundary lines that he described as having an inherent capacity to "deter" without reference to surrounding characteristics, such as the force that mans them or the weapons that they contain. A contemptuous view of Arab history and culture, which was one of the weaknesses of classical Zionism from its origins, prevented Israelis from believing that an operation as brilliant as the amphibious Egyptian water crossing of October 6, 1973, could be within the power of such a decadent adversary.

Some Israelis were troubled by the prevailing military euphoria. And yet, all the evidence seemed to support the optimistic mood. For several years whenever Israel's power had been put to the test, it had come out triumphant. Israeli forces could wrest a Sabena airliner from armed hijackers, cross into

---

[4]*Ha'aretz.* September 20, 1973.
[5]Professor Yehoshofat Harkabi. *Between Israel and the Arabs* (Ma'arachot, 1968), p. 101.

Egypt to bring back a new Soviet tank or radar installation, enter Beirut in April 1973 to seek and kill PLO officials and spokesmen, and inflict heavy casualties on the Arab aircraft that they met on patrol. Whenever the Israeli army or air force moved, there was always a sense of mastery and command.

All was quiet west of the Suez Canal, where Sadat had not revived Nasser's futile "war of attrition." King Hussein, acting in his own interest, but to Israel's consequent advantage, was blocking any westward movement of Palestinian terrorists across the Jordan. All in all, Israelis in their own mind were clothed in power and majesty and there was none to make them afraid. In part, this was a justified reaction to the extraordinary resilience displayed by our forces in the Six Day War and in some subsequent operations. Missing was the common soldierly prudence of not underestimating the enemy.

It was in an uneasy frame of mind that I set out early in August on a series of official visits to South America. There had been signs of hostility toward Israel among African states, including some that Israel had helped on the road to development. Latin America, on the other hand, was not vulnerable to Muslim solidarity and was much less exposed than Europe to Arab oil pressures. My visits to Brazil, Peru, and Bolivia ended with strong reaffirmations of support. The Bolivian capital is 14,000 feet above sea level, but I managed to live without much oxygen for three days despite the exertions involved in Spanish oratory. My Latin American journey had been planned some months ahead and could not have been postponed without giving offense, but as I got farther from home, my enjoyment of new landscapes and friendly people was marred by the feeling that the distance between my colleagues at home and myself was growing wider. I was in a hotel in Rio de Janeiro when I got two reports that made me wonder if our government was still in full contact with international reality.

On August 10 a Lebanese airliner had taken off from Beirut on a scheduled flight to Teheran. On reaching cruising altitude, it was intercepted by Israeli jet fighters and ordered to land at a military airport. The pilot complied. For some hours Israeli security officers interrogated the puzzled passengers. Finally the airliner was allowed to go on its way. Our intelligence services had believed that the most savage of the Palestine terrorist leaders, George Habash, was aboard the plane. The intention had been to arrest him and, presumably, to bring him to trial before an Israeli court.

Apart from the fright and risk of interception, the passengers and crew of the airliner had suffered no injury. And yet, a shock went through Israel and the world. Here was a civilian aircraft subjected to an act of force, not by terrorist "revolutionaries," but by a sovereign government. Until then we had always been passionate crusaders for aerial freedom. In condemning Arab hijacking, we had sought to place civil aviation on a special peak of immunity, removed from all vicissitudes of political conflict. And now a planeload of travelers, representing a cross section of innocent and vulnerable humanity, had been placed at risk. There was a feeling across the world that but for the pilot's compliance, there might have been a tragedy similar to the Libyan aircraft incident in 1972.

It turned out that the interception had been approved in a rapid consultation between three ministers: Golda Meir, Moshe Dayan, and Yisrael Galili. It had opened Israel to a hostile reaction in world opinion, especially in the United States. I felt that our decisionmakers might have made a wrong calculation about the techniques of antiterrorist combat. What could we have done with our "success" even if Habash had been aboard? He would surely have used an Israeli court as a forum for expounding the "Palestine revolution" in a mood of martyrdom to a world audience. His very presence year after year in an Israeli jail would have provoked a new series of kidnappings with the aim of getting him released.

I sent a telegram to the prime minister from Brazil strongly criticizing the interception. I expressed the fear that the principles defended by Israel in its struggle against hijacking would now be undermined and that even our closest friends would condemn our action. Golda's only reaction was a request to avoid publishing my vehement criticism in order to safeguard our electoral prospect, but nothing becomes more widely known in Israeli politics than an unpublished fact or rumor.

All these forebodings turned out to be well founded. In discussions of the Security Council and the International Civil Aviation Organization, Israel reached the nadir of her isolation, while Arab governments exulted. In Israel, there was more press criticism of the interception than of most other security decisions since 1967. One of the nation's most fervent "hawks," the novelist Moshe Shamir, wrote trenchantly against the attempted hijacking.

On the home front too, there was disarray. The Labor Party was formulating its plans for development in the West Bank and Sinai for the next four years. Most Labor ministers were reluctant to go beyond the selective and cautious policies that we had followed since 1967. Only a few thousand Israelis had established themselves beyond the old armistice lines, most of them in Jerusalem or close to the previous borders where we seemed to have a prospect of limited territorial change under a peace agreement. There was no objective need to make noisy formulations of long-term settlement goals. The Israeli government had full control and could always move empirically as conditions dictated. But as de Tocqueville once wrote: "Democracies only do external things for internal reasons." In this case, the judgment was well founded. Dayan was hinting that he might not be a Labor Party candidate in the election unless commitments were made for an accelerated "creation of facts" in the territories. Galili was accordingly asked to draft a document that would bridge the gap between the views of Moshe Dayan, who favored increased settlement in the West Bank and Sinai, and those of Finance Minister Pinhas Sapir and others among us who did not.

The Galili document was published on August 23, and the next day I anxiously telephoned Sapir in Kfar Sava from Rio de Janeiro. He gave me the impression that he had emerged victorious from the engagement. He told me that very few binding commitments were contained in the Galili text and that everything was hedged in with political and financial reservations. He thought that the document by itself would not generate any additional settlements and that everything still depended on individual Cabinet decisions. This was literally and formally true, but while the document said very little in substance, its psychological effects were far-reaching. Sapir may have triumphed on the strict language of the document, but Dayan had won in its spirit and impression. Internal politics, not for the first time, had laid a heavy burden on our diplomacy.

The Dayan-Sapir compromise as drafted by Galili was interpreted across the world as a reinforcement of annexationist tendencies. In my conversation with him from Rio de Janeiro, Sapir told me he was afraid that if Dayan left the Labor Party and fought on a separate ticket, he might pick up twelve to fifteen seats in the Knesset at the expense of the Labor Alignment. He said that I ought to bear this in mind and judge the document as a domestic necessity even if there was some international inconvenience.

Between 1967 and 1969, Dayan's administration of the newly conquered areas had been supervised by a ministerial committee under the chairmanship of the prime minister. But with Eshkol's death, when Golda Meir took over, this committee was disbanded, and Dayan, in effect, held solitary control over the million Arabs under military rule. It was, of course, possible to defeat some of his proposals by a Cabinet majority, but there was always an apprehension that if this was done too often, he might resign with the support of enough Knesset members to destroy the government's majority. One influential minister, in private conversation with me, used to say that "a large Cabinet majority without Dayan is not really a majority."

By the summer of 1973, the charge of Israeli "expansionism" was giving us particular trouble in Africa. At the conference of the Organization of African Unity in Algiers in early September, President Sadat made a strong impression. We expected that Muslim African nations would act in solidarity with Egypt; and we knew that some poor countries in West Africa were being simultaneously threatened and tempted by the opulent governments of Libya and Saudi Arabia. But even our loyal friend President Mobutu of Zaire was now reported to be contemplating a rupture of relations. This was not because of any failure in our diplomacy, but because, unlike Egypt, we were not members of the African "club" and had no claim on continental solidarity.

I felt that time was now working against us. Accordingly, in an interview with the newspaper *Davar* on September 29, I revived my assault on the solidity of the status quo. I said that deadlock is not an American ideology and should not be an Israeli objective. We should be concerned to unfreeze the situation, not to perpetuate it.

But there was nothing to indicate that most of our political and military leaders saw anything wrong in the idea of deadlock. The New Year editions of our newspapers were saturated with cheerful statements about our impregnable security. On September 26 the *Jerusalem Post* editorial stated: "There was never a period in which our security situation seemed as good as now." The same mood was reflected in an interview with General Rabin in *Yediot Aharonot* on September 18. The familiar headline was: "Golda has better boundaries than King David or King Solomon." The text was a warm celebration of the cease-fire lines and of the existing stability. The lesson seemed to be that patience and strength together would bring their due reward.

All this time, the rhetoric of confidence continued to be backed by military superiority. On September 13, Israeli and Syrian aircraft clashed just off the Syrian coast. Thirteen Syrian aircraft were brought down with the loss of one Israeli plane. Amid all the jubilation, I recalled our air victory against Syrian MiGs in April 1967 and the growing Soviet hostility up to the eruption of the Six Day War. With this memory it was hard for me to celebrate this last triumph wholeheartedly.

Prime Minister Golda Meir was then on a visit to Strasbourg to address the Council of Europe. This was a relatively modest chore for a prime minister and it illustrated how far the Israeli government was from any premonition of crisis. She decided to go personally to Vienna. Arab terrorists had attacked a train carrying emigrants from the Soviet Union on their way to Israel. Golda wished to urge the Austrian chancellor, Bruno Kreisky, to rescind his decision to halt the use of the Schonhau transit camp, which he deemed too vulnerable. The world's newspapers, including those of Israel, were giving their central attention to this drama—none at all to the troop concentrations on the Egyptian and Syrian cease-fire lines.

It is very hard to recapture the serenity of my first meeting with Henry Kissinger in his capacity as secretary of state. It was October 4. He had met Arab foreign ministers at a dinner party a few days before. In the American ambassador's suite at the Waldorf Towers, he was jocular and relaxed. He recalled our conversation in the Israeli embassy residence in Washington the previous August when we had spoken of the need to replace the diplomatic vacuum by "some form of negotiation." He now came back to this theme, but there was no panic or urgency in his mood. He told me that he knew of Egyptian and Syrian troop concentrations. He asked me what our intelligence services had to say. I replied by reciting the military intelligence appraisal that I had sought from Jerusalem that morning. Our experts confirmed that the concentrations in the north and south were very heavy, but they gave no drastic interpretation of their purpose. They spoke of "annual maneuvers" on the Egyptian front, and of a hypochondriac Syrian mood, which might have made Damascus apprehensive of an Israeli raid. Syria was the base of the terrorist movement whose members had attacked the train bearing Russian immigrants to Vienna: Damascus might well have expected to punish the Vienna outrage by striking at the Syrian base. It would thus be normal for Syrian troops to be in heavy defensive posture.

Our military advisers believed that without a prospect of aerial advantage, Egypt would not risk storming the Suez Canal and the Barlev fortifications.

It seemed that American intelligence experts confirmed the Israeli view, and Kissinger was tranquil. Nevertheless, he doubted that Israel could indefinitely enjoy a stable cease-fire, occupation of all the administered territories, and freedom from international pressures. This seemed too unrealistic for comfort. It was in this meeting that he said, "Well, you have your election soon. In any case, nothing dramatic is going to happen in October. Can you be back here sometime in November? I have reason to believe that the Egyptian foreign minister will be here. I would then like you both to come to Washington so that we may discuss how a negotiation may be set afoot."

Kissinger has never been a worshipful follower of the Israeli annexationist school. In his memoirs he has formulated a cogent summary of the issue:

Israel put forward a demand as seemingly reasonable as it was unfulfillable: that the Arab states negotiate directly with it. In other words, Israel asked for recognition as a precondition of negotiation.[6]

Secretary Kissinger's idea that Egypt should be the first candidate for negotiation was also congenial to us. Any Egyptian-Israeli negotiation would, of course, require concessions in Sinai, but these would not evoke the passionate reaction involved in territorial concessions in Judea and Samaria. I told Kissinger that if our party was returned to power, I expected to come back to the United States in early November and would welcome the opening of a "negotiating process."

I remember leaving Kissinger's apartment in the Waldorf Towers in a mood of relief. At last there was some promise of movement. Israel's international position could only be improved by a process of negotiation. The contagion of hostility in Africa might be checked. Our credibility in Europe would be restored. And the atmosphere of our own national life would be transformed if our essential military power was supplemented by an active diplomacy in which we and the Arabs would be talking about mutual compromise.

From Kissinger's suite I went to that of President Félix Houphouët-Boigny of the Ivory Coast, one of Israel's most faithful friends. He was worried about the effects of Muslim pressure on Israel's position in Africa. But his own attachment to us seemed unimpaired. He was also concerned that Washington was leaving Africa to Muslim and Communist influence without any balancing assertion of American interest.

---

[6]Kissinger, *Years of Upheaval*, p. 199.

I hardly found time to change into formal clothes for the dinner party marking Kissinger's assumption of office as secretary of state. It was held, unexpectedly, in the Metropolitan Museum of Art. It was hard to imagine any of the secretary's predecessors choosing such an environment. But Kissinger was not a conventional politician, and he was celebrating his new eminence with candid relish. His mind had been shaped in Europe, but it was only in the atmosphere of American pluralism that a Jewish immigrant could rise to such sudden prestige. He was now the leading statesman in the world community, and the foreign ministers and ambassadors passing along the receiving line seemed to be united, whether reluctantly or willingly, in a tribute to American predominance.

None of the after-dinner speeches was brief and few contained any particular radiance of thought or expression. Kissinger himself spoke dutifully about the importance of the United Nations. I felt that he was allowing courtesy to triumph over candor, since I knew him to be as skeptical as any man could be about the pomposities of conference diplomacy. All in all, there was little tension in the air that evening, and certainly no warning of possible shock. The Soviet representatives, led by Gromyko, were stretching their faces sideways very hard to convey a determined amiability. China was not yet a United Nations member, but we knew that it was on the threshold. The traditional Cold War was giving way to new attitudes and vocabularies. Such talk as there was of the Middle East that night was mainly about the outrage at Schonhau and the prospect of checking the terrorist movement. Not a single minister or diplomat spoke to me of the Egyptian and Syrian troop concentrations.

Nor did my agenda the next day give any indication of an approaching storm. I had scheduled meetings with foreign ministers of African states, of which the most important for us was Nigeria. President Mobutu of Zaire had gone directly from the liner at New York Harbor to address the United Nations in a fervent speech, at the end of which he announced that Israel had been a loyal friend of his country—and that he was now breaking relations with it. His explanation: A man can choose his friends, but he cannot choose his brothers. It was the same with nations—the Arabs had been unfriendly to Zaire in its ordeals but they were African kinsmen, whereas Israel had been a staunch friend but was not one "of the family." He must therefore put kinship above friendship and do what the Arabs wanted.

The next day, October 5, while I was with Foreign Minister Orikpu of Nigeria at his mission, my political secretary, Eytan Bentzur, was called to the telephone. A message had come to me from Jerusalem saying that I might have to request another talk with Secretary Kissinger in New York that day. Nothing was said about the issue to be discussed, but I assumed that it had something to do with the troop concentrations in the north and south. I was asked not to fix the interview until material on the subject of our talk reached me through our embassy in Washington. If Kissinger was in Washington, the material should be conveyed to our chargé d'affaires, Mordechai Shalev. Our ambassador, Simcha Dinitz, was in Tel Aviv mourning the death of his father.

Hours went by and no reports arrived. Finally a telegram came from Mordechai Gazit, the director-general of the prime minister's office, saying that it would not be necessary, after all, to trouble Kissinger for another meeting; it would be enough if our appraisals were brought to his knowledge in writing.

It was nearly six o'clock when Shalev called me to say that the "new material" had come in. It turned out to be a more detailed version of the intelligence appraisal that I had received the day before, ascribing the Egyptian troop concentrations to "maneuvers," and those in Syria to a fear of Israeli action. This document was accompanied by a personal message from the prime minister to Kissinger, asking the United States to assure Cairo and Damascus that Israel had no intention of attacking. If the Arab troop concentrations were based on anxieties about an Israeli attack, said Mrs. Meir, the United States could set them at rest, but she added that if Egypt and Syria or both intended to attack, Israel was vigilantly posed for a response. Shalev did not recite or send the whole text of the cable to me in New York before Yom Kippur. In any case, the decisive weight of Mrs. Meir's communication seemed to be in the enclosed intelligence document. This gave an accurate description of how Egyptian and Syrian troops were aligned, but it concluded with the official Intelligence judgment that "the probability of war is low."

I understood in strict logic why it had been decided by Jerusalem to cancel my proposed talk with Kissinger. He was a busy man whose closest friends have never praised him for monumental patience. He would not like to be asked for an emergency meeting twice in two days simply to be told that our government in Jerusalem did not see very much to worry about. Like all foreign ministers at the United Nations, Kissinger was in almost constant movement from one meeting to another. Shalev told me that he had passed the Jerusalem reports to Kissinger's deputy at the National Security Council, General Brent Scowcroft, who was in permanent communication with the secretary from the White House. We could assume that Kissinger would get our documents before nightfall. (I later learned that he had received them very soon after 6:00.) With hindsight, I believe that it may have been a mistake for Jerusalem to have canceled my proposed meeting with Kissinger. The confident tone of our documents may have reassured him, but a personal probing by both of us together might have provoked some twinge of concern and led to an earlier American decision to find out what was going on.

Several months after the Yom Kippur War, I asked Kissinger how he had reacted to the documents that were submitted to him on the eve of the outbreak. He replied that he had gone to sleep peacefully. He had naturally asked American Intelligence agencies to give their own appraisal, but they tended to concur with Israel's judgment. Mrs. Meir's cabled suggestion that the United States make soundings in Damascus and Cairo seemed reasonable, and Kissinger intended to act on it the next day. In the meantime, the evening closed in on Israel—and on Israelis in New York—in the somber tranquillity of the Day of Atonement.

Yom Kippur is a unique day in the calendar of the Jewish people. In Israel all secular activity is suspended while the nation turns inward for prayer and reflection. Television and radio stations are closed, and no vehicles are heard or seen on the streets. Most Israeli soldiers can count on a day's leave except in the most crucial positions at the front, and even there the lines are usually lightly manned.

Something of this repose affects the lives of Israeli representatives abroad. I remember saying to Suzy late on October 5 that we could count on not being disturbed for twenty-four hours—a rare prospect for us. This optimism was mocked when I heard a firm knock on my door at the Plaza Hotel very early the next morning. I opened the door to find Eytan Bentzur holding a telegram just received from Jerusalem. It was signed by Yisrael Galili, on the prime minister's behalf. It stated bluntly that "to our certain knowledge" the Egyptians and Syrians would launch a combined and coordinated attack later that day with the aim of seizing positions at the Suez Canal and on the Golan Heights.

It was clear that what we faced was not a "contingency plan" but an act of war timed precisely for October 6. A violent armored and air assault would be made simultaneously from the north and south. The time of the assault was not specified, but there was an implication of early evening. For reasons that have never become clear, several hours seem to have passed between the receipt of this hard intelligence in Tel Aviv and the official communication of it to the United States through Ambassador Kenneth B. Keating and myself. The report from Israel added that Golda had told Ambassador Keating that our government had decided "not to pre-empt" the attack by a strike of our own.

I called Kissinger at his headquarters in the official residence of the U.S. heads of mission to the UN. He had received Keating's message about the impending attack and had alerted the Egyptian foreign minister, Muhammad el Zayat, who was in New York. Zayat had invented a story of an Israeli naval provocation at a place on the high seas that had not been included in any map. I dismissed this from Kissinger's mind and told him of our decision not to pre-empt. He said that he thought that this was a wise decision, but he wanted it to be recorded that it was an independent Israeli decision, not a response to anything that the United States had ever requested. I confirmed this understanding. It has not prevented the creation of a copious bibliography informing readers that Kissinger personally twisted Israel's arm and miraculously engendered an Israeli decision not to pre-empt.

Two hours later, at 7:30 A.M. in New York, my telephone rang again. The message from Gazit was that fierce fighting had erupted on both the Egyptian and the Syrian fronts. Almost simultaneously the TV set in my hotel conveyed the same news.

A cable drafted before the outbreak of war reached me ten minutes after the war erupted. It told me that on Friday, October 5, four ministers—Golda Meir, Yigal Allon, Moshe Dayan, and Yisrael Galili—meeting with senior military officers, had discussed the Egyptian and Syrian troop concentrations for over two hours. They recalled how in May 1973 similar Egyptian concentrations had dispersed without firing a shot, so that millions of shekels had been wasted on Israel's massive mobilization. This episode had a deterrent effect on those who would otherwise have wished to advocate a mobilization of reserves in the October crisis. The Egyptians had not moved in 1973 and Dayan was not going to be fooled again.

Under the emphatic persuasion of our own military intelligence, the four ministers had accepted the appraisal that on this occasion the probability of war was "minimal." They concluded their meeting by accepting Allon's proposal to discuss the security situation at the regular Cabinet—on Sunday, October 7!

On Friday, Mrs. Meir had briefed those ministers "who happened to be in Tel Aviv." It was a strange criterion for a ministerial meeting. Golda did not wish to disturb those who lived in Jerusalem, Haifa, or the kibbutzim. The gist of the meeting was that the probability of war was "very low."

At 4:00 A.M. on October 6, General Zeira was startled to receive a message that moved him to call Defense Minister Moshe Dayan, Chief of Staff General David Elazar, and Deputy Chief of Staff General Israel Tal with the information that war would certainly break out on both fronts, probably toward sundown. Two hours later General Elazar asked the minister of defense to authorize general mobilization and a pre-emptive strike. Dayan refused the strike and authorized a more limited mobilization than Elazar demanded: one division for the northern and one division for the southern commands.

Since Elazar was tenaciously advocating more stringent measures than Dayan was willing to approve, the matter was referred to the prime minister.

Dayan still opposed the general mobilization that General Elazar emphatically requested. He said that the United States or world opinion would regard this as provocative. This argument is described in the official report on the war—the Agranat Report—as "cogent." I have rarely heard that word more strangely misapplied. I do not recall any cases in which a precautionary mobilization of our forces has ever had any adverse international effects or has ever been opposed by a foreign minister, let alone a defense minister on those grounds.

Dayan yielded reluctantly even to Elazar's precaution. He said that he did not intend to lie down in the middle of the road to prevent the reservists from reaching their targets. He was clearly convinced, as were most Israeli leaders, that the Israeli forces already on the ground would be adequate to stem the first assault, so that massive mobilization could safely be postponed until after an attack took place. Elazar made a proposal for a pre-emptive air strike against Syria. Dayan rejected this on grounds more cogent than those that had impelled him to oppose the mobilization of reservists. He said that nobody would believe the "pre-emptiveness" of a strike when only a few hours before Israel had been telling the United States that the Egyptian and Syrian concentrations did not portend war at all.

This had all become pre-history by the time that I received the telephone call announcing the outbreak of the war. Duties now pressed upon me so heavily that I had little time to reflect on the collapse of all the appraisals that had dominated the Israeli security doctrine for over six years. The war that our Intelligence experts had defined as of "low probability" had erupted in sensational violence. The perfection of surprise, the seizure of initiative, and the early success of a complex amphibious operation all proved—as we later discovered—that there had been effective preparation by Egypt for many weeks before. The Israeli deterrent had simply not deterred, and the Israeli Intelligence had detected but misunderstood. The idea of driving Egypt to a polarized option between accepting the status quo or negotiating on Israel's terms had proved baseless. There had been a third option—that of military assault—and it had been seized by Sadat in an operation that showed originality and flair.

And yet, in the first few hours these hard thoughts were balanced by more sanguine hopes. After all, the Israeli security doctrine had been based on two assumptions: that our adversaries would hesitate to make war unless they had a prospect of victory, and that even if the Arabs took military action, the Israeli response would be so crushing that they would be suing for a cease-fire within a few hours. The latter was the more important of the two elements in the Israeli security doctrine, since it was the one over which Israel had direct control. We could not ensure that the Arabs would not make war, but we could ensure that they would lose it heavily. The memories of 1967 were still vivid in our minds. Everything that had occurred since then had confirmed the impression of Israeli superiority. Thus, my first impulse on receiving news of the war was to console myself for the shock of its eruption by the expectation that it would be short and triumphant.

Not many hours passed before this hope, too, fell to the ground. The ticker tape on my television set spoke of conflicting claims—by Egypt of having crossed the Canal in force, by Israel of having "resisted" the first wave of Egyptian attack. In the north, it was confirmed, the Syrians had made a slight encroachment on our position, but there was no impression yet of deep penetration. I drove down to the Israeli delegation at the UN to meet press representatives and give television interviews. As the day went by without convincing news of Israeli success, my apprehensions mounted high.

News of the war was by now passing from mouth to ear, especially in synagogues in America, while less observant Jews across the country were drinking in every word and picture from the television screen. The choice of Yom Kippur for the Arab attack seemed at first to be diabolic; it added the crime of sacrilege to the sin of aggression. Yet in the secular atmosphere of modern international life, it carried very little odium for the Arab governments. Nor did that particular choice of date give them any military advantage. In fact, it later emerged that the Arab leaders who planned the war had not been aware of Yom Kippur at all. They had thought of such things as the full moon, the rate of flow in the Canal, and Israeli preoccupation with the election. While our Day of Atonement was not in their consciousness, it was in fact imprudent of them to choose the day in which Israeli mobilization would be quicker than at any other time. The call-up of Israeli reserves faces two logistic difficulties: delay in locating reservists and congestion of communications. On Yom Kippur, an Israeli reservist can be found either in his home or in a synagogue; and the roads are open and free. Sadat had not done us any disservice by his choice of date.

By midmorning many delegations at the United Nations were anxiously asking me for news. To Sir Donald McIntyre of Australia, the president of the Security Council, I gave all our information, which he acknowledged in laconic tones through which I caught a hint of anxious sympathy. The Arab delegates, mindful of 1967, were reticent and confused. They had learned from experience that it was unwise to be exuberant too soon about prospects in the battlefield.

I was now receiving news from the front, not all of which I felt inclined to share with anyone else. I learned how in the first few hours of the war the Barlev Line, too lightly manned, began to crumble; how the Israeli tank force in Sinai became diminished beyond the point of national safety; and how scores of Israeli aircraft, attacking in mass formation, were brought down by new missiles of unexpected accuracy. By nightfall Egyptian helicopters carrying commando troops had seized strategic points east of the Canal. Boats and bridges had begun to carry 70,000 troops and 1,000 tanks across the water. In the north, 40,000 Syrians with 800 tanks had driven deep into the Golan Heights. Soon they would be able to cross the river and fork out toward Safed and the lower Jordan.

Some of these disasters were obscurely hinted in the first Israeli official broadcasts to a stunned and confused nation. In a television address Mrs. Meir announced:

The army is fighting back and repelling the attack. The enemy has suffered serious losses. Our forces were deployed as necessary to meet the danger.

Dayan pretended to be even more sanguine:

> In the Golan Heights perhaps a number of Syrian tanks penetrated our
> line, but the situation in the Golan Heights is relatively satisfactory. In
> Sinai, on the Canal, there were many more Egyptian forces. The Egyp-
> tian action across the Canal will end as a very dangerous adventure for
> them.

Meanwhile I had the impression that it was a very dangerous adventure
for us. The question in my own mind was not how it might end, but how it
had begun. Israeli military specialists had clearly overrated the difficulty that
the Egyptians would encounter in crossing a water obstacle with heavy
equipment. Months of Egyptian preparation had obviously gone into amphibious training. The so-called maneuvers were being expanded into a total
assault. By the end of the first day, everything in the field had gone against
us, and the shadows were growing long.

On Sunday, October 7, Secretary Kissinger and I continually compared notes
on the military situation. Kissinger asked me what instructions I had received
about a cease-fire, which was being discussed at UN headquarters as a matter
of routine. I said that I had no guidance yet from the Tel Aviv military
headquarters where the prime minister and her staff were following the maps.
I told Kissinger that I had a specialized experience on cease-fires: "If Israel
is doing badly in the field, we won't be offered a cease-fire, and if we are doing
well, we won't need a cease-fire." Kissinger replied: "If you're capable of
aphorisms, it means either that you are doing well or that you don't know the
situation any better than I do." I deduced that the distance of the battlefield
from Cairo had caught the U.S. by surprise and they had not yet set up a
monitoring procedure. I did not imagine that they would have a successor to
the ill-fated signals ship SS *Liberty* in neighboring waters.

We concluded that we should leave the UN alone for the present. I said,
"The Security Council only brings hostilities to an end if the belligerents have
a mutual interest. I've never found much philanthropy there."

By noon on Sunday I was becoming somber in my evaluation of our
fortunes at both fronts. I cabled back home: "Nothing could be more disastrous for Israel, or corrosive of its deterrent power, than to cease fire with the
Egyptians and Syrians well beyond their previous lines. The Arabs would
wish to pursue their advantage, and we would want to cancel it."

In my talks with Kissinger, we developed a joint policy of making our
agreement to a cease-fire dependent on withdrawal to the positions that had
existed before the Egyptian and Syrian attacks. This would be quite unrealistic unless we had some military success. The Soviets were still in a buoyant
mood. Their official policy was to refuse a cease-fire unless Israel evacuated
the whole of Sinai, Golan, the West Bank, Gaza, and East Jerusalem. I told

Kissinger that this attitude, ridiculous as it sounded, had a good chance of being adopted by a majority of the Security Council. Kissinger's reply was: "Adoption of such a resolution would be impossible; we are against it."

On Sunday evening, October 7, it was plain that we were in military disarray. There was no Israeli denial of Egyptian claims to have moved massively across the Canal with tanks, guns, and missiles. News reports of heavy Israeli losses in aircraft and tanks were coming on the air without being denied. American Jews were catching these indications with sharp sensitivity. The previous evening Jewish leaders, led by Sam Rothberg, had come to my office at the Israeli delegation where I recorded a broadcast to Jewish communities, calling for solidarity in a difficult hour. My listeners must have noticed that I did not claim any victory in the early fighting. On Sunday hundreds of Jewish leaders assembled in the Plaza Hotel to hear my account of the Israeli struggle. A mass demonstration of New York Jews and sympathizers had been called for the next day.

A message from Mrs. Meir on Sunday asked me to remain in the United States for possible action by the Security Council. That evening I experienced the harshest psychological blow that Israelis had endured in recent years. We saw films from Damascus on television showing dozens of young Israeli soldiers sitting dejectedly on the ground, blindfolded, with their hands on their heads in the demeanor of surrender. Many of them were in slovenly dress, as though they had been taken unawares. Some were wounded, with bandages covering their heads, faces and arms. How different this was from the image of Israeli soldiers who had established a reputation of invincibility in 1967.

In the next forty-eight hours the cables from Jerusalem came to me thick and fast. Dayan had flown to the front by helicopter and had returned to Tel Aviv to meet the Cabinet and to brief the committee of newspaper editors. It was only a few days later that I learned that he had unfolded a somber vision of Israel's danger and had recommended a withdrawal to the Mitla Pass in the south and to a position several miles within the Golan Heights. I later heard that he had spoken apocalyptically of "the destruction of the Third Jewish Commonwealth." The majority of the Cabinet, led by a calm Mrs. Meir, overruled defeatist proposals. The decision was to contain the Egyptian bridgehead until it could be attacked, and in the meantime to transfer the main Israeli counteroffensive to the Golan Heights.

This was the correct priority. The battle front at the Suez Canal was remote from Israeli centers of population. Sinai offered room for a war of movement, and an Egyptian advance of a few kilometers here or there would not threaten vital Israeli targets. On the other hand, a further Syrian thrust of more than five kilometers would put the most savage of our enemies in control of roads leading to Safed and Haifa. They would also be able to bring the settlements in Upper Galilee and the Jordan Valley under fire. So it was the Syrians, not the Egyptians, who now threatened the security of our state.

The battle of the Golan Heights had first urgency, and as long as it was being waged, there would be no surplus of strength to uproot the Egyptian bridge head. It took some time for our forces to regroup against the Syrian tanks, since they had to remove the old people and women and children away from the line of fire, and then get the chickens and cows out of their way. The fact that thinly populated civilian settlements close to Arab armies are a security burden, not an asset, is well established by the experience of Israel's wars in which tanks are decisive.

At a tense meeting of the United Nations General Assembly on Monday I said that it was our intention "to throw the attacking forces back to the cease-fire line whence they had come." Twenty-four hours later this appeared to be a remote ambition. When the Israeli Cabinet and defense chiefs surveyed the scene after three days of war, they found a position that would have seemed fantastic to any Israeli a week before.

The Arab success could not be denied. Our military command had, incredibly, left no more than about four hundred troops and thirty tanks at the front line to face hundreds of thousands of Egyptians in full array a few hundred meters across the water.

It turned out that any fear of premature Security Council action was unfounded. The Egyptians and Syrians had their tails up and were in no mood to call a halt. The optimism that our commanders had expressed to the prime minister was not yet confirmed by military results. The operations of our forces on Monday, October 8, were immensely heroic, but when night fell, the Egyptian bridgehead was still in place. In the north the Syrians had been checked, but not thrown back, and Israeli losses were high.

Tuesday, October 9, was the black day, made darker for us in New York by a sense of impotence. We could not ask for a cease-fire with Arab forces deep into our lines, and we had no clear political aims as long as our military fortunes were low. So, for many hours, I alternated with Ambassador Tekoah at fruitless meetings of the Security Council in which we discussed Arab complaints about Israel bombing raids near Damascus, Ismailia, and Port Said. This reached a high peak of paradox even in the quaint jurisprudence of the United Nations: The Arabs were waging war, refusing a cease-fire—and loudly complaining that Israel was hitting back!

In the first seventy-two hours of the war, we made no ambitious arms requests from the United States. Since we were telling Washington that the Egyptian and Syrian advances were going to be crushed in a few days, there was no reason for Washington to prepare an emergency supply operation. This condition changed only when the disappointing results of Monday's engagements became known. Once our reserves had been moved into position, the Israeli commanders on both fronts ordered massive attacks with huge waste of planes and tanks; they were clearly concerned to make up for the days of unpreparedness. The initial Israeli tactic was to fling the Egyptian and Syrian forces back by the sheer intensity of armored and air counterattacks.

But they were now confronted with a surprise. The Soviet Union had supplied Egyptian and Syrian forces with antitank and antiaircraft missiles of such mobility and simple deployment that they could be effectively used even by troops not specially qualified in advanced weapon techniques. The Egyptians were now equipped with lethal antitank and antiaircraft missiles that could be operated from the shoulder, like a somewhat bulky rifle or machine gun. These new devices, and men trained to use them, were deployed in such mass that the Israeli air and tank forces wilted under the intensity of the Arab assault. The Israeli assumption had been that soldiers in a country where the level of general education was not high would find it difficult to use sophisticated weapons. The opposite was the case. As with modern cameras, it is sufficient to point a weapon of this kind in the general direction of a target and to hope that the target will be found by the electronic "brain."

By the fourth day of the war, Israel's losses both in first-line planes and in tanks were so heavy that our commanders were inhibited from throwing further forces into new attacks. The slender shield of steel that stood between the nation and its direst peril had quite simply become too thin. It was now essential to ask the United States for immediate reinforcement of lost material.

No preparations had been made for such a contingency. For several years the expectations had been that if war broke out at all, it would be swiftly ended by the action of the Israeli forces. On Wednesday, October 10, Kissinger said to Dinitz, recently returned to his post: "You thought you would have won the war by Wednesday; what went wrong?" Dinitz now embarked on an energetic campaign to have the airlift implemented.

President Nixon has told me how he gave the order, "Israel must be saved," as soon as he heard of Israel's losses on Tuesday, October 9. Kissinger strongly favored this course: Without an Israeli military success there would be no cease-fire and no negotiation for an Egyptian-Israeli settlement. The Defense Department, led by Secretary James Schlesinger, had reservations. It feared Arab reactions with repercussions on the American oil flow. The Pentagon wanted the president to limit himself to the dispatch of three huge Galaxy aircraft. Nixon had said dramatically: "We have twenty-five; send them all in at once—everything that can fly. As for the Arabs, I'll have to pay the same political price for three as for twenty-five."

Before the planes could take off, we were faced by an unexpected decision in Israel to accept an immediate cease-fire in place. This would mean that the fire would cease at a time when Egypt and Syria had established salients beyond the positions that they had held when the war broke out. This would have meant that the Egyptians and Syrians had won the first round of the war. From these new positions they would have pressed for Israel's return to the pre-1967 lines.

I went to Washington on Friday, October 12, and arranged to see Kissinger with Ambassador Dinitz the following day. Both Dinitz and I were
shocked by the readiness of our government to cease fire in conditions
favorable to our Arab assailants. We could only assume that the decision had
its origin in the dejection created by the first few unsuccessful days of the war.

To our good fortune, it proved to be difficult to get the UN Security
Council to adopt a cease-fire resolution! Kissinger telephoned in our presence
to Sir Alec Douglas Home, the British foreign secretary. After consultation
with Prime Minister Edward Heath, Sir Alec expressed regret. The British
government had approached Sadat and had received a negative answer; the
Egyptians were doing very well in the war and were not thinking of pocketing
their gains and going home. They wanted another fling on the wheel.

Kissinger meanwhile phoned the Portuguese government and addressed
them very strongly with a preemptory request to allow an American airlift to
make a fueling stop at the Azores.

Kissinger told Dinitz and me that the president had authorized an airlift,
and we replied that this news had given immense satisfaction to our government and our military commanders. But Tuesday was Tuesday and it was
now Saturday, and the subject was the implementation of the president's
pledge. This was all the more urgent since European countries, paralyzed by
an oil panic, were imposing embargoes on the dispatch of arms to Israel. This
applied even to spare parts of tanks that the British had sold to us. The
quantities at stake were not vast, but the British example affected other
countries in Europe. We gave Kissinger details of the large Soviet transports
that were reaching Egypt.

Kissinger lifted the telephone and urged the Pentagon and other departments to take rapid action. He was visibly urgent. He found the present
military position inimical to American interests. It gave no incentive for a
cease-fire, still less for a negotiating process. He said that "before the night
is out, I shall know if we have broken through."

Toward Saturday evening I flew to New York to deal with any possible
cease-fire scenario in the Security Council. A few hours later, a call came
through to me from Kissinger. He said that he would repeat what he had just
told Ambassador Dinitz: The interdepartmental debate had been settled by
President Nixon and dozens of huge transport aircraft were now in the skies
on the way to Israel. I gave the information to an anxious meeting of Jewish
leaders meeting under the chairmanship of Jacob Stein in New York.

Kissinger had suggested to me that when I got back to New York I should
try to get the Australian delegation to propose the cease-fire resolution.
Before I could locate Sir Donald McIntyre, a cable arrived from Jerusalem
asking Dinitz and me to halt the effort for a cease-fire. We breathed with
relief. A capital mistake had been avoided. The background was the successful opening of a military campaign led by General Arik Sharon to capture
Egyptian territory and build an Israeli bridgehead west of the Suez Canal.

This brilliant operation transformed both our military and our political position. Henceforward a cease-fire "in place" would signify that Egypt's most successful military operation in its military history had failed to change the territorial status quo.

I rejoiced in the lucky chance that had enabled us to benefit from Egypt's refusal to accept a cease-fire when the lines would be to its advantage. On its part, Egypt had lost another opportunity through excessive maximalism.

Nixon and Kissinger had shown a sensitive understanding of the fact that a balance-of-power system sometimes works when collective security does not. Kissinger had never ceased to express his conviction "that an Israeli defeat by Soviet arms would be a geopolitical disaster for the United States." The fact that a massive airlift was in full operation three days after Israel had acknowledged the need for it indicates that the United States had performed a bureaucratic miracle. Kissinger was entitled to write:

> So much for the canard that the Nixon administration deliberately withheld supplies from Israel to make it more tractable in negotiation.

Nixon has revealed with pride that the airlift to Israel from October 13 onward was more massive than the Berlin airlift in 1950.

As if in response to a wave of better fortune, we abandoned the bleak pursuit of a cease-fire. From October 15 onward we followed the forward thrust of our armies. Egypt's planning had been very precise up to October 16, but it had taken no account of the prospect that Israeli troops under Sharon and Adan (Bren) would leap over the Canal with heavy pontoon bridges to reinforce Sharon's bridgehead. The Egyptians could no longer pretend that Sharon's operation was a mere "commando raid."

On October 18, Golda cabled me to say that we were clearly approaching the political phase of the war. There would be important decisions to be made about when to cease fire and it was essential that I should come home. I called Kissinger, who said that he had enjoyed our work together and that the "principles that have guided us for the last two weeks will guide us in future. . . ."

On the flight to Paris I learned that Asher Ben-Nathan, our ambassador, had been told that his son had been killed in action. I was poignantly reminded of the human anguish that underlay our battle descriptions.

Dinitz now reached me and reported what Kissinger had only hinted to me a few hours before over the open telephone: Kissinger had been invited by Brezhnev to come for a few days to Moscow to work out a joint policy for ending the war.

There is no doubt that Brezhnev's invitation to Kissinger arose in the context of Egypt's declining fortunes in the war. Kosygin had traveled to Cairo and made great efforts to liberate Sadat from the euphoria that still persisted from the early days of the Canal crossing. Kosygin had learned that Egyptian forces were facing a debacle. Moscow's choice was to wait fatalistically for a crushing Egyptian defeat, with Israeli forces closing in on Ismailia and Suez—or to work for a cease-fire on realistic terms. The Soviets would have to climb down from their lofty sermons about the need to "grant" Israel a cease-fire on condition that we withdraw all the way back to the June 4, 1967, boundaries. The United States would settle for a cease-fire "in place," leading to a peace negotiation soon after.

It was late on Friday, October 19, when Suzy and I reached our home in Herzliya. Less than four weeks had passed since I had set out for what promised to be a routine meeting of the UN General Assembly. The Israel to which we were returning was living in a new era. The streets were blacked out, able-bodied men were nowhere to be seen, cafés and movie houses were empty, and the list of casualties reaching my ministry each day threw up one name after the other with poignant closeness and familiarity. The prime minister and her senior colleagues were in continuous session. I was astonished by her resilience and energy, but I saw a sharp difference in the demeanor and rhetoric of the defense chiefs. The shock of the first few days was clearly marked in their muted expressions and what they were saying was in sharp contrast to their discourse four weeks before.

The blackout in our streets was matched by the blackout of news during Kissinger's stay in Moscow on October 21. Dinitz was repeatedly asked to come to the White House to receive reports, and on arrival was told apologetically by General Haig or General Scowcroft that the White House was receiving blank pages. Later we learned that the Soviets had begun, as expected, with a demand to link a cease-fire with an Israeli withdrawal to the pre–June 4, 1967, lines. When Kissinger invited them tactfully to begin talking seriously, Brezhnev proposed an immediate cease-fire in place and a call from the Security Council to "all the parties concerned" to start to implement Resolution 242 in all its parts. Resolution 338, which embodied this doctrine, also called for the first time in a UN document for "negotiations between the parties under appropriate auspices aimed at establishing a just and durable peace in the Middle East."

Kissinger's deputy, General Alexander Haig, called Dinitz to the White House, gave him the text of Security Council Resolution 338, and added that its words were graven on stone and could not be changed.

The prime minister's first reaction was stormy. She had a strong case on the procedural aspect. After intimate and sustained cooperation on a matter affecting Israel's security, the United States had signed a document with the Soviet Union and presented it as an immutable text. It was not a triumphal moment for the sovereignty of small states. Some of our ministers assumed that if the powers had allowed us a few more days of fighting, we could capture the besieged Egyptian "Third Army," humiliate Sadat, and inflict a resounding and unprecedented defeat on Egypt. How this would contribute to any affirmative purpose such as peace or eventual coexistence was not one of the questions that received an answer in this dramatic scenario.

While I joined my colleagues in expressing criticism of the Moscow procedure, I ventured to remind them that on substance Resolution 338 was a staggering victory for Israel. We had created a military result that astounded all those who had begun to recite funeral prayers over our bodies. We had secured the stabilization of the cease-fire in an international document and had won the bonus of a cease-fire in an advantageous position, as well as the first international confirmation of the duty to negotiate peace. I suggested that we accept the cease-fire on those terms before anyone changed his mind.

A Cabinet meeting was called for 10:00 on the evening of October 21. It unanimously endorsed the cease-fire that was to go into effect on October 22 at 18:52. If experience was a guide, that would be the only hour at which the cease-fire would not go into effect.

We were waiting for news from Moscow. After three days in the Soviet capital, Kissinger touched down at Lod Airport in the morning of October 22. He seemed apprehensive when I told him that Golda was waiting for him. It sounded like a summons to a stern headmistress. His typical good humor returned as we sped through the white concrete agglomerations that herald the approach to Tel Aviv. It was evident, he said, as he responded to the friendly waves and shouts of passersby, that the Israeli people view me with favor. I confirmed his impression and added that by coincidence he had used the phrase "views with favor" in the exact form of the Balfour Declaration. I had written somewhere that the Balfour Declaration was the only document in diplomatic history in which anyone had viewed anything with favor.

He was closeted alone with Golda for an hour. Having seen her anger that morning, I did not envy him that experience. Later I joined Golda and Kissinger together with Allon, Dayan, and Galili. Some of our generals entered to report with stark realism on the situation at the fronts.

In the limousine on our way back to the airport, Kissinger was in jovial mood. He told me that he had felt good in Moscow because Brezhnev was obviously feeling bad. The Soviets had been leaning on broken reeds. Their Arab clients had offered no support on which anyone could rely. Kissinger told me of the intention of the United States and the Soviet Union to convene a Middle East Peace Conference. He would wish to see me in Washington in November to work out the details. He would insist on representation at the foreign-minister level. He was impressed by the Israeli generals whom he had met, but he thought that they looked as if they had done enough fighting.

As I anticipated, the fighting in the Suez area did not cease at 18:52 or even at 18:53 on October 22. It went on for three days at the end of which the conflict had escalated from its Egyptian-Israeli context into a global confrontation of the most dangerous kind.

The first stage in the escalation was a perception of the United States that Israel intended to continue the battles until the Egyptian Third Army capitulated. Kissinger, back in Washington, was sending insistent messages through Dinitz that the United States did not intend to allow the Third Army to be captured a few days after an American-Soviet cease-fire. As Israeli forces continued to tighten the squeeze over the Third Army, Brezhnev sent a message to Nixon on October 25 suggesting that the two major powers use their forces in the Middle East to "keep Israel in order." The Soviet communication indicated that if the United States was unwilling to play this role, the Soviets would be willing to do it themselves.

The wording was extraordinarily casual. It was as if Brezhnev was a kindly neighbor offering a baby-sitting role to relieve a harassed couple for an evening. This offer of helpfulness passed through the White House like an electric shock. It was believed that the Soviet Union was preparing to land supplies by helicopter to relieve the Third Egyptian Army. There were rumors of Soviet troop concentrations in Hungary and East Germany preparing to be flown to the Middle East. The Soviet Union would then be physically involved in the war against Israel and the United States would have to think long and hard about what its "commitment to Israel's security" really meant. The globalization of the Arab-Israeli conflict had always been the American nightmare. This time, after many hours of tormented consultation in the White House, it was decided to stand up to Soviet threats.

None of us who took part in the all-night meeting of the Israeli Cabinet on October 25–26 will ever forget the tension that gripped us. Would the United States really defy Soviet threats? Or would it prefer to join the Soviet Union in direct pressure on Israel? When we knew that Nixon and Kissinger had decided on a deterrent alert, we were heartened and impressed.

On the other hand, our need to take American wishes into account was now more acute. American-Israeli relations were clearly in the balance. Kissinger had told us that, while the United States had shown readiness to go to the brink, "it was not prepared to go over it."

So each of us had to vote for a clear choice: Should we attempt the destruction of Egypt's Third Army at the risk of Soviet intervention, or should we ensure American support and the saving of Israeli lives by accepting the cease-fire and allowing the Third Army to be saved? Once the issue was clearly seen in this light, our options were narrowed. It was hard to believe that the destruction of the Egyptian Third Army was an aim sufficiently vital to justify military confrontation with the Soviet Union with no parallel support from the United States.

As our forces approached the suburbs of Suez, Kissinger's messages became more insistent. He was frank enough to state clearly that the United States could not allow the Egyptian Third Army to be starved out by military action several days after a cease-fire had been agreed to between the United States and the Soviet Union. If this was Israel's policy, he said, the United States would have to "dissociate itself from it."

Brezhnev's warning of unilateral action had impelled the United States to move on two fronts; every pressure would be put on Israel to accept the cease-fire and to open a supply line to the Third Army. At the same time, threats of Soviet intervention would be met by a tough American posture, including a military alert.

The Washington meeting at which the alert was discussed had convened under the chairmanship of Kissinger. The president was reported to be in a mood of stark depression inspired by his approaching downfall through the Watergate affair. At 12:25 A.M. on October 25, a message went around the world: American forces everywhere were put on DEFCON III (defense condition 3), short of full readiness but higher than a normal alert status.

Kissinger's warnings and the danger of Brezhnev's action were not the only impulses that led the Israeli government to accept the cease-fire. Although we were in a dominant position in the Suez area with the Egyptian Third Army surrounded, our own commanders were not unanimously in favor of another round.

Our Cabinet session lasted through the night and adopted the cease-fire unanimously at 4:00 in the morning of October 26. The Yom Kippur War was "officially" over, although there was, as usual, an aftermath. It was enough to recollect the dangers from which we had emerged to understand that we now faced a new kind of challenge. The accent had passed from the tanks and guns—to the diplomatic table.

There is no truth in the legend that all Israelis mourned the loss of an opportunity to subdue and capture the Egyptian Third Army. In the Cabinet sessions, our military commanders showed no such inclination. They had passed through great ordeals with honor, and had seen much death among their men on the way. When some of us interrogated them on the number of Israeli soldiers who would fall in an effort to storm the Third Army's encampment, terrifying statistics were heard. One of the estimates was that it would cost a thousand casualties.

I reflected that if we captured the 20,000 Egyptian soldiers of the Third Army, we would have to return them quickly to the International Red Cross. The thousand Israelis would not return.

I raised my hand as emphatically as I could.

The cease-fire was a great salvation. It was not a defeat.

```
┌─────┐
│     │
│ 26  │
│     │
└─────┘
```

GENEVA: 1973 AND AFTER

By NORMAL MILITARY calculations, Israel had won the war. When the cease-fire came into effect on October 26, 1973, Israeli forces were deep into Egyptian territory near the city of Suez. The Israeli positions on the Golan Heights had been fully restored. The Egyptian Third Army was encircled and embarrassingly dependent on the United States for food and eventual extrication from siege. Israeli forces were twenty-five miles from Damascus. No Israeli city was in similar proximity to Arab forces. The Israeli Army and Air Force had been restored beyond their previous strength by the American airlift.

Yet hardly anyone in Israel spoke of "victory." That word had been drained of its meaning. Israel had won the war but there was no mood of celebration. Egypt had lost the war but had not been humiliated. A new psychological balance had been established. It seemed to augur well for negotiation.

The cost to both sides had been high. In absolute terms the Arab armies lost many more men than Israel, but in relative terms, Israel's losses in dead and wounded were a much heavier blow. Two thousand five hundred Israelis had died in a war that the Israeli Intelligence Services had defined as of "low probability." The shock of this disaster and the consequent demand for political penalties were not immediately felt, but they were not far away in the future.

For me the central reality was that the cease-fire lines could not be held without early explosion. Hundreds of thousands of Israeli, Egyptian and Syrian forces, masses of artillery pieces, tanks, aircraft and missiles, were all tangled up in a confused medley of intersecting positions. My hope of negotiation was stirred by the perception that the Israeli and Arab forces were mutually vulnerable to each other. But whereas Egyptian vulnerability was focused on distant Sinai and the Third Army, the whole Israeli nation and society were paralyzed by mobilization. Israel was in a weak tactical situation. Our need of disengagement was more acute even than that of the Egyptians.

While our parliamentary opposition led by Menachem Begin was criticizing us for accepting the October 26 cease-fire, the hard truth was that Israel had no hope of further military gains. It would have been madly suicidal for us to pursue a subsidiary and sterile aim such as the capture of the Egyptian Third Army at the risk of Soviet intervention, American diplomatic hostility and a huge Israeli casualty list. Kissinger had done Israel a great service in Moscow by transferring the crisis from the military domain, where there was nothing for us to gain, to the diplomatic arena, where new prospects seemed to beckon.

While the battle raged, I had been defending our interests in speeches directed toward the Arab states, the United Nations and the two superpowers. I had become disquietingly aware that there was a substantive difference between the atmosphere in 1973 and that which I had known in 1967. The Egyptian attack on Israel on Yom Kippur aroused no international revulsion. Not a single government accused Egypt of "aggression." Few governments and even fewer newspapers and radio stations believed that we should have expected belligerent Arab states to observe Jewish religious festivals.

The difference between world reaction in 1973 and in 1967 reflected changed perspectives of Israel's role. In 1967 the Egyptians and Syrians were seen by the rest of the world as threatening Israel's security, and indeed its very existence. In 1973 Egypt was deemed to be fighting for the restoration of its own territory after fruitless attempts to achieve that aim by diplomacy. The Egyptians, and even the Syrians, had skillfully avoided defining their aims as the destruction of Israel. They had won further points in world opinion by a military campaign that in its initial stages had shown Arab armies as capable of executing complicated amphibious operations. In 1967 Israel had been regarded throughout the world as a nation protecting its own lives and soil; in 1973, it was widely portrayed as defending an occupation of Egyptian and Syrian lands.

The years of complacency and the rhetoric of excessive self-confidence in 1973 had taken toll of Israel's credibility as a victim of aggression. At one moment our military heroes had been boasting of the deterrent effects of King Solomon's boundaries and of our inherent capacity to capture all the territory between Khartoum and the Taurus Mountains. Less than two weeks later we were manifestly unprepared to meet an assault by 800 Syrian tanks swarming across Golan and an even larger Egyptian force that overran our vaunted fortifications with contemptuous ease. The reputations of our military prowess and of our Intelligence services plummeted abruptly from the heights of 1967. Nor were our measures for ruling the occupied territories generally admired. Their accent was punitive and the lack of rapport between rulers and ruled was no less marked than in colonial regimes. The tide of international opinion, to which Israelis are more sensitive than they like to admit, was flowing against us.

By early November I thought that it was wrong to preoccupy Israeli opinion exclusively with an analysis of the military campaigns. I began to turn my comment inward to express the pervasive trauma of the Yom Kippur War and the need for sharp change in Israel's view of itself. I said and wrote that the war had

shaken Israelis out of the images and ways of thought in which we have lived for over six years. Since all these have become suddenly obsolete in a single week, the intellectual and emotional shock is hard to sustain. We are summoned almost overnight to a far-reaching reconstruction of our conceptual world.

I urged that we discard the illusions underlying Israel's security doctrine since 1967. I wrote that "Israeli policy should be directed not only to making the enemy unable to fight us again but also to the hope of making him unwilling to fight us again. Deterrence and conciliation are not incompatible." In many articles and interviews I listed some of the illusions and fallacies that should now be thrown overboard:

The illusion that the cease-fire can exist indefinitely in a diplomatic vacuum;

The illusion that a million Arabs can be kept permanently under Israeli control without corrosive effects on our own society and our international relations;

The illusion that we could ever have peace and security without substantial changes in the map created by the 1967 war;

The fallacy that Zionist principles are enhanced by refusing to share territory and sovereignty between two nations in the former Palestine Mandate area;

The illusion that the 1967 boundaries have an inherently deterrent effect and make war less likely;

The fallacy that a nation cannot be strong unless it demonstrates and proclaims its toughness in every emergency.

The diplomatic scene now had many points of action. One of them seemed exotically unexpected. One day in early November while Prime Minister Golda Meir was in Washington, I received an urgent request from the Romanian Ambassador in Israel, Ian Kovaci, to be received in my home in Herzliya. He carried a message from President Nicolai Ceauşescu, urgently requesting me to make an official visit to Bucharest. The ambassador pointed out that what was at stake was not only the further development of our bilateral relations but the need to hear the Romanian president's account of larger dangers and prospects. Romania had been the only member of the

Warsaw Pact to maintain diplomatic relations with Israel since 1967, and I did not feel we could rebuff this approach.

Despite the awkwardness of leaving the Cabinet table in Israel, at which emergencies were arising every hour, I made the journey to Bucharest. Apart from the need to avoid an abrasive refusal, I had been interested in reports about the close links between Romanian and Arab leaders.

When Suzy and I arrived in Bucharest, courtesies were exchanged at lavish banquets. We were the objects of warm Romanian hospitality. We were shown industrial enterprises that were unimpressive by Israeli standards. We spent an enforced vacation of thirty-six hours in the neighboring mountain area, but my own peace of mind was disturbed by the consciousness that more central events were unfolding that involved Jerusalem, Cairo, Washington and Geneva. Yet in a conversation of four hours with President Ceauşescu, enlarged by translations that always seemed longer than the original text, I was able to gain new insights.

He had recently met Anwar Sadat. He was in touch with PLO representatives. He was aware that the proximity of the Egyptian and Israeli armies on the ground made a stable cease-fire improbable. He supported the Egyptian proposal for an Israeli withdrawal from the area west of the Canal. What he wanted to tell me most urgently, however, was that in his view Anwar Sadat was ready for permanent peace. If for technical and logistic reasons we were to allow the disengagement idea to fail, we would be losing the opportunity for a permanent peace and not only for a technical military accord.

I carried this message back to Jerusalem, where Mrs. Meir received it with skepticism. She even wondered whether the Romanian visit rated a Cabinet report and discussion. It would soon emerge that Ceauşescu was reading Sadat's mind accurately.

Later events make it difficult for me to reconstruct the strange story of Israel's relations with Romania for the seven years between 1967 and 1973. After the breakdown of our relations with the Soviet bloc during the 1967 war, the decision of Romania to maintain and later to broaden its relations with Israel had a consoling effect. The Bucharest relationship left us with some insight into the dark Communist world. There was also an important dividend in the form of immigration to Israel by Romanian Jews. There was, however, a price for this gain. We found ourselves in the position of supporting Romania's pleas to Washington for trade concessions. And on each anniversary of Romanian "independence," at a celebratory meeting in Tel Aviv, I or one of my colleagues would have to praise President Ceauşescu's practice in maintaining contacts across the entire range of the international system, irrespective of Cold War psychology.

The savage nature of Romania's internal politics was kept at a discreet distance from our minds. The courage of Romania in maintaining simultaneous relations with the United States, the Soviet Union and China, with the Arab states and with Israel, indeed with all the actors in the international drama irrespective of the conflicts between them, was worthy of international emulation. Yet the events of 1990 put our speeches of 1967 and thereafter in a strange light. For many years Israel was so starved for friendship that it had to look for it wherever it could be found. We could not have maintained even a restricted foothold in world diplomacy if we had made the acceptançe of Israel's social ideals a condition of our friendship.

One of the exhausting phases of a visit to a Communist country in those days was the necessity for me to adapt myself to a Marxist dialogue. Under Communist rules it was inconceivable that one's interlocutor could ever present himself as being impressed by the arguments of a non-Communist heretic. At one point Ceauşescu fixed me with a disapproving glare and said, "I understand that you are against Resolution 242." I disclaimed that attribution emphatically and pointed out that I was an ardent supporter of that text and could even be regarded as one of its formulators. The Romanian president looked again at his brief and said, "No, your Excellency is mistaken. You are against Resolution 242."

Mrs. Meir had returned from Washington, where her contacts with President Nixon had been generally reassuring. Yet she had to fight hard to prevent the United States from advocating unilateral Israeli withdrawal. A further point at issue were the prisoners of war. The record of Arab governments, especially Syria, in the treatment of prisoners had caused horrified reactions in Israel at many stages of the conflict. There was no chance that an Israeli government would sign an agreement beyond the cease-fire unless it received assurances on this point. To bring about a unilateral withdrawal from the cease-fire lines without any concession from Egypt and Syria was beyond our domestic possibility or our international duty.

Mrs. Meir had suggested that some of the most urgent problems in the field should be addressed by direct meetings between commanders. These took place at a high military level in a tent at Kilometer 101 on the Suez-Cairo Road in Sinai, sixty-three miles from Cairo. The text of the six-point agreement appears in retrospect to be technical and even subsidiary, but it had great importance at the time. It reversed the cycle of conflict and set up a process of dialogue. The very spectacle of Major Gen. Aharon Yariv for Israel and Lt. General Muhammad Gamasy for Egypt in hard but courteous bargaining seemed to augur a more rational order of relations in the Middle East.

Once the Kilometer 101 talks had been initiated, I set out for the United States with two primary aims. The first was to make contact with American Jewish communities that had passed through a period of unprecedented ferment with sharp alternations of anxiety and relief. American Jews now saw the toll that the war had taken primarily of young Israeli lives, but also of our morale and of our economic resources. The 1967 euphoria had collapsed, and our nation was scarred and tormented by bereavement. I thought this a good time to deepen our sense of common purpose with the Jewish Diaspora. The occasion was to be the annual convention of the Council of

Jewish Welfare Funds meeting that year in New Orleans. Neither before nor since have I ever addressed American Jews in an atmosphere of such intense and anguished solidarity.

Another of my aims in the United States was to talk in detail with Secretary Kissinger about the forthcoming Geneva Peace Conference. In Washington on November 14 I found Kissinger in an anxious mood. There was danger that the Kilometer 101 talks would collapse and that this would mean a renewal of war. The main issue was an Israeli proposal under which we would withdraw from positions west of Suez in return for a liquidation of the Egyptian bridgehead east of the Canal. Our American friends did not believe that Sadat would agree to remove Egyptian troops from their cherished gains in western Sinai, but that some compromise by way of reduction of forces on both sides might be feasible. It was evident, however, that it was useless for General Yariv to ask General Gamasy to give answers to these questions. Affairs in Egypt were simply not run at that kind of level. Kissinger was therefore on firm ground in advocating that the issues that were not solvable at Kilometer 101 should be transferred to the forthcoming Geneva Conference.

The upshot of my conversations in Washington was that I would seek Golda's agreement for the Geneva Conference to convene before the Israeli elections in an open session that would be maximally publicized. At this session all the participants would be invited to state their general positions on a comprehensive settlement. The very inauguration of the conference would arrest and deter any tendency to resume military action. The conference would be convened by the Secretary General of the United Nations, who would, however, not play an active role on any substantive issue. The convening parties would be the United States and the Soviet Union. Henry Kissinger and later Golda Meir were surprised by my advocacy of this procedure. My rationale was that the Soviets would have a dominating influence in any case by virtue of their military power and their intimate relations with the Arab world. I thought it would be better for this influence to be overt and therefore subject to public criticism rather than to be allowed to work behind the scenes with corrosive effects.

Kissinger and I agreed that the participants would be member states of the United Nations. Any proposal for additional participation, for example by a Palestinian organization, would be subject to ratification or veto by the original sponsors. In the expected event that the opening speeches would not reveal a consensus for a comprehensive settlement, the conference would concentrate on disengagement agreements involving Egypt and Israel and Syria and Israel. These agreements would be conducted with the mediation of the United States.

Flying straight from Washington to Israel on November 23, I made immediately for Golda's Jerusalem residence, which I reached in the late evening. She was now remarkably calm, as she went about the business of making coffee for the two of us. I had the impression that she was recuperating rapidly from the shock that she had suffered through the outbreak of the Yom Kippur War and the ensuing disasters of the first week. In a single hour she had decided that we ought to accept the procedures and principles that Kissinger and I had developed. She had originally wanted to postpone the opening of the Conference until after our election. She now realized that a spectacular peace occasion in late December symbolizing a new era in the life of our region would do no harm at all to our electoral prospects.

All this was possible because Golda had developed an attitude of trust toward Kissinger. Within a very short period, he had masterminded the American airlift of arms to Israel. He had successfully resisted hostile Soviet pressure in his October meetings in Moscow. He had inspired the American nuclear alert and had enabled us to obtain prisoner exchanges with Syria at an unexpectedly early stage. We were now moving swiftly away from the atmosphere of the Yom Kippur War into a new era to be dominated by diplomacy. Opposition to the Geneva conference was growing in Likud circles, Menachem Begin's resistance was strong and even Golda began to ask more from Kissinger than he could realistically achieve. Kissinger has recorded that when Nixon heard of Golda's negative attitude to the conference he wrote a note to Kissinger on December 13 saying, "Tell Eban and the others. If this demand on their part brings another war, they go it alone."[1]

The issue on which Golda balked was the participation of the Palestinians. The very existence of this nation seemed to cause her difficulties. The intensity of her opposition to Palestinian participation did not mean that she was particularly enamored of Jordan's role. But neither Kissinger nor I expected that mentioning "Palestinians" as people who could only take part in the Geneva Conference with Israel's consent would be a problem for an Israeli government.

There was now no other course for Kissinger except to set out for the Middle Eastern capitals. He had not secured any agreement from any of the parties. On December 13 he receded completely from our view. When he surfaced in Jerusalem, the journalists who had accompanied him regaled us with "Arabian Nights" experiences. I would have given a great deal to watch Henry Kissinger reviewing a military guard composed of Saudi soldiers with bristling black mustaches standing at attention in white uniforms across which there flashed a seemingly inexhaustible number of daggers and swords. Kissinger had refuted Faisal's assertion that Jews controlled the American press. The journalists in his party had told him that this was not the case. Marilyn Berger, Marvin Kalb, Bernard Gewirtzman and Martin Agronsky had all testified to the relative paucity of Jewish influence in the U.S. media.

□   □   □

---

[1]Kissinger, *Years of Upheaval*, p. 759.

After the solemnities of Riyadh, Kissinger must have found some relief in the relatively modernistic style of discourse in Damascus. Kissinger has written with surprising respect about President Hafez Assad of Syria:

> I developed a high regard for Assad. In the Syrian context he was moderate indeed. He leaned toward the Soviets as the source of his military equipment, but he was far from being a Soviet stooge. He had a first-class mind, allied to a wicked sense of humor. I believed that I was the first Western leader with whom he had dealt consistently. . . . he never lost his aplomb. He negotiated daringly and tenaciously like a river boat gambler to make sure that he had exacted the last sliver of available concessions. I once told him that I had seen negotiators who had deliberately moved themselves to the edge of a precipice to show that they had no further margin of maneuver. I have even known negotiators who put one foot over the edge, in effect threatening their own suicide. He was the only one who would actually jump off the precipice, hoping that on his way down he would break his fall by grabbing the tree that he knew to be there. Assad beamed.[2]

As the date for the Geneva Conference was drawing near, Kissinger had urgently probed Assad on the conditions for convening the Geneva conference. He had told Assad that the Israeli conditions for attending the conference were very complex. The Israelis wanted the Conference date to be postponed. They wished the PLO to be specifically excluded. They required the agenda to be limited to a general review and not touch substantive issues until after the Israeli election. They insisted that the United Nations not have any intrusive role.

To Kissinger's astonishment, Assad had replied that as far as he was concerned there was no reason for objecting to any of these demands. This electrifying response induced Kissinger to remark that President Assad had a reputation for obduracy and militance, yet here he was acquiescing in a whole series of Israeli positions. Perhaps his image had been wrongly understood in the West? At that stage Assad had clarified his position: Since he would refuse to allow Syria to attend the Geneva Conference, he did not really care whether the United States decided to accept the Israeli conditions or not.

Henry Kissinger devotes more than fifty pages of his memoirs to the Geneva Conference and sums up by saying: "The Geneva Conference of 1973 opened the door to peace through which later Egypt and Israel walked and through which it is to be hoped that other nations of the Middle East will walk in the

---

[2]Kissinger; *Years of Upheaval*, p. 781.

fullness of time." No such sense of importance characterizes most of the bibliography about the Geneva Conference. Yet it is important to recall the seriousness with which it was taken at the time. Both the Israeli Labor Party and the new Likud Party had made Geneva the primary plank of their platforms. The Geneva Conference has suffered in the media because of the somewhat technical appellation Disengagement Agreements. It would be more accurate to call the conference a conference for the prevention of war, which after all is not a small or ignoble objective. When I set out for Geneva on December 19, I made full preparation for what might have become a historically memorable occasion. Although I doubted whether we would be able to get much beyond the idea of disengagement, I worked with my Foreign Ministry colleagues to establish files and briefings for a full peace conference. Interdepartmental committees had been established to study the problems of a peace treaty—its juridical provisions, its political and economic implications, and above all, its territorial aspects. I took to Geneva a draft of a peace treaty that I would be prepared to sign with Egypt, Jordan and Syria after no more than a perfunctory consultation with my colleagues. My aim was not merely to add a new document to the archives but to establish a new order of regional relations with free movement across an open frontier. In view of our internal domestic situation I decided to submit the main points of my speech for the prior scrutiny of my colleagues. They all reacted with total silence, which in the Israeli tradition is the nearest one can get to praise. I thought it unlikely that any of the foreign ministers of the Soviet Union, the United States, Israel, Jordan and Egypt would change their policies because of speeches by other delegates, but I also felt that beyond the Palace of Nations there was a great world of opinion, imbued with a basic friendship for Israel and yet anxious to see the quest for peace pursued with greater vigor.

A day after arriving at Geneva, I went to the Palace of Nations to spy out the land. It was midafternoon on December 20. I found the building to be inhabited by ghosts. I cast my mind back to the mid and late thirties, when I had first developed an interest in diplomacy. Nostalgia seemed to cry out from every brick and stone. It was as though the League of Nations heroes— Eden, Briand, Litvinov, Beneš and Smuts—were about to arrive. There was a sense of occasion in the air. Nobody believed that a conference by itself could overcome the deep rancors that had scarred Arab-Israeli relations for so long, but an innovation had been made. It was now certain that the peace conference would open on December 21, 1973.

That morning at breakfast with Kissinger, I told him that I hoped to resume contacts with the Soviet Union, from which we had been cut off since 1967. It seemed grotesque that the chairman of a peace conference should boycott any contact with one of the participants. He promised to help arrange this with Gromyko.

The anomalies in Arab attitudes came to light very early. Here we were at what was called a Middle Eastern peace conference and yet the Egyptian delegate had stipulated that he and I would not shake hands or be photographed in any other posture of cordiality. Moreover, he would not sit next to me at the conference table. He even wanted an empty table and chair to separate me from him. I told Secretary-General Waldheim that although I was not very interested in protocol I felt that a political principle was at stake. Could anything be more ridiculous than to open a peace conference with a visual message that the two countries that were supposed to make peace with each other could not even sit normally around a table? I told Secretary-General Waldheim and Henry Kissinger that I would refuse to accept any seating arrangement that gave an impression of ostracism, as if we were afflicted with a contagious disease. After an agitated consultation among the participants, Eppie Evron drew various hexagons on a piece of paper and came up with a solution. The secretary-general of the UN as presiding officer would, sit in the middle with me on his left and Egypt on his right. My left-hand neighbor would be Gromyko, while Kissinger would sit to the right of the Egyptian foreign minister. Beyond the Soviet delegation would come the empty Syrian chair. And finally the Jordanian delegation, headed by prime minister Zaid al-Rifa'i.

When I entered the conference chamber on my way to the Israeli seat, I saw Gromyko standing in my path. I approached with an outstretched hand, while cameras clicked frenziedly from all over the room. I was taking a risk. If Gromyko had turned his back and rebuffed my approach, the peace conference would look ridiculous, the incongruity of the Soviet chairmanship would be revealed and Israel would be humiliated in full public view. I also knew that although it was Saturday morning, the Israeli television was focused on our meeting and there was scarcely an adult Israeli who was not following the proceedings. To universal relief, Gromyko seized the situation with professional speed. He rose, shook my hand more lengthily than was strictly necessary, removed a diary from his pocket, perused it as if he were undertaking a complex process of research, and invited me to come to his headquarters in the evening at 8:00 P.M. with as few or as many of my colleagues as I would wish to bring.

The speeches began. Henry Kissinger has described them:[3]

Gromyko opened with what was by Soviet standards a restrained presentation. He repeated standard criticisms of Israeli "aggression" and called for a return to the 1967 frontiers, but he also emphasized that the Arabs needed to accept Israel's sovereignty and its right to national existence.

Kissinger goes on:

---

[3]Kissinger, *Years of Upheaval*, pp. 796–7.

I spoke next and made four principal points. The importance of maintaining the cease-fire, the need for some realistic appreciation of what could be accomplished in a short period of time, the imperative of early disengagement, and the necessity of realistic negotiations between the parties themselves.

I also amused the assembled dignitaries by attempting to quote a Proverb in Arabic.

Fahmy was next. With an eye to Damascus, he gave an oration uncompromising on substance.

The most hard-lined rhetoric came from Jordanian Prime Minister Zaid Rifa'i whose actual views were in fact the most moderate. Afterwards Rifa'i admitted to me privately that his tone reflected the necessities of Arab politics.

Kissinger's comment on my speech in *Years of Upheaval* is generous:

A statement punctuated by the oratorical flourishes for which he had become renowned, Eban gave the longest and clearly the best speech of the conference. Moderate in tone, firm in substance, it stressed the importance of legal obligations of peace and asked for patience in what was bound to be a prolonged effort.

The main substance of my speech was to indicate that Israel was ready for a territorial compromise that would serve the legitimate interests of all signatory states. There must be a basic readiness on all sides to make such concessions as do not threaten vital security interests. I then outlined my vision of a Middle Eastern community of states.

The ultimate guarantee of a Peace Agreement lies in the creation of common regional interests in such degree of intensity, in such multiplicity of interaction, in such entanglement of reciprocal advantage, in such mutual human accessibility, as to put the possibility of future wars beyond rational contingency.

I ended by quoting Isaiah in Hebrew and the Koran in Arabic. Kissinger had created the philological momentum by citing a popular Arabic slogan of which the literal meaning was: "That which has passed is dead." I did not begrudge Kissinger his linguistic precocity, although I was struck with wonder at the fact that a renowned historian had diagnosed the past as having no influence on the present. My own experience until that moment and even thereafter was that the past predominated so emphatically in the Middle East that the present was irrelevant and the future clouded in impenetrable mystery.

I made my way to our delegation headquarters to brief the press. I told the astonished gathering of journalists that I would be meeting Gromyko at 8:00 P.M. The result was that the television bulletins in Israel that evening opened with the news that the Moscow-Jerusalem dialogue broken off seven years before would be resumed.

The Soviet embassy in Geneva is the most impressively luxurious of all the missions in that city. I found Gromyko surrounded by his ambassador to Egypt, Vladimir Vinogradov, and three other officials whose names and identities I was never to learn. I was accompanied by Eppie Evron, Eytan Bentsur and Zeev Shek, a holocaust survivor who later became our ambassador to Austria.

I had always wondered whether Soviet policy with its special rigidities ever allowed its spokesmen to develop a personal sentiment. For me Gromyko was a special case. It was he who in 1947 and 1948 had electrified the Jewish people by suddenly abandoning Soviet anti-Zionism in favor of unswerving support of Israel's independence and admission to the international family. This had lasted for four years. It seemed impossible that he would have been unaware of this lineage or that he could have forgotten the hours of common counsel that he and I had spent together in the decisive stages of Israel's national struggle.

In my remarks to Gromyko the keynote was the opening sentence: "Israel wins its wars but would much prefer to prevent them." Gromyko replied as though he were making a response to a lengthy accusatory attack. He said that he welcomed my explanations but it would be wrong to assert that the Soviet policy consisted of blind adherence to the Arab cause. "First: We take an independent and logical line. The Soviet Union recognizes that Israel has an undoubted right to exist like any other independent state in the world. If anybody violates this principle, we will oppose that with great force since that would be against our basic policy. Second: the Soviet Union believes that security ought to be sought not by the acquisition of the territories of other states."

Gromyko added: "The Soviet Union regards the June 4, 1967, lines as the only secure and recognized boundaries of Israel. If Israel would agree to withdraw to them, we can expect important progress."

I reflected silently that Gromyko had said nothing that would arouse enthusiasm in Israel, since our security required some changes in the June 4, 1967, boundaries. Nevertheless this was the first time that a leading member of the Soviet Politburo had recognized the boundaries that, but for the 1967 war, would have been acceptable to Israel. The Soviet Union was thus departing from its previous position, according to which Israel's legitimacy was confined to the area recommended by the 1947 Partition Plan. Gromyko told me that, "in principle," he saw "no bar to diplomatic relations between the Soviet Union and Israel." When I heard the words "in principle," my heart fell. To approve something in principle is diplomatic language for an intention not to fulfill in practice what one knows to be right in principle.

Gromyko said that the U.S.S.R. had been the first country to establish full diplomatic relations with Israel. But to renew them now would only become possible if there was "important progress in the work of the Geneva Conference." My effort to clarify the term "important progress" met with no response.

Gromyko and I parted courteously, with the decision that whenever foreign ministers of Israel and the Soviet Union met in an international assembly they should discuss their respective positions, as well as their hope of bilateral relations. It would turn out in the ensuing years that compared with the totally sterile atmosphere since 1967, the Soviet Union and Israel were embarked on a cautious, if sporadic, dialogue.

This was welcome as far as it went, but there was no change in my impression that an attempt by a non-Communist spokesman to have any impression on a Marxist's system of belief is a forlorn exercise. When Gromyko said with an air of puritanical virtue that it was inadmissible for a state to seek security by encroaching on existing frontiers, I thought that since the room was warm, the atmosphere genial and nobody seemed to be in a hurry, I would attempt to outflank Gromyko by analogy. I said that his nation had understandably sought a better boundary with Poland on the ground that it had been repeatedly invaded from the west. Why should Israel not have a similar emotion after attacks from the east? Gromyko: "Polish problem interesting. . . . Different . . ."

Undaunted, I resumed the fray: "Did not the Soviet Union push its frontier with Finland westward so that Leningrad would not be vulnerable to artillery from the ferocious Finns?" Gromyko (with great solemnity): "Finnish question very interesting. . . . (after long pause) Different!"

It is difficult in cold print to convey the triumphant certainty with which the magic expletive "Different . . . !" resounded in the room. A formula of panaceac efficacy had been discovered. It could cure every dilemma and be mobilized in every cause. Soviet interests and justifications were simply "different" from all others.

Gromyko made an unexpectedly emphatic plea to me to ensure the continuity of the Geneva Conference. I later learned that he was responding to pressure from Fahmy. The Egyptian suspicion was that they had been lured innocently into a peace conference for the express purpose of being humiliated in the Arab world. Egypt had to prove that something concrete was emerging from its readiness to sit around a table with us. What Egypt and the Soviets wanted from us would be symbolized by the presence in Geneva of an Israeli military officer so that military talks could be seen to be taking place in the interval. When Kissinger pressed me on this, I acceded and an Israeli officer appeared in Geneva on the day after Christmas.

The speeches made on December 23, despite evident divergences, were well received across the world. The physical proximity of the participants, the formality of the convergence to a single table, the evidence however slender that some new contacts were at work, encouraged the general belief that the Geneva Conference was a transforming event. I myself, however, have always attached more importance to the working session that we held on December 24. The five foreign ministers and their assistants were meeting alone around the table. The television cameras and the press correspondents had vanished. The absence of the news media gave birth to a visible relaxation. This confirmed my impression that much of the virulence in Israeli-Arab exchanges at international meetings results from publicity. Faced by the bright light and the hovering pencil, statesmen are more likely to strike poses of heroic virility than to be revealed in compromise and reconciliation. It was at our meeting on December 24 that agreement was reached by the United States, the Soviet Union, Israel and Egypt to establish a joint committee to work out disengagement agreements. The intention was to begin with the Egyptian-Israeli front and then to seek disengagement in the Syrian-Israeli sector.

The only discordant note at the December 22 working meeting came from Jordan, whose prime minister, Zaid Rifa'i, suddenly realized that he was being isolated from a process in which everybody else would take part. He pointed out with convincing logic that if Jordan was to be excluded from the disengagement process it would in fact be penalized for not having made war against Israel. This of course was accurate. If Jordanian and Israeli forces had been as close to each other as those of Israel and Egypt, or of Israel and Syria, there would have been a necessity to disengage. Since all was quiet across the Jordan, there was no incentive for the major powers to seek disengagement. When Rifa'i said that Jordanian and Israeli forces were indeed close together since he himself could jump over the River Jordan, I congratulated him skeptically on his athletic prowess. Looking back, I confess that it was an error on everybody's part not to take the Jordanian aspect of the peace conference more seriously.

I made for the airport, leaving General Gur and Colonel Tsiyon in Geneva to establish the symbolic link between the Geneva Conference and the subsequent disengagement negotiations. When I arrived home I could see that the Geneva Conference was the central issue in the electoral contest. The tragic opening of the Yom Kippur War had discredited the complacent rhetoric of ministers and of the leading officers. Many political observers anticipated a collapse of the Labor Party's leadership. As soon as I touched Israeli soil I could see that the Geneva Conference had given an infusion of strength and hope for my party.

Before leaving for Geneva, I had been more active then ever before in formulating the Labor Party's platform on peace and security. I had agreed to accept this role only if I could initiate the first draft that would form the basis of the platform. I said that I would neither draft nor support a text that gave any support whatever to the Galili document or that made any specific statements about the territories that we would not renounce. For the first time, therefore, the Labor Party adopted a flexible test. It asserted the principle of territorial compromise "in all sectors." It spoke specifically of the Geneva Conference as the main arena in which Israeli diplomacy would be deployed, and for the first time the Labor Party in its platform gave recognition to the rights of the Palestinian Arabs, not only to economic benefits or autonomy, but to the "expression of their national identity" in the state that would arise on Israel's eastern border in an Israeli-Jordanian peace settlement.

On December 31, 1973, when the election results became known, the Labor Party had lost six seats partly through the defection of a new party founded by Shulamit Aloni. She was a vigorous Labor member who had been excluded from our list of candidates by Sapir's committee on the grounds that her appearance on the list would irritate Prime Minister Golda Meir. Aloni had been a constant critic of our rule in the territories and of the concessions that Golda was reluctantly making to the religious parties. We paid a heavy price for her exclusion. Mrs. Aloni received over 30,000 votes, most of which would have accrued to our party if she had not been driven to establish her separate list. Golda Meir had many great qualities, but these did not include tolerance of diversity.

Nevertheless, with fifty-four members in our parliamentary party, Labor's supremacy had been maintained. In an inquest on the election results at the party's leadership bureau, I said that the results were worse than we had hoped but much better than we had feared. It was astonishing for a party in continuous office for twenty-five years to receive a vote of confidence after such a period of anguish and travail.

The Labor Party had won a respite, not an escape. There had been intense public pressure for the resignation of Moshe Dayan. In Israel's constitutional theory there is collective responsibility for the acts, the successes and the failures of governments. In theory all ministers were equally responsible for the failures in the first week of the war, but it is ludicrous to believe that other ministers had any basis on which to reach a different conclusion than that which the defense minister and the chiefs of staff had diffused. The logistic failures that were nearly fatal certainly had their origin in the Defense Department alone. The conception that Egypt's military weakness, especially in the air, precluded any serious military option was Defense Department doctrine fed assiduously to the public on the basis of information that no other ministry was equipped to challenge. The notion that a State of Israel extending from the Golan Heights to the Suez Canal had no need to modify its structure or its attitudes was Dayan's conviction and had therefore become a national doctrine.

If Dayan had resigned, the Meir government could well have survived. I saw a respectable precedent in Winston Churchill's resignation from the Asquith government in Britain in 1916 after a failed expedition in the Dardanelles. The government had survived and Churchill had returned to public office less than two years later. Dayan, however, was not a man from whom Churchillian gestures could be expected. If he were to go he would take all of us with him. The justice minister, Ya'akov Shimshon Shapira, had publicly proposed Dayan's resignation, but it was he and not Dayan who had been requested by Golda to resign. Charisma had confirmed its reputation as the mother of all stupidities.

When it appeared that there was no intention by anybody to resign, a public protest movement arose. It was kindled by those who had been officers in the Army during the traumatic first few days of the war. The Israeli Cabinet responded prudently by appointing a commission headed by Chief Justice Shimon Agranat. The other members were Justice Moshe Landau, who had conducted the Eichmann trial, General Yigael Yadin, and General Chaim Laskov, who had been chief of staff of the Israel Defense Forces in the early 1960s.

The terms of reference were defined absurdly. The Agranat Commission was directed to examine the unpreparedness and failure of the first phase of the war. There was something wantonly masochistic about this definition. Here was a war that had begun in failure and that had ended in triumph, and yet the government, which had shared both the failure and the triumph, decided to investigate the former and not the latter. I thought that this might well be unprecedented in judicial history. It was part of the paradox that was to make the Agranat Committee a disruptive episode in Israel's political history and a controversial episode in the development of our juridical traditions.

However, in the existing circumstances, it was an achievement to get any form of inquiry at all, and there was some hope that, in response to sheer logic, the Committee would take its examination beyond the first phase of the October war and would also be fearless and without deference to power. Neither of these hopes was destined to be fulfilled. The limited terms of reference caused me to reflect that it was as if the British government after the Middle Eastern campaign in the Second World War had appointed a commission to examine the Middle Eastern campaign up to the fall of Tobruk without the subsequent and redeeming triumph at El Alamein.

The election result seemed to augur the continuation of the Meir government's leadership. There had certainly been no landslide or collapse. The electorate had refuted the drastic idea that we were a government of failure. Pinhas Sapir said publicly that the Geneva Conference, with its panoply and symbolism, and in the aftermath of my televised speech, had rescued Israeli minds from the tragic memories of war. To that extent, I had been a leading participant in my party's relative electoral success. It would, however, have been naive for me to conclude that there would be any reward for the artificial respiration that I had supplied. In political life nobody ever forgives you for having done him an important service.

27

DISENGAGEMENT

THE FIRST HALF of 1974 found my preoccupation swinging in a wide arc between domestic politics and the diplomacy of disengagement. The explosive tensions on the ground impelled me to give priority to the pursuit of a disengagement agreement with Syria. The hazard to my political career was inevitable. The signs were already on the wall.

The word "disengagement" has a technical sound and cannot rival the simple effect of such terms as peace and war. The aim of Kissinger's shuttle was to prevent what would otherwise have been a certainty of renewed war; this was not a trivial objective, and the publicity that attended it was not exclusively a function of Kissinger's dramatic personality.

Dayan visited Washington as soon as the results of the December 31 elections in Israel became known. The fact that his own political self-preservation was at stake does not detract from the importance of his initiatives. Dayan, being a realist, did not make a fetish of "direct bilateral negotiations." He later wrote that "it was essential that the United States be involved in the negotiations so that it would share responsibility for its implementation."[1] Touval has written that "Dayan sought a mediator because he wanted a guarantor."[2] Golda Meir and I were similarly skeptical of any prospect that Egypt and Israel could achieve a binding agreement without the aid of a third party. We therefore urged Kissinger to come to the Middle East to set a disengagement process in motion. He had intended to stay in the region for a few days, but was persuaded by Sadat to remain until the conclusion of an agreement two weeks later.

We knew that the cease-fire would not exist by mere inertia. Sadat would not be able indefinitely to play down the fact that Israeli forces were close to his major cities; nor could Israel hold territory in the heart of Egypt without

---

[1] Moshe Dayan, *Story of My Life* (Tel Aviv: Steimatzky, 1976), p. 458.
[2] Saadia Touval, *The Peace Brokers* (Princeton: Princeton University Press, 1982), p. 243.

a certainty of eventual war. We were prepared to give up our newly captured positions west of the Canal despite the calculation that many Israeli lives had been lost in capturing them. But we could not possibly move out of the area west of the Canal while allowing the Egyptians to remain in strength east of it.

Kissinger was in his element. By nature and temperament he always preferred limited goals to visions of perfection. Saadia Touval, in the standard work on mediation in the Middle East, has noted that "the distinction between the gradualist and the comprehensive approaches to international problems had attracted Kissinger's scholarly attention many years before he became secretary of state."[3] In exalting the role of the "statesmen" and deriding the contrary approach of the "prophets," Kissinger had written:

The statesman's view of human nature is wary; he is conscious of many great hopes which have failed. He will try to avoid certain experiments not because he would object to the results if they succeeded, but because he would feel responsible for the consequences if they failed. To the statesman, gradualism is the essence of stability.[4]

Touval perceptively points out that Kissinger sympathized not only with the statesman's philosophical perspective, but also with his pessimism. He sought to attain relative stability and did not try to "solve" the conflict in a single thrust.[5]

The policy statements by Egypt, Israel and Jordan at the Geneva Conference on December 23 were not so discordant as to preclude an intense effort to explore a comprehensive agreement. Kissinger has been criticized for setting his aims too low. He could not wait long enough to get the peace rhetoric off the table and to proceed to the delineation of limited agreements. Those of us who might have thought it worthwhile to explore wider visions of peace were obliged to go along with Kissinger because of the explosively urgent need to disentangle military forces from each other on both sides of the Suez Canal and subsequently in Golan. It was a situation that forbade patience.

Since both Israel and Egypt were in urgent need of disengagement it is not surprising that agreement was reached on January 17, 1974, after two weeks of shuttling Kissinger from one capital to another, supplemented by lengthy negotiation between him and the Israeli and Egyptian teams. The final agreement provided for Israeli withdrawal from all the positions that we had occupied west of the Canal in 1973 and from some of the positions that we had held east of the Canal since 1967. Egypt had initially asked for Israeli

---

[3]Touval, *ibid.,* p. 273.
[4]Henry A. Kissinger, *A World Restored* (Boston: Houghton Mifflin, 1957), pp. 315ff.
[5]Touval, *ibid.,* p. 273.

withdrawal from most of Sinai with a fallback position to a demand for a line east of the Mitla and Gidi Passes. In the end, the Israeli withdrawal west of the Canal was more limited, leaving the passes in our hands.

Our delegation decided to demand a formal abolition of the legal state of war between Egypt and Israel. I did not object to this as a tactic, but I warned that it was unrealistic. Egypt was sustained by the traditional view that the elimination of the state of war was part of a comprehensive peace treaty and not of an interim military arrangement. If Egypt had abolished the state of war in the disengagement agreements of 1974, it would have been left without any bargaining power in subsequent peace negotiations and would have been reconciling itself to continued Israeli occupation of most of Sinai, Golan, the West Bank and Gaza.

One of the Israeli gains in the negotiation was Egypt's agreement to clear and reopen the Suez Canal by unilateral decision and to rehabilitate the shattered villages in the area. Egypt would also allow Israeli cargoes, though not yet with Israeli flags, through the Canal. The rebuilding of Egyptian towns and villages in the Canal area sounds like a concession by Egypt to itself. Yet I believed that it was also an essential benefit for Israel. Peace agreements are not zero sums in which one party loses what the other party gains. Egypt was not likely to invest millions of dollars in the rebuilding of the devastated area if it intended subsequently to risk fierce exchanges between Egyptian artillery and Israeli aircraft as it had done until the 1970 cease-fire.

Whenever agreements are discussed between Israel and an Arab state, the question "Can they be trusted?" always arises on our side. In such agreements Israel renounces concrete possession in return for behavioral assurances. Nor could we forget the 1970 violation by Egypt of its obligation to keep its new Soviet-made missiles at an agreed distance from the cease-fire line. To meet our distrust, the United States now guaranteed our right to free passage at every point in the Red Sea, including the Bab El Mandeb Straits, and also undertook to monitor the disengagement agreement by overflying the whole area and bringing the air photographs to the attention of both signatory parties. The buffer zone separating Egyptian and Israeli forces was to be wide enough to ensure that neither party would be able to reach the other party with artillery fire.

The last stage of the negotiation dealt with the reduction of Egyptian forces. The entire agreement would have become intolerable unless we could be assured that the evacuated areas would not become jumping-off grounds for sudden assault. Therefore the question of how far Sadat would be prepared to go in reducing his forces in Sinai was crucial. This issue nearly led to the failure of the negotiations. Sadat was sensitive about Egyptian sovereignty, and even the optimistic Kissinger had not believed that he would get Egypt to accept fewer than 250 tanks facing Israeli forces in Sinai. It would have been impossible to convince an Israeli public and parliament that this was real "disengagement." The moment at which I believed in Kissinger's success was when he returned from Cairo to tell me that Egypt had agreed to no more than thirty-two tanks in Sinai. He had induced Egypt to reduce its tank force in Sinai from 700 to a few dozen, and its military manpower from 70,000 to 7,500, with corresponding reduction of artillery, missiles and other arms. He had virtually secured not only disengagement, but also the virtual demilitarization of areas in Sinai that Egypt had proudly captured in the Yom Kippur War.

The final agreement was drawn in simple lines, but the approach to it was tortuous. The Israeli background was turbulent. Likud sympathizers organized street demonstrations, which became increasingly virulent. Kissinger was depicted as an emissary of evil, skillfully hypnotizing Israel into a betrayal of its security interests. One day a large demonstration outside the Knesset carried banners and slogans with the word "Jew Boy" prominently emphasized. This was an allusion to one of the uglier expressions in Nixon's taped conversations. I found it strange to see anti-Semitic invective purveyed by Israeli nationalists. Israel paradoxically became the first Middle Eastern country in which Kissinger was invidiously reminded of his Jewishness.

The disengagement agreement did not make an attack by Egypt impossible, but it certainly ruled out any chance of a surprise attack. The kind of frightening situation that endangered us on Yom Kippur 1973 would have been inconceivable with the American monitoring system and the separation and limitation of forces enacted in the 1975 agreement.

After every session with our team, Kissinger would make his way back to Lod Airport for a visit to Alexandria or Cairo—that is, to whatever palace inherited from the royal regime that Anwar Sadat was occupying at that time. Sometimes his itinerary would be Egypt, Israel, Egypt, Israel, within a single day. And since there were many crosscurrents of policy within the Arab world, he would often make tangential jumps to Riyad, Damascus or Amman. There were always cameras, tape recorders and microphones massed outside the building in which our disengagement negotiations took place. The demonstrations throughout the country were usually inspired by General Arik Sharon. At that phase in his career, some years before the Lebanese War, his security credentials were impressive. The public recalled his intimate knowledge of the Sinai terrain as well as the audacity and sweep of his crossings of the Canal. His case was that positions captured by Israel at poignant expense of life were being bartered away for little benefit.

It was not difficult to make this case, since the negotiation was never symmetrical. The visible result was the transfer of territory by Israel to Syria. Israel's benefits were greater but less tangible: the saving of Israeli lives, movement away from war, the ability to release our productive manpower from military tasks and the laying of foundations for Arab-Israeli coexistence. As became usual in such agreements, Israel benefited also in its relations with the United States. We received not only a large measure of credit in governmental and public opinion in America, but also a substantive increase in weaponry. The United States is indispensable in mediation in the

Middle East because it is called upon to compensate the parties for the concessions that U.S. representatives persuade us to make. A Swedish mediator, however skillful, could not have built a new Israeli air defense system in the Negev when Israel relinquished Sinai in 1979, and a non-American mediator could not have concluded a massive arms transaction with Egypt when that country accepted advice to make peace with Israel and thereby lost its Soviet arms supply.

It remained for Kissinger and me to reflect seriously on the horizons that now faced us after the accord with Egypt was completed. The end of the negotiations in January came amid unusual blinding snowstorms that swept through Jerusalem. In order to reach Kissinger at the King David Hotel from my own residence a few blocks away, I had to ride with Dayan and General Elazar on a snowplow, which made me feel that I was involved in the last stages of the Russo-Finnish War. On January 18, the snow had melted and so had the positions of the parties. I held a television and radio press conference at the King David Hotel in precise synchronization with announcements from Alexandria by President Sadat, and from Washington by President Nixon.

The next day, the roads from Jerusalem to anywhere else were obstructed by ice on the road. We Israelis have never come face-to-face with the idea that Israel sometimes experiences North European weather. I traveled with Kissinger on a train from Jerusalem to the airport at Lod. It would be no disrespect to the Israeli Railway Authority if I were to say that our carriage did not have any of the lavish amenities attributed by Agatha Christie to the Orient Express. During the unusual train journey we compared our political impressions. Kissinger was convinced that Egypt had made a dramatic shift in its policy. It was now determined to move away from dependence on the Soviet Union toward a closer relationship with the United States. Sadat had refused to sign the disengagement agreement at Geneva, where a Soviet presence would have been inevitable, whereas at Kilometer 101, in the heart of the desert, Israel and Egypt could sign with no one except the United Nations' chief of staff as witness.

Kissinger was convinced that although our agreement with Egypt was unconditional, Sadat might not be able to remain isolated as the only Arab leader to have entered a contractual relationship with Israel. It would be necessary to negotiate a parallel agreement between Israel and Syria early in 1974, and then to turn to the Jordanian-Israeli sector. Kissinger and I recalled Zaid Rifa'i's speech at the Geneva Conference. The Jordanian prime minister had hinted that if King Hussein was left out of the disengagement process he would be discredited as a negotiator on the future of the West Bank. The result would be an increase of prestige and status for the PLO leadership. But the main brunt of Kissinger's exposition amid the rhythmic sound of railway wheels was the need to use the momentum of the Egyptian agreement to achieve a disengagement agreement with Syria.

I was impressed with Kissinger's persuasive power. I felt that if he wanted to sell us a car with a wheel missing he would achieve his purpose by an eloquent and cogent eulogy of the three wheels that remained. As we left the train and walked to Kissinger's aircraft he said, "And now we can all relax."

This was a rare flight from realism. Relaxation was not on the cards for either of us. The Watergate crisis was approaching boiling point and would claim Kissinger's anxious attention. And I would have to descend from the celebration of the disengagement agreement in Jerusalem to the harsher reality of our domestic political struggles. Between January and the end of May 1974, I lived turbulent and mournful days. The major themes were the rise and fall of Golda Meir's last government; the election of a new Israeli leadership; and the negotiation of an Israeli-Syrian Disengagement Agreement. All were overshadowed for me by my mother's illness and death.

From the Lod airport Kissinger had flown not back to Washington but to Damascus. On his return journey he made a stopover at the airport, where Allon and Dayan I awaited him. He showed us a map on which President Assad had delineated a disengagement line in a hypothetical Syrian-Israeli interim agreement. In any area except the Middle East, Assad's map would have been regarded as the collapse of a negotiation with Syria before it had even begun. Assad had sought a disengagement line somewhere between Safed and Tiberias. When I said to Kissinger, "Surely this means that the man doesn't want an agreement, otherwise he wouldn't have sent us such an absurd map," Kissinger replied, "I think that basically he does want an agreement. Otherwise he wouldn't have given me a map at all. I believe that this is bazaar bargaining." My interpretation of this Delphic hint was that I ought to put my opening position somewhere between Istanbul and Baghdad, and that Kissinger would get Assad to be content with Kuneitra.

Six months later, Kissinger's newly acquired understanding of Middle Eastern negotiating techniques would be vindicated. Meanwhile, we set out from the Lod airport to distant preoccupations. He to the Watergate imbroglio, and I to the Israeli political arena, which can best be described as a beehive without honey.

The relatively favorable electoral result for the Labor Party on December 31 had been illusory. Between January and March, the protest movement against Moshe Dayan, and to some extent against the whole government, intensified. The successful negotiation with Egypt did much to restore the government's prestige, and by early March, Mrs. Meir was dealing with the intricate task of forming a coalition. The difficulties were immense. It began with an announcement by Moshe Dayan that he would not join the new cabinet that Golda was trying to put together. This was widely and not inaccurately interpreted as a familiar gambit whereby Dayan habitually attempted to influence the party platform by threatening a parliamentary crisis. The next obstacle was the National Religious Party, which announced that it would not join Golda Meir's government unless its composition was widened to include the Likud opposition. I recognized that this would paralyze our diplomacy. We would not even be able to offer the territorial concessions, which were called for in the Labor Party's platform and which the Arabs and Americans deemed inadequate.

Nevertheless in early March, Mrs. Meir was able to constitute an administration with a slender statistical basis. The assured support for the government in the Knesset would consist of only fifty-eight supporters so that it would have to rely on abstentions in order to survive. Golda was still relentless in excluding Shulamit Aloni and her three Knesset members from the list. When she presented her cabinet for confirmation by the party's central bureau, Yitzhak Rabin appeared as minister of defense, and Aharon Yariv as minister of transportation. Dayan was excluded at his own request, and Shimon Peres stood loyally by his side.

After reading out a list of potential ministers, Golda Meir delivered her bombshell. She proposed one other "minor" change. She suggested that a new prime minister be found.

The traditional pandemonium broke loose with ministers and party leaders making pilgrimage to Mrs. Meir's house in Jerusalem, urging her to stay in office, and emerging to tell the television cameras about their persuasive efforts. I decided not to join the procession. This was not my habit. Nor did I think that it was all that deplorable for the party to understand that it would soon have to give its support to a younger leader. On the other hand, I reflected that we were in the midst of crucial negotiations with Syria and that we ought at least to ensure continuity until a Syrian agreement was concluded. Unless this happened, we could not actually say that the Yom Kippur War had ended, or that the simmering volcano would not again erupt. I sent a personal letter to Mrs. Meir expressing this view, and she responded with a cordial telephone call to my home.

Meanwhile Dayan and Peres had become scared by the announcement that Rabin would become minister of defense. This was the department that Peres and Dayan had dominated in one or the other capacity through all the years of Israel's independence. It was apparent that the role of backbenchers in opposition was not their supreme ambition. They suddenly announced that they had received news of great tension on the Syrian front, which amounted to a national emergency. Accordingly, they would overcome their distaste for public office and join Mrs. Meir on patriotic grounds.

There was not the slightest basis for Dayan and Peres's assertion that a new emergency existed. There had been no new developments on the Syrian-Israeli boundary. Never has a smaller fig leaf been invoked to cover a larger area of naked pretense. Nevertheless, Mrs. Meir, aware that without Dayan and Peres her parliamentary support would be fragile, received the news of their repentance ecstatically and amended her proposal for the ministerial team. Dayan would be defense minister. Peres would be minister of information, and Rabin would become, somewhat incongruously, minister of labor. On receiving this news, the National Religious Party announced that it would join the government, which would therefore have a relatively stable majority.

There had been some gossip about the possibility that I would be excluded from the new Cabinet because of my well-known reservations about the conduct of the government during the era of complacent rhetoric when I had declined to be dazzled by King Solomon's boundaries. This prediction turned out to be unfounded. Golda appointed me to the Foreign Ministry in all her governments.

Meanwhile the imminent publication of the Agranat report brooded over our scene like a hot, humid sky waiting to explode.

When the cloudburst came, all the elements of stability in our society were flooded away. If the intention in appointing the committee had been to bind up the nation's wounds, the exact opposite occurred. The effect was disruptive in every way. The committee had words of stern rebuke for the Intelligence failure, for the complacency about the enemy's military options and for the "conception" that Egypt would abstain from war so long as it was conscious of its inequality in air strength. It also asserted culpable unreadiness even after it was known that war was imminent.

These findings, submitted to the Cabinet on April 2, were the basis on which the committee recommended the dismissal of the chief of staff, General David Elazar, the chief of Intelligence, General Zeira, and the commander of the southern front, General Gonen. The condemnations of the military chiefs were drafted with stern rigor. But when the committee came to discuss the defense minister, the language became deferential and acrobatic argumentation was adduced to acquit him from responsibility.

The case against General Elazar was that he should have proposed the mobilization of reserves several days before the war, and that the tank forces should have been put in an appropriate alignment when it was known that war was imminent. But the committee acted as though the minister on whose orders Elazar acted had no responsibility for having endorsed the decisions of his subordinate. It portrayed the chief of staff and his fellow officers as final arbiters whom it would have been unreasonable for any minister to overrule. It stated without any evidence or argument that "it was not the Committee's task" to express an opinion on parliamentary responsibility. No such specific provision existed in the Committee's terms of reference.[6] Having

---

[6] In 1973 a similarly constituted committee of inquiry under the chairmanship of Chief Justice Kahan went deeply into the question of ministerial responsibility and recommended the removal of Defense Minister Ariel Sharon from his position.

thus circumvented the need to associate any minister with the errors of his subordinates, the committee declared:

> By the criterion of reasonable conduct, the minister of defense was not obliged to adopt additional precautionary measures, other than those recommended to him by the general staff.

This must rank as one of the most extraordinary sentences in political literature. The word "obliged" is hair-raising. The implication was that a minister had no duty to make a wise rather than a reckless decision if his senior subordinates made a wrong recommendation for which they were dismissed. The committee was portraying the defense minister, an ex-chief of staff, as a rubber stamp for whom "the criterion of reasonable conduct" offered no option except to ratify whatever was recommended to him by his military advisers.

This committee was alert to the assumption that the minister at issue in this case was a man of versatile military experience who might at least have been deemed to share General Elazar's culpability. It moved to close this window as well. It stated that the committee would not ask itself whether the special qualifications of a minister—in this case, Moshe Dayan, a former chief of staff and now minister of defense—"should lead that minister to arrive at a conclusion opposed to what was unanimously presented to him." Here was the rubber stamp theory all over again.

The Cabinet deliberated on the Agranat report intensively during the first week of April. General Elazar resigned after stoutly asserting that his minister should share responsibility with him. Most of us around the table could not forget that in 1967, the credit for triumph had gone to the minister and not to the officers who had formulated and executed the triumphant plan. Charisma seemed to mean that its owner could be praised for success but never blamed for failures.

Another illogicality was that General Elazar's recommendations had been characterized by a greater vigilance and urgency than had those of Defense Minister Dayan. Yitzhak Rabin, now in the Cabinet as minister of labor, suggested vainly that the Agranat report be returned to its authors in an atmosphere of rebuke and rejection.

The head of the law faculty at Tel Aviv University, Amnon Rubinstein, wrote an article of vehement criticism in the daily newspaper *Ha'aretz* criticizing the excessive indulgence shown by the commission for Dayan, compared with its severity in dealing with his subordinates.

The ensuing uproar indicated that the Israeli public found it hard to accept the committee's eccentric view on the distribution of responsibility between a minister and his subordinates. Its coddling of Dayan was popularly and reasonably regarded as unacceptable favoritism. It seemed to have surprised Dayan himself.

With Parliament and her own party in turmoil and Golda still mourning its dead, Golda decided to resign. This time, she put her resignation into effect without waiting for counterpressures. In accordance with the peculiarities of our constitutional system, she remained in interim but fully effective control of the Cabinet for several weeks during which she, I, and other ministers including Dayan successfully negotiated the disengagement agreement with Syria.

Within a few days of Golda's resignation, Shimon Peres and Yitzhak Rabin had submitted their candidacies for the prime minister's office. The party's Central Bureau seemed evenly divided between their supporters.

There was another paradox here: the Labor Party was not monolithic. Its historic divisions still dictated the distribution of allegiances among its members. It was, in fact, a federation with three components: Mapai, descended from Ben-Gurion in his prime ministerial days; Achdut Ha'avoda, a small party based on the kibbutz movement, and Rafi, the party descended from Ben-Gurion, which was in effect Dayan's political bodyguard. Mapai had an overwhelming majority among these components. It would have been natural for one of its leaders to inherit Mrs. Meir's mantle. The obvious candidate would have been Finance Minister Pinhas Sapir, the dominant leader of the party faithful, and a successful and dynamic architect of its prospering economy.

Sapir, however, was adamant in his refusal. His major reason for this, as he confessed to me, was that Golda Meir was passionately hostile to Sapir's ascent. She even made contemptuous references to that prospect in *Time* magazine. Another possibility was Chaim Zadok, who had succeeded Yaa'cov Shimshon Shapira as minister of justice. Sapir, acting apparently on Golda's behalf, exerted strong pressure on him to reject the prestigious office.

At that stage, Aharon Yadlin, the secretary-general of the party, and Moshe Baram, the leader of our parliamentary party, turned desperately to me. They spoke in the name of the Mapai wing of the party, which by its very numbers was qualified to claim the central place. After consultation with family and friends, I decided to examine the idea of presenting my candidacy for the premiership. To my surprise, Pinhas Sapir swept into my office with all his physical and political weight, and adjured me in threatening terms not to put my candidacy forward. Later, at a meeting attended by Suzy, he waved an admonitory finger in her face.

There were two reasons which he adduced for this action. First, nobody unacceptable to Golda Meir could, in Sapir's view, be regarded as a candidate to succeed her. Second, Sapir explained that the most important and vital necessity was for the Peres candidacy to be defeated: He thought that Rabin could achieve this, whereas I might not be able to do so. Sapir told me that it would be beneath my dignity to enter a contest in which I was unlikely to get more than twenty-five percent of the votes. I also had some reservations of my own, since I had given all my time to foreign affairs and had not built a prime ministerial image.

Nevertheless, I made a mistake in regarding Sapir's excuses as valid. It was a major error. If Sapir believed that I would get twenty-five percent, it could easily have become thirty percent once my candidacy was in the ring and I was able to sustain it rhetorically. In Western political tradition thirty percent of support in one's own party is an inadequate basis for a prime minister to bring to his candidacy. In Israeli terms, however, that percentage of party loyalists could sustain a political career for many years and even decades. This would be proved in 1981 when Rabin secured thirty percent of the central bureau's vote for the leadership of the party in a contest with Peres, and carried his percentage with him for many years as his immutable share of the party's patronage in every governmental, parliamentary, and trade union institution.

On April 21, the party's central committee met against the background of the Peres-Rabin rivalry. I addressed the meeting and, to everyone's surprise, including my own, elicited strong and even fervent applause. In my speech, I said that the party should rid itself of its oligarchical habits and present itself anew to the voters. There had been much talk of the need to renovate the government. My proposal was that the central committee should first renovate itself. It had been elected many years ago and had stagnated. What right, apart from formal jurisdiction, did it have to dictate the party's future, when its own competence was in question? I said that the electorate had voted for a ministerial team composed of Meir, Allon, Eban, Dayan and Sapir. If the party intended to change that leadership, it should first go back to the hundreds of thousands of those who had voted for it.

The *Jerusalem Post* of April 22 spoke of the audience as "spellbound." The evening paper, Yediot Achronot, commented that if I had spoken as vigorously as this before in party meetings, the leadership issue would have been decided in my favor. At midnight, the television was still including me among the candidates, but a few minutes later, I formally announced that I was not running and that I would support Peres's candidacy.

The next morning, Peres came to breakfast with me at the Dan Hotel and spoke soberly and imaginatively of the innovations of policy and style that he would try to introduce if he was elected. He said that he would regard me as his senior partner.

While I thought it natural that Rabin should be given ministerial office, it seemed to me that his elevation to the central and highest role would be premature. I was only partly influenced by his political inexperience. At that time he had never held ministerial office, or even been a member of parliament. General Ezer Weizmann had caused a sensation by circulating his memories of Rabin's depressive reaction to the sudden crisis of May 1967. Weizmann made too much of this, since Rabin quickly recovered and exercised real command during most of the period of the war. Rabin clearly had leadership quality. Indeed, it was this attribute that prevented normal cooperation with me in a subordinate capacity. During his service in Washington, he had shown incomprehension of the ambassadorial role. He considered that the hierarchical principle on which he had relied in the army career was not applicable to the relations between an embassy and a foreign ministry. A study of his cables to Jerusalem showed periods of thoughtfulness and moderation interrupted by sudden outbursts of aggressiveness. These eruptions would target members of my own staff or myself or other ambassadors or, on occasion, the Israeli government or the army command, which he had recently led.

After a daring raid against Egypt under his successor's command, a Rabin cable poured scorn on the operation as inadequately intensive and added that even the Americans expected stronger military action than our forces were taking. On one occasion, a telegram from the Washington embassy recommended for simultaneous action, (a) intensification of air attacks on Egyptian targets, (b) preparation to intervene in Jordan in the event that King Hussein was superseded, (c) actions in the air that would induce Syrian aircraft to present themselves for elimination by Israel. On Rabin's frequent conversations with Assistant Secretary of State Joseph Sisco, a veteran Israeli diplomat has written:

> Rabin ventured to suggest that the Israeli Army might have to march on Cairo. In his report, he described Sisco's reaction—"he did not fall from his chair"—concluding from the secretary's sedentary stability that the United States was in sympathy with such far-reaching Israeli action. This assumption was received in Jerusalem with considerable skepticism.[7]

The difficult dialogue between Rabin and me was not undignified; it often turned on substantive issues that cut across Israeli opinion. When I spoke in the UN General Assembly and, in a transparently tactical gambit, invited the Egyptian foreign minister to confer with me during the current UN session, Rabin complained that I had undermined our request for more aircraft by creating an atmosphere for peace. A few days later President Johnson approved our arms request with a specific reference to my speech as one of the reasons for his ability to approve it! The argument that our arms requests would prosper most if tensions were high was not only abrasively expressed; it was simply wrong. The United States has always given us arms in the hope of their not being put to use.

In one of the ambassador's cables, directed at his colleague the ambassa-

---

[7]Gideon Rafael, *Destination Peace* (New York: Stein and Day, 1981), p. 205.

dor to the United Nations, Yosef Tekoah, Rabin suggested that Israel should close down its UN mission and effectively cease to be a member of the world organization. I replied that this was a result that our Arab enemies would have spent endless days and millions of dollars to achieve. Every year the Arabs attempted to secure our suspension from participation in the UN General Assembly. Why should we fulfill their ambition?

I was concerned by the views and strictures that I have selected for mention above not only because they caused departmental demoralization, but because they were not sustained by international or national experience.

The main reason for the selection of Rabin as the Labor Party candidate had been his detachment from responsibility for the errors of the Yom Kippur War. I found this to be true in the formal sense, but it was not the whole truth. His writings and speeches since his relinquishment of the Washington embassy had been very similar to those of Dayan: confidence in Israel's military supremacy, an enthusiastic celebration of Israel's expanded ("King Solomon") boundaries as a deterrent against attack, and dogmatic certainty that the Arab oil weapon was ineffective and that an Arab attack would not win even a temporary or partial success.

Looking back, I see no reason to believe that I was wrong in any of these controversies, and I doubt that Rabin would take the same attitudes today as those he took when military command was his only experience and vocation. This episode strengthened my preference for professional diplomacy and my skepticism about the habit of appointing ambassadors who do not accept the limitations as well as the wide opportunities of their function. Diplomacy with its necessarily strong emphasis on hierarchy was not his natural field.

Nevertheless, I had always adhered to my view that I should vote for whatever leader the Labor Party would select, since the real domestic adversary is not Rabin or Peres, but the right-wing parties led by Begin and later by Shamir.[8]

But in 1974, I felt that the Rabin-Peres duel would be a serious obstacle to our party's electoral success. On April 23, the day before the Central Bureau was due to vote on the party's candidate for the prime ministership, I sent an urgent letter to Sapir, imploring him to reconsider his rejection of what would have been the supreme challenge of his career. I did not accept Sapir's lack of international experience as a valid argument for his rejection. I could cite many governments in other nations, including those of Europe, in which a prime minister concentrated on maintaining his administration in good order and his party in strong support, while entrusting his foreign ministers and other advisers with international tasks. Levi Eshkol had assumed the premiership without previous international experience, but he was

---

[8]This is still my attitude now after Rabin's election to our party's leadership in February 1992. When Rabin became prime minister in the summer of 1992, my enthusiasm was sincere.

able to win warm support and friendship amongst other heads of government, especially in the United States.

My letter to Sapir indicated that his failure to fill the void created by Golda's departure would lay a heavy responsibility upon him. I had previously warned him that unless we ensured a prudent succession, our party would not win an election for a long time. This prediction was fulfilled; the Labor movement did not win an election between December 1973 and the election of Rabin as party leader in February 1992.

I took an active role in support of Peres's candidacy. His weakness was that his main support came from the minority, Rafi, sector of the party. I brought together in my home a gathering of nearly one hundred stalwart Mapainiks. From that time onward, Peres was regarded as a serious candidate with a potentiality of victory in the Central Committee.

On April 24 the party's central bureau elected Rabin as its party leader and prospective prime minister by a vote of 289 to 245. Rabin had defeated Peres by a modest margin, so that the two of them were locked together in mutual dependence. Since the alienation between them was deep and passionate, the country and our party were not destined for an easy road.

Looking back, it would have been normal for me to take myself out of the reckoning for Cabinet membership as soon as Rabin had been invested as the candidate for prime ministership. Shimon Peres, however, dissuaded me from this course. He asserted that, in the virtual deadlock of distribution of power, he would be able to nominate at least half of the number of ministers from his "camp." He even once gave the impression that he would not conclude an agreement with Rabin unless he had me at his side.

It was presumably anxiety about the narrow base of his government that caused Rabin to make two attempts to appoint me to the Cabinet team: first, as minister of information, and later, in a visit to my home, with a vague offer of Cabinet membership and a request for me to decide what I wished to do. Meanwhile, however, he had offered Yigal Allon both the post of foreign minister and that of deputy prime minister. In other words, he had slammed the door of the foreign ministry in my face and had prudently sealed the window against any possibility of my entering from another direction.

I rejected the ministry of information, which I have always regarded as a mischievous and illusory gimmick. As Aharon Yariv and Shimon Peres were later to discover, a ministry of information is a snare and trap. The very name is redolent of totalitarian regimes, and the function of becoming a spokesman for policies fashioned by others becomes a humiliation.

When Rabin came to my home in Balfour Street, only a few hours remained before our party was due to ratify the list of its representatives in the Cabinet. Rabin said that he would like me to be in his Cabinet, and then asked me if I had anything to suggest about what I would do. I replied that it was surely for him to make specific offers and not for me to make requests.

It was clear to me that it would be both personally abrasive and nationally disadvantageous for me to accept his proposal. At the most, I would hover, vulture-like, over the international arena, causing confusion to Allon, who was later affronted by the fact that during all the years of his tenure at the Foreign Office, the national polls presented me as preferable to him and all others in that capacity.

I turned with relief from the political jungle to the more orderly diplomatic battleground. The Syrian-Israeli negotiation was naturally more prolonged and difficult than that which had ended with the Egyptian-Israeli disengagement. With Israeli forces twenty-five miles from Damascus, Syria had no choice but to overcome its anti-Israeli obsessions. At the very least, it would have to recover the territory that it had lost in 1973. Without this, Assad's status, in relation to Egypt, would be humiliating.

Israel had four reasons for wanting an affirmative result: Our economy could not sustain the existing level of military preparedness; we doubted whether the Egyptian-Israeli disengagement would endure if it were not matched by a similar accord with Syria; and the United States was offering both its pressure and its offer of Kissinger's unique statecraft; and overriding even these considerations was the urgent need to get our prisoners back.

We Israelis are so familiar with the difficulties that we encounter with mediators that we do not often give thought to the infuriating spectacle that we sometimes represent for them. Kissinger was later to write: "All our sympathy for Israel's historic plight and affection for Golda was soon needed to endure the teeth-grinding, exhausting ordeal by exegesis that confronted us when we met with the Israeli negotiating team." He must have been disconcerted by the way in which our team seemed to expand at every encounter. In fact, we were a team only in the sense of being numerous, not in the sense of being united.

The Israeli side of the negotiating table was occupied by Golda Meir, Allon, Eban and Dayan. After the Labor Party conference that nominated our candidates for the next government, Rabin and Peres were added. Together with Chief of Staff Mordechai Gur and his colleagues, we were an imposing phalanx.

While the Israeli team was a debating society, the American mission was a papacy in an age of dogmatic rigor. There was only Kissinger. On the dozens of occasions when I traveled with him from Lod Airport to Jerusalem, he would report on his recent meeting in Cairo or Damascus, without noticing biblical or modern landscapes along the route. On one trip, however, his eye seized the verdant landscape in the approach to Latrun. The central landmark is the monastery where excellent wines and cheeses are produced and marketed by the community of monks. I said, in reply to his query, that the monastery was based on Trappist principles: "One man is allowed to speak to the outside world and the rest have to maintain total silence."

"I see," said Kissinger, "just like the State Department." He was not exaggerating.

This particular visit must have had a special significance for him because, at his request, he visited the Holocaust memorial, Yad Vashem, with me. By mutual agreement, it was decided that the press would not be invited. The staff at the memorial library produced one file after another in which a Kissinger was recorded amongst the Holocaust victims. Henry and his parents and brother had escaped in time, but many Bavarian Kissingers were left behind to their desolate fate. As he and I traveled in a helicopter from Jerusalem to the coast, we maintained the only silence that has ever existed between us. I could see that his emotions were too deep for expression.

The negotiation with Syria was not only impeded, but even endangered, by the persistence of terrorist assaults. On May 15, three armed terrorists of the most extreme Palestinian organization, PFLP, burst into the village of Ma'alot from Lebanon, captured four teachers and ninety schoolchildren, and threatened to kill them all by exploding the house unless Israel liberated dozens of Arab guerrillas. We left Henry Kissinger languishing in the King David Hotel in profound anxiety, while our Cabinet meeting lasted through the day.

In spite of efforts by the French and Romanian ambassadors to work out a compromise, the decision was taken, on the initiative of Dayan, to storm the building and capture or kill the kidnappers. As our soldiers smashed their way into the building, there were the inevitable few seconds of hesitation while they surveyed the intermingling of the terrorists with the hostages. The three kidnappers were killed, as was one Israeli soldier. But, amid the tragic exchange of fire, no fewer than twenty teenagers—most of them girls—were killed. It was one of the most savage cases of Israeli suffering and Arab cruelty.

The next day we faced a question whether to go on with the Syrian-Israeli negotiation at all. The three terrorists had crossed from Lebanon, but nobody doubted that the assault had been a clear case of Syrian-based terrorism. Kissinger was deeply impressed when Golda told him that we would allow ourselves only one day of suspension before proceeding with the negotiation. Her logic was immaculate: Terrorism was a symptom of the fundamental disease of peacelessness. Negotiation was the only remedy. It would be illogical to renounce the cure and to allow the fever to pursue its deadly course. "We had all better get back to peacemaking," she said.

It was one of her noblest moments.[9]

There were far more obstacles to be surmounted than Kissinger had encountered in the negotiation with Egypt. Apart from the necessity of dealing with

---

[9]Kissinger, *A World Restored*, p. 1076.

tho parties directly involved, Kissinger invoked the influence of Egypt and Saudi Arabia and, on one occasion, even flew to Cyprus to prevent Gromyko from playing a spoiler's role. His chief weapon in Damascus was to remind the Syrians that the alternative to a disengagement would be constant confrontation with Israeli power. Syria had never been so imprudent as to face Israel's entire strength without the knowledge that Egypt was attacking us from the south. The Soviet Union had shot itself in the foot by not having relations with us; it had awarded all initiative and prestige to its superpower rival. At their Cyprus meeting, Kissinger had no trouble in putting Gromyko in his secondary place.

For Israel, the chief pain lay in the fact that, in any disengagement, we would have to give up control of the town of Kuneitra. This did not strike me as a fatal loss. When Geulah Cohen, a passionate rightist, said that it was like the surrender of Jerusalem, I replied, "If I forget thee, o Jerusalem, may my right hand lose its cunning."

Toward Israel, Kissinger employed both pressures and incentives. The pressure was the threat by the United States to withdraw and leave us alone with an active state of war in the north. The incentive supplied by President Nixon, despite his embattled condition at home, was to convert one billion of the promised aid program from a loan to a grant. There was also a new infusion of weaponry, especially of aircraft.

In the end, Syria not only gained Kuneitra, recovering the ground it lost in 1973, but also made a small but symbolically significant encroachment on the previous Israeli position in the Golan Heights. Syria's face had been preserved; Israeli interests had been respected; and Kissinger emerged in the public domain as a diplomatic superman. He absorbed the praise without manifest display of embarrassment.

When Syrian and Israeli officers sat down in Geneva, under the chairmanship of the UN Chief of Staff, General Ensio Siilasvuo, on May 29, 1974, the theory of irreconcilable conflict had been breached, this time in the most unexpected context.

The time had come for me to conclude my period of office as foreign minister. My last appearances in my familiar capacity were valedictory. At a press conference at Lod Airport, where I appeared jointly with Kissinger to celebrate the Syrian-Israeli disengagement, Kissinger daringly said that the Israeli establishment and the Labor Party must be crazy if they renounced my services. (A few years later, I would say the same about him, when the Ford presidency expired.)

The final Cabinet session that I attended was ceremonial. There were nostalgic speeches attending Golda Meir on her departure, and there were some references to my own Cabinet career, mostly from ministers who had not always been in accord with my views. Shimon Peres said of me briefly and surprisingly: "The Jewish people has had many voices in its history, but it has never had a voice that reverberated from one end of the world to another with such resonance as this."

There was another nostalgic moment on June 4, when I assembled the personnel of the Foreign Ministry on the lawn outside our modest buildings. Many of those assembled there had long been my disciples in international politics and diplomacy. I told them that Israel's cause could be represented either with moral incisiveness and intellectual elevation or with routine prosaic dullness. In the former case, our policies would have a strong resonance among the Jewish people and throughout the world. "It matters very much, not only what Israel's policies are, but how they are expressed." I wished the ministry success in its future responsibilities and then walked away. It was over two years before I was emotionally capable of entering it again.

How could my mind not go back to 1946, when I first harnessed myself to the Zionist cause? I had spent eleven years in senior diplomatic posts and fifteen years as a Cabinet minister. I had played an intense role in our party's electoral struggle on four separate occasions. From 1947, right through to the Geneva Peace Conference, I had been a leading participant in Israel's international battles. I had traveled the world in this cause.

The satisfactions had come from the bite and thrust of conflict and from the general upward curve of our national history. The price had been paid in human terms: in long family separations, in an implacable series of tensions, in the strangling effects of security precautions and protocolar fuss.

I had also lacked the real freedom of self-expression. At every stage, I had to remember that I was speaking, not for myself alone, but for a country, a government, or a party that might not want to be committed to everything I believed or pronounced. In compensation, I had been able in my books *My People, My Country* and *Voice of Israel* to expound my views as a writer without any sense of official reservation. But these works all dealt with matters in which most Israelis were in harmony. On issues held in controversy, the image of my thought and character had been blurred by the restraints of office and collective responsibility. I could now bring it to light.

Opposition is an honorable function in a democracy, but it is the only honor that politicians do not actively pursue. I had always admired Walter Bagehot's explanation in his classic work on the English Constitution that: "The Cabinet system is the only system in which criticism of the government is just as much a part of the system as is the government itself." My problem was that I was neither in the government nor in opposition, since I had been elected as part of the Labor Party, whose task it was to sustain Rabin's administration.

I faced other difficulties of a more prosaic kind. Former presidents and former prime ministers in Israel have their path to the opposition wilderness paved by a few courtesies. Parliament accords them offices, a vehicle with a driver, and a small but crucial secretariat. A foreign minister enters his new condition without any such alleviations. From June 1 onward, I had no office and was obliged by precedent to vacate the official residence within a few weeks. Fortunately, I had the foresight some years before to use the royalties from my first book toward building a house on a small plot of three-quarters of a dunam in Herzliya. Suzy pooled some of her resources with mine to make this possible. The road was unpaved and there were no houses to the left or right. Our home was not large, but it had a view on the sunset and at dawn over the sea. This has now been blocked by a highly developed neighborhood of villas, some of them belonging to foreign embassy personnel. Israeli cities are not the paradise of the environmentalists.

The chief affliction attending those departing from public office is the sudden drying up of information. This is mitigated, in Israel's case, by the circumstance that the most widely published items in the press consist of secret information derived from cabinet meetings and official documents.

Nevertheless, the withdrawal symptoms were even sharper than I had experienced when I left my two embassies in 1959. There was, however, not a single moment of risk that I was passing into oblivion. Within a week of my departure from office, I received offers of chairs or long-term lectureships in Israel and American universities. I also signed up for the very first time with a lecture agency, which I had refused to do when I had been an ambassador.

Among all the offers, I selected the invitation of the president of Columbia University, William McGill, to spend a whole year as distinguished visiting professor. To accept this invitation in its full scope would have meant resignation of my Knesset seat. I saw no reason to give all that comfort to my rivals and adversaries. I therefore agreed to teach at Columbia for one semester, between September and mid-December 1974. More than half of that period would, in any case, fall within the Knesset recess. I decided to teach a postgraduate course on multilateral diplomacy and to hold a seminar on "Deterrents and Miscalculation in War as Illustrated by the Middle Eastern Conflict of 1948 to 1973."

Before setting out, I experienced my first activity as a former foreign minister still laden with a residuary memory of the past. President Nixon visited Israel in June. He was the first American president to visit Israel while in office. (Since then, he has been succeeded on that route only by President Carter, in the course of his mediation in 1978–1979.) As I passed Nixon at the reception in the Knesset, he said: "You tried for years to get me to come here. I remember your suggesting that at my first dinner in your home in Washington, more than fifteen years ago. Now that I come here, I don't find you as foreign minister." I had a presentiment that his political future would henceforth be shorter than mine, but he had a strange air of confidence for one so close to the brink.

More substantive was my talk the next day with Henry Kissinger, who was accompanying his president. Henry expressed concern that the new Israeli government, with its very small parliamentary majority, would adopt an even less mobile diplomacy than its predecessor. He thought that the test case was an interim agreement with Jordan. Israel would have to decide whether we wanted King Hussein as our partner in negotiating the future of the West Bank and Gaza. "If you are not willing or able to make a favorable decision," said Kissinger, "you will have to deal with the PLO and not with Hussein." He made it clear that there was a strong American preference for a Jordanian-Palestinian negotiation. But he exercised no strong pressure. Watergate was enfeebling American diplomacy in every sector.

Prime Minister Rabin's first statements had concentrated on the theme that the heart of the Middle Eastern problem was the relationship between Israel and Egypt. In that conception, Jordan and the Palestinians were subsidiary, and agreements with them were not urgent.

This provoked me into writing articles in *Ma'ariv* and *Ha'aretz,* taking issue with this analysis. It was, of course, true that the decisions on behalf of the Arab world to make war, to cease-fire, and to sign armistice and disengagement agreements had all been initiated by Egypt, which is the natural center of Arab culture and politics. Yet, I had always believed and still believe that the core of the dispute lies in the unresolved conflict between Israel and the Palestinian Arabs. Egypt and Syria entered the arena, not through any concern for their national interests, but in obedience to Arab solidarity focused on the Palestine people.

In my articles, I suggested that we now give equal priority to a Jordanian-Israeli agreement on a par with those concluded with Egypt and Syria, even if this meant giving Jordan a foothold across the river at Jericho, so as to create an analogy with the Syrian gain of Kuneitra. I wrote: "If our government says that it is impossible to make the transition to peace with Egypt and Syria in one leap without going through intermediate stages, why does this logic expire when we come to the problems of Jordan and the West Bank?" I added that, even if there was no military justification for a disengagement with Jordan, we should pursue that aim so as to prevent the PLO from monopolizing responsibility for the Palestinian cause.

I later learned that Yigal Allon, as foreign minister, had pressed views similar to my own. When he reached Camp David for talks with President Ford and Secretary Kissinger, he had been instructed by Rabin to keep off the subject of Jordan on the grounds that we could not have an election just because of Jericho. The complication here was that, although the National Religious Party had not entered Rabin's Cabinet, the Labor Party wished to keep that entry open in the future. It had therefore signed an agreement that there would be no cession of territory in the occupied areas without facing the electorate.

In Washington, Kissinger was telling the Senate Foreign Relations Committee:

The sensible next step . . . would be Jordan, for two reasons, one because it is the most moderate of the Arab governments . . . and secondly because the best way to deal with the Palestine question would be to draw the Palestinians into the West Bank. . . . On the other hand, Israeli domestic politics does not permit a disengagement on the Jordan River right now because they need the National Religious Party in order to support the government. . . .

This was the last realistic possibility for a Jordanian solution. It foundered on the rock of our domestic politics, which gave the balance to a small religious splinter party. The lost opportunity has not yet been restored.

The "Egypt first" doctrine was now advanced in every official Israeli speech, the "noncentrality" of the Palestine issue became an article of official faith, Geneva was shunned, and diplomacy slowed down. Fourteen months were to elapse before a new interim agreement with Egypt was concluded. This was little more than a renewal and enlargement of the 1974 agreement, with the addition of extremely valuable new understandings between the United States and Israel. In March 1975 Rabin had declined to give up the Abu Rudeis oil fields and the Mitla and Gidi passes without an Egyptian declaration ending the state of war. In September he accepted those very terms. I supported this decision in the Knesset vote although Moshe Dayan voted against it, thereby negating the very policy that he had initiated in the 1974 disengagement agreement.

While all attention was concentrated on Egypt, the PLO was leaping forward to international recognition. Jordan's role was eclipsed, and the UN adopted resolutions in favor of the PLO. When the National Religious Party, now under fundamentalist leadership and dominated by its radical wing, entered the Cabinet and two moderate ministers, Shulamit Aloni and Aharon Yariv, resigned within a year, these events—together with the appointment of General Sharon as the security adviser to the prime minister—accentuated a subtle drift toward hawkishness.

In August 1974, Suzy and I took a two-week vacation in Europe, and returned home to Herzliya to prepare for our new adventure. We arrived in New York on the eve of Labor Day 1974 and prepared for my professorial career. From my peaceful point of vantage at Morningside Heights I watched developments at home with anxiety that became intense on November 13, when Arafat was invited to address an obsequious General Assembly of the United Nations. The pistol and the pseudo-military appearance of his clothing stripped the United Nations of any pretension to dignity. The Arafat speech itself would have disgraced a patient in a psychiatric clinic. The very principle of international organization was polluted by the inebriated atmosphere in which the strange ritual was conducted. It was clear that the Palestinian cause was making the worst possible entrance on the international stage, and yet it was being acclaimed as if it were Jeffersonian democracy in its purest form. We had the feeling that the world belonged to our enemies.

In mid-December 1974, I relinquished my visiting professorship at Columbia, declined an even more tempting proposal to accept a chair on multilateral diplomacy at the Johns Hopkins University under the auspices of its Center of Advanced International Studies, and returned home.

Henceforward, the Knesset would be my political arena.

28

DISENGAGEMENT AND
PEACE: 1974–1980

A CABINET MINISTER in a democratic country wakes up each morning and asks, "What shall I do today?" An ex-minister asks himself, "What shall I say today?" I found that the frustration of leaving office lies in the gap between these two questions. Parliamentary duties are often time-filling and they deal with much the same issues as those that arise in Cabinet meetings. Yet my first sentiment on leaving my Cabinet post in 1974 was that a career revolving entirely around the parliamentary building would combine maximal activity with minimal results.

The Israeli political culture deals generously with former prime ministers, offering them cars, secretaries and offices for the rest of their lives. This is a greater measure of deference than is accorded by most other governments to former prime ministers. No such amenities could possibly be offered to the populous ranks of ex-ministers, and the status gap between the ministerial team and "backbenchers" is exceptionally wide. The structure of the Israeli government apparatus was determined by David Ben-Gurion in the late 1940s. He saw himself as a permanent prime minister and he had no affection for the checks and balances whereby a democracy restrains executive power. Knesset members who are not Cabinet ministers or chairmen of Knesset committees are not even accorded a private room in the Knesset building. They are divided into pairs who inhabit tiny roomlets furnished so sparsely that any additional austerity would justify the concern of the International Red Cross.

The Knesset rules afford unlimited speech to ministerial spokesmen, while other members are condemned to a brevity of utterance for which Israeli politicians have no previous training. The Knesset is extraordinarily parsimonious in the research facilities that it offers its members. Normally, a parliamentary assistant is a young student who is preparing for a degree in law or international relations and is willing to put in a few easily forgettable hours in the Knesset on a pittance far below the minimum wage decreed by honorable members on the floor of the House.

The Knesset library discredits the idea of the Jewish people as "The People of the Book." The periodicals regularly received are minimal in number. A Knesset member traveling abroad is filled with envy and wonder at the capacious and well-staffed offices and libraries in other parliaments.

The deflationary effects of ceasing to be a minister are softened in Israel by the intensity of parliamentary combat. But the consolation is far from complete. Ex-ministers suddenly feel themselves remote from the scenes of executive action and with only limited access to the information on which foreign policy judgments can be made. In these conditions, the cafeteria and dining room are the most frequented rooms of assembly. It is there that waves of gossip generate an energy that, if only it could be harnessed, would suffice to illuminate entire cities.

Nevertheless, membership of the Knesset Committee on Foreign Affairs and Defense comes nearer than anything else to giving a few former Cabinet ministers a sense of continuing official dignity. I became a member of that Committee in 1974 when I was not included in Rabin's Cabinet. I took part in its debates during the entire period of Menachem Begin's tenure as prime minister from 1977 to 1983. I became committee chairman from 1984 until the end of my Knesset membership in 1988. This chairmanship traditionally empowers the incumbent to take the floor early in debates on defense matters and international politics.

On the surface, the powers of the Foreign Affairs and Defense Committee are considerable. The prime minister, the defense minister and the foreign minister are obliged by tradition to appear before it each month. The army chief of staff, the head of military Intelligence and the commanders of all the military formations provide the committee with accurate, precise and exhaustive reports. Many military chiefs welcome the exercise of reporting to the committee, since it gives them chances to think methodically about their functions instead of reacting to daily events. The committee members visit the headquarters of all of the major military and Intelligence formations in the course of each year. Thus, a committee member of long tenure amasses a spectacular quantity of knowledge and insight into the workings of the defense system. Members of this committee devote more time to defense and foreign policy than do Cabinet ministers, whose agenda is charged with more varied and urgent concerns. Together with the finance committee, the Knesset Committee on Foreign Affairs and Defense determines the military budget, which is immune to discussion in the plenary Knesset.

In theory, the government of the day would have to tremble if there was a clear majority against its policies in the Foreign Affairs and Defense Committee. In practice, however, the composition of the committee reflects the balance of parliamentary strength. If Likud or Labor has a majority in the Cabinet, it will have a majority in the committee as well.

The Rabin government began its career with a mouth full of silver spoons. Everything seemed to be going for it. It was headed by a Sabra born in

Jerusalem who had achieved the highest rank in both the military and diplomatic establishments. The average age of its members was lower than in any previous Israeli administration. Yet it was never able to bring these advantages to fulfillment. One of its weaknesses was the narrowness of its parliamentary backing. Its survival from month to month depended on the National Religious Party, which joined Rabin's administration in 1975. This party, with its annexationist policies, inhibited the cabinet from dealing seriously with the Palestinian and Jordanian relationships.

In the late 1960s the National Religious Party had lurched toward a fundamentalist interpretation of Israel's right to the Land of Israel. In this vision, everything belonged to Jews, nothing to Arabs. The pragmatism of Moshe Shapira and his colleagues, Yosef Burg and Yitzhak Raphael, was replaced by the ardent and undisciplined ardor of the younger leaders, Yehuda Ben Meir and Zevulun Hammer. Both of these men have since outgrown their militant passions, but in their return to realism they have lost the control of their party. The NRP is now a shadow of its former self.

The small margin of votes supporting the Rabin government in the Knesset was not its only burden. Overshadowing the normal inter-party tensions was the antagonism between Rabin and Peres. This mutual hostility was so implacable and comprehensive that it qualified as one of the wonders of the political world. While I believed that Peres was an imaginative statesman, I felt some discomfort at the fact that he was attempting to subvert the Rabin regime while continuing to be a member of Rabin's cabinet. When the time came for an election, prematurely induced by Rabin's imprudent decision to break with the National Religious Party, I thought that Peres should have resigned in order to make his bid for succession from outside the Cabinet. As it turned out, the prime minister's office and Peres's defense ministry became, in effect, rival campaign headquarters.

Being unable and even unwilling to tackle the central core of the Palestinian problem, the Rabin administration was able to concentrate sharply on the development of relations with Egypt. It did this with tenacity and success. The willingness of Henry Kissinger to expand his involvement reinforced the prospect of a new breakthrough.

A new Israeli-Egyptian agreement, later called Sinai Two, was reached in September 1975. The area of separation between Israeli and Egyptian forces was widened, but the main importance of the new agreement lay in a development of American-Israeli relations that far overshadowed its territorial and security provisions. The process of reaching the agreement was abrasive and truculent on both sides. Attempting to strike a militant pose that went beyond his administration's real strength, Rabin at one time held out hopefully for an abolition of the legal state of war and the retention by Israel of the Abu Rodeis oil fields and of the Mitla and Gidi passes. When Kissinger became irritated by what he saw as unrealistic demands and was sustained by President Ford, the Rabin administration prudently yielded and was denounced not only by Begin's Likud Party but also, inexplicably, by Moshe Dayan. Over seventy-six senators had objected to the severity of the Ford administration's attitude to Israel's neogtiating stance, and their support helped the American-Israeli dialogue to move back to harmony.

My own belief was that the large concessions Rabin had made were fully compensated by remarkable stipulations in a separate agreement with the United States. Washington offered to make long-term appropriations for military equipment and other defense requirements as well as for the energy requirements and economic needs of Israel. The United States also offered to supply Israel with oil from its own resources in the event that Israel lacked supplies as a result of boycott by other oil-producing states. The United States committed itself not to recognize or negotiate with the Palestinian Liberation Organization so long as the PLO did not recognize Israel's "right to exist" and accept Security Council Resolutions 242 and 338. The United States further announced that it would oppose any initiative in the Security Council to alter adversely the terms of reference of the Geneva peace conference or to change Resolutions 242 or 338 in ways incompatible with their original purpose. Israel now had a security alliance in everything but name.

In articles in the world press, I took sharp issue with the Israeli and American demand for PLO "recognition of Israel's right to exist." I considered this to be demeaning for Israel. Under the UN General Assembly Resolution 273 admitting Israel to membership in the United Nations, we were a peace-loving state equal in sovereignty to the United States, the Soviet Union and all the other Charter signatories. How could we solicit an organization of vastly inferior international standing to recognize our right to exist? Our government was asking the Palestinians for what was the hardest thing for them to do and the least useful thing for us to receive. I wrote that Israel's right to exist was independent of anyone's recognition of it and that no self-respecting nation had ever put its own legitimacy to challenge long after the world community had recognized its sovereignty. Later, when Menachem Begin announced his cabinet to the Knesset in June 1977, I had the satisfaction of hearing him support the view that Israel should never ask anyone to "recognize its right to exist."

The reinforcement of the American-Israeli relationship by the 1975 Sinai agreement was the major achievement of the Rabin government. A year later a different kind of success electrified the world and gave Israel an immense boost of self-confidence. An Air France plane bound from Tel Aviv to Paris made a scheduled stop at Athens where additional passengers joined the flight. A few hours later the new passengers revealed themselves as hijackers acting under the command of the extremist Palestinian organization, the PFLP[1]. They ordered the captain and crew to land in Libya and, after

---

[1]Popular Front for the Liberation of Palestine

refueling, to proceed to the Entebbe airfield in Uganda, where the egregious President Idi Amin, Israel's implacable enemy, appointed the 250 passengers, including the 85 Israelis, as his "guests." The hijackers' terms for the release of the kidnapped crew and passengers were the "liberation" within forty-eight hours of forty Arabs held in Israel and thirteen incarcerated in European countries for terrorist acts.

The Israeli response was deliberated in the full Cabinet with parallel consultation in the Knesset Foreign Affairs and Defense Committee. It was evident that a unified national stance was imperative. Defense Minister Shimon Peres and the army chief of staff General Mordechai (Motta) Gur were firmly resolved on a military solution and totally opposed to the very idea of negotiation and compromise. Prime Minister Rabin raised the realistic possibility that a rescue act across the distance between Israel and Uganda might not be feasible and that a tactic of delay leading to negotiation might become inevitable.

There was nothing wrong in both contingencies coming under discussion. The dark consequences of the May 1974 decision to storm the building at Ma'alot where our hostages were being held must have been in Rabin's mind. Twenty schoolchildren had died during the Israeli Army's attempt to free them. But in the case of Entebbe the prospect of a military rescue was pressed by Peres and Gur with such single-minded confidence that this option clearly had majority support and eventually won Rabin's approval.

Before an Israeli reply could reach Uganda, the hijackers, less heroic than they seemed, extended their previous ultimatum to allow a further seventy-two hours for deliberation. Their aim was to isolate the Israeli passengers and to release the non-Israelis. In the interval our Intelligence service was able to interrogate the released passengers on the precise structure of the building in which the Israelis were held, as well as the location of the Ugandan guards and of the aircraft that held the promise of escape. Peres had felt so strongly on the necessity to deny any comfort or reward to the kidnappers that he had sent the military rescuers under the leadership of the parachutist commander General Dan Shomron on their way to East Africa, noting that if the Cabinet and our committee recoiled from confrontation the plane could be called back.

They were not called back. Peres and Gur won their debate. An aircraft bearing the military rescue team flew unbelievably to Nairobi and thence to Entebbe, where the Israeli passengers had the astonishing experience of seeing an Israeli soldier in the doorway of their prison saying, "We've come to take you home." Only a minute earlier, they had almost despaired of survival.

Israel had lived an exalting moment. When the hijacked Israelis, liberated from the shadow of death, landed at Ben-Gurion Airport they found an ecstatic nation looking at itself with new eyes. In New York on July 4, 1976, Americans were celebrating the two hundredth anniversary of their nation's independence. There were many reasons for ships to let their sirens be heard in salvation and praise. Israel had risen above its own highest ambitions of valor and good report. But, as usual, the joy was not unconfined. There was a strong undercurrent of grief. The Entebbe triumph carries the memory of two valiant souls. There was Lieutenant Colonel Yonatan Netanyahu, killed in action. And there was Dora Bloch, a simple citizen, who was taken to a hospital for treatment during the detention of the hijacked Israelis and who was evidently murdered by Idi Amin's henchmen. I shared the grief of her son, Danny Bloch, now an editor of the daily newspaper *Davar*.

While the Entebbe rescue was being celebrated in fame and story, little else was going right in other fields of action and struggle. The most disquieting development was the erosion of domestic authority. A test case with historic consequences took place almost as soon as the Rabin government was constituted in June 1974. A group of militant religious Zionists settled without governmental authorization in the Arab village of Qadum, near the biblical site of Elon Moreh. There was a brief assertion of governmental authority during which Rabin promised to make an example of the illicit settlers by ordering their removal. Yigal Allon, the foreign minister, actually proclaimed his intention to resign if this decision was not implemented. The decision was not implemented and Yigal did not resign.

On the other side of the barrier, Defense Minister Shimon Peres supported the settlers and worked assiduously to keep them in their place without injury to their prestige. In the end, the Rabin-Peres-Allon government found it more convenient to satisfy the ambitions of the settlers than to buttress the authority of the government that they headed. The subsequent, uncontrolled proliferation of settlements in the West Bank is largely the bitter fruit of the seed sown in June 1974 at Elon Moreh.

The Rabin government did not survive its full term. Weakened by the internecine relationship between its two major figures, assailed constantly by Begin's opposition as deficient in national devotion, lacking a guiding and a sustaining vision, it lived out its three years from 1974 to 1977 in declining fortune. Toward the end of its career it had to compete with a new center party called the Democratic Movement for Change (DMC). This party had a moderate policy on Arab-Israeli relationships and a strong reformist impulse in domestic affairs. It was headed by the prestigious Professor Yigael Yadin, who had commanded Israel's forces in the war of independence and had won further fame as the scholar who developed the site of Masada.

Yadin's chief associate in his new political career as a party leader was Amnon Rubinstein, the head of the Tel Aviv University Law School. One by one, prominent members of the Labor Party, unwilling to participate in the savageries of the Rabin-Peres tension, abandoned the Labor Party. Rabin sent them on their way with a resigned greeting—"good riddance."

The decisive step in the erosion of the Rabin government's authority came in 1977 when he dismissed the National Religious Party ministers from his administration. A ceremony had been held at an air base on a late Friday afternoon to receive new American jet aircraft. Members of the National Religious Party abstained on a vote of confidence presented by the ultraorthodox Poalei Agudat Israel on the ground that the Sabbath had been violated. Rabin used his statutory powers to dismiss the religious ministers, effectively liquidating his own administration. I thought that it was legally correct but politically wrong to break up a coalition on an issue of conscience.

The result was to be momentous in Israel's domestic history. The radicalization of the National Religious Party, which had already begun, became dramatically intensified. The NRP not only withdrew its members as it was obliged to do; it also swore eternal vengeance against the Labor Party. For the past fifteen years it has been impossible to form an administration under Labor leadership except for the two years of the Peres premiership between 1986 and 1988; without a religious party there is no majority for a coalition led by Labor.

To these troubles were added accusations of corruption against the Labor Party. These were based principally on the attempt to appoint Asher Yadlin, the head of the Histadrut Sick Fund (Kupat Cholim), as governor of the Bank of Israel. This involved an investigatory process that might otherwise not have been necessary, revealing that Yadlin had appropriated public funds for party and, perhaps, for individual gain. The final blow was when Rabin himself resigned as prime minister as a result of the prosecution of his wife on a currency issue.

One day in May 1977, I sat in the upper room of the Labor headquarters in Tel Aviv with Golda Meir and others while the election results were announced. They were unprecedented. Begin's Likud Party swept to a landslide victory. Likud had won forty-three seats while the Labor Alignment fell from fifty-one to thirty-two. Never had such a tidal wave struck the entrenched social democratic majority. Fifteen years would pass until an arithmetically similar landslide brought Labor back to power in June 1992. Although Begin had emphasized his devotion to the principle of an undivided Land of Israel under Jewish rule, this had not been the brunt of his campaign. He, and especially his campaign manager, Ezer Weizmann, had observed the growing discontent of the Oriental Sephardic community, whose standards of life and representation in national leadership were below those of European immigrants and native Israelis. Thus, the dismissal of the Labor Party was paradoxically the result of a populist revolt. Begin's purple rhetoric, which had previously caused embarrassment and derision, appealed to the passionate mood of the disinherited part of our citizenry—those who wished to protest against what they regarded as the paternalistic and condescending attitudes of the European Jewish leadership.

The conventional view that the Labor leadership had neglected the Israeli immigrants from Oriental lands was largely unfair. The manner in which a population of 650,000 with meager resources had doubled itself in a few years and trebled itself within two decades reflected immense credit on the nation's founders. No child was without schooling, no citizen was without food and health care, and the population of the squalid ma'abarot soon moved to modest but weatherproof dwellings. Even the ma'abarot with their flimsy tents were a great achievement in objective terms, but those who had been sheltered by them against famine and social disaster recalled their ugliness and discomfort with a resentment that seemed to grow with time.

Israeli society had come to consist of "us and them"—those who had established relatively solid patterns of life during the pre-state years and those who had to meet scarcities head-on. The fact that there had been countless acts of social concern in the record of Labor governments did not mitigate the tensions. The new populations were humiliated by being the objects of benefaction. They aspired to equality. Status meant more than welfare.

Menachem Begin had no understanding of Sephardi culture, but he expressed the condition and mood of the Sephardi masses. He had been the outsider. He had lost seven electoral contests. Ben-Gurion would not even mention his name or stay in the Knesset to hear his speeches, and speeches were Begin's crowning glory. As recently as June 1974, I recall how discomfited Begin looked during President Nixon's state dinner in the Knesset building when protocol placed him at the head table nearer the end of the line than its center, while the lights moved restlessly from one Labor celebrity to another. During the 1973 election campaign, Labor propagandists published what most of us thought to be a successful commercial: It portrayed an ancient, run-down battered car with an "L" learner's plate on its rear fender and a caption: "Would you ride with a driver who had failed the driving test seven times?"

The public had said "yes"! It admired Begin's perseverance and felt that it would be inhuman for him to end his political life without even a taste of the bright lights, the resonant applause and a surrounding atmosphere of deference and command. He had an essentially histrionic sense of history. He saw Israel's career as a drama, dominated by tragedy, but illuminated by occasional moments of redemption in which he would appear center stage as the defiant champion of his people and the defender of its affronted dignity. He would totally dominate Israeli life for the next six years in a way that no one except Ben-Gurion had done before him, and no one yet has done since his resignation.

It was a moment of truth for the Labor Party, but truth is not always the welcome ally of political parties. Most Labor leaders saw the end of their rule as a violation of the natural political order. All of them, including Rabin and Peres, were now in opposition. In a strange way this enhanced my own position. I was no longer a dissident member of a government party, but one of the thirty-two Knesset members who were the standard-bearers of a defeated movement. I seemed better equipped than most of them to bear the deprivations of the political "wilderness."

It was Menachem Begin's hour. My own relations with the triumphant Likud leader had been ambiguous. I could not accept his view that Israel could permanently hold a hundred percent of the sovereignty and territory between the River Jordan and the Mediterranean Sea without explosive consequences. This would only become possible if the Palestinian people would one day be coerced or persuaded to accept a status without equal rights in Israel or a separate national identity outside it. But it was unrealistic to imagine that the Palestinians would accept this when world opinion was so emphatically in favor of their freedom from Israeli control.

No national movement has ever won anything like the universal international recognition ahead of statehood that the PLO has secured. This was one of the few tangible benefits that the PLO had obtained for the Palestinian cause. The very immensity of Arab resources beyond the Palestinian context elevated their pride. The Arabs were a minority in Israel but a crushing majority in the region, and it was the region, not the Israeli state, that defined their weight in the world balance. All the factors that had worked in favor of a separate status for the Jewish minority in 1947–1948 now cried out for some fulfillment of Palestinian rights in what remained of non-Israeli Palestine. The more pragmatic Palestinians were now confirmed partitionists.

Like most of my party colleagues, I was offended by Begin's insistence on describing the golden period of Israel's emergence to sovereignty as a record of failure. He was depriving the Israeli nation of its historic pride and dragging the generation of the Founding Fathers into the mire. On the other hand, his attitude to me was one of unremitting courtesy. Shortly after my return from the UN debate in 1967, Begin called on me in my Jerusalem residence. He came straight to the point. "I suggest to you, my friend, that you publicly join the supporters of the movement for a Jewish State with sovereignty in the whole area of Judea and Samaria." He added that he had read the *Ha'aretz* poll that proved that our UN victories had made me suddenly popular with an eighty percent rating. "You are the chosen of Israel," he said. He added that I could be the decisive element in changing the balance of Israeli opinion and power. I replied with some embarrassment that what he was suggesting was very imaginative, but inconceivable. I would lose all credibility if I took attitudes contrary to my well-known and real convictions. I simply did not believe that permanent Israeli rule over all the populations and territories in the West Bank and Gaza was either feasible or desirable. He greeted this answer with respect and without surprise, and after a courtly exchange of comments took his leave with the utmost courtesy.

Begin was impressed by what he regarded as some of my successes in the international arena. He was sensitive to form, and his public persona was based on a strange convergence of Polish aristocratic mannerisms with British parliamentary dignity. Despite his relentless fight against the British

Mandate in its declining days he, like his mentor, Zeev Jabotinsky, admired the stateliness with which the British nation conducted its affairs. He once stopped me in a corridor outside the Knesset committee room and said, "Did you notice the exceptionally cordial and warm tone with which Callaghan[2] worded his invitation to me to come to Chequers?" I did a little research and discovered that the British Foreign Office has been using a standard text for invitations since the reign of George IV. Begin got the same invitation as the president of Gambia.

Begin combined an unworldly innocence with a capacity for virulent cunning and intimidation. Since one could never predict his mood, I found every encounter with him to be an "occasion," never a routine. My personal relations with him were better than those that I "enjoyed" with some of my colleagues in the upper reaches of the Labor movement. One of the sources of his friendship toward me was that he knew no other Knesset member who could understand his Latin quotations. Instead of the truism that agreements ought to be kept, he would say sonorously, "Pacta sunt servanda," and cast a disdainful eye on the uncomprehending audience.

I was not surprised when Begin responded positively to a speech by Anwar Sadat in November 1977 in which the Egyptian leader offered to go to Jerusalem and address a peace appeal to the Knesset. Having watched Begin closely in the Knesset Committee on Foreign Affairs and Defense, I had no illusions about his motives. He believed that if he could neutralize Egypt and offer the Palestinians minor functions of administration, it would be easier for him to enforce rigid Israeli sovereignty over the whole area between the River Jordan and the Mediterranean Sea. From my point of view, therefore, Begin was about to do the right thing for the wrong reasons. He could be flexible in Sinai in order to be obdurate in the West Bank and Gaza. Yet I felt, mistakenly, as did many others, that his flexible policy toward Egypt might create a spontaneous dynamic for similar compromises in other sectors of the Arab-Israeli conflict. In any case, I thought that a peace between Israel and Egypt would be a momentous achievement if it were part of a comprehensive peace settlement, but that it would also be a considerable asset if it stood alone for some time.

Nevertheless, when I stood on the tarmac at Ben-Gurion Airport on November 19, 1977, and saw President Anwar Sadat, with his ministers and military officers, descend from an Egyptian aircraft to the sound of the Israeli national anthem, I turned to my neighbor in the line, Transportation Minister Gad Yaacobi, and said, "I don't believe what I am seeing." Yaacobi was mouthing the exact same words. Sadat passed down the line, shaking hands with his former enemies with an air of one who was surprised to discover that we were not little green men from another planet with antennas sprouting

---

[2]James Callaghan, the British prime minister from 1976 to 1979.

from our ears. When he shook my hand he said, "You look just like you do on television!" This did not strike me as an aphorism of great potential resonance; it seemed to illustrate the difficulty of starting a dialogue after years of unnecessary separation.

Israelis would not have been surprised on Yom Kippur 1973 if they had not deluded themselves with the belief that the 1967 map described a stable condition. Even those of us who believed that our military occupation was fragile and explosive had no inkling of the circumstances in which it would collapse. Since Sadat himself did not know all the details of his subsequent actions, there was no shame in our ignorance of his exact plan. But there was a legitimate intellectual division between Israeli leaders who fell for the absurd glamour of the "King Solomon" map, and those who were convinced that the military results of the 1967 war could not endure without grief, loss and danger. In that respect I was on one side of the barrier between truth and illusion, and the Likud leaders were on the other, more heavily populated, side.

I did not expect that the drama of Sadat's visit would lead to a swift conclusion of a peace treaty with Egypt. But I was convinced that once Begin and Sadat had agreed on the principle of trading Sinai for peace, the treaty was only a matter of short time. There was great value in the work of Dayan, Weizmann, Attorney General Aharon Barak, U.S. Secretary of State Cyrus Vance and others who drafted formulas that lay halfway between substantive clarity and face-saving obscurity. But the irreversible breakthrough resulted from the decisions of the heads of state, not from the formulatory skills of the draftsmen. There is inaccuracy as well as injustice in partisan attempts to ascribe the major success of the Egyptian treaty to Dayan and Weizmann. If Dayan had wanted to put through a program based on exchanging Sinai for peace, he could have done so from his position of strength in the Labor Party, which had already espoused that principle through the Eshkol government in June 1967. This would have prevented the Yom Kippur War.

Ezer Weizmann, while justly proud of his own role at Camp David, has never denied Begin's decisive part in the revolutionary breakthrough. The resignations of Dayan and Weizmann from the Begin government in 1983 were motivated by their understanding that Begin's flexibility in Sinai was going to be counteracted by his retreat from the Camp David accords, which had envisaged a predominantly Arab destiny for the West Bank and Gaza.

Before 1973, Anwar Sadat had never been regarded as a statesman capable of large decisions in the mold of Nasser. His election to the presidency had been greeted with skeptical derision in Egypt and the world. He had held none but representational and protocolar positions with the revolutionary regime over which Nasser had presided as the directing spirit. Yet within a few years Anwar Sadat was to shake the Middle East out of its inertia with two decisions of staggering audacity. They were: to attack Israel on October 6, 1973, despite Israel's well-known military superiority; and to go all out thereafter for a peace treaty instead of playing with another round of "interim agreements."

Sadat's decision for military action in October 1973 refuted the conventional assumption that no state knowingly starts a war unless it has a strong belief in its own victory. Sadat began a war that he knew he could not win, in the knowledge that the war itself would serve his design, irrespective of its result. The October war would unfreeze a deadlock that worked solely in Israel's favor. It would compel the superpowers to address themselves to the Arab-Israeli situation toward which Nixon and Brezhnev were evincing total apathy as late as in the summer of 1972.

Sadat's second revolutionary decision was to recognize that the Arabs would get nothing from Israel by war and that Egyptian and Arab ambitions could be largely fulfilled in peace accords. The disengagement agreement of 1974 and the Sinai Two agreement of September 1975 were stages in a carefully graduated approach. Sadat was reading the Israeli attitude to Egypt correctly and the Likud attitude to the Palestinian issue incorrectly. He thought that he could get more out of Begin than he had obtained in the 1979 treaty on Sinai. In any case, he did not attach anything like equal importance to the two parts of the Camp David accords: He was, first and foremost, an Egyptian nationalist passionately resolved to recover his territory. All that he promised the Palestinians was to do his best to support their cause, for which the Egyptian people had already spent a vast amount of its blood and treasure. He opened new doors wide for them but could not force them to enter.

Both as a spectacle and as a political event, Sadat's astonishing voyage to Jerusalem and his address to the Knesset stand out as one of the climactic experiences of this generation. It was immediately clear that the Middle East was set on a new course and that nothing in the region would ever be the same again.

The Arab and Israeli nations had both been paralyzed by the weight of their historic experience. Our two nations give great reverence to the past; we are saturated with history. But our past is the enemy of our future. There is nothing in the images that the Arabs derive from their past that prepares them for the idea of a Jewish sovereign state in what they call "the Arab region." For them, the Middle East is a monolith of a single Arab color, so anything in it that is not Arab or Muslim reflects itself in Arab minds as artificial, transient and disruptive of regional continuity. Jews appear in Arab history as subjects of Muslim societies, members of a heretic faith, doctors, scholars, advisers, merchants—but never as the bearers of an independent political and territorial identity. The intellectual torment of Arabs in coming to terms with Israeli statehood is authentic and should not be taken lightly.

For Israelis, on the other hand, the Middle East is a tapestry of many colors of which the salient thread was woven by Jewish experience centuries ago. The idea that Israel is alien to the Middle East is not something that people of Jewish consciousness can absorb, even as an eccentric and deviant illusion. The encounters between Egypt and Israel in history have been memorable for mankind. Most of them have been encounters in conflict to which Israelis are endemically inured.

Sadat's immense achievement was to make a simultaneous breach in the walls of Arab rejection and Israeli suspicion. For the first time the Arab world was presented by one of its leaders with a vision of the Middle East that did include the sovereign state of Israel. The rhetoric and literature of rejection would live on in parts of the Arab world, but in November 1977 it lost its dogmatic force and could no longer claim to be the only normative Arab doctrine.

On the same day, Israelis came to look on peace not as a utopian fantasy, but as a concrete and vivid reality. The Israeli consensus about the indispensability of large territorial gains had already been weakened by the failure of Sinai to give us any real security on Yom Kippur or in the war of attrition. Once Sadat offered peace, demilitarization and stringent monitoring, the Israeli center immediately adjusted its attitudes. Sadat was the first to put a peace prospect to a test, and his reward was immediate and dramatic. Israel made territorial changes that nobody would have previously imagined, and these have turned out to be advantageous. Sadat also offered the Palestinians an avenue of escape from deadlock. If the PLO had accepted the Camp David formulas the Palestinians would now be celebrating the fourteenth anniversary of their independence, either as a mini-state or as a state in a confederation with Jordan.

Israeli leaders had been misled by some of our own orientalists who had made an academic discipline out of analyzing Arab war speeches to prove the "never, never" theory about the alleged impossibility of peace between Arabs and Israelis. They had assumed that Arab propaganda was an authentic expression of irreversible emotions. My own view is that governments first decide on their interests and then seek the vocabulary most congenial to their policies. I found a parallel with Churchill, whose war speeches had expressed an almost chemical hatred of Germans, whom he would call "Boche" and "Huns" as if to exclude them from human society. Yet a short time after the war, the great man was making speeches all over continental Europe in support of a united Europe in which a postwar Germany would be the central participant. Americans were undergoing a similar transformation of their attitude to Japan.

The notion that Arab culture is unable to absorb the reality of Jewish statehood has been inculcated in Israeli minds through decades of brainwashing. It is true that the Koran offers no encouragement to the seekers after Muslim-Jewish cooperation, but there is a ferocious strain of anti-Gentile passion in traditional Jewish writings as well, and Joshua's conquests did not observe the restraints of the Geneva Convention. I have never detected much Koranic influence in the makeup of the elites who control the policies of our immediate neighbors.

Another lesson to emerge decisively from the Camp David experience in 1978–1979 was that pre-negotiation rhetoric often loses its sharpness under the transforming effects of negotiation. A deathblow was dealt to the theory of irreconcilability according to which the dispute between Arabs and Israelis, unlike all others, is permanent, implacable and inherently insoluble. In the Arab world this theory had become axiomatic, and in Israel it had been elevated into an academic discipline that made deep inroads on the nation's mood.

The refusal of other Arab leaders to follow Sadat's journey and to reap similar fruits is one of the mysteries of the years that followed the Egyptian-Israeli peace treaty. Jordan, whose monarch had been the first Arab leader to understand the permanence of Israel's existence, paradoxically launched a campaign of criticism against Sadat for having followed his own example. Much of this acrimony was due to a diplomatic error; Carter and Sadat had drawn up a blueprint for the West Bank and Gaza involving detailed provisions for Jordan's participation without doing enough to ensure Jordan's presence. The United States underestimated the factors of pride and sensitivity that govern the reactions of Middle Eastern leaders.

The opposition of Jordan and the PLO to the Camp David agreement was especially ironic, since it gave the impression that Sadat had secured Egyptian interests while abandoning the Palestinian cause. Any objective reading of the Palestinian section of the Camp David agreement would refute this impression. Sadat had obtained the adherence of Menachem Begin to formulations that constituted a breakthrough similar to the Balfour Declaration in Jewish history. The Camp David agreement treats the West Bank and Gaza as an area of indeterminate status. It goes on to make clear that the status of those territories may not be determined unilaterally by Israel alone but only by agreement between Egypt, Israel, Jordan and the elected representatives of the inhabitants of the areas. It would be difficult to conceive of a body composed of four members, three of them Arabs, deciding to incorporate the Arab-populated areas of the West Bank into Israel. In the case of such an unlikely event, the agreement stipulates that any accord would have to be endorsed in a plebiscite among the Palestinians in the West Bank and Gaza. The agreement lays down that the permanent solution of the problem of the West Bank and Gaza will have to satisfy the "legitimate rights of the Palestinian people and their just requirements." Pending the negotiation of the permanent status of the West Bank and Gaza, there is to be a transition period of three to five years, during which "the elected representatives of the inhabitants of the West Bank and Gaza shall decide how they shall govern themselves, consistent with the provisions of the agreement." There must also be a "withdrawal of the Israeli military administration" and a "withdrawal of Israeli armed forces . . . and their redeployment into specified security zones."

Not one of the statements and provisions quoted above could possibly have been written about the sovereign territory of Israel, as defined in Knesset resolutions. The non-Israeli status of the West Bank and Gaza cries aloud from every salient formulation in the Camp David agreement. Henry Kissinger, in an interview with the London *Economist,* wrote that in accordance with the dictionary meaning of words, Begin was proposing what would inevitably develop into the embryo of a Palestine state that would be recognized as such by all the nations of the world except Israel. Kissinger wrote: "Begin's proposal (Camp David) is incompatible with his strategy." My own opinion was that anyone who wanted an undivided Land of Israel under exclusive Israeli rule should not have signed the Camp David accord at all.

My own observation that the Palestinians have never lost a chance of missing an opportunity chalked up an additional "success" when the PLO and Jordan rejected the Camp David accords.

The Egyptian treaty has been presented, absurdly, as a victory for direct, bilateral negotiation. It was nothing of the kind. The necessity of encounter between the contracting parties at the same table was accepted, but without mediatory assistance, they would have gone on indefinitely glaring at each other and reciting their respective unilateral ambitions. Direct, bilateral negotiation collapsed at Ismailiya on December 25, 1977, when Sadat and Begin parted after two days during which they demonstrated their total incompatibility with each other. Eight months elapsed without meetings involving the heads of state. U.S. Secretary of State Cyrus Vance and his deputy, Ambassador Atherton, shuttled vainly between the Middle Eastern capitals. Sadat and Begin then gratefully accepted the invitation of President Carter, who fixed the time, the place, the agenda, the procedure and the media policy and eventually drafted the compromise paragraphs. It is a law of negotiation that each party can accept a compromise from a third party that it could never accept from its adversary or initiate itself.

In a discussion in which sanity had even a marginal status it would be hard to see the Camp David proposal as anything but a Palestinian Charter. Yet it was rejected vehemently by the Palestinian organizations and by most Arab states, opposed by the Soviet Union, ignored by the United Nations and received coolly by the European governments. Instead of being hailed for creating new opportunities for Palestinian nationalism, Sadat was reviled by Arab propaganda and eventually assassinated by Muslim fundamentalists. The European skepticism toward Camp David was inspired by a strange narrowness of spirit; it was pointed out that the treaty concluded between Egypt and Israel was not a "comprehensive settlement" embracing the entire region. This came ill from a Europe in which a new peace and security system was negotiated over three decades with separate treaties involving Germany, Italy, Poland and the East European states, as well as Finland and the Soviet Union. Comprehensiveness in the attainment of regional settlements has no European history.

An Israeli treaty with one Arab state is preferable to a treaty with no Arab states. To make unanimity a condition of progress would be tantamount to giving a veto power to the most obdurate party and the most intransigent issue. If we all have to wait until all the twenty-two Arab states and the Palestinians are ready to move forward together on the Israeli issue, it will be necessary to suspend all action until President Qaddafi of Libya experiences a unique spasm of lucidity.

I lobbied intensively for the Egyptian-Israeli treaty and the framework agreement on the future of the West Bank and Gaza. My articles appeared in *Foreign Affairs* and *Foreign Policy* magazines and in most of the major newspapers over the world. I derived encouragement from the fact that the international media were accessible to me. I began to develop charitable thoughts toward those who had excluded me from Cabinet office.

The sudden accessibility of Egypt had important personal results for me. I had felt psychologically deprived when the Arab world was closed to me. I felt more capable than many Israelis to achieve a degree of understanding with Arab leaders and intellectuals. I also feared that the physical remoteness of Israelis from Arab lands and scenes contributed to the ideologies of irreversible antagonism. A situation in which it was more feasible for me to visit Japan or New Zealand than to make an hour's flight to neighboring Cairo seemed grossly artificial.

My resumption of contact with the neighboring world arose through a chance conversation between Menachem Begin and Suzy. On our way back home from a visit to the United States we stopped over in London because of a snowstorm that had kept planes grounded. The plane that we joined at the London airport was carrying Begin back from an official journey to Washington. Shortly before we were due to land at Ben-Gurion Airport, Begin entered the part of the aircraft in which Suzy and I were sitting and told me with evident satisfaction that he had conversed with the British prime minister, James Callaghan, who had expressed approval of Begin's autonomy plan.

I felt awkward, since the nature of the conversation decreed that he was standing and holding on to the ledge of the baggage compartment while I was seated. Begin even banged his head lightly on the baggage shelf and courteously said to Suzy, "As you see—for you I would even lose my head." Traditional gallantry of this kind was ascribed by biographers to the habits of Polish gentlemen. Begin then turned to Suzy and asked her to join his party on the journey that he planned to make to Ismailiya later in the week for a historic meeting with Anwar Sadat.

"I hear that you were born in Ismailiya," he said. "How is it possible for Jews to be born in Ismailiya?" Suzy explained that procedures leading to birth are practiced with regularity in the Nile Delta, no less than in America and Europe.

A few days later, Begin carried out his promise and Suzy landed in the city of her birth on December 24, 1977. She participated in a luncheon hosted by Sadat and attended by only a dozen Israeli and Egyptian leaders. She visited the house of her childhood, which she found in ruins, but her Egyptian hosts could hardly be reproached for this distressing sight, since the damage had been inflicted by the Israeli Air Force. A short time thereafter, Suzy's description of the Ismailiya meeting was appreciatively accepted for publication in *The New Yorker* magazine.

I made full personal use of the free access to Egypt that was one of the advantages of the peace treaty. I visited Cairo once with Prime Minister Begin, who, in a gesture of bipartisanship, included me in the Israeli delegation to Cairo a few days after the signature of the Egyptian-Israeli treaty in Washington. I went to Cairo twice with Peres and Barlev as a member of the Labor Party's delegations, and once in the declining days of Peres's premiership in 1986 when he was received by President Mubarak in Alexandria. I also went alone to Cairo twice to deliver lectures to the Egyptian "diplomatic center" where candidates for the foreign service are trained. I was impressed by their literacy and competence.

There were enough enemies of the peace treaty in Cairo and Alexandria to make free movement in the capital impractical, and my colleagues and I were for the most part confined to contacts with our official hosts and the residents of the hotels where we stayed. Nevertheless, there was a liberating feeling tinged with nostalgia in the experience of opening a window on the Nile, gazing at the bridges, driving along the Cairo streets with their kaleidoscopic tumult of ancient automobiles, donkeys and Egyptian crowds. Even the ability to read *Al Ahram* at my breakfast table took me back to the recollections of 1942.

I did not regard the Egyptian-Israeli peace as a cold peace. In the context of Egypt's position in the Arab world I thought that Sadat and, later, Mubarak showed unexpected courage. The planes landed, the oil flowed, statesmen and officials exchanged visits, Israeli tourists flocked to the bazaars of Cairo and the Israeli flag was aloft our Cairo embassy, challenging other African and Arab capitals to emulation. Beyond these fundamentals there was still a great wall of Egyptian reserve, but on the larger issues, I was astonished by the tenacity with which Egyptian leaders resisted Arab sentiment in Egypt and the neighboring region. If anyone had previously told me that Egypt would maintain its basic treaty obligations toward Israel while the Begin government sought military confrontation against Lebanon, Syria, Iraq and the Palestinian bases and carried its intimidating power as far as Tunis, Beirut and Baghdad, I would have dismissed this as a pipe dream.

In Egyptian policy the treaty with Israel proved stronger than Arab solidarity. Israel's renunciation of Sinai was a "painful concession" at the time but it later turned out to be a godsend. It vastly increased Israel's logistic security. How could our occupation of Sinai be called a "security asset" when it cost the lives of three thousand Israeli soldiers and made the eruption of war inevitable? With the Egyptian threat removed from Israel's South, Israel's forces were automatically doubled and trebled in the overall regional balance. Israel's gain in security was even greater than its gain in peace. The Likud government had a free hand for building new settlements in the West Bank and Gaza and could wield its military power all over the Middle East, with American vetoes protecting it against serious international rebuke. Sadat had virtually given Begin a separate peace.

There was no equality of sacrifice between the signatories of the Camp David agreements. Sadat was riddled with bullets in a Cairo boulevard, while Begin proudly went alone to Oslo for his Nobel prize. Since his breakthrough in 1977, his fortunes had changed as dramatically as his moods. From the outer darkness or an opposition role, he had sprung into the center of the world arena. He was enjoying himself prodigiously.

In 1980 the United States under Ronald Reagan made anti-Sovietism the heart and center of American policy. This meant that Israel's new rulers, as steadfast devotees of the Cold War, would have a relatively clear international field. An American Establishment that no longer tormented itself with discomfort about occupations, administrative detentions, apartheid, "wars of choice" and other moral subtleties would give militant Cold War governments their place and time in the sun. By the end of the eighties an Israeli strategy built on the myth of permanent Soviet threat and permanent Palestinian extremism would look frayed and obsolete. But for a few joyous years, the Reagan administration in the United States and the Likud-led government in Israel could base their alliance less on pioneering memories and democratic values and more on the new hardheaded notion of "strategic cooperation." The Soviet Union and the PLO "cooperated" in this change of emphasis from values to interests—the Soviets by maintaining their strategic threat and the Palestinians by preferring rhetoric and ideology to the more prosaic language of realism.

Sharon had seen nothing unseemly in describing Israel as a gigantic aircraft carrier available to the free world for combat against Soviet penetration. Begin asserted that the United States gained more from its alliance with Israel than did Israel from its relationship with the United States. I thought that this was excessively self-righteous. I suggested an intellectual exercise: Imagine that some natural disaster were to cut America and Israel off from contact with each other; there would be no telephones or postal services, no commerce or tourism, no monetary transactions between the two countries.

Who would notice it first?

In Knesset debates in the late seventies, Yitzhak Rabin and I were reserved in our comments on the strategic emphasis in American-Israeli relations. Our case was that cooperation between the two defense systems could be implemented without strident Cold War rhetoric; and that the enduring basis of the American-Israeli friendship was the system of values that had brought our two countries together in Israel's youthful years.

A full decade would pass before this calm logic would prevail. The 1980s would be the last lease on life for the international system that had endured with every sign of permanence since 1945.

29

TUMULTUOUS DECADE:
THE 1980S

AFTER THE CELEBRATIONS of the peace treaty, including the award of the Nobel Peace Prize to Menahem Begin and Anwar Sadat, I had a feeling of discomfort. My interpretation of Begin's motive in concluding the Egyptian treaty restrained my exuberance. Begin's interpretation made it quite clear that he was not supporting the principle of "territories for peace," which is the central theme of UN Security Council Resolution 242. He was not exchanging territory for peace. He was exchanging Sinai for absolute Israeli rule over the territories and populations of the West Bank and Gaza.

His logic was simple: With Egypt's military strength neutralized by the peace treaty, Begin would be free to initiate operations against Syria, Iraq or the Palestinians in their Lebanese bases. Anwar Sadat inadvertently became a convenient element in the success of Begin's design. Sadat often repeated that he would not approve a "separate peace": He sincerely wished to embrace the Palestinians in a new regional order. But in fact he was thinking of Egyptian interests alone. His devotion to the Palestinian cause was perfunctory and unconvincing. In all the journeys in which I accompanied Peres to Egypt, Sadat always reacted with irritation to our mention of King Hussein of Jordan as an essential partner to any peace settlement. For a few months after signing the treaty he continued to send his representatives to discussions with Israel on Palestinian "self government" and "full autonomy," but Egypt showed little interest in the West Bank and Gaza. Egyptian ambassadors in Israel avoided involvement in the areas under Israeli military rule.

In 1979–1980 the negotiations on autonomy between Israeli and Egyptian missions became farcical. Egypt interpreted the Camp David accords as an interim arrangement that would eventually lead to Palestinian statehood. The language of Camp David gave strong support to this idea. Begin's assumption was that the Palestinians would exercise a few minor administrative functions while the real sovereignty and power, with all their emblems and prerogatives, would remain in Israel's hands. Security, regional defense, foreign policy, land, water and the custodianship of abandoned property would all be reserved for the Israeli rulers while the Palestinians, as the "lesser breed without the law," would have neither equal rights in the Israeli parliamentary system nor a separate national identity no matter what the Camp David agreement said. Since the signing of the Camp David accords, no member of a Likud government has ever quoted the Camp David provisions about "the legitimate rights and just requirements of the Palestine people." The autonomous body proposed by the Israeli delegates in the negotiation with Egypt was defined in such a way as to exclude any right of legislation or enactment.

Ambassador Sol Linowitz, the eminent architect of the Panama Canal Treaty, had been appointed by President Carter to represent the United States in the autonomy talks. He consoled himself by enumerating the large number of departments that would be subject to the autonomous Palestinian body. The truth is that the "few" powers reserved to Israel amounted to unreserved sovereignty. The Israeli delegations appointed by Begin rejected the idea of Palestinian elections and insisted on freedom to establish new Israeli settlements in the areas which the Camp David agreement designated for Palestinian "self-government." The independent powers allotted to the Palestinians in the autonomy talks were less than those that the American colonists had rejected as inadequate in the eighteenth century and that the Israelis in 1948 had regarded as meaningless when offered by the British.

The "danger" from Begin's viewpoint was that Dayan and Weizmann would take self-government seriously and agree to transfer real power from the Israeli administration to a Palestinian administrative body. To preempt this danger, Begin appointed Interior Minister Yosef Burg, to head the committee negotiating the autonomy proposal. He achieved a double aim. By designating the minister of the interior for this purpose, he was hinting that the West Bank and Gaza were a permanent part of Israel's domestic jurisdiction and not a subject of foreign policy. And since Dr. Burg was unlikely to suggest anything original or daring, the maintenance of the negotiation in his hands would ensure deadlock. In 1982, when Moshe Dayan, and eventually Ezer Weizmann, understood that they would have no role in the implementation of the Camp David agreement, they resigned at intervals of a few months. They passionately denounced Begin for what they called his obstructive interpretation of the Camp David accords. Dayan accused Begin of "oppressing" the Palestinians.

The Palestinian leaders, acting as usual against their own interests, created their own deadlock. They attempted to shorten what was envisaged as the interim period and to drive straight for Palestinian statehood. This negated the central purpose of the Camp David agreement, which was to avoid a premature determination of final status. The PLO professed to ignore the fact that even the most moderate Israelis would require them to prove their readiness for coexistence. This was the minimal price that the Palestinians would have to pay for their virulent rhetoric and terrorist assaults over more than thirty years.

The Jerusalem municipality, under the imaginative direction of Teddy Kollek, was more disposed than the Israeli governments to accord substantive administrative powers to the Palestinian inhabitants of the city. But the Palestinians weakened Kollek by refusing to take part even in municipal elections.

In July 1980 Jerusalem became the focus of the regional tension when the right-wing parties, led by Geula Cohen of the Techiya party, secured the adoption of a Knesset resolution establishing the indivisibility of Jerusalem under Israeli rule. This was a superfluous measure, since it added nothing to the enactments already made by the Knesset in June and July 1967. The Labor Party, in obsequious response to the Likud camp, decided to support Cohen's measure. I absented myself from the meeting in order to avoid supporting the provocative legislation. Nobody was doing anything to limit Israel's total freedom to govern both Jerusalem and the Golan Heights. Letting well alone would have been the ideal solution, but the Israeli Right was not built temperamentally for gradualism.

It was a painful issue for me, since I had traveled to Latin America several times to persuade Nicaragua, Guatemala, Costa Rica and the Dominican Republic to establish their embassies in Jerusalem. When the Knesset adopted a new annexationist resolution on July 30, 1980, all these governments, together with that of the Netherlands, which had never moved from Jerusalem, dismantled their embassies and took their flags to Tel Aviv. The absence of embassies weakened Jerusalem's character as an international capital. Other results were a strong expression of American displeasure and an impulsive decision by Sadat to suspend the autonomy talks for what turned out to be an indefinite period.

To Sadat's embarrassment the position of the Palestinians in the West Bank and Gaza became progressively worse after Camp David. In efforts to suppress Palestinian demonstrations, detention centers were established in Israel, which it became my duty to visit in my capacity as chairman of the Knesset Committee on Foreign Affairs and Defense. Thousands of detainees were arrested without due process and without formal accusation. Many of them were teenagers. A subsequent report by a committee headed by Justice Landau, a former president of the Supreme Court, stated that the security authorities "normatively" subjected detainees to the extraction of false confessions by what was euphemistically called "moderate physical pressure." The spectacle of the grim detention centers strengthened my conviction that ruling the Palestine nation would have a corrosive effect on Israeli life without solving the Palestinian problem. There were only two democratic options: Either the Palestinians must be integrated into a united Israel with the right to exercise their full weight within the Israeli parliamentary system; or they must be allowed to express their separate national identity as a mini-state or as part of a confederation with Jordan. If they were destined to be ruled permanently by Israel without enjoying civic equality or separate political status, our democracy would be eroded and we would be condemned to the task of suppressing a permanent national revolt.

Against all the evidence of the text, Begin continued to interpret the Camp David agreement as if it were compatible with Israel's retention of all the territories in the West Bank and Gaza. This was a misrepresentation of what he had signed. The Camp David accord in fact is the most renunciatory document that any Jewish leader has ever signed in relation to any part of the Land of Israel. It treats "the West Bank and Gaza" as an area of indeterminate status unconnected to the sovereign territory of Israel. The permanent status of these territories is to be decided, not by Israel alone, but by an agreement involving Israel, Egypt, Jordan and the residents of the West Bank and Gaza. Israel is to be outnumbered by three to one in the decision-making body. Israel's military and civil administration are to be "withdrawn and replaced" by a Palestinian authority. The elected representatives of the Palestine people are to "decide how to govern themselves." The agreement must satisfy the "legitimate rights of the Palestinians and their just demands." Nothing is said about Israel's legitimate rights or just demands. There is even a provision according to which the Palestinian residents could override a decision of Israel, Egypt, Jordan and the representatives of the Palestinians in the four-power decision-making body. The Camp David agreement is more favorable to the Palestinian nation than the Balfour Declaration was to the idea of a Jewish National Home. Yet Begin's hypnotic authority in his own camp was so absolute that he could present it as a victory for the Greater Israel movement. He "interpreted" the agreement as if President Carter and President Sadat had become adherents of the Likud manifesto.

The sincere devotees of an undivided Land of Israel under Israeli rule were not deceived. They seceded from the Likud and formed the Techiya party, denouncing the Camp David agreement as the forerunner of a Palestinian state. One of the Techiya leaders, Shmuel Katz, published a crushingly convincing article proving that the Camp David agreement was a prescription for renouncing the West Bank and Gaza, not for retaining it. No less an authority on the interpretation of diplomatic documents than Henry Kissinger cogently pointed out that if language was given its normal implication, Begin had virtually signed the West Bank and Gaza away. He wrote:

Paradoxically the Begin government, against its preferences and ideology, was really proposing what all other nations were certain to read as an embryo Palestinian state and, to compound the irony, within the 1967 border since none other was under discussion. Once there was an elected, self governing authority on the West Bank, an irreversible political fact would be created on the territory over which its authority was supposed to run. However limited this authority it would soon turn into the nucleus of something like a Palestinian state, probably under PLO control. It would be so treated by almost all of the countries of the world, except Israel.

Kissinger went on to summarize:

The Israeli government's proposal was incompatible with its strategy. The only way the Israeli government could avoid the implications of its own proposal was to deprive the word autonomy of its dictionary meaning, for example, by elaborating a distinction between autonomy of persons and autonomy of land. Deadlock between Egypt and Israel, and later tensions between the United States and Israel, were thus built into the definition of the problem.

Kissinger concluded:

So long as some form of Israeli sovereignty over the entire West Bank was the objective, the autonomy negotiations could not be brought to a conclusion acceptable to all parties. A point would have been reached at which either the United States would have had to put forward its own definition of autonomy or there would have been a blow-up of the negotiations.[1]

Menachem Begin received his Nobel Prize just in time. Within less than two years of Anwar Sadat's triumphal visit to Jerusalem, the parts of the Camp David accord that dealt with the Palestinian problem were collapsing, with Moshe Dayan and Ezer Weizmann, Israeli war heroes, ascribing the main fault to Begin rather than to their Palestinian interlocutors. This was true, but not the whole truth. If the Palestinians had taken the text of the Camp David agreement at its face value and had called persistently for its meticulous implementation, Begin's semantic acrobatics might have failed. As it was, the best that Dayan and Weizmann could achieve was to prove that Begin was defaulting on an international agreement, which the Palestinians themselves had also refused to accept.

The democratic principle would allow only two alternative solutions to the Palestinian problem. One way would be to apply the doctrine of "territories for peace" in strict accordance with UN Security Council Resolution 242. This would mean a territorial compromise on the Golan Heights and an agreed division of sovereignty in the West Bank and Gaza, with the bulk of the Arab-populated territories passing into Palestinian hands. The other way

---

[1]Henry A. Kissinger, *Observations* (London: Weidenfeld, 1984), p. 94.

would be to regard the Camp David agreement against its own letter and spirit as an opportunity for a dynamic military policy for Israel, with the comforting assurance that Egyptian power had been neutralized. Today, thirteen years after the Camp David accords, it is clear that the second line of policy has triumphed.

Prime Minister Yitzhak Shamir, who opposed the Camp David agreement and the peace treaty with Egypt in 1978–1979, has now stated that he is no longer committed even to "all the provisions" of the Camp David accords. Menachem Begin's semantic legacy does not commit his successors. The Camp David agreement became a prescription for peace in one sector and embittered confrontation in others.

Many Israelis were even dissatisfied with the limited nature of cooperation between Egypt and Israel after the conclusion of the peace treaty. A more sanguine view was expressed by Ezer Weizmann and by me. We noted that, in spite of tensions and reservations, "the trains run, the oil flows, the aircraft land, the newspapers and publications of Israel and Egypt reach readers in each other's countries and Israel's flag flies in an embassy in the capital of the most important Arab state." We pointed out that the ideological breakthrough implied in this condition was well worth all the concessions that Begin had made in Sinai.

But Israel gained more from the Egyptian treaty in terms of security than in terms of recognition and legitimacy. Begin had skillfully made peace without reducing security. Together with the peace agreement went a prodigious reinforcement of our logistical defense. In three decades between 1956 and 1982 we had lost 3,000 of our young men in capturing, defending and restoring Israeli rule in Sinai. From 1982 onward, with Sinai under Egyptian rule, our losses of human life were zero.

With Sinai under Israeli rule, war was always inevitable: The only open question was when it would actually erupt. On the other hand, with Sinai under Egyptian rule and with effective American monitoring, the outbreak of war between Israel and Egypt was and is almost inconceivable.

I have often asked myself what the American people would think if 180,-000 American soldiers had been killed in an effort to retain possession of a territory that the United States had no intention or capacity to hold. If a diplomatic way had been found to release itself from this nightmare, would the United States really believe that it had made "a painful concession"?

The unpleasant truth is that the Egyptian-Israeli treaty undoubtedly facilitated the Israeli war in Lebanon and strengthened the capacity of Likud administrations to do exactly what they liked with the Palestinian population in the occupied territories. Even the bombing of the Iraqi nuclear reactor in June 1981, which nobody should now regret, would not have been possible if the threat to Israel from Egypt had not been neutralized. By the summer of 1981 it must have been evident to Sadat that Begin, with his electoral mandate narrowly renewed, would be able to prevent any significant self-government for the Palestinians. On October 6, 1981, the anniversary of what the Egyptians called "the October victory," Anwar Sadat was assassinated while reviewing what he had ironically called "a victory parade" in Cairo.

It is an extraordinary tribute to Begin's dominance in domestic politics that he was able to carry out an audacious policy at home and abroad with a parliamentary majority of one. This was because of his success in winning the allegiance and support of the religious parties. Rabin's decision in 1977 to cut the link between the Labor Party and religious Zionism recoiled upon the Labor Party with boomerang effect. Begin was not a fully observant Jew, but his frequent use of biblical imprecations, his obsessive reiteration of "please God" and "thank God" slogans, the dexterity of wrist with which he would put a skullcap on and off his head, in and out of occasion, all created an image of contrast with the more austere secularism of the Labor movement.

One effect of the alliance between Likud and religious Zionism was the placing of the entire Israeli education system under the control of the National Religious Party. During my tenure at that ministry, I noted that thirty percent of the Israeli schools had been effectively removed by my predecessors from ministerial jurisdiction and were administered by party bosses at NRP headquarters. Now even the nonreligious majority in the educational system had come under a strange mixture of egocentric nationalism and orthodox religious ideology. Religious Zionism has a stronger position in the education system than in the Knesset.

The structure and texture of Israel underwent a sharp change during the 1980s. The effect has been to create a society in the West Bank and Gaza based on the principle of ethnic separation. As president of the "International Center for Peace in the Middle East," I joined in drafting a memorandum, in 1981, of which the key sentence was:

> Two legal systems have been created for the two nations living in these territories: One system is intended for the Palestinian residents of the area and the second for Israelis.

In the West Bank and Gaza a Jewish settler is protected by stringent democratic safeguards. He cannot be expelled from the country in any circumstances. His house cannot be blown up on the grounds that his father, uncle or cousin is suspected of crime. He cannot be arrested without warrant or detained without accusation. He cannot be ordered to climb up a telegraph pole to bring down a flag, planted there by somebody else, with danger of electrocution. He cannot be placed under curfews for dozens of days or weeks every year. His right to demonstrate peacefully against an unwanted political situation is unconditional.

Arabs in those territories have none of these rights and immunities. They are under a jurisdiction that serves the rulers and not the ruled. Their condition recalls the famous Greek dialogue in which the Athenians described their own rule over a conquered nation: "The strong impose what they can and the weak suffer what they must."

The Palestinian population is not even allowed to develop a free economy. It may not manufacture anything that might compete with Israeli industry. Arab workers from the territories do not have the right to stay overnight and their wages are far below the Jewish levels. There is mutual utility in the flow of workers each day from the territories into Israel, but there is no dividend of pride or satisfaction.

Gravest of all for the Arabs is the self-confidence that enables Gush Emunim and its allies to challenge the Israeli legal system. Religious zealots, fired with fundamentalist zeal, have taken it upon themselves to maim and cripple the mayors of Arab cities; to place bombs on buses destined to carry West Bank Arabs about their business to and from Israel; and even to plan the destruction of the Muslim holy places with the certainty that punishment would either not be meted out at all, or would be abbreviated by procedures of legal pardon. A historian has written of the 1980s:

No one claims that the nation's existence was yet in peril; its character as a viable democracy, on the other hand, unquestionably was approaching the threshold of its acutest vulnerability.[2]

Israel has advanced into its fifth decade with an immense accretion of material power, but in deep confusion about its structure and values.

There is also the hard legacy of the Lebanese War.

For me that war began on May 8, 1982, when Shimon Peres, our party chairman, convened a meeting of a dozen party leaders in his Tel Aviv office. Peres reported on a plan conceived by Defense Minister Arik Sharon for a massive military operation in Lebanon to be carried out in stages. The plan was designed to "change the map of power and authority in the Middle East by creating a new political order."

The operation would have five aims:

First: to remove all the PLO bases and headquarters to points more than twenty-five miles from the Israeli-Lebanese international boundary.

Second: to eliminate all Palestinian presence and influence from Lebanon.

---

[2]Sachar, *ibid.,* p. 165.

Third: to secure the expulsion of Syrian troops from Lebanon.

Fourth: to establish a Lebanese-Christian Maronite government that would, in effect, be an Israeli protectorate responsive to Israeli interests and policies.

Fifth: to destroy Palestinian nationalism in the West Bank and Gaza, thus directing Palestinian nationalist ambitions to Jordan. Sharon believed that the sweeping momentum of his assault would make it possible to define Jordan as the Palestinian state, leaving the West Bank and Gaza under the permanent and exclusive control of Israel.

Shimon Peres based his account of Sharon's plan, not on secret information, but on candid briefings that he, together with former Prime Minister Rabin and the party secretary-general, Chaim Barlev, had received from Prime Minister Begin and Defense Minister Sharon. This had become Sharon's policy and intention as soon as he became minister of defense in August 1981. It was not a "contingency plan" because Sharon had decided to implement it not as a response to Arab actions but as a deliberate act of choice on his part. It may have been the only war in history that derived from a ministerial appointment. Neither Rabin, nor Arens, nor Weizmann, nor Peres, nor Begin, had any one of them become or remained defense minister, would have considered undertaking the operation on which Sharon embarked in Lebanon.

The plan was not conditioned on any provocation from the Arab side. Sharon believed that he could get United States acquiescence in this grand design, since one of its consequences would be the erosion of Soviet influence, which drew its strength from the PLO and Syria.

In June 1982 Peres told us that he and his colleagues had expressed their unanimous opposition to what Sharon had called "the Big Plan." Rabin had pointed out that Israeli interests did not require any wide-ranging military action in Lebanon. The Labor leaders were especially skeptical about the capacity of Israel to create a Christian government in Lebanon. Christian predominance in Lebanon was a historic memory, not a present reality.

Soon after participating in this consultation in Peres's office, I met the American ambassador, Samuel W. Lewis, in my home. I had a tradition of receiving Lewis, and later his successor Thomas Pickering, at least once a month on a Friday afternoon. Sam Lewis said, without detail, that Sharon was expounding an extraordinary plan in Washington but that there was no need to worry. No Israeli government, let alone any American government, would ever dream of taking the plan into serious consideration.

The 1982 Israeli action in Lebanon was always a possibility so long as PLO forces threatened our northern regions from artillery posts within twenty-five miles of the border. But, oddly, the entry of the IDF into Lebanon actually came not in response to PLO action but rather in response to

PLO passivity. For nearly a year a cease-fire agreement, negotiated between Israel and the PLO by the United States emissary Philip Habib, had been generally respected. This did not alter the fact that Israeli villages were permanently under threat of PLO artillery even in periods in which the threat was not put to work. But the belief of the army general staff was that PLO action against our northern villages could be deterred by our capacity of reprisal and that as long as the cease-fire held there was an Israeli interest in maintaining it.

The defensive nature of the PLO's attitude at that time was a result, not of its virtue, but of its weakness. Fully aware of the disparities in the balance of power, Arafat and his senior aides were desperately anxious to maintain their Lebanese foothold without incurring a major Israeli strike.

During all the meetings of the Knesset Foreign Affairs and Defense Committee in May 1982, I emphasized that just as war has a dynamic so does the absence of war create a dynamic of stability. This is especially the case where there is a large disparity between the power levels of the contending parties. Meanwhile, Israeli residents in the areas previously exposed to Palestinian attack enjoyed a welcome release from the agonizing tensions under which they had lived before the cease-fire.

Sharon had come to our Knesset committee every week since his assumption of office as defense minister. He gave irritable replies to members who asked him whether the cease-fire was holding fast. His grand design depended on the PLO violating the cease-fire agreement, not on the PLO preserving it. What Sharon needed was a casus belli. The American secretary of state, Alexander Haig, had urged Sharon not to enter Lebanon "unless there is an internationally recognized provocation." Since the PLO was not a pacifist organization, something that could be interpreted as a "provocation" was bound to occur. Haig's definition left Sharon with the power to define the time and circumstances of an Israeli invasion.

The opportunity came on June 3, 1982, when our ambassador in London, Shlomo Argov, was shot in the head by a Palestinian assailant outside the Dorchester Hotel in London. There was no Lebanese or PLO context to this brutal assault, which has left Shlomo Argov crippled for life. The assailant was a member of the Abu Nidal group that objected to Arafat's acceptance of the cease-fire. Sharon had decided to act as if the attack on our ambassador by Arafat's opponents in London constituted a cease-fire violation by Arafat's followers in Beirut.

When we gathered at our party headquarters on the day after the assault on Ambassador Argov, Peres raised the possibility that, for reasons of camouflage, Sharon would now secure authority only for the first phase of his grand design, namely the clearing of a zone of twenty-five miles between the Israeli and Lebanese boundary. Sharon would expect to receive authorization for this step and would carry the other items of the program to fulfillment on a wave of momentum. This, in fact, is what had become evident in the Cabinet meeting on the morning of June 4: Nothing except a limited local assault on the PLO artillery base was discussed.

Early on June 6 our radio reports told us that Israeli armored columns were rolling into Lebanon. This time five opposition members were invited to meet Begin: Shimon Peres, Yitzhak Rabin, Chaim Barlev, Victor Shemtov, the Mapam leader, and myself. This time Sharon gave us no intimation of a "Big Plan." He modestly sought the understanding of the Labor leadership for an operation that would be based on a twenty-five-mile-deep penetration into Lebanon, the destruction of the PLO's infrastructure and an Israeli withdrawal in favor of an international force. We were told specifically that there was no intention to reach Beirut and that Israeli forces would do everything to avoid a clash with the Syrians.

Sharon, who was in an exuberant mood, even told us that he would order the Israeli forces not to come within four kilometers of the Syrian forces at any time or place. As we were moving toward the door, Begin said, "Friends, if the operation takes a little more than forty-eight hours, I hope that you won't raise a fuss."

The Knesset was late in discussing the movement of our forces into Lebanon. The Knesset speaker, Menachem Savidor, did not use his prerogative to call a meeting to discuss the war. During June 6–7, when savage fighting was taking place across the Israeli-Lebanese boundary with an imminent threat of Syrian involvement, the Knesset went on—ludicrously—with a discussion of the budget of the agriculture ministry. The only motion put to the House was by the Communist member, Meir Wilner. He attacked the Begin government's decision to put its forces into Lebanon with such extreme invective that no Zionist member of the Knesset could possibly support him.

The Labor opposition was quiescent. When the time to vote came, the only possibility for me, or anyone else, to express reservations on the invasion of Lebanon would have been by voting for a Communist text based on the assumption that the United States was invading Lebanon and the Israeli government was giving obsequious support to an American design. The Labor Party and allied groups would have been willing to vote for a simple motion supporting the initial decision to remove the PLO threat and calling upon the Begin government to restrict its operation to the limits that Begin himself had laid down.

The reason why such a moderate text was not voted is that nobody thought of presenting it. The result was that those who were against the Big Plan did not have a parliamentary opportunity to express their reservations. Even Yossi Sarid and his colleagues did not vote against Begin on June 8. They developed their intense and courageous criticism in the ensuing days.

Two days after the outbreak of the hostilities in Lebanon, the Knesset Committee on Foreign Affairs and Defense took a trip to the northern frontier, near Safed. We held a meeting to define the Committee's position.

We also wanted to meet our young soldiers who were geared for a battle that we knew would be savage and would exact many casualties.

As Knesset members mingled with the troops I found myself surrounded by young soldiers who wanted to know whether I thought that the war, in which they would shortly be involved, was the kind of operation that they could carry out in clear conscience. Here I came up against a dilemma. I was by no means sure that it had been wise for our government to move its forces into Lebanon when there was an alternative option to maintain a cease-fire. Yet, faced by the young faces of soldiers, some of whom could hardly contain their fears, I found it emotionally impossible to do anything but give them the feeling that the enterprise on which they had embarked was worthy of their support and, if necessary, their sacrifice. I could not imagine that any Israeli leader with normal sensibilities could have given any other answer.

The brilliant standard work, *Israel's Lebanon War,* by Zeev Schiff and Ehud Ya'ari,[3] two of the most respected political and military commentators, is quite clear on two points: First, that there was an unused option for a more prolonged cease-fire; second, that the United States, represented by Secretary of State Alexander Haig, conveyed a credible impression that the U.S. would acquiesce in Sharon's "great design."

Schiff and Ya'ari have written:

Sharon was clearly pleased with the results of his meeting with Haig. The Secretary had confirmed Israel's right in principle to respond to acts of terrorism as long as they were indisputable provocations on the part of the PLO. Haig had spoken of a significant violation of the cease-fire without stopping to define what he meant by that concept. His remarks could be, and were taken to mean, that he expected Israel's response to take the form of an action that, while moderate in scope, would be marked by the éclat that the Israelis had displayed on the battlefield so often in the past. To Sharon's way of thinking Haig's response could be construed as tacit agreement to a limited military operation. From Israel's standpoint this was sufficient. Neither during the Yom Kippur War nor the Six Day War before it, had Israel enjoyed such hearty understanding from Washington.

Schiff and Ya'ari continue:

To say that the American government was prepared to wink at an Israeli move in Lebanon is far from accusing the two governments of the brand of collusion that Israel practiced with France on the eve of the Suez campaign. Yet it was clear that the Israeli government had

---

[3]Zeev Schiff and Ehud Ya'ari, *Israel's Lebanon War* (New York: Simon and Schuster, 1984).

grounds for believing that Washington had indeed bestowed its tacit approval on a limited military action in Lebanon. It was all part of a cagey dynamic prompted by Sharon in which ears strained to hear what was not said rather than what was; in which style was deemed more meaningful than substance; in which one side spoke in veiled language and elusive gestures that made it possible for the other to understand exactly what it wanted to.[4]

In the early phases of the war, while Haig conducted American foreign policy, we kept hearing American representatives telling us that the Lebanese War was a disaster but that sometimes disasters give rise to improved situations. The common metaphor that we heard from them was: "You can't make an omelette without breaking eggs." This was very similar to saying that it is worth breaking eggs in the hope that an omelette will emerge.

Schiff and Ya'ari correctly linger on the extraordinary briefing that Haig gave to the world press on Monday, June 7, a day after the full scale invasion had begun. Haig stated that he knew that the Israeli government had no intention of attacking the Syrians. He accepted at its face value Begin's announcement that the Israeli government's only ambition was to clear terrorists from a forty-kilometer strip in Lebanese territory. Haig added that Israel was not interested in holding on to any part of Lebanon.

While Haig was assuring the Arab world and the international community that Israel was resolved to avoid any engagement with Syria, Sharon was planning to eliminate the Syrian presence in Lebanon. A few hours hence, Ariel Sharon would ask, but fail to get, the Israeli Cabinet to approve an overt attack on the Syrian force in Lebanon. Within two days Sharon would achieve his goal of bombing the Syrian missile batteries in Lebanon out of existence. Schiff and Ya'ari conclude, "Haig was not the only American diplomat to come out of that week looking, at best, like an Israeli dupe."

I must not give the impression that Sharon was having everything his own way. He encountered two principal obstacles: The Israeli Cabinet was not accepting his reports with credulity and Sharon had clearly lost confidence amongst a large sector of the Cabinet. Some ministers, including Deputy Prime Minister Simcha Erlich, Minister of the Interior Yosef Burg and Minister Yitzhak Moda'i, constantly expressed their strong opposition to an expansion of the war. The dissentients were joined, on some occasions, by Minister of Communications Mordecai Zippori, who constantly argued that it would be impossible to destroy the PLO forces and headquarters in Lebanon without this leading to a war with Syria. The minister of development and energy, Yitzhak Berman, like his party colleague, Simcha Erlich, opposed Sharon's war before it broke out and continued to express criticism of its execution. He later said:

---

[4]Schiff and Ya'ari, *ibid.,* p. 67.

When our interest in a twenty-five-mile strip was discussed there was already a plan that included much wider aims, conquering Beirut, establishing a pro-Israel government, and exerting influence over presidential elections in Lebanon. But all this was not brought to the ministers' attention when they were called upon to approve "Peace for Galilee."

The only force that might have restrained Sharon would have been a clear expression of dissent by Menachem Begin. This never came. Nor were things going Sharon's way in the battlefield itself. By June 13, a week since the outbreak of the war, Israel had already lost 130 soldiers killed in action.

By the first week in August, Cabinet opposition to Sharon was blocking his action. On that day there were eight Cabinet votes against endorsing Sharon's plans. These votes were cast by Ministers Berman, Hammer, Zippori, David Levy, Burg, Uzan and Aridor. Sharon's response was to take action without Cabinet approval. These actions included the mobilization of reserves and, above all, massive air bombardments of Beirut on August 11 and 12.

By that time, Prime Minister Begin, when asked if he was really kept informed of every stage in Sharon's plan, could only say sheepishly, "I am kept informed either before or after action has been taken."[5] By that time the skeptical ministers were beginning to form a coherent group, with Deputy Prime Minister David Levi standing above his colleagues in resolution, vigilance and courage.

By the eleventh day of the war Israel's military casualties exceeded three hundred. Objections to the war had spread from the Cabinet to the Israeli High Command. It was, in fact, among senior officers that revulsion from the war first became a serious obstacle to its execution. One Israeli commander, Colonel Eli Geva, asked to be liberated from his command rather than to lead his brigade into Beirut. He said that as a matter of conscience he couldn't expose his troops and Beirut's civilian population to the horrifying casualties that were sure to ensue.[6]

There is no doubt in my mind that what Sharon had called "the grand design" defined his purposes from the very beginning and determined the action that was taken in the field. By the end of August the chief of staff, General Rafael Eitan, settled once and for all the question about the origins of the war and responsibility for its conduct. He said:

We were the initiators in this war, we initiated it, we determined the plan in advance, we determined the timing and the forces in advance. This is the first war in which the war's ends were determined from

---

[5] *Yediot Ahronot,* August 13, 1982.
[6] Sachar, *ibid.,* p. 193.

beginning to end in the General Staff master plan, subject of course to Cabinet approval. In no previous war were the purposes determined from the moment of initiation to the moment of declaration or recognition of the war's end.[7]

By mid-July I had attracted much public attention by the vigor with which I was analyzing the catastrophic results of the war. I wrote in *Ma'ariv:*

Nobody who listened to Begin's initial projected warnings could have predicted that within seven weeks the war would be in full swing, hundreds of Israelis would be killed or maimed, thousands of civilians in Lebanon have lost their lives, a moral torment would have seized many Israelis in and out of the army, a series of bombardments of civilians would have transformed Israel's reflection and consciousness of this generation. The Egyptian peace treaty would be in question, world opinion would have been lost, the United States, without whom the military victory cannot be translated into political gain, would be so sharply alienated. The shattered bodies in the Beirut hospitals, the buildings fallen on scores of mangled civilian corpses, the piled-up garbage breeding rats, the children with amputated limbs, above all the Israeli soldiers on their endless stretchers and funeral biers. These six weeks have been a dark age in the moral history of the Jewish people.

I wish I could say that the Labor leadership had a distinguished record in the Lebanese War. When Peres addressed the Knesset on June 8 he gave the impression of being totally identified with the action that Sharon had taken. Yet I myself heard him say to the Knesset committee on foreign affairs two days previously: "There were differences of opinion on the eve of the operation and there will be differences of opinion in the future. However, all of us are patriots and as long as the operation continues no one should raise any other thought."

It is unfortunate that Peres's reservations were not expressed publicly in the Knesset plenum. When he addressed the Knesset on June 8 he appeared as if he saw the war as an excellent idea and only wished that he thought of it first. This illustrates the extraordinary difficulty of a political leader when the armies of his country are already on the move. The question in those conditions is not whether the government had acted wisely but whether we wish for the success of our own troops or for those of the enemy.

As the war escalated, Labor opposition became less ambiguous and more incisive. In our Knesset Committee on June 13 the former chief of staff, General Motta Gur, called the war in Lebanon "prolonged and needless."

---

[7] *Yediot Ahronot,* September 17, 1982.

Knesset Member Gad Ya'acobi, a former minister, asked the prime minister to explain to the Knesset why the government had deviated from its original commitment that the fighting would cease after the twenty-fifth mile was reached.

In an analysis of the war, Shai Feldman and Heda Rechnitz Kigner have written in a report by the Jaffee Center for Strategic Studies:

> Almost from the very beginning Israel's legislators were deeply divided as to the merits of invading Lebanon. Dissent by Israel's parliamentary opposition became sharp and more vocal after the twenty-five-mile limit was exceeded and even more so after the June 11 cease-fire was established. Labor MKs continued to be torn between their opposition to Sharon's goals in Lebanon and their wish to avoid giving vocal expression to such dissent as long as the IDF was in battle. This led to considerable inconsistency in their public expressions exemplified by a number of statements given by Labor Party leaders during the first weeks of the fighting which could be interpreted as expressions of support for the war. Once the siege of Beirut began they faced an even more difficult dilemma.

This statement underestimates the ambivalence in the Labor Party record. On July 24, Knesset Member Gur was offering to serve as an adviser to Sharon. He stated that the release of some reserve forces may have been premature and that once the siege of Beirut had begun, "it should have been made tighter."

The recommendation to tighten the blockade arose from a purely professional and clinical approach. The aim was to expedite the end of the Israeli involvement, not to continue it indefinitely. It was similar to the U.S. decision to bomb Haiphong in order to create an "honorable" atmosphere for exit.

This was also the case with a resonant statement by Yitzhak Rabin on July 24. On the one hand, Rabin had stated that "expressions such as 'not a single terrorist will remain in Lebanon' or 'a strong Lebanese government will sign a peace treaty with Israel' or talk of the expulsion of all foreign forces from Lebanon, including the Syrians, are objectives which cannot be realized . . . and I think I would not have gone to war for the purpose of obtaining them."

This sounded well. On the other hand, Rabin went on to say: "The first priority in my view is to get out of the Beirut quagmire where, if the terrorists do not come out, or will not be brought out, Israel would suffer a serious blow. Two methods must be used: tightening the siege, including the selective bombing of terrorists and water and electricity cut-offs."

The disastrous idea of tightening the siege reached the public at a time when heartrending pictures were being published in the world's press showing women and children with empty water cans standing in line hoping to avoid the terrors of famine and thirst. The press gave prominence to a statement of mine:

> MK Abba Eban, a former foreign minister, joined the forces of those calling for withdrawal: Israel lost nothing, he said, by restricting its Lebanese presence through the evacuation of Beirut and it will lift a squalid burden from Israel's shoulders by moving in similar unilateral fashion out of the Shuf Mountains toward the belt that commands the safety of the Galilee.

It was not until the summer of 1983 that the Labor Party emerged with a sharply defined profile and definitive aims. It refused to support a draft agreement reached between delegations of Israel and Lebanon on May 17, 1983. After negotiations on both sides of the common border, Lebanese and Israeli delegates had signed an agreement that would have given Israel a paramount interest in Lebanon, and no place at all to the Syrians. This was a wildly unrealistic document. It had no relationship to the situation on the ground or to the power equation in Lebanon itself. It was absurd to believe that Lebanese signatories, directed by Bashir Gemayel and the Phalangists, could possibly represent a Lebanese consensus in the form of a peace treaty. U.S. Secretary of State George Shultz, who succeeded Haig in late June 1982, was mislead in believing that the Lebanese signatures to the May 17 agreement had any validity. Instead of becoming an ally of Israel, Lebanon became the center of anti-Israeli assaults by both Shi'ites and Palestinians.

On June 8, 1983, Peres presented a resolution to the Knesset calling for Israel's unilateral withdrawal from the central and eastern regions of Lebanon. This resolution was rejected by the Knesset in a relatively balanced vote of fifty-five against forty-seven. This was one of the few occasions when the vote of the minority was more significant than the vote of the majority. This was obviously not the kind of position on which a government could base the prolongation of a war. It was a big victory for the Labor Party.

It was not until 1985, when Peres was prime minister in the national coalition with Rabin as defense minister, that they were able to get a cabinet majority for withdrawal from Lebanon, subject to Christian Lebanese military control in the security zone. It was a big victory for the Labor Party.

It was the only war that ended without any victors. It is also the only war in military history that has no affirmative bibliography. The magisterial account by Schiff and Ya'ari stands almost unchallenged except by Sharon, whose role in the war caused him to step down as defense minister, and the chief of the army general staff, Rafael Eitan, whose term of office was allowed to expire. Schiff and Ya'ari summarize:

> Born of the ambition of one willful and reckless man, Israel's 1982 invasion of Lebanon was anchored in delusion, propelled by deceit and

bound to end in calamity It was a war for whose meager gains Israel has paid an enormous price that has yet to be altogether reckoned. A war whose defensive rationale belied far-reaching political aims and an unconsciously myopic policy. It drew Israel into a wasteful adventure that drained much of its inner strength and cost the IDF the lives of over 650 of its finest men in a vain effort to fulfill a role that it was never meant to play. There is no consolation for this costly senseless war. The best one can do now is to learn its lessons well.[8]

It seems that every nation has to get an unsuccessful war out of its system before it can face its destiny with any degree of realism. The United States has its Vietnam, France its Indochina and Algeria, Britain its Suez, the Soviet Union its Afghanistan. In the Lebanese War, Israel went through a familiar gamut of emotions. It began with military pride and public confidence, it passed through all the stages of uncontrolled euphoria, it arrived at a period of military deadlock and political frustration with our young men finding themselves inexplicably in the slums of Beirut, in the Shuf Mountains and all along the Beirut-Damascus highway. Within a short period of its conclusion, the Israeli public was voting in the polls: sixty percent thought that it had been a failure from the very beginning. The political establishment was convulsed and the main brunt of demoralization fell undeservedly upon an army whose senior ranks had taken a negative view of Sharon's aims from the very beginning.

Sharon's supporters are on strong ground when they question whether their hero should bear the full responsibility for the defeat. In formal terms he was one of several ministers subordinate to the prime minister's will, and when the fortunes of the war were running high Begin gave ecstatic expression to his joy. He predicted that Israel would have tranquillity for a whole generation, with all its neighbors bound by peace treaties with Israel, and with a Christian government firmly installed in Beirut. The harsh truth is one that Begin's admirers have never fully faced: Without Begin's support, encouragement and acquiescence, Sharon could never have carried his enterprise through its varying stages. Schiff and Ya'ari conclude:

Whether Sharon deliberately misled Begin about certain facts we have not been able to determine, nor can we say that Begin simply deluded himself. Either way, however, as prime minister his responsibility for the war is beyond question.

In a study published in 1987, the cabinet secretary at that time, Aryeh Naor, establishes that Begin did not know of the specific decision to send the

---

[8]Schiff and Ya'ari, *ibid.*, p. 301.

Phalangists into Sabra and Shatila. Sharon even confessed this in his testimony to the Kahan commission. But Naor's defense leaves Begin under the shadow of having learned vital information from the radio and not from his own defense minister.

No one may ever know with certainty whether Begin's resentment at Sharon's treatment of him was one of the factors that led him to the drama of his last seven years: a period of dark cosmic brooding in self-inflicted silence on what might well have been avoided.

Many months before Peres and Rabin secured the withdrawal of Israeli forces from Lebanon, it had been evident that nothing of the "grand design" had been achieved. The Syrians whom Sharon aspired to evict had been strengthened. The Lebanese Christians whom he wished to enthrone had been shattered. The PLO, to be sure, had been driven out, but enough Palestinians remained to reach our northern settlements with rocket fire. In addition to Palestinian armed assaults we would now have to face Shi'ite violence. The word "fiasco" is not an exaggerated description of the Lebanese war. Not a single one of the aims for which so many lives were sacrificed came to fulfillment.

The other non-victors included the United States. The Reagan administration had complete control of its own degree of involvement. It persistently made erroneous judgments. It did not exercise its full authority to keep the hostilities within the promised limits of twenty-five miles and forty-eight hours. It is certain that Reagan himself and, in the early stages, Alexander Haig were captivated by the prospect of a vicarious triumph whereby America would gain a victory without effort by exploiting the anticipated triumph of its Israeli ally. Washington gave no attention to the idea that the year of tranquillity between 1981 and June 1982 should have been prolonged. Then came the period of winks and nudges in which Secretary Haig gave Sharon to understand that there might be virtue, and even good issue, from the breaking of a few eggs in the quest for the proverbial omelettes.

In September 1983, President Reagan sent a marine force into Beirut in reaction to the tragedy at Sabra and Shatila. Their strength was sufficient to make them a target and not great enough to make them a serious military factor. When Secretary of State George Shultz took over from Haig, he seemed to accept the idea that Washington and Jerusalem together could preside over a new period of Christian-Phalangist rule in Lebanon under the direction of Bashir Gemayel. These American errors were compounded when lack of vigilance led to a terrorist attack that cost the lives of 241 U.S. marines in an exploded military headquarters. All in all, the Lebanese war gave no more glory to the United States than to Israel.

The Christian Maronites, who were slated by Begin and Sharon to be the beneficiaries of the war, became its most dejected victims. They suffered their worst defeat in a tragic history. They had put their trust in an Israeli invasion, just as they had previously put their faith in France and later in America.

They failed to understand that Christian Maronite hegemony had long ceased to rest on any political or demographic reality. They have now become marginal in a power game that they once dominated.

Syria also was a loser in a war that it had initially wished to avoid, but from which it did not have the resolution to disengage itself. The PLO was visibly routed, ending in 1986 with a dramatic sailing from Lebanon under the protection of France. On the surface, the Palestinians seemed to have been the most abject losers of all, and yet they survived to play their strongest card. They proved that no peace process can proceed without them and that their lack of a geographical base does not signify a lack of influence. Israel, under Shamir's leadership, negotiated directly with PLO interlocutors who received their instructions from Tunis.

Lebanon, the eternal loser, found itself unable to extract a coherent structure out of any situation. None of these, however, could exceed Israel in the depth of the trauma bequeathed by the war. The central grief was the loss of over seven hundred men and the wounding of thousands. For the only time in its history, Israel bore cruel sacrifice without any compensatory result. When Sharon launched the fiercest of all Israeli attacks on Black Thursday in August 1981—with three hundred people, mostly Lebanese, dead in West Beirut—Begin had the experience of receiving a telephone call from Reagan describing the bombings as "unfathomable and senseless." This belated American sermon was not necessary. Israeli opinion had already moved against continuing the war.

The national passion for disengagement from Lebanon was accentuated by the fearful slaughter in the refugee camps of Sabra and Shatila on September 16, 1982. Sharon had evidently lost touch with his own country's character and mood. He seemed unable to grasp that the State of Israel had never ceased to be a moral reality and that there was a breaking point beyond which Israelis would not give their trust even to those who bore their uniform. On that dark day, Bashir Gemayel's soldiers had been allowed by the Israeli authorities to enter the camps. They had behaved like wild hungry beasts, shooting, knifing, smashing the bodies of undefended men, women and children with sadistic fury. The sense of crisis seized the whole of our society. President Navon threatened to resign if a properly constituted inquiry commission was not established. He had almost taken the same decision earlier, after Sharon had ordered a ferocious raid on Beirut in August 1982, when apartment houses were bombed on the assumption that Arafat was in one of them. Shimon Peres celebrated one of his effective moments as an opposition leader when he shouted to a crowded Knesset: "Who were the fools who let the Phalangists into the refugee camps at Sabra and Shatila?" It was the kind of phraseology that would have been inconceivable in the euphoric days of June 1982.

This does not mean, however, that the Labor opposition had a successful record in the Lebanese War. It went through a bewildering series of phases.

It began with lucid criticism, lurched into obsequious endorsement, returned briefly to a measure of criticism and, at a certain stage, experienced its worst hour when Peres called a meeting to discuss the advisability of jumping on the bandwagon of what then seemed a successful enterprise.

It was strange how little durable effect the failure of the Lebanese war had on the entrenched Israeli political establishment. There was only one resignation of conscience, by Minister Yitzhak Berman, who refused to shoot women and children and to endanger his troops senselessly by breaking into Beirut. Only one resounding military protest, by Colonel Eli Geva. Sharon was deposed from the defense ministry only to pop up again as an influential minister without portfolio and later as minister of trade and industry. The chief of staff, Rafael Eitan, who had been virtually dismissed from office as a result of the Kahan Report, sat proudly a few months later as a member of the Israeli Cabinet and leader of one of the right-wing parties.

The only institution in Israeli society that emerged with enhanced credit was the commission appointed under public pressure by Begin after the Sabra and Shatila tragedy. It was appointed in a wave of public indignation that found expression in the largest demonstration ever held in Tel Aviv, with anywhere between 250,000 and 350,000 participants united in an expression of social and moral anguish. The chairman of the commission, Chief Justice Kahan, and his colleagues, Justice Barak and General (Reserve) Yonah Efrat, showed greater courage than the Agranat Commission in their willingness to express criticism evenhandedly among the prime minister, the foreign minister, the defense minister and officers responsible for the area in which the outrage was enacted. International indignation at the massacre was largely counterbalanced by admiration for the frankness and honesty with which it was castigated, and Begin regained many points by the speed with which he accepted the report, despite its reflections upon him and his closest colleagues. No democracy can ever avoid making mistakes, but the courage of confessing them can have a partially mitigating effect. Begin himself had initially described the episode as "goyim killing goyim," forgetting that the goyim on this occasion had been under the jurisdiction of Israeli officers.

Today, seven years after the end of Israel's Lebanese campaign, the negative effects on our country's image of itself has only partially healed.

The two central memories of the 1980s are linked to a single theme: Sharon's "grand design" sought to eliminate Palestinian nationalism. The intifada was the Palestinian attempt to prevent this from happening.

Political memoirs are an excellent way of telling the truth about other people. Sometimes, however, they are self-revelatory. As I look back on the story of Israeli rule in the occupied territories, I cannot find a single instance in which I shared the illusion of permanence, or even stability. Political nature does not allow anything more intrinsically squalid or explosive than the spectacle of one nation ruling over another while preserving for itself all effective control of the nation's resources. I was one of the most constant Cassandras in my predictions on this point. I was convinced that military occupation and diplomatic deadlock cannot long exist without deforming our very nature as a democracy.

In the euphoria that seized the nation immediately after the Six Day War, there was a tendency to believe that the open bridges policy would cause Arab nationalists to submerge their national aspirations under the influence of increased employment and economic stability. Moshe Dayan indulged his pragmatism to the extent of believing that both Israelis and Palestinians would come to be content with their new "coexistence." He thought that the Israeli economy would benefit from the torrent of cheap labor, while the Palestinians, despite their lack of political or civic freedom, would be consoled by a constant rise in living standards. This theory conveniently ignored the fact that employment in its present style does not create any aftermath of Palestinian pride or satisfaction. The Arab migrants from across the old border labor hard as the sweepers of streets, the cleaners of toilets, the tenders of gardens and, paradoxically, as workers in the construction industry who are, in effect, building the Israeli settlements that foreclose their own future. Pinhas Sapir, the leader of our economic policies, was first to point out that the Arabs from the territories were becoming "the hewers of wood and the drawers of water," without any access to the economic activity that would give them social mobility or national pride.

The entire process is without dignity. The workers are harried by the police if they are seen sleeping in Israel overnight. Their duty is to go to their homes in the West Bank and Gaza at night and then to rise at dawn, when they line up at the checkpoints for searches. The effect on Israel's social ideals causes concern. Jews no longer cover the whole spectrum of the labor market. Thus the labor market is creating a class system with the line between Arabs and Jews coinciding with a frontier between dignified and cheap labor. The Histadrut does not have a proud record. It has attempted too little in the protection of the rights of Arab workers from the territories.

Here we come to one of the paradoxes in Israeli politics and society. Our nation's links with Judea and Samaria are so strongly rooted in national and universal history that it would be absurd to describe Israeli rule as colonialism. The land itself sends out more intimate associations with Israel than with any other people. However, when we turn our eyes away from the land to the people, there is no escape from the fact that a condition in which one social group exercises total domination over another social group, by military power and economic control, comes to resemble the relations between colonial powers and their subjects. This disagreeable analogy is, of course, deepened and strengthened if the ruling power refuses to admit that its domination is temporary. In the Labor Party, the conviction that Israeli rule was provisional and would be replaced one day by a reality based on consent safeguarded Israel against colonialist analogies.

No less a figure than Yigal Allon, Israel's foremost strategic thinker, was the first Israeli leader to utter the word "colonialist" in an Israeli context. Referring to proposals that would grant autonomy to the Palestinian Arabs within a limited scope, while denying them full participation in the Israeli parliamentary system, Allon likened this prospect to the Siskei model. He was drawing an analogy with a situation in Africa where the Africans in the so-called "homelands" had a certain degree of autonomy without being citizens of the South African Union and without being allowed to determine their own central interests.

Allon sharpened the alternatives. If Israel wished to assert and protect its democratic image, it would either have to annex the Arab areas and grant the Palestinians voting rights and full participation in the Israeli political system or, if Israel wanted separation, it would have to release the Palestinians for a separate identity.

The constitutional aspect had less effect on me than the concrete results of an occupation that tended to become more and more permanent in the world's consciousness as the years went on. There is nothing in international experience, especially since the revolutionary events of 1990 in Europe, to support the idea that the rule of one people over another can endure without prejudicing the values of the society that holds the power.

The most trenchant example of the occupational syndrome in the relations between Israelis and Arabs was the career of Menachem Milson as the administrator of the occupied territories from 1981 to 1983 during the regime of Arik Sharon in the defense ministry. Milson, as a professor of Arabic at the Hebrew University in Jerusalem and a graduate of Cambridge and Harvard, appeared to be ideally suited for the task of moving Israeli-Palestinian relations out of deadlock. Apart from his academic eminence, he had an imposing military career as a parachutist and commander of a commando platoon. Milson became, in my eyes, a kind of Dr. Strangelove. He lived in a world of illusion that belied his reputation for disciplined rationality. He believed that he, with the power of the Israeli state behind him, could fashion the structure of life and politics in the occupied areas.

He began by denouncing the action taken by Defense Minister Shimon Peres in permitting free municipal elections in the territories back in 1976. This had predictably given municipal power, and therefore political influence, to Arabs who combined their pragmatist temperament with a basic allegiance to the PLO. Milson believed that it would be important for leadership in the West Bank and Gaza to be directed, not by the PLO, which based its strength on the intellectuals and activists in the cities, but on rural Arabs who had been remote from political action. His eyes fell on a group called the "Village Leagues," whose members sprang from an agricultural background and whose lives revolved around the affairs of small cities. Despite their social weakness, Milson believed that he could transform their stature by injections of authority and patronage derived from Israel. He declared virtual war upon all Arab leaders with PLO roots, denied them import licenses, deprived them of any ability to distribute patronage and subjected them to such harassment and impotence that he expected them to be spurned by the Arab public in the territories. On the other hand, he would get Arab populations to understand that the leaders of the Village Leagues would grant entry and exit permits, driving licenses and business permits. Milson also considered that he could give pro-Jordanian Arab notables a measure of supremacy that would be denied to what he called the "inciters" of the PLO.

A particular target of Milson's hostility was a group called the National Guidance Committee, composed of mayors of cities, teachers, academics and others who were ideologically connected to the PLO. These were the natural leaders of Palestinian nationalism, and Milson worked assiduously to clip their wings.

Milson deposed elected Arab mayors, such as those in Nablus and Ramallah, arrested Palestinian activists for inciting demonstrations and ensured that they would lack the capacity to distribute economic benefits.

The more militant Israeli religious settlers were heartened by the sensation of having Milson on their side, despite his conspicuously secular outlook. In May 1980, before Milson's appointment, the mayor of Hebron, Fahd Qawasmeh, had been deposed and exiled. A few weeks later a group of Jewish settlers placed explosives in the car of the mayor of Nablus, Basam Shak'a, and in the car of the mayor of Ramallah, Karim Khalaf. Basam Shak'a lost both legs and Karim Khalaf one leg. In the same context of carnage a bomb had been placed in the car of the mayor of Bireh, Ibrahim Tawil. An innocent Druse expert of the Israeli army examined the mayor's car and, in the ensuing explosion, lost his sight completely for life. Menachem Begin, despite his general sympathy for the right-wing settlers, found it morally necessary and politically advisable to condemn their action. President Herzog went further and, in a rare statement on a political issue, exclaimed that such actions "lower us to the subhuman level of murderous terror organizations that act against us."

Throughout 1981 and 1982, Menachem Milson worked to sharpen the severity of the administration in its attitudes to elected Arab mayors and members of the National Guidance Committee. In the first half of 1982, riots and killings multiplied, as Milson worked to eradicate all remnants of prestige and status that reposed in mayors and officials whom the Arab urban populations regarded as their leaders. I could almost see the white-plumed hat of a colonial governor shining resplendent on his head as he went about the job of deposing mayors, appointing others, denying permits to orange growers with the "wrong views," distributing favors and penalties and accompanying the entire process with classical Arabic oratory on a high grammatical level.

Milson's error was to believe, with astounding naïveté, that military control of a population endowed a ruling government with an ability to define leadership in the community over which the government ruled. He failed to come face-to-face with the hypothesis that a national movement, persecuted by a military authority, would become more and more popular in the measure that the persecution became more severe. All that Milson achieved was to make the Village League look like quislings and the PLO activists look like national heroes.

Meanwhile the Palestinians were drawing their own conclusions from their own deadlock. The result would be—intifada.

The Arabic word "intifada" means "shaking off." It denotes an attempt to break shackles, to sunder chains, and to relieve the mind from self-imposed restraints. In that sense, the intifada began in December 1987. The proximate causes were trivial and subsidiary. On December 6, 1987, an Israeli industrialist was stabbed to death in the Gaza Strip. On December 8, an Israeli truck collided with two Arab trucks, killing four residents of the Jabaliya camp. A rumor spread throughout Gaza that the death of the four Arabs was deliberately inflicted by the driver of the Israeli truck. From that day on, the Arabs of Gaza begun a rampage: burning tires, throwing stones, raising Palestinian flags and developing what had always been a simmering kind of tranquillity into a routine of street demonstrations and commercial strikes. All this was accompanied by a fiery rhetoric, of which the central theme was not so much the destruction of Israel as the need to bring an immediate end to the military occupation.

At first there was very little violence among the demonstrators, and the Israeli reaction based itself on the assumption that a massive military presence and a few punitive curfews would bring the outburst to an end. Our administration called in the army, which, under Rabin's orders, carried out mass arrests. By the end of December, more than twelve hundred Palestinians, many of them teenagers, were being held in detention camps. Dozens of them were held without accusation or trial. The toll at the end of the month showed that some 23 Palestinians had been killed and 170 wounded.

Throughout the whole of December the official military view was that no such thing as "an uprising" was taking place. I recall a meeting of our Knesset Committee on Foreign Affairs and Defense on December 13, to which the chief of staff, Dan Shomron, reported that it would be wrong, and even counterproductive, to define the demonstrations as a "civilian uprising" since he was certain that calm would soon be restored. A minority in our committee, led by Yossi Sarid, insisted that the events could and should be described as "an uprising" and treated mainly as a political phenomenon. Many Arab newspapers even compared their own insurrection to that of the Jews against the British in the mid-1940s.

Rabin's response was punitive. "The goal is to make sure that we teach them the lesson that through violence and terror nothing will be achieved. Their suffering will be increased and instead of creating conditions that allow them to live peacefully, as long as the political situation has not been resolved, they will suffer more and more."

During the early months of 1988, the leaders of both parties, principally Rabin and Shamir, went beyond the diagnosis of "uprising" and stated, in somewhat farfetched terms, that "the issue is whether there will be Jewish existence in the whole of Eretz Israel." As I examined this diagnosis I asked myself whether there was ever a case in which a state with thousands of tanks, hundreds of aircraft and dozens of missiles had ever lost its "existence" owing to street demonstrations and throwing of stones. In all my speeches I pointed out that Palestinian violence could threaten the lives of Israeli individuals, but could not possibly have an existential influence on the destiny of the Israeli state itself.

More significant than the street demonstrations and occasional acts of violence was the tendency of the Palestinians to institutionalize the rebellion. What we faced were not individual outbursts of rhetoric and violence but a tendency of the young generation of Palestinians to create institutions. By methods that indicated a high level of managerial talent, an institution called "The Unified National Command of the Uprising" began to develop a quasi-governmental authority, issuing orders for strikes, closures and demonstrations, most of which were spontaneously obeyed. I did not consider that the semantic issue was trivial. If a new reality could be described as acts of violence inspired by "inciters," it was clearly a matter for police action. If, however, the situation was described as a "national uprising," it was clear that suppressive action by the police and soldiery would make sense only in the context of a political dialogue enhanced by diplomatic activity.

By now, any suggestion that Israel's existence could be eliminated was scrupulously kept out of the intifada documents and of subsequent Palestinian rhetoric. The Palestinians were advocating a Palestine state side by side with Israel. This slogan had a potent appeal: It sounded as though Israeli founding father doctrine. The intifada was clearly aiming at a specific target—public opinion in the world, and especially in Europe, where military occupations still had the negative connotations derived from the Second World War. Another indication that the intifada authorities knew what they were doing in ideological terms was the decision to abstain from lethal violence and to symbolize the rebellion by the throwing of stones. It must have been evident that even a stone, if it hit a sensitive target, could bring about severe injury and even death. The assumption, however, was that these would be rare instances, while the great bulk of the deaths and woundings would be absorbed by the Palestinians themselves.

It would not be long before this new rhetoric and these new tactics would be proved effective. Television viewers across the world, ignoring the past record of Arab aggression against the State of Israel, showed authentic pictures of bulkingly equipped soldiers, armed to the teeth with clubs, machine guns and tear gas, chasing youngsters in the slums of Gaza and the

Casbah of Nablus, subjected only to stones thrown by the skinny hands of youngsters. As these television images multiplied, a kind of panic began to seize Jewish communities across the world. The idea that the intifada was sheer terrorism was losing ground. By now General Shomron was saying bluntly that it was wrong to require the army to eliminate the intifada by military force, since "this is a problem of nationalism."

The origins of the intifada lay not in the events of December 1987 but in the accumulated despair of a whole decade. The bonfire had taken many years during which its inflammatory ingredients were brought together with the match ever ready to light the flames. The Palestinians had indulged their talent for lulling themselves into a false sense of security ever since the 1967 war had brought them under Israeli rule. In the early part of this period they hoped that they would be liberated from Israeli rule by the General Assembly of the United Nations, by the Security Council of the United Nations, by cooperation between four powers as de Gaulle had recommended, by cooperation between the two superpowers that held their periodic meetings at the summit. These were illusions. Shortly after the Camp David agreement was signed, many Arab nationalists in the West Bank and Gaza believed that Sadat, having achieved the evacuation of Sinai, would go on to "liberate" the Palestinians from their servitudes. They invariably placed their trust in the manifest superiority of Arab geopolitical weight compared with that of Israel. The Palestinian expectation was that the Arab governments would utilize the weight of their status and the reverberation of their voice in the world to bring about the freedom of the Palestinians, who would not be called upon to do very much except to organize demonstrations. Their chief aim was to avoid negotiations with Israel and to seek salvation from outside forces.

I have described in an earlier chapter how, in my first encounters with Arabs in the territories and in East Jerusalem, I found them skeptical of their own power to change their condition. Almost every Arab leader with whom I spoke made a journey to Amman or Cairo or Beirut in order to ask instructions either from the Egyptians or the Jordanian monarch or the Palestinian headquarters in Beirut. They had now begun to rely on themselves. The official Israeli reaction to the demonstrations was unimaginative. The leadership of the two major parties continued to believe that the revolt, unlike similar revolts in other countries, could be suppressed by force without the enhancement of diplomacy. Rabin had spoken of "force, might and beatings." He had distributed special flagellatory instruments to the troops. The beatings evoked more indignation than the shootings. The consequences are described painfully by Schiff and Ya'ari:

> Considering that whole corps of soldiers were battering away at defenseless civilians, it is hardly surprising that thousands of Palestini-

ans—many of them innocent of any wrongdoing—were badly beaten, sometimes to the point of being crippled. The clubs descended on limbs, joints and ribs until they could be heard to crack—especially as Rabin let slip a "break their bones" remark in a television interview that many soldiers took as a recommendation. . . . Palestinians turned to sabotage and terrorism in return for having been humiliated by the Israelis; fathers who had seen their sons battered and children who watched in terror as their fathers were clubbed. . . . The reaction to the beatings was stronger than to the shooting of demonstrators, demolition of houses or deportations. The office of Israel's president had difficulty coping with the swell of letters on this issue. . . . What had happened, sad to say, was that the troops were brutalizing the Palestinian population because the intifada had brutalized the IDF. . . .⁹

The irony is that the floggings were sincerely conceived by Rabin and others as an alternative to the multiplication of deaths from the fire of soldiers' weapons. It turned out that the killings of demonstrators with a chilling preponderance of teenagers were not substantially affected. The beatings were therefore conceived as an aggravation of the suppressive measures taken by the army and not as an alleviation or as an alternative to opening fire.

The intifada never approached the realization of its unrealistic aim to dislodge the Israeli army from the occupied areas, but it was not a total failure from the Arab point of view. It inculcated a sense of Palestinian solidarity, and caused embarrassment to Israel in the focal points of its international relations. It had a demoralizing effect on our own soldiers. Many in their hearts felt a grudging respect for the young Palestinians who were putting their lives in hazard with the aim of ridding themselves of a coercive military occupation. In a talk that I gave in one of our high schools, I received the impression that Israeli youngsters were in favor of every intifada except the one that was directed against us. When Israelis hear of a distant land in which armed police are shooting or beating civilian demonstrators, their sympathy normally flows toward the demonstrators, not to the police. Here, and here alone, they are called upon to be devotees of a "law and order" mentality. But modern international law recognizes the idea of national insurrection against external force, and the spectacle of Israeli soldiers bursting into an Arab village to tear down its flags and invade its homes confuses our own Israeli emotion.

Since Begin's ascent to power in 1977 I had been working in the unfamiliar guise of a member of the opposition. I found no lack of policies and actions worthy of criticism, but I frankly chafed at the experience of not having any positive role in the country's policy and diplomacy. This condition changed

---

⁹Schiff and Ya'ari, *ibid.,* pp. 150, 153.

to some extent after the election in 1984. The two major parties were virtually deadlocked in complete equality. It was agreed that Shimon Peres and Yitzhak Shamir would each hold the premiership for two years beginning with Shimon Peres in 1984.

During his seven years of exile, Peres's style and outlook had undergone a considerable change. He was no longer bound to the severe territorial conceptions of Moshe Dayan. During the wilderness years he had moved frequently in the company of leaders of the social democratic movements such as Helmut Schmidt and Willy Brandt in Germany and Bruno Kreisky in Austria. His outlook on the Palestine question was now expressed in his 1981 declaration: "Labor has no interest in becoming masters of 1.3 million Arabs against their will." And again in 1984: "Our goal is territorial partition rather than to be perpetual rulers over others."

Peres's other priority, which was far easier to bring to fulfillment, was to end the ludicrous rate of inflation, which made a joke out of the Israeli economy. The Israeli shekel was rocketing far above the celestial levels of the drachma and the Italian liretta. One of Peres's reforms was to harmonize his political outlook with his economic program by a considerable reduction of settlement activity in the West Bank. A large part of the area that had been confiscated had changed hands on paper alone, without ever having been put into civilian use. Indeed, when Peres took office, the number of Israelis who had taken up residence beyond the 1967 line, except for East Jerusalem, did not exceed thirty thousand. Many Israelis prudently recalled that it had been necessary to evacuate the Sinai settlements and they were not sure that this would not happen again. At least half of those who settled in the West Bank had done so for secular, utilitarian, pragmatic reasons and were not devout adherents of the religious fundamentalists. The numbers of those expressing themselves in the polls in favor of territorial compromise rose steeply.

One effect of the intifada was to sharpen the conflict between the Israeli settlers and the Israeli Defense Forces. The settlers, inspired by Gush Emunim, were devoted to an ideology that did not give the Israeli government or army a particular deference. In its original manifesto of September 1967, the Movement for an Undivided Land of Israel had stated clearly that the status of the territories lay outside and beyond the jurisdiction of the elected Israeli parliament and government. This meant that even when settlers, using violence, were prosecuted by the State they lost no status or prestige among their own followers. One of them, Rabbi Moshe Levinger, could even be carried shoulder high by a cheering crowd of supporters on his way to serve a prison sentence for killing an Arab. He could also be certain that his stay in jail would be astronomically shorter than that of anyone murdering a Jew for robbery or passion in a Tel Aviv street. At one stage during the 1980s the National Religious Party actually proposed a resolution in the Knesset to the effect that anyone who killed "with intention to serve Zionism" would be automatically qualified for presidential pardon.

If we were going to be a state in which the penalty for any crime of violence would depend for its severity on the ethnic identity of the perpetrator and the victim, our pretension to call ourselves "the only democracy in the Middle East" would be undermined. The settlers were so insatiable in their demands for violent suppression that the relatively moderate and restrained reactions of the IDF drove them to mutiny and rage. In the mid-1980s they were actually demanding the award to themselves of police powers in order to usurp and replace the authority of the Israeli Defense Forces. They called for far longer prison sentences for stone throwers; the destruction of refugee camp houses very near main roads; the automatic deportation of known instigators; the easing of regulations regarding the use of live ammunition; permission for settlers, not only security personnel, to enter Arab schools from which a stone had been thrown; and the imposition of hermetic curfews on trouble spots.

Public opinion developed in Israel against the methods whereby curfew breakers were punished. In the instructions issued by the chief of staff, Rafael Eitan, anyone found in the streets during a curfew could be beaten before any questions were asked and, if he sought to escape detention, could be subjected to live fire. This meant that someone on the way to see a doctor would be risking his body, and even his life. These recommendations were not accepted.

Peres's leadership of the Labor Party brought no alleviation of the severity with which demonstrations or protests were suppressed. Despite his titular authority as prime minister over all other Labor ministers, Peres left the ministry of defense, under Rabin's direction, completely alone. When I addressed a letter to him in 1988 suggesting that he influence the IDF in the direction of preventing measures of repression that would shock public and even Jewish opinion, he replied by throwing up his hands and stating that repression was preferable to "anarchy."

On the other hand, Peres was actively pursuing a peace settlement with Jordan, which in its turn was coordinating its action with PLO moderates. During the years that were a prelude to the intifada, the main thrust of the advice that my colleagues and I gave in the Knesset was that, in addition to the need to preserve minimal order, the best hope of mitigating the turbulence in the Arab refugee camps and urban centers was to create a diplomatic process in the success of which they would have an interest. Our prisons were overflowing with young people, some of them so young that the very spectacle of their being photographed in the foreign press was bound to alienate international sympathy. In the early months of 1987, Rabin ordered the closure of all Palestinian universities without distinction. Years passed before they could be opened, and in the meantime the Palestinians complained of what they saw as a deliberate attempt to spread illiteracy and intellectual backwardness in a sophisticated community.

There was a glimmer of hope when, after careful and gradual preparation, Peres reached an agreement in London with King Hussein, not only on the procedures for an international conference but also on the principles that should govern its work. Peres, as foreign minister, had gone about the preparations for this agreement without reference to what he seemed to regard as the trivial fact that Shamir, and not he, was the prime minister. Foreign governments were baffled and frustrated by the experience of receiving the prime minister and the foreign minister of Israel in swift succession, bringing totally divergent pictures of what they wanted the world's governments to do.

During this period the American Secretary of State Shultz, whose sympathies for Israel were ardent, manifestly hoped that Peres's strategy would succeed. He soon, however, came to the realization that prime ministers are not merely "first among equals": They invariably have the final word.

In the Likud there was a refusal to regard the uprising as having any connection with the reality of occupation. Likud spokesmen asserted that if Arab stone-throwing could not be deterred, the threat would be not merely to individual life but to the very existence of the Jewish state. In *The New York Times* I urged Israelis and the friends of Israel in the influential media not to present Israel as though it were a negligible state like Monaco, faced with a Palestinian enemy in the military lineage of Alexander the Great, Genghis Khan, Napoleon and the Russian and German dictators of the twentieth century. I pointed out that, in fact, reality was on the opposite side of the debate. The PLO could no more destroy Israel with its stones and bottles than Denmark could destroy the Soviet Union. I found that weakness had been such a constant characteristic of the Jewish reality that Jews were not coming to terms with Israel's strength. We had the kind of military defense and deterrent that used to be associated only with the great continental and imperial powers and yet we had a tendency to shiver with existential fright whenever a hostile stone or firebomb was thrown at us. One of the paradoxes of Israel is the gap between the reality of our power and the psychology of our vulnerability.

The Reagan administration was sparing in its peace initiatives. President Reagan had sent a proposal to Begin in September 1981. It called for a settlement based on Resolution 242. It envisaged a considerable, though not a total, renunciation of the West Bank and Gaza. The evacuated areas would not form a separate state, but would be "associated" with Jordan. The United States would make far-reaching contributions to Israeli security as well as to our economic development. Begin had rejected this proposal with vehement indignation and the United States had not pursued the dialogue. All that Begin wanted from the United States was massive amounts of money and arms and strict nonintervention in the question of what he would do with the money and the arms.

Reagan projected himself to Israel, not as a brother or father figure who might make disciplinary suggestions with good intent, but as a compliant uncle who gives the kids candy that spoils their teeth and stomachs but leaves them with a good memory of avuncular benevolence.

George Shultz seemed to be made of sterner stuff. On his appointment after Haig's resignation, he attempted a last-ditch effort to put a peace process into motion. Overcoming an initial reluctance to give the Soviet Union a foothold in our region, Shultz worked closely with Peres and King Hussein to elaborate a plan for an international conference to be convened by the United Nations. The plenary meeting of the conference would set the stage ceremonially, after which it would split up into committees in which Israel would negotiate with each Arab state on a bilateral basis. There would be a brief interim period like that envisaged in the Camp David accords, after which there would be an attempt to define the permanent status of the territories and the populations. There would be rigorous timetables for implementation.

This initiative came to a head in February 1988. The American election was only nine months ahead. Shamir knew clearly that all he had to do was to play for time. He told Shultz that he should not believe that Peres, his own foreign minister, committed him in any way. He denied that Resolution 242 required any withdrawal from the West Bank and Gaza. He had expressed a readiness to negotiate with the Arab states, but he now revealed that the negotiation would be held merely in order to hear Shamir's refusal to give up a single inch of territory! Shamir added that Israel under his leadership would not attend any international conference, however innocuous the formulation of its powers.

Meanwhile, Shultz was bursting out of his previous amiable passivity into a surge of candor and truth. In September 1988 he told a meeting of the Israeli lobby that "the status quo between the Arabs and the Israelis does not work; it is not viable. It is dangerous. Israel's security is paramount, but Palestinian political rights must also be recognized and addressed. The principle must be land for peace, and negotiation between Israel and the Palestinians." He had delivered himself of similar views in February at a meeting of the Knesset Committee on Foreign Affairs and Defense under my chairmanship. He had entered into a confrontation with Eliahu Ben-Elissar, a Likud militant, to whom he said that the Palestinians had *political* rights and were not merely individuals who should be humanely treated. Shultz had absorbed Shamir's rejectionist response to his peace plan, but he was determined to embody it in his legacy. In my view, the Shultz plan and the Hussein-Peres document were the most serious documents revolved among the parties in the 1980s.

When Shamir rejected the Shultz-Peres-Hussein formulas and scorned the very idea of an international conference, he added that "the only worthwhile words in the Shultz plan are his signature." (Shamir had extraordinary good fortune in his ability to insult American statesmen personally without evoking any reaction.) Shultz further illustrated his courage when he orchestrated a movement in which the PLO would announce its recognition of Israel, and the United States would open a dialogue with the PLO. To reach this result, he had worked skillfully with the Swedish foreign minister and with a group of Jewish leaders headed by Rita Hauser, the American chairman of the International Center for Peace in the Middle East, of which I am the international chairman. After tentative gropings in Stockholm, Arafat had chosen a highly publicized United Nations Assembly in Geneva to say the magic words about 242 and the recognition of Israel that virtually compelled the United States to abandon its boycott.

I drew encouragement from these new approaches by Secretary Shultz. He had immense credit with Israel as a result of his support of our central interests, his pressures on the Soviet Union to allow emigration of its Jews and his indulgent effort to avoid an escalating crisis when an American, Jonathan Pollard, spied energetically for Israel, made off with documents of extreme sensitivity and delivered them to Israeli defense ministers who asserted that they did know whence they came. Shultz was now willing to spend some of this accumulated credit for the highest cause.

It was too late. The United States wasted the dialogue with the PLO by conducting it at the very lowest level of authority (the U.S. embassy in Tunis!) and breaking it off when many Israelis thought that its continuation would be valuable. The excuse for the break was that Arafat had obtusely refused to "condemn" an outrageous terrorist attack by a dissident member of a Palestinian fringe group. The underlying reason for the break was that Israel's friends in the U.S. Congress and in some pro-Israeli groups had been trying to prevent and thereafter to annul the American-Palestinian dialogue which was an indispensable element in any serious peace process. Love for Israel sometimes takes turns in which good intentions and disastrous consequences go hand in hand. Our pro-Israeli friends sometimes enjoy the intentions and Israel suffers the consequences.

I took heart from the success of the United States in inducing the Palestinians to accept a more realistic appraisal of their position, which was a remarkable achievement. It was received by the Likud with cries of alarm, by Shimon Peres, strangely, with sadness.

The trivial gesture of drinking tea in Tunis as a first step to engaging the United States in a serious exploration of the Palestinian reality gave birth to apocalyptic visions among frightened columnists in the most prestigious East Coast media. Israel's media friends are more ferocious in defending radical Israeli positions than are most Israelis. *Commentary* magazine even published an editorial dirge in which Israel's demise had already taken place and the requiem was intoned over its departed spirit. The language of these effusions is uniformly redolent of the published handouts of the senior Likud propagandists.

Shamir, thus encouraged, now stipulated that the physical repression of our enemies and their unconditional surrender could be the only prelude to peace negotiations. By the end of 1988, even the disillusioned United States was joining Security Council resolutions condemning our deportations. The policy of suppressing the intifada by force alone had reached a dead end. But so also had the intifada itself. There is such a thing in physics as fusion at high temperatures. In politics also, the very intensity of a crisis sometimes brings the contending parties into a mutual quest for innovation. By the end of the 1980s, the Palestinians were reiterating their acceptance of Israel's "right to exist," entering a dialogue with the United States and urging a "two-state solution" based on the partition idea.

At a crucial stage in his negotiations with Hussein, Shimon Peres had convened a very small decision-making group of our party in the foreign ministry. I felt the tension in the air. He told us that if Shamir blocked the international conference and the Hussein-Peres program, he would resign, break up the coalition and go to the country to seek a peace mandate. He had made this pledge to King Hussein, Margaret Thatcher, François Mitterrand, Felipe Gonzales and to Shultz himself. When Peres brought his plan to the ministerial committee, there was a tie vote, which meant that Peres's initiative was blocked. Peres, however, continued in office without the confrontation with Shamir that had been threatened. His domestic and international image were gravely impaired.

Those of us whom the deadlock had driven close to despair had failed to take account of a new factor in our national calculations. It sometimes happens that the fate of nations is affected not so much by what they do themselves as by the interplay of larger forces outside their control. The sense of choking deadlock in Israel's situation was destined to be relieved in the wondrous years 1990 and 1991, by three revolutionary developments that lay beyond our own field of vision. These were the Desert War, the collapse of Soviet communism and the consequent beneficial flow of mass immigration. In these conditions even the terms of the Arab-Israeli dialogue would be transformed. Israel was propelled by forces greater than itself into what could well become a new era—with hope on its wings.

We did not know it at the time—but the nineties were going to be sensationally different.

30

RETROSPECT AND PROSPECT

WHILE THE COLD War lasted, we were not exactly serene, but we knew where we stood. Then came the 1990 Desert War and the Communist collapse. All our certainties and assumptions were suddenly overturned. Nothing was unthinkable anymore.

The Soviet Union has been the subject of a vast literature in scores of languages. The study of Soviet history, the analysis of Soviet motives, the discussions on how to cope with Soviet policies have become a recognized academic discipline. Hundreds of chairs, faculties, seminars and institutes have sent their insights into a great ocean of learning and public debate. Yet there has not been a single prediction that could prepare anyone to believe that the Communist empire would end its life in the way that it did.

What would I have thought of anyone who would have predicted in early 1990 that within a year I would be attending a dinner in New York, organized by a Jewish organization in honor of "ex-President Mikhail Gorbachev"? Yet here I was shaking his firm hand and furtively contemplating the birthmark on the much-photographed bald pate.

He had spoken lucidly, but without eloquence, against anti-Semitism and had taken due credit for restoring Soviet relations with Israel without giving the impression that he saw this as his most cherished achievement. A flood of rhetoric from his Jewish hosts had exalted him as the victor in an epoch-making struggle against despotism. The tributes, as is usual on such occasions, were repetitive and not excessively brief. Yet they were substantially true. His life had mattered to the world.

Nevertheless, as I shook hands with him for the first time, I was afflicted by a sense of desperate compassion for him. There was nothing revolutionary, or even dignified, in the spectacle of an ex-president of what had been a superpower, disdained by his own nation, scrounging in capitalist fashion for a few million dollars in a gathering of black-tied notables and bejeweled women, who were simultaneously extolling a successful American businessman.

In his wrinkled brown suit, Gorbachev looked haunted. He seemed surprised by the frequency with which rabbis called us to our feet while they harangued the Creator a little more insistently than the Heavenly Host might have wished. He may have been wondering how he would look in the home newspapers if they could see him now. Only a year before he had been the idol of adoring European crowds, the central figure in the international gallery. His decline of power had a Shakespearian proportion:

Oh! what a fall was there, my countrymen;
Then I, and you, and all of us fell down,
Whilst bloody treason flourished over us.[1]

Bloody treason had not quite flourished over him in the Russian coup, but there had been an alarming attempt at it, and Gorbachev had been saved only by the transformations that he himself had generated in the massive body and stolid mind of his compatriots. Nobody may ever know what went through his mind in the Crimean dacha while his opponents deliberated on his fate. He must have believed for several hours that his hour of death was near. Since he emerged, pale and tentative, from the aircraft that took him to safety in Moscow, the light in his eyes has never had the previous glow.

Was Gorbachev a great man? The answer that comes to mind is based on a definition by Isaiah Berlin:

A great man is one who deliberately causes something important to happen, the probability of which seemed low before he took up the task. A great man is a man who gives history a turn which it could scarcely have taken without him. They give history a twist which nobody would have predicted. . . . Great men leave permanent effects.[2]

As I contemplated the scarred landscape of Russian politics, I had concluded that Gorbachev was the highest tree in the forest. It is true that it was Boris Yeltsin who had stood heroically on a tank, but he could not have stood there for a single minute were it not for the changes wrought by Gorbachev in the psyche of the Russian people.

The Berlin Wall had fallen and the Soviet satellites in East and Central Europe were already revolving in their independent orbits by the time the effects of the 1991 Russian Revolution were felt in the Middle East. The Soviet attitudes toward Israel had begun to soften in 1989. Access by Israelis to the Soviet Union and meetings with its leaders were no longer exceptional. There had been a time when an Israeli ambassador who managed to say

---

[1] *Julius Caesar* (Act III, Scene ii).
[2] Ramin Jahanbegloo, *Conversations with Isaiah Berlin* (London: Peter Halban, 1992), p. 201.

"good evening" to a Soviet diplomat at a cocktail party would send an excited telegram to the foreign office in Jerusalem and would leak the sensational news to the Israeli press. I was never impressed by such "achievements."

By the end of the 1980s, the boycott of Israel by the Soviet Union was almost ended. The agreement that I had made with Gromyko in 1973 for our Foreign Ministers to meet regularly at UN sessions was ignored once by Allon in 1974, and then by Dayan in 1977 and 1978. Dayan never regarded the Soviet Union as one of the countries worthy of his interest and attention. The Soviet-Israeli ministerial meetings were renewed by Shamir and Peres when each of them in turn came to head our Foreign Ministry. I myself received an invitation from the Soviet Peace Movement in 1989 to give lectures in Moscow, Leningrad and Kiev, but I did not consummate the plan, owing to the disappearance of Mr. Bogdanov, the official who had tendered the invitation. The way in which Soviet officials vanished from sight and sound had often disconcerted me. My curiosity about the fate or destiny of Dmitri Chuvakhin, who was the Soviet ambassador when Moscow broke relations with us, remained unsatisfied until the end of May 1992, when he suddenly emerged from twenty-five years of anonymity to send me a greeting from a dacha near Moscow.

Despite the virulent rhetoric of Soviet leaders in denouncing Israel during the twenty-five years of broken relations, the Soviet Union had never repudiated the principle that Andrei Gromyko had formulated to me at Geneva in December 1973. He had said that he opposed our policies, not our existence, and that the Soviet Union had been the first to see the Middle East as an area that must contain a Jewish State.

As the 1980s drew toward their close, nobody in Israel foresaw the awesome breakthrough that eventually occurred, but the prediction that the U.S.S.R. would not permanently violate international stability did not seem far-fetched. I had never been one of the extremist Cold Warriors who trembled before Soviet power. Back in 1983 I had written:

> The Soviet Union has been transformed by the end of the Brezhnev area. From being the center of world revolution dedicated to the downfall of the existing social order, it has evolved into a mature global power whose interest in stability balances its revolutionary zeal.[3]

At that time, no one in Israel or in the Western world foresaw the intensity of the forces that were already corroding the federal power that gave coherence to the Soviet system. The Soviet Union was never anything like a nation,

---

[3]Abba Eban, *The New Diplomacy* (New York: Random House, 1983), p. 399.

but the use of the term "union" conveyed the impression that it had a structure more or less similar to that of the United States. Georgia was deemed to be Pennsylvania and the Ukraine was something like New York State.

The reality was different. Behind what Churchill had memorably called the "iron curtain," "from Stettin on the Baltic to Trieste in the Adriatic," the elements that had held the bulky superpower together for seven decades were dissolving rapidly. It turned out that the U.S.S.R. had never really been a "union" at all. The traditional symbols of the individual republics had always excited the sentiment of the masses more passionately than the Western Sovietologists had ever perceived. How many of us until very recent years could even recite the names of the fifteen republics? Moscow, the capital, had apparently evoked little respect among the diverse nationalities. By 1990 the central government had neither dignity nor effectiveness, and it was not even inspiring as much fear as in its heyday. Seweryn Bialer has added the interesting insight that younger people in the Soviet Union had become so ashamed of the incompetence and grayness of Chernenko, the leader who reigned briefly between Andropov and Gorbachev, that they were driven by sheer self-respect to require a different sort of leadership.[4] Gorbachev with his Western habits, sophisticated rhetoric and well-dressed wife was so different that one tended to forget that he was the product of the same Marxist education and Leninist loyalties as all his predecessors.

We now groped in the dark. Occasionally, reports by immigrants reaching Israel from the Soviet Union hinted at a disintegrative process within the Soviet system, but we tended to attribute their warnings to the normal rancor of émigrés toward the society from which they were taking flight. There was also the embarrassing fact that Israel had grown up, as it were, in the shelter of the Cold War, and our anti-Sovietism, paraded more ostentatiously by the Likud than by Labor, had become materially and politically useful in every political and material sense. It seemed to offer a permanent assurance of American support.

The turning point was August 2, 1990. Iraq invaded Kuwait.

Historians will always speculate whether George Bush's belligerent response was influenced by the presence of Margaret Thatcher as his guest in Colorado; it was an opportunity for her to pose as the reincarnation of Churchill reacting to Hitler's invasion of Russia in 1941. No less momentous was the fact that U.S. Secretary of State James Baker was traveling in Russia on August 2 with his Soviet opposite number, Eduard Shevardnadze. On August 3 they jointly condemned Iraq and announced the suspension of the military aid by which both superpowers were vigorously reinforcing Saddam

---

[4]*Foreign Affairs* (Winter 1991–2), p. 167.

Hussein's regime in Baghdad. The Soviet signature on the August 3 statement was sensational. The formulation was vintage Soviet style: The Iraqi invasion was described as "an act of perfidy and a blatant violation of international law and the UN Charter." A few hours previously, Iraq had been a close ally of the Soviet Union. Over a thousand Soviet advisers were actively enhancing Saddam Hussein's power at the very moment when the punitive American-Soviet declaration was published. The Baker-Shevardnadze communiqué of August 3, 1990, is the documentary epitaph of the Cold War. Curiously, the only previous occasion when American and Soviet representatives had jointly denounced an aggression was in the UN Security Council on July 15, 1948, when their culprit was the group of Arab states whom I had charged with responsibility for rejecting the continuation of the truce with Israel.

Between early August and mid-January 1991, we Israelis were made aware of our marginality in the new international alignment. From Washington and Moscow came entreaties to Jerusalem to adopt a low profile, which has never been a characteristically Israeli posture. Saudi Arabia, not Israel, was going to be the place where the great coalition of power would assemble and the Bush administration was already planning a massive force and a huge concentration of firepower in the desert sands. The UN Security Council was now an American arena, and illusions of a "new international order" proliferated as the United States accumulated resolutions endowing it with a legitimate right of intervention. An essentially unilateralist American policy was basking in the sunlight of the exaggeratedly revered doctrine of collective security.

The notion that Israel would be marginal to the imminent war had never secured the assent of Saddam Hussein. He made it clear that he would exploit the Zionist scapegoat in an effort to detach Egypt and Syria from George Bush's coalition. The embarrassing complexity of our position had now become manifest: We were going to be the target of an aggression to which we were forbidden by iron circumstance to respond. Moreover, the bilateral American-Israeli honeymoon was evidently over. The United States in every decision would henceforward balance Israel against the pro-Western Arab states that had joined the American military forces.

The fact that Israelis suffered fewer casualties from the Desert War than anyone could have predicted does not reflect the depth of our anguish. In the weeks leading up to Saddam's debacle, the certainty that he would attack our civil populations filled our minds and hearts.

The Israeli ordeal in its sharpest form began on January 15, 1991. Suzy and I spent the "Scud weeks" commuting between Herzliya and Jerusalem. The whole nation worked by day and waited for the Iraqi Scuds by night. In Herzliya, I tried to add some pages to *Personal Witness* and to the TV scripts of a new PBS series. Our home would have been lonely during the expected Iraqi air raids and had no shelter facilities, so we would drive between Jerusalem and Herzliya in the afternoons. The most acute sense of vulnerability afflicted us on the congested roads when an air-raid warning could have been heard at any time. One Scud fell perilously close to the Herzliya main road. In Jerusalem, we were surrounded at the Laromme Hotel by Jewish visitors from abroad who came to demonstrate solidarity. At the Jerusalem Hilton Hotel, I accepted the request of our Foreign Office to brief many of the newspaper and TV representatives who came to "cover" the war.

It soon became apparent that Jerusalem was not one of Saddam Hussein's designated targets, but his Scuds nearly always fell on places that he did not intend to hit, and missed places that he did want to injure. Most alerts were therefore countrywide, and the nontargets had most to fear. The actual sufferers were mainly the residents of Ramat Gan and Tel Aviv. At one stage, Mayor Shlomo (Chich) Lahat of Tel Aviv protested against citizens who sought refuge outside Tel Aviv. He called them "deserters." This puzzled me, since I recalled that in the 1941 London blitz, the authorities were grateful to Londoners who looked after themselves instead of throwing their health and welfare on to the shoulders of the hard-pressed authorities. The very invocation of this precedent reminded me that few Israelis other than I had actually experienced prolonged aerial assaults.

The luck that saved us from mass casualties has led many people to underestimate the traumatic psychological impact of the Desert War for Israelis. Since 1967, many Israelis believed that the post-1967 frontiers gave us permanent assurance of safety from enemy fire. I had never supported this view. In 1990 it became evident that we would now be vulnerable to devastating aggression from places beyond the range of our response by tanks and artillery. We would even be limited in our capacity of reacting by air, since few of our aircraft were equipped to get to Baghdad, perform an intricate operation and get back without refueling. We had lost our capacity of conventional punitive reprisal. We were forced to understand that we now had an adversary whom we could not reach with our major weapons. This made the 1967 talk about "King Solomon's frontiers" even more frivolous than I had always considered it to be.

The spectacle of our children donning gas masks evoked poignant recollections when we recalled the gas chambers in which hundreds of thousands of Jewish children had been asphyxiated in the Nazi decade. Saddam Hussein had assaulted us without any provocation, and we had been unable to return his malice and his fire for fear of disrupting the coalition of which Egypt and Saudi Arabia were integral members.

Many Israelis accepted our enforced military passivity with embarrassment. I did not altogether share this emotion. It is not strictly accurate to claim that American pressure or coalition sensitivities alone prevented us from taking our own action to eliminate the Iraqi Scuds. The truth is that we had no capacity to avenge our few tragic deaths without incurring losses of human life far greater than any that we had suffered. When Pentagon officials were shown the kind of military "options" that had been considered in Jerusalem, they congratulated themselves and us for not having risked them. To enter western Iraq looking for Scuds and launchers would have been an endless search for mobile needles in concealed haystacks. If there were any devices or strategies or weapons suitable for resisting the Scud danger, the American and British forces had them in greater numbers than we. It is only now that the United States and Israel are cooperating in the development of the Arrow missile, which will be more effective than the American "Patriots" in destroying sophisticated ground-to-air missiles.

A strange feature of Israel's limited role in the Desert War was the discomfort with which many Israelis reacted to our exclusion from the UN coalition. I found this to be paradoxical. For years we had lamented the circumstance that we always had to stand against our enemies alone. Now we were suddenly affronted by the fact that one of the greatest military forces in world history was acting in its own interest to inflict enormous damage on our most dangerous foe. We had always complained that nobody else ever punished our enemies. We were now complaining that great forces in the world and in our region were smashing our enemy's power with deadly blows, without giving us a chance to reciprocate and thus to fulfill our principle of independent self-defense. Our historic experience had not accustomed us to the notion of alliance, in which each ally plays its role in its own time, not always simultaneously. We felt a strange guilt at observing that others were doing work from which we would reap large benefits.

I felt none of these qualms. I could recall occasions in which other powers had benefited tangibly from contests in which we Israelis had done all the fighting and taken all the losses. Had not the United States derived a sharp lift of prestige and confidence from Israel's successes in the 1967 war? The Soviet Union had then been humiliated by the military failure of its Egyptian and Syrian allies, and Americans, after the shame of Vietnam, could now say: "Our side is winning." I do not recall that the Americans were conscience-stricken in 1967 because they were benefiting from the lonely sacrifice of their Israeli ally.

Ben-Gurion had once said that what mattered to Israel was not what the *goyim* said but what the Jews did. I had never regarded this as his most felicitous utterance, and it did not echo his authentic doctrine, for no Israeli leader ever attached more importance to Israel's position in the world. In 1990–1991 our destiny was potently affected by processes that were external to what Jews either said or did. Our security was enhanced by the Desert War from which we had been excluded and by the collapse of communism of which we, with the rest of the world, were astonished spectators.

By the end of 1991, our sense of success was growing fast. Our most savage and dangerous enemy had been crushed In the battlefield and was suffering humiliating intrusions into his enfeebled weapons system. Syria had always been careful not to attack us except when it could be sure of two conditions— parallel Egyptian action and the existence of a safety net of Soviet protection whenever President Assad got himself into trouble with Israel. Neither of these two conditions now existed, and Assad moved into the winning American side with astonishing nonchalance. Saudi Arabia, as the pivot of the Desert Storm operation, began to see Israel as a fellow victim of Saddam Hussein's Scuds and as a potential collaborator in postwar economic enterprises. A year later, it even proposed a transaction whereby Israel would freeze new settlements and Saudi Arabia would cancel the Arab boycott regulations. If Shamir had accepted this proposal, as any other Israeli prime minister would have done, Israel's economy would have taken a forward leap. But Mr. Shamir did not give first priority to the Israeli economy. Or to the Israeli education system. Or to Israel's social problems. Or to Israel's relations with the United States. He was entirely obsessed by the perceived need to sacrifice every other interest to the unique obsession with putting caravans on Samarian or Judean hills. The words "Medinat Yisrael," the "State of Israel" as defined in Knesset legislation, was never heard on his lips. "Eretz Yisrael"—Israel plus the West Bank and Gaza—was now the fashion, a historic and geographical expression that holds our democracy and our occupied territories in a single phrase. The trouble is that "Medinat Yisrael" is a democracy and "Eretz Yisrael," on the contrary, is a land of separate and unequal jurisdictions.

The change in the structure and orientation of the Soviet Union had massively positive consequences in Israel's international relations. Gorbachev decreed the resumption of diplomatic relations, Yeltsin appointed his envoys, as did the heads of most of the other republics. The Baltic states offered a normal relationship with Israel. Nothing except their enforced subservience to Moscow had ever separated them from us. This was true of Poland, Czechoslovakia, Hungary and Bulgaria. Even Albania became a scene of rapprochement with Israel. Countries, such as India and China, that had spurned Israel in the name of "nonalignment" discovered that there was no sense in this alienation. Competitive nonalignment was no longer a doctrine or a practice. There was nobody with whom not to align.

The Bush administration, in a high moment of vision, saw a peace opportunity in this new international context. It is to Baker's lasting credit that he tore himself away from the current obsession with the war and allowed himself a glance over the wall into the postwar future. By this he placed himself squarely into the lineage of Kissinger and Carter, who had served Israel greatly by transcending a popular Israeli preference for the status quo. As soon as the ground war against Iraq was over, Baker crisscrossed the Arab countries and Israel, indefatigably promoting the idea of encounter. The old taboos that had inspired the Arab refusal to have any contact with Israel were in discredit. Shamir had no alternative but to accept the precise pattern of an international conference that he had denounced as subversive when Peres and Shultz had proposed it in easier circumstances two years previously. The Madrid conference presented a unique spectacle of Israeli, Palestinian, Jordanian and Syrian delegates around a table, with American and Russian foreign ministers as chairmen and sponsors.

Later, a network of meetings in Moscow, Brussels, Ottawa, Tokyo and Rome took diplomats from Israel and the Arab states on far-flung journeys across the globe in new combinations to discuss the hypothetical consequences of a peace that Israel and its neighbors had not yet decided to conclude. Even Saudi Arabia shared a table with us. Little or nothing was agreed in any of these meetings, and the bilateral talks were trapped in a deadlock through the American decision to avoid active mediation. But it was clear that the Arab dehumanization of Israel by treating us as a lepers' colony was now the relic of a forgotten age. It was easy to dismiss these conference encounters as mere "symbolism," but the Arab-Israeli dialogue of the deaf has always been haunted by such intangibles as recognition, non-recognition, prestige, pride, secret encounters followed by denials of their existence, the shaking or non-shaking of hands, and theological distinction between Arabs who called us Israel and those in whose fevered imaginations we were still the Zionist entity. I calculated that if the refusal of the Arabs to sit with us had been a legitimate cause for condemnation, their sudden readiness to overcome their inhibitions could not be as worthless as many in the Israeli Right pretended them to be. On the other hand, I predicted that if the "peace process" continued to consist of noncommittal seminars in scattered cities, it would become ridiculous before becoming effective.

The most sensational innovation in the Madrid talks was the posture of the Palestinian delegation. It was composed of Arabs from the West Bank and Gaza, many of whom were serious academicians and professional people. For some weeks the United States and Israel were engaged in handpicking Palestinian members. I thought and said that this was a grotesque spectacle. Secretary Baker had informed the Shamir government that Israel would not have to negotiate "with anyone that we did not want to negotiate with." This platitude was communicated to us alone, though it should in all civility have been addressed to all members of all the delegations. Baker had also stipulated that Israel was entitled to negotiate with "satisfactory Palestinians." It was as if a heavyweight boxer had asked to defend his title against a "satisfactory" opponent—someone with a glass jaw and two broken arms. My own conviction was that the essential quality for a negotiating partner was not amiability, but representativity—and the capacity for fulfilling an agreement in the test of action.

I had no doubt that Mr. Shamir would eventually have to negotiate with the PLO or its surrogates, or with nobody at all. He would probably have preferred the last-named option, but in the post–Desert War climate, this was no longer available. His tactical skill, which was formidable, would be devoted to the opening of a dialogue from which he could ensure that nothing substantive would flow.

At one time it really did appear that the question of Israel's right to legitimize or disqualify members of the Palestinian delegation would be the make-or-break issue of the peace process. A reasonable and compact proposal made by President Mubarak late in 1989 for a conference with Israelis and Palestinians in Cairo had broken down on this issue on a tie vote in the inner Cabinet.

As I surveyed recent history, I concluded that there had been no long-term successes for the wish of ruling powers to handpick the representatives of subject nations. In the long run, the French had to talk to the FLN, the British to Gandhi, Nehru and Makarios, the Rhodesian leaders to Mugabe and the South African nationalists to Mandela.

When the Israeli soccer squad had dreams of participating in the World Cup encounter in Rome if it could, improbably, defeat Colombia, I went on the air to suggest, sarcastically, that Mr. Shamir should insist on Israel's right to appoint the Colombian goalkeeper. This went down very well. Soccer is so popular in Israel that even the most rigorously religious parties have never suggested that Sabbath games be forbidden.

Eventually, Israelis and PLO leaders met on the basis of a fiction. In reality we would be negotiating with Palestinians who were passionate adherents of the PLO. They would go to Tunis for instructions, at first furtively, and later openly. The Shamir government would be allowed to pretend that the Palestinians were "representatives from the territories" who had never heard of the PLO and whose visits to Tunis were press speculations. This is the kind of transparent pretense that alienates diplomacy from public understanding, but I agreed that negotiation by a subterfuge was better than not having a peace process at all.

The important innovation was that the Palestinians had changed their policies, their rhetoric and their image. Since this had happened without the pomp and circumstance of the Sadat-Begin encounter, many Israelis failed to grasp the momentous nature of this change. The aim of our diplomacy and our military organization had always been to get the Palestinians to change their attitudes, and when this occurred, we seemed unable to adapt ourselves to the change.

The Palestinians were now willing to accept an interim period of self-government in which their status would still fall short of sovereignty. This was the very Camp David doctrine that they had previously rejected. The more perceptive among them understood that they were unlikely to achieve real independence without a transitional phase in which they would have to reassure Israel of their good faith. They might even have noticed Henry Kissinger's analysis,[5] which suggested that the momentum of the Camp

---

[5] Kissinger, *Observations*, p. 96.

David accords, if its text is taken seriously, is more likely to lead to Palestinian statehood than to anything else.

The rhetoric of the mainstream Palestinians is now in harmony with their proposals. They speak of Israel in adversarial but formally courteous terms, avoiding the frenzied invective that alienated most of world opinion in previous years. As a result of the new policies and rhetoric, the Palestinian delegates at Madrid won friends during the conference. It is difficult to portray Dr. Haidar el Shafi, who resembles the kindly family physician in a Hollywood movie, as one of those wild terrorists with knives between their teeth and bombs ticking away in their pockets. Hanan Ashrawi, whom Moshe Arens had implausibly designated as the authority who sanctions murderous raids, looked to TV watchers more like a headmistress of a British finishing school in Switzerland where traditional values are inculcated. Hanan Ashrawi and Feisal Husseini, the leading Palestinian in the negotiations, were able to dissociate themselves from the murderous outrages committed by their rivals in the Muslim "Hammas" party. Even the Syrian negotiators, without changing their militant tone, have been assiduous in attending the meetings prescribed in the American "peace process." Their demands continue to be stringent in Israeli eyes, but the fact is that they are asking for the return of the Golan Heights in exchange for peace, which is not all that far from the solution that the Eshkol government (of which Menachem Begin was a member) empowered me to offer the Syrians on June 19, 1967, with the crucial condition of demilitarization.

The sense of new opportunity obscured by old prejudice emerges even more strongly from the Jordanian attitudes since Madrid. Jordanian ministers openly fraternize with Israeli officials and dream of the horizons that they see over the hills, with nothing but an Israeli decision separating them and us from a peace that was once the Israeli goal. The question "do they want peace" was asked in the world more frequently about Israel than about our adversaries. Is it too farfetched to conclude that Zionism may have reached its historic goal—and is tragically reluctant to take "yes" for an answer? Our aim was never the destruction of the adversary. Arab nationalism is indestructible by the sheer weight of a massive human reality. The Zionist aim in its central expression has always been not to eliminate the Arabs but to change their way of thought; to bring them to an understanding of what is possible and what is unnattainable.

The presence of Arab delegates in civilized discourse with Israelis, at a higher level of formal authority than that of their Israeli counterparts, indicates that we may be celebrating a Zionist triumph. It was achieved, first of all, by the attritional effects of our consolidation. For more than forty years, the Israeli air was vibrant with the sound of hammers knocking towns, villages, roads, schools and houses together. The Arab world eventually saw the Israeli enterprise as a growing organism within its recognized boundaries and were too intelligent to believe that Israel in the 1990s was a candidate for "destruction." They could see for themselves how little the rhythm of Israel's development was affected by the chaotic, fragmented and explosive environment in which Israel managed to grow. The Israeli military triumphs would not have counted for anything permanent if they were not achieved amid an irrepressible urge to build. The sense of having a new creation entrusted to our hands glorified the Zionist enterprise in its better years, when the object of our settlement policy was to serve a human cause and not to impose our muscular defiance on impotent neighbors.

While Israel counted its gains after the Desert War, the Palestinians inspected their wounds. The PLO had absorbed many blows. It lost its gains in the West through its own folly in embracing Saddam Hussein. Its friendships in East Europe vanished when the members of the Warsaw Pact preferred to seek reconciliation with Israel, rather than serve as arsenals and training grounds for the PLO. The challenge for the Palestinians is not to get what they have always wanted, but to save what little they can in a world context where their traditional advantages have melted away.

There is a tragic paradox in the fact that while pragmatism moved forward in the Arab world, fundamentalism had been making progress in Israel. Despite the massive gains for Israeli security as a result of the Desert War and the collapse of communism, the Shamir government responded apprehensively to the challenge posed by the peace process. There were prime ministerial statements every week affirming in loud decibels that Israel will never relinquish a centimeter of Arab-populated land in the West Bank and that we would insist on deciding with whom "not to talk" in negotiations with the Palestinians. His coalition partners were even more emphatic in their rejection of trading land for peace. The arrival of Secretary Baker in the Middle East was often greeted with the demonstrative establishment of a new settlement in the West Bank or Gaza, as if Mr. Shamir had some interest in humiliating the United States and discrediting its mediatorial role. While the Israeli government declared that the permanent status of the West Bank or Gaza would have to be negotiated, it counteracted this principle by refusing to admit the issue for negotiation for at least three years until the boundary question would reach the table after a period of autonomy. Shamir's intention appeared to be to create an irreversible situation in which there would not be any continuous area of predominantly Arab habitation in any part of the former Palestinian Mandatory area. The partition logic that enabled Israel to be born as a Jewish state, recognized by the world community, was to be rendered obsolete by unilateral action with the enforced acquiescence of a docile United States. Shamir did not object to what the Americans said so long as they did not restrain him from doing what he wanted.

The consequence of this policy was that the establishment of new settlements in the occupied areas had become the central priority of the Israeli government. This aim was held to be more important than the absorption of Russian Jews, than the development of the peace process and than the maintenance of a cooperative relationship with the United States. This policy could only be implemented as a direct or indirect result of massive financial assistance from the United States. The alleged "crisis" in U.S.-Israeli relations in the spring of 1992 arose because Shamir required the United States to finance a policy to which American policies and interests have always been unanimously opposed. If Washington balked, an Israeli minister could be relied upon to accuse the United States of racism and anti-Semitism. Many Israelis and most American Jewish leaders were offended by this extremism, for the Bush administration had accorded Israel fourteen billion dollars in four years, thus overtaking all previous presidencies in the scope of the reinforcement that it offered our economy and our defense system.

There was no chance that the settlement policy could be acceptable to the United States or to the Arab world, or even that it could be the basis of an Israeli consensus. When Yitzhak Rabin was elected to the leadership of the Labor party in the early part of 1992, he declared that he would abandon Mr. Shamir's "priorities." The funds that Shamir was expending at a prolific rate in the West Bank and Gaza would be devoted by a Rabin administration to the absorption of Russian Jews with the corollary aim of salvaging the peace process from deadlock and collapse. Never have the policies of the two major Israeli parties been defined in terms of such sharp confrontation. The Likud belief that annexation and peace are compatible is not shared by mainstream Israelis.

In his first contact with the Arab-Israeli conflict after the 1967 war, Kissinger had defined the conflict in terms of parallel illusions:

> Israel chased the illusion that it could both acquire territory and achieve peace. Its Arab adversaries pursued the opposite illusion, that they could gain territory without offering peace . . .[6]

The balance is now changing. None of the Arab governments or peoples represented in the peace process any longer declares or believes that it can "gain territory without offering peace." The parallel illusion—that Israel can keep all the Arab-populated territory and achieve peace—is entrenched more strongly than ever before in the mind of the Israeli government, though not in the central arenas of Israeli opinion.

In his book on the Yom Kippur War,[7] Chaim Herzog has a moving passage describing the desperate situation faced by Israel on October 6, 1973, when the Syrian tank assault began. The Israeli commander had to argue with the settlers on the front lines for several hours to persuade them to carry out the order to evacuate their settlements so as to enable the Israeli tank forces to take up their positions! Precious hours were being lost. The civilians, with their children and senior citizens, their cattle and chickens, were

---

[6]Kissinger, *Years of Upheaval*, p. 199.
[7]Chaim Herzog, *The War of Atonement* (London: Weidenfeld and Nicolson, 1975).

targets; they were not sources of strength. In tank battles Israel needed tanks and guns, not farm produce or civilian debates. The notion that civilians at points of armed confrontation are anything but a burden on Israel's security has long been discarded by professional military opinion. In the Elon Moreh case in the Israeli Supreme Court in 1975, the military witnesses described them as "a burden." Security is not what the settlements are about.

Mr. Shamir replied with a simple formula: In his vocabulary the territories, namely Nablus and Jenin, Ramallah and Tulkarem, are not linked to security, but they quite simply "belong to us. They are ours."

Do Nablus and Ramallah really "belong" to Shamir? This is clearly not the case in international jurisprudence, up to and including the Camp David accords that bear Begin's name. These accords define the West Bank and Gaza as areas of undetermined sovereignty of which the permanent status cannot be determined without Palestinian consent. Shamir was in perpetual revolt against Begin's signature.

There is a deeper human sense in which the territories do not "belong" to Mr. Shamir. We Israelis did not build the streets of Nablus; we did not erect its mosques and its town squares; we did not study in its schools; our parents and grandparents are not buried there; Shamir cannot read its street signs or understand what comes out of its transistor sets. And his prospect of ever walking its unprepossessing streets is close to zero. We face the disparity between the claim of Israeli power and the silent, stubborn evidence of a rooted Palestinian reality. There are 1.8 million Palestinians who will not go away. The dilemma that they pose for Israel has been vividly illustrated by Amos Oz, modern Hebrew literature's most resonant voice:

> I study the elusive cunning of the Biblical charm of this landscape; and isn't all of this charm Arab through and through? The lodge and the cucumber garden, the watchman's hut and the cisterns, the shade of the fig tree and the pale silver of the olive, the grape arbors and the flocks of sheep—these picturesque slopes that bewitched from afar the early Zionists; these primeval glades that reduced the poet Bialik to tears . . . the tinkle of the goats' bells which entwined, like magic webs, the hearts of the early Zionist settlers who came from Russia thirsty to don Arab garb and to speed on their horses toward the Arabic biblicality, the enchanted groves of Amos Kenan[8] and the longed-for cisterns of Naomi Shemer,[9] yearning for the bare-faced stony mountains, for merger into the bosom of these gentle, sleepy slopes so very far removed from Yiddish and the ghetto, right into the heart of this oriental rock-strewn tenderness. Are these not the landscapes of those whom Yael Elitsur[10] sees as "the life and death enemy"? You with your bulldozers,

---

[8]A Hebrew writer and a leading advocate of Israel-Palestinian co-existence.
[9]The songwriter, author of "Jerusalem the Golden."
[10]The wife of the leader of the settlers' movement in the West Bank.

will spread your factory-built houses with their asbestos roofs and solar water-heaters and symmetrical rows of white houses and security fences and antennas across the hills and vales. Thou shalt see the land from afar but thou shalt not go thither. For if you should enter, the penetration will not be one of harmony, but of occupation and capitulation and destruction. Where shall we turn our ancient Biblical longings if Samaria is filled with prefab villas . . . ?"[11]

These word pictures are too idyllic for my liking, yet they do prove that Zionism in its pre-Likud era had a reluctant respect for the rootedness of the Palestinian rural landscape. There was no illusion that this rooted community would disappear, even though much of it was ravaged by wars that Arab leaders themselves had willed. Oz cries out for coexistence with an Arab society that has lost its capacity to be an existential threat to Israel. I echo this cry of the heart. What is wrong with accepting the existence of this neighbor with which we, the Israelis of the first generation, vowed to live in adjoining societies, each in national freedom? Why should our Founders' vision be crushed in the debris of a neighboring people's memories and dreams when we are strong enough to sustain their proximity?

This was the precise question that was put to the Israeli electorate on June 23, 1992. The pollsters sadistically predicted a hung Parliament in which none of the major parties would be able to form a majority without what the French government, in a similar quandary, had called "uneasy cohabitation." I faced this prospect in a mood of apocalyptic fear. Around the world, the air was alive with change, not all of it favorable, but none of it making provision for the tenacious stagnation to which Shamir's rule seemed to condemn us. Would I never see even the first glow of a post-Likud dawn?

I went to the Dan Hotel on the Tuesday evening where the Labor leaders were assembled in the quadrennial ritual of expectation. Tradition decrees that as soon as the polling stations are closed at 10:00 P.M. a celebrated TV commentator, Chaim Yavin, in the mold of Walter Cronkite, declaims the computerized findings taken from a few dozen stations that have proved exemplary, in the sense of always having anticipated the destined result within an error margin of two seats. The mood was tense, the sweat prolific and the nerves taut. I expected nothing good to ensue. In our party we had been conditioned for fifteen years to believe that democracy was more noble in its procedures than in its results. The Labor Party had conducted the election on the basis of hero-worship of Yitzhak Rabin, who had narrowly defeated Shimon Peres in the primaries. The primaries themselves were an innovation: 160,000 paid-up members of the party could vote for the candidate for the premiership and, subsequently, for the forty faithful who aspired to membership in the Knesset. Rabin was not an easy candidate for charis-

---

[11]Amos Oz, *In the Land of Israel* (London: Fontana, 1983), pp. 239–40.

matic treatment. He was the sort of man who, if anyone stopped him in the street and asked him politely for the time of the day, might well reply, "Why don't you buy a watch?" He regarded the bulk of the human race with apprehensive suspicion. The consequent lack of the conventional graces was ascribed by most Rabinologists to abrasiveness. Strangely, I, who had no reason for more emollient appraisals, considered that it might be no more than shyness and therefore not to be censured out of hand.

Rabin had run on a platform of castigatory menace toward our Arab neighbors, who at that time were notably mild of attitude and diction, so that it was never clear against whom Rabin was brandishing his clubs. Yet behind these punitive scowls, he showed a disciplined obedience to the Labor Party platform, which spoke of freezing the establishment of new settlements in the West Bank and Gaza and negotiating with Arab states on the basis of "territorial compromise," which is a code word for restoring Arab rule in the occupied territories, subject to peaceful relations and provisions for demilitarization and other security arrangements. Rabin gave a somewhat harsh expression to his moderate territorial proposals. He gave the impression that he wanted to rid our state of Arabs, not because it was wrong to rule another nation, but because Arabs are awkward folk to have around the home and are intrinsically disagreeable.

Nevertheless his formulations were a welcome change from the Likud's insistence on holding 1.8 million Palestinians under what Rabin himself had called "the iron fist." The United States was only one of the 160 governments that ardently desired Rabin's accession. For one thing, he had an almost deferential attitude to America, which he identified with American power rather than with a Jeffersonian legacy. Hard-headed leaders in the world community called Rabin "a man with whom other men can do business." Nobody had ever heard Shamir so described.

Some time before election day it had transpired that the Israeli nation did not see itself as authentically represented by Shamir's defiance. Porcupines are not the most sensuous bedfellows, and Israelis had begun to wish for the pristine glow of popularity. Moreover, Shamir was multiplying his enemies across a wide field. He was asking the United States for three things. First was ten billion dollars, in the form of loan guarantees for the absorption of immigrants from the former Soviet Union. Second, he wanted the continuation of a "peace process," which consisted of marking time so vigorously as to give the impression of forward movement, thus giving Shamir the appearance of peaceful virtue without any of the pain and tears inherent in real compromise. And, third, he wanted unlmited license for establishing Israeli settlements in the territories, which were the only remaining arena for "fulfilling the legitimate aspirations of the Palestine people." This phrase from the Camp David agreement of 1978 had been signed by Menachem Begin, only to disappear from his prime ministerial lips as soon as the ink was dry.

There was a brief moment in which I feared that the Bush-Baker team would indulge Shamir's appetite for unearned benefits, in order to keep him within the peace process and to avoid an inconvenient clash with a Jewish electorate that then seemed to admire hawkish shrieks rather that dovish melodies. If the U.S. had been willing to shower its billions on an Israeli regime that was eroding the foundations of an American peace process, Shamir would have proved that he, not the president of the United States, was the real architect of American foreign policy. Approving the loans and settlement freedom would have been a blatant intervention by the United States in the Israeli elections with an intention to secure permanent Likud rule. As things turned out, Bush himself seemed alert to the consequences of his policy. He resolutely held the line in demanding a sharp diminution of settlements activity as a natural environment for granting the loans. He understood that Shamir was like a man who negotiated the sale of an automobile while unobtrusively removing the tires and steering wheel from the scope of the transaction.

While Bush and Baker sometimes gave indiscrete expression to their exasperation with Shamir, the mass of Israeli opinion, led by the Labor Party, believed that Shamir, not Bush, was responsible for the disruption of a relationship that was crucial for the security of Israel and for its economic welfare. After all, Begin had no hesitation in accepting a settlement freeze while negotiating with Egypt. If he had not been pliable on this issue, Israeli forces would still be in Sinai exchanging murderous fire with Egyptian forces. Shamir had opposed Israel's withdrawal from war to peace with Egypt and had also opposed Israel's withdrawal from the blood bath in Lebanon. Shamir did not want war; he only wanted its fruits.

The Israeli nation, despite its instinctive respect for existing authority, was becoming impatient with its government's scowling, fist-waving demeanor. It seemed to feel that a new spirit ruled the world, and that it touched even such unlikely segments of humanity as F. W. de Klerk's administration in South Africa. Shamir was offering Israel the opportunity to succeed South Africa as an apartheid state with a whole disenfranchized nation subservient to its power. I was convinced that five more years of Likudism might end in a Palestinian revolt, with most of mankind in sympathy with the Palestinians and with a missile exchange as its ultimate and not so distant prospect.

Another feature of Shamir's regime was a rampant McCarthyism. Shamir believed that dissent was treachery and that opposition to annexationism was a form of subversion. Neither tolerance nor diversity of opinion nor democracy figured high in Shamir's quaint hierarchy of values. He delivered tirades against the Labor movement, accusing it of disregard for the national security, forgetting that ninety percent of the nation's military commanders had sprung from Labor soil. The forty-four elected Knesset members on the Labor side included six generals, while the Likud benches were notable for legislators who could not include a uniformed photograph in their youthful memories. Likud spokesmen were more notable for biblical pontification than for individual military prowess.

I thought that it was effrontery for Shamir and Arens to give stern lectures on national security to Labor leaders who had immersed themselves in professional military experience—such as Rabin, Gur, Kahalani, Barlev, Uri Or, Weizmann, Sneh, Ben Eliezer—or who had been the architects of Israel's strategic deterrent, such as Shimon Peres. I saw the Likud leadership after fifteen years as stricken with the sin of "hubris."

My readers can therefore imagine my rapture when Chaim Yavin came on the TV screen with an incredulous cry of *"mahpach"*—"upheaval"—and went on to declaim the incredible figures: Labor 47, Likud 33, Merets (Labor's ally) 13 and Techiya—bastion of the extreme right—zero. Labor and Likud had almost the same parliamentary strength as Likud and Labor had had when their positions were reversed in 1977. It was the end of the Likud era for years, perhaps a decade. The Zionism of the founders had returned. It would be pragmatic, visionary, terse in expression, concrete in affairs and alive to the movement and the impulse of the modern age. Rejoice, beloved country! Israel had come home to itself.

It was true that I was more enthused by the decline of Likud than by the rise of my own party. But politics like diplomacy is entitled to be judged more by the dangers that it avoids than by the gains that it achieves. Relief rather than exuberance greeted the new government. Among those who welcomed the change were a majority of the Jewish immigrants from the former Soviet republics. The joy of their arrival had been mitigated by the hardships that they had faced. Instead of having the first priority of the national concern and resources, they found themselves relegated to a secondary role. American and other Western Jews gave money for Russian Jews, a great part of which enabled the government to spend its own resources on caravans in Gaza and Nablus. The absorption of Russian Jews was no longer the dominant mystique. A huge sector of them were unemployed and those who had work were employed far below their levels of competence. Shamir had said with engaging candor that he could not understand the fears expressed by his right-wing allies about the talks with Arabs. "My intention was to talk about autonomy for ten years and meanwhile to fill the territories with Jews so that no room would remain for Arab self-government." He left his office and emptied his desk without ever explaining how he expected to maintain a structure in which 4 million Jews would enjoy all the rights and immunities from which 1.8 million Arabs would be excluded.

Rabin has a wide area of action and maneuver. American friendship beams down at him by the very act of his accession. Free of a Greater Israel obsession, he will have resources for the development of neglected urban centers. Russian Jews will come back to the center. Peace negotiations will focus on principal issues, not on badges and rules of procedure. There is hope of an early phase of self-government. Here the challenge will be for the Palestinians. They will have to grasp that a half loaf is better than no bread at all, and that the half loaf could bring a better nourishment into view. A confederation between Israel in more secure boundaries and a Jordanian-Palestinian Confederation with the West Bankers and Gazans in the Arab part of the community is not a certainty, but neither is it pure fantasy. Nothing in political structures is a fantasy if it is based on consent. Coexistence by consent and separation by consent are both legitimate values in the new confusion of nationalisms. The Palestinians will have to face their ordeal of choice.

The task of Likud, as of Labor a decade and a half ago, is to cleanse itself of excessive pride. As a Jew, I have never refuted the Christian prediction that "the meek shall inherit the earth." The question is whether, having inherited it, they will continue to be meek.

Is there a stable solution in sight?

Twenty-five years have passed since I addressed the Council of Europe in Strasbourg in the aftermath of the Six Day War. I had reached the conclusion that Europe's most important offering to Israel should be the force of its own example. Sovereignty must be both respected and transcended. I suggested a community arrangement on the European or Benelux model under which Israelis, Jordanians and Palestinians could each enjoy independence in agreed territorial spheres while offering each other free access and trade, and accepting community obligations in matters of security. The main security provision would be a demilitarization of the West Bank and Gaza. Israelis have been exposed too long to violence from those places for any of us simply to go away and trust to luck. The precise delimitation of boundaries between Israel and the demilitarized West Bank and Gaza would have to be negotiated. Curiously, the Camp David agreement signed by Begin and Sadat spoke of the "boundaries between the West Bank and Gaza and its neighbors." Some people called the idea of Middle Eastern community "Utopia." I find it hard to believe that the structure that I have advocated is any more fanciful than that proposed by Jean Monnet and the Europeans of the first generation, when they created a community of states whose previous wars were infinitely more prolonged, frequent and destructive than those waged between Israelis and Arabs in the past decades. It is precisely because the background is inflamed that a community or confederative structure is needed.

The governments most intimately concerned, including the United States, seem to believe that the question of interrelated state structures should be taken up after such matters as boundaries and security guarantees are decided. They are wrong. An agreement on structural relationships could have an alleviating influence on the contentious issues of boundaries and security. A Palestine state that could do exactly as it liked would arouse serious reservations in all sectors of Israeli opinion. But a Palestine self-governing entity, perhaps confederated with Jordan, that would accept community constraints and a coordinated security policy would pose a lesser threat than

Israel faces in the present volcanic situation. The idea that national freedom is indispensable for Bosnia Herzegovina while military rule is reasonable for the Palestinian people defies all logic. Since 1967 the issue has always been how to reconcile Israeli security with Palestinian freedom. This cannot be achieved without an integrative process in the relations between the peoples that inhabit the Land of Israel.

This issue is particularly acute in the mood and atmosphere of the 1990s. It is extraordinary that any large body of Israelis should not take heed of what the Hebrew phrase calls "the spirit that hovers over the generation." The Europeans call it "zeitgeist" or "l'esprit du siecle." The central theme of the last decade of this century is not nuclear war, but the structure of states and the interplay of nationalities. When Jefferson announced that "governments derive their just powers from the consent of the governed," he was expressing a moral vision, not a living reality. The world of Jefferson was a hierarchic world. Consent of the governed was a very rare commodity.

Two centuries later, Jefferson's dictum is the theme and spirit of the age. The world is closing its mind against coercive jurisdictions. Power retreats before freedom. Rulers yield to their erstwhile subjects. It has happened in Moscow and Warsaw, in Budapest and Sofia, in Bucharest and Tirana, in Prague and Vilnuis and Riga and Estonia. Even in Croatia and Slovenia. Yes, and above all, in South Africa. How will Israel claim to be the "only democracy in the Middle East" if it remains one of the diminishing number of states in which 1.8 million people under its jurisdiction cannot vote or be elected, have no control over the government that rules their lives, cannot move freely, cannot manufacture anything that might compete with Israeli produce, are not allowed to sleep at night inside the country where they go to work at reduced wages, and are subject to penalties, curfews, detention and other rigors that would not be applicable to them if they were Jews or even Arab citizens of Israel?

To be or not to be is not Israel's question. How and what to be is the question. The existence of statehood was never the whole of the Zionist ambition. The nature and quality of the new society occupied the minds of our founders more obsessively than its constitutional forms. There is no other state anywhere whose structure is marked by such sharp discontinuity as that which describes the relations between the area of Israeli democracy and the areas under military rule. How can a society aspire to any degree of social harmony if it rules over an alien nation more than a third of its own size without a single mutual bond of flag, tongue, faith, historic experience, national solidarity, common allegiance or juridical and civic equality?

Throughout my diplomatic career I have taken for granted that nationhood is still the dominant theme of international politics. There is paradox in this fact. Never was the world more united in its destiny—and more fragmented in its structure. In theory the individual nation-state should be in eclipse. It is not a viable unit of security. It does not function as an autonomous economic system. It cannot solve environmental problems within its own limits. Yet there has never been such a swift proliferation of nation-states as in the last quarter century. The multiplicity of nation-states in a world where sovereignty has lost a great part of its meaning is the central political anomaly of our age. The need for men and women to be identified with a social group seems to be as elemental as the need for food, shelter and the perpetuation of the species. Despite the growth of regional and supranational institutions, there is no sign that the individual nation-state is about to be superseded as the focus of allegiance and social pride.

The world is integrating and fragmenting at the same time. The Middle East must think of itself as a community of nation-states, not as an agglomeration of peoples, populations or tribes.

Israel's vulnerability is much increased by the fact that we have not won any degree of international legitimacy for the present territorial and administrative structure. The realistic school of diplomacy held that military power was the dominant theme of interstate relations. It has now been proved that the eclipse of legitimacy is today a more potent issue. The vast changes in the world map have owed more to changing ideas of legitimacy than to the results of military confrontations. Colonialism and imperial rule were once legitimate even in terms of international law. Karl Marx was a devout supporter of the British role in India. So was the great liberal John Stuart Mill. When peoples and regimes ceased to believe that the subjection of nations to other nations was legitimate, a vast crumbling of accepted stabilities took place without much reference to military causes. First, the eclipse of British and French colonial regimes occurred with relatively modest changes in military balances. We then observed the dismantling of the Warsaw Pact, the end of the Berlin Wall and the disintegration of Soviet rule without any change of any kind in the balance of military forces. The delegitimization of apartheid in South Africa had little to do with military force. Movements of ideas are becoming more potent than movement of armies.

In these conditions the tendency of rightist movements in Israel to ignore the importance of legitimacy and to put continued trust in military facts becomes a dangerous source of vulnerability.

On the one occasion in which territorial compromise was tried in our area, it increased our sense of security. The Egyptian-Israeli treaty made us safer by sparing Israeli lives and increasing the relative weight of Israel's existing military power. Nobody concerned with Israel's security would now agree to return to Sinai even if there were a gilt-edged invitation. The idea that security is advanced by seeking maximal proximity to your adversary collapsed under the weight of experience in Sinai and Lebanon. The Sharon doctrine, which told us that if you put your head in the crocodile's mouth, you cause anxiety to the crocodile, was discredited in the Lebanese war.

I have no reason to regret that so much of my diplomacy was concerned with the establishment of international legitimacy for Israel's statehood. The provisionality of military results, the tendency to find the winners of wars swiftly losing the exaltation of victory, has been one of the chastening impressions of my half century in international politics. There is a realm of diplomacy that lies beyond realism. It is a world in which nations seem compelled to express their own vision of a human order even if there is little chance of attaining it. Voluntary cessions of power in the post-1945 world have been so prodigious in their scope that the denial of a visionary element in world politics becomes factually absurd.

The most promising feature of modern diplomatic literature is its restrained mood. There is little self-delusion. Those who seek Grand Designs for the immediate transformation of the human condition are likely to suffer disappointment. Yet the traditions and institutions of diplomacy, developed in a long sweep of history, may have a protective role if they are put to work wisely and well. Problems of war and international rivalry may never be "solved," but there is a rational hope that they can be kept in restraint. War prevented is a kind of peace, perhaps the only kind of peace that nations will ever know. This may sound unambitious and unattractively sober in comparison with the messianic yearnings for perfect peace that fill many of the noble chapters of literature. Diplomacy is not theology; it does not promise salvation. But diplomats, scarred by their own experience, have few choices but to inhabit a middle emotional ground between excessive skepticism and exaggerated hope. Once we come to terms with the fact that international politics is fundamentally different from any other kind of politics, we shall at least enjoy the shelter of realism. The central fact about international politics is that power is not controlled, since there is no authority capable of controlling it. It is only in this generation that a secretary-general of the United Nations has made a concrete suggestion for endowing international law with a modicum of force, albeit as the service of agreement not of coercion.

Diplomacy, therefore, has to be empirical, pragmatic and intuitive, since it cannot rest its assumptions on any rigorous mathematics. It depends, in the last resort, on the way in which its practitioners react to opportunities and dangers as they arise. The fact that it was possible to organize a great coalition of force to prise Iraq out of Kuwait does not mean that this kind of enterprise can or will be emulated in other conflicts and thus establish collective security as an international norm. The failure of international action to restrain Serbia in 1992 proves that a new international order based on collective resistance to aggression has not yet dawned.

Memory brings me full circle. My political career began when I sat with the aging Chaim Weizmann and we drafted his last speech before a Zionist

Congress. The theme was that Masada had been a disaster in Jewish history since it ended in heroic death, not in life. It should be studied for avoidance, not for emulation. There is a tendency among Jewish historians to measure heroism by self-sacrifice. But the ancient rabbis condemned Bar Kochba, who rebelled against the Romans in conditions that were bound to result in the destruction of Jewish statehood and a long exile of the Jews. The fallacy of military force unrestrained by a sense of prudence and consequence was a terrible lesson on which the Jews had many centuries of powerlessness to reflect amid tears.

Life is the theme. My own has been lived intensely and its spiritual and intellectual rewards have abundantly surpassed its griefs. The national cause that has illuminated my path has prospered, although I cannot forget that its triumphs have been snatched out of the ashes of disaster. My fortune placed me in the turbulent center, not on the external fringe, of this drama. It is for others to evaluate the attitudes that I took and the service that I gave.

There is no doubt that the pervasive theme of Israel's performance is triumph. And yet the victorious State of Israel has more unsolved marks of interrogation hanging over it than most other political units in the modern world. Israel's structure, dimensions, boundaries, human composition, political regime, Jewish vocation and moral quality all became uncertain once the underlying principles of the early years were abandoned. Our founders envisioned a situation in which we would live in peace side by side with a neighboring nation in a context of democratic freedom. Israelis and Palestinians are now living in physical proximity but in spiritual alienation. Neither of these two human worlds seeks harmony with the other through any compromise of its separate nature. They can only achieve peace in separate identities. Achievement has been abundant, but we are still involved in an unfinished quest.

For most of my half century of public life, I have been concerned with Israel's relations with its external realm. I have helped to create a tradition of response to a nation's struggle in revolutionary situations. The documentary evidence confirms my impression that I have had an influence on the way that Israel is regarded and regards itself in the perspectives of history. I have had an unequaled opportunity of communication. My platforms have been those with huge listening constituencies. My PBS series had an accumulated rating of tens of millions of viewers, and my new TV production on the history of Israel and the Middle East bids fair to reach an even larger audience. My arenas have been international organizations at the height of tensions, television and radio news programs, and—on two occasions— access to the world of public television where I have interpreted the currents of Jewish civilization and the struggle of my country for survival and peace.

My audiences have been counted in many millions, and their willingness to hear me has exceeded every rational hope. I have sometimes wondered whether, in my urgency of appeal and advocacy, I may have committed Israel to levels of virtue and achievement beyond anything that could fairly be asked of it in the light of the environment in which it arose.

I have found intellectual satisfaction in my preoccupation with diplomacy, quite apart from the specific national ends to which I devoted my endeavor. The diplomatic drama is now played out with the whole world as stage. I began with a skeptical attitude toward those who exalt the personal role in negotiation. In most cases, nations make accommodations to each other, not because they are impressed by their adversary's rhetoric but because they believe that making a concession will be more useful or less harmful than refusing it. Thus the business of a diplomat is not so much to be eloquent in defense of his nation's rectitude as to define incentives and deterrents so convincingly that his rival will identify a concession with his own self-interest. This seems to mean that a diplomat must rely for his effect not so much on his gifts of personality as on the inducements and pressures that his government can mobilize outside the negotiating room. It follows, I thought, that elegant books sparkling with anecdotes that define diplomacy in personal terms tend to be more entertaining than realistic.

However, this austere view of the diplomatic process does not fit in this post–World War generation, and I have abandoned it. Publicity, summitry and habits of intense expression of opinion have invaded the sheltered sanctuaries in which small groups of mandarins used to arrange the affairs of nations. The modern negotiator cannot escape the duality of his role. He must transact business simultaneously with his negotiating partner and world public opinion, including his own. This involves a total modification of techniques. The communications revolution has altered the tone of diplomacy to an extraordinary degree. Whether the eclipse of reticence is a favorable development or not is immaterial. It is, in any case, moot. On the one hand, it is asserted that political solutions require skills and knowledge that come only from long training and experience. How can such issues, it is asked, be left to the public, whose only training is the reading of newspapers and an occasional glimpse of a television debate? On the other hand, the pathos and tragedy inherent in peace or war strike at the very heart of the human condition, and no living human being would be safe from an erroneous choice. How then can it be said that these issues should be left for decision to small groups of experts?

Public diplomacy worked in favor of Israel's cause, and certainly added an important dimension to my own ministry in Israel's cause. How the emissaries of nations express themselves has become a matter of importance and urgency. Moreover, Israel's appeal to the world resounds to so many emotions, sentiments, memories and passions that its cause was much more likely to succeed in wider audiences than in the rooms where a few statesmen used to fashion the ways of the world. I did my best to take advantage of these opportunities for public repercussion. I consider that in today's conditions, an Israeli representative would be crippled without it.

Diplomacy has become more exciting than it used to be. Sovereignty is more respected and also more encroached upon than ever before. International relations must now be studied in the context of a vast expansion of its scope. There are many more actors in the drama, more issues to be wrestled with, more functions performed, more specialized skills mobilized, more methods of analysis and research invoked and put to work, more materials available than in the days when diplomacy was a compact exercise in which relatively few people in a few sovereign countries dealt with a few strategic problems, while the masses of humankind went on their way unheeding. The task, as it has always been, is to keep the future open for life and, if possible, for peace. But the understanding of this task requires more complex and strenuous labor by men and women who can see the soil below as well as the vistas ahead.

Those who have shown an interest in the movement of my policies and attitudes have sometimes observed reproachfully that I have not been consistent in my attitudes to the use of force. I have been far less ferocious than the hawks deserve, but also not so contemptuous of force as the doves would have liked.

This is the last thing for which I would ever apologize. Consistency amid the ebb and flow of crises is an advanced form of intellectual sloth. It replaces empirical wisdom by dogmatic fallacy. It is as silly to be invariably against power as to be tenaciously in its support. To rush to forceful actions with knee-jerk spontaneity is as foolish as to renounce force when the refusal to use it would endanger the highest ends of freedom and independence. When I asked Anwar Sadat why he made the astonishing transition from the denial of Israel's existence to the conclusion of a peace treaty, he said simply: "Because you had my land. I tried every way to recover it without the hazard of making peace: I tried UN action, four-power, three-power, two-power pressure. I tried war, armistice, international condemnation. I reached the answer that only by peace could I recover my land."

He was unwittingly confessing that a certain degree of tenacity in Israeli positions led him to a far-reaching conviction that peace was his best option. Something of this spirit is stirring in other parts of the Arab subcontinent. The important thing is to know when the hour is ripe to be seized. I believe that the time is now. In the last resort, harmony comes when interests converge—not when one interest overcomes and crushes the other. Convergence means reciprocal movement. It is sometimes necessary to build a wall of resistance, but if there is no open door in the wall for peace to enter, opportunities will be squandered in repetitive violence. I have reviewed the decades and concluded that, in the general perspective, I have not been wrong in the oscillation of my attitudes between flexibility and obduracy.

□　　□　　□

In the end I can only salute the hero of my story—the Jewish people, battered by the tempests of a tragic history but still endowed with an incomparable recuperative power.

My particular tribute is to the Israelis of the first generation who have few spokesmen left to record their ambition and achievement. We were young and fragile in those early days and our prospect of survival was a matter more of faith than of reason. But we were sustained by a clear and lucid vision. We knew how to distinguish between fantasies and realities. We understood that our task was not only to assert our own rights, but also to bring our rights into harmony with the rights and interests of others. We had no illusion that we could live outside the universal human order in which the interaction of destinies mocks the pretensions of unilateral power. We were inspired by our history without being enslaved by it. We realized that in statecraft, as in all pursuits charged with any degree of nobility, the key to success lies in the disciplined use of reason in pursuit of understanding. We recalled that our land was twice ravaged and our freedom destroyed because we sometimes gave rein to a suicidal zealotry that did not give survival its due priority of concern. We took these warnings to heart. And so, in our first decades, we gave a new impulse and direction to Jewish history and set Israel on a path in which the opportunities transcended the dangers.

As a witness and actor in that drama, I can only bequeath my memories, in the hope that a dim light from the past will illuminate Israel's onward journey. Most nations exhort their new generations to fix their eyes resolutely on the future. Young Israelis would do well to spare a thought and memory for the poignant, early days when our Founding Fathers first put our flag into the winds of history.

INDEX

Barak, Aharon, 588, 617
Baram, Moshe, 565
Barbour, Walworth, 282, 397–99, 489
Barenboim, Daniel, 224
Barker, Evelyn, 73, 77
Barlev, Chaim, 504, 594, 605, 607, 648
Bar-Siman-Tov, Yaa'cov, 486–87
Battle, Lucius, 363–64, 383, 438
Bauer, Yehuda, 43–44
Bedell Smith, Walter, 207, 224, 277, 281
Beeley, Harold, 103, 108
Begin, Menachem, 191–92, 299–300, 333, 334, 489–91, 514, 568, 583, 584, 641; Camp David accords, 466, 588, 591–95, 597–98, 600–603, 640, 644, 646, 649; described, 586–87; Irgun, 62, 69, 100–101, 163, 182; Lebanese War, 605, 607, 609–12, 614–17; Nobel Prize, 200, 595, 597, 601; as PM, 230, 579, 581, 585–88, 591–95, 597–98, 600–603, 605, 607, 609–12, 614–17, 620, 624, 627, 640, 644, 646, 647, 649; Six Day War, 362–63, 367, 402, 403, 406, 412, 437, 440, 452; Yom Kippur War, 541, 546
Belaunde, Victor, 15, 180
Belgium, Israel and: to 1948, 89, 90, 120, 121, 129; 1948–1956, 179, 196; 1956 Suez-Sinai War, 265; 1967 Six Day War, 407; 1967–1973, 510, 511; 1974–1992, 639
Ben-Aharon, Yitzhak, 477
Ben-Bella, Ahmed, 352, 424
Ben-Eliezer, Arieh, 367, 439, 648
Ben-Elissar, Eliahu, 628
Ben-Gurion, David, 33, 40, 45–49, 56, 57, 63–64, 71–72, 78, 79, 86, 88–89, 94, 99–101, 106, 107, 117, 124, 126, 147, 150, 154, 157, 161, 163–64, 169, 176, 201, 327, 328, 331, 332, 336, 448, 462, 476–77, 511, 565, 585, 637; as defense minister, 239, 245–48; described, 317–18; Haganah, 69, 136; Lechi, 63, 100, 182; as PM, 174–75, 181, 182, 191, 202–4, 207, 209, 211–12, 217–19, 221, 227, 228, 230, 231, 233, 235, 248–51, 254–58, 261, 263–65, 268–69, 273, 275–82, 284, 287, 288, 290–95, 299–304, 307, 309, 311–13,

315–16, 318, 321, 323, 333, 334, 351, 396; resignation (1953), 227, 230, 235; resignation (1963), 239, 250, 315–16, 321–23, 333; "retirement," 235, 237–38; Six Day War, 362, 363, 403, 411; Suez-Sinai War, 253–58, 261, 264–65, 268–69, 273, 275–82, 284; Weizmann compared to, 47, 81, 83, 174–75, 181–82; at Zionist Congresses, 22, 23, 47, 82–83
Ben-Gurion, Paula, 63–64, 181–82, 238, 336
Ben-Horin, Eliashiv, 512
Ben Meir, Yehuda, 580
Ben-Nathan, Asher, 335, 535
Bentzur, Eytan, 524, 526, 551
Ben-Zvi, Rachel Yanait, 462
Ben-Zvi, Yitzchak, 313–14
Berendsen, Carl, 15, 210, 345
Berlin, Isaiah, 19, 38–39
Berman, Yitzhak, 609–10, 617
Bernadotte, Folke, 148, 164, 165; assassination, 175–77, 182, 192, 193; report, 170–71, 175, 177–78, 197, 212
Bernstein, Peretz, 107
Bevin, Ernest, 14, 63, 66, 179, 218, 260, 377, 457; Zionism, 67–69, 71, 72, 76, 78, 79, 81, 85–87, 91, 95, 96, 98–100, 102–3, 107, 119, 125, 131, 136, 143, 145–46, 155, 168–71, 173, 184–86, 190, 206, 213
Bialer, Seweryn, 634
Birrenbach, Kurt, 334
Bitan, Moshe, 397
Blaustein, Jacob, 219
Blom, Nicholas, 90, 97
Blum, Léon, 120, 123
Bohlen, Charles (Chip), 376
Bolivia, Israel and, 130–31, 519
Bourges-Maunoury, Maurice, 257, 277
Brandt, Willy, 511, 512, 625
Brazil, Israel and: to 1948, 115, 121, 123; 1957–1967, 312–13; 1967 Six Day War, 358, 417, 457; 1967–1973, 519, 520
Brezhnev, Leonid, 487, 509, 535–39, 589, 633
Britain, Israel and: to 1948, 15, 19–25, 34–35, 37–48, 49–51, 54, 56,

58, 61, 62, 64–69, 71–74, 76–105,
107–9, 111–13, 119, 124–27, 129,
130, 131, 133, 135–37, 140–46, 148,
151, 154, 155, 182, 199, 200, 206,
213, 227, 228, 232, 289, 457, 465,
494, 586–87, 591, 598, 600, 621;
1948–1956, 153–56, 165, 168–73,
176, 179, 183–87, 190, 196, 199,
202, 208, 209, 212, 214, 218, 228,
237–42, 245–48, 252, 346; 1956
Suez-Sinai War, 228, 252–65,
267–70, 272–79, 282, 286, 287, 297,
333, 366, 368, 378, 404, 442;
1957–1967, 267, 288, 289, 316, 324,
338, 345, 347; 1967 Six Day War,
357, 358, 361, 371, 373–75, 377–79,
381–82, 387–90, 394, 396, 398–401,
404, 406, 409, 420, 429, 431–32,
439, 444–47, 449, 455–59;
1967–1973, 477, 480, 481, 484–85,
488, 497, 509, 511, 517, 623; 1973
Yom Kippur War, 534; 1974–1992,
587, 593, 637; 1990–1991 Gulf War,
637; Balfour Declaration, 15, 19,
21, 25, 49–50, 66, 77, 84, 105, 213,
227, 456, 537, 591, 600; Peel
Commission, 22, 56, 88, 108–9
Brown, George, 378, 379, 400–401,
439, 456
Bulgaria, Israel and, 341, 426, 429,
439, 638
Bull, Odd, 409–10
Bullock, Alan, 68, 168, 169
Bunche, Ralph, 14, 96, 100, 101, 105,
186–89, 199–200, 273–74, 472
Bundy, McGeorge, 423
Burg, Yosef, 580, 598, 609, 610
Burla, Yaakov, 462
Burma, Israel and, 267, 304, 325–26,
343, 345, 506
Bush, George, 634, 635, 638, 643,
646–47

Cadogan, Alexander, 14, 129, 172,
173, 175, 179
Callaghan, James, 587, 593
Cambodia, Israel and, 343
Cameroon, Israel and, 305, 506–7
Camp David accords, 466, 502,
588–95, 597–603, 611, 623, 628,
640–41, 644, 646, 649, 651, 655

Canada, Israel and: to 1948, 97, 105,
115, 117, 120; 1948–1956, 179, 186,
187, 190, 209, 227, 236, 244; 1956
Suez-Sinai War, 253, 267, 272–75,
277, 339; 1957–1967, 339–40, 345;
1967 Six Day War, 358, 394, 398,
401, 417; 1974–1992, 639
Caradon, Lord, 455, 457–59
Carmel, Moshe, 399
Carter, Jimmy, 574, 638; Camp David
accords, 502, 591, 592, 598, 600
Casey, Richard, 58, 345
Ceausescu, Nicolae, 343, 542–44
Chamberlain, Neville, 17; White
Paper, 34, 56, 62, 63, 82, 109;
Zionism, 22, 23, 34, 56, 62, 63, 82,
109
Chamoun, Camille, 118, 123, 211, 288
China, Israel and: to 1948, 96, 129;
1948–1956, 179, 190, 205–9; 1956
Suez-Sinai War, 264; 1967 Six Day
War, 393; 1974–1992, 638
Christian, George, 386
Church, Frank, 474
Churchill, Winston, 14, 21, 27, 28, 34,
42, 46, 49, 57, 61–64, 90, 93, 230,
234–35, 286, 293, 321, 400, 407–8,
436, 455, 466, 554–55, 590, 634;
Zionism, 22–23, 25, 38, 58, 61, 62,
65–66, 68, 78, 80, 85, 87, 100,
107–9, 145–46, 184–86, 190, 228,
239, 245
Chuvakhin, Dmitri, 347, 353, 354,
361, 396, 425, 427, 633
Clark, Dickie, 66–67
Clay, Lucius, 224
Clayton, Iltwyd, 58, 64
Clementis, Walter, 232
Clifford, Clark M., 135, 149
Clurman, Dick, 423
Cohen, Benjamin V., 178
Cohen, Geulah, 572, 599
Cohn, Joseph, 139, 149
Colombia, Israel and, 129, 179,
324–25
Comay, Michael, 114, 154, 253
Cornford, John, 17–18
Cornut-Gentile, Bernard, 263, 264
Costa Rica, Israel and, 599
Coupland, Reginald, 22, 108–9, 117
Couve de Murville, Maurice, 338–39,
372, 375, 376, 379

Crossman, Richard, 103, 379
Cuba, Israel and, 149, 264
Cunningham, Alan, 145, 146
Czechoslovakia, Israel and: to 1948,
  98, 105, 115, 130, 136–38;
  1948–1956, 159, 163, 232, 241;
  1957–1967, 341; 1967 Six Day War,
  426; 1974–1992, 638

Dafni, Reuven, 51, 242–43, 272
Dalton, Hugh, 65, 66
Dayan, Moshe, 44, 257, 260, 281,
  301, 307, 315, 322, 331, 377, 468,
  476, 477, 487, 490, 496, 499–500,
  503–5, 515, 520–21, 556, 560–63,
  565, 566, 568, 570, 571, 576, 581,
  588, 601, 625, 633; Palestinians,
  462–66, 470, 598, 618; Six Day
  War, 362, 367, 396, 403, 406, 412,
  423–24, 427, 432, 436, 437, 440,
  442, 462, 618; Yom Kippur War,
  527–28, 530, 531, 537, 554–55,
  563–64
Dean, Arthur, 224, 282
De Gaulle, Charles, 90, 176, 230, 261,
  279, 293, 316, 321, 323–24, 339,
  480, 481, 623; Six Day War, 361,
  370–79, 387, 389, 396, 399, 407,
  431–32, 447–48
Denmark, Israel and, 130, 196, 202,
  394, 417, 511
Dewey, Thomas E., 177–78, 180–81,
  214
Dillon, Douglas, 385
Dinitz, Simcha, 468, 525, 533–36, 538
Dixon, Pierson, 264, 265
Dobrynin, Anatoly, 452
Dominican Republic, Israel and, 195,
  599
Dori, Ya'akov, 157–58
Douglas, Lewis, 136, 143
Douglas, Paul, 222, 223, 295
Douglas Home, Alec, 377, 517, 534
Dugdale, Blanche (Baffy), 21, 24
Dulles, Allen, 277
Dulles, John Foster, 177–79, 209, 224,
  234–35, 240–42, 244–48, 252, 276,
  288–91, 295, 323, 340, 359, 363,
  385; described, 297; Suez-Sinai
  War, 220, 253–55, 257–58, 267,
  269–70, 272, 277, 278, 280–87

Eden, Anthony, 25, 58, 61, 62, 140,
  228, 237, 245–47, 282, 548;
  Suez-Sinai War, 254, 256, 257,
  260–62, 264, 274–76
Efrat, Yonah, 364, 617
Egypt, Israel and, 198, 295. See also
  Gaza; Sinai. To 1948, 16, 32, 136,
  139, 145, 146, 151, 152, 404;
  1948–1956, 158, 162–63, 165, 166,
  179, 183, 186–90, 205, 218, 233,
  234, 236–39, 243, 245–49, 251–52,
  254–55; 1956 Suez-Sinai War,
  210–11, 220, 252–87, 291–93, 297,
  298, 324, 328, 332–33, 338, 339,
  351, 356, 366, 368, 369, 378, 394,
  404, 408, 418–19, 426, 442, 444,
  449, 482, 608; 1957–1967, 287, 288,
  290, 316, 322–25, 328–31, 333,
  346–48, 352, 502; 1967 Six Day
  War, 33, 278, 279, 343, 352–459,
  461–63, 468, 482–84, 486, 492–94,
  500, 519, 522, 541–43, 564, 566–67,
  608, 618, 623, 637, 643, 649;
  1967–1973, 478, 482–91, 494–96,
  498–509, 512, 516–19, 521–23, 527,
  558; 1973 Yom Kippur War, 33,
  146, 286, 380, 465, 470, 482, 487,
  493, 501, 505, 516, 518, 522–55,
  557, 559, 560, 562–64, 568, 572,
  573, 581, 588–90, 603, 608, 617,
  633, 643–44; 1974–1992, 466, 472,
  473, 483, 492, 502, 556–61, 567,
  570–72, 575, 576, 580–81, 587–95,
  597–603, 611, 635, 638, 640–41,
  644, 646, 647, 649, 651, 655;
  1990–1991 Gulf War, 635, 638;
  Camp David accords, 466, 502,
  588–95, 597–603, 611, 623, 628,
  640–41, 644, 646, 649, 651, 655;
  Geneva Conference, 334, 545–55,
  557, 560, 573, 581, 633
Eichmann, Adolf, 312–14, 555
Einstein, Albert, 69, 228–29, 242–43
Eisenhower, Dwight D., 51, 224, 225,
  229, 230, 233, 234–35, 240, 242,
  244, 246, 288, 289, 295, 297, 330,
  340, 380, 381, 385, 387, 392, 473,
  478, 493; described, 297–98; Nasser
  appraisal, 247, 252; Suez-Sinai War,
  253, 258, 263, 268, 274–76, 280–82,
  284, 286–87, 298
Eitan, Rafael, 610–11, 613, 617, 626

Goldmann, Nahum, 47, 88, 116–17, 143–44, 192, 219, 221
Golomb, Eliahu, 38, 40–41
Gorbachev, Mikhail, 631–32, 634, 638
Granados, Garcia, 98
Greenberg, Uri Zvi, 462
Gromyko, Andrei, 14, 157, 168, 176, 435, 439, 440, 452–54, 572; Geneva Conference, 548, 549, 551–52, 633; Zionism, 95, 103, 112, 123, 143, 154, 160, 172, 551
Guatemala, Israel and, 98, 105, 115, 599
Gulf War (1990–1991), 446, 631, 642, 652; details of, 634–38
Gur, Mordechai (Motta), 411, 553, 570, 582, 611, 612, 648
Gush Emunin, 462, 468, 469, 604, 625

Habash, George, 519–20
Habib, Philip, 606
Hacohen, David, 367
Hadow, Michael, 409
Haganah, 367; to 1948, 34, 40–42, 44–45, 51, 55, 69, 71, 125, 128, 131, 135–39, 147, 182; 1948–1956, 157, 162
Haig, Alexander, 536, 606, 608, 609, 613, 615, 628
Haiti, Israel and, 123, 124
Hakim, Taufiq al-, 59
Halevi, Yehuda, 53
Hall, George, 81
Halper, Neville, 64
Hammarskjöld, Dag, 188, 209, 237, 256, 264–67, 273–74, 282–83, 306, 359
Hammer, Zevulun, 580, 610
Harel, Isser, 313, 333
Harkabi, Yehoshofat, 518
Harman, Abe, 363–64, 373, 381–86, 392, 393, 397, 398, 404, 438, 455, 479
Harmel, Pierre, 510
Harvey, Oliver, 25
Hauser, Rita, 629
Hausner, Gideon, 313, 314
Haykal, Hassanein, 375, 395, 408
Hazan, Ya'acov, 468
Hazaz, Chaim, 462

Heath, Edward, 377, 534
Heeney, Arnold, 244
Heikal, Muhammad Hassanein, 487
Henderson, E., 382, 390
Hentig, Otto von, 62
Herter, Christian, 282
Herut Party: 1948–1956, 161, 191–92; 1957–1967, 322, 332, 347; 1967 Six Day War, 439
Herzl, Theodor, 20, 40, 74, 200–201, 316
Herzog, Aura Ambache, 59
Herzog, Chaim, 23, 59, 74, 163, 216, 217, 340, 442, 465, 620, 643–44
Herzog, Ya'acov, 276, 277, 288, 468, 475
Hildring, General, 120, 121
Hillel, Shlomo, 485
Hitler, Adolf, 17, 23–26, 38, 41, 42, 44, 48, 53, 55–57, 109, 125, 169, 196, 222, 226–27, 253, 272, 286, 313, 334, 434–35, 512, 634
Holmes, Oliver Wendell, 70
Holocaust, 48–49, 51, 59–61, 65, 67, 69, 73, 81, 90, 145, 146, 171, 221–22, 224, 239, 334, 341–42, 349, 368, 404, 406, 434, 511, 551, 571, 636
Hoo, Victor, 96, 188
Hood, John D. L., 97
Hoopes, Townsend, 383
Hoover, Herbert, 294
Hoover, Herbert, Jr., 276
Horowitz, David, 96–97, 100–108, 110, 116, 119–20, 127, 188, 221–22
Houphouët-Boigny, Félix, 439, 523
Hourani, Albert, 58, 79
Humphrey, Hubert H., 474–75, 478
Hungary, Israel and, 341, 426, 638
Hussein, king of Jordan, 200, 251, 331, 346, 347, 494, 495, 498–99, 512, 519, 560, 567, 575, 591, 597, 623, 626–28; described, 496–98; Six Day War, 401, 404, 408–10, 420, 438, 439, 446–47, 457
Hussein, Ahmed, 252
Hussein, Saddam, 446, 634–36, 638
Hussein, Taha, 31–32, 59
Husseini, Feisal, 641
Husseini, Haj Amin al-, 56, 57
Husseini, Jamal al-, 173

Ibn Saud, king, 80
Iceland, Israel and, 113, 122–24, 510
Idrisi, king of Libya, 196
India, Israel and: to 1948, 98, 105;
   1948–1956, 208, 209; 1967 Six Day
   War, 358, 413, 417, 418, 420, 429,
   439, 455, 458, 459; 1974–1992,
   638
Iran, Israel and, 98, 105, 256, 264
Iraq, Israel and: to 1948, 146;
   1948–1956, 195–96, 204; 1956
   Suez-Sinai War, 256, 258;
   1957–1967, 287, 288, 316, 328; 1967
   Six Day War, 357, 368; 1967–1973,
   494, 496, 497, 517–18; 1974–1992,
   446, 594, 597, 602, 631, 634–38,
   642, 652; 1990–1991 Gulf War, 446,
   631, 634–38, 642, 652
Irgun: to 1948, 62, 66–69, 71,
   100–101, 131, 137–39, 182;
   1948–1956, 157, 163–64, 182;
   disbanded, 157, 164, 182; King
   David Hotel bomb, 72, 73
Israeli Intelligence, 33; 1948–1956,
   186; 1957–1967, 313, 315, 333, 352;
   1967 Six Day War, 356, 357, 362,
   367, 380, 383, 395, 396, 406;
   1967–1973, 516–19; 1973 Yom
   Kippur War, 380, 522–23, 525, 526,
   528, 540, 563; 1974–1992, 579, 582
Italy, Israel and, 511, 639
Ivory Coast, Israel and, 439, 523

Jabotinsky, Zeev, 316, 322, 587
Jamili, Fadhil al-, 15, 204
Japan, Israel and, 343, 344, 347, 417,
   639
Jarring, Gunnar, 458, 471–72, 480,
   482, 483, 489, 490, 493, 500–507,
   509
Javits, Jacob, 290
Jebb, Gladwyn, 14, 208, 209, 218
Jessup, Philip C., 149, 172, 186
Jewish Agency, 18, 24–25, 42–44, 74,
   76, 88, 91, 93, 96, 99, 101, 113, 114,
   119, 122, 124, 142, 155, 172;
   Information Department, 77, 79;
   Political Department, 94
Johnson, Hershel, 111–12, 119–20, 123
Johnson, Lyndon B., 149, 176, 277,
   279, 281, 294, 297–98, 324, 325,

478, 479; military aid, 339–40,
   473–75, 567; Six Day War (1967),
   361, 368, 369, 371, 373, 381,
   383–84, 386–94, 397–98, 400, 401,
   404–6, 409, 417, 420, 422–24,
   431–33, 435, 438, 441, 449, 453,
   455–56, 458–59
Jordan, Israel and. *See also* West
   Bank. To 1948, 136, 145, 146, 151;
   1948–1956, 158, 164–66, 170, 176,
   188, 200–206, 234, 236–37, 245–46,
   249; 1956 Suez-Sinai War, 254–58,
   286–87, 408; 1957–1967, 288, 289,
   328, 329, 346, 347, 364; 1967 Six
   Day War, 352, 357, 367, 368, 376,
   395, 401, 404, 408–12, 419–20, 423,
   427, 428, 434, 437, 439, 446–47,
   450–52, 457, 463; 1967–1973, 472,
   478, 489–91, 493–99, 502, 509, 512,
   515, 519; 1973 Yom Kippur War,
   546, 548–50, 553, 554, 557, 560;
   1974–1992, 559, 560, 567, 574–76,
   580, 590–92, 600, 605, 620, 623,
   626–28, 639, 641, 649–50; 1982
   Lebanese War, 605; Geneva
   Conference, 546, 548–50, 553, 557,
   560; Jerusalem proposal, 200–206
Joseph, Dov, 76
Josephtal, Giora, 307, 315

Kahane, Mordecai, 105–6
Kahan Report, 617
Kahn, Richard, 18, 39
Kaplan, Eliezer, 76
Katz, Shmuel, 600
Katznelson, Berl, 38–39
Keating, Kenneth B., 526
Keightly, Charles, 261
Kemal, Mustafa, 384
Kenan, Isaiah L. (Si), 154, 219, 223
Kennedy, Jacqueline, 336
Kennedy, John F., 294, 297–98, 316,
   322–24, 383, 393, 415, 473, 474
Keren, Moshe, 216
Khalaf, Karim, 620
Khalidi, Walid, 495–96
Khoman, Thanat, 344
Khomeini, Ayatollah Ruhollah, 98
Khoury, Faris al-, 15, 129
Khrushchev, Nikita, 415
Kidron, Mordechai (Reggie), 210

Kigner, Heda Rechnitz, 612
Killearn, Lord, 31
Kissinger, Henry, 220, 330, 471,
    479–81, 488, 493, 499, 500, 502,
    504, 515–16, 574–76, 580–81, 592,
    600–601, 638, 640–41, 643;
    described, 480; Geneva Conference,
    545–50, 552; shuttle diplomacy,
    556–61, 570–72; Yom Kippur War,
    522–26, 530–31, 533–39, 541,
    545–50, 552
Klerk, F. W. de, 647
Knesset, 40, 62, 638; 1948–1956, 199,
    202, 245, 334; 1956 Suez-Sinai War,
    253, 286; 1957–1967, 304, 307, 308,
    311–12, 315, 320, 321, 329, 333–35,
    340, 346, 347, 476–77; 1967 Six
    Day War, 364, 367, 370, 397, 408,
    411, 412, 433, 438–39, 459;
    1967–1973, 491, 516, 521;
    1974–1992, 559, 562, 565, 573,
    576–82, 585–87, 589, 592, 595–96,
    599, 606–8, 611–13, 616, 621, 625,
    626, 628, 645, 647–48; 1982
    Lebanese War, 606–8, 611–13, 616
Knowland, William F., 277, 281, 290
Kohler, Fay, 383
Kohn, Leo, 105–6
Kol, Moshe, 475
Kollek, Teddy, 29–30, 63–64, 78, 216,
    223, 246, 311, 427, 599
Kook, Zvi Yehuda, 469
Kosygin, Aleksei, 396, 420, 431–38,
    441, 451, 453, 458–59, 484–85,
    535–36
Kreisky, Bruno, 522, 625
Krock, Arthur, 224
Kuwait, Israel and: 1957–1967, 328;
    1990–1991 Gulf War, 446, 631,
    634–38, 642, 652
Kuznetsov, Vasili, 459

Labor Party, 475, 480, 483; to 1948,
    38, 40, 43, 44, 66, 83, 124, 131–32,
    142; 1948–1956, 191, 248, 250;
    1957–1967, 299–303, 307, 315–16,
    320, 331–32, 336, 348, 377; 1967
    Six Day War, 367, 403, 407, 430,
    433, 437, 450; 1967–1973, 460, 465,
    466, 470, 476–79, 486, 490, 493,
    499, 515, 520–21; 1973 Yom

Kippur War, 518, 553–54;
    1974–1992, 561–70, 572, 573, 575,
    579, 584–88, 595, 599, 603–5, 607,
    611–13, 616–18, 625, 626, 634, 643,
    645–49; 1982 Lebanese War, 603–5,
    607, 611–13, 616–17; described,
    301–2
Lahat, Shlomo (Chich), 636
Landau, Caim, 367
Landau, Moshe, 313, 555, 599
Laski, Harold, 70–71, 103
Laskov, Chaim, 555
Latvia, Israel and, 638
Lauterpacht, Hersch, 18
Lavon, Pinchas, 235, 238, 239,
    315–16, 318, 321–22
Lawson, Edward B., 258
Lazarus, Fred, 224
League of Nations, 87, 92, 101, 105,
    548; Zionism, 19, 49–50, 87, 91, 96,
    145
Leavis, F. E., 18
Lebanese War (1982), 482, 559, 597,
    652; details of, 604–19; Kahan
    Report, 617
Lebanon, Israel and: to 1948, 125,
    128, 138; 1948–1956, 158, 165,
    188–89, 195–96, 210–11; 1956
    Suez-Sinai War, 210–11; 1957–1967,
    288, 331, 346; 1967 Six Day War,
    357; 1967–1973, 494, 495, 509, 515,
    519–20; 1974–1992, 211, 472, 482,
    559, 571, 594, 597, 602, 604–19,
    623, 647, 652; 1982 Lebanese War,
    482, 559, 597, 604–19, 652
Lechi (Lochamei Herut Israel): to
    1948, 62, 63, 68–69, 71, 80, 100,
    107–9, 131, 137, 139, 175, 177, 182;
    1948–1956, 157, 175–77, 182, 192,
    193; Bernadotte killed, 175–77, 182,
    192, 193; Moyne killed, 62, 63, 80,
    107–9, 175, 177, 182
Lee Kuan Yew, 344
Levavi, Aryeh, 440
Levin, Daniel, 414
Levin, Shalom, 314
Levinger, Moshe, 625
Levy, David, 610
Lewis, Samuel W., 605
Liberia, Israel and, 121, 123, 124, 306
Libya, Israel and: 1948–1956, 196;
    1957–1967, 328; 1967 (Six-Day

War), 453–54; 1967–1973, 514,
517–18, 520, 521, 593
Lie, Trygve, 14, 91, 95, 105, 115, 123,
135, 143, 149, 154, 163, 176, 188,
266
Likud Party, 161, 191, 470, 483, 518;
1967–1973, 460, 493; 1973 Yom
Kippur War, 546, 548; 1974–1992,
559, 562, 579, 581, 584, 586, 589,
595, 598–600, 602, 603, 628, 629,
634, 643, 645–49
Linowitz, Sol, 598
Linton, Ivor, 151
Lippmann, Walter, 224, 474
Lisicky, Karl, 98
Lithuania, Israel and, 638
Lloyd, Selwyn, 25, 256, 257, 265
Lloyd George, David, 81, 105, 245
Locker, Berl, 24
Lodge, Henry Cabot, 263, 264,
273–74, 284, 359–60, 385
Lopez, Alfonso, 129
Lourie, Arthur, 18, 133, 151, 154,
155, 183–84, 210, 405, 409, 420
Lovett, Robert H., 149
Luxembourg, Israel and, 89, 90, 113,
510, 511

Ma'arri, Abu-l-Ala al, 32
MacArthur, Douglas, 150, 229, 274,
389, 493
McCarthy, Joseph, 223, 229
McCloy, John J., 222, 224
McCormack, John, 223
McDonald, James G., 190
MacDonald, Malcolm, 25
McGill, William, 574
McGillivray, Arthur, 105
McIntyre, Donald, 529, 534
Macmillan, Harold, 176, 239–40, 248,
316
McNamara, Robert, 340, 384–87, 390
McNeil, Hector, 179
McPherson, Harry, 409
Madrid Conference, 639–41
Malaysia, Israel and, 344
Mali, Israel and, 429, 439
Malik, Charles, 15, 118, 210–11, 288
Malik, Yacov, 14, 154, 205–6
Malraux, André, 311, 372
Manuilsky, Dmitri, 172–73

Marcos, Ferdinand, 345
Marcos, Imelda, 345
Marcus, Mickey, 159
Marshall, George, 14, 111, 124–25,
136, 144, 149–50, 177, 178, 180–81,
214
Martin, Joseph, 223
Martin, Paul, 339
Mayhew, Christopher, 169–70
Meir, Golda, 72, 83, 145, 146, 201,
210, 305, 584; described, 336–37; as
foreign minister, 250, 251, 258, 263,
267, 268, 273, 276, 281, 282, 284,
289, 292, 316, 319, 320, 323, 324,
331–34, 336–37, 343; as PM, 230,
468, 476–78, 481, 485–87, 489, 490,
501, 504–6, 515–16, 518, 520–22,
525–27, 529–31, 535–37, 542–46,
554–56, 561–63, 565, 566, 569–72;
resignation, 565, 569, 572; Six Day
War, 367, 369, 433, 439, 440; Yom
Kippur War, 522, 525–27, 529–31,
535–37, 542–46, 554–55
Mendoza, Raoul, 130–31
Meroz, Yochanan, 258, 334
Mexico, Israel and, 96, 209, 324–25
Middle East Center of Arab Studies,
58–61, 66, 70, 73, 74, 76
Milson, Menachem, 619–21
Minervi, Isaac, 511
Minorsky, Vladimir, 23
Mitterrand, François, 100, 630
Mobutu, Joseph, 506, 521, 524
Moch, Jules, 14
Moda'i, Yitzhak, 609
Mollet, Guy, 253, 257, 264, 274–75,
283
Molotov, Vyacheslav, 23, 240, 247–48
Montgomery, Bernard, 51, 131
Morocco, Israel and, 328
Morrison, Herbert, 62, 218, 261, 377
Morse, Wayne, 474
Mountbatten, Louis, 42, 457
Moustafa al-Nahas Pasha, 30
Movement for a Greater Israel,
460–62, 469, 493, 600
Movement for an Undivided Land,
625
Moyne, Lord, 58; assassination, 62,
63, 80, 107–9, 175, 177, 182
Mubarak, Hosni, 594, 640
Mugabe, Robert, 640

Soviet Union, Israel and: to 1948, 88, 95, 103, 112, 113, 115, 118, 123, 125, 126, 136–37, 143, 551; 1948–1956, 154, 157, 159–63, 165–66, 172–73, 179, 189–90, 205–6, 227, 231–33, 235–36, 240–43, 245, 247–48, 251–52, 254–55, 426, 635; 1956 Suez-Sinai War, 255–56, 264, 265, 269–70, 274–79, 284–85, 426, 444; 1957–1967, 324, 330, 341, 347–49, 352, 522; 1967 Six Day War, 352–54, 357, 361, 362, 365, 368, 369, 373–76, 378, 379, 383, 387, 392, 393, 396, 401, 407–9, 413, 415, 418–20, 422–27, 429–41, 444–45, 447–55, 458–59, 637; 1967–1973, 473, 480–93, 506–9, 512, 516, 519, 524, 552, 558, 623, 633; 1973 Yom Kippur War, 530–31, 533–39, 541, 545, 546, 548, 549, 551–53, 589, 633; 1974–1992, 560, 572, 592, 595, 605, 628, 629, 631–35, 638, 639, 646, 648; 1982 Lebanese War, 605; 1990–1991 Gulf War, 634–35, 638; Geneva Conference, 545, 546, 548, 549, 551–53, 633

Spain, Israel and, 196
Stalin, Joseph, 14, 112, 154, 231
Stevenson, Adlai, 14, 225–26, 294, 393
Strauss, Franz Josef, 332, 333
Sudan, Israel and, 328
Suez-Sinai War (1956), 210–11, 220, 228, 286–87, 291–93, 297, 298, 324, 328, 332–33, 338, 339, 351, 356, 366, 368, 369, 378, 394, 404, 408, 418–19, 426, 442, 444, 449, 482, 608; details of, 252–85
Sukarno, 352, 424
Sweden, Israel and: to 1948, 97, 100, 102, 105, 116; 1948–1956, 176–77, 202; 1974–1992, 629
Switzerland, Israel and, 511
Symington, Stuart, 290
Syria, Israel and. *See also* Golan Heights. To 1948, 125, 128, 136, 146; 1948–1956, 158, 165, 179, 188, 199, 235–36, 248–49; 1956 Suez-Sinai War, 286–87; 1957–1967, 290, 316, 328–31, 346–49, 352, 364, 522; 1967 Six Day War, 352–53,

356–57, 361–62, 364, 367–68, 373, 395, 404, 407, 408, 411, 412, 419, 423–25, 427, 434, 437, 444–47, 450, 463, 541, 637; 1967–1973, 494, 496–98, 509, 515, 641; 1973 Yom Kippur War, 522–34, 540, 544–50, 553, 562, 572, 643–44; 1974–1992, 556, 559–62, 565, 567, 570–72, 575, 594, 597, 605, 607, 609, 612–16, 635, 638, 639, 641; 1982 Lebanese War, 605, 607, 609, 612–16; 1990–1991 Gulf War, 635, 638

Tabor, Hans, 411, 415, 418
Taft, Robert, 222–23
Taimour, Mahmoud, 59
Tal, Israel, 419, 527
Talmon, Ya'akov, 316–17
Tawil, Ibrahim, 620
Techiya Party, 599, 600, 648
Tekoah, Yosef, 411, 501, 532, 568
Thailand, Israel and, 122–23, 343, 344
Thatcher, Margaret, 378, 630, 634
Thompson, George, 379, 381–82, 390
Thors, Thor, 122, 123
Touval, Saadia, 556, 557
Tov, Moshe, 89, 101, 104–6, 124, 154, 180, 205, 324
Truman, Harry, 63, 67, 68, 71, 73, 85, 111, 114, 119–21, 124–26, 136, 137, 141, 145, 150, 159, 177, 178, 180–81, 213, 220–23, 225, 229–31, 233, 274, 294, 321, 383, 474, 478; Eban meets, 214–16; Weizmann and, 84, 119, 133–35, 139–40, 144, 147, 149, 151, 156–57, 169, 174, 212, 221, 227, 295
Tsarapkin, Semyon, 95, 112, 125
Tsur, Yaacov, 248, 255–56
Tunisia, Israel and, 328, 616, 629, 640
Turkey, Israel and, 178, 205, 340

Uganda, Israel and, 33, 380, 582–83
United Nations, 304, 310; beginnings of, 13–15, 65; Korean War, 208–9, 216, 218, 228, 229, 232, 234, 274, 298, 389; League of Nations compared to, 87
United Nations, Israel and, 303, 314, 343, 344; to 1948, 14–15, 84–136,